For Grandma Anna and Grandpa Louis
With love, gratitude, and apologies

THE MIDWIFE'S ADVICE

❮❮❮ BY ❯❯❯

GAY COURTER

A SIGNET BOOK

SIGNET
Published by the Penguin Group
Penguin Books USA Inc., 375 Hudson Street, New York, New York 10014, U.S.A.
Penguin Books Ltd, 27 Wrights Lane, London W8 5TZ, England
Penguin Books Australia Ltd, Ringwood, Victoria, Australia
Penguin Books Canada Ltd, 10 Alcorn Avenue, Toronto, Ontario, Canada M4V 3B2
Penguin Books (N.Z.) Ltd, 182–190 Wairau Road, Auckland 10, New Zealand

Penguin Books Ltd, Registered Offices:
Harmondsworth, Middlesex, England

Published by Signet, an imprint of Dutton Signet,
a division of Penguin Books USA Inc. Previously published in a Dutton Edition.

First Signet Printing, January, 1994
10 9 8 7 6 5 4 3 2 1

 REGISTERED TRADEMARK—MARCA REGISTRADA

Printed in the United States of America

PUBLISHER'S NOTE
This is a work of fiction. Names, characters, places, and incidents either are the products of the author's imagination or are used fictitiously, and any resemblance to actual persons, living or dead, events, or locales is entirely coincidental—except for historical characters briefly mentioned.

A wise person hears one word and understands two.

To be in on a secret is to be under no blessing.

Man thinks, God laughs.

—*Yiddish proverbs*

Contents

Problem 1:
Anna-Maria Tartaglia
Wants a Son

◆

1913

Life begets life. Energy creates energy. It is by spending oneself that one becomes rich.
                                        —SARAH BERNHARDT

∽ 1 ∽

BEFORE the outrageous act, Hannah Sokolow knew she abhorred violence and would not tolerate it on her midwifery service. Arriving for duty on that brilliant January morning, the head midwife had no inkling of the blow soon to fall. Later, when she traced the upheaval in her life to those swift seconds of brutality, she would decide that barbarous deeds, while unacceptable and to be avoided, did serve a purpose. Assassinations of archdukes and czars, senseless acts of madness—even a bellicose phrase—shattered governments and innocents alike. Yet they also led to change.

With no knowledge this was the turning point in her life, Hannah began her day with nursery rounds. The glistening sun slashed through the windows on the East River side of Bellevue Hospital, creating puddles of warmth in the postpartum ward, which hummed with the sounds attending the newest lives in the city. Her eyes scanned the fresh, crisp sheets smoothed on the wheeled infants' cots, mounds of folded diapers stacked on tiled counters, soft, sweet-smelling blankets tucked around squirming arms, and hesitant, squinting eyes opening to the wonders of their new world. Pausing, Hannah watched one set of pink lips as they parted, and out came a mewing sound that so surprised the hour-old boy that he bellowed in fright. In a few moments his neighbors wailed in unison, but the orderly glanced wryly at Hannah, for the noise belied the fact that actually everything was in order. Nurses, calm in their steady progress down the row, tended their charges one by one, and no chart indicated the midwife needed to tarry there.

Hannah took a deep breath. The first hour was always an adjustment. Emma's cough had been worse this morning and Benny had been difficult to awaken. She had left her husband, Lazar, with instructions for what to do if the boy became feverish, but he had seemed unconcerned. No, that was unfair, Lazar just did not fuss over the children, but what man ever did? At least Mama was nearby if he needed help.

"Sixteen women were admitted on the third shift," announced the ward clerk, "but only four babies so far."

"Then we'll have a busy morning," Hannah commented as she refocused on her task. She took a moment to flip through each new chart in case she needed to alter any orders before making her way to see the expectant mothers at the south end of her pavilion.

Bellevue was an imposing structure that had begun in the early 1700s as a six-bed infirmary in New York's Public Workhouse and House of Correction. In 1811, the city purchased a large farm called Belle Vue and began to build the immense establishment that would eventually take up the entire area from 25th to 30th Streets and from the East River across to First Avenue. To a visitor, the place was a maze of floors, wings, and pavilions—containing beds for more than a thousand—a power plant, a police station, teaching facilities, a riverfront park, kitchens, libraries, meeting rooms, nursing quarters, a morgue, even its own wharf and tubercular ward on a ship. To the midwife, however, it was merely the place where a mother could come to be safely delivered of her baby with the most modern and considerate care.

A long tiled corridor stretched between the maternity and nursery ends of the pavilion, and a glance at the amount of congestion there was an indication whether all was functioning smoothly. As Hannah approached, agitated student nurses, their high, sheer caps bobbing, were scurrying about carrying pans and rattling trays. Too many blue aprons could be glimpsed from a distance as the midwives on the day shift made the clumsy transition into the midst of a night duty's case. For some reason, mothers often decided that a change of shift was the moment to deliver the prize they had withheld through the bleak night. Was it the sunrise over the river that spurred them on? Hannah wondered obliquely as she began her preliminary check of each laboring or recently delivered mother.

Five labor wards were staggered on either side of the long, dark passageway, and in Ward A, Sarah Brink, a capable woman with ten grandchildren of her own, had just about brought everything from the evening before under control. Two women who already had delivered were tucked securely into their high iron beds, while their babies were being observed in the nursery. Three more were in early labor, and two of these were walking the hallways so that gravity could help the process. A primigravida, a sweet-faced child who could have been no more than sixteen, was the focus of Sarah's gentle but firm coaxing. "The worst part is over," she cooed to the frightened first-time mother. The girl's moans were diminishing as Hannah left to view Wards B and C. Hattie Donovan and Millicent Toomey had only four patients each, although Mrs. Toomey was concerned about a breech in Bed Twelve.

"Shall I send in a reserve to cover it for you?" Hannah asked as a matter of form.

"That won't be necessary," Mrs. Toomey replied in the light lilt that suggested her Irish background. "A nurse will be enough for now."

Hannah backed away. "I'll check back later," she said as a courtesy. Mrs. Toomey's breech technique was flawless, so it was to her Hannah steered new graduates for lessons in manipulations of difficult presentations.

With a perfunctory nod at young Miss Wylie in Ward D, Hannah walked around and examined the chart at the foot of each bed. No problems yet, but this room was bound to become lively in a few hours. Hannah decided she would spend most of her time here later in the day.

Shortly after rising to the position of head midwife, Hannah had systematized the labor wards quite differently than her predecessor, who had admitted patients to a given ward based on how far their dilatation had progressed. By separating those who were several hours from delivery from those whose time was imminent, the latter supposedly would receive the most diligent attention from the staff, who would congregate where they would be kept busiest. The flaw in this system was that predicting the course of any single labor was impossible. Some mothers would come in at two centimeters and deliver eight hours later, while another would present with the same exact progress and expel a child within the hour. Chaos was Hannah's speciality. Her ability to sort out the screamers from the truly suffering, to find dangerous signs in the stoics, to offer comfort to the frightened, was why she had come so far so rapidly. But once she was in charge, her attack of the problem involved a more analytical placement of patients.

The twelve beds in each ward were set in an awkward but recognizable circle, which her midwives could refer to as numbers on a clock. New patients were admitted to any ward with available beds, but usually at a number that most closely approximated their stage of cervical opening. Since ten centimeters was the maximum, numbers eleven and twelve were reserved for complications that might include twins, breech presentations, or abnormal bleeding. While one midwife could handle an entire ward most of the time, if Beds Eleven or Twelve were filled, another was sent in to cover those. This watchfulness had rapidly reduced both infant and maternal mortality, and credit had been given to Hannah's "Maternity Clock" plan.

That morning Ward E had nine patients in active labor, although none in the critical beds. Either someone had been allocating beds between the wards unfairly, or more likely, nature had played her usual tricks, with some women delivering more rapidly than expected. Hannah surveyed a few charts as the midwife, Norma Marshanck, a husky woman her same age, gave a brief summary of each case.

"Only one primip among the experts," she said in her scratchy voice. "Bed Six is having her tenth. Don't think I'll be needed there, do you?" She gave a low, guttural laugh.

Hannah did not hesitate to advise caution. "Could be a bleeder. Expect a boggy uterus. And have cold compresses at hand as well."

Beds Four and Seven were rushing to the finish line simultaneously, with both at eight centimeters. "Everything seems normal with these two. Would you accept a student to assist you?" Long ago Hannah had learned to ask—rather than tell—another midwife what she would prefer.

"Certainly. They're conventional cases, but I'll keep an eye out, just to be certain."

Hannah stood in the center of the room and waited to see if anything worried her. On this side of the building, away from the river, there were few windows. Thus the lights that swung down from the high ceilings burned day and night. As Midwife Marshanck went about her duties, she cast an elongated shadow across the floors and beds of the vast chamber. Something did not feel quite right, Hannah realized. She pivoted to review each bed. A small, dark woman with a long braid of thick black hair was curled on her side in Bed Three. Hannah approached the foot of her iron-bedstead and glanced at the chart: Anna-Maria Tartaglia. Six centimeters. No change for two hours.

"Para five," she said to Norma Marshanck. She noted one child had died. Pointing at the chart, she asked the midwife, "Which one?"

Mrs. Marshanck shrugged. Obviously she had been too busy to worry about such a detail, but this might be a clue as to why dilatation had stopped. If it had been her last child, for instance, she may have been unconsciously holding back on letting this one go. Hannah came up to the patient from the side turned away from her. She bent over and placed a hand in the small of her back and pressed. The mother-to-be groaned.

"Does that feel better?" Hannah asked sympathetically. She checked the records to remind herself of the name, then added, "Mrs. Tartaglia."

"Ahhh ..." Mrs. Tartaglia expelled a long sigh. "Yes."

"Pressure in the back?"

"Yes, yes."

Hannah continued to rub the spot above the crack in the buttocks, which often ached when a baby had not rotated to an anterior presentation. After Mrs. Tartaglia had begun to relax, Hannah said matter-of-factly, "So, you should be an expert by now. This is your fifth baby, isn't it?"

"No, my sixth."

Hannah waited.

"One died."

"At what age?"

"Two months. He was my first."

That theory was shot. After four more healthy babies, she should not be so tense. Hannah tried again. "All the others are living."

"Yes, thanks to Jesus, Mary, and Joseph."

Sometimes it helped to divert someone by having her tell about her family, so Hannah asked, "What are their names?"

"Claudia, Antonia, Cecilia, and Oriana."

"What a nice family," she responded mechanically, then absorbed what she had been told. These were all girls. The one who died, the firstborn, had been the only son. Tartaglia. The family was Italian. "You want another boy." It was a statement, not a question.

"I must have a boy!" Mrs. Tartaglia cried imploringly. "You can't imagine what will happen if I don't!" A wave of pain rolled through the woman, and she thrashed forward on the bed so violently Hannah held onto her so she would not fling herself to the floor.

Norma Marshanck rushed over and assisted Hannah in rolling the trembling woman onto her back. "Is she seizing?" Norma asked with alarm.

"No, no," Hannah said, efficiently tucking the covers and organizing the pillows.

Midwife Marshanck felt the woman's abdomen with her fingertips. "That's more like it. That's what will bring this baby along."

"Why don't you examine her?" Hannah asked. "I could stand by to assist you if she gets too upset." Hannah need not have been so courteous with Norma, who was much too practical to worry about the niceties that some other midwives fussed about, but she did prefer to consult rather than criticize.

"Nine," Midwife Marshanck crowed. "You're almost there, Anna-Maria." She patted her patient. Mrs. Tartaglia's gaunt, determined face did not relax at the news.

"How's the presentation?" Hannah asked.

"Still posterior, but the pelvis is huge. I don't see any problems."

Mrs. Tartaglia was taller than Hannah had first realized because her legs had been curled around her belly. Now stretched out, she seemed skinny except for the huge mound of her overripe belly. Nevertheless, the tall ones often had big bones, and anyone who had given birth to five babies already was hardly at risk for a tight fit.

"I'll send in one of the senior students, probably Lenore or Alice, and I'll be in Ward D if you need me."

"Fine," Norma Marshanck mumbled as she made a notation on Bed Three's chart.

Hannah hurried to the door, then turned quickly. Mrs. Tartaglia's long, pallid face puckered in a frown. Her cheeks reddened with the force of the latest contraction, and she cried out. "Good," Hannah murmured. At least she was making progress. As Hannah hurried across the hall, she made a mental note to inquire whether Mrs. Tartaglia had given birth to a son.

 **2**

Hesitating in the corridor, Hannah glanced to her left and right. Now everything was humming along. Only a few people were making purposeful strides in the hall. The sounds from the wards were the familiar ones of labor with no extraneous chatter or hysterical shrieks. Why did it always take the first few hours to settle everyone down? she wondered idly. What changes might be made during the night shift to effect a more graceful transition?

At the approach of Mrs. Hemming, the midwifery supervisor, Hannah's moment of self-satisfaction was curtailed swiftly. Three years earlier, this compact woman with a military bearing had objected to Hannah's appointment as head midwife, asserting that not only had Mrs. Sokolow been in charge of her shift for less than a year after completing training to renew her midwifery license in New York, but also her command of written English was not up to the hospital's standards.

"Let us not confuse secretarial with case-management skills," Mrs. Giles, director of the Committee on Maternity Affairs for the Board of Managers had stated. "The most competent technicians should have responsibility over the patients, and Mrs. Sokolow is the best clinician we have to offer."

No other midwife had the depth of training Hannah had

received at Moscow's Imperial College and Lying-In Hospital, or the breadth of experience acquired by delivering babies alongside the community midwife, Bubbe Schtern, in Odessa, yet Hannah had suspected that no matter her excuses, Mrs. Hemming objected to having an immigrant Jewish woman in a managerial position, especially one who did not have an impeccable command of the English language.

"Good morning, Mrs. Sokolow," Mrs. Hemming began. She had an unnerving manner of being able to speak without hardly moving her lips. She tapped a sheaf of folders. "The end-of-the-month reports."

Hannah's heart skipped a beat: hers were incomplete. "I'll have mine to you tomorrow . . . if the expectant ladies cooperate." She forced a little laugh.

"See that you do, because I wouldn't want to explain to the board why you were delinquent again," Mrs. Hemming said. Abruptly she turned back in the direction she had been headed.

As Hannah listened to the clipped tattoo of her heels walking away, she determined to tackle the records at the first possible moment, but one glance around Miss Wylie's hectic ward frustrated her resolve. Quietly she stood to one side while supervising a major perineal repair. "Nicely done," she complimented as Miss Wylie washed up. "Why don't you show me what we've got here and let me know where I can assist you."

Dorothea Wylie lowered her gaze. "Well . . ." Her large brown eyes widened as she turned in the direction of Bed Twelve. "I had to leave her to attend to this birth, but she came in bleeding."

"How much?" Hannah asked with some urgency.

"More than spotting, less than gushing, so I knew there would be time for a more complete evaluation . . ." Her insecurity caused her voice to thin as it trailed off.

Without comment Hannah went to the woman's bedside, but stepped back to allow Miss Wylie to continue to handle the case. "How are the pains, Mrs. Kovacs?" Dorothea asked.

The woman replied in monosyllables. The recently certified midwife removed the drape entirely and checked not only the pad but the sheet. Then Hannah followed Miss Wylie to the midwives' desk in the center of the room.

"After my initial examination, I didn't confirm a placenta

previa, but now ..." Hannah waited. The young woman would never learn to trust herself if she jumped in too quickly. "Frankly, I'm worried," Dorothea said more firmly. "The placenta may be beginning to separate."

"How do you wish to proceed?"

"I could call for a consulting doctor, but if she could be monitored more closely, I'd feel comfortable waiting."

"What would you like?"

"Pulse every five to ten minutes, fetal heart every ten to fifteen minutes, blood pressure every fifteen minutes, a watch on her fluids, and, ah, of course, the usual pad check."

"Certainly, Miss Wylie," Hannah said, grinning. "I think I can manage that."

While Dorothea returned to a woman who had entered the pushing stage, Hannah remained with Mrs. Kovacs. The second time she checked, it seemed the blood flow had increased slightly. Hannah changed the pad and saved the old one for comparison. She noted the time: 10:44. She would check again in ten minutes. While waiting, she allowed her fingers to hover lightly across the patient's abdomen during an intense contraction. Immediately after it was over, she checked for bleeding and noticed a worrisome fresh spurt. Now a placenta previa—a potentially hazardous condition in which the internal uterine os is totally or partially covered by the placenta—seemed the most likely explanation. The time had come to make some decisions. Just as she tried to catch Miss Wylie's attention, however, a howl, like an animal suddenly caught in a trap, erupted from Bed Two. "Get it out! Out! Ow! Ow!" As if summoned by a buzzer, a circulating nurse came in to assist Hannah was turning back to monitor the bleeder when a crash startled her. The patient in Bed One had fallen.

"Oder gor, oder gornit!" Hannah whispered in Yiddish. It was one of her favorite phrases, as a mother as well as a midwife, because it meant: all or nothing at all. Either it was too quiet or too crazy. Reluctantly leaving Mrs. Kovacs, she confirmed that there were no serious injuries to either the mother or her fetus before tucking the hysterical woman tightly into bed. Without further consideration of who should handle the complicated case, she announced her decision to Miss Wylie, who was gently massaging the last bit of cervix over the scalp of an almost born baby. "Mrs. Kovacs is di-

lating nicely, but if we are to prevent surgery, I must manage the case more aggressively."

"Yes, please do," Miss Wylie agreed just as a slick orb of cranium plopped into her waiting hands.

Immediately Hannah made the preparations to puncture Mrs. Kovac's membranes and proceed with a complex procedure. A midwife at Miss Wylie's level would have called for a physician, but Hannah abhorred the alternatives they would employ. The older ones would recommend rapid stretching with a Bossi dilator, but she had once seen someone bleed to death from the lacerations it inflicted. The younger surgeons would insist on a cesarean section. While this might produce a safe outcome for the infant, infection and other complications often compromised the mother's life. Hannah had confidence that this was an excellent case for a less invasive technique, if only Mrs. Kovacs would cooperate.

She bent over the woman and spoke in a calm yet adamant tone. "I must make you more uncomfortable for a short while, but it is an absolute necessity to prevent injury to you or the child. Do you understand?"

"Yes. Do what you must."

Heartened by the resolve in her patient's clenched jaw, Hannah placed a colpeurynter in the uterus and filled it with sterile water. Then, after making a Spanish windlass from an abdominal binder twisted tight with a tourniquet handle, she tamponed the vagina with cotton, and bound the abdomen with as much counterpressure as the patient could tolerate. This procedure to stanch bleeding required her full attention, so she did not notice two people standing in the doorway. One was Dr. Dowd, a fine gynecological surgeon, the other was Mrs. Hemming. They were whispering to each other.

Hannah concentrated on her patient. Almost as if she sensed the urgency, Mrs. Kovacs allowed the contractions to ripple through her at a rapid pace. Hannah patted her and rubbed her back. "Yes, you're doing nicely . . . better than expected . . . that's it . . . you're very brave . . . not too long now . . ." she said soothingly.

When one of Dorothea Wylie's ladies let out a yelp, Mrs. Kovacs grinned at Hannah conspiratorially, as though they were handling matters in a far superior fashion. This union, formed with a patient after only a short while in labor, was one reason Hannah enjoyed her profession. Underlying this camaraderie, however, was a deep concern for the welfare of this trusting woman. Had she made the right decision? She inspected the pads. The bleeding had almost ceased entirely. She checked her progress. The mother was ready to push! Looking over her shoulder, she saw the doctor had departed. He was probably nearby, waiting for her summons, but now she was certain that would not be necessary.

The circle of head that appeared with each downward compression widened from the size of a quarter to that of a soup bowl. The furrowed forehead emerged and then the head turned to reveal once again the miraculous form of a human face. Hannah's heart quickened, as it always did when a new person entered this world. Blue and still one second, he was stimulated by the cold air and bright light. A quiver started at the base of his spine. His eyes clenched tighter. And then, as if on cue, his lungs filled, his mouth opened, and he made his presence known.

"A boy!" Hannah chimed as she handed the squirming newborn up to the mother, who clasped his slippery body with trembling hands.

"He's a good one?" Mrs. Kovacs asked, tears streaming down her face.

"Yes, a good one, a very good one," Hannah said, wiping the tears from her own without shame. "How many is this?"

"Five, five boys!"

"You're a lucky woman," Hannah said, then was reminded of the Italian lady in Ward E. Funny how some have all boys, others all girls, she mused. I wonder if the other lady got what she wanted.

"I didn't know anyone was still using the Spanish windlass." The voice that interrupted her meditation was that of Dr. Dowd.

"I wouldn't recommend it for everyone, but this was a textbook case," Hannah replied without looking up as she tidied up the delivery area.

"Not the beginner's manual," Midwife Wylie replied. "I'll finish up here," she offered deferentially.

"A good outcome for mother and child, that's what counts," Hannah commented evenly.

"Not always the case, unfortunately . . ." Mrs. Hemming's words trailed off with a hint of a warning and she pursed her lips as though tasting something sour.

"Even after more than a thousand, I'm always ready for a surprise." Avoiding her supervisor, Hannah spoke those words in the doctor's direction.

"Indeed. That is why obstetrics never bores me," he replied.

"Nor me," Dorothea added, beaming. "I only hope it's the same when I'm your age."

As Mrs. Hemming gave a perfunctory nod and headed in the opposite direction, the doctor and Hannah laughed in unison. "I am sure you will." Hannah managed to restrain her urge to add that thirty was hardly as ancient as the girl intimated. "If you have any other complications, I'll be in Ward E."

The doctor followed her out into the corridor. "My students could learn some surgical alternatives from you, Mrs. Sokolow," he complimented, then his tone sobered. "It would have been a tragedy to leave five boys behind, when there are advanced techniques that can save lives in cases when the most noble attempts fail."

Before Hannah could frame a reply, he had hurried off. At least he didn't say it in front of Mrs. Hemming, she thought gratefully, then muttered, "Oder gor, oder gornit."

3

Taking a moment for herself, Hannah ducked into the midwives' changing room, really no more than a closet with a bed, chair, and shelf space for personal articles. Behind a curtain there was also a private toilet and a small sink. Hannah ran cold water across her wrists, a trick that always revived her, then scrubbed her face, and rinsed her mouth. From her section of the shelf she took a tortoise comb and tidied her hair. Thirty! She leaned closer to the mirror, its silver dim with age, and scrutinized her image. Was she deceiving herself or did she really look at least five years younger than Norma Marshanck, who already had gray hair around her temples? Her figure was far trimmer—at least that was for certain—and it even eclipsed many of the younger students', who had neither her high, round bosom nor her sleek waistline. Except for a slight sagging under her vivacious green eyes, her face remained unlined. And even these pouches smoothed after a long sleep, but these days that was a rare luxury.

Thinking about a long morning in bed with Lazar, her heart gave an involuntary lurch. At the cafés her husband frequented daily he beheld the bright, earnest faces of young women—who probably hung on to his every word—and he must have found some more appealing than his wife of eight years. Yet he was still interested in her. Why even last night—

Giggling in the hall startled Hannah. She tightened the combs that held her hair taut so no loose strands would annoy the likes of Mrs. Hemming, then tucked in her shirtwaist, and retied her apron securely. When she opened the door, the nearby nurses scattered. Showing no concern, Hannah headed for Ward E.

Norma Marshanck was sitting with her feet up on a footstool, her eyes closed. At Hannah's step she turned slowly. "You were right," she said at once. "Bed Six was about to gush, but I was ready. I made her take a dram of fluidextract of ergot within a few seconds of the placenta and kept up a brisk uterine massage until the uterus firmed up. Otherwise everything was routine."

"What about the Italian lady?"

"She went to postpartum hours ago."

"Good work. If you need me, that's where I'll be."

The sun had long ago passed from the east side of the building, but reflections off the river mirrored a delicate flicker from the lofty windows onto the plastered walls of the ward facing the broad East River, where the beds were lined up in parallel rows of twenty. Beside each mother's mattress was a smaller iron cot for the newborn. This was the time of day visitors were permitted, and by many beds were the silhouettes of fathers or other relatives bending over a baby's basket. Considering that more than thirty women and newborns were present, the hall was unusually tranquil. Sensing the hushed mood in the ward, people whispered in a polyglot of languages: Russian, Yiddish, German, Italian, Polish, Armenian, Serbo-Croatian, Hungarian, Czech, as well as a variety of American twangs. After the din in the labor rooms over the last few hours, Hannah drank in the orderliness.

If it hadn't been so quiet, Hannah might not have heard the slap. Or if she had, she might not have known what the brief crack had meant. As it was, she heard it—and saw it.

Out of the corner of her eye she had observed the man and thought him just another father bending over to examine his child. She had watched him raise the folds of the blanket, the flannel corner lit from behind by the glow of a lamp. The gash of light on the father's face had illuminated a dark arch of thick eyebrow, wavy black hair, and thick lips that dominated a receding chin. He had made a peculiar grunt, which Hannah, in her innocence, had taken for satisfaction with his latest child.

Then the woman had leaned forward as if to take the child from the man, but the man had not lifted the infant, though the hands had advanced toward its crib. Now the mother's ivory face was bathed in the same subtle sheen. Hannah recognized the angular profile of Mrs. Tartaglia, who seemed hardly more relaxed than she had been in the throes of labor. In an instant Hannah sensed something was wrong, yet could never have predicted that the muscular arms approaching the frail woman were about to strike her. But they did.

First the right palm slapped her cheek, then the left fist pummeled the side of her deflected head. The crack and subsequent pop echoed through the room, propelling the dormant scene into a frenzy of recoils and gasps. Since Hannah was the closest staff member, she rushed to the bedside and placed herself squarely between the man and his wife.

"What is the meaning of this?" Hannah bellowed.

"She is my wife," Tartaglia replied flatly, then grunted again.

Hannah swiveled to see Mrs. Tartaglia hunched over and holding the left side of her face. A nurse ran forward with a wet compress.

"This is outrageous!" Hannah continued harshly. "What sort of man strikes his wife, let alone one who has just delivered him a fine—?" she stumbled, then made a profound mistake. Knowing of the family's wish for a boy, she assumed the next would be a male. "—healthy boy."

She realized her error as soon as she saw his pig eyes squint. His lips curled nastily. "All Anna-Maria can produce

is worthless girls!" He spat the words so forcefully he
sprayed Hannah's face.

She backed away, realizing there was no use talking to
this barbarian. "Get out of my ward! And don't you dare return until it is time for Mrs. Tartaglia to be released."

"Please . . ." she heard from the bed, "he'll be fine. It's
just a shock . . ."

Hannah ignored the woman's pathetic plea. Her hand
pointed toward the archway. Mr. Tartaglia grunted, then
turned without a word.

"Giovanni!" his wife cried.

As if on cue, their infant shrieked a long wail. Hannah
lifted the child, who pinked from her toes to brow with the
exertion of filling her lungs. She was a hefty newborn with
a perfectly formed head covered with shiny black hair that
was long enough to conceal the nape of her neck. A perfect
child. Only a few temporary marks around her eyes—
commonly called stork bites— marred her delicate face. How
could anyone spurn such a blessing?

The midwife handed the baby to the mother, half thinking
she also would reject her. But Mrs. Tartaglia clutched the
child and finally hushed it by offering one of her large
brown nipples. When the baby was sucking rhythmically,
she leaned back and sighed. An angry welt, almost a match
of a handprint, marked her cheek, and a lump was forming
on her opposite temple.

A nurse brought an ice pack, which Hannah held to the
left side, and when that area became too chilled, switched it
to the other. The tension in the ward had not decreased.
More babies cried, many mothers squirmed under their covers, and most visitors were saying farewells and departing.
Even the pace of the nurses had picked up. It was as if the
earlier scene had been a photograph of flawless serenity
slashed by the furious father.

Hannah was amazed at how rapidly the flesh under the
compress was swelling. A lump the size of an egg had
popped out above Anna-Maria's right ear, and yet she had
not uttered one word of protest.

"What is . . . your name?" she asked softly.

"Midwife Sokolow."

"I meant your Christian name," she said apologetically.

Hannah masked her offense. "My first name is Hannah."

"Hannah," Anna-Maria repeated. "That's what I'll call her." She touched the baby's hand. "Hannah Tartaglia."

Hannah forced herself not to wince. To have her name linked to that monster was an insult, but what could she say? Besides, there were so many Hannahs named after her—because the mothers had planned on having a boy—that she had ceased to find the idea flattering. However, in this case it was worse: a throwaway name for an unwanted infant.

Anna-Maria looked at her for a response, and out of pity Hannah forced herself to say, "I am glad you find my name pleasing." She put down the compress. The swelling seemed to have reached its maximum size, and she needed to tend to others. "Keep this on the bruises as much as you can. I'll be back after my rounds."

In the postpartum ward there were a puerperal infection, a breast abscess, two post-hemmorhage patients to manage. The next time she passed by Mrs. Tartaglia's bed, Hannah had her coat on to leave. Thankfully, the woman was asleep.

4

Tompkins Square was covered with a patina of powdery snow. In the golden glow of the gaslights the shimmering park seemed an oasis of calm. Though pushcarts, pedestrians, horses, even a few automobiles had pulverized the surrounding sidewalks and streets into a muddy slick, not a single person walked the park's freshly dusted paths. This neighborhood was not nearly as fine as her sister Eva's or even as pleasant as the area around the university, where the Sokolows had lived for several years, but it was close to Bellevue and certainly an improvement over the filthy East Side tenements they had been crammed into as immigrants fresh off the boat.

After crossing through the sludge at the curb at Avenue B, Hannah hesitantly picked her way through the forming crusts along 7th Street. Simultaneously she saw both that a lamp was shining in Mama's parlor and that her rooms on the top floor were dark. Lazar, who taught German at New

York University, had a class that night, so he would have sent the children to have supper with Mama. Hannah instantly regretted staying late on her shift. Now she would have to listen to her mother chiding, "You know I never mind having the children, but I would prefer to have some notice." And later, when Lazar came home, he would let her know that before he left for work he had been lectured about something that they were not doing right with the children. "You promised, Hannah, to be the go-between with your mother." Also Benny and Emma might start in about how the other mothers were always home after school . . . Hannah sighed as she prepared to meet the onslaught.

"What happened to you?" were her mother's first words.

She shrugged at this burst of Yiddish. Her mother spoke not a word of English, and sometimes Hannah wished she would at least try for the sake of her grandchildren.

"Ma!" Emma shouted gaily from the sofa, where she had been working on her stitchery. Hannah went directly to her daughter and gathered her in her arms. A whiff of her sweet hair and the child's rewarding hug made her heavy heart soar.

She touched the child's forehead with her lips. Cool and dry. Good. She had recovered. "Where's your brother?"

"On the pot," she grinned.

Her grandmother glared at the child's crudeness, then asked Hannah pointedly, "Another emergency, I suppose?"

"Something terrible happened," she began slowly, then flinched as Mr. Tartaglia's slap reverberated in her mind.

Mama Blau's eyes widened with both shock and curiosity. *"Nu?* What was it?" She placed her plump hands akimbo on her rotund hips and leaned forward. "Nobody we know, I hope."

Hannah briefly related the attack.

"Who hit who?" asked seven-year-old Benny as he entered the room.

"Who hit whom?" his sister, who at five thought she knew everything, corrected.

Benny made a fist, but one look at his mother's face caused him to withdraw it behind his back.

"Have you eaten?" was Mama Blau's initial response to the tale.

Hannah bristled at her mother's lack of empathy. "That man, that brute, walked into my ward and hit one of my patients. And for what? Because she had not delivered him a male child!"

"This was why you could not be home to feed your family? I would have thought someone was dying."

Hannah welled with resentment at being cornered the moment she returned home, but she checked herself from saying anything.

"There's borscht with a potato and—"

"Thank you, Mama," Hannah said grimly as she made her way into the kitchen to fix herself a bowl. She felt the pot: it was still warm. She found the ladle and served herself.

Her mother bustled into the room, not done with her yet. "What?" Her eyes, the color of burnished steel, were sharp with criticism. "You're going to eat it cold?"

"It's fine, Mama."

"You take care of the whole world but forget you have to take care of yourself . . . and your family." She said the last in a harsh whisper that pretended to be private but could easily be heard by the children.

"I know," Hannah admitted. She eyed her mother for a moment, then decided not to start a fight. Without her mother's help with the children, she did not know how she could maintain her position at the hospital. A professor's salary was barely enough, and for some reason the university had cut back Lazar's classes this semester.

Her mother also realized she had pressed too hard. She cut Hannah a thick slice of bread, buttered it, and set it on the table before pulling up a seat. "Hannahleh," she began in a voice so soothing her daughter was disarmed, "just because you hold a new life in your hands every day does not mean you can change the world, nor should you try. Besides, '*A patsh fargayt, a vort bashtayt.*' " The smart of a blow subsides, the sting of a word abides.

The retort that leapt to mind at the Yiddish saying was something about how her mother's words often stung, but fortunately Hannah was too busy chewing her potato.

Mama sat across the table, stirring her tea. "Did I tell you Eva's news?"

Hannah shook her head.

"She's buying another whole suite of furniture for their new apartment and going to give me what I want for here."

"That's nice, Mama. But I thought you didn't like fringes and tassels."

"I could make do, or even change the trimming. The color is fine. That Napthali"—she beamed at her son-in-law's name—"every year he is doing better and better. He's not satisfied with second best. What a *mentsh!*"

Hannah was irked by this unspoken comparison with her own husband, but she could not deny that from the moment Napthali Margolis had passed through Ellis Island's portals, he had been the most single-minded of men. If America was the Golden Land, then he was going to amass his portion of the bounty. He had come alone, with no family to fetter him. His fiancée was to follow later, when he could set her up in style. As a laborer on the railroads and then in the oil fields, he worked extra shifts and starved himself to save every penny. With his first stake he leased an entire tenement building on the Lower East Side, then rented out the rooms to itinerants by the week because that way he could get the most money per square foot. Later he was able to arrange to purchase that building and lease another. Within five years he had a dozen buildings to his name.

Hannah let her mother prattle on about Eva's redecorating plans while she finished her soup. She had not even seen her youngest sister's latest residence, but was now treated to a room-by-room inventory. After they had lived in larger and larger apartments on the Lower East Side, the Margolises had moved first to West End Avenue, and now were in a huge apartment on Riverside Drive. Even so, most of their holdings were in the old neighborhood. And one of them was the Tompkins Square building where Hannah and Lazar resided.

Hannah took her dishes into the kitchen and looked around. This flat was Mama's idea of heaven. The kitchen was a bright yellow with a white gas range, a large round table, and an ice box. Eva had given her their first three-piece parlor suite in leaf green plush, and she had her own bedroom with a double iron bedstead. Then, when Hannah had decided life would be easier if she were nearer to Bellevue and Lazar closer to the Lower East Side cafés, Napthali had offered them the third-floor front at a reduced rent. At first he had suggested Lazar collect the rents, but Hannah knew what her husband would say. Landlords were the object of many of his political tirades. After all, he had been a revolutionary in Russia before they emigrated. At first Hannah assumed she would collect the rents, but then Mama had volunteered. She prided herself on being self-sufficient. For extra money she still took in piecework from a garter factory.

"It will get me out, give me something to do," she had insisted.

Hannah had agreed, for it was much more difficult for a tenant to turn down a little old lady's polite request. Also, it made her mother feel as if she were earning her keep, since Napthali had given his mother-in-law the apartment rent-free.

There was a knock on the door. Hannah wiped her hands on the dish towel and started out.

Benny got there first. "Pa! You're home early."

"Class was cancelled. The trolleys weren't running. Frozen lines or something."

Hannah looked up and smiled at her husband, who grinned back at her. Even after eight years of marriage, their daily reunions brought a moment of contentment. In his wide eyes and strong jaw she still saw hints of the dashing yeshiva student who had covertly flirted with her.

"Tell Pa what happened!" her son coaxed.

Hannah recounted the story, and her mother filled in as her daughter skimmed over some details.

"Don't you think he must have been the most horrid man?" Emma exclaimed to get a word in.

A bit annoyed at the interruptions, Hannah went on, "If that is the way he behaves in a public place, can you imagine how he terrorizes her in private?"

"Who's going to police her parlor?" Lazar asked somberly.

"I admit there's nothing we can do," Hannah said, deflating from her outburst. "The marriage license gives him all the rights."

"To think freely, a woman would first have to be free." Lazar's gaze was filled with resolve. "The whole concept of marriage was based on the laws of private property, with the woman as the property. This one is but one sad example of the unfair bargain in which a woman gains a measure of economic security, while a man purchases himself a domestic, a sexual object, a breeder."

Hannah shook her head in agreement. Her husband had a singular way of distilling an issue to its essence. As she watched him standing there in the lamplight, she was drawn to his broad shoulders and slender flanks. She reached out for him and he took her hand.

Warming to her reaction, he went on, "Your Italian gentleman sees himself as merely prodding his chattel to perform her duty of providing him with a son and heir, but he is too ignorant to realize she cannot control the result." His sky blue eyes flickered with his zeal and Hannah noticed the others were all gazing at him. Here was the Lazar she adored: the champion of the oppressed. While many radicals worried about the workers, they were ignoring the plight of women. Not Lazar. "In recent years women have banded together to unravel these issues, but they'll hardly be solved soon enough for your poor patient."

"I wish more men . . ."

"How true," Lazar affirmed.

The two knew each other so well they did not have to finish their thoughts.

Hannah sighed deeply. "If more people would avoid petty quarrels and unite together in a common purpose, everyone would be more content."

Lazar nodded and for a long moment the world of the Tartaglias and Bellevue, the unfinished paperwork, even her mother's scolding faded away.

❧ 5 ❧

Within a few days, word of Giovanni Tartaglia's attack on his wife spread through the hospital. Some were disappointed that Hannah had barred him, for they were curious to see the brute in person. Mrs. Hemming had asked for an explanation of the unusual chart notation, but accepted Hannah's justification.

"By the way, I want you to know I appreciate having your folder in more promptly this time," she said with the faintest hint of a smile, although her voice remained accusatory.

"That's why I came in early this morning to make certain the records were updated by the midwives. They don't al-

ways give me what I need on time either." Now she returned
the taut grin.

"Yes, well . . ." Mrs. Hemming paused to give an apologetic shrug. "I hesitate to ask you this favor, but with some
of the trolleys being out, two midwives won't be able to
make the night shift. Will it be a problem for you to stay
on?"

Hannah almost laughed aloud. This was the last Friday
night of the month, the one day Mama's entire family had
supper together. Not only that, this particular Friday was the
day before her mother's birthday and this was to be her celebration. "It's impossible for me," she stated flatly.

"A supervisor, who has perspective on the problem, is expected to rise above petty inconveniences." Mrs. Hemming
folded her muscular arms across her chest and waited.

Hannah had to swallow to control her inflection. "I don't
consider my children 'inconveniences,' " she said, slightly
altering the circumstances since Mrs. Hemming would
hardly be sympathetic to the dilemmas a family reunion
could pose. "Of course, in a true emergency, I would make
the sacrifices," she hurried to add so she would not seem obstinate.

"I would hope so."

"In any case, I'll see if anyone can rearrange her schedule."

"If not?" Mrs. Hemming asked in a challenging tone.

"Then I shall do my duty," Hannah answered, returning
the woman's unwavering stare.

After Sarah Brink and Norma Marshanck volunteered to
work that evening in exchange for three days off in a row,
Hannah was asked to approve someone in the postpartum
ward who had requested an early discharge. A routine maternity stay was ten days, but some were anxious to return
home. To rule out infections as well as to give detailed instructions for both mother and child, the head midwife on
the day shift was required to sign an early discharge form.

When Hannah picked up the chart and read Tartaglia, she
almost dropped it. She wanted to return to her husband
early? Why, to further safeguard her, Hannah had put her
down for a few extra days, using as an excuse the woman's
profuse vaginal discharge. "Did she say why she wanted to
leave?" Hannah asked.

"She mentioned other children at home."

"She should rest."

"You can tell her that."

With some reluctance Hannah went to confront Mrs. Tartaglia. "I do think you could use a few more days of solitude," she began.

"No, it will be worse for me if I stay."

For a moment Hannah wondered exactly what she meant, then realized she did not want to ponder Mr. Tartaglia's retribution. In fact, Hannah's reaction to his blows may have incited him further, and his wife might be victimized more because of it. "All right, but you are to keep off your feet as much as possible."

Anna-Maria laughed heartily, and as she did so her face reddened, revealing the traces of the discoloration from her bruise. "Don't you understand what it's like with children?"

"Yes, that's why I wanted you to rest longer. Is there anyone to help you?"

"Oh yeah, Giovanni's mother will be cooking, but she leaves the kids to me, and the girls will be all over me anyhow."

Hannah nodded emphatically. "Just try."

She went on with her instructions for bathing and umbilical cord care, but before she finished her usual list, Anna-Maria tugged her arm. "Tell me the secret. I must know!"

Hannah was surprised by the urgency in her voice. She also didn't understand the question. "Know what?"

"How to have a boy next time. Giovanni will kill me if I don't."

With anyone else Hannah would have thought the woman was exaggerating, but now she was instantly contrite. "Nobody knows why, but some people have more boys, others more girls. Anyway, it all evens out in the end."

"That's not true!" Anna-Maria cried vehemently. "You Jews just want to keep the answer to yourselves!" Inexplicably her anger turned to tears. She wept for a few minutes before turning back to Hannah accusingly. "Why won't you tell me? What would it hurt for me to know?"

Hannah sat on the bed and took her hand. "I can't help you. If I could, I would." She saw that the woman was not appeased. "There are ways to prevent having another. I could assist you there," she muttered under her breath, thinking this might have been where the conversation was leading the whole time.

"I could never do that!" Anna-Maria said righteously. "Neither would any of the Jewish ladies in my neighborhood. But they always have boys."

"That's not true. Look at me," Hannah added with a tinge of amusement. "I was a girl, at least the last time I looked."

Mrs. Tartaglia's mouth did not soften. "Of course you people have girls now and then to keep your numbers growing, but I have counted. There are three or four boys to every girl."

At last Hannah realized the woman was deluded. There was no reason to continue, so she folded the baby's linen and waved for a nurse to take over..

The balance of the day was without incident. Hannah did not deliver a single patient, but coached an awkward student through several, pleased that the young midwife's hands had finally begun to remember where they needed to be to manipulate the baby's head, shoulders, and torso for maximum effect during each phase of the birth process. After Hannah was convinced of the trainee's competence, she backed out of the room to permit her to manage an uncomplicated delivery without an overseer. Because everything was running so smoothly, she even managed to sneak away from the hospital earlier than usual.

✆ 6 ✆

Her good humor was buoyed further when the trolley arrived only seconds after she reached the corner, preventing a long wait in the brisk wind. Beating the rush meant she had a seat, which she sank into gratefully. The promise of a quiet weekend at home was a welcome prospect. She needed some time to draw Lazar out. While he had been warm and affectionate on the surface, she had sensed some distance from what he was thinking. Since it always took time to extract his true feelings, and since their time together was usually limited, Hannah looked forward to a long chat that might begin with inconsequential matters, yet might lead to what was troubling him.

Of course the children would come first, as always. Emma wanted to make a skirt, a project that she could tackle only with her mother's assistance. Benny had said something about skating in a flooded area of the park if it was cold enough. If it wasn't, she would play checkers with him. He always won, even when she tried her hardest, but she enjoyed being beaten by her son, if only to appreciate the acuity of his mind, which—in games at least—was always a step ahead of hers.

In an energetic mood Hannah hurried down First Avenue, making a few last-minute purchases for supper. In the waning sunlight the scene of merchants closing their stalls and mothers calling their children seemed infused with a familiar warmth. Against the grayness of the slushy streets and tenement buildings, the ruddy faces and gaily colored scarves and mittens brightened what some would have thought were dreary surroundings. Many of these residents were Jews who continued to celebrate the Sabbath by attending the synagogue and having a ritual meal. A devout socialist, Lazar had rejected much of this as religious nonsense, but her mother honored the old traditions, as did her sister. Her brother, Chaim, and his wife, Minna, were even more radical than they were, but at least they respected Mama's wishes, and once a month went along with the simple observance for her sake. By arriving just after the candle lighting and blessings but before the meal, Lazar managed to satisfy his conscience and maintain peace with the family.

Feeling contrite about her recent disagreements with her mother, Hannah was determined that this party in her honor would be one way of making amends. When she entered the front hall, she noticed the door to Mama's apartment was closed. Good, she thought. Nobody else was here yet. They would congregate downstairs later, with each daughter bringing food.

Of course, Minna wasn't asked for a donation, Hannah thought darkly as she climbed the stairs. Chaim and his wife lived behind a printing press, where they worked for its owner. With only a single burner and not even an oven, how they survived was a constant source of concern between Mama and Eva. Even Hannah had been known to cluck her tongue over Minna's total disdain for making a home, but Chaim did not seem to mind, and Lazar told Hannah it was none of her business. "Still," Hannah murmured as she reached the third-floor landing, "it's fine for Minna to be so committed to her causes, but I end up doing the cooking."

Hannah called a greeting to her family while going directly into the kitchen to start her contribution for the meal.

"You're early, Ma," Benny said, pecking her cheek.

"I slipped out while nobody was looking. Don't tell on me," she responded in a mock whisper.

"You went in early, remember?" Lazar muttered as he came out of the bedroom. "They don't own you body and soul."

"Of course they don't, darling," Hannah replied sweetly.

Lazar opened his mouth to say something, but settled on an expellation of air and a shrug of his shoulders.

"Where's Emma?"

"Taking a bath," Benny replied.

"At this time of day? I need her to help me." Hannah's voice rose in a tense pitch, then it was her turn for an exasperated sigh. Furiously she began to peel the potatoes.

Benny and Lazar decided it best to leave the room. "I'll get dressed, all right, Ma?"

"Sure, sure." She watched Lazar move toward his favorite chair and was about to say something about changing from his stained slacks, but decided not to badger him.

For a moment she surveyed the scene, welcoming its peace. The two-bedroom apartment was less than half the size of the one her sister Eva had just given up as too small, but it was more than most had. The children shared the larger of the two bedrooms, with a curtain between the beds, because Emma was beginning to demand more privacy from her elder brother. The bath had a separate heating pipe which, when the door was closed and the hot water turned on, made it the warmest room in the house. The parlor was small, with the dining table in the center, but the four of them had plenty of space—or would have had if she could ever get Lazar or her children to put away their books and papers promptly. Mama had a larger, more up-to-date kitchen, thanks to Napthali, but hers was fine for what they needed, and someday they would replace the chipped sink, get an icebox with two shelves, maybe even a larger stove. "But with our money," she reflected, "not Eva's."

As she began to grate the potatoes for the pancakes, she planned the rest of the menu. Eva would be bringing the meat dish, probably a brisket she'd cooked the night before,

as well as her usual rhubarb pie. Hannah had already made
the soup stock and there was plenty of applesauce, plus the
bread and macaroon cookies she'd picked up from
Liebovitz's stall. All she had to do was boil the carrots for
the soup and heat it downstairs at the last minute. As soon
as the last potato was shredded, she felt the meal was under
control.

Lazar strode into the kitchen, took the heel of the bread,
and began to chew on it. "Can't you wait?" she asked good-
naturedly. "You're as bad as Benny."

"I'm not going downstairs tonight."

"What?"

"You can go without me."

"Lazar! It's Friday night and Mama's birthday."

"You know I can't tolerate Napthali."

"He's been good to us. The least you could do is—"

"I won't go," Lazar said stubbornly, and stomped out of
the kitchen.

What's eating him? she wondered. Most evenings he was
filled with stories or interesting asides on the issues of the
day. When he snapped at her and she had done nothing to
provoke him, it was often because he was worried about
something. What was it now? If there had been time, she
would have sat next to him, held his hand. Hannah kept
molding the pancakes, though, for they had to be fried
quickly before the potatoes discolored.

"You don't have to come down until the meal starts. Eva
and I will have some cooking to do beforehand. The children
can help me and you can join us at the last minute." She refrained from tagging on "as usual." Hannah was accustomed
to making excuses for her husband; her family was accustomed to his moods. Napthali was particularly forgiving.
Why not? she asked herself irritably. He could afford to be.

While she was cutting the carrots, she thought to bring
one out to her husband to munch on. "I forgot how badly it
went last month," she commented, probing, "and if it
weren't Mama's birthday—"

"Damn your mother's birthday!"

Hannah felt a churning in her belly. Something was very
wrong. "What is it?" she asked gently. "Are you ill?" She
touched his forehead.

He pushed her hand away. "I can't face him this month."

"Why?"

"The rent."

"The first of the month isn't until next week."

"I know!" he shouted. "I can count!"

Hannah forced herself to remain silent.

"I owe him for last month already."

"But we had the money . . ."

"I held it back."

"Why? There was plenty and—"

"I'm not teaching this semester, that's why!" he exploded. "My classes were canceled before the winter recess. I thought that after the new registrations were in, I would be called back, so I didn't want to worry you. Now it seems permanent." He gave her a challenging stare.

"You aren't teaching . . . ? But your classes? You went uptown and . . ."

"I had to finish up work at my office."

"You don't have a job?" Hannah asked tensely.

"Now you are getting the picture."

"What are we going to do?"

"Well, I'm not planning to march downstairs and announce it to your family."

The smell of burning *latkes* caused Hannah to rush back into the kitchen. Salvaging the meal occupied her mind for a few minutes. She remembered the carrots and cut them in smaller pieces so they would cook more quickly, wiped the spattered counter, tossed out the burnt pancakes, and tried to determine if she still had enough.

Satisfied she did, she began to digest the import of Lazar's news. Her husband did not have a job. Why? Didn't students study German anymore? Were there more popular professors? Lazar had a reputation for being exacting, but in the past he had been praised for the high achievements of his students. Anyway, there was a constant need for professors. Lazar could teach German at another university or at a high school, for that matter. He also was equally proficient in Russian, Hebrew, and Yiddish, though not many studied these languages. In a few weeks he could get another job. In the meantime her wages at Bellevue would keep them going.

The only problem was the rent, but Napthali would wait. This was not the first time. She understood why Lazar did not want him to know, but he would be charitable. He had been through hard times himself, and he was a member of the family.

The last of the latkes quivered as they were dropped in the fragrant oil. The aroma attracted Benny, who lifted one off the towel and popped it in his mouth. "You'll burn yourself!" Hannah chided. "I want you to carry them downstairs. Are you ready?"

Benny grinned and slipped another before accepting the platter from her. Emma came into the room.

"You take the bread and macaroons and see if you can help Aunt Eva when she arrives."

"Do you like my dress?" Emma asked.

Without looking up, Hannah said, "It's fine."

"Ma!" Emma protested.

Hannah noticed that the sash wasn't tied, did the job, and gave her daughter a loving pat on her behind to send her on her way. "I'll be down as soon as the soup is ready."

When the children had gone, she went into the darkened parlor and perched on the arm of Lazar's chair. "I had no idea you weren't working. I wish you had told me." She gulped and quickly added, "I understand why you didn't. But it's not the end of the world, there are other— "

"I don't want to talk about it."

The pot on the stove was boiling so hard, spatters of soup sizzled on the range. "I have to take the soup downstairs." She stood and gave him a pleading look. "Can't you come down for a few minutes later? I'll say you have a headache."

"That's the truth."

"So, that's even better. Come for Mama's sake, and then you can leave anytime."

He did not respond.

"Please, Lazar . . ."

"Ya, ya" was all he would mutter.

As Hannah hefted the kettle, her groan could have been taken for the result of the effort, but it was really her relief that he had agreed to come down.

Slowly, with the soup sloshing precariously, she made her way downstairs to Mama's flat, where Eva and Sophie Feigenbaum, Napthali's sister, were managing the kitchen.

"I had to rescue the latkes from the children," Eva clucked, "or there wouldn't have been any left."

"We'll hardly need them," Sophie said thoughtlessly, "since Eva brought a brisket *and* a chicken." She shot Hannah a superior look, and Hannah had a momentary urge to wring her neck.

"Don't you think that's more than we need?" Hannah asked grumpily.

"My Napthali prefers a nice piece of beef, but I know it disagrees with Murray. Why shouldn't everyone have what they want?" Eva replied in a patronizing voice.

"And where are the men?" Hannah inquired to change the subject. "I only saw Chaim with Mama."

"Murray had an emergency, frozen pipes. He should be here soon."

"Isn't Napthali coming?" Hannah wondered, for a moment wishing he would be occupied elsewhere.

"My husband had to see his manager a few houses down on this street," Eva said smugly. "He dropped me off so I could warm the roasts." She stirred Hannah's soup and tasted it. "Hot enough, but maybe more salt?" The question was rhetorical, for she spiced it to her taste without waiting for Hannah to reply.

Hannah busied herself by rinsing the soiled cutlery while Eva continued a topic she had begun earlier, a discussion of the latest movie she had seen. With her lavish hand gestures and fluttering eyes, she did a fine job of recounting the plot of *Tillie's Punctured Romance* and Hannah found herself amused. At times like these she was surprised to find that her younger sister had grown up.

While many girls are at their best before they are twenty, Eva had blossomed late. Her pregnancies had filled out her hollow cheeks and padded her once skinny figure. Her squinting eyes had been cured with spectacles that gave her a pleasant, intellectual appearance. Nobody would rave about her looks, but she made an attractive enough companion, as well as a good mother to Isabel and Doreen. Even Napthali, who easily might have dallied about, seemed content. And why shouldn't he be? Eva adored him.

Hearing someone arriving, Hannah went into the parlor, hoping that Lazar had decided to come down sooner. Her face fell when she saw Napthali and Murray. Minna was taking their coats. At least she's doing something, Hannah thought. Certainly it would be a big surprise if she ever set foot in the kitchen, if only to carry a platter or pitcher. Minna was about to take her seat on the sofa when she caught Hannah's somber glance.

"Hello, Hannah," she said brightly. "Sorry I didn't greet

you earlier, but I didn't want to upset your balance with the heavy pot."

Of course, you couldn't have helped me with it, could you? was Hannah's unspoken thought.

"How's Lazar?" Minna asked to fill the silence.

Not "Where's Lazar?" Hannah noted suspiciously. "Actually, he has a headache, but if the powders take effect, he'll be down later."

"He's been through a lot lately," Minna said with exaggerated sympathy.

"What do you mean?" Hannah challenged while steering Minna into a corner of the room where they would not be overheard.

"Woll . . ." Minna rolled her eyes upward, not sure how to proceed.

"You mean about losing his job, don't you?" Hannah coaxed.

"Yes," she said with a crooked smile of relief. "So you know."

"Of course I know! Why wouldn't I?"

"He didn't want to worry you."

Since when had Lazar started confiding in his sister-in-law before his wife? Hannah wondered. "I realize he expected that after this semester's enrollments were in they would need him, but . . ." Something in Minna's expression warned her that she did not yet have the entire story.

"It's unlikely they would have had to *double* the classes. Once they hired Rolf Hoffman to replace him, he must have known."

Who else besides Minna knew about this? Chaim? Their mother? Eva and Napthali? The waiters at Sach's café? Hannah forced herself to remain calm, thereby not revealing the extent of her ignorance. "I can't understand why they would have done that."

Minna's eyes roamed the room, looking for an excuse to escape. At last she allowed, "You should be proud of him."

"Proud? You can't eat pride."

"Nor can you teach a language without talking about the culture, the history behind the words, any more than you can ignore the political reality of the present. His stand was courageous, and the university behaved like feudal lords instead of enlightened educators in a free country."

What was Minna talking about?

"Ah, he didn't explain that part . . ." Reading her confused expression, Minna continued, "No, of course not. When it happened, he made us promise not to tell you—it was the day before Chanukah—but we told him he'd have to confess everything to you before he had to reappear in court."

Hannah blanched and her hands began to tremble. In response, Minna put her hand on Hannah's shoulder, but she jerked away from it. "He was arrested?" she choked.

"I suppose so, at least technically, but he didn't spend any time in jail," Minna said in a rush to placate her. "Chaim and I came for him."

"What did he do?"

"He stood up for what he believed. A lesser man might have ignored the students' harangue, but not Lazar!" Minna said admiringly.

"I still don't understand how the police became involved."

"I don't have the details—you'll have to ask him—but apparently some of the students started to throw books at him and he took matters into his own hands—literally. Some furniture was broken, even a few windows."

Hannah did all she could to suppress a groan. Lazar must have been giving an awfully fiery lecture if students had started tossing books at him. "What's the charge?"

"Disturbing the peace. They'll probably hold him accountable for the damage to the classroom—"

"Come to the table, everyone!" Eva called in a high, musical voice.

With a glance Hannah warned Minna to remain silent. Her sister-in-law's quick nod indicated her tacit acceptance.

In the parlor, Napthali was talking to Murray and Uriah, a cousin of Sophie Feigenbaum. "The main point to remember is that somewhere someone wants to sell even more than you want to buy." Napthali paused, letting his words sink in. "Only sell when you aren't ready to sell. Be seduced, but if you want to get the best price, don't seem to care."

Eva slipped behind her husband and patted his shoulder. "Dinner's ready, gentlemen," she announced with syrupy sweetness.

Napthali shifted his weight and groaned as he stood. The slender young man who had married Eva had filled out under her ministrations, and his belly looked like that of a much older man. Still, it was hard to dislike him. His broad smile and crinkling eyes had a way of putting everyone at ease. Once he had settled in his place—which he had picked at the head of the table, opposite Mama—he continued with his lecture. "You see, the world can be divided into two categories: buyers and sellers."

Inwardly Hannah sighed. Why did men want to simplify everything? Even Lazar was forever breaking things into two parts. No wonder there is so much animosity between them, she decided. They are more alike than they know.

Hannah busied herself serving the soup. But once she was able to sit down and taste it, she found it far too salty. Pushing it aside, she turned to Minna, who as usual was sitting by her husband. Her legs were crossed and her dress hitched up, revealing the shapely turn of her slender legs. The girl was too bony for her own good, not that her husband would have noticed. Seeing them chatting softly, Hannah wondered for the hundredth time what spell this angular, plain woman had cast over her brother. Was she telling Chaim what had transpired? This had happened before Chanukah, more than a month ago! The idea that the three of them had conspired to keep a secret from her was enraging.

"Evaleh," Mama cooed to her daughter, "your soup is delicious."

Hannah whipped her head around.

"But Hannah made the soup," Eva admitted in a way that had her taking some sort of credit, if only for honesty.

"Oh, yes?" her mother replied without another word.

The soup was too salty, and everybody knew it, for they were drinking lots of water. "Eva helped with the spices," Hannah added impetuously.

"Mm, just the way I like it," Napthali complimented.

"Me too," Mama said with a smile. "An old lady like me doesn't get much spice except at the table."

Eva laughed too loudly. "Oh, Mama! Please, even if it is your birthday. Besides, the way you run up and down the stairs collecting those rents proves you're younger than the rest of us."

Hannah suddenly found herself pondering the problem of the unpaid rent. Lazar usually gave Mama his last pay envelope of the month for their share, so she had to know it was overdue. Had she told Napthali or covered it by saying someone else had not paid, hoping it was only a temporary oversight? Why hadn't Mama told Hannah about it? By now perhaps even Eva had been informed. If Lazar had any idea the problems he had caused with his silence ... And he thought he had been protecting her! Protecting her from what?

Just then the door opened and Lazar walked in. He squinted as he entered the bright room from the dank foyer. He looked so pale and drawn his headache excuse would be believed. Emma patted the empty chair beside her. "Want some soup, Pa?" she asked.

"Don't bother," piped Benny, "it's way too salty. Save yourself for Ma's latkes."

For the first time that evening Hannah felt cheered. Her husband had not let her down, and her children were defending her. She jumped up. "I'll get them."

Mama patted her snowy white hair and straightened her lace collar. She had not noticed friction about the soup or anything else. "Well, now, isn't this nice," she pronounced, beaming. "Everyone's here! All my children, my friends."

After doling out the latkes, and watching them disappear before she got around the table, Hannah sat, pleased that her contribution was a success.

"Save some room for the meat," Eva warned. "There's a chicken *and* a brisket, you know."

Napthali began talking more loudly to Murray and the other men. "Yes, we're almost caught up for last year, and the January collections are better than ever." He wiped his mouth after finishing the last bite of pancake. "Anyway, it's easier to get tenants to pay in the winter than in the summer. You know why? Because they don't want to get thrown out in the cold," he finished, chuckling.

"And you are proud of that?" Lazar asked.

Everyone turned and stared at him. At first Hannah sighed, wishing he had let well enough alone—it was Mama's birthday after all!—but then she saw something else in the eyes of Sophie and Minna. Lazar always stood up for the oppressed, and they admired him for it.

Eva sneered at Lazar. "There's nothing wrong with what Napthali does. He's an honest businessman, but he has a right to collect what is his due. After all, we have payments to make too!"

"My dear sister-in-law, that is an entirely different matter. One man is trying to keep a roof over the heads of his children while another buys buildings with borrowed money, uses collateral from other holdings to establish credit, and takes the workingman's dollar to rule a private empire. Could there be a more unethical route to earn a living?"

"That's the American way," Eva said.

"The American way is corrupt," Lazar spat.

"Then why don't you go back to Russia?" Napthali retaliated.

"They'll send him back if he keeps up the way he's going—" Eva burst out, but then stopped. Hannah's head began to pound. So she did know about the arrest, but had decided against mentioning it in front of Mama.

"What were you going to say?" Lazar asked foolishly.

"That this nonsense is your way of covering up for not paying us what you owe."

Hannah's mouth fell open.

"Now, children," Mama began, "this isn't the moment—"

"Why isn't it?" Eva said in a voice that became more and more strident. "Lazar thinks he can insult my husband and get away with it. We have been patient with him before and we are being patient with him this time. Nevertheless, my husband must pay his mortgage whether the rents are in or not, yet does anyone feel for us? No!" Her face purpled. "But Lazar wins you over with a few eloquent phrases!"

"In this world principles are more essential than profits," Chaim said, but nobody responded to him, for simultaneously Napthali rose in his seat.

"Now, now," he began in a tone that sounded conciliatory, but had a self-righteous edge. "Lazar is merely misguided by those *meshugeneh* friends of his."

"Who are you talking about?" Lazar muttered.

"That maniac Alexander Berkman, for one."

"Sasha's not a maniac," shouted Chaim, entering the fray more aggressively.

"What else would you call that futile attempt on Frick's life?"

"He made a stand for the workingman," Chaim answered forcefully as he brushed back the long, unruly lock of hair that often covered his left eye.

"That's ridiculous! He was living out some anarchistic hallucination. And the poor bastard couldn't even shoot straight. Frick survived, and where did it get Berkman? Fifteen years in prison, that's where."

"I can see I should have remained upstairs," Lazar said, pushing back his chair.

"That's it, run away from the truth. I wish I could run away from responsibilities, but I have a family to support, a big family," he added with his arms sweeping the room to encompass everyone present.

Lazar yawned broadly.

"I'm tired too. I'm tired of your condescension," Napthali retorted. "You think me an idiot. Well, I know all about Proudhon and Bakunin and Kropotkin as well as your darling Sasha Berkman. I know all about them and I spit on them and your blind worship of their fashionable but useless anarchist doctrines! In a single day I feed more people than they did in a century."

In a flurry Sophie Feigenbaum hurried to serve the rest of the meal, but the party mood had soured. Emma clasped her father's hand, but he pulled it from her and moved away. Noticing this, Hannah then saw how her brother's face had turned stony. It was not his style to confront Napthali the way Lazar did. Five years older than Hannah, Chaim had been a clever student. Like Lazar, he had been groomed for a life of religious study until he had been caught up in the radicalism of the university in Odessa. Maybe because the grisly massacre of his family in the Kishinev pogrom, Lazar had been the most volatile member of the group. He had acted as their spokesman and had been the one with the most grandiose schemes, while Chaim had always taken a cooler, more intellectual approach. Her brother became the planner, the detail person, and the one who made the secret contacts with other cells of dissidents. Even now nobody was certain what role Chaim had played in the plot to kill the hated Russian Minister of the Interior, Von Plehve. All they knew was that Chaim had been in St. Petersburg on that fateful day and that, under torture, one of his comrades had implicated him. Looking at his shock of black curly hair and dark, brooding eyes, Hannah was reminded of the miracle of her brother's escape. If only Lazar could appreciate how far they both had come, and realize it was better to leave well enough alone, at least in the family.

Nobody had much appetite for either the brisket or the chicken, the macaroons tasted stale, and even Chaim said he did not want coffee. "We've an early morning tomorrow. The press run starts at four."

"And we've got to get the little ones to bed. It will be a long ride uptown tonight," Napthali boomed.

"I'll bundle everyone up," Eva called as she removed her apron.

Minna stood to leave too. That way she would not have to help in the kitchen either. As she went for her coat, she gave Hannah a peculiar glance that caused her to follow to the door.

"I'm sorry about what happened," Minna began generously, although the words came out anemically.

Seeing Hannah's disbelief, she added, "You know, you should give him your support on the book idea. Tell him he should do it."

Refusing to admit that once again Minna knew more than she, Hannah retorted, "I think I know how to support my husband better than you do."

Ignoring the last remark, Minna went to stand beside Chaim. She placed her arms around his waist and gave him a loving squeeze. Hannah winced. Didn't they know this was not the time or place for that? Then Chaim opened the door, allowing Eva and the children to step into the foyer. For a moment Hannah was relieved the evening was over. Then she had another surprise.

In a gentle, almost offhand way, Chaim turned to Napthali, then tossed his head to whip the hair from his forehead. "Like you, my dear brother, I have come to despise the term *anarchism*. Some socialists who swear by Marx and Engels insist on it meaning chaos and disorder, which shows how ignorant as well as dishonest they are."

Hannah jumped slightly. Here was Chaim's retort, indirect, but meeting its mark.

"Since you seem confused, let me tell you what anarchism is not," he continued. "It is not bombs, not robbery, not murder, and certainly not a war of each against all, for that would mean a return to barbarism. In truth, anarchism is the opposite of that. It means that we should be free; that no one should enslave you, boss you, rob you, or . . . impose upon you. It means you should be free to choose the kind of life you wish to live without anyone interfering. So, my esteemed brother-in-law, as you make your way through the next hours and days, think about what I have said and think about who around you is really free—and who is not."

❧ 7 ❧

Saturday was blustery and seemed interminable. Hannah and Lazar went round and round, but the facts were facts and nothing could change the situation.

"What's this about a book?" Hannah prodded.

"Who told you?"

"Minna."

Lazar's mouth opened, then shut.

"I know you have always enjoyed writing down your thoughts," she began encouragingly.

"I can't sell my thoughts!" he replied defensively.

"What's it about?" Hannah coaxed.

He cleared his throat. "The Russian uprising of 1905, an essential topic for the comprehension of the roots of the conflict to come."

This did not sound profitable either, but for the moment there was no point in pushing him further. One of the secrets of their marriage was that if not for her, Lazar would never have left Russia. A young leader in Odessa's Jewish self-defense movement, he might have risen to become one of the men leading Russia to revolution—not that such a thing seemed likely to ever take place, despite the continuous rumbling of the Lower East Side radicals. The fact was Lazar not only believed his career had been aborted, but that she was the cause of his failure. In choosing to uphold her honor, he had to leave Russia and thus remain out of the fray. Since then he had always felt like less of a man because many of his friends, including Chaim, had been jailed for their principles. For some crazy reason, Hannah reflected, Lazar actually resented that he had never gotten in trouble for a cause. In Odessa he had written inflammatory pamphlets and had been wanted by the authorities, but since he had used a pseudonym, he had never been caught. Many would have thought this clever; he believed he had never stood up to be counted.

"Well," Hannah began with more confidence than she felt,

"at least my job is secure. If we cut back on expenses, we can manage for many months so long as you can bring in a few dollars a week."

"Can we talk about this later? I have a pounding headache."

From previous experience Hannah knew that her husband would never openly seem to comply with her, but her words would not be forgotten. He was probably looking for work teaching or tutoring, but had been unsuccessful so far. Give him a few days, she told herself as he went to their room to lie down.

A few minutes later he came out to complain. "How can I rest with all the noise the children are making?"

Emma and Benny, who were playing a game in their room, could hardly be expected to be silent. "I'm taking them to visit Rachael," Hannah announced as though that was what she had planned all along.

The children, who were delighted to have an outing, cooperated in putting on their coats and galoshes. In a few minutes they were on their way to visit Hannah's dearest friend, Dr. Rachael Jaffe, whom she first had met during midwifery training in Moscow. She and her physician husband, Ezekiel Herzog, lived above his office just off Washington Square.

Dr. Herzog greeted Hannah and the children warmly. "Just what we needed. Nora's been pestering me all day and I'm trying to get some reading done." Although his face was covered with a thick black beard, his impish grin was easy to read.

Emma sailed directly to Nora's room, which Hannah knew she envied because Nora did not have to share it with a brother. Benny lingered behind, unsure, but Herzog came to the rescue. "Want to look through my microscope?"

"You have your work to do . . ." Hannah demurred.

"If Benny won't chatter, he can spend the whole day sorting through my collection of terrifying microorganisms."

At that Benny's eyes shone, and he followed the doctor like a docile pup. More a drawing room than a clinic, Herzog's plush office had a desk, chairs, a sofa, even a card table, but other than the microscope, few medical accoutrements. He had a devoted group of well-to-do patients who liked to hobnob with radicals, and they paid what even he admitted were exorbitant fees for his services. Ezekiel, who claimed he was still as political as when he had been incarcerated in Russia, was beginning to practice what he termed "intellectual medicine," which involved more theoretical discussions with his patients than hands-on care. Because he had special training in diseases of the eye, he often did *pro bono* work in several hospitals, but lately he was concentrating on the elite who found it worthwhile to pay a doctor to talk about their troubles, both real and imagined.

Benny went right to the microscope and peered through the lens. "What's this?" he asked excitedly.

"I'll show you in a moment," the doctor replied.

"You're sure he'll be no trouble?" Hannah inquired.

"Absolutely! Rachael's upstairs. We'll be fine here."

After studying his coal black eyes for any shadow of annoyance, Hannah decided Herzog really didn't mind having the boy around, and as she climbed the stairs, she wondered idly if he and Rachael might ever have a son of their own. Rachael was in the second-floor parlor. Once a grand, formal room, the Herzogs made no pretense of entertaining there. Nor did they apologize for the clutter of books, scrawny ferns in cracked cache pots, dusty lamps with straggly fringed shades, unfinished paperwork, stacks of professional journals, stereopticon cards and viewers, glass and porcelain knickknacks Rachael referred to as her "*tchotchke* collection," and Herzog's latest fancy: mechanical music boxes.

Realizing how different Rachael's life was from her own, Hannah sometimes marveled that their friendship had endured. Here was the one person whom Hannah wholeheartedly admired. She was brilliant and beautiful, kind and compassionate, and no other woman she had ever met knew as much about science and politics as well as people.

Rachael was stretched out on a chaise surrounded with medical literature. "Don't get up," Hannah insisted. "What are you studying?"

"Actually, I'm absorbed by *Madame Bovary,*" she said with a repentant smile. "In fact, I was just thinking you would agree that Flaubert has made it impossible for any woman who has had a child to be sympathetic to his heroine."

"Why?"

"She farms out her daughter to a repulsive wet nurse and cares hardly a whit for her. Disgusting!"

"What about the husband?" Hannah asked as she sat on

the piano bench, the one seat not covered with books or clothing.

"He's a doctor, so he's not much help!" Rachael gave the high, uninhibited laugh that Hannah found so appealing. She sat up without caring that she scattered several papers. "Anyway, what's going on?" she said, switching to a more intimate Yiddish.

"In my life or medical management?" Hannah quipped. For the first time in days she felt herself relaxing.

"Either, so long as it's food for thought."

Her first instinct was to mention Lazar's predicament, but decided it less disturbing to skip to Mrs. Tartaglia. As she repeated the incident, Rachael's face registered every nuance of curiosity, excitement, alarm, then revulsion.

"Vile man! Poor, poor woman. If only this was an isolated case!" Her lively brown eyes flecked with gold glanced about the room, indicating she considered that topic was over, so Hannah did not mention the woman's odd request. "Anything interesting clinically?"

"Well, there was a partial placenta previa this week," Hannah answered in Russian.

Oddly, the two of them intermingled Russian, Yiddish, and English, sometimes using words from all three in a single sentence. They preferred Russian for medical discussions, for both had received their training in that language; Yiddish for friendly and intimate concerns; English when others were around. Rachael was equally at home in German, and even knew French.

The doctor ran her hands through her unruly mass of auburn curls, which she pulled back only during medical procedures, and gave the midwife an encouraging smile. "And the outcome?"

"Actually, she was an ideal candidate for the Spanish windlass," Hannah continued with enthusiasm. Any residual tension began to ebb as she launched into the clinical details that were rewarding to share with such an educated listener. Besides, her tongue was loosened as soon as she spoke in Russian, for she never felt she could find the precise word, especially a technical term, in English.

She had finished explaining why, in her opinion, cesareans should be the last option when the doctor interjected silkily, "How's Lazar?"

"Home with a headache."

"He doesn't usually get those. Do you want me to look in on him?"

"Only if you need German lessons."

Rachael furrowed her brow, but let Hannah continue with the explanation, including her outrage that Minna had known more than she.

"Minna makes up in commitment what she lacks in tact," Rachael said as she watched for Hannah's reaction out of the corner of her eye. Noting the downturn of her friend's lips, she glossed it over. "Lazar was stifled at the university anyway. After all, those Prussian poets can wear a little thin . . ." From Hannah's glum expression she saw this was not helping. Her voice softened. "If Lazar is distressed, he must be difficult to live with."

"You don't know the half of it," Hannah allowed with a long sigh. "I wish there was something I could do . . ."

"I know what you mean. When we spend our day fixing up strangers, we think we can work the same magic in our homes. But we can't, can we?"

"I hoped you would have a pill that would put everything right," Hannah said while trying to dissolve the lump in her throat.

"If I did, you'd be the first one to get the prescription. Just remember that you cannot take care of everyone else unless you take care of yourself." Before Hannah could frame her sarcastic reply, Rachael abruptly shifted the subject back to where they had begun. "So what do you think will happen to the Italian lady?"

"Don't know. The poor woman is desperate," Hannah replied, grateful to return to the safer realm of the hospital. She went on to tell of Anna-Maria's plea. "What did she think, there was some potion that would create only boys?"

Rachael shrugged. "Why didn't you give her your recipe for chicken soup?"

"If I thought it would help her, I would have. What upset me was that she really believed I was lying to her. If only she had been more open to a few suggestions for family limitation."

Rachael acted as if she hadn't heard the last phrase. "Tell me again what she said about more boys than girls."

"She insisted that in her neighborhood there are three or four boys to every girl."

"Where does she live?"

"Who knows?" Hannah held her hands up. "Besides, what does that have to do with it?"

"Could you find out?"

"I suppose," Hannah replied, irritation creeping in her voice, "but why?"

"I just wondered if the Jews she lives near might be Orthodox because, as you know, I treat many in my practice." Hannah nodded, for these women preferred to be seen by a female physician. Rachael closed the book she had been reading and placed it precariously atop a stack of books already teetering on the end table. "I also have had the impression that they have more boys than girls, or maybe it's only because the boys are always running about."

"You don't think she could be right?"

"Stranger things have happened."

"But what could be the reason?"

"We all know that God prefers men to women, at least ours does."

Women were excluded from so much in Judaism that Hannah did not dispute this. "So he gives the devout more boys?"

"Easier to have a minyan that way," the doctor replied, referring to the requirement of having ten men present for any religious observance.

"All right," she said with resignation, "since you're so curious, I'll find out where she lives."

&ers; **8** &ers;

When they met a week later, Hannah had the address. After making a visit to a woman who wanted to be delivered at home, the midwife made her way north in a light snow to Rachael's clinic on St. Mark's Place, knowing that she was usually in late on Wednesdays. Depending on her mood, Hannah was by turns oppressed and invigorated by the noise and confusion of the crowded avenues of the Lower East Side. Coming around the corner to Orchard Street, she made her way down the middle of the street. Every building had an awning extending over the sidewalk, with as many tables set outside as in. At the curb was another set of sellers in stalls, which were flanked by the pushcarts of the most impoverished merchants. And among them roamed still a lower rank, those whose wares were carried on their persons. Every pair of searching eyes was filled with raw inspiration. Someday I'll have a pushcart, thought the soft drink peddler with the brass urn strapped to his back. Someday I'll have a covered stall, imagined the apple seller. I will have a storefront I can lock, wished the tobacco man. My family will live far away from this clatter, not above the shop, trusted the grocer. And my children, they will never break their backs like me! was each man's secret hope.

Hannah's thoughts turned to her own children. With a pang she realized that Wednesday had been the one day Lazar used to be home until suppertime and she didn't have to worry about the children, but now he had nowhere else he had to be. Of course, he might be going to a café to discuss politics, but he would wait for her to arrive home. He knew how much she hated having to ask her mother to take over, and right now, with the rent two months overdue, he was not about to ask his mother-in-law for more favors.

Hearing the bell jingle, Rachael poked her head out of an examining room. "Good to see you. Carrie's cleaning the other room, where we had a bit of a mess, I'm afraid, and I'm with a patient."

"I can wait."

"I would like your advice."

Hannah walked into the examining room, where an expectant mother lay on her back. Rachael was measuring the fundus to determine how far along the woman was. She showed the midwife the tape and told her the woman's last menstrual dates. Hannah realized the patient's abdomen was too small for the time she said she was pregnant. Although many women had their dates wrong, this one was way off the chart. Hannah nodded at Rachael to confirm a complication.

"Please get dressed, Mrs. Baum, and I'll be back shortly," Dr. Jaffe said briskly.

As she ushered Hannah into her disordered office, Rachael shook her head. "Not good, is it?"

"Do you think she has the dates right?"

"Well, she's Orthodox, as you may have noticed from the

wig, and they are more accurate than the rest because they mark everything down so they know when they are unclean."

"Then I'd worry about preeclampsia, and also a placental dysfunction."

"That's what I thought. I'll have her stop in every day to have her blood pressure checked. Now," she said, smiling, "what brings you here?"

"Oh, I just came by with Mrs. Tartaglia's address."

"Who?"

"The Italian lady who wanted a boy."

Rachael instantly glowed with expectation, although Hannah couldn't imagine why she had been so curious in the first place. "Well?"

"Elizabeth Street, a few doors away from the San Salvatore church."

Rachael nodded. "Just as I thought. Lots of Orthodox Jews in that neighborhood."

Hannah gave her a quizzical look. "So?"

"If you have a few minutes . . ." Rachael rummaged around on her desk. "Here's a stack of charts I pulled. They are Orthodox families with the names and birth dates of all the children. There's about forty of them, so that should account for a hundred or more offspring. Could you make a tabulation: how many boys, how many girls, in each family?" She handed Hannah the papers. A few fluttered down, but she didn't stop to pick them up. "I'll have to see Mrs. Baum now, but I'll be back." She shut the door, then it opened a crack. "Mrs. Baum has three boys, no girls—yet." Then she was gone.

Hannah shook her head as she picked up the fallen papers. Making space on a crowded table, she settled in with a pad of paper and a pencil. She lifted the first file: three girls, one boy, then ticked these in columns on her page marked male and female. Adler, two girls, two boys. Twerski, four girls, two boys. "See? Already Rachael's wrong," she muttered prematurely.

The next file indicated that the mother had lost two children, then the mother had died, the father remarried, and had three more. How should she account for that? Hannah wondered. Well, the point was how many children of each sex a family had, living or dead, one wife or two, so she made more columns to indicate deceased males and females. She worked rapidly, just listing the numbers and not bothering to add them up.

When Rachael reappeared, Hannah was finishing the last of the stack. "What's the result?" she asked, looking over Hannah's shoulder.

"I'm just totaling them." After Hannah rechecked a column, she stared up at her friend with genuine astonishment. "I would never have believed—"

"What?" the doctor asked as she inexpertly pinned her loose hair wisps back with tortoise shell combs.

"There are a total of one hundred and sixty-six living children. One hundred and fourteen are male; only fifty-two are female. How can that be possible?"

Rachael did some calculations on the back of an envelope. "That's sixty-nine percent male and thirty-one percent female."

"Wouldn't that be considered a significant statistical finding?"

"It's a very small sample," Rachael complained.

"Do you have a comparison group of non-Jews, or at least non-observant Jews?"

"Carrie!" Dr. Jaffe called. Her assistant poked her head in. Her hat was on and her coat was over her arm. "Were you about to leave?"

"Yes, Doctor, but I could stay if you need me."

"Only for a few minutes. Can you pull forty or fifty files for me? Pick them at random, but leave out any Jewish names." She turned to Hannah. "Observant or not, let's look at an entirely different group. And, Carrie, select any Italian names you see first."

While they waited, Rachael showed Hannah the mortality figures. "You counted twenty-two children who had died, either in late pregnancy or early childhood, right?"

Hannah nodded. "I picked any that had a sex listed, although there were seven of unknown sex, and probably more than that since, from my experience, not everyone is forthcoming about the deaths of infants or miscarriages."

"Let's assume that will be true of our control group as well," Rachael continued. "So, if we combine the numbers, we have a selection of one hundred and eighty-eight children. But only three girls died, compared to nineteen boys." She paused and bit her lip thoughtfully. "Do you realize what that means?"

"That girls are stronger than boys."

"Exactly. At least in this example. Perhaps there is a biological reason to have more boys, since more are apt to succumb."

"If you think about it, though," Hannah began slowly, "it would make more sense for there to be more females, since women die of complications of childbirth."

"That's true, but you and I both know that in the general population the sexes are more evenly distributed, or this unusual preponderance of men would be well known."

"Are you saying that Mrs. Tartaglia was right? That the Jews are the chosen people made in God's image—his male image?"

"Not exactly. I think there is a less inflammatory reason."

The nurse came in and handed the doctor a fresh stack of folders. "Where shall I put them?"

All flat surfaces of the room were filled, so Rachael pointed at the floor. The assistant shook her head, but did not seem surprised. Carrie said good night and left the two ladies on their knees to sort the papers.

"It will go faster if I read them off and you write," the doctor said in a sudden burst of efficiency "Corona had two boys, two girls living, and three boys deceased; Pennington has one girl; Petrucci, two boys, two girls, one girl deceased . . ."

They stopped when they reached one hundred and seventy-five and began their calculations. "Ninety-one living males, eight-four females." Hannah looked down at Rachael, who was sitting cross-legged on the floor.

The doctor made some swift calculations. "That's fifty-two percent male, which is more what one would expect, isn't it?" Her faced flushed with excitement. "Quite a variation from the sixty-nine percent of the Orthodox Jewish sample, wouldn't you say?"

"There must be something wrong here. What about the deaths?"

Rachael worked the numbers out several different ways. "Look at this, fewer males died than the other group, but it's close enough to account for the natural difference between boys and girls." She looked up at the clock that ticked on her office mantel. *"Gevalt!* Seven already! Herzog's lecturing tonight. I've got to get home to Nora."

"Mama's probably feeding mine already. If I don't arrive

by six, they hurry downstairs to see what's on the stove, Lazar included."

"The best decision you ever made was to come back to this part of town."

"I can't depend on Mama forever, though, or so she keeps telling me. She thinks I've forgotten how to cut noodles and chop fish."

"Well, I'll admit that I was never any good at either of those."

"I can do it, I just don't have the time," Hannah replied defensively.

"You don't have to explain to me," Rachael retorted a bit too harshly. Then realizing how much strain Hannah was under, she softened her voice. "I shouldn't have kept you so late. We'll share a ride, my treat."

No automobiles were about, but they did find a hansom cab. As the horse trotted toward Tompkins Square, Hannah and Rachael mulled over whether Mrs. Tartaglia was correct. "You know that Lazar was brought up to be a religious scholar, following a long tradition in his family," Hannah began in Yiddish.

"Let's speak in English, you need the practice."

Hannah frowned, but knew she was right. If she spoke slowly the words flowed more easily. "I once remember him telling me that there was a passage in the Talmud that said the determination of sex takes place during sexual relations, and that when the woman emits her seed before the man, the child will be a boy. Since the woman's egg isn't released by the sexual act, Lazar used this as an example of the ignorance that religion disseminates."

"How apt," Rachael commented slyly.

Hannah cuffed her lightly. "Others more uneducated, though, might have taken it to mean that there was a special factor in the fluids a woman secretes during her—" For a few moments Hannah struggled to find the right English word for *excitement*. Finally she gave up and substituted a Russian one. "But Lazar went on to say that the book advised a man to hold back if he wanted a boy, and he assumed it meant to wait until a woman had her pleasure. What do you think?"

Rachael was thoughtful for a few minutes. "I can't see what difference that would make, except to keep the woman happier about having relations with her husband. To me, this is another example of religious laws having some basis in the health of a community. For instance, the rules for keeping kosher contain important sanitary considerations, especially for people who lived in hot climates without the ability to store food safely. Also, a circumcised boy has fewer problems keeping himself clean. If we assume that most men want a son, and if they believe that satisfying their wives will lead to that end, then they will put aside their selfish considerations. The result—more contented partners—protects the family unit in the end."

"Have you considered that circumcision may also influence the consequence?" Hannah asked.

"In what way?"

"Well, I've heard that a circumcised man can control his desires better, thus prolonging the act to pleasure his wife. So, if it is true that a female orgasm creates male children, and if the patriarchs who ordained circumcision thought more males desirable to the tribe, well . . ."

Before they had settled anything, the carriage drew up to Hannah's house at the corner of the square. "Let's both give it some more thought," Rachael suggested as Hannah stepped down. She was almost at the door of her building when the doctor called out, "I hope your mother cut some nice noodles today."

∽∾ 9 ∽∾

No time was better than the first moments home with her children, who were as eager to see their mother as Hannah was to be with them. Emma had brought home from school a very good drawing of a horse, with the word written neatly underneath, and a list of sums her parents were to help her memorize. Benny had already finished his sheet of numbers and had set up the checkers board. Hannah warmed herself a bowl of soup left over from the party, diluting the brine. There were plenty of carrots left, because nobody else in her family liked them. Some hard bread tasted fine soaked in the fatty broth, and for a final course she had two pickles from the barrel under the sink.

Lazar was more than ready to leave for the café when she appeared. He had not gone downstairs for supper, making do by cutting up some chicken and reheating it with rice. Hannah was so grateful he had not bothered Mama she did not show her desire for him to remain home. For a moment he seemed ready to challenge her if she did, and when she merely kissed him warmly at the door, he gave her an extra squeeze and whispered in her ear, "I'll be home early enough ..." knowing she would catch his meaning. That was all Hannah needed to feel warmed by him. Despite his problems, he loved her, a fact she never had to question.

Emma did very well with the sums, which she had learned more easily by turning them into a little song with a tune of her own creation. Benny put his fingers in his ears, but he was only pretending, and ended up applauding when his sister managed a flawless run-through. "So, Ma," he called, "want to be beaten in checkers?"

After Hannah was in fact soundly routed, she sat back and mulled over the intriguing sexual problem. How could delaying the climax affect the sex of offspring, and if it did, how could she discover whether these Orthodox families followed this directive in the Talmud faithfully enough to produce such lopsided results in favor of boy children? What did one ever know about what happened in another couple's bed? Of course, she was as curious as the next person, but these were private matters that nobody shared.

Nevertheless, one did know what happened in one's own bed. Here she was with a boy and a girl, and since she usually enjoyed lovemaking with Lazar, she supposed she experienced a climax with the conception of both of them. But had it been before his? Usually that is how it worked out. If they had gotten anything right in their marriage, it had been their sexual relations. As they developed more competence, they had synchronized matters. She knew how to indicate her satisfaction and to signal so he could proceed with his, often with the consequence of hers repeating once or twice more before he was finished. Sometimes it happened that they consummated the act in unison, but that was not a special goal, it just happened, or maybe her spasms triggered his. Considering her professional knowledge about the pelvic anatomy as well as nearly ten years of practical experience with a man (men, she amended mentally—but never to anyone else), she actually knew a paltry amount.

Putting the matter aside, she turned her concentration to the children. After they were bathed, she sat first on one and then the other's bed, massaging each one's neck, shoulders, and back. Benny liked to feel her nails scratching his skin; Emma preferred softer, longer strokes. Sensing each one relaxing, hearing their breathing slow, she felt an intense closeness coupled with a twinge of regret as they departed into the sphere of sleep.

Lazar was later than she expected. She hadn't inquired when he would return or where he was going. Probably to the Café Boulevard or Sach's, the usual haunts, where his friends congregated to drink schnapps and argue some question of the revolution-to-come. She knew how restored she felt after spending time with Rachael and admitted he had the same need—now perhaps an even greater one—to schmooze with his companions. Besides, talking to friends might be the most rapid way for him to find new employment.

"Ah, you are not sleeping," he said as he tiptoed into the bedroom.

"I waited for you." She patted the bed.

"And why is that?" he teased as he removed his shirt. In the amber light of the single lamp the firm muscles of his back and shoulders gleamed like polished stones. A few inches shy of six feet, he was by far the tallest member of the family, but as he stretched he seemed even more formidable—and more exciting.

"Because I have been wanting you all evening." Now, that was the truth! As much as she had tried to apply an intellectual approach to the problem of choosing a sex, she had found herself becoming physically, as well as mentally, aroused during her contemplations.

"Is that so?" he said with a twinkle in his clear blue eyes. Curls of sandy hair framed his face charmingly, but she would have to remember to trim it before he went to see about any job possibilities. At least his firm jaw and wide smile always made a good first impression. He was the sort of person people immediately liked and trusted.

Lazar glimpsed her over his shoulder as he went to wash himself, and Hannah hoped she appeared as inviting to him as he did to her. Her long chestnut hair, which she normally wore swept up in a braided bun, cascaded across her shoulders and down the front of her gown. Instead of buttoning it so the collar warmed her neck, she had left it open to the cleft of her breast. Usually she shivered until he joined her under the comforter, but that evening she was infused with a warmth that penetrated her bones. In a few moments he climbed in. Despite the frigid night he was naked. She reached out to him.

"Ah, you're like a furnace," he crooned. His hand stroked her gently rounded hips. "I love your skin . . . so smooth . . ."

"Come closer, unless you're afraid you'll catch fire."

"I'll take my chances."

As a signal she wanted him, she fondled his muscular thigh until Lazar's hand covered hers and pressed it to stop. Her heart lurched. "Are you feeling all right?" she whispered.

"Yes, I'm just too agitated to relax."

"Do you want to tell me about it?"

"Of course I do. When is there ever time? You came home so late tonight and then the children pounced on you."

With a great effort Hannah refrained from voicing her annoyance that he should resent that the children came first. Still, she could not resist a gentle reproach: "You did not have to rush out to the café."

"I was meeting Chaim, who was bringing someone who is interested in my book idea. The sooner I select my topic, the sooner I can begin the research."

"Will they pay you to write this book?"

Lazar sat up sharply and turned so he was no longer in her embrace. "That's not the way it's done. I will only make money when the copies of the book are sold."

"That could take months, maybe longer. And what are we to do until then?"

"We're not going to starve."

No, Hannah thought, thanks to me. She shivered at the fleeting remembrance of their first years in America, especially one bleak winter when they had gone hungry. Buttoning up her gown to stave off a growing chill, she realized nothing was secure. Not professorships, not midwifery positions either. She looked into his eyes. A moment earlier they had flashed with zeal, but now they cringed with an acute awareness of their predicament. Affected by his sadness, she reached over and touched his cheek.

Clasping her hand, he spoke in a strangled voice. "You cannot fathom how it has been. I looked into the eyes of the young men in my classes and what did I see? Vacant, empty souls. These children of privilege have no idea what is going on in the world. They learned German with no comprehension of Germany, or even Europe. Everything is by rote, everything is mechanical. But the world today is perched between good and evil, the oppressors and the oppressed. These are not stirrings of my imagination, these are certain truths. They need to know them. Somebody has to tell them. And not in an abstract way."

"Yes, that's very true," she said encouragingly. Lazar had never accepted the simplistic or facile. A visionary, he saw beyond the pedestrian daily events. Because of his immense store of learning, which he was always replenishing, he was impatient with others too indolent to do the same. At his side she often felt inadequate, retreating to her native pragmatism if only because it was easiest.

"Darling," he said in appreciation for her understanding. He rubbed her shoulders and kissed her lips. As he pressed his body to warm her, she felt his arousal. A few minutes ago she would have accepted him eagerly, but now her stomach churned with anxiety. Lazar seemed unaware of her altered feelings. His hand caressed her breasts with exquisite tenderness, rolling the dusky nipples first gently, then more firmly, until her thoughts were fogged by the mounting sensations.

Now the concerns she had mulled over earlier began to reassert themselves. What was the question? Something about whether a woman had a climax first and the sex of a baby . . . It was an intriguing idea . . . she mused as his fingers parted the moist flesh between her thighs. How she loved his body still! Lazar was as slender as the day of their marriage. She clasped his buttocks, enjoying the way they squeezed as he probed her. She should concentrate on the sequence of events . . . she needed to understand more about what happened when a man and a woman merged . . . if only she could . . . Her gown was lifted up . . . no time for the buttons . . . no time for anything else . . . not even remembrance.

⤜ 10 ⤛

No answers were forthcoming that night. Or the next. And on the evening after that Lazar laughed as Hannah fondled him. "Have they been spicing the coffee at Bellevue?"

"What do you mean?" she asked in feigned ignorance.

"Don't remember when you've been so demanding." His voice was tinged with humor, so Hannah did not bristle at his choice of words.

"Would you prefer to sleep alone?" she inquired, pouting.

"Absolutely not," he said, slipping a leg over hers. "I like you this way."

Good, she thought as she readied for another "research trial."

Admiring his broad shoulders and lean flanks, Hannah felt lucky to have him. Despite all their difficulties, he was a wonderful lover. As before, she tried to concentrate on what was happening to him and to her. This time she analyzed her feelings. Arousal was almost instantaneous. Lazar knew just where to touch—and when—and yet there was a hollowness in her heart that she had not identified before. Was it because she knew him so well, or did it have something to do with their latest difficulties? Still . . . how could she complain? she reflected as the sensations began to dissolve her sense and she relinquished her mind to desire.

At the end of the week her monthly flow started, thanks to the French device with which Rachael had fitted her three years before. Since they preferred to wait until the worst had subsided, in the interim she gave some thought to what she had learned. Nothing new, she admitted. Certainly she was not about to be an experimental subject on having a boy or a girl, since she had decided that her two children were ideal, especially for a woman who worked long hours at a hospital.

It was Rachael, however, who discovered some research first. One afternoon several days later, Hannah was having a glass of milk with Norma Marshanck in the training school's lunchroom when Rachael appeared. Pretending to be annoyed, she asked, "Is this the way midwives spend their day?"

"Of course, it's what we are qualified for," Hannah quipped. "Why are you here?"

"Several cases are in the house. I had to hospitalize Mrs. Baum—remember the woman with the undersized uterus?" Dr. Jaffe frowned momentarily, then went on, "Now, Hannah, isn't your shift almost over?"

She checked the clock on the wall. "Just about."

"Could you join me for a kibitz at Sach's café?"

"What's a kibitz?" Mrs. Marshanck asked. "Sounds like something delicious."

Hannah and Rachael laughed. "It is, especially if you think giving each other advice is as tasty as we do."

"I'll cover for you with Mrs. Hemming," Norma Marshanck volunteered.

"I don't know ... I always think she's waiting in some corner ready to pounce on me if I make a mistake."

"Why would anybody do that?" Rachael asked.

"It's hard to explain, unless you know her," Mrs. Marshanck allowed, "but I think Mrs. Sokolow might be exaggerating."

"Not really. I think she would like to knock me down a peg, if not get rid of me entirely." Seeing Rachael's disbelief, she hurried on. "It's true. She's never wanted me to have this position. In her book I'm not qualified."

"But your training is far superior to anything—" Rachael started to protest, but Hannah cut her off.

"My training has nothing to do with it. As far as Mrs. Hemming is concerned, I was not born to the right parents in the right part of town in the right country, and no matter how much I try, she always finds a way to correct my speech."

"Well, you can trust me to keep her calm today," the other midwife insisted.

Hannah gave her a grateful smile. "As Benny would say, you're swell."

The winter afternoon was sunny but quite windy. Even so, Hannah and Rachael walked the whole way downtown to Suffolk Street, which was not far from Hannah's apartment. Sach's Café, which really came to life after sundown, was almost empty that afternoon, but in the smoky haze Hannah recognized a few of her husband's cronies. Josef, the elderly waiter who knew hardly anybody's name but everybody's order, brought them steaming glasses of tea, placed the sugar cubes on Rachael's side, the milk pitcher on Hannah's, and without a word having been said, offered an apricot strudel cut in four slices for the two ladies to share.

"Spasseeba," Rachael thanked him in Russian.

"As usual?" he asked.

She nodded, which meant he would charge her husband's account.

If strangers had observed the two women, they might have thought Rachael the harried housewife of a professional man, for though her clothes were of fine cloth and fit her tall frame snugly, she always seemed in disarray, as though the demands of household chores and children had led to her confused state. On the other hand, while Hannah's garments were not nearly so fine, she presented a far more competent image. When she wasn't wearing her midwife's blue apron over a white uniform, she selected a tailored suit, usually in a worsted wool that flattered the jade green of her eyes. For her shirtwaists she preferred an ivory shade, so "I don't look like a corpse on a pillow," she had once confided. Rachael had only shaken her head. She thought Hannah's pale skin a hallmark of her delicate beauty.

Rachael took a quick sip of the steaming tea, then a bite of strudel. "I've been doing some research on sex selection," she said, licking her lips in approval. "Apparently your Italian lady isn't the first to want to shift the odds in her favor."

"What have you found?" Hannah asked.

"There are some illogical ideas. A Greek fellow, Parmenides, thought that males are formed in the right chamber of the uterus, females in the left. His followers suggest having a woman turn on one side or the other to permit semen to flow the desired direction. And do you know what's odd? Even today stock breeders stand their cows on one side of a slope or the other for the same reason!"

Hannah was not convinced this was necessarily wrong, but did not want to appear stupid. Rachael continued on with several other far-fetched concepts about left and right testicles, and a mathematical formula based on odd and even numbers of ovulations.

When she paused, Hannah handed the doctor another sliver of pastry. "What about the fact that the Orthodox women abstain from intercourse until at least a week after the finish of their menstruation?" Hannah asked. "Doesn't it make sense that this would place their first opportunity to have relations each month close to a similar point in their cycle, and maybe it is this particular time that the egg is more receptive to a boy than a girl?"

Rachael chimed in breathlessly. "I've been thinking along the same lines, but from the perspective of the other sex. Let's assume that their husbands also abstain, as I suspect most of the Orthodox do. Wouldn't the number of sperm have increased in density, and might not this contribute to a reason they have more boys?"

"There are so many alternatives. How could we possibly determine the answer?"

"We can't, at least not us and not now, but that wouldn't stop you from telling Mrs. Tartaglia the secret."

"You just said we couldn't know the reason."

"That may be true, but evidently that doesn't prevent the Orthodox from having more boys."

"That would mean—" Hannah's voice caught and she began to chortle. "Can you see Mrs. Tartaglia in the *mikvah?*" She laughed so hard at the image of the stern Italian woman in a Jewish bathhouse she began coughing.

Rachael joined in, holding her side when she could not stop laughing. "That's not a bad idea. Those women who run the ritual baths know the rules. You could see an attendant and then tell Mrs. Tartaglia exactly what the dates are so she could abstain until the right moment."

"I can't imagine her telling Giovanni when he could and couldn't."

"Why not? Wasn't he the one who wanted the son?"

"Do you think it would work?" Hannah asked, suddenly taking Rachael seriously.

"Only sixty-nine percent of the time and only if she follows the rules—all the rules."

Hannah caught her meaning. "Her husband would have to give her pleasure first."

"Exactly. And he would have to stay out of her bed almost half the month."

"Anna-Maria might appreciate the respite," Hannah said thoughtfully, "and I wouldn't mind knowing the bastard's balls ached."

At first Rachael flinched at these harsh words, then managed to add, "I have a feeling his wife wouldn't either."

"I'll do it," Hannah said, pushing away from the table. "I'll get the details on the Mosaic laws and give them to Mrs. Tartaglia. She can use them however she wishes."

∝ 11 ∝

Hannah was already familiar with the *pukherin,* or attendant, who ran the Rivington Street bathhouse because she had delivered Mrs. Rosenblatt's daughters. From the first moment she stepped into the mikvah's dank hallway, though, Hannah felt she was in an alien land. Long ago she had rejected the world of her Orthodox grandmothers, and this archaic rite, while probably a sensible rule to insure hygiene in more primitive times, had no place in a modern milieu of running water and educated people.

Walking across the puddled floor, she lifted her long worsted skirt to keep the hem dry. Already her linen blouse stuck to her skin and her tailored jacket felt itchy in the clammy room. Her stiff hat seemed ridiculous. Hesitating slightly, she opened the door to the room with the pool. Sunlight poured into the bathhouse from small round windows a foot below the ceiling. The bars at the windows threw a shadow of crosses across the shimmering water, which shattered into ripples each time a bather descended the stairs. With only sheets draped around their naked bodies, women waiting their turn sat on wooden benches. A few were shivering, though the room was filled with steam from the heated pool. A woman with stretch marks on her thighs and abdomen entered the pool and crouched down slightly. Holding her nose, she submerged. When she surfaced, the matron pressed her down again, saying, "Some hair floated up. The whole body must be under at the same time." The bather, who looked as if she was a mother many times over, sighed and took a second plunge.

She surfaced, saw the pukherin nod, then, while standing in the water that lapped at her arms folded over her breasts, chanted the prayer, *"Boruch atoh adonoy eloyhainu melech ho'oylom asher kidshonu bemitzvoysov vetzivonu al hatviloh."* After submerging one more time, she scurried out of the pool.

Mrs. Rosenblatt waited until the next in line, a scrawny child with a flat chest and even flatter rear end, entered the water. Hannah had to look twice to be certain the bather actually was female. A few comments from the women on the bench indicated this girl was about to be married, which was the reason she was having the ritual bath that morning. Putting a towel on the bride's head, Mrs. Rosenblatt helped her through the appropriate prayer, then wished her well. *"Mazel tov."*

When the group was finished, Mrs. Rosenblatt smiled at Hannah. "I've never seen you here before. Are you going to bathe today?"

Since Hannah was wearing her street clothes, she thought the answer was obvious, but she declined politely. "I need to advise a woman on the laws of *nidah,* and I do not recall all the points to tell her."

"Nu? Send her to me."

"She . . . well, she doesn't want to come to the mikvah."

"Without the bath she will never be pure."

Hannah was not about to launch into the specifics of her experiment, but she did not want to insult Mrs. Rosenblatt, so she agreed with her. "Yes, you are right. Why don't you tell me the part about the clean and unclean days, and then I'll suggest she come to you for the rest?"

This seemed to satisfy the pukherin. "Come up to the front," she said, closing the heavy metal door to the bathing room behind her and locking it. Just outside the dressing area was Mrs. Rosenblatt's desk. Here she had a stack of cards printed with the rules in Yiddish and Hebrew as well as a chart, which made them simpler to follow.

She had Hannah sit and she went over each point. "When a woman sees even the slightest bleeding during her regular period—or at any other time for that matter—she becomes a nidah and must be separated from her husband. They must stay apart through the days of bleeding until after the *tviloh*—the ritual immersion—in a mikvah." She went on with clinical descriptions of what constituted staining and how to test with a special cloth. "If she believes that all bleeding is over, she then can don the white by preparing a piece of completely white cotton cloth, which must be soft and fine—not new, not coarse—and washed freshly clean. Nothing else must be used for this purpose."

Hannah wanted to tell the attendant that she did not require all these particulars, but since she couldn't explain, she let her prattle on. "Tell her to wash the lower part of her body, place one leg on a footstool and, while standing, insert the cloth turned around her finger as far into her body as possible. Then she should move it back and forth into every slit and fold. When she removes it, it should be absolutely white. If there is any question of the color, she should take it to her rabbi for consultation."

Unable to restrain herself, Hannah asked incredulously, "Women take the cloths to their rabbis?"

"That's what they are supposed to do," Mrs. Rosenblatt replied in a resigned tone that indicated she might be less stringent. "If she is clean, she must put a fresh white sheet on her bed and also change the rest of her bed linen. From then after, during her clean days, she must not use any linen or undergarments that are not white."

How could any woman follow these procedures? Hannah speculated silently, but said, "So once she does that, she can begin counting the seven clean days."

"No," Mrs. Rosenblatt replied firmly, "the counting begins the day following the donning of the white. But remember, in Jewish law the day actually begins the evening before."

Hannah nodded numbly, thinking that none of this would matter to Mrs. Tartaglia.

"Now at the conclusion of seven clean days, she prepares herself for the bath by cutting her fingernails and toenails . . ." Just as Rachael had suggested, the Jewish laws were grounded in sensible hygiene. "Now if this occurs during *yomtov* . . ."

Impatient to leave the steamy hallway, Hannah waited for a pause to review the points that most concerned her. "So, if a woman has five unclean days, she waits a day—making it six days—then adds seven white days, has her bath, and then can resume relations with her husband."

"Wish it were that simple," Mrs. Rosenblatt said, sighing, and showed Hannah the chart that dealt with irregular periods and other special circumstances. In some cases, when a woman had a short cycle, it seemed almost impossible for a husband and wife to get together. Smiling, Hannah realized that hers, which averaged thirty-three to thirty-five days, gave the maximum of clean days, as if it mattered in her marriage, but still if she and Lazar had lived in a different time or place . . . Anyhow, she had what she needed. Now all she had to do was explain it to Anna-Maria.

∽ **12** ∽

Finally, the first week of March, Hannah was able to make a visit to Elizabeth Street during a time she was fairly certain Mr. Tartaglia would not be at home. Although the journey from Tompkins Square to Elizabeth Street was hardly more than a mile, Hannah passed through several different worlds. Not only did signboards change from Hebrew to Polish to Italian, the faces, clothes, and language were as varied as the motley multitude packed into the processing hall at Ellis Island. Even odder were the variations in aroma: from pickle brine and pastrami to the piquant scent from the hot sweet-potato wagon, leading up to stronger and stronger scents of onion and garlic. Since she had missed her noon meal, Hannah munched on a knish, a dumpling filled with barley and liver, she purchased at a pushcart.

Hannah could not help noticing the boys, some even younger than Benny, who roamed the streets when they should have been in school. A few were selling newspapers, others carried bundles of piecework bigger than they were, ran errands, offered to shine shoes, or were manning stalls. She passed a pathetic group of bootblacks who were hunched over a charcoal fire thawing their numb fingers. Their smooth faces had a hardened edge. One of the boys looked up and called, "Hey, how's your knish?" Hannah forced herself to keep going. Behind her she could hear the boys guffawing because *knish* was also a crude slang for "vagina." Such toughness was a requirement in these streets, she knew, but the loss of their innocence plucked at her heart. Approaching her destination, Hannah felt even more dismay. The alley beside the tenement was hung with criss-crossing lines of frozen laundry that crackled in the gusting wind. On a broken cart five children too small for school were bundled so that only their eyes were visible. Frost formed on their delicate lashes. At the sight of Hannah one child reached her bulky arms out in a plea to be taken indoors.

Hannah went over and patted the girl's chapped cheek. "What's your name?"

"She's Cecilia," answered an older child sitting behind her.

"And yours?"

"Antonia."

That sounded familiar. "Antonia what?"

"Antonia Tartaglia."

"Are you cold? Do you want to come inside?"

Both girls nodded. "Come with me, I'm here to see your mama." She lifted the larger one down and took the smaller one in her arms. "Show me where your flat is."

As they walked away, a child abandoned on the wagon began to wail. "I'll find your mama too," the midwife promised.

Cecilia pressed her icy nose against Hannah's neck and shivered. Hannah followed Antonia up the rickety stairs slowly, watching for broken slats and holding on firmly to the unsteady banister. The older child's legs were so swaddled she had to bring both feet together on a step before she could attempt the next. The higher they rose, the more intense became the scent of garlic simmering in oil. They passed a haggard woman carrying a bundle of laundry, and Hannah said to her, "There's a child crying outside."

"I'm going down, aren't I?" she snapped.

As Hannah stopped to let her pass, she happened to look down into the stairwell at a mound of rags and papers. A firetrap! How could people live like this? she fretted, shaking her head. Even when her family had been reduced to conditions not so different, she had seen that the hallways were free from debris, if only to keep the vermin from breeding there.

"Here it is," Antonia said in a chiming voice.

"Mama, Mama!" Cecilia called.

Someone coughed, then shouted, "I told you to stay outside. Who let you in?"

"I did," Hannah said as she pushed the front door open.

Mrs. Tartaglia, who was surrounded by pillows on a day bed in the dark, cluttered room, stared at the midwife without recognition. Hannah's long coat covered her dress, which wasn't her uniform in any case—and the brim of her hat hid most of her face. "It's Mrs. Sokolow from Bellevue, the head midwife."

Before the two little girls had pressed themselves against their mother, Hannah noticed she had been nursing baby Hannah.

"Hannah Sokolow." The midwife accented her first name.

Anna-Maria's face was transformed from apprehension to congeniality. "I did not expect you to come to my house," she said apologetically, pushing the little ones away. They then clustered around Hannah, who reflexively began to remove their scarves, hats, and leggings.

"I don't usually, but—" She caught herself from bringing up the real reason she had come for a moment, and prevaricated slightly. "I was curious to see how little Hannah was getting on."

"She eats, she sleeps, she eats some more."

Hannah stepped closer to see the baby, who was not as plump as a child of six weeks should have been. Out of the corner of her eye she saw a pillow on the bed stir. A little white hand poked out. Mrs. Tartaglia pulled up this baby, who could not have been much more than a year old, and put her on her other breast.

Little Hannah had relaxed her grip on the nipple and seemed asleep. "May I hold her?"

Anna-Maria nodded, and as Hannah lifted the baby, the toddler squirmed for a better position across her mother's lap.

"What a fine family," Hannah forced herself to say in a sunny voice, although the weight of this family's poverty pressed upon her, making her want to flee. The small rooms, the bathtub in the kitchen, the sound of the toilet flushing in the hall, were all reminders of a not-so-distant past. "Tell me their names and ages again."

"Antonia is three, Cecilia almost two, and Oriana was just one. There is also Claudia, who started school this year."

As she spoke, Hannah surreptitiously gave the baby an examination. Except for a crusty scalp, she seemed normal. "You still would like a boy."

"Not me. I don't want any more, but what I want has nothing to do with it."

Hannah looked up to see if Anna-Maria was smiling. She wasn't, so Hannah didn't laugh. "There might be a way to increase your chances of having a son," Hannah began in a tentative tone.

"Ha! I knew it." Anna-Maria threw her head back and sniffed. "Why do you tell me now?"

"I only just discovered it myself."

"Aren't you Jewish?"

"Yes, but just as some Catholics go to mass every day and others only on Easter, there are also Jews who adhere to every commandment and those who don't."

"And you don't," Mrs. Tartaglia said with a voice that was slightly accusatory.

In her excitement over the discovery of sex-selection ideas, Hannah had forgotten the unpleasant aspects of this woman's personality. However, one glance around at the family's privation and the woman's burdens—not to mention the crass husband who shared her bed—softened Hannah. "No," she said. "My husband and I do not practice the religious rituals associated with marriage, but apparently those who do have a much higher chance of having more boys than girls, as you already have noticed."

A clatter made the two women jump. Oriana screeched as the breast was jerked away. Hannah looked toward the small kitchen area, which was nothing more than a board over a wash sink, a few pans and kettles, and a broken table propped up on bricks. Hanging from the peeling wall were a box of matches and a cross. Antonia had been eating spaghetti out of a pot when Cecilia pulled on her skirt, causing her to lose her balance. The children were covered in spaghetti and sauce.

Mrs. Tartaglia propped the toddler on the bed, and Hannah placed the infant on a blanket on the floor. Both women rushed to the spattered children to prevent them carrying the mess into other parts of the house.

"At least it was cold," Hannah said, thinking the accident could have been far worse.

This didn't seem to console Anna-Maria, who didn't need another chore that day. Almost a half hour passed before the older girls and the kitchen were presentable.

"Thank you for helping," Anna-Maria said.

"I'm still hungry!" Antonia whined.

"Take Cecilia to the bedroom," she directed the child, "and I'll feed you later." Her daughter pouted, but did as she was told.

"Have you eaten?"

"Not really," Hannah admitted.

"I am going to have something while the babies are quiet. It won't last long," Anna-Maria predicted and made them two plates.

Until Hannah dipped a piece of bread crust in a spicy bean soup, she did not realize how famished she had been. Mrs. Tartaglia finished some pasta that had been recovered from the floor.

"Are you going to tell me how to do it?" Mrs. Tartaglia asked sharply as she took Hannah's bowl.

Hannah bristled, but then after seeing the anxiety in the woman's expression, softened. "Yes, but you may not wish to follow the rules. And your husband will have to cooperate."

"What do you mean?" Anna-Maria asked cautiously.

"Well, first there are certain days he may come to your bed and certain days he may not."

Mrs. Tartaglia's face darkened as she mulled this over. "How many?"

"That depends on how many days you have between bleedings."

"But I haven't had my monthly in three years!"

Hannah had not thought about this eventuality. When a woman fed a baby by breast, menstruation usually was absent until the child began to take a considerable amount of solid food. This was responsible for a certain level of natural birth control, but was by no means foolproof, as was evidenced by the Tartaglias' closely spaced children.

"When you did have your cycle, was it regular?"

"Yes."

"How many days?"

"Twenty-eight or nine. Like a clock."

Hannah sighed. There was no way to establish a count.

Seeing Hannah's bewilderment, the woman offered, "If it helps, I've always had twinges in the middle of the month."

The middle. Mittelschmerz! Hannah thought. For some women the sharp pains that accompany the release of an egg from the ovary were so severe that they sought medical advice. Hannah could always pinpoint this as a normal phenomenon when it occurred precisely two weeks before menstruation began. Even if a nursing mother was not having a normal period, she would have to ovulate to be fertile. And if she normally experienced these pangs, she should feel if she could become pregnant that month.

"Is it the sort of pain that shoots through you when you sit on a hard chair?" the midwife asked.

"Yes, how did you know?"

"And you always have them?"

"Yes. Once, before I was married, it was so severe that I fainted. My mother thought I had a side sickness and took me to the hospital."

"It wasn't your appendix?"

"No, but they couldn't tell me what it was. When it happened the next month, I told my aunt and she said not to worry."

"Have you felt it since Hannah was born?"

"No, thanks to the blessed Virgin."

Hannah opened her purse and took out the card with clean and unclean days she had prepared. She numbered a month from one to twenty-eight and put an *X* on day fourteen. This was about when an Orthodox woman with a typical cycle would begin relations with her husband anyway.

"Now I will tell you the secret," she said.

Anna-Maria leaned forward expectantly as Hannah gave her the instructions for what to do if menstruation commenced, but then warned, "Since you might conceive your next baby before the bleeding begins, the pain can be your signal." She pointed to the *X*.

Mrs. Tartaglia seemed confused. "Are you saying that my husband must sleep somewhere else for two weeks?"

"Yes, that is what the Jews do."

"Giovanni will never agree."

Hannah shrugged. "Even if that is the only way to have a boy?"

"He would never believe! He would—" she gasped. "Well, you saw him when he was angry. In bed he is different. He needs it. Almost every night unless he has too much to drink."

Without thinking Hannah said, "You could serve more wine."

Anna-Maria giggled in response. "I'd have to knock him

out for two weeks." Then she shook her head. "No, he'd never wait that long."

Hannah stood up. "Then I cannot help you." She started for the chair on which she had draped her coat and hat. "Unless . . ."

When she saw that Anna-Maria had tears in her round dark eyes, Hannah decided to offer one final suggestion. "You could do everything he wants, except allow him inside you." She watched the woman's face to see if she understood.

"Use my hand or mouth?" she whispered.

"Whatever you would prefer," Hannah responded in a purposefully offhand manner.

Anna-Maria flushed. "Would you do that to *your* husband?"

Hannah did not reply at once. What did it matter what she would or would not do? If Mrs. Tartaglia was not made to feel ashamed of the act, she might consider it. "As long as both the man and the woman agree, there is nothing wrong," she answered, hoping it would get her off the hook.

This seemed to satisfy Anna-Maria. Now she became more animated. "So, I put Giovanni off as much as I can, or do the other for the first two weeks, and after—?"

"And then as much as he wants for two weeks," Hannah replied, then added, "and you want."

She reached for her hat again, but then remembered the Talmudic charge for the woman to be satisfied. Was this something she dare mention? Not every woman experienced fulfillment with her husband, yet hadn't Anna-Maria said that her husband was different in bed? Did that mean gentler, more considerate? Anyway, Hannah had gone too far already to leave out this point. She didn't believe it would really matter in the determination of sex, since what impact could a woman's pleasure have on biology? Still . . . there was much they did not yet know.

Little Hannah was stirring. She made a mewing cry that shortly would become more forceful. Hannah spoke quickly. "Another thing, the Jewish man is told that if his reward comes before a woman's, a girl will result, but if a woman's precedes his, there will be a boy. Do you understand what I mean?"

Anna-Maria's mouth puckered, but she didn't reply.

"The man must wait until the woman is satisfied," Han-

nah reiterated. "That is, if the woman is able to . . ." Now
she was lost. She probably shouldn't have brought this up.
There were no guarantees that the system would even work.
And what right did she have to alter the woman's expectations? There was probably a fifty–fifty chance she would
have a son the next time anyway.

Anna-Maria turned away from Hannah to gather up a diaper and a wet cloth. "I will have no difficulty with that
command," she murmured.

Hannah's chest heaved with relief, not only because she
had been understood, but because some measure of delight
had momentarily alleviated this woman's wretchedness.

∽ 13 ∾

One broiling afternoon in late June when Hannah and her
daughter stopped by to rest in Dr. Jaffe's office on their way
home from Emma's dance class, they found Rachael working on some calculations.

"Ever since your Italian lady asked for the secret, I've
been keeping up with the numbers. For some reason my Orthodox ladies have been having babies like crazy."

"It's always like that nine months after the high holy
days."

"Well, they must have been praying for boys. There are
more than ever this month."

Hannah fanned herself with a Yiddish newspaper, the *Tage-
blatt*. When she realized what she was using, she dropped it.
"What are you doing with this dreck?" she cursed at the anti-
Socialist paper.

"A patient must have left it." She quickly changed the
subject. "Have you heard anything more about 'our little experiment'?"

"I'm not about to monitor that particular bedroom for
compliance with Talmudic injunctions," she said more abruptly than usual, then apologized. "Sorry, the heat . . . Anyway, I doubt that it will work. Her husband is more an

animal than a person. He'll never put aside his needs for something as elusive as this."

"Who's an animal?" Emma asked.

Ignoring her, Hannah said, "Show Aunt Rachael what you are learning in class."

Emma, who was the only one not wilting, twirled around, her long braids flying behind her. Hannah could not help but admire her daughter, who was light on her feet and had a natural, seamless grace. Ever since she had been a baby, whenever she passed a musician or heard a song, her face had brightened. "Some people breathe air, she breathes music," Lazar had noted, an apt assessment Hannah had never forgotten.

"Very good," Rachael said, clapping.

"Mrs. Roosevelt said I was the best in the class."

"Where does she go?"

"Rivington Street Settlement," Hannah said, mentioning one of the social service centers that provided the community with everything from health care to sewing, music, and dozens of other classes. "You should enroll Nora. It would be good for her." Rachael's daughter was almost exactly a year older than Emma, but was pudgy and shy.

"Nora wouldn't like the teacher," Emma said quickly.

"Yes, she would," Hannah disagreed. "She is wonderful with all the girls, even the ones who aren't quite as talented as you."

"Like Nora?" Emma added thoughtlessly.

Hannah flushed as Rachael deftly steered the conversation into another channel. "I wonder if your lady is pregnant yet."

"You mean Mrs. Tartaglia?"

"Who else?"

"I'd be surprised if she wasn't, but I am not in the mood to walk over to Elizabeth Street to find out." Tired by the whole subject, Hannah sagged.

"Do you think she tried the system?"

"Maybe, but in my experience women are much more likely to put aside their selfish concerns for a larger good— like the needs of her children—than a man. And this is the last man in the world I would expect to be selfless for a second, let alone two weeks of every month."

"She could still have a boy."

"For her sake I hope she does."

"But possibly not for yours."

"Why?"

"If your Italian lady has her son, every member of San Salvatore is going to be at your doorstep begging for advice."

"Then I'll send them all to you," Hannah said with a laugh.

"In any case I hope you hear the result."

"If she doesn't come to Bellevue on my shift, or doesn't come to Bellevue at all, we'll never know."

⤜ 14 ⤛

But they soon would. The rainy August day Mrs. Tartaglia arrived at Bellevue to parade her swollen abdomen, Hannah had been told that a former patient wanted to see her downstairs. Though mothers frequently wanted to show off the babies she had delivered previously, they did not understand that she had more allegiance to the laboring patients in the wards. So when she heard about this woman she sent the usual message, "Tell her I am busy with a delivery and wish her well."

Two hours later, the nurse came by to say the patient was still waiting. Hannah's brow furrowed. "Something must be wrong," she said. "Nobody would stay that long unless they needed me. How did she look?"

The nurse held her arms out in a circle in front of her. "Huge, but she said she wasn't due until October."

"Why didn't you tell me she was pregnant? Was anyone with her?"

"Just two small children. A fat baby about nine months and another little girl who has been running from one end of the hall to the other and back like a rabbit."

"Then it might be important," Hannah said, giving some instructions before leaving the ward.

Thunder boomed outside and a fresh torrent of rain pounded the sidewalks. Hannah chided herself for worrying about the woman, who was probably only waiting out the storm. Lightning splintered the slate sky and the great gold gash lingered longer than expected. In the doorway to the main entrance an obviously pregnant woman was outlined by the pulsating light. Her toddling daughter clung to her skirts, while a baby rested on a jutted hip.

"You wanted to see Mrs. Sokolow?" Hannah queried.

The woman turned around.

"Mrs. Tartaglia!"

With her free hand Anna-Maria patted her abdomen. "How can I ever thank you?"

Hannah swallowed hard. What could she say? It was true the woman had conceived for the sixth—no, seventh—time, which was hardly a feat for her, but there was no guarantee the child she carried was male. All Hannah did was smile warmly and reach for the baby. Here she could fuss appropriately, for little Hannah was a beauty with apple cheeks and long black ringlets that framed a flawless ivory face.

She kissed her namesake and stroked her luxuriant curls. "Such a big girl! What a beauty." Not forgetting Oriana, she bent down and asked, "How old are you now?"

The gaunt child, who would always be overshadowed by her younger sister's loveliness, held up two fingers proudly. Hannah made the appropriate fuss.

"I did everything you said. Everything," Anna-Maria added, pausing meaningfully. "Giovanni was easier than I expected. I gave him much more wine, my whole portion, and lots of extra onions—that upsets his stomach—so he was often either too drunk or too gassy to be interested, if you know what I mean." She prattled on. "Besides, as you can see, he's a fast worker, so he wasn't denied much for very long."

"When do you think you are due?" Hannah asked.

"Just after my Hannah's birthday. They'll be a year apart. Giovanni is so excited. He's telling everyone that it's a boy."

Hannah frowned. "There is no assurance . . ."

Anna-Maria moved the baby from one hip to the other and shifted her weight. "I *know* it is a boy because this one is out front, while the others made me fat around. And there are lots of other signs."

Not wanting to discourage these daydreams, and also running out of time for chatting, Hannah replied, "I hope you are right, and even if you're not, it must be agreeable to have a contented husband." She gave Anna-Maria a sympathetic smile and gestured that she had to be going.

"You'll deliver him, won't you?" Anna-Maria's voice was less positive than before.

"Here we work in shifts. If you come in when I am on duty, I will try to be there for you, but I cannot promise."

Mrs. Tartaglia dropped her eyes. "I understand."

Backing away, Hannah called, "Good-bye, little Hannah, good-bye, Oriana."

"See you in October," their mother added wistfully.

❦ 15 ❦

That summer Lazar made some attempts to secure employment, but not on a regular basis. There were some fees from tutoring students who had failed the previous semester, a task he felt was onerous. "It's like pushing them uphill with a broom," he complained. Chaim also asked his assistance with some large runs at the press, and then after the regular carter had been hit by a runaway automobile, he found Lazar a job delivering printing supplies. Hannah was afraid her husband would decide that work was too demeaning, but was amazed to find him buoyant.

"Why?" she asked Chaim.

"He gets out, sees what's going on in the world. Uptown at that university, he never saw anything but four walls of a classroom. Also, this gives him a chance to schmooze with his friends."

Even so, his irregular contributions were not enough to keep up with the rent. In addition, Mama was complaining because Lazar was never home during the day anymore, which meant she had to watch the children the whole summer. Reluctantly, Hannah saw the only choice was to accept the higher-paying night shift, a side benefit of which was that Mrs. Hemming would rarely be on duty when she was.

By September, Hannah thought she would be accustomed to the schedule, which once the children were in school, gave her long hours of uninterrupted rest during the day, but

it did not work that way. There was still the house to keep
up, the shopping, the laundry, the cooking. The best way to
accomplish everything was to cheat on her sleep. That way
she could make certain that Emma, Benny, and Lazar were
well taken care of. Even if she denied herself by waking the
moment the children returned home from school, she enjoyed sharing the news of their little triumphs and defeats. If
she hurried, Hannah could make them an early supper, eat
with them as well as her husband if he were home in time,
and still manage a full shift. This meant Lazar had to limit
the time he spent at the cafés, but since he could fit his fra-
ternizing in between his other activities during the day, Hannah was hardly sympathetic to any complaints on that score.

The wards of Bellevue, usually a welcome refuge from
political turmoil, began to throb that autumn with dissenting
opinions about the right of women to vote. Most of the midwives applauded when President Wilson was able to secure
the release of the English suffragist Emmeline Pankhurst and
were appalled when she was ordered deported on grounds of
moral turpitude.

"Over there they may even register to vote next year,"
Norma Marshanck, the most vocal of the team, said before
a staff meeting.

"It's more than we're doing," Lenore, one of the brightest
midwifery students, commented. "All they did in New York
last week was to hold that baby show to prove we're good
mothers, as if that has anything to do with women's rights."

"Without good mothers we'll never have good citizens,
and without good citizens woman suffrage is a moot point,"
Norma noted wisely.

"It's so frustrating!" Lenore said more forcefully. "Last
year my mother would not permit me to walk in New York's
first woman suffrage parade. This year my husband is the
one who won't hear of it. But he can't tell me what to do,
can he?"

Hannah looked at the young bride and wanted to warn her
that peace at home was worth any price, but she could not,
for this would undermine everything she believed.

Still waiting, Lenore challenged, "Well?"

"If you march, you will be too tired to work," Hannah
said, using her status as the girl's supervisor to duck the issue. Then she had brought the staff meeting to order.

Hannah had almost forgotten the discussion until one

morning a few weeks later when Lazar was fixing himself a
glass of tea. "Do you want one?" he asked.

"I'm going to bed, remember?" she said irritably, for the
damp morning was making her bones ache and she yearned
to lie down.

"But you can't, not today."

"I'm not a machine," she snapped. "I need to rest sometime."

"But this is the day of the women's parade. You must join
in. All your friends will be there."

"Like who?"

"Minna, for one."

"Minna! Was she up all night catching babies and washing ladies' rear ends?"

"You sound exhausted," he said soothingly. "Why don't
you sleep for a few hours? If I wake you at noon, there will
be plenty of time . . ."

Too tired to argue, she went to lie down. A few hours
later, Lazar was kissing her awake. She sipped the tea he
brought to her bedside. Then he climbed in beside her.
"Maybe we should practice some equal rights before we go
out," he suggested in a slightly gruff tone. He had removed
his slacks and pulled her gown over her head before she
could protest. Since they were rarely in bed at the same
time, their lovemaking had diminished and she found she
was as anxious as he for the encounter.

Returning his kisses vigorously, she murmured, "What
rights?"

Lazar lay on his back, his arms pinned to his side. "It's
time that women did half the work."

Understanding at once, Hannah raised herself on top of
him and took charge while he urged her on with a wry smile.

∽ 16 ∽

"We're late already," he said as he stirred after drifting off
to sleep.

"I won't have time . . ." Hannah protested.

"You don't have to join in, but come and watch your sisters march. Besides, it's a beautiful day. You never get out in the fresh air anymore."

That much was true, and anyway, she was so content with her husband, she wanted to enjoy his companionship awhile longer.

By three o'clock on that glorious October day, every band in New York was striking up "Tipperary" as the groups of women formed around Washington Square. Hannah watched with amusement as after many false alarms and shouts of "Make ready!" and "We're moving out!" the marshals took charge, straightened out the kinks in the lines, then began to chant, "Left, and left, left!"

Led by women musicians on horseback, thousands of women, arm in arm, began to move up Fifth Avenue. Right after the band came Mrs. Carrie Chapmann Catt, President of the International Suffrage Association. Next came the first float, a facsimile of the Liberty Bell, carried by the Pennsylvania Suffrage Society, whose marchers were all dressed as Quakers. The next group wore great yellow chrysanthemums, and after that marched college women in caps and gowns followed by foreigners in their national costumes. Automobiles crept along conveying the pioneer suffragists. Behind them marched uniformed nurses carrying a banner that read: "CLARA BARTON WAS A SUFFRAGIST."

For a moment Hannah was sorry she had not consented to join that great stream of women, all flowing in the same direction, all moving toward the same goal. Their cause was so simple, so just, it seemed ludicrous that so many had to chant and march to make themselves heard. Yet, as unbelievable as it seemed, on the sidelines there were those who shouted against them. And many of the detractors were women!

"Go home to your children!"

"You'll burn in hell!"

One waved a placard asking, "Who will rock the baby?"

Hearing a scarlet-faced woman next to her yell, "Misguided fools!" Hannah became incensed. "We couldn't make a worse mess of it than the men, and we might do better."

"You'll see where this will lead," the woman raged at Hannah. "Decadence, blasphemy and decadence!"

"Leave her be," Lazar said, steering his wife away. "There's no cure for ignorance."

   As they approached the next intersection, policemen held
the encroaching throng back from the marchers. "What a
day!" Hannah heard one officer on horseback complain to
the other as they waited for a break in the parade.

   "Yeah, I thought we were going to go home early!" the
other laughed. "Fat chance!"

   The sun was falling and the wind had risen. Women who
had been in line for hours found holding aloft their banners
increasingly strenuous. Already a few had torn from their
moorings and were soaring with the breeze, carrying the
message of women's freedom up and away. Others in the
front lines were sagging under the long garlands of laurel,
which bound them into a united flank. Hannah held on to
Lazar as they crossed the avenue after the mounted policeman. They were almost to the curb when they heard someone cry, "Oh, no!"

   Lazar's head whipped around in time to see a woman in
the Collegiate Equal Suffrage League, who had been holding
a banner pole, trip and tumble forward. Someone ahead of
her broke her fall, but the pole flew out of her hands and
threatened the heads of the oncoming marchers. Lazar
surged toward it, but it eluded his grasp. Instead he stumbled
into a group of women, who began shrieking as he landed on
top of them.

   The whole section was brought up short. Hearing the
commotion, three policemen charged to the spot where
Lazar was tangled among banners and skirts. Two leapt
down to drag him roughly to the curb opposite where Hannah was waiting. Between them the tide of marchers advanced forward, dodging the fallen and confused in their
determination to continue the protest.

   Hannah could barely see what was happening until she
climbed on the base of a lamppost. Across the sea of marching bosoms with ribbons across their chests, she glimpsed
Lazar in the grip of two burly policemen. He gesticulated
wildly, shaking his head at some accusation, then was
pinned against a building and had his clothes examined for
weapons. This is too much! Hannah thought. She had to
reach him. She jumped down and tried to step off the curb.

   "You can't cross until this section has finished," a marshal
said, restraining her.

   "But . . . my husband—"

   A firm hand pushed her back on the sidewalk. On the tips

of her toes she looked but could not see Lazar. She tried the lamppost again. He had gone! Frantically she searched the opposite corner. A glance down the side street brought a constricted cry from her throat. Someone was being shoved into a paddy wagon, but because she saw only the legs, it was impossible to be certain if it was him. She looked back at the avenue. There was a gap between groups and the marshal's back was turned. For a long second she plotted her move, then dashed between the lines. Someone shouted at her, but she was on the far side of the street before she turned around. Nobody was coming after her. She rushed to the spot where she had seen the police vehicle, but it had disappeared. Then she dashed back to the corner where Lazar had last been seen. He was nowhere in sight!

❦ 17 ❦

What if he were taken to jail? What if they found out about his previous arrest at the university? Would he be branded a troublemaker? How could they afford the bail money? She would have to ask help from someone like Napthali!

In a daze she walked a few blocks until she saw another policeman. "I think there's been a mistake," she began. "My husband, he may have been arrested, but he was only trying to help!" Staring up into his cold, blank eyes, she burst into tears.

"He's probably just lost in the crowd," the officer replied soothingly, then raised his eyes to heaven in a silent plea that he be spared assignments with ladies and their causes.

"Where would they have taken him?"

"This far south it would be headquarters, Two-Forty Centre Street."

Hannah was unsure whether to get help or to go there directly. If she went to find Chaim or Herzog, she would surely be late for work, so she made her way to the trolley and headed downtown.

When she found Lazar in the holding room, he was pressing a bloody handkerchief to his mouth. Nervously she struggled to open the clasp on her pocketbook and handed him her clean one.

"Is this your husband?" the policeman who had shown her to the room asked unnecessarily.

"Yes, we got separated in the crowd." She dabbed his mouth until she saw the extent of the damage. A large gash had split his lower lip and another had sliced his chin. "He's hurt. He'll need stitches."

"There's no doctor here." The policeman signaled another to witness the discussion.

"I'll take him to Bellevue, where I'm on the night shift," she said more forcefully.

"A doctor, are we?" the officer asked arrogantly.

"I am the head of the midwifery service," she responded in the coolest voice she could muster.

She felt herself being appraised, from her shiny patent shoes to the satchel she carried.

"What are the charges?" the first officer asked the second.

"None yet. They've just brought in the troublemakers to prevent any incidents."

"He's not a troublemaker. He was helping with a falling banner!" Hannah insisted.

The first policeman perused the room. Compared to this lot of beefy thugs and disreputable women, Lazar and Hannah seemed quite respectable.

Shrugging, the officer gazed sternly at Lazar. "Be more careful," he warned gruffly.

As soon as they were on the street, Lazar spun around and spat a mouthful of blood on the sidewalk. "This country needs more than a revolution in women's rights!" he sputtered.

A few hours later, after the doctor had determined that Lazar required only a bandage and a "strong whiskey," Hannah was sitting at her desk, trying to do some paperwork, but she was too upset to accomplish much of anything. At last she realized she had missed her supper and decided she would be more effective if she found something to eat. On her way, though, Hattie Donovan intercepted her. "I know you're not on duty yet," she said apologetically, "but I wonder if you'd see a patient."

Hannah looked up with surprise. Hattie had just been made head midwife for the second of the three shifts and was perfectly competent to handle most anything.

"The woman keeps asking for you. You must have delivered one of her children. I know this happens all the time," Hattie continued with deference, "but Lenore told her you'd be on duty soon and now she's most insistent."

Putting down her pen, Hannah sighed. "Lenore meant well, don't be too hard on her," she said, since she didn't want this student's eagerness suppressed. "Besides, you know I'd rather do anything than finish reports. Mrs. Hemming will have to wait."

Hannah followed Hattie to Ward A, where she said, "Bed Six. She came in at six centimeters, but she's almost there. Just a rim of cervix was left when I went for you, so she's probably—"

From the door both midwives could see the sweating, disheveled woman purpling from the strain of pushing. They rushed to the foot of the bed. While Hattie lifted the drape, Hannah cupped her hands underneath just in time for the warm, wet head to plop into them. "Stop pushing. Just breathe," she said to prevent the patient ripping the delicate perineal tissues.

The woman did as she was told. Hattie handed Hannah a square of cloth to wipe the child's nose and mouth. As they waited for the next contraction, Hannah glanced up and recognized the strong angles of the woman's drained face. "Mrs. Tartaglia?"

"Yes," she grunted. "I knew you would come. I waited for you." A pain gripped her, and her abdominal muscles tightened. Just then her perineum bulged with the final expellation of her baby.

The child slipped into Hannah's hands upside down. Her concern was to make certain the infant's airway was open, but Anna-Maria strained forward. "What? What is it?"

Hannah looked down at the baby but only saw the backside. It was a big baby, larger than little Hannah, yet slender and delicate, much more like a girl than a boy. Her heart plummeted. She stared at the buttocks, which were mottled white and pink as oxygen began to flow into the child with every fresh breath. A long time seemed to pass, though it was only seconds.

Impatient with Hannah's silence, Mrs. Donovan lifted up the child and handed it to Anna-Maria. "A boy," she said, oblivious to the significance of her comment.

Mrs. Tartaglia crossed herself and began to wail. Long

sobs, which anyone else would have taken for tragic keening, echoed through the ward.

"She's happy." Hannah felt she had to interpret. "She already has five daughters."

Mrs. Donovan nodded as if she understood.

Hannah closed her eyes and took a long breath. Fresh in her mind was the sound of the slap, Giovanni Tartaglia's brutish face, and his wife's pathetic cringing. She could smell the garlic wafting into Elizabeth Street and envision the freezing children on the cart. She thought of little Hannah, who would be forever displaced by this prince of the household, and felt an even greater pang for the homely Oriana and her older sisters. A boy or a girl, what difference did it make? It was just another child to feed in a household that could barely manage already. It was just another child requiring the time and love of a mother with little left to apportion. Had her interference made matters better or worse for the Tartaglias? She opened her eyes and appraised the new mother. Tears stained Anna-Maria's cheeks and her cries had softened into coos meant for the baby.

"Here comes the placenta. Do you want me to finish?" Hattie asked.

"Yes, please, I don't even have my uniform on yet," Hannah said, anxious not to linger.

∽ 18 ∽

All the credit went to Hannah, much to her mortification. Mrs. Tartaglia began her exulting right in the maternity ward, which became so disruptive that she was moved to postpartum with dispatch.

"Mrs. Sokolow is a genius," the patient boasted to her bed mates. "She knows the secrets. This baby would not be here if it weren't for her!"

When Hannah got wind of this, she tried to tease Anna-Maria into a respite. "You must stop giving me the credit. Your husband is the one who cooperated." She lowered her voice. "And in more ways than one."

Unfortunately, Anna-Maria had a wide audience for her story on how to ensure a boy, though she would give no specifics. All she would say was that the Jews had a system, Mrs. Sokolow knew it, had told her, and Giovanni, Jr. was the result.

Because of the commotion, Hannah avoided the postpartum ward during Mrs. Tartaglia's stay, which was fairly easy on the night shift since most of the new mothers and babies slept. Also, this was not a time Mr. Tartaglia was permitted to visit, so Hannah avoided seeing him again. The night before Mrs. Tartaglia was discharged, Hannah was off. When she returned, Hannah was not disappointed to find the name "TARTAGLIA" removed from the census. A few evenings after that, when she took over from Hattie Donovan, the women spent fifteen minutes together during the shift change walking the wards and discussing any conditions that might require special handling.

"By the way," Midwife Donovan said, "your Mrs. Tartaglia asked me for your address."

"You didn't give it to her?" Hannah asked with alarm.

"I d-didn't think you would m-mind," Hattie stuttered. "She wanted to send you a token of her gratitude."

Hannah's face drooped, but she couldn't chastise the woman. "I'm sure you did what you thought best."

If any expression of gratitude was ever sent to Hannah, she never received it. Instead, dozens of women—and not only Italian friends of Mrs. Tartaglia—began to visit her house, asking how to have a boy instead of a girl. Even worse, many arrived when Hannah was sleeping. Since it was easier to get up and talk to them than send them away to return at an appointed time, she saw every one of them. Her generosity soon took its toll.

Because Mama Blau lived downstairs, she soon realized that the building stream of visitors was depriving her daughter of her rest. "You sleep at my place, and I'll keep them away," she offered.

In other circumstances Hannah would not have been able to relax under her mother's ministrations, but she was too exhausted to protest.

"Don't ask her to watch the children in the evenings so much," she cautioned Lazar.

"She needs to keep busy, it's good for her," he replied. *"Jeder nach seinen Fähigkeiten . . ."* he quoted Marx.

"Ya, ya," Hannah responded with resignation. "From each according to his abilities . . ." Still she worried how she would ever even the score with her mother.

Occasionally Hannah did counsel the women, but it was time-consuming. She had to take down a menstrual history, plot a calendar of days, explain about keeping their husbands out of their beds—which usually caused such a *tumel* she had to calm them down. Sometimes she mentioned having an orgasm first, sometimes she didn't. After a few consultations, it became easy to read who could handle what level of information. If they flinched about checking themselves for blood, or seemed confused about counting the dates, she offered the simplistic version and sent them away with admonition this probably wouldn't succeed. If they asked questions that pertained to their bodies and took the clinical details as a matter of course, Hannah would continue. Always she told them she didn't work miracles, but they did not believe her.

One afternoon just before Chanukah, Hannah met Rachael at her husband's "consulting room," as he preferred to call it. She wanted him to look at Emma, whose eyes had a crusty discharge. While he was seeing Emma, Rachael and Hannah had a chance to catch up.

"I've been trying to get here all afternoon," Hannah complained. "But the women are lined up. I don't know if I can keep this up much longer, especially since there are no guarantees."

"If a woman can control the sex of her offspring, she might feel more in control of her existence," Rachael began thoughtfully.

Hannah knew the doctor had said something profound, but exactly what it meant she would have to sort out later.

"Just a case of pink eye, Hannah, nothing to fret about," Dr. Herzog said as he came out to greet her.

"Herzog," Rachael said, "don't you think the world would be a better place if women could control the sex of their children?"

"That's not the point!" Hannah snapped.

"You would prefer not to assist women playing God," he stated flatly, stroking his wiry beard.

"There's no way of knowing if I am helping, and even if I am, the point is senseless, and I wish I didn't have to worry about the whole matter," she said, slumping with fatigue. "I just can't do what everyone wants twenty-four hours a day."

"Why don't you cut back on your Bellevue schedule or return to days?"

"Only if I can also cut back on food and clothes and . . ." She gave a hollow laugh. "You know what Mama says? She wants me to charge a dollar for every lady and ask for a bonus if they get a boy."

"Not a bad idea," Rachael said.

"You think they would pay me?"

"People will pay for anything they think they need."

"If they pay me, they will feel cheated if they don't get what they desire."

"People pay doctors even though they can't be cured," Dr. Herzog replied smoothly. "The secret is to leave them feeling better than they did before they came in."

"Yes, I agree," Rachael inserted. "And you are already doing that by making them think they can have more of a choice. Besides, if they fail, they are most likely going to blame themselves for being irregular or getting the dates wrong or not waiting long enough."

"But if you succeed . . ." Herzog grinned. "And you will at least half the time, maybe more."

"That's not all they want to know. You should hear the questions they ask! I thought I'd heard it all as a midwife, but when you start to talk to people about what they do in their beds, well . . ." Hannah reddened.

"What do you tell them?" he asked.

"I try to steer them back to the original point, otherwise it takes too much time. If I charged them, they would demand explanations I do not have."

"I'm often asked questions I cannot answer. What you do is listen and seem sympathetic, something you are skilled at anyway. If worse comes to worst and you have nothing else to offer, repeat the woman's words back to her. It's a trick, but they never catch on. They just think you are very insightful."

"I don't understand what you mean."

"Ask me a question," Dr. Herzog said, leaning back against the door frame. "Something about your children," he coached.

"What should I do with my daughter?" Hannah asked tentatively. "She won't do her schoolwork."

"Your daughter won't work in school."

"No. She would rather dance than study."

"You think she's wasting her time dancing when she should be studying."

"Yes. If she's going to get ahead in the world, she should follow her brother's example."

"Your daughter is a worry to you."

Hannah threw up her hands. "We're getting nowhere."

"That's because you're analyzing everything to take back and use yourself. However, if you were really in enough distress to tell me about it, and I responded just as I did, you would find relief in talking it over with someone."

Was this true? What harm could come from testing it? Besides, the idea of charging for her trouble was appealing.

Later that evening, she asked Lazar what he thought about the scheme.

"Well, my opinion is that it is absurd to give advice to anyone," he said, looking up from his newspaper.

"Even for money?"

"Especially for money. Money is not everything."

Now she was sorry to have initiated the conversation. "That may be true, but it is something, or has it been so long since you've held any in your hand you have forgotten what it's for?" she countered.

"That is not the point," he said airily, then turned back to what he had been reading.

Exasperated, she planted herself in front of him. "Then what is it?"

He did not respond until she batted down the shield of paper. "Wise men never need advice and fools never heed it."

"So? Who cares?" She stomped across the room, then spun around. "If the wise ones and the foolish ones will pay me, isn't that enough?"

"Why ask me if you don't care what I recommend?" he snarled as he tried to find his place in the crumbled paper.

Indeed, she thought in a huff. I won't ask you, and I won't worry about them. If people come to me for advice, I'll tell them what I think, and take their money as fair compensation for my effort. And then they can do with it what they want!

Problem 2:
Rachael Jaffe's Secret

◆

1914

Observe, probe
Details unfold.
Let nature's secrets
Be stammeringly retold.
— GOETHE

∽ 1 ∽

HANNAH began to read. Even if the English was difficult, she had to find answers to her questions before she could help others. Lazar got her started. He had been frequenting the university library in preparation for his book project, and in a spare moment had looked for something that might interest his wife. The first volume he discovered was by Havelock Ellis.

"Havelock," Hannah said as he put it on the dining room table with the pile he had borrowed from the library. "An odd name. What does it mean?"

"It's just a name."

"Yes, but 'have' and 'lock' are together."

Lazar scowled and removed his shabby brown sweater. "Names aren't supposed to make sense. I just thought you'd find him interesting because he writes about sexual matters."

Hannah hung up his sweater, then sat at the table, opened the book, and stared at one of the chapter titles: The Phenomena of Sexual Periodicity. "What does that mean?"

"I suppose it has to do with rhythms and cycles. Isn't that

what you spend so much time talking to women about?"
Her husband looked over her shoulder at the introductory
paragraph that outlined the chapter's contents and read,
" 'The various physiological and psychological rhythms—
menstruation—the alleged influence of the moon—frequent
suppression of menstruation among primitive races—mittelschmerz—' "

"Mittelschmerz!" Hannah interrupted.

"That's German for pain in the middle."

"I knew that."

Lazar flipped the pages until he found the reference.
"Read it for yourself, then," he said as he cut himself a slab
of bread.

With trembling hands she took the volume. Her finger
found the paragraph beginning with the familiar word and
she read on until only a few sentences down Ellis referred to
"règles surnuméraires" and in the same paragraph a book
by Fliess called *Die Beziehungen zwischen Nase und
weiblichen Geschlechts-Organen.* Tears flooded her eyes.
"The English is difficult enough. Who knows French, at
least I think it's French, and German and—?" she stammered. Matters of language had always confounded Hannah.
Maybe if she were younger. As a child she had easily mastered Yiddish, which was spoken at home, and Russian, the
language of her education, but a few lessons in German had
daunted her and English had been a strain from the beginning. She knew she often made mistakes when she spoke,
and even more when she wrote. Sometimes one of the American midwives would have to rewrite her notes if she made
too many errors, and her children often laughed when she
made a stupid slip.

"Oh, Ma," Benny would say, "you're *tsemisht.* It's not a
letta, it's a lettuce you want."

"I don't want a whole head, just a piece."

"Yeah, but it's still a lettuce, a *piece* of lettuce."

"So give me a piece, if you're so smart," she'd respond in
an offended tone.

Now here was a book that she longed to read, but this
Mr. Havelock had not provided the key. Noticing her distress, Lazar finished his bread and put his arms around his
wife. "You don't have to understand every word to find it
useful." He turned to the last page of the section. "Here's an
idea! Read the end first. A good writer summarizes his find-

ings. Then, if you think what he is saying might be applicable, you can study it in more depth."

"Is that proper?"

Lazar shook his head and grinned. "Who cares? There are no rules."

Hannah turned to the next part. The title, "Auto-Erotism," was unfamiliar, but a quick glance at the list of subjects revealed some interesting subheadings: "masturbation—abuse of implements and objects of daily life —the frequency of hairpin in the bladder—the influence of horse-exercise and railway traveling—the sewing machine and the bicycle . . ." She snapped the book closed. "Yes, I think you may be right."

"I'll help you translate anything that troubles you," Lazar offered.

Hannah was surprised to feel her face flushing. There had never been any shame around him before, but for some reason she was reluctant to have his assistance, at least on this section. "Thank you, but this will be good practice for me."

For many years he had been trying to interest his wife in bettering her language skills. "Good, that will kill two birds with one stone."

"Why would anyone want to kill two birds?"

Lazar laughed heartily. "To make a soup."

Hannah knew this was some sort of joke. "Then I suppose I must get our supper ready," she said with a light laugh to cover her confusion.

2

The business was steady. As few as five or as many as twelve women consulted with her each week. Hannah decided to charge by the chart instead of the time taken. That way she could quote a figure and the customer could determine whether she could afford it or not. For some she spent more than an hour explaining, others returned when they were confused, but most women were so average that a ready-made graph sufficed. It all equaled out, the midwife decided. Besides, she was doing it in her spare time and the money—at fifty cents a chart—was very welcome.

Both Hannah and Rachael were early risers, a result of their medical training. So while their families slept in on Sunday mornings, they would each walk halfway to meet at the Copper Kettle, a tea room near Astor Place. One unusually dreary morning, the third Sunday in February, the air was so icy and damp Hannah's bones ached. Arriving before Rachael—as usual—she picked a table as far away from the door as possible and did not remove her coat.

"Are you coming or going?" Rachael asked as she flung her wrap on a spare chair.

"I think I'll stay," Hannah said, unbuttoning hers.

Rachael looked around at tables covered with blue-checkered cloths as if seeing them for the first time. "I do like it here. It's so . . . comfy."

"Yes, comfy," Hannah agreed with her friend's choice of words. As she poured the tea into the delicate cups, Hannah realized how much she preferred the Dutch plates with scenes of old New York, the cobalt blue pots with hand-knitted cozies to keep each pot warm, and the other dainty touches to the starkness of the cafés the anarchists frequented. How pleasant it was to have a saucer on which to place her spoon and to feel the porcelain lip next to her mouth instead of the thicker rim of the Russian-style tea glasses. Most of the well-dressed ladies, who would soon be on their way to church services, were speaking in hushed tones. Not a single voice was arguing a political point.

Rachael passed the basket of muffins. Hannah took one banana and one bran. "I love these."

"Me too. They're so . . . so American!"

Hannah laughed. She knew exactly what Rachael meant. The curls of sweet butter, the bowl of white sugar, the little pots of fruit preserves, were symbols of how far they had come.

Rachael put down her teacup. "Now, tell me, how's it been going for you?"

"The same as usual."

"Good usual or bad usual?"

"Well, Mrs. Hemming has started an 'infraction list,' whatever that means. Basically it's a way to report to the Board of Managers anything I do wrong or to blame me for any mishap on the wards."

"That doesn't sound fair, especially if it is not your fault."

"She says that she accepts full responsibility for my failings, and thus I must accept the same from those under my guidance."

"And who writes up her infraction list?"

"I wanted to ask her that, but I didn't have to. She says she answers to the Lord."

Rachael rolled her eyes. "Poor woman. She sounds terribly lonely."

"Whose side are you on?" Hannah asked with a smirk.

Rachael deflected that question with another of her own. "And Lazar?"

"Trying to stay out of trouble. I think the incident at the suffrage parade worried him more than he would admit. Anyway, he supports the advice-seekers. And why shouldn't he? The more money I take in, the less guilty he feels about not contributing."

"I doubt that," Rachael responded too quickly, then seeing Hannah's sour expression, changed direction. "Who's coming to you for advice, anyway, and what do they want to know?"

"Well, it's mostly the same business about having a boy, but what I find interesting is how the women react when I tell them that, if possible, they should climax before their husbands." Hannah tried to ignore Rachael, who was licking the berry jam from the spoon.

"How is that?" Rachael asked, nonplussed.

"Some nod or indicate that they comprehend what I am saying; others blush or turn away."

"So? This is not something most of us discuss with anyone—not even our spouses."

"I realize that. These are the normal reactions I would expect. The ones that concern me are those that have no idea what I am talking about."

"They've never heard of an orgasm or they've never experienced it?" she responded loudly enough for Hannah to grimace. Two gray-haired ladies nearby either hadn't overheard or dared not indicate they had.

"Both, I suppose," Hannah said in an obvious whisper.

"Then what do you say?"

"Usually I skip over it. I sense that many of these women know they are missing something, yet are powerless to do anything about it."

"And I presume that these women have a majority of female offspring," Rachael said in an oddly facetious manner which put Hannah on guard.

"Would you care for anything else?" the waitress in the primly starched flowered apron asked.

"No, thank you," Hannah replied, for this place was quite expensive.

"Don't be silly. We'll both have another pot of tea, plus another order of muffins and jam." Rachael grinned mischievously. "Don't forget the jam!"

Hannah waited patiently until the waitress had left, then bent closer to her friend. "I just don't buy the whole orgasm theory of sex determination. The menstrual dates are much more responsible for the outcome, at least that's what I believe."

"Believing and knowing are two different kettles of fish."

"Look, Rachael," Hannah said with her voice rising, "I have a boy and a girl. I love my husband, and that includes sleeping with him. So what does that prove?"

"I have a girl," the doctor replied under her breath.

Hannah threw her head back and laughed, then spoke in a forced whisper. "I thought you believed in the orgasm hypothesis."

"I do." Rachael stared ahead at a point above Hannah.

Oblivious to her friend's mounting distress, as well as anxious to win the round, Hannah babbled on. "But if you knew the exact day you conceived Nora, we could tell if you were within the period mostly likely for a boy or not." She giggled at her next thought. "Besides, I doubt that you and Herzog restrained for the weeks before or—"

At last Hannah focused on her companion. What she saw bolted her lips. Tears streamed down the doctor's pale cheeks. What was the matter? Hannah's heart began to beat hard in her chest. What had her friend been trying to say? That she never had experienced an orgasm? No. Not Rachael, who always seemed so flamboyant, so free with her body. It was not possible. And yet once before, about seven years ago, when Hannah had confessed some indiscretions to the doctor—thinking she would understand because she was a woman of the world—Rachael had admitted that she was far more conservative than she seemed and had never been with a man before her wedding night.

The doctor had removed her wire-rimmed spectacles and

was blotting back the tears with her napkin. She had almost brought her angular face under control. Was Rachael really saying that her marriage was incomplete, or only that she hadn't had satisfaction when Nora was conceived?

"You haven't . . . ?" was all Hannah could manage to ask.

The droop of Rachael's chin and the slight shake of her head was the reply.

Hannah's face, which had been about to laugh at Rachael's jest, contorted into a confused grimace as she tried to comprehend the enormity of the confession. "I'm sorry, I—" rang hollow. Hannah gulped and tried again. "I couldn't imagine what you meant . . . stupid of me . . ." Giving up on speech, she reached for Rachael's hand.

The women were silent together. There was so much that Hannah wanted to know. Had Rachael ever experienced an orgasm, even by masturbation or fondling? Did she enjoy any part of the sexual act? Was her husband a competent lover? Or was there a medical reason for the difficulty? She recalled a lecture by Dr. Petrograv in Moscow. "There is a habit that practitioners break at their peril. At first we think each symptom unique, until we have so much experience with the various abnormalities that cross our paths, we begin to believe pathology is a given, when more often than not, we have merely been presented with variations of the usual. Save the big bullets for the most deviant, treat everyone else as a most ordinary and—dare I say it?—boring case. But never, never be lulled by weeks or months of the typical into thinking that nothing untoward will happen, for the true anomalies arrive when you least expect them."

During this interval the second round of muffins had been served and a fresh pot of tea had been delivered, but the women had touched neither. As if awakening, Rachael buttered one and poured the tea. Then she sighed and gave a crooked smile. "What are you thinking? I can almost see the wheels spinning."

Looking up, Hannah saw no malice in her friend's clear eyes, but she was afraid to reopen the tender subject.

"I'm not angry with you," Rachael said as an offering.

"You should be, if only for laughing at you."

"Don't. I should have told you—or at least hinted to you—many years ago. I just never could find the right time . . . or words."

"You never have . . . ?"

"No."

"Not even by yourself?"

"Well . . ." Rachael's eyes fell. "There were times at school when I would awake from a dream to find my hand between my legs and . . ."

"You felt a gratifying sensation."

"Yes, but it was fleeting, and I never could make it happen for myself, or with my husband."

"What does he say?"

"He gets what he wants, not that he cares that much about it. Usually he is too tired. We're really very well suited." The stridency of her last statement belied her conviction, but Hannah let it pass.

"You don't find doing it, ah, distasteful, or painful?"

"No. Even though I could live without it, I don't mind gratifying my partner. Isn't that the role of a woman?"

"What role is that?"

"To accommodate men—and children—so they may proceed through life with their needs met."

"And not receive anything in return?"

"There is always give and take. Usually the husband is the breadwinner and in many cases—certainly in mine—he is a companion through life. As a mother, though, you'd have to agree that while the rewards may be subtle, they are there."

Hannah did not know what to say. Motherhood and marriage were very different conditions. Yet while she vehemently disagreed with the doctor, this was hardly the time to be contentious. Passion, though usually submerged in the daily routines of life, united her and Lazar more than economic bonds. Even the children, who delighted them both, were no match for the purity of their physical union. Without that release life would be much more tedious.

"Don't you agree?" Rachael challenged more aggressively.

Hannah forced a chuckle. "You know I never conform with you. That's why we like each other. Haven't we agreed to disagree?"

"Not always," she replied diffidently.

"You're right. I remember the one time you went along with anything I said."

"When was that?" Rachael challenged.

"When you were in labor with Nora."

"*Zorg zich nit.* Don't worry. That's not likely to happen again."

Did she mean that she wasn't likely to agree with Hannah or have another baby because of the infrequency of her sex life? Hannah wondered but did not ask. She wanted desperately to steer the subject to something less consequential, but Rachael persisted.

"Sometimes . . ." she began so softly, Hannah could barely hear her at first, ". . . sometimes I don't agree with myself."

"That's because you don't know everything," Hannah blurted without thinking. She looked up at Rachael and saw an openness in her golden eyes. "Do you want to experience it?"

"Of course I do!"

"I think it should be possible to figure out how."

"I've read about it, but that hasn't helped."

"I've read about playing tennis, but I still wouldn't know what to do if you put a racket in my hand."

"It's not as though I don't practice."

"Maybe you need a better coach."

"I've thought of that," Rachael whispered, "but who might volunteer?"

Hannah recalled the other two men she had known: the Russian obstetrics professor to whom she had given her virginity, but had found more electrifying in the classroom than the bedroom; and the scion of a prosperous Jewish family in New York, who had seduced her by asking her help with his impotence problem. She had cured him, but her reaction to his advances had been lukewarm. Neither man could hold a candle to her husband. If Herzog lacked some basic appeal, perhaps Rachael would be more responsive to someone else. But who? No! The idea was inconceivable. There was too much at stake to risk that bond for the sake of experimentation. Some way had to be found to help them to find fulfillment together.

"Perhaps that's the wrong approach. Someone else might help you in a different way."

"Who? After all, Herzog and I are both doctors."

There was a self-righteousness in her expression that galled Hannah. Sometimes a midwife bristled when physicians pulled rank, but no time more than when the midwife knew the doctor was wrong and still had to allow him to have his way. "I think I could be of more use than anyone," she blurted before reflecting that she had no idea what she meant.

"I think you could too. That's why I told you," Rachael replied in a most uncharacteristic tone, one that could best be described as acquiescent. "You know more than you think, and you know how to get answers to what you don't know. Not the solutions found in textbooks, but the practical ones. I realize something is missing in my life, something as basic as the key to a lock. You know how scatterbrained I can be. I've probably overlooked the obvious. I was hoping you might help me find it."

What could she say? After her unintentional affront, she had to make it up to Rachael. Anything she could do, anything she could discover to help her friend would be done. Rachael was right. The solution had to be simple, like locks and keys. Sex was the most basic of human transactions. Besides, if most healthy men could do it, any woman should be able to as well! Locks ... keys ... Havelock Ellis ... Yes, the solution seemed within her grasp.

"I'll find the answer," she replied breathlessly. "I promise I will."

Rachael tilted her head to show her skepticism. "Don't promise what you can't deliver." She passed Hannah the last muffin. "Just try."

3

Hannah was adrift. Where would she turn for advice? Certainly not to the Herzogs, even though in the past Rachael and Ezekiel had been her primary sources of information outside the hospital. She looked over at her husband, who was translating something from an American paper into Yiddish and scowling. "What's wrong?" she asked.

"Now they've gone and done it!"

"Done what?"

"One thousand United States Marines have seized the

Mexican seaport of Veracruz, with four killed and twenty wounded."

Knowing her husband's fury at the American involvement in the war to the south, she wisely decided to change the subject. "You know that book you found for me?"

"The one you complained you couldn't read?"

"It was difficult, but I found some interesting points. Could you get me another book by him, or someone else on the subject?"

"You could go to the library yourself."

"With what time?" she challenged.

Lazar backed down. "I'll see what I can find."

His next contribution was even more perplexing. The name of the author had been bantered about, especially by Herzog and some of his associates, so she knew something about Mr. Freud, but reading his *Three Essays on the Theory of Sexuality* posed more questions than it answered. The first section, which dealt with aberrations, made Hannah wonder why these doctors spent so much time trying to understand what was abnormal, but then, after she put the Freud book down, she decided that people went to doctors only when they were worried about something. Just as medical doctors had to try to cure the deviations in health called sickness, so these new mental doctors had to treat the results of sexual sickness first. After all, Rachael wouldn't have a problem if her relations with her husband were satisfactory. Telling herself this helped Hannah to relax and pursue the book further.

Dutifully she read each word. Although many were unfamiliar, she could generally figure them out. *Libido,* for instance, had to do with one's drive to be sexual. The discussions on the sexuality of childhood confirmed what any midwife—and any mother—knew. Many boy babies were born with erections; little girls rubbed themselves between the legs and seemed to derive pleasure. So what else was new? As she read on, however, she kept wondering how it could apply to real people who might not be content with their circumstances. When she reached the third section on "Transformations of Puberty," Freud became ambiguous. Thinking she had misunderstood, she began again, muttering to herself in her effort to make sense of the text.

"It is not until puberty that the sharp distinction is established between the masculine and feminine characters." All right, that's true. So? "The development of the inhibitions of sexuality (shame, disgust, pity, etc.) take place in little girls earlier and in the face of less resistance than boys ..." Well, if boys could get pregnant, their mothers would inhibit them!

She continued aloud: " 'The leading erotogenic zone in female children is at the clitoris, and is thus homologous to the masculine genital zone of the glans penis.' " What else was new? Her Russian anatomy professor, Stepanoff, had stated that the similarities between men and women were greater than the differences, and also that the variations among individuals of the same sex were more vast than one imagined they could be.

"Puberty, which brings about so great an accession of libido in boys, is marked in girls by a fresh wave of repression, in which it is precisely clitoridal sexuality that is affected. What is thus overtaken by repression is a piece of masculine sexuality." Now, wait a minute, Mr. Freud! The boys and girls both start to get more excited by the opposite sex. The boys go and try it, but the girls—just when they have these sensations—feel bad about them, so hold them in, and cut off the maleness within. Could this be true? Had she felt that way?

She once had liked to sleep with the pillow under her belly and sometimes would put it between her legs and rub back and forth. How old had she been? Twelve or thirteen. The first sensations of pleasure had been mild but relaxing. But sometime before morning she would move the pillow up to her head so that nobody would know. Was that how she repressed the masculine side of her sexuality?

Maybe the answer was somewhere in the next part of the text. "When at last the sexual act is permitted and the clitoris itself becomes excited, it retains a function: the task, namely, of transmitting the excitation to the adjacent female sexual parts." That seemed consistent with her experience with her husband. During the act she would rub against him or he would fondle her so the external genitals were excited, and then other areas would respond until during a climax she felt delicious ripples from deep within her uterus to the tips of her toes. But then came the most troublesome part of the theory.

"Before this transference can be effected, a certain interval of time must often elapse, during which the young woman is anesthetic. This anesthesia may become perma-

nent if the clitoridal zone refuses to abandon its excitability."
Did this mean that Rachael had entered the anesthetic period
and had never been able to open the door to depart it? And
if so, was it possible to find the missing key?

There was no time to read more before she had to start
dinner. Later that evening, Lazar was helping Benny with his
sums while Emma drew a picture of a row of houses along
the edge of his newspaper, so she turned back to the book.

To get her attention Lazar patted her arm. "I have some
good news."

"Oh?" she said, drifting back to the family. "What?"

"The university dropped their charges against me."

"Will they give you back your job?"

For a long moment he did not respond, then began again
in a fresh voice. "What are you doing next Wednesday
night?"

"What do you think?" she snapped. "I'm always on duty
then, aren't I?" His face fell. "I'm sorry," she apologized. "I
guess I'm a bit unsettled by this book."

"Really? Then it must be very good. The dull ones never
pinch a nerve, the brilliant ones always do." His smile ab-
solved her harshness. "Anyway, the reason I asked is that I
wanted to take you somewhere with me." He smiled warmly.
"There is this rich lady who invites interesting people on
Wednesdays. Herzog is one of her doctors and he has taken
me once before. I think you'd like it. Why not see if you can
exchange the night with someone else?"

"That's difficult to arrange," she protested.

"I'd like you to come with me," he said in a voice that
commanded her attention.

"Who is this woman?" Hannah said, suppressing the suspicion in her tone.

"Mabel Dodge. A very wealthy lady, but she likes to sur-
round herself with people who challenge her mind."

"I thought you reviled capitalists."

"She may be the daughter or wife of one, but she has
given that up."

"You mean she's given away her money?"

"Not exactly, but she helps her friends."

"And who are her friends?"

"Come with me and you'll see," he said to tempt her.

Intrigued, Hannah agreed she would try, then she tensed.
"What will I talk about to these people?"

"Don't worry. Anyone who is reading Freud will fit in there."

"I may be reading him, but I am certainly not agreeing with him."

"Say just that and see what happens."

∝ 4 ∝

For the next few days Hannah mulled over what Freud had written. Sometimes she felt he was absolutely wrong; other times she was almost convinced by his arguments.

One Friday, her one night off, they sat up in bed reading. "Lazar, what do you think of this?" She pointed to some confusing paragraphs.

He read them aloud. " 'When erotogenic susceptibility to stimulation has been successfully transferred by a woman from the clitoris to the vaginal orifice, it implies that she has adopted a new leading zone.' I'm not certain what he means . . ." Lazar muttered, then jumped down the page. " 'A man, on the other hand, retains his leading zone unchanged from childhood.' That makes more sense to me."

"Not to me," his wife fumed. "What's the big difference here? Is shame—that has to come from the family and the community, not from some gland—able to create a whole different range of feeling in girls at some point?"

"What about you? You're certainly a normal woman." He gave her a provocative smile.

Hannah mulled over the question. If she herself had felt anesthetic, she had never known when. Certainly there must have been a time she had not been as interested in touching herself, but what she remembered most acutely was that crucial week in which she had lost her virginity to Dr. Petrograv and then given herself to Lazar. She had experienced no special sensations with the doctor, or at least nothing that had resulted in a climax, but then she also had been afraid of being found and guilty about what she had been doing during their one rushed encounter. The next man she had permitted to touch her had been Lazar, who had aroused her passionate response.

"Nu?" he prompted by stroking her thighs under the covers.

If months or years had passed between the two encounters, she might have allowed that the first had been the result of her youthful anesthesia and the second, which had been far more fulfilling, had been because of her more mature— what had Mr. Freud called it? transference, but in actuality it had only been a matter of days!

"What's the big mystery?"

Hannah blurted, "I've never been anesthetic with you."

This seemed to satisfy him, much to her relief. Even after all these years only Rachael knew her secret. Lazar was thoughtful for a moment, then he offered one of his political analyses. "The whole premise is logical. After all, children develop and go through predictable patterns from turning over to crawling to walking to saying no to learning to read to wanting to be with their friends in much the same way that a society passes through stages from feudalism to capitalism to socialism. So why shouldn't a young girl go through phases about her body?"

"Then why don't boys experience parallel changes as they become men?"

"Maybe they do, only Freud has not yet found out what they are."

"Then how will I ever discover what is right?" she asked with exasperation.

"You won't. It's like a new form of government. You don't know what will work until you try it. Besides, since this is theoretical, why brood about it?" With that, he closed his book and let it drop to the floor. His hand began to stroke her neck and the cleft between her breasts.

Hannah leaned back and closed her eyes, but her thoughts remained with Rachael. Of course, she could bombard Rachael with possibilities, have her try them, and see which proved successful. Was there one right way to give birth? No. Each mother and each attendant sorted it out, trying a bit of this, a bit of that until the baby came. Whatever worked.

Yes . . . she sighed as Lazar's fingers began to probe between her legs. That first time so long ago with Dr. Petrograv, she had been tense, but even so either the doctor had been a poor lover or rushed by his unruly excitement. Also, while she had been impressed with his brilliance at the lying-in hospital, his naked body had not appealed to her. She slid down and wrapped her arms around her husband, whose touch always could dissolve her, like a lump of sugar in a glass of tea.

"Remember that time you took me to your rooms in Odessa," she murmured.

"How could I forget" came the reply muffled by his kisses.

During that initiation, Lazar had been impetuous but gentle, and his touch had seemed educated—at least as far as to what she required. She had climaxed under his initial ministrations. Not that the feeling hadn't intensified as they had learned more about each other. The meager spasms she had felt then had been eclipsed by the deep, meteoric shudders their love was capable of producing today.

Was this finding contrary to Mr. Freud, or did it prove his point? Hannah's mind was spinning. Her memories were vague. Most mothers forgot the agonies of birth shortly after the baby was placed in their arms, for if they recalled it they might never have another. Did it follow that they probably forgot the joys of conception as well?

Without much luck Hannah tried to sort her mental images from the insistent sensations Lazar was encouraging. His tongue reached deep into her mouth and she lifted herself to meet him more than halfway. Maybe her early responses had been more muted—like those when she fondled herself—so this might mean she had merely skipped the anesthetic phase and had moved from the clitoridal to the vaginal, although it was difficult to isolate where her satisfaction began or terminated. Perhaps this was the moment when she would discover the truth. . . .

5

Once again she learned nothing. In the morning, the book lay upside down and opened to where she had left it. She began again. "The fact that women change their lead g erotogenic zone in this way, together with the wave of repression at puberty, which, as it were, puts aside their childish masculinity, are the chief determinants of the greater proneness of women to neurosis and especially to hysteria. These determinants, therefore, are intimately related to the essence of femininity."

This was the conclusion? Did this mean Rachael was more masculine and she more feminine? Although Hannah wanted to refute this, there were elements that she had to agree might be true. Rachael was slender in the hips, had fairly small breasts, and was as tall as a man—taller than many, in fact. Yet she had produced a daughter, nursed her, nurtured her . . . In other ways she was decidedly feminine. Her walk was graceful. Her long arms were those of a dancer. And her genitalia were absolutely normal. Hannah strained to remember any odd configuration. She had done many pelvic examinations for her friend and had never found anything unusual. Rachael's uterus might have been a bit tilted and her womb had dropped slightly since the birth. What else? Hannah smiled to herself. Rachael's pubic hair was a beautiful color: a rich, burnished hue like sunset on a Ukrainian wheat field. Probably the hair on her head had been that tone when she was a child, but it had darkened over the years. Of course, Hannah hadn't checked the labia or clitoris with this matter in mind, but anything too small or large or distorted would have made an impression. Besides, Rachael had said that she had experienced some sexual sensations, just not during intercourse. Had she not moved into the more mature phase because of a physical reason, or did shame rule her passions? Hannah recalled that Rachael had come from a long line of rabbis, who would have frowned on her whole way of life. Next time Hannah spoke to Rachael she would see whether this line of questioning might unlock the door.

❦ 6 ❦

"I am delighted that you decided to come with me," Lazar said as he wrapped his arm around her and hurried Hannah across Fifth Avenue. The evening air was filled with the fragrance from a blossoming bush in a churchyard.

Hannah paused to catch her breath. "So few blocks, so much difference," she said as she looked at the fine houses that lined the wide avenue, comparing them with the humble tenements a few blocks to the east. The sidewalks were clear of pushcarts and peddlers, loungers and urchins. "There's not a child to be seen, even on such a mild night."

"Is that a complaint or a sigh of relief?" Lazar asked lightly, then so as not to start a discussion added, "We're almost there." He walked briskly to the corner of 9th Street. "This is the place."

At first Hannah was disappointed by the somber square building with the brown painted bricks. As she approached 23 Fifth Avenue, however, she saw that the front doors were inset with clouded glass engraved with Greek or Roman faces and the knobs were forged from silver. Lazar rang the bell. Hannah's hand flew to her hair to straighten the wisps that had straggled free. Lazar smoothed them for her. "Don't worry. You look very lovely." The warmth of his words gave her confidence as the doorman let them in. Without asking where they were going, he pointed the way up a long flight of vermilion carpeted stairs.

As they walked slowly along the hall with vaulted ceilings, following the voices that spilled out and echoed off the darkened wood, Hannah whispered, "Who else might be here?"

He spoke in Russian. "Alexandra Kollontai's coming to speak. She wants to distribute a pamphlet she wrote for Lenin on 'Who Needs the War?' I hope Mrs. Dodge will agree to support its American publication."

"You're going to ask her for money for the Bolsheviks?" she responded in Yiddish.

"No. If she likes the idea, she will offer it," he said quickly, then with a touch of annoyance added, "Drop the Yiddish here."

"Lazar, we will not sit in the woman's parlor and beg for money!" Hannah retorted, then was about to ask why Russian was more acceptable than Yiddish when the door to the apartment opened at their approach.

Hannah almost gasped as she walked from the gloom into the blazing light. The ornate woodwork was painted white and the walls were covered with a thick, textured paper also in white. "Good evening, Vittorio," Lazar said, as if to prove that he had been there before. They were ushered into a corner room with three soaring windows that looked out both on Fifth Avenue and 9th Street. The draperies were straight, handwoven linen curtains, the same vivid white as the walls. A carved white marble mantelpiece glistened as the focus to the room. The light came primarily from a huge white porcelain chandelier, its curved arms encrusted with birds and flowers. People provided the color to this purposefully monochromatic backdrop, and it seemed as if the whole setting had been designed to set off the striking faces and outlandish combinations of garb. Immediately Hannah felt her gray suit and eggshell shirtwaist made her seem far too ordinary, and wished she had never agreed to come.

"What do you think of my home?" was the first question a woman in a flowing white dress asked.

Hannah presumed this was her hostess. "It's very cheerful," she murmured, hoping the choice of words was safe.

Mrs. Dodge seemed pleased. "Isn't it, though? It seems I cannot get my fill of white. I suppose it is my repudiation of grimy New York. Mr. Sokolow, what do you think of my latest addition?"

Hannah was amazed that she recalled her husband's name. Mrs. Dodge had pointed in the vicinity of the mantel, but Lazar stared at the floor. Several people moved to reveal an enormous white bearskin rug on which reclined a girl with very short hair wearing a tight black skirt. She seemed asleep despite the din, oblivious to the fact that most of the male eyes in the room could not keep their eyes off her protruding rear.

"The girl or the rug?"

"I meant the carpet, Mr. Sokolow. I had it sent to me from the villa." She smiled at Hannah in a way that almost made her feel at ease, and winked, which Hannah took to mean she was not going to introduce the shapely girl. "You are the midwife, am I right?"

"Yes."

"Emma also studied midwifery, and she'll be here, and I especially want you to meet Margaret because that's her field too." She leaned closer to Hannah and spoke as though she were sharing a confidence. "I do so love people who manage intimate matters on a daily basis. They are so much more in touch with the truth than the rest of us, don't you think?"

Fortunately, some people had come in behind them, diverting their hostess, so Hannah did not have to respond. Lazar steered her into the room.

"Who are Emma and Margaret?" she murmured.

"Emma Goldman and Margaret Sanger."

"Oh."

The furniture, an odd combination of delicate French chairs and more chaise lounges than were ordinarily found in a parlor, were arranged in clusters. Almost every one was taken by men and women who seemed to know each other well enough to have dispensed with pleasantries and had moved directly into forceful arguments. For a while they hovered by a more serene group, who were commenting on the furnishings.

"Les plusieurs nuances de blanc," one of the most elegantly dressed ladies was saying in what even Hannah could tell was a badly accented French.

"Wait until you see the bedroom," her companion replied as she poked the air with a cigarette holder. "It's divine."

"I'd go to any bedroom with you, Marie," the man beside her replied so that everyone could hear, but the girl didn't flinch.

As Lazar steered Hannah closer to the fireplace, the girl in the black skirt was sitting up, brushing back her loose hair. She was remarkably pretty, but nobody was paying particular attention to her.

A man leaning against the fireplace smiled at Hannah in a friendly manner. Lazar gave his wife a little push. "Talk to him," he muttered in Russian. "His book, *In the Spirit of the Ghetto,* is about the Lower East Side and he is fascinated by Jews."

"In Yiddish?" she asked facetiously.

There was no time to check her husband's reaction, for the man's trusting blue eyes flickered their welcome. "Hello!" he called heartily, then offered his hand. "Might you be Mrs. Sokolow?" Hannah nodded. Immediately she was drawn to this man's expressive mouth and forlorn jowls. "I'm Hutch Hapgood and this is my wife, Neith."

A woman with a face powdered as white as the wallpaper stretched languorously on the chaise. She gave Hannah an enigmatic smile. This made Hannah feel even more at ease, for a man would not be flirting with her in front of his spouse. She took the chair that he offered. Lazar was no longer in sight, but she didn't want to strain around to see where he had gone, so she tried to listen politely to the heated discussion on the build-up of the German navy.

There was a shuffle as Mr. Hapgood noticed someone across the room waving and went to him. His wife sat up and patted the thick loop of braids wound around her head. "Come sit here and rest your feet," she called to their passing hostess.

"Isn't this better than moldering in Dobbs Ferry, Neith?" Mrs. Dodge said as she slid beside her. "Ah, there's Margaret!" She gestured to a woman with a beautifully curved back. "I would like to introduce her to you."

"I know Margaret Sanger, thank you very much," Neith replied archly.

"I meant that Mrs. Sokolow might enjoy meeting her," Mabel replied as though she were explaining to a rude child.

Hannah's heartbeat amplified. She had followed Mrs. Sanger's work ever since New York's leading English-language socialist paper, the *Call*, began printing her columns entitled "What Every Girl Should Know." The Bellevue midwives— even Catholics like Mrs. Brink—unanimously had approved of Sanger's suggestion that women needed to educate themselves about the procreative act. But they had been bitterly disappointed when Mr. Comstock, a fanatical member of the New York Society of the Suppression of Vice, had the Post Office Department denounce her article on gonorrhea as violating the boundaries of good taste, and threaten the *Call* with the revocation of its mailing permit if it printed the next article on syphilis.

As Mrs. Dodge waved the woman forward, Hannah was amazed at how different her demure appearance was from her formidable reputation.

"Margaret, do you know Hannah Sokolow? Although it is her first time here, you might have met her professionally. She's a midwife at Bellevue."

"No, we haven't met," Mrs. Sanger replied starchily. "But you must know a good friend of mine, Wendell Dowd."

"Yes, we work together," Hannah replied awkwardly. Then, with forced casualness she added, "I've read the *Call* articles, of course."

Margaret Sanger tilted her head. "Sokolow. I've heard of you . . ." she said as if recalling something. "You're the one with the system."

Hannah flushed. The sham of her sex-selection counseling was about to be exposed.

"You are doing the women a great service," Margaret Sanger continued forcefully. "A woman will never accept the concept of family limitation until she has finished her family. The sad fact is that most will continue to procreate until they have that all-important boy. If there is a way to make certain they have a male child among the first few, you will contribute more than the devices we are working to procure for the masses."

"The system isn't foolproof," the midwife responded warily.

"You must tell me more about it."

Hannah looked over at Mrs. Dodge and Mrs. Hapgood. Both were leaning forward. The girl on the rug and another, also with bobbed hair, came closer. For some reason the men had shifted elsewhere. "It's merely a chart that helps a woman to pick the best day of the month for conceiving a male child."

"I heard it is more complicated than that," Mrs. Sanger said as if to coax a confidence. "Don't I recall someone mentioning that you advise women to climax before their husbands?"

"Is that best?" Mrs. Dodge asked breathlessly.

"Nobody knows for certain," Hannah began testily, "but there is some indication that the secretions that accompany the contractions might affect the sex of the baby by altering the 'climate' of the vagina."

"This sounds like my kind of system," Mrs. Dodge said, giggling slightly.

"Why not ask this midwife the big question?" Mrs. Hapgood wondered.

Mrs. Sanger baited their hostess. "Well, Mabel?"

"Don't be coy, Margaret," Mrs. Dodge retorted. "Why, only a few weeks ago you were expounding on how sexual congress—not for procreation, but for pleasure—was the first duty of men and women. You made such a fine case for the conscious choice of a mate and the responsibility to ennoble the union with unfettered self-expression that I have been following your advice ever since." Mrs. Dodge gave a little pout. "Still, even though I am pleased to say I am the mother of a male child, I will admit I have not yet achieved my goal in the search for the perfect orgasm."

Nobody gasped. Nobody cringed. Mrs. Dodge had not even lowered her voice.

"My wife is an expert in that department," boomed Lazar, who must have been nearer than she realized.

"How forthcoming you are, Mr. Sokolow!" Margaret complimented.

"Yes, well . . ." He was flustered, then recovered. "But I meant she's a professional." Mrs. Dodge's eyebrows raised perceptively. "All midwives are," he blurted to cover the gaffe.

"I wish that were true," sighed Margaret Sanger. "Of course, Emma Goldman has been teaching classes about sexuality at the Ferrer School, but she can't begin to influence the number of women that someone who treats them every day can," she continued. "You might find her lectures of interest, Mrs. Sokolow." She smiled up at Lazar. "And you too." Lazar seemed captivated, and Mrs. Sanger did not miss his regard. She turned to face him. "Tell me, do you think the Labor Revolutionary Movement is only an excuse for a saturnalia of sex?"

"Why not? We can use all the excuses we can get," he retorted so swiftly, Hannah was proud of him, even if he was indulging in risqué repartee with another woman.

Mrs. Dodge drew the attention back to herself. "Well, you *professionals* can go out and fight the great wars, but I'd like to have a trifling victory of my own."

"Now, Mabel, I know you're not frigid, so what's all this about?" Margaret inquired impatiently.

"I could use some expert advice." Mrs. Dodge took the midwife's hand. "I'd like to hear what you know."

Hannah thought of Rachael, who she supposed met the

definition of frigid, and of her readings of Ellis and Freud, and considered what she could possibly offer.

"Go ahead," Mrs. Sanger said with a pleasant taunt, "she's asking for it."

"We could speak privately at another time."

"Why?" asked her hostess. "We're all curious."

Hannah swallowed hard, then plunged in. "There are some who believe that before a woman can achieve the ultimate fulfillment, she must make the transition from the childish pleasures that a young girl feels to the mature sensations of an older woman."

"Who says?" Margaret Sanger challenged.

"Mr. Freud," Hannah replied boldly.

Mrs. Sanger's eyes widened. "Really? And what else does he say?"

Hannah glanced around as she contemplated her response. Out of the corner of her eye she saw a familiar face enter the room: Ezekiel Herzog. Rachael was not with him, which made her less self-conscious. "In his essay on sexuality, he speaks of three stages."

"And what are they?" Mrs. Dodge asked eagerly.

So, if this is what they want, this is what they'll get, Hannah resolved. After a quick inhalation she sputtered, "The clitoridal, the anesthetic, and the vaginal."

Mrs. Dodge blanched as white as her chiffon. Mrs. Hapgood's mouth slackened, but she remained still.

Hannah was now in command. "However, I don't think his theory makes any sense, at least from an anatomical point of view. Personally I prefer Mr. Ellis on the subject."

"You are reading Havelock Ellis as well?" Mrs. Sanger asked reverently.

"I told you my wife is an expert."

Mrs. Sanger gasped in surprise. She had forgotten Lazar's presence. "Well, I'm going to meet Mr. Ellis in London at the end of the year."

Hannah was impressed, but she restrained herself, sensing that a certain coolness was the correct way to proceed with these influential women. "You might ask his opinion on this point, then let Mrs. Dodge know his conclusion."

"And you might want to talk to Emma Goldman about Freud. When she was in Vienna she attended a series of his lectures, and she says that he helped her understand herself better. She believes his theories about sexual repression may explain why we have to contend with this nonsense about birth control being sinful."

Hannah wished Lazar had not said that she was an expert. Having read a few books she barely understood hardly put her in a class to argue with women who had met or were meeting the authors themselves. Most probably Mr. Freud was right and her experiences—or interpretations of those experiences—were incorrect. But at that moment everyone was waiting for her response. She felt as though she was about to leap a chasm, but had no alternative. "Although these men may have given the matter much thought, they still cannot know what a woman feels, any more than a woman can understand what a man feels."

Mrs. Sanger's mouth drooped, but she did not sound offended when she said, "An excellent point, but if we cannot understand one another, how can we help each other?"

"Maybe we shouldn't strive to understand," Mrs. Hapgood said, rising to her feet. She smoothed her satin gown, a delicate cream color that was a perfect foil for her loops of braided red hair. "Wouldn't that destroy the secret, the mysteriousness, the forbidden something that is the essence of everything erotic?"

For the first time Mabel Dodge seemed flustered with the discussion. She also stood up from the chaise and mumbled something about finding out if Max had arrived. When she moved away, the group dispersed slightly.

"I wish you hadn't said so much about me," she mumbled to Lazar in Yiddish.

"You were wonderful!" he said sincerely, ignoring her slip into the familiar language.

Feeling overwhelmed, Hannah turned away. "It's getting late. Shouldn't we be going?"

"Herzog just arrived. Besides, we can't leave before midnight. That's why we're here."

Hannah was perplexed.

A man crossing behind them understood their Yiddish, much to Hannah's chagrin. "You mean your wife doesn't know about Mabel's famous suppers?"

"I didn't mention it." The man raised his eyebrows, then excused himself. "It's worth the wait," Lazar said.

Hannah spent much of the last part of the evening with Herzog, which was a relief since she was too tired to tackle anyone new for a while.

"You should come again next week," he said. "It won't be nearly so dull."

"This is your idea of dull?" Hannah gave a purposeful shudder. "I hate to think what your idea of lively is."

Herzog laughed. "Well, E. G. should be here and John, if he recovers from his back pains." Seeing her confusion, he explained, "John Reed and Emma Goldman." Then he went on to give her some background on two of the salon's more colorful figures until the midnight supper was served.

At last Lazar was ready to leave. After the tiring walk they finally reached Tompkins Square. Lazar paused at the front step. "Tell me you are glad we went."

"Lazar, I'll be glad when I see my bed."

"Come now, you met Max Eastman and Lincoln Steffens and not only spoke with Margaret Sanger and Mabel Dodge, but you held your own with them."

"That's hardly true."

"They were impressed with you. I know they were, because when someone bores them they know how to cut them dead."

"Well, the last time I looked I was very much alive."

"Indeed you are," he said with an affectionate squeeze, "and I'm very proud of you."

"I am pleased to have been there, but not for the reasons you think."

"Then why?"

"Because it was important to you. I know you will not be happy until you are in the center of things again."

"Again?" Before he could reply she opened the front door and started up the stairs. "What did you mean by 'again'?" he said as he rushed up behind her.

"Shush!" Both knew anything said on the stairs could be heard elsewhere in the building, and at that time of night might wake someone.

He opened the door to their flat. Mama Blau was lying on her back on the divan in the parlor, snoring loudly. Hannah covered her mother with an afghan and checked on the children. Emma was sucking her thumb. Hannah removed it from her mouth and tucked the moist hand under her pillow. Benny twitched at her approach, but was settled by her cool hand smoothing the hair from his forehead. In the kitchen she poured herself a glass of milk to soothe her stomach after so much rich food so late in the evening. When she reached their bedroom, Lazar was washing. Good. There was no point dredging up the political work he had relinquished by marrying her to legitimize Benny.

He was in bed first. When she slipped in beside him, she could tell by his rhythmic breathing he was going directly to sleep. She put her arm around him and caressed his chest. He seemed so content. She had been mistaken in her reluctance to go to Mrs. Dodge's salon. He had wanted to share it all with her: his new friends—who were among the movers and shakers of the day, the glorious setting, the lavish buffet, the tantalizing talk. What she should be doing was prompting him more in that direction, although she had little desire to return to that place where she had not felt comfortable for a single moment. Even if there were people like Lazar there, it was clear that they were invited as part of the entertainment. She would never be able to feel at ease with the likes of a Mrs. Dodge or even Neith Hapgood. You had to be born into that world to know how to lift a spoon—or an eyebrow—at the right moment.

Lazar stirred, then turned over. He cupped her breast and continued into a deeper phase of slumber. It dawned on her that if he went alone, he might get in far more trouble, and not just with luscious young girls who lay around on fur rugs. Had he made any contacts that might help him with his book? she pondered, then berated herself for not asking him. No wonder he had been cross with her. She had been thinking more about feeling ill at ease in that rarefied environment than his professional plight.

Hannah suddenly was struck with a sense that something was about to change their lives. Was it somebody they had met that evening? Possibly, but she fell asleep before an answer presented itself.

7

The next day Hannah's petty concerns were obliterated by the news that the Archduke Ferdinand and his wife had been assassinated in Sarajevo. The cafés of the Lower East Side bustled with interpretations of the event. Their table at the Café Boulevard was no different.

"This brings Mayerling to mind," began Rachael.

"How right you are, my dear," complimented Ezekiel Herzog, stroking his beard. "Leave it to you to link this with the romantic suicide of one of the archduke's predecessors." His warm smile in his wife's direction reflected his obvious respect.

Chaim had monopolized the other end of the table with a stack of English-language newspapers. He sputtered, "The curse of the Hapsburgs," and he tossed one to the floor in disgust. "I can't believe nobody cares about this assassination. The latest episode in *The Perils of Pauline* concerns these capitalists more than the removal of a man who stood in the way of peace in Europe."

"I don't know about that," Herzog began in a purposeful attempt to stir the pot. "Some believe the archduke was a friend to the Jews."

Chaim rose to his feet. "Since when do you read dreck like the *Morgen Zhurnal?*"

Minna reached out to placate him, but he brushed her hand away. "He's only trying to provoke an argument," she said gently.

"I think it important to know what everyone—from the most Orthodox to the most liberal—is thinking," Herzog replied steadily.

For once Lazar mediated. "The point is that the killing has prevented the accession to the throne of a man who would have begun a period of the worst reaction for Austria, which then would have escalated into a violent people's war."

"And what is wrong with that?" Chaim barked. "Since when are you for tranquility and moderation?"

While Lazar leapt into the fray, Hannah became lost in her own thoughts. Politics held little fascination for her. The men would go around and around, pummeling each other's points. Even though they might sound angry, she knew that none of them would take the discussion personally, and their friendship would remain secure. More than anything it was an exercise for the mind. Usually she assumed that Lazar was so well informed that his opinions must be right. Although they often disagreed, this was one area Hannah deferred to her husband's greater knowledge. The larger universe of political strife she would leave to Lazar; the smaller world of the women and their babies was vast enough for her.

As the summer wore on, Lazar became more and more irate. When the war broke out in Europe the first week in August, he was home for hardly more than an hour a day. With no courses to teach that summer, he devoted his time to his political activities. "This war effort is being plotted by plutocrats and spawned by munitions makers," he began as he sat down to supper one night.

Ignoring the remark, Hannah pointed to his plate. "Don't you like it?"

Lazar stared at his brisket without taking a bite. "If the working class collaborates against them, it can be prevented, but I don't think unity can be achieved in time."

Hannah didn't know what to say, so she parroted something she had heard in the hospital. "President Wilson has urged us to remain neutral."

"How long do you think that will last?" Lazar threw down his napkin.

Hannah knew better than to even comment further. Best to listen, to let him talk it out. That way she would know what he was thinking, for Lazar usually acted on his thoughts. And when he did, the family was bound to be affected.

By September it was obvious that Lazar would not be rehired by the university, or anyone else, as a German teacher, since the language was decidedly unpopular. More and more of his time was spent with Chaim as the two helped draft a Socialist statement on the war. From the paltry sum he was contributing to their expenses, she was certain he was making fewer deliveries of printing supplies.

Lazar was forever trying to explain his position to Hannah. "Don't you see how important it is that we demonstrate that we are not presuming to judge the conduct of our comrade parties in Europe? We realize that they are victims of the vicious system, and that they did the best they could under the circumstances . . ."

Hannah only half listened to this diatribe while she calculated how much they would have to live on through the fall and winter. At this rate she would never be able to get off the night schedule and probably would have to add extra shifts to provide the family with essentials.

"Well?" he prodded.

"Any way I calculate it, we need more money."

"With everything going on in this world, is that all you can think about?"

Hannah took her pocketbook from the drawer. She spilled out her purse. A few coins plunked on the table, others scattered to the floor. "That is what's left for the rest of the week, unless you have something to add."

Lazar's eyes wandered over the room, then returned and fixed steadily on his wife. For a moment she thought she saw a naughty glimmer in his sky blue orbs, so she turned away, unwilling to be charmed out of her stance. "You're right," he began, disarming her completely. "I'll be bringing in several dollars by the end of the week, but if wc are that low I could get them in advance."

"From where?" she asked warily.

"Chaim suggested that I submit my commentaries on the war to some of the Yiddish papers. The fees are not much, but if I vary my slant to align with the editorial policy of the paper, I can offer different versions of the same material to various ones."

"Is that ethical?"

"Ethical, schmethical, why should you care so long as it fills your purse?"

"I'd never want you to go against your conscience."

"I'm not about to submit anything to the *Morgen Zhurnal,* if that's what you mean."

"What about your book?"

"It's coming, it's coming, but if my name gets known from the articles, it will make it that much easier to sell."

Hannah's chest heaved with relief. "For now I'll stay on the night shift. You can write while I sleep and we won't disturb each other," she said, thinking that at least she would know that he was home and working, not schmoozing with his friends in the cafés.

On a particularly warm day for October, while the world turned its attention to the Germans' race to the sea across Belgium and the cafés were abuzz with the effect of the fall of Antwerp and the casualties at Ypres, Hannah arrived at the hospital an hour early to catch up on her paperwork. There was no point in trying to accomplish anything at home, for more and more women would stop by to ask a "quick question." If Hannah had learned one thing, it was that there were no quick questions, only the excuse not to pay for the service. More than anything, even the extra dollars, Hannah needed her rest. When Lazar was home, he would send them away, but the knocks on the door would disturb her enough that she could not get back to sleep. Lately, when Lazar was out talking to editors and other writers, she ended up answering the door.

"You'll have to send them away," Lazar warned.

"What difference does it make? Once I hear the knock I get up anyway."

"Look at you! You can hardly drag yourself through the night shift. Maybe I should stay home and guard the door."

"No! If the editors don't know you're around, you won't get the work."

"That's true," he admitted a bit too agreeably. "I am building my reputation."

For a moment Hannah speculated how he had managed to convert her exhaustion to his advantage, but let it pass because he could easily win a war of words. He should have offered to stay home some of the time, but he hadn't. If she pointed out how little he was earning, she would be condemned as a money-grubbing capitalist before he would admit his failure to provide. Once in a while he did have an assignment that paid a few dollars, although hardly more than enough to feed the family a few meals a week. Nevertheless, when he received his wages, he brought the money directly to her in an envelope—with a slip showing the amount due and the assignment it was for—to prove he was keeping nothing back for himself. Even though he was seeing his name in print more frequently, his fees were minimal; sometimes he didn't even expect payment. Perhaps he was "building his reputation," but then his reputation was as a Socialist radical opposed to the war, and those who would compensate for those thoughts usually did not have much to spend. Either he would have to be paid better, or find a more lucrative line of work, but the best way to manage Lazar was to let him see the consequences of his actions. She only hoped his myopic vision would clear before she collapsed from fatigue.

∽∾ 8 ∽∾

One day in early November Lazar asked Hannah if she could take a Monday night off ~~to~~ ~~go~~ ~~to~~ ~~Mrs.~~ Dodge's. "We've changed the night because there will be certain guests who are wanted by the authorities," he explained with a lopsided grin. "Mrs. Dodge wants a confrontation. She believes that free speech is championed best if the opponents meet on a friendly playing field."

Hannah's spine felt like it had been washed in seltzer. This was the sort of idea that sometimes came to a bad end.

"Well? Will you try to arrange it?" Lazar prodded. "Chaim, Minna, even the Herzogs are coming."

"I bet Minna will have some spicy comments about that mixture of agitators and society types," Hannah said with a grin, which also indicated her assent.

Once again they ambled into the blazing whiteness of the famous drawing room. "I see some of the sentimental rebels are here already," Lazar said to Vittorio as he handed the butler their coats.

"Yes, sir," Vittorio replied blandly.

Against the stark walls Hannah noticed that many, including Lincoln Steffens and Hutchins Hapgood, had arrived in full evening dress. She glanced at her husband's shabby slacks and sweater and winced. "What did you mean?" she whispered.

"What do they have to rebel against?" Lazar continued in a voice that should have been more modulated. "What injustice have they suffered?"

Knowing better than to hush him, Hannah merely changed the subject. "I don't see many people that I recognize from before."

"So you'll make new fans this time."

"What if I don't want to talk about Mr. Freud?"

"No matter what you say, I'm sure you'll be a hit. Or if you want, just listen in and you are bound to hear something titillating."

Hannah wanted to ask him what he meant, but Lazar merely steered her closer to those congregating in front of the fireplace, then drifted off on his own. She was disappointed not to see any sign of the Herzogs or even Chaim and Minna yet.

"Hello!" the voice came from behind Hannah. She turned and recognized Neith Hapgood's milky skin and brooding eyes.

"Mrs. Hapgood," she responded in a tone that might have been too breathy with relief.

"You're the midwife, am I right?"

Hannah tried not to show her disappointment that the woman had not remembered her name. "Yes, Hannah Sokolow."

"And your husband's the professor."

"These days he is more of a writer."

"Good, then maybe he could referee a little dispute my husband is having with Max."

"Mr. Eastman?" Hannah asked earnestly. It was Lazar's fondest wish to be published by his magazine, *The Masses.* "What sort of argument is it?" she ventured, thinking that her husband was apt to take the wrong side and ruin his chances.

Just then Lazar glanced over to see how she was faring. She waved to him, but he seemed too engrossed to be moved. Rolling her eyes in a pleading gesture finally won his attention. "They need you as a referee," she explained.

"For what?"

"Ask her," Hannah said, deferring the question.

Behind Neith was a man Hannah believed she had met before. Although she couldn't recall his name, she did remember he had slighted Lazar. Neith turned and asked, "Hipp, how would you explain Hutch's dispute with Max?"

"In a word: bourgeois" came the scratchy reply of the moon-faced man with mischievous eyes. "At their publication meeting yesterday they voted on the poems to include in the new issue. How can you vote on poetry? How can you vote on something from the soul?"

"Well, Hipp, I think Max was probably being diplomatic," Mrs. Hapgood interjected in a voice that was not quite as sweet as her expression. "Would you rather he made autocratic decisions on his own?" Her husband came up alongside her and slid his arm protectively around her slender waist.

"In this case, yes," Hippolyte Havel answered, but Hannah doubted his sincerity.

"Besides, if the people can't help select what appears in *The Masses,* the title is a mockery, isn't it?" Mr. Hapgood responded smoothly.

"What do you think, Mrs. Sokolow?" Mrs. Hapgood asked politely.

"That's my husband's department," Hannah hedged as she looked to Lazar to fill the gap.

"The idea of voting to take the pulse of an audience makes sense so long as the group doesn't dictate what is published," Lazar began confidently. "Every editor must strive to strike a popular chord so the material will be purchased and read, but he also must have the audacity to print pieces that will incite and inspire."

Mr. Havel had taken off his glasses and was wiping them on his shirt, but when Lazar finished, he put them on and took a long look at the speaker. "What do you write?" he asked.

"Political commentary," Lazar replied steadily.

Mr. Havel tossed his shoulder-length hair. "For whom?"

"Mostly the Yiddish press."

"Do you know Max Eastman?"

"Yes, but he doesn't know me," Lazar replied with just enough of a lilt to charm the group.

"You'll introduce him to Max when he arrives," Mr. Hapgood said.

"Of course," Mr. Havel answered with a naughty grin, "if you'll introduce him to Mr. Wright at the *Globe.*"

Hannah's heart leapt. It was good they had come again! People who had forgotten his name were now interested in his work. Lazar needed to meet people like this, people who could help him succeed.

Purposefully Hannah moved away. Lazar now had their attention and it would be better if he didn't need to concern himself with her. She took the opportunity to see if the Herzogs or Chaim and Minna were there yet.

"Mrs. Sokolow?" The voice was familiar, but for a long moment Hannah could not place the man in a perfectly fitting cutaway coat. "I usually wear white, not black," he said with some amusement at her startled expression.

"Dr. Dowd," she replied with the nervous stammer of someone caught in a compromising position. Then, with a quick recovery, she added, "You're a friend of Mrs. Sanger's, aren't you?"

"We've met . . ." was all he would allow.

Hannah's eyes shifted around the hallway where they faced each other. Was the doctor alone? She knew he was married, but had never seen his wife.

As if sensing her thoughts, he asked, "Are you by yourself?"

"Of course not!" she blurted, then blushed. Why did she feel she had to prove she had an escort?

"I thought you were on the night shift."

Hannah felt herself stiffen. Was this going to be an interrogation? "A rare night off as well as a rare night out," she replied with forced nonchalance. "It's supposed to be an especially good show tonight."

"So I hear. Do you come to Mrs. Dodge's evenings often?"

"As often as my schedule permits."

The doctor's thick eyebrows raised and lowered provocatively. Was he a regular? If so, he would know she had exaggerated. Or perhaps he came infrequently and was impressed that one of Bellevue's lowly midwives fraternized with this illustrious crowd. He gave a wry smile, tossed his head slightly, then spoke as though she were an old friend.

"Well, Mabel has done it, hasn't she? All the 'dangerous characters' are assembling. Won't this be fun?" The doctor steered her into the main salon, where everyone was gathering. "Never thought I would see Emma Goldman and Sasha Berkman, English Walling and more of their followers in the same room with Lincoln Steffens, Bill Haywood, Carol Tresca, Elizabeth Gurley Flynn, and Arturo Giovannitti, even Walter Lippmann, did you?"

Before she could respond, a gong rang to signal the formal proceedings were about to begin, but it silenced nobody. Since Lazar was an organizer, he was standing next to Mrs. Dodge. Hannah took a seat in the overheated room next to the doctor. The one vacant seat on her other side was filled by Minna. Fortunately, there was not time to introduce her to the doctor because Mrs. Dodge was clapping her hands to get everyone's attention.

"Tonight what I have in mind is that we should take the

first part of the evening to listen to each other's positions, then rebut them, but only if you wish." The crowd roared. "Then, during supper, there will be time for a bit more socialization and—"

"You did mean socialism, didn't you, Mabel?" called a man in the back.

Everyone laughed again. Mrs. Dodge threw up her hands. The handkerchief that had been wadded in her palm fluttered to the floor.

"Let the lions into the coliseum!" Mr. Havel shouted.

Hannah pretended to pay attention as Lincoln Steffens opened the fray, but glanced sideways at her sister-in-law, who, in her sleek black dress with gray trim, looked more like a regular than Hannah in her best tweed suit.

When Bill Haywood stood up, the doctor nudged her and whispered, "Now, this is what I've been waiting for."

His voice caught Minna's attention and even without turning Hannah felt her sister-in-law leaning closer, as though that would help her discern the identity of the stranger. Even Hannah felt herself paying more attention to the speaker because she wondered why the doctor was so interested in him. Haywood's impassioned call to sabotage brought cries of dissent as well as cheers from his supporters, but Hannah couldn't keep her gaze away from his one eye that was sunken in and didn't move.

"Is he blind in one eye?" Hannah asked Dr. Dowd during the fray that followed his remarks.

"Yes, an interesting story . . ." the doctor began, but stopped when Alexander Berkman commenced his plea for direct action instead of propaganda as the only way to change society.

Soon people became more restless and less attentive. Hannah glanced at a clock on the mantel. Still fifteen minutes to midnight. Then English Walling gave a theatrical yawn. "I dare say that socialism is triumphing, if only by default." This seemed the signal for the group to disperse.

Minna pulled at her arm, so Hannah went in that direction. Dr. Dowd moved down the row of chairs on his side without another word to her.

"Who was that?" Minna demanded.

"A doctor from Bellevue," she said without emphasis to avoid any more probing, but she could not prevent Minna from following her through the supper line. At the other end

Rachael was waiting for her. "I have a table over there." Hannah's smile was one of relief.

"Did you get the red glaze for the turkey?" Minna inquired as she came to sit with them. "It's divine."

Divine? She had never heard Minna use that word before. "No, I must have missed it."

"At least she didn't miss the biscuits," Rachael said protectively. "See if it doesn't melt in your mouth." Hannah did as she was told. "Wasn't I right?" Hannah nodded as she chewed. "And here"—Rachael plopped a few black olives that glistened like jewels onto her plate—"try these."

"Where's your husband?" Minna asked in a tone that set Hannah on edge even further.

"Around here somewhere," she said, pretending not to care.

"Max Eastman wanted to talk to him. He thought Lazar might have a story to submit to him. You must know the one."

Once again Minna was better informed than she was. "He's been working on several," Hannah hedged.

"I think Eastman's interested in the one about the prostitute—the one you delivered."

"I delivered?" Hannah gasped.

"Don't worry about revealing identities," she said, misreading Hannah's confusion, "because it's supposed to be an allegory about the exploitation of the proletariat told from one victimized woman's viewpoint."

"The state as the ultimate pimp," Rachael commented.

Lazar had just joined them, so Hannah explained. "We heard that Max Eastman wants to see that story you wrote. You know, the one about the prostitute I delivered." Her voice was thick with indirect rebuke.

"Needs some polishing first," Lazar replied tautly. Then, realizing the import of what she had said, he glowed. "Eastman? Are you sure it was him?"

"Ask Minna. She seems to know all about it."

Minna pointed to the room where she thought Eastman was having his dinner.

"I'll track him down," Lazar said with enthusiasm.

"Isn't it time to leave?" Hannah asked.

Lazar smiled benevolently. "Yes, of course. Let me just see to Eastman."

"We need to be going too," Rachael murmured.

"I'll ask Vittorio for our coats." Minna used the butler's name as if they were old friends.

At the door they chatted with Mabel, who seemed muddled by the dissension she had fostered that evening. "Yes, the midwife's little sister," she said absentmindedly to Minna, then turned with eyes shining in Hannah's direction. "Tonight's agenda did not leave us a moment for one of our more personal talks. Last time you had so many fascinating things to say. I would dearly like to continue where we left off."

"I'm certain Lazar will bring me again, although I'm usually on the night shift."

"Wouldn't it be better if it was just us girls?"

"Perhaps . . ." Hannah allowed.

"And during the day?"

"Yes."

"You must come for lunch on Friday next—both of you," she said, nodding in Minna's direction.

When Hannah and Lazar finally stepped out into the windy night, she asked her husband, "How long have you been thinking of that story?"

"For a while."

"How long have you been writing it?"

"Not long." He took a quick breath, then stared at her. "Who were you sitting with?"

"What do you mean?" she asked, even though she knew the answer.

"During the debate. I saw you chatting with someone I did not recognize." Then, misreading her rigid expression, he shrugged. "Glad to see you can make friends on your own, that's all."

"He's not a friend, just a doctor from Bellevue. Never expected to see him there."

"Mabel does like to collect doctors. Never knows when she might need one." There was a long pause, then: "What's his name?"

"Dr. Dowd. He's a gynecologist."

"Perfect!" Lazar threw back his head and laughed, but something about it set Hannah off. This was just a diversion from his problem.

"You haven't written a single word, have you?"

He winced. "You know me too well."

"Which woman were you talking about?"

"A girl from Allen Street. Her name was something like Janie?"

"Jenny ..." Hannah recalled slowly.

"Remember you told me that some schmuck had hired thugs to beat her, then had stepped in to take care of her. When she was grateful, he taught her to whore for him. Once she was used to the money, she couldn't accept factory work."

"I remember."

"Just as the proletariat is first made to suffer before the government comes in with their puny offerings, soon they are seduced into thinking that is the only way to make it in life."

Hannah wasn't listening to the diatribe. She was remembering the pimp coming for the baby—he had taken it away so Jenny could go back to work—and Jenny's disappearance.

"Did you ever see her again?" Lazar asked as they approached their front door.

"No," Hannah said as she fumbled for her key.

"What do you suppose happened to her?"

"She probably returned to Allen Street."

They walked as quietly as possible up the flights of stairs to their rooms. "Could she have killed herself?" Lazar mused.

"Why do you ask?"

Lazar opened their door. "It would make a better story."

〜 9 〜

On the appointed Friday, Minna and Hannah returned to Mrs. Dodge's. They had made no attempt to travel together, but they arrived at the building at the same time, coming from opposite directions.

Vittorio took their wraps before leading them to a room that Hannah did not remember seeing before. She followed behind Minna, who was wearing a peach silk frock, which though shabby if one looked closely at the collar and cuffs, fit her so handsomely, she managed a genteel elegance. Once again Hannah thought her sensible shirtwaist, wool skirt, and jacket made her appear dowdy by comparison.

Margaret Sanger and Mabel Dodge sat opposite each other on the blue damask chairs that flanked a carved marble mantel in a sitting room off the master bedroom. Mabel wore a pink silk gown, which flattered her pale skin, while Margaret was dressed much as Hannah in more tailored attire.

Hannah wondered who else was coming, but after the introductions, realized that it would only be the four of them that day, which relaxed her guard.

"You have met Mrs. Sanger," Mrs. Dodge said to Hannah, "but I don't believe your sister has."

Hannah decided not to correct her.

"My pleasure." Margaret Sanger offered her hand.

"Minna Blau." She had assumed Mrs. Dodge did not recall her full name. "I was one of the first customers at your Amboy Street clinic."

"A satisfied one, I hope," Mrs. Sanger replied. Her voice was soft, yet every word was enunciated in a way that even Hannah understood each nuance.

"Entirely. Thanks to your work we have been able to choose to not have children until the world is a better place."

"How wise, especially in these difficult times," Mrs. Sanger noted.

So that was the secret of Minna's childless state! Nobody, not even Mama, had been able to understand why Minna had never conceived, yet she had been willing to divulge this to two strangers.

"How long have you been married?" Mrs. Dodge asked.

"Seven years," Minna responded proudly.

"There are so few clients who have been practicing restraint as long as you have, I would be curious as to your habits, if you would not mind sharing them with me."

"Not at all."

"Do you merely follow the calendar or do you use a device?"

"I have tried several quinine pessaries."

"Any difficulties?"

"A few, until I found the best-fitting one."

"Do you use it every time?"

"Yes, it's the only way, isn't it? At least for someone who counts as poorly as I do."

As they laughed, a gong was sounded.

Lunch was served in the dining room. Despite the frigid December weather, a rosebud in a silver vase was placed to the right of each plate, the rim of which matched the flower's color. A creamy vegetable soup was served with crisp rolls curved like crescents.

Mrs. Dodge buttered her bread and turned to Hannah. "I know you are wondering why I have invited you here. You think you have nothing in common with a woman like me." Shocked by her directness, Hannah was relieved that no reply was expected. "Both Margaret and I wanted to talk with you again, but I understand you are a very busy woman with your occupation as a midwife as well as a mother and wife." She smiled at her little play on words. "But look at us: we are all women of about the same age. Yes, we come from different social backgrounds and lead divergent lives, but here we can converge on the most equitable playing field."

"What year were you born, Mrs. Dodge?" Hannah asked in the same tone she would use with a client. At least she had managed to stop sounding deferential.

"Eighteen seventy-nine."

"The same as I," Mrs. Sanger added. "And you?" she asked Hannah.

"I'm thirty-one, four years younger."

"I'm thirty," Minna replied with a crooked smile. "So you are right, we're not very far apart."

At that Hannah wanted to laugh aloud. Not far apart? Even if Minna had forgotten her peasant origins already, how could she compare her sparse quarters behind the printing press with this luxurious room?

Sensing some tension in the air, Mabel asked Mrs. Sanger, "Didn't you work on the Lower East Side a few years ago?"

"Yes. When I first began to take obstetrical cases, I never expected to end up with the poorest clientele, but it was as if I were being drawn downtown by a force outside my control. Even so, I hated the work."

Minna's spoon dropped. She did not try to cover her gaffe, but waited for Margaret to explain herself.

"The conditions were wretched. I despised the hopelessness. Soon I came to see that a woman in childbirth was the sum of her upbringing, which also ordained her children's future in this bleak world."

Minna was nodding. "That is why my husband and I have refrained."

Hannah wished Minna did not keep bringing the subject back to herself. Fortunately, they were diverted as the waiters served plates of baked fish on a bed of rice and almonds, and topped with a swirl of melting butter. After observing which fork Mabel selected, Hannah picked up the same style and tasted the delicate fish.

"What really changed my whole perspective, though, was one woman," Margaret continued. "Her name was Sadie Sachs. One day her husband found her unconscious from the effects of a self-induced abortion in her Grand Street tenement."

The clatter of silver around the table halted. Gently Hannah balanced her fork on the plate.

"Three tiny children were in a panic, crying hysterically. I sent for a doctor and the two of us worked for a week fighting the septicemia. During her illness, her husband washed the children, ran up and down the stairs carrying ice and medicine and laundry. Two weeks later she was much improved, although I would not have given her a ten percent chance in the beginning."

As the story took a happier turn, all the women, except the storyteller, continued their meal.

"When I returned for my final visit, Mrs. Sachs said the doctor had told her that another baby would finish her off. 'What can I do to prevent it?' she had asked him. 'You can't have your cake and eat it too. Tell Jake to sleep on the roof' was his reply." Margaret lifted her fork and took several bites of the fish. Nobody disturbed her with questions. After finishing her filet, Margaret queried, "How do you think the story ends?"

"She became pregnant again?" Minna offered.

Margaret nodded.

"And she tried to abort herself?" Hannah added.

"Only three months later." Margaret took a sip of water. "When I arrived she was in a coma. She died within ten minutes. And that is when I determined I would do something that the doctor would not."

The fish course was removed and a lamb chop with mint sauce was served. Minna, who looked as if she could use the extra nourishment, declined, but Mrs. Sanger and Mrs. Dodge accepted the serving. Hannah had not expected another course, but the rich aroma of the meat tempted her. She pointed to a small one on the silver tray.

Mrs. Dodge turned the conversation in another, unexpected direction. "Do you see Dr. Dowd very often?"

Hannah and Margaret looked up at the same moment, and both began to speak. Margaret laughed and deferred to Hannah. "Not often on my shift."

Mabel glanced toward Margaret, who shrugged. "I've consulted him for my column, but not lately."

"Well," Mabel said, batting her eyes to make her point, "I wish I had an excuse to consult him as often as possible."

Hannah felt obliged to comment. "He's an excellent surgeon."

"But . . . ?" Margaret parried.

Best to put a stop to these gossipy speculations once and for all, Hannah decided, especially since Minna was hanging on every word. "We midwives think he's too quick with the knife. 'To cut is to cure' is one of his favorite mottos."

Mabel giggled. "Any others?"

Hannah was happy to oblige. She gave Margaret a conspiratorial glance. " 'When in doubt, slice it out.' "

All four joined in the laughter until Mabel pushed back her chair. "Coffee and petit fours will be served in the living room." She stood and led the way.

"You'll be comfortable there," Mrs. Dodge said, urging Hannah to take the armchair, while she sat on the edge of the chaise. Margaret and Minna remained standing on either side of the fireplace.

Margaret's expressive hands fluttered as she spoke. "I know that most of what I say shocks people, and I apologize if my story about Mrs. Sachs was not appropriate luncheon chatter, but if we are reluctant to talk about the natural aspects of our functions, as well as the consequences of them, we cut ourselves off from what makes us human."

"How true!" Mabel exclaimed.

Hannah leaned forward in her seat and raised her coffee cup. Margaret walked over to a sideboard and poured herself a glass of sherry from a decanter. Minna followed her lead, much to Hannah's dismay.

After taking a sip, Margaret continued. "If we cannot be honest in this setting, when can we ever be?" She stared at Hannah, but apparently her question was rhetorical, for she continued in an urgent tone. "The body has an infinite number of levels for sexual expression. At the bottom is the basest opportunity afforded by the plumbing. I wonder how many people accept this as all that there is, never reaching beyond to what ecstasy can be attained?"

Mrs. Dodge was enraptured. "Yes, Margaret, go on."

"Physical love has so many layers of mystery that one can spend a lifetime uncovering them," she continued with dramatic emphasis. "With the infinite connections that are possible between the nerve fibers, no sensation is ever the same twice. Each time we make love we channel the sum of this mighty power and reawaken dormant sensations that infuse our very bodies with vitality."

"Yes!" Mrs. Dodge exclaimed. "Somehow you have managed to make the act seem sacred and scientific at the same time."

"You have known love . . ." Margaret prompted.

"I will admit I have not been denied the pleasures of the flesh," Mabel began slowly, "but I always have the feeling that I must make compensation for every delight. What you said makes me think that I have gone about it all wrong, that sexual congress may be a means to a high plateau. Even if it does not lead to procreation, it nurtures the growth of the soul."

Mrs. Sanger beamed the smile of a teacher to an exceptional pupil. "Then you will agree that sexual health, which means mutual satisfaction, is the first duty of every man and woman."

"Duty?" Mabel asked with a throaty chuckle.

"Duty may sound like too pedestrian a word, but I mean to be taken seriously. One does not just practice it anywhere or with anyone, for promiscuity is irresponsible."

"Are you saying this may be accomplished only in the context of a marriage with a single partner?" Minna asked with a tinge of condescension.

"No. Your choice may be for an hour or a lifetime, but it still must be honorable."

"What do you think, Hannah?" Margaret inquired.

"In theory I am in total agreement . . ."

"Yes?" Margaret urged.

Hannah took a deep breath. "The problem is that while we may enlighten our minds, our bodies require more practical training. It's like—" Her mind raced ahead of her language proficiency, and she started to speak in Yiddish.

Minna had to translate. "Like swimming."

"Yes, swimming," Hannah continued now that she grasped the word. "While you may talk the whole day about how one is supposed to move the arms and legs, until one has the sensation of being in water and balancing one's own weight, one can never learn."

"Exactly!" Mrs. Sanger clapped her hands in delight. "I could show women a way to heighten the pleasure and prolong it. I could demonstrate how we can move away from what have been marked the sexual zones and show how the whole body can be sexualized so that every pore is sensitive and alive."

"Could you teach me?" Mrs. Dodge asked, her eyes widening in anticipation.

"If everyone was given instruction in the art of sexual intercourse, our whole society would be healthier."

For a moment there was a pause, and Hannah contemplated what this might mean to Rachael. Should she send the doctor to Mrs. Sanger, or might something as simple as the swimming metaphor produce results?

"What do you think?" Mrs. Dodge was asking Hannah.

"Something in the back of my mind keeps worrying me."

"Yes?" Margaret Sanger prodded with some impatience.

"In the Bible it says that Eve was made from Adam's rib, so that is the way everyone has looked at the question ever since. We are taught that the woman's clitoris is a smaller version of a man's penis. Mr. Freud says that as she grows into a woman, a girl must move away from these masculine sensations and find her satisfaction in her vagina. Well, what if it is the other way around?"

Mrs. Dodge knitted her brow. "I don't understand . . ."

"I think what Mrs. Sokolow is saying is that nobody has given any thought to the chance that men's genitalia may be an exaggeration of a woman's. Is that it?" Margaret asked.

Hannah nodded but did not continue, for the theory had just begun to form.

"What a curious idea!" Mabel exclaimed.

"I like it," Margaret said, although Hannah sensed an undercurrent of annoyance that she had not originated it herself.

"I must give it some thought," Mrs. Dodge said, standing and stretching. "I am so impressed with both you and your sister."

"Sister-in-law," Minna corrected.

Mrs. Sanger looked at her wristwatch and compared it with a crystal clock on the mantel. "I can't believe it's so late." She reached for her shawl.

"When do you leave, Margaret?" Mrs. Dodge asked.

"For Europe? Next week."

"Are you still going to meet Havelock Ellis?" Hannah asked, her eyes shining at the prospect.

Mrs. Sanger's cheeks filled with color. "I hope so. Perhaps he will be interested in your Adam-out-of-Eve theory."

Something facetious in her expression caused Hannah to wince inwardly. Mr. Ellis would find her ideas laughable. Now she regretted her impetuousness. It was always better to listen than to speak out.

"There is one problem," Margaret was saying. "My little effort, *Family Limitation,* is so successful I have no idea how to keep up with the requests while I'm away."

"It shouldn't be a problem to have someone fill the orders," said Mabel.

"But it is!" she groaned. "Since there is risk associated with the dissemination of this information, I am having trouble finding courageous workers."

"I'll help you," Minna offered without missing a beat.

"Perhaps you should discuss this with your husband first," Mrs. Dodge suggested in a sugary voice.

"Considering how firmly my husband has stood up for his principles, he could hardly object if his wife lives by hers," Minna answered.

Mrs. Dodge looked doubtful. "In my experience, what men say and what men do are entirely different."

"You don't know my brother." Hannah glanced to see if Minna appreciated her support, but her flashing eyes were concentrated on Mrs. Sanger.

"I think it is only fair to warn you that Mr. Comstock, that self-proclaimed head of the New York Society for the Suppression of Vice, is a formidable man," Margaret said in a seething voice. "He has already ruined the lives of some fine doctors."

"How does he affect you?" Mabel inquired.

"There is a rider in the Comstock Law that brands anything about birth control as lewd and lascivious, including having a doctor give information to a woman in the privacy of his office. One of Comstock's favorite tactics is to write to a suspected practitioner claiming he is a desperate woman living in poverty. Sometimes a doctor is won over by the appeals and writes back with suggestions on family limitation. Last year Comstock was able to put several doctors away for five-year terms."

"You haven't frightened me off yet." Minna replaced her glass. "If it suits you, I'll be at your clinic tomorrow." She stood and smoothed the folds of her skirt. "Unfortunately, I have another engagement."

Hannah glanced at the clock. It was past three.

"I hope you can stay, Mrs. Sokolow," Mabel said sincerely.

There was no reason for Hannah to leave, and she didn't want to seem to be following Minna, so she said, "No, I am in no hurry."

"The children?" Minna reminded unnecessarily.

"They'll be with Mama," Hannah replied firmly, even though she had taken Minna's point.

"I thought this was Mama's afternoon out."

Minna was right. This was her rent collection day. Hannah stood as well.

"A pity you cannot stay longer," Mabel said sincerely, then winked. "Please give my regards to the dashing Dr. Dowd when you encounter him next."

"I don't expect to see him unless we have an emergency in the middle of the night."

"He must be masterful when he takes charge," Mabel said wistfully.

"Oh, Mabel!" Margaret chastened like a schoolmarm. "Take it from this old nurse, there's nothing romantic about a midnight rendezvous in an operating theater, I assure you."

"What a pity!" Mabel sighed as she said farewell to her guests.

∽ 10 ∾

It had to be an emergency! Something was wrong with one of the children! Or Mama! When the nurse said her husband was waiting in the midwifery office, Hannah's heart plummeted. Lazar never came to the hospital. He couldn't tolerate the smell, he said. What could not wait an hour or two until she came home? She would have rushed out to him at once, but there was a serious complication in progress on Ward B.

The midwife on duty had called for a consulting physician, and Hannah had stayed into the morning shift to monitor the desperately ill mother's vital signs until he arrived. This was one case which even Hannah had agreed the gruesome fate that the woman faced was worse than the risk of cesarean surgery. The baby's pulse was so weak it might not last more than an hour, and the mother wasn't doing much better. Even so, Hannah's anxiety for the wretched woman was suddenly overshadowed by the personal disaster that she would surely be facing.

As Dr. Wendell Dowd rushed in with Midwife Donovan, who had been briefing him as they hurried into the ward, Hannah had a fleeting thought: Margaret Sanger had been right. When lives were at stake the medical staff had no time for anything more than the clipped abbreviations of medical jargon. And Mabel should see her "dashing Dr. Dowd" now, for he looked much too harried and distracted to care about anything besides the crisis at hand.

They went directly to Bed Twelve, where Hannah stood with her fingers on the mother's wrist. Without even a civil greeting he did a quick examination. "You might have called me sooner!" Shaking his head, he spoke harshly to Hannah, even though she had not been in charge of this case. "This pelvis is so contracted, probably due to childhood disease, that normal delivery is impossible. Now, considering her condition . . ." The patient's eyes fluttered open, so he spoke in technical terms. "I agree with the findings of Reynolds and Newell in Boston that in a case like this, a surgical delivery is far less invasive than an instrumental one." His brusque manner clearly conveyed his dismay at the way the case had been managed. "I'll meet you in surgery," he said.

This time, however, Hannah not only agreed with the diagnosis, but also that Hattie had waited too long even to call her in on this one. Already she was seeing this at the top of this month's infraction list.

"She was dilating so well and the baby is small," Hattie said apologetically.

This was no time to chide the woman, who had made an educated guess but had been wrong, and somehow she would have to make Mrs. Hemming see it this way when the time came. "I'll send Rosa in to help you get her ready and I'll be down in fifteen minutes. Start without me if I'm not there," Hannah added, then rushed to hear what Lazar had to say. If worse came to worst she could leave with him and Hattie could assist Dr. Dowd without her.

"Mr. Eastman is going to print it!" Lazar burst out the moment she walked through the door.

"Print what?" Hannah asked. Her heartbeat had drowned out his words.

"My story about Jenny, the prostitute." Suddenly weak, Hannah slumped against the wall. "Are you all right?" Lazar slid a chair under her. She sat and held her head between her hands.

"Yes, but I thought . . ."

Oblivious to what had worried her, Lazar rattled on impetuously. "I knew you would be excited, but I didn't think you'd turn white. Anyway, I had a message to go over to Twenty-one Greenwich Street—that's where his office is—and when I walked in this man said, 'You must be Lazarus Sokolow,' and showed me right in."

"Lazarus?"

"I thought it sounded more literary, like Emma Lazarus." Hannah sighed and stood up. "I have a patient who—"

"Wait, let me tell you the rest."

This was an important moment for him, she reminded herself. Shifting from one foot to the other, she acquiesced. "Nu?"

"Eastman said, 'You know *The Masses* is the only publication in New York that would touch a story like this. Everyone else would treat the subject sanctimoniously.' "

"That means he liked it?"

"Of course it does!"

Lazar was acting impatient with her, which under the circumstances she found infuriating. "Good, very good, but I'm expected in the operating theater." She took a few steps away from him.

He grabbed her arm. "He said what he liked about the story was that I had written it with 'unlabored grace'—which means that I made it look easy." Lazar beamed expectantly.

"How much will they pay?"

Lazar's face fell. "I didn't ask." For a second he seemed apologetic, then he brightened. "They didn't like my title. I was going to call it 'The Last of Jenny,' but Eastman said it was too saccharine. He is changing it to 'Allen Street.' What do you think of that?"

Hannah pushed past Lazar. "I'm happy it's good news, but I have to go."

He followed her down the corridor. " 'Allen Street,' is it strong enough?"

"Yes, Lazar, yes." Hannah hurried away. "I'll see you later."

∾ 11 ∾

The acceptance of Lazar's story by *The Masses* gained him more assignments from the Yiddish papers. Mostly they wanted different perspectives on the war, for which they would pay a dollar or two more. Still he was discontent, for nothing he submitted interested Max Eastman again.

"He rejects everything I offer him," Lazar complained as he prepared for bed on Friday, the one night they went to sleep at the same time.

"Keep trying," Hannah encouraged.

"It's no use. A million people have died and he couldn't care less about my viewpoint."

"I don't think that's it." Hannah slipped beside him and clasped his hand. "You can read statistics in any paper."

"Not the way I am writing them. He's fickle." Lazar tossed the latest issue of *The Masses* on the bed. " 'Read this piece by John Reed,' he told me. John Reed this, John Reed that! Just because the man covered the Mexican War for the *Metropolitan* and went to Europe this year doesn't make him Shakespeare!"

"Why not ask him what he wants?"

"I did, but he will only tell me what he doesn't want." Lazar turned away from Hannah and stretched out with his back to her. "He said he will not print anything that smacks of commercial journalism, and that he was determined to give a voice to creative literature like 'Allen Street.' "

"So, find another Jenny." Hannah leaned over to rub his back. If she could calm him, they might make love, something she had been looking forward to all day.

He sat upright in the bed. "You think that's so easy?"

"Well, you might begin by looking at what has been appealing to Mr. Eastman recently," she said as she tried to bolster his back with a pillow.

"Last month he published a story about a man who makes money by eating live rats in public."

Hannah grimaced. "I see people like that—people torn apart by life—every day," she replied more stridently than she intended, but he already was far too inflamed to get into a sexy mood.

"That's not very helpful," he groaned, then rolled out of bed.

"Where are you going?"

"To get some peace and quiet!" he snapped as he picked up a book and left their bedroom.

A week later, she had almost forgotten the argument when he came home and slapped down the most recent issue of *The Masses.* "He calls this dreck 'the place where radical intelligentsia and revolutionary labor meet on a common ground.' Ha!"

"What's wrong with it?"

"Not a single interesting story. What he needs are character sketches about real people with problems symbolic of society's weaknesses."

"What about a woman tyrannized by her husband?" Hannah offered as an idea formed. "Like the Italian lady, Mrs. Tartaglia, whose husband slapped her. Why don't you write about her desperation to have a boy?" Hannah was becoming enthusiastic about her idea. "You could call it 'Elizabeth Street.' "

"I don't want to do another story about a woman who had a baby, or that is all they will think I can do. You don't understand what he requires."

"Tell me."

"He wants the magazine to be a forum for agitation. Whatever is printed has to stir the mind and the soul into action."

"Nu? Look around. Look out on the street. There's a story walking out every door."

Lazar moved to the window. Snow was falling softly on the park in the square, where a man dressed in rags was sitting on a wagon, two children were sliding in the slush, a woman carrying a basket was heading up the stairs of the stoop next door. Around the corner came a car moving too fast for the slippery conditions. The rear of the vehicle went one direction, the front another, and the car slithered out of control for a few seconds until it came to a stop in front of their building. A man in a fur hat stepped out, then helped his wife and two children.

Lazar groaned. "Your sister and her brood are here."

"It's Friday night, remember?"

"I wish I could forget it."

Hannah did not jump to the bait. After many unpleasant confrontations, the sisters had not encouraged their husbands to be together. One or the other had missed the last few months of Sabbath meals. If Mama realized that Lazar was usually occupied elsewhere when Napthali was around, she had refrained from mentioning it. The truth was, she was mostly interested in seeing her daughters, her son, and her grandchildren.

"Last time Eva mentioned your story. She had a copy and was showing it around. She was proud of you."

"Now she'll think that just because I'm getting published, I can pay the overdue rent."

"If you keep up like this, it's not impossible," Hannah said encouragingly, although they had never been less than two months in arrears since he had lost his professorship.

"Not at Eastman's rates."

"Don't worry, the right idea will come along."

He shook his head morosely, then suddenly became animated. "I know what I'll write about!" He came up behind her and gave her a squeeze.

"Good, now that is settled, are you coming downstairs, staying home, or going out?"

Lazar kissed her cheek. "Don't you want to know?"

"I suppose," she said, moving away from him and toward the door.

"You were right. The idea was right outside the window."

"What do you mean?"

"Your sister's tale is almost as good as Jenny's."

At the spark of comprehension Hannah gasped. "No!"

"And Minna's," he went on, too preoccupied to notice her distress. "It's obviously a true story. Nobody would invent anything that coincidental."

"You can't!"

"The contrast will make the point. Here were two lovers in the old country devoted to each other and the same ideals. Then fate intervened. Everybody will adore it, especially the part where Minna reappears and—"

"Lazar, I forbid you!"

The children came into the room. "Go downstairs!" Hannah shouted. Emma shrugged at her brother, but they did as they were told. "Tell them to start without me," she said as she locked the door behind them.

"It would make a good story—no, a great story!" he said. "Besides, I wouldn't need to use their names."

"But you will use your name, so everyone will know."

"Nobody will care. It happened a long time ago."

"That's true, but Napthali has never been told about that bastard at the cigar factory."

"He had a right to know."

I suppose he did, Hannah thought, but at the time the words could never have been spoken. Even now the quirk of fate that had matched her sister and brother so well seemed incredible. In the old country Napthali had been betrothed to Chaim's wife, Minna. He had come to America first. After Hannah had saved the life of one of his sister's premature triplets, Sophie Feigenbaum had told Hannah how her brother's intended had been killed. To ease his pain, they were hoping to find him a match. At once Hannah suggested her sister, Eva, who had just been made a manager at the cigar factory where she worked. Napthali had been impressed with the young girl's ambition. From there, everything had gone smoothly until Eva balked at the marriage.

Hannah could not bear to remind herself of the terrible secret that Eva had revealed, or what she had done about it. They had vowed never to mention it again, and Eva had gone on to marry Napthali. Everything would have been perfect, but then Minna had reappeared. She had not died in the pogrom after all, but had been rescued and hidden by peasants. When she arrived at the Feigenbaums only to discover that Napthali had married Eva, the distraught woman was befriended by Chaim, who not only admired the frail girl's indomitable spirit, but fell in love with her.

"Well?" Lazar asked impatiently.

"Eva may have been wrong not to tell him everything, but after so much time it's best buried in the past." Hannah closed her eyes as she remembered the day Rachael discovered that Eva had been impregnated by the owner of the cigar factory, and that her rise to manager had been her reward for her silent compliance with his abuse. When Eva had threatened suicide before she would have the illegitimate child, Rachael and Hannah had shared the responsibility for the abortion. "Please, Lazar," she pleaded, "there are children who could be hurt, innocent children!"

"Don't you see this is my chance to establish a name for myself, even earn some more money? Isn't that what you wanted? If not, I'll go back to working on something important like my book about Stolypin, even though that won't pay the grocer."

Staring at him coldly, Hannah raced to find some way to convince him. All right, maybe it was a good tale, maybe it would appeal to the fickle Mr. Eastman, but what aspects were important for his purposes anyway? Eva's story was the melodrama that set the stage, but she knew Lazar would more likely point up the current contrast between the former lovers, Napthali and Minna. Eva's involvement was secondary. After Minna had lost her case in the rabbinical court, she had diverted her anger into political causes. Chaim had introduced her to the most radical elements. Then, without telling anyone, the two had married and joined up with the most fanatical sect that espoused anarchism and atheism. Here was the crux of Lazar's story: Minna and Chaim were pledged to destroy the world in which Napthali and Eva thrived. The two thwarted lovers became a symbol for the polarization of the plutocrats and the populace. It was irresistible—and impossible! Shaking her head at her inability either to sway Lazar or protect her family, she left the room without another word.

"What's wrong, Hannahleh? Are you ill?" her mother asked as she took her place at the table.

"No, well . . . I'm not feeling quite right."

"Don't eat the bread," Eva warned. "Wheat is difficult to digest."

"Don't mind me." Hannah stared at her sister with a mixture of revulsion and pity.

Eva shrugged at Mama and continued talking about her excitement at hearing the Russian Jewish writer, Solomon Rabinowitz, who was better known as Sholem Aleichem.

"Eva saw him at Cooper Union," Mama said proudly.

"He had the audience in pain from so much laughter. We're going to take Mama next time."

"It will be good to have something to smile about in these terrible times," Mama agreed.

"Sholem Aleichem understands that," Eva said somberly. "Before he began to read from his stories, he had the audience stand for a minute as an expression of sympathy for the war sufferers. A great man," she concluded respectfully.

Mama nodded. "A great Jew."

"Your Lazar should write more like him, show the humorous side of life. People pay attention if they can laugh first."

If you only knew . . . Hannah thought miserably. Even more than humor, everybody loved gossip. That's why everyone would read Lazar's story. Even if people figured out it was about Napthali, he was too rich to be harmed by it. Eva's feelings might be hurt, and Minna—well, she would probably side with Lazar and his political aim. Only if the abortion were mentioned could a disaster happen.

"Don't you agree?" Mama asked.

"Yes, yes," Hannah murmured slowly, then more forcefully, "Yes!" as she had the answer to her dilemma. If Lazar wrote about the abortion, people might assume she had something to do with it, even if that was not specifically mentioned. Midwives were always being accused of performing this illegal act, and she knew some who, out of charity or conviction or a way to supplement their meager incomes, did just that. But any taint associated with Bellevue's head midwife would be brought to the attention of Mrs. Hemming, who would not hesitate to take it to the Board of Managers. Surely this was precisely the fuel her supervisor would relish, and she would be dismissed. While they might manage without his salary, hers was the family's lifeline. As soon as Lazar realized these consequences, he would change his mind. Another idea would come along. She turned around and glanced out Mama's window. The snow was falling heavier than before. Yes, there was always another idea right outside your door.

Problem 3:
Christina Czachorwski's
Examination

◆

1915

Knowledge is like a sphere in space; the higher it rises, the more it balloons.

—PASCAL

❧ 1 ❧

EIGHT hundred thousand Russian army troops were heading toward Prussia in a new offensive at the end of January, despite the fact that the czar had tried to propose arbitration at The Hague. Lazar and his friends were consumed with the meaning of this development, while Hannah's concerns were more immediate. Benjamin was ill.

"Ma?" he called plaintively on the first afternoon he had spent in bed.

"Yes, I'm here."

"When are you leaving?"

"Leaving for where?"

"The hospital. I can tell by the light on the water tower that it's almost time for you to go."

Hannah felt a pang that her child was so acutely aware of when she left him. "I'm not going anywhere."

"But—"

"They'll have to do without me tonight. You need me more."

This was the truth. His fever had increased during the day.

His skin was dry and hot to the touch. He needed fluids, but claimed his throat was too raw to swallow them. He would need to be coaxed with honey-laced teas and broths cooled to the perfect soothing temperature. Lazar or her mother might manage, but she had seen too many mild infections turn into virulent diseases to be able to leave her son in his condition.

The next morning, she received this message from Mrs. Hemming: "Might I prevail upon you to return to your duties this evening? An outbreak of contagion amongst the staff has left us shorthanded."

For a few hours it seemed that Benny's fever was responding and so she thought she might be able to return to work that night, but by the time the sun had slipped behind the water tower on the tenement across the street, it had peaked to a new high. She sent Emma downstairs to sleep at her grandmother's, and remained in the room with her son. Between tending his vomiting and applying compresses to quell the raging fever, she did not sleep more than an hour. The next morning, Hannah felt her throat becoming raw and began to gargle with salt water, followed by a vinegar rinse. This seemed to cure the first symptom, but by the next day she too had become febrile. Even so, the women came to the door. When she would not let them in, they were anxious enough to ask their questions in the hall, sometimes slipping pieces of paper with their menstrual dates on them. Too weak to protest, Hannah sat bundled in her kitchen, sipping tea mixed with honey and responding between her racking coughs.

"This has got to stop!" Rachael demanded when she bustled into the apartment to check on Benny and Hannah. "Do you know there are four people sitting on the steps waiting their turn? And look at you!" She touched Hannah's forehead. "You belong in bed."

Sternly Rachael informed those waiting to see the midwife that she would be unavailable for at least a week. Deaf to their mutterings, the doctor closed the door and firmly latched the bolt. "I saw Lazar at the Café Boulevard yesterday, but he didn't tell me you were this sick. How long has it been going on?"

"A week, more or less. I forget when Benny came down with it."

Rachael took her temperature and felt the glands under

her arms, alongside her neck, and behind her ears. "Any rashes?" She listened to her chest. "Cough. Again. Once again."

Just having Rachael pressing and fussing made Hannah feel better. "It's just the grippe. I'm going back to work tomorrow."

"You are not!"

"But—"

"You need a week of complete rest. In bed. Your mother can make the meals. Emma should stay with her, and as soon as he is back in school, Benny should join her downstairs."

"But Mrs. Hemming—"

"Hand Lazar your Bellevue cap and put him to work."

"Delivering babies or answering the ladies' questions?" Hannah laughed, then broke into a fit of coughing.

"He'd enjoy the latter, but somehow I think they'd end up with more political than practical responses." Rachael pulled up a chair and faced Hannah squarely. "Anyhow, that's something else I must talk to you about."

Hannah trembled as she realized she had not made any progress with Rachael's problem.

"You must lie down," Rachael said, taking her response for another symptom.

Hannah allowed herself to be arranged on the sofa with pillows at her head and under her knees, and an afghan tucked around her. While Rachael made another pot of tea, she considered why all her talk with Mabel Dodge and Margaret Sanger, all her reading, had brought her no closer to solving her best friend's difficulty. When the tea was served, Hannah warmed her hands over the steaming glass, but did not drink. She waited for Rachael to broach the subject.

"You can't continue to have these women coming to your house at all hours."

The criticism was a relief. "I try to tell them when to come, but who listens?"

"It's unprofessional. Also, it's not good for the children. There are some things they shouldn't hear."

"What do they know about days of the month?"

"More than you think."

"How can I send them away? Anyway, we need the extra money."

"I'm not suggesting you stop. You are performing a valuable service. Most physicians don't have the time to talk to women the way you do, and where else can they turn for advice?"

Hannah was too exhausted to parry with Rachael.

"I'm sorry to bring it up now, but I've been thinking about this for several weeks. I wonder if you could work in my office."

"I'm not a doctor," Hannah said with resignation, since Rachael had encouraged her to go on to medical school in Russia, and had prodded her to consider it again in America.

"That's not the point. When I am out at the hospital, the patients still come, especially now, when so many are sick. Carrie sends them away. She lacks the judgment to sort out the serious cases—which ones should be seen immediately, which ones could wait for a future appointment. Last week she turned away a sick child who then had a convulsion outside the door. If you had been there, you might have known what to do, or could have referred her directly to Gouverneur's or Bellevue."

"I wouldn't be able to manage most of your cases."

"Yes, you would. I could leave you a list of what type should be sent to an emergency service. Mostly I see women and children anyhow, and you know almost as much about that as I do. Also, you can speak Yiddish to the Orthodox and help me with some of the prenatal care."

"And when am I to do this? I still work nights at Bellevue and I try to get some sleep at least every other day, whether I need it or not."

Rachael laughed and shook her head. "You'll soon find this will give you more time, not less. I'd put your name and hours on the door. They could be as few or as many as you like. Carrie would make appointments for you." Even before Hannah did, Rachael knew that the idea was being accepted. "Think about the times you would like and tell me next Thursday when you come to be checked *before* you return to Bellevue." She tied her woolen scarf around her neck and buttoned her long coat. "Don't move!" she said as Hannah stirred. "I'll see myself out. On the way down I will sweep any desperate creatures off the steps, as well as talk to your mama. She's going to stand guard for me."

Hannah closed her eyes. She lacked the strength to argue. Sleep washed over her before she heard the last of the doctor's descending footsteps.

2

The war news in the next month was a blur as Hannah slept all day and worked all night. The icy weather had deterred her advice seekers, who were never certain they would see her or not, and one day a sign—in English and Yiddish— appeared beside her doorbell advising:

APPOINTMENTS TO CONSULT HANNAH SOKOLOW
MAY BE MADE AT THE OFFICE OF
DR. R. JAFFE, 78 ST. MARK'S PLACE.

Although Hannah was unsure how she could sit behind Rachael's desk and dispense information that was not entirely based on fact, as soon as she had her next month's schedule for Bellevue, she made a visit to set up some hours that would be convenient. Dr. Jaffe's clinic had expanded to include the entire first floor of the building, which was a few doors in from the corner of First Avenue and St. Mark's Place. There were two waiting rooms, one for women and children, one for men, to satisfy her Orthodox clientele. In each was a small sign, which showed the payment schedule for usual services and the line: *"The above are customary fees. It is expected that those unable to pay will give what they can afford, and those who can will pay what they feel the services are worth."*

Hannah supposed that few paid more, but nevertheless, Dr. Jaffe's practice had prospered. Even families who had moved away from the Lower East Side continued to see one of the only women in general practice in the city. However, Hannah suspected that the mainstay of her friend's income came from her husband's contribution.

Hannah looked around the women's waiting room and saw a gaunt woman who surely had a terminal wasting disease, a bright-cheeked child with feverish eyes, and a boy whose skullcap could not hide a crusty scalp infection. A lot of good Herzog's talking cure would do them! Hannah thought.

"Hello, Mrs. Sokolow" came the husky voice of Dr. Jaffe's nurse, Carrie, a chocolate-skinned woman Rachael had cured of consumption, then had trained to assist her. "I'm really pleased to see you!" she said with genuine warmth as she showed her the list of more than twenty women who already wanted appointments with the midwife. "When might I schedule them?"

"I can come in Tuesdays and Wednesdays from three to five, if that would be convenient."

"The doctor goes to the hospital after two, so that would be fine for her as well. Can you come any other day?"

"Maybe on my way home from the hospital for an hour or two on some mornings. I'll have to see."

Carrie lifted a black appointment book. "Let me show you Dr. Jaffe's days in Gouverneur's clinic." Just then two women came in the door. Both faces were streaked with tears. "Which of you needs to see the doctor?" Carrie asked in a reassuring voice.

"I do," said the smaller of the two, who was dabbing her eyes with a frayed handkerchief.

"The doctor isn't in. Is this an emergency?"

"No," she said with a trembling lip.

Carrie gave Hannah a perplexed glance. Then the one who wasn't ill began to weep even more copiously. "Isn't it horrid? To think it happened to her?"

"To whom?" Hannah asked gently.

"To Sarah!" she gasped.

Hannah turned to the one who was to be the patient. "Are you Sarah?"

"No. I'm Christina."

"Hello, I'm Midwife Sokolow. Dr. Jaffe won't be back for several hours. Might I help you?"

"I dunno," she mumbled between sniffs.

Placing her hands on her hips, Carrie asked loudly, "Who's Sarah?"

The women looked up, their noses raw from weeping in the cold. "You didn't hear about Sarah Bernhardt? They had to amputate her leg in Paris!" moaned Christina.

Hannah could not repress a smile of relief that she did not have to face a medical emergency. The papers had been filled with details of the surgery on the French actress's leg due to an infection from a ten-year-old injury, but Hannah was taken aback by so emotional a response to someone they did not know. "Would you prefer to come back another time?" she asked Christina.

"Yes, but I am terribly uncomfortable."

"Tell her the problem," her companion hissed. The woman nodded for the other to speak on her behalf. "My sister's womb has fallen," she whispered.

Hannah knew exactly what she meant, but was unsure of what to do. This was not a critical situation, but depending on the severity could be debilitating. Should she wait for Rachael or check the woman herself? She didn't want to appear to be taking away the doctor's patient, but then decided if she didn't keep any part of the fee, she couldn't be criticized. From the overly emotional entrance and its cause, Hannah supposed the woman may have exaggerated this difficulty also, and it would be a service to Rachael to manage the minor complaint. "I could check you and then consult with the doctor when she arrives, but only if you want me to."

Again the sister responded. "Why not get it over with?"

"But, Magda, I don't want to go through with it more than once if I don't have to."

"I understand," Hannah said, now sorry she volunteered.

"That's not it . . ." She gave her sister a beseeching look, but Magda seemed preoccupied. Christina stared up at Hannah and something in the midwife's composed expression must have decided her. "Could I speak to you in private?"

"Of course. Come with me."

Hannah led the way to an examining room. She might have felt more comfortable talking to Christina in Rachael's office, but was unsure of its state of disarray and she did not want to have to apologize for the doctor's habits.

Carrie followed with a chart, asked the patient to be seated on the stool, and took down her vital statistics. The woman's name was Christina Czachorwski. She was thirty-six years old, a widow with four children, the oldest twenty with a child of her own. The youngest child was six, so the current predicament was not a direct result of a confinement.

"Thank you, Carrie." Hannah went to the basin to scrub her hands.

"Are you going to look at me now?" Mrs. Czachorwski asked in a high, panicky voice.

Hannah wondered how the woman expected her to cure her without an examination to view the extent of the prolapse. Even during childbirth some women were vigorous in their attempt to preserve modesty. However, when a baby was determined to be born, the last vestiges of shyness melted with the necessity of the moment. "No, not yet. How do you think this happened?"

"I was sick for a few weeks and was coughing so hard it fell out."

Hannah was immediately sympathetic. "I had the same grippe. A very nasty one." She smiled at Christina, but the woman's face was becoming harder and more inflexible. Her lips were drawn in a tight line, and she chewed the lower one as she waited. In her mind Hannah pictured diagrams that illustrated various displacements of the uterus. She knew that strong exertions, like breathing and straining, coughing and sneezing, created pressure on the organ, affecting its position. If everything was fine, the ligaments and muscles which supported this structure snapped it back into its normal anteflexion, but sometimes, when the firm underpinning of the pelvic floor was weakened by the stresses of childbirth, the uterus slipped part of the way into the vaginal vault. While uncomfortable and embarrassing, there were some simple solutions that Hannah might employ—but only after a close examination.

"Would you like me to leave the room while you undress?" she asked solicitously. "Or do you require help with your fastenings?"

"There's another problem . . ."

"The wrong time of the month?" Hannah asked. Although she could still examine her, Hannah could not fit a pessary, the device used to prevent the uterus from descending farther, if the flow was too heavy.

"No, it's not that."

Hannah's patience was faltering, but she was experienced in checking herself and merely waited until Christina felt compelled to fill the silence.

"I think I am unusual."

Now she had Hannah's full attention. "I have examined hundreds of women," she began slowly, then added, "thus it's unlikely you have anything that I have not seen."

"You mustn't tell anyone . . ." she gasped, "not even Magda."

"Of course not," Hannah said. Now she was even more perplexed. Maybe the problem was some sort of growth or recent disfigurement. A tattoo? Hannah was anxious to discover this woman's secret, yet something warned her not to become too enthralled. After all, here was a lady whose reaction to an actress's misfortune had been extreme. This lonely widow, a Polish girl whose raw hands and swollen feet indicated she had led a difficult life, not only found refuge in her fantasies about stars of the theater, but believed she had unusual attributes as well. "I'm only interested in alleviating your problems, not how you appear."

"It's not what I have—" she stumbled "—it's what happens when someone touches me there."

"I'll be very gentle, and I'll stop whenever you say." The poor woman had probably suffered under some callous practitioner who had poked her harshly.

"I'm not worried that you'll hurt me," Christina responded, then forced a queer laugh.

Now Hannah thought the woman's mind might not be balanced. "If you don't tell me the obstacle, I cannot assist you," she snapped, finally unable to control the irritation creeping into her voice.

In her mind she could see Lazar, after hearing one of her hospital tales, throwing up his hands and saying, "Women! How can you work all day with *meshugeneh* women?" Wait until she told him about this one ... she thought as she handed Mrs. Czachorwski an examination robe and turned her back. Not that she would ever tell him. Because he would never have believed what happened next.

∾ 3 ∾

When Mrs. Czachorwski realized she had gone too far to halt the progress of the visit, she became more passive. This sort of acceptance happened during the late stages of labor, and from experience Hannah knew that the best way to win cooperation was to change from her authoritative stance to one with the right degree of deference, while still maintaining a professional posture. This is where male practitioners refused to bend and why women preferred another woman at a time like this, although there were few Dr. Jaffes or even midwives available for gynecological work. Many would rather suffer than submit. Hannah resolved to make this experience one Mrs. Czachorwski would remember in the most positive light.

She assisted the woman, who was fairly heavyset, onto the table and gave her a sheet to preserve her modesty. Taking the speculum from the drawer, Hannah warmed it under the examining light, since vaginal tissues were sensitive to temperature.

"Could you spread your legs?"

Mrs. Czachorwski complied, although Hannah noticed her knees trembling. "This won't take long."

"Are you going to touch me?" came a whiny voice.

"Not yet, but I'll tell you before I do."

For the moment Hannah merely observed the woman's vulva for any sign of open sores or injured tissue. Everything appeared normal. The uterus did not protrude all the way, which was a relief. Whatever the degree of prolapse, it should be correctable with a simple device.

"Now I am going to spread you with a metal tool, but it is warm and it should not hurt you."

"All right, but . . ."

"Yes?" Hannah looked up. The woman's strained face made it appear that she was bracing for an assault. "It will be easier if you can relax. Take a few deep breaths. Good. Good."

Hannah introduced her finger between the pubic arch and the anterior lip of the prolapsed cervix that poked halfway down the canal, probably giving a cramped but not unbearable sensation of fullness. "Here's the problem. It's not severe."

"Are you almost—" she gasped.

Hannah looked up again. The sound was worrisome, almost that of someone choking. Christina's head had snapped back, her eyes had closed, and her mouth grimaced. Hannah withdrew her hand and prepared to deal with a seizure. Wasn't that what Rachael had mentioned? A child who had had a convulsion when she wasn't there?

But this was no convulsion.

In a few seconds Mrs. Czachorwski's eyes opened. She

turned her head to the wall. "Have you finished?" she mumbled.

"Did I hurt you?"

"No," she whispered.

Hannah looked between the woman's trembling legs. Her vulva glistened. The skin of the tissues glowed with a healthy ruddiness. The muscles of the perineum seemed to be bulging, then relaxing spontaneously. Probably only a few seconds had passed, but it seemed like much longer as Hannah processed what she was witnessing. Could this woman have attained some form of climax from her mere touch? Was this what she had been mortified about? Never having witnessed a woman's sexual response from that particular viewpoint, Hannah was confused but fairly certain about what had taken place. Suddenly she felt a peculiar shame at having caused it. Was this woman some sort of an invert who enjoyed contact with her own sex? Even so, how could anyone react so quickly? Didn't most women require some loving stimulation before they could be fulfilled? Or was Mrs. Czachorwski on the opposite pole from a frustrated Dr. Jaffe? Hannah's head pounded with confusion, then she reminded herself that this was exactly what the patient had feared would happen, so others—including men—had caused the same reaction. Her husband was dead. Was this what ensued when a sexually mature woman was deprived of a partner for too long? That seemed unlikely. Then why was Mrs. Czachorwski able to be aroused so swiftly when most people required much more stimulation, and others—like Rachael—were utterly denied what they most desired?

"May I get up?" came a faraway voice.

Hannah's heart began to race. Here was a chance to observe a woman's excitement! The answers for which she had been searching might be in front of her. But did she have the right to use the woman for an experiment? She could ask her permission, but how could she explain what she wanted? She couldn't very well touch her in different places without seeming to be her partner, and yet considering how much she owed Rachael, how could she let this opportunity disappear?

"I need to continue," Hannah replied as emphatically as she dared.

This was true. She had not completed the exam. Usually, though, she did not need to scrutinize the exterior as she reached into the vagina—her education was in her fingers. This time she strained to observe every nuance in Mrs. Czachorwski's responses. Initially she had lubricated her finger, but now she was certain the natural fluids were sufficient to allow painless penetration. With a purposeful and efficient maneuver, Hannah neither attempted to stimulate her nor tried to accomplish anything more than a full comprehension of the medical problem. Avoiding the clitoris, she merely introduced two fingers until she felt the neck of the womb and the uterine body that was present. The vagina tensed and relaxed, and the minor lips' color changed from pink to a rosy red, then to wine color. Christina writhed for a moment. Hannah removed her fingers, for she had no reason to keep them inside any longer. The whole episode hadn't lasted more than a minute and Hannah had been too attentive to the outer structure and her sense of touch to have noticed the early changes in the clitoris. When she glanced at it, she regarded the swelling, but had no idea if this was reacting during an orgasmic phase. Perhaps Christina represented an extreme example of maturation into the vaginal stage Freud described. Did this mean Freud was correct? While her mind rushed ahead, trying to absorb what she had learned, Hannah managed to place the sheet over Christina's legs and assist her in sitting up.

"Can you help me?" Mrs. Czachorwski asked in a cottony whisper.

Hannah could barely look at the woman, but fortunately her eyes were averted as well. "Your problem can be solved with a device inserted in the vagina to hold your uterus in place. The doctor has some, but they come in different sizes and she should assist in the fitting."

"Can't you do it?"

Hannah's mind raced with what would be best—as much as for Rachael as for the patient. "I thought you might prefer to return another time . . ."

"I've been so uncomfortable," Christina lamented.

"Of course you have." She made up her mind that Rachael would be even more disturbed by this woman than she was. "There are rubber pieces that will help hold up your womb. I could try to give you one today, but it will take many attempts to fit you with the right size and shape. I don't know if you would want . . ."

"The worst is over," Mrs. Czachorwski said, supporting herself on one elbow.

In what way? Hannah wondered. Had the sexual excitement diminished, the way it did after a satisfying encounter with her husband? Or did she mean that now the midwife knew what to expect—and had not shown obvious astonishment—the woman felt less shame? It mattered not. All Hannah could do was care for the patient when and if she requested it.

"Shall we do it now?" Hannah asked again to be certain.

"Please."

"All right," Hannah said. She went to the cabinet where Rachael kept a small selection of pessaries. She decided to begin with the simplest form, technically called the ring, although the round type was no longer considered as practical as the ones that looked like variations on a circle, which had been squeezed into eccentric shapes. She handed Christina one to examine. "These are the easiest to keep clean." Hannah stopped herself. Usually a woman who wore a device came to have it removed monthly. A nurse—probably Carrie—would extract it, wash and sterilize it, then the doctor would reinsert it. It was doubtful Hannah could be there every time, nor should she, since this was Rachael's business, not hers. Also, how would Mrs. Czachorwski react to other people manipulating her? Hannah was about to explain this, but decided to wait until she achieved a reasonable level of support with the equipment first.

The first two shapes—the Hodge and the Thomas modification—were poorly adapted to this woman's anatomy. Hannah became so engrossed in trying to determine which of the remaining might be best, she was able to ignore Mrs. Czachorwski's sexual reaction, although she was fairly certain that the excitement had not lessened. The insertions were becoming more complicated because her natural moisture was making the rings slippery. Hannah began to perspire.

The hell with propriety! the midwife decided. There was too much to learn here. "I am going to have to see what the difficulty is," Hannah said tensely. She readjusted the examining table light so it afforded the best view of the genitalia. Since a dainty touch seemed to stimulate her as much as a harsher one, Hannah decided not to treat her any differently than she would an everyday patient. She separated the labia with her left hand until the os uteri could be viewed without obstruction. Here the woman's prolapsed condition was beneficial, at least for scientific purposes. Lifting the third ring, with two curving arches instead of one, she tried to fit the posterior bar behind the cervix while the anterior bar stemmed itself against the symphysis just behind the vaginal entrance. Hannah swept her right forefinger across the space between the cervix and the pubic arch and then around all the surfaces of the porcelain ring to check the fit. An orgasm began. This made the fitting impossible, for the contractions several times each second altered the spaces. Hannah kept a grip on the edge of the ring while she observed the os opening itself almost an inch, then made five or six successive gasps—if that is what one could call them—drawing the external area of the cervix inside itself in the regular, rhythmic action that any woman who has felt the same pulse inside herself would recognize for what it was. In a few seconds the cervix prepared to lose its hardness. Hannah touched the rim. It was quite soft. The color went from a livid purple to an unremarkable pink. Inured to the woman's writhings, she watched to see if the ring was displaced when the contractions subsided. It seemed to conform well with the posterior end of the pessary raising the cervix and tilting the uterine body forward. The anterior end lay behind the symphysis in what seemed a comfortable position.

Mrs. Czachorwski was breathing normally. "I think we have a good fit," she told her. "If you reach inside, you will be able to touch the end with your fingers. This is how it should be, so don't worry that it has slipped. You will continue with that 'full' sensation, but it should not be as great as before. At least you won't have to fear that anything is about to fall out." Hannah pulled Christina's gown over her knees. "If you would like, you can walk around to see how it feels."

Hannah supported the woman's back and helped her sit upright. Mrs. Czachorwski sighed. Her face was flushed, her lips drawn and tense. The ordeal was over.

After Christina took a few tentative steps around the room, she grinned at the midwife. "It's working!"

Carrie knocked on the door. When Hannah opened it, Carrie whispered something about a woman who thought she was pregnant, but was bleeding.

"I'll be right there. Put on a fresh pad so we can see how much it is."

Quickly Hannah gave Mrs. Czachorwski a few directions about sanitary care, then asked her to return in two weeks to be checked.

In the next room the bleeding woman was aborting a six-month fetus and had to be taken to the hospital. Hannah accompanied her to Bellevue, and became so involved in the case she could not ruminate on Mrs. Czachorwski that day. Even if reflections about her penetrated Hannah's thoughts throughout the week, she managed to sweep the disturbing images aside. More study was required before she could decide whether Mrs. Czachorwski was suffering—and Hannah was not certain if that was the right word—from a pathological condition or merely an exaggeration of regular sensations.

That Friday Hannah was asked by Mrs. Hemming to accompany Mrs. Clayborn Church, one of the youngest members of the Board of Managers, to a new pavilion that was under construction for a discussion about the floor plan for the proposed maternity suite.

"We've requested more electrical outlets than any other division." Mrs. Church stepped gingerly around workmen uncoiling huge snakes of electrical cable. "Even if we don't need them now, it's best to have more than you require for the future than less."

Hannah murmured something in agreement, but her mind had wandered to the connection between wires that brought electrical current to a lamp and the nervous system that connected energy in the human body. Could Mrs. Czachorwski have extra coils of nerves, or were hers merely excited more easily than another person's? Hannah was unable to separate her experiences from each deliberation, or the idea that she saw herself at some level of "normal" and Rachael and Christina as opposite ends of "abnormal." Yes, sometimes it was easier for her to become excited than others. There were physical reasons, such as illness, or pain, or the time of the month. There were emotional differences based on how her day had gone, the mood her husband was in, and permutations in how loving she felt when they were alone. Sometimes her thoughts could not be dissociated from her children or her laboring mothers long enough to focus on sexual needs. Other times she actively ruminated about her physical desires, plotting to have Lazar home early and the children tucked away. Hadn't Mrs. Czachorwski seemed a little hysterical over Sarah Bernhardt? Perhaps she dwelled on mating excessively and this is what kept her ablaze. Had she been like this during her marriage? Hannah was annoyed with herself for not asking enough questions. The problem would have exasperated her more, however, if the next few weeks had not been so eventful. As it was, she would have little time for deliberation.

The first difficulty concerned Minna. While Margaret Sanger was in Europe, Minna managed the office. One day a shabbily dressed man came to the office and introduced himself as Mr. Collier. "Is this the place that can tell me how to prevent my wife from having more children?" he asked deferentially.

"I would be happy to speak to your wife," Minna replied as she had been instructed.

"She cannot leave the children. She's just had our seventh child. Another one would kill her—and me!" he said beseechingly.

Recalling Margaret Sanger's story about Mrs. Sachs, Minna took pity on the man and gave him a copy of the pamphlet, *Family Limitation*. She put the matter out of her mind and went back to neatly copying Margaret's notes on the methods of birth control she had been learning in Dr. Rutgers' clinic in Holland.

The next afternoon, a tall man with gray hair and side whiskers burst through the door, shouting, "I am Mr. Anthony Comstock and have a warrant for your arrest." The man Minna recalled as Mr. Collier entered. This time he was wearing a business suit and carrying a search warrant. "Where is Mrs. Sanger?" Mr. Comstock demanded.

"She is not here."

"When will she return?"

"I do not know."

Mr. Comstock had misunderstood how Minna would react. "Now, miss, I want you to realize that we are not interested in you. We know you are not the author of the filth that originates here. Anything you tell us will not be used against you. All we want is to locate Mrs. Sanger."

"She is not in the United States," Minna stated firmly. "If you want to arrest somebody, I suppose you shall have to arrest me."

"Did you write the pamphlet?"

"No, but I believe in the principle of family limitation."

"Are you asking for trouble, young woman?"

"I did not think that in America you could be in trouble for believing in principles."

Comstock's face became mottled with angry red patches. "Then we shall see about that."

When she arrived at the jail, an official took her aside and told her, like a friendly uncle, that he understood how a sweet girl like her could have been duped by Mrs. Sanger. None of this was her fault. Jobs were hard to find and she had done right to protect her employer, but lawyers were costly and could only impede the case. "Plead guilty, and we will recommend you be given a suspended sentence. You can be home before supper tonight."

Minna refused. She was arraigned and bail was fixed at five hundred dollars, an extraordinary sum for someone of Minna's means. Mrs. Dodge was contacted, but she could not be located until Minna had spent two nights in the filthy cell.

Mama Blau was distraught, but Chaim was sanguine as he calmed her. "Mr. Comstock has done everyone a favor. All the newspapers are printing stories about *Family Limitation*. Now more people than ever before will know about it."

"Your wife slept with vermin and this is how you talk!" Mama scolded.

Hannah had mixed feelings. In one sense she was proud of Minna's stand, but she felt that she had gone too far, as usual. For Chaim's sake, if for no other reason, she should have modified her position. When Lazar agreed with her about this initially, Hannah was heartened. "So you see she's been through enough. Anything more would be too much of a burden."

"What do you mean?"

"That article about her past." Even though Hannah had

told him her fears for her job, he had discounted them, claiming her apprehensions were groundless. Since he certainly did not care about Eva's feelings, she had hoped that Minna's current predicament might deter him.

"I don't agree about that," he muttered.

For a moment Hannah was going to resurrect the old argument, then seeing the stern set of his jaw, dropped it like a child with a piece of ice. "What's going to happen to Minna?" she asked to bring them back to the issue.

"It's like a dance, everybody must do their part, but in the end, when the music stops playing, nobody will remember what happened."

Hannah, who had experienced an unpleasant brush with the law many years earlier, doubted the matter would be as trivial as he indicated, yet hoped his words were true.

Nothing happened on that front for many weeks, nor did Lazar seem to be working on the worrisome story, which she learned was titled "The Landlord." Her instinct not to press him had been right. If Lazar began something new and that took root, he might discard the old idea on his own. But if she provoked him, he might continue with it just to win his way. As she bustled about making a compote from bruised fruit she had picked up for a cheap price, she tried to figure out what the topic might be. Her eye was drawn to some notes and newspaper clippings spread on the kitchen table. "What is this about?" she asked warily.

"An interesting obituary. Count Sergie Witte died of influenza in Petrograd yesterday."

"That's too bad," Hannah said, stirring cinnamon into the fruit. Considered a progressive by some—if not Lazar's group—Count Witte had been Russia's first constitutional prime minister.

"Do you want to hear what I've written?" He waited for her nod, then began in Yiddish. The obituary, while neutral on the surface, contained the barbs the readers of the radical Yiddish press expected, as well as the proper note of respect for a man who had been a friend of the Jews.

"Very nice, very nice," she murmured. Hannah did admire her husband's choice of the apt word, also the way a reader was left to interpret the matter-of-fact story in light of the political climate without feeling the author had told him what to think. Too bad you couldn't eat words. "You should write more about Russia." Lazar raised his eyebrows provocatively. "And your feelings about the war," Hannah added in a rush.

"But not my feelings about your family." Hannah willed herself not to rise to the bait. Lazar's lips curled in a wary smile. "By the way, I finally sent 'The Landlord' to Max."

She finished tasting the fruit, then added more sugar before she replied levelly, "When?"

"About a week ago. I have an appointment to see him tomorrow."

Torn by her desire to see her husband succeed—or at least to protect him from the pangs of rejection—she momentarily hoped the response would be favorable. Yet for the sake of Eva and Minna—all of them, in truth—she wished Max Eastman would reject it.

When Lazar did not return by the time Hannah left for the hospital the next evening, she ruminated whether he was out celebrating or moping. She would learn soon enough, she decided.

⤙ 5 ⤚

Early that evening Hannah met a most agitated Lenore Harvey in the midwives' changing room. She was going off duty just as Hannah was coming to work. "Watch out," the other midwife warned, "Mrs. Hemming is on the warpath."

Hannah was unfamiliar with the idiom. "The what?"

"You know, she is trying to make certain everything is shipshape, ah, absolutely perfect."

"That's all I need!" Nobody ever knew when Mrs. Hemming would appear on a ward or what she would ask to see. One day it would be the linen cupboard, the next the drug cabinet.

"I think she has had it in for me ever since I was in nurses' training school because my hems were never even enough to suit her eagle eye."

"I often feel the same way, but I don't think it's because of my clothing."

"I know how you feel, but I have to keep remembering that she always wanted the best for us."

Hannah understood it would not be prudent to condemn Mrs. Hemming, but she knew Lenore was glossing over how vigorously the student nurses were worked. Bedside care at Bellevue was entirely provided by current training-school students, who actually paid for the privilege of working seventy-hour weeks to prepare for careers managing cases in the home setting, where any person of means remained for most medical treatments. A few, like Lenore, went on to do midwifery training, and then were offered staff obstetrical positions; but most served their time to get a diploma, then left.

"You don't like her, do you?" was Lenore's response to Hannah's silence.

"I do respect her," Hannah hedged. The problem was that no matter how hard anyone tried, Mrs. Hemming found there was always room for improvement. Worse was Hannah's sense that Mrs. Hemming did not trust her. Why? Because she had received most of her training in Moscow? Because her English was often fragmented? Or because she was not Christian? Everyone was aware that Mrs. Hemming had not supported Hannah for the position of the most senior midwife, but the rest of the Board of Managers had determined nobody else was as qualified. Fortunately, most of the doctors also liked Hannah, especially Dr. Wendell Dowd, who was thought to be next in line for chairman of the obstetrical service because of his progressive stance.

"She's had a tragic life," Lenore said in Mrs. Hemming's defense. "You know what happened, don't you?" Hannah shook her head. "She once was married—well, her name is *Mrs.* Hemming, isn't it? They were together less than a year when her husband developed pernicious anemia. He died the morning of their second Christmas together. Since then she has dedicated herself to her work."

Hannah was tiring of this topic. "If there isn't anything else of a clinical nature that I better know about," she said, centering her blue apron, "I must get out on the floor."

"The preeclamptic in Ward C might be going sour."

"Sounds like a good one for Dr. Dowd."

"He's in surgery."

"Who's on call?"

"Dr. Mariceau." Lenore rolled her eyes expressively. The

doctor with the French accent was considered very handsome and charming by the nurses, but his flamboyance annoyed the midwives, who had much more respect for Dr. Dowd.

Hannah groaned, but hurried directly to Ward C and studied the problem patient's chart before the doctor arrived. Severe headache was Mrs. Weed's first complaint, followed by loss of appetite and general lassitude. In her mind Hannah reviewed the conditions that indicated eclampsia, or toxemia of pregnancy, potentially one of the most dangerous complications that may befall a pregnant woman.

She rechecked the notations. Pulse: 110, which was fine, but the temperature had gone from 100° an hour ago to 102.2° a few minutes earlier. The sharp elevation was worrisome, but the chart indicated everything was well with the baby, and Hannah had no reason to distrust the readings. Still, to satisfy herself, she would have to listen to the baby's heartbeat.

She lifted the woman's gown and placed her stethoscope above the navel. This was not the best place to hear this particular baby's heartbeat, so she moved the cup a few inches higher. Something in the periphery of her vision caused Hannah to raise the gown farther. What had seemed the small red dots of nipples placed too low came into focus as a rash. More circles—some lighter, some darker than others—studded the landscape of her chest.

"Had you noticed this before?" she asked Midwife Wylie.

The young midwife was shocked. "No, not when I examined her, and nobody else said anything about it."

"Remember Dr. Dowd's lecture last month on illness in pregnancy?"

"Yes, of course!" Her face lit up. "He said that while pregnancy is not in itself an illness, pregnant women do become ill."

"Exactly, although Dr. Jeffers argued that parturition was an abnormal state for a woman and that she needed to be 'delivered' of her ill health as well as her baby."

"He hasn't changed his tune in fifty years!"

"At least he's been put out to pasture. But Dr. Dowd's point was that just as pregnancy does not convey spontaneous disability, it also does not offer immunity against the perils and plagues that infect the rest of the population."

"And you think this might be one of those cases?"

"Very possibly."

Just then Dr. Mariceau arrived with two students in tow. All three found the rash curious and speculated on the cause. "Quite an allergic reaction, isn't it?" His assistants nodded deferentially. "Really should get someone down from skin service on this one," Dr. Mariceau concluded.

"Do you think it might be derived from the toxemic process?" Hannah pressed.

"Unfortunately, we have not yet discovered whence these toxins originate." Dr. Mariceau directed his speech to his students. "Many theories have been advanced. Halvertsma maintained that the uterus compresses the ureters, thus producing a uremia. Various bacilli have been found in the bacteria by Dolèris, Blanc, and Favre. Nevertheless, I believe that the febrile nature of the disease, accompanied by the fact it occurs oftener in cold and damp weather, would argue for an extraneous microbic origin."

"Yes, but I have never seen a rash in a toxemic patient before," Hannah asserted.

"Nor I, but then skin disease is not my specialty."

"How shall I proceed?" Hannah asked bluntly.

"Make hourly observations and advise Dr. Dowd to consult in the morning. Take the routine precautions for a preeclamptic, which goes without saying." His students nodded sagely, then turned in unison with him when he strutted from the ward.

"Don't put anyone in Beds Nine through Three," Hannah said to her assistant. "I want vital signs every hour and word if she has any labor contractions, no matter how minor."

The night wore on with a steady stream of ordinary births, but there was never a break. Finally, when she had a chance to sit and work on her notes, she again was summoned to Ward C.

"They've sent for the doctor, but they want you to come too," said the excited nurse.

Hannah leapt up and ran down the corridor. Rushing in, she fully expected to begin treating a convulsive woman, but the patient in Bed Twelve was calm. "It isn't Mrs. Weed?"

"Yes, it is," the midwife on duty said with unaccustomed agitation. "Her fever's up to one hundred and five."

"Where is she?" came a booming voice.

"Over here, Doctor," Hannah replied steadily.

Dr. Dowd moved across the room with decisive yet unhurried strides. "What's been happening?" he asked with a hint of a friendly smile, then began flipping through the chart.

Hannah gave him a quick reprise of Mrs. Weed's condition. "Dr. Mariceau thought it might wait until morning, but once the fever spiked—"

"Texas!" he boomed. "Is that where she's from?"

Hannah was silent. She had paid no attention to the woman's place of origin.

"Do you know how long she's been in New York?"

"She told me she had arrived only a week ago," Dorothea Wylie managed in a wispy voice.

The doctor lifted the gown and inspected the rash. "Arrange for a transport to the contagious-disease pavilion at once!"

"What seems to be—?" Hannah began.

The doctor was shaking his head at his discovery. "This looks like Rocky Mountain spotted fever, carried by a tick they have out west."

"Then it has nothing to do with the pregnancy?"

"Of course not."

Hannah was impressed with the diagnosis. She would like to see the expression on the faces of Dr. Mariceau and his cohorts when they heard the news. "I didn't think so," she allowed.

"Good to see someone around here has some common sense." The doctor's tone was complimentary.

"Thank you, Doctor." Hannah watched as he made some rapid notes on the chart, admiring the man's graceful hands.

"By the way, I haven't seen you at Mrs. Dodge's lately."

"My schedule . . ."

"Ah, yes." For a long moment he stared at her as if contemplating what to say, but then his demeanor became more serious. "Now that I've signed the transfer, I'll take over from here."

For the first time in many hours Hannah felt a sense of relief. With this case out of her jurisdiction the rest of the night would pass uneventfully, but then why did she have the lingering desire to have to work with Dr. Dowd awhile longer?

6

It was not until Hannah made her way home on the Second Avenue line the next morning that she thought of Lazar again. If he was pleased about his discussions with Mr. Eastman, she was bound to be distraught. If he was depressed, she would be relieved, but then she would have to console her husband. Yet as she tried to prepare herself for any eventuality, her mind kept returning to Mrs. Weed's odd rash, like a tongue probing an aching mouth sore. The train stopped at 14th Street and did not budge. Hannah closed her eyes. Usually the outcome for her patients had already occurred before she left the hospital, or the result was obvious. She knew nothing about this disease, and she had been so happy to have the responsibility lifted she had not even asked for the prognosis on Mrs. Weed. Surely there was a cure, but perhaps there were complications. The fever had been treacherously high, and that in itself could have harmed her or the baby. Rarely did she leave a person in such dire straits, and yet many doctors did. That was why she was a midwife, she reminded herself as she wearily climbed the long final flight of stairs to her front door.

Lazar had already left the house. The children were in school. Good. She needed to rest because she would have to be up early enough to see a few women who had appointments that afternoon at Rachael's office. Whatever concerns remained about Mrs. Weed or Mr. Eastman were soon washed away by a welcome wave of sleep.

A torrential downpour woke her. The darkness of the room had fooled her and she would now be late. Hurriedly Hannah dressed in her navy blue suit, downed a glass of tea, ate some spoonfuls of pot cheese, before rushing through the storm. The whistling wind and drumming rain were infuriating. No public transportation covered that particular crosstown route. Despite her wool coat and umbrella, she would be soaked. Perhaps she should cancel the clinic and stay home until it was time to go to Bellevue. By then the storm should have abated. Rachael would understand. Nobody there was about to have a baby. But then she recalled her second reason for working at Rachael's office: helping Carrie when Rachael could not be there. What if she were truly needed? Hannah sighed and bundled up. At the doorstep the wind whipped at her umbrella. It would be useless. She found a babushka in her pocket and wound it around her head in the peasant style and turned up her collar.

"You're not going out in this, are you?" came her mother's voice behind her. "You'll catch your death."

"I'll be fine, Mama."

"Did you see Lazar?" Mama asked.

"No. He was gone before I came home."

"I don't know when you two ever get together," she clucked.

"It's not as bad as that." She laughed to deflect the criticism.

"Isn't it time you started taking your own advice?" Mama countered.

"Maybe, if you would stop giving it," she said in what she hoped sounded like a teasing tone, although she was partially serious. Lately some advice seekers, not finding her home, had decided the mother might be a second-best source and had asked Mrs. Blau for her opinions—opinions which Mama freely gave. Oh, well, what could she do? After all, her own counsel was based more on assumptions than scientific fact. If people were foolish enough to seek information from Mama—and to utilize it—why should Hannah stop them? Besides, they were more likely to get a harmless Yiddish aphorism like: *"An aynreydenish iz erger vi a kreynk,* an imaginary ailment is worse than a disease," for Mama believed that many people invented their problems. Well, at least it was better than handing out medical prescriptions.

"If you see Lazar, tell him I'll be home around four. We can have an early supper before I go in later."

"I thought you were off tonight," Mama said as she looked out the foggy windowpanes on either side of the building's front door.

Hannah blanched. "I forgot!" For a second she felt a pang of disappointment.

"It's a wonder you know whether you're coming or going with your crazy life." Mama shook her head. "Go now, it's not raining so hard."

Hannah hurried along in the lull. As she passed the children's school, her heart lurched. Mama was right. This schedule had cut her off from them. What were they thinking? Who were their friends? If Lazar sold articles more regularly, she could go back to the day shift, and then everything would be so much easier. Tonight she would comb all the knots out of Emma's hair, clip Benny's nails, and give them each a massage. And yet she had wanted to see Dr. Dowd about Mrs. Weed. She rushed across First Avenue and almost into the path of a small dark car that hadn't seen her. The wheels screeched, a raucous horn clarioned, and a voice screamed at her. On the other side of the street she ran from the curses.

Shivering, Hannah opened the door to Dr. Jaffe's offices. Rachael ducked her head out at the slam of the door. The waiting room was empty. "Oh, it's you!" she said, her smile warming the drafty room. "Nobody else has shown up. I sent Carrie home early. I hope you don't mind."

"No. I can handle my ladies myself."

"If anyone comes. My regulars have canceled."

"I suppose we'll have to examine each other," Hannah said, then regretted her words. Mrs. Czachorwski's perineum flashed before her eyes. What made her so different from Rachael? Hannah had not checked her friend since a few months after Nora's birth, and Nora was now nine. Of course, she was absolutely normal physically. To think otherwise was absurd.

Hannah followed Rachael back into her office, leaving the door open so they would hear if anyone came in. Rachael took the stuffed chair and offered Hannah the only space on the flowered sofa that was not covered with medical books.

"Now, what seems to be the problem?" Rachael asked with a slight smirk on her full lips.

"Not enough sleep," Hannah said, realizing this was the truth. "And not enough time in the day—or is it the night? I get so mixed up."

Rachael looked serious as she peered over her glasses. "You're right. This isn't healthy. You can't get flowers to bloom in the dark. You must go back to a regular schedule. Doctors' orders."

"Not until Lazar brings in more on his own."

"When will that be?"

"He talked to Max Eastman yesterday."

"Oh? Perhaps they might put him on staff there."

She hadn't thought about that, but maybe that was the direction Lazar should take. If only he had a regular salary . . . But then he might be too contentious to work under anyone like Mr. Eastman, who had a peculiar set of ideologies. "I doubt it, but he's been working on a long story he hopes Eastman will like."

Rachael took the cue. "I almost forgot," she said, jumping up. She went behind her desk and pulled out a leather pouch. She counted out thirty dollars and handed the bills to Hannah.

"What's this for?"

"Carrie says twenty dollars is half the fee for the patients you have seen when I haven't been here, and the rest is what she's collected from your people."

"I was helping you as my way of reimbursing you for the space and Carrie's wages."

"I have to pay her and the rent whether you are here or not."

"I can't take it. I haven't done anything to earn it."

"Nonsense. You've saved me a great deal of trouble on some minor cases that didn't require my attention at all. And Carrie says you spent more than an hour with that Polish lady who needed to be fitted for a pessary."

"She's very shy." Hannah was apologetic. She felt she needed to protect Rachael from Mrs. Czachorwski, but she didn't want to seem as though she was taking money from Rachael's practice.

"I'm pleased you are seeing her. That's a monthly appointment Carrie could not manage, and I'd rather not have to do it. My skills are best served by attending those who are truly sick." Rachael shook her head. "I don't know who is worse, you or Lazar." She held out her hand and waited for Hannah to accept the money. "Do I have to give it to him?"

Hannah dropped her protest and accepted the bundle. "Well, I'm cured. What about you?"

"I wish my problem were that easy," Rachael said wistfully.

Hannah swallowed hard. "I am working on it, but frankly the research seems to have been done by men. They have lots of theories but no solutions."

"I know." Rachael's voice was scratchy with emotion.

"It's not that I think the problem is hopeless . . ." Hannah proceeded slowly so she could keep thinking the matter through. No matter the illness, it was always best if the patient—even if someone as intelligent as Rachael—could believe that a cure was on the horizon. In her speculations on how to assist her friend, Hannah continued to face the wall of how little she knew.

"Maybe if you would answer a few questions, I might be able to offer some suggestions from what I have learned."

"All right," Rachael said, forcing a smile, "but they say that doctors don't make very good patients."

"How often?"

"How often what? Do I clean my teeth?"

Hannah shook her head, but understood what Rachael was doing. "How often do you and Ezek—" She caught herself. Best to be as impersonal as she would with any client. "How often do you and your husband have marital relations?"

"Once or twice a month, I guess."

Is that all? Hannah thought, but did not betray her shock. Despite the fact that she and Lazar frequently did not sleep during the same hours, they managed to make love several times a week.

Rachael filled in the gap. "We're so busy . . ."

"How long a time do you spend?"

"Counting from when?"

"From . . ." Hannah considered how to phrase this. Most people would have assumed from the joining of the organs to the ejaculation of the husband and subsequent uncoupling, yet Rachael's question contained a hint. Hannah had the sudden sense that if she asked the right questions and listened hard enough that some answers would be forthcoming. "From when you both know you are beginning to when you both know it has ended."

Rachael smiled, and at the same time tears filled her eyes. The mentor was congratulating the student, yet the import of the words had moved her beyond intellectual analysis and into private emotion. She blinked as she attempted to respond. "Not a half hour, probably much less."

"And in that time your partner usually achieves satisfaction."

"Yes."

She visualized Mrs. Czachorwski's well-lubricated organs. "Are you moist and receptive?"

"A little, depending on the time of the month."

"Do you ever try it during your monthly?"

"No, I'm Jewish, remember."

"Not that Jewish," Hannah bantered, then was sorry she did, for the mood had been broken. She struggled to regain her place. "Do you ever feel like you might get your wish?"

"Yes, but it never happens."

"But you feel something mounting or pressing you forward?"

"Once in a while."

"Freud talks of anesthesia, which I would assume means a total lack of sensation. That's not it for you, is it?"

"As I said, I feel something most of the time."

"What do you do when it is over?"

"Usually Herzog rolls over and snores, but I lie awake. I don't find the act as relaxing, I suppose." Her voice caught. "Sometimes I cry."

Oh, Rachael! Hannah's heart began to pound. She felt so sorry for her friend, but what could she offer? She thought about how wonderful it was to curl up against Lazar after they both were fulfilled, how they would sigh and touch each other, usually offering one last, long, lingering kiss in gratitude. Was it something Herzog was doing wrong? Or was he not trained in how to stimulate her? A man with his knowledge should have been an outstanding lover, but who knew what he was really like? Just as Hannah began to frame a tactful question about him, a door groaned. Both women jumped.

"I'll get it," Hannah said. A man held up a bleeding hand. "I got cut with some falling glass." Blood pooled along with the water from his dripping clothes, making crimson circles on the waiting room floor. "You the doctor?"

Hannah tried to mask her annoyance at the inopportune interruption. "No, but come with me."

7

The sky cleared at sunset. As Hannah walked home, she thought about the superb job Rachael had done stitching

three almost severed fingers. How could someone so knowledgeable be so unfulfilled? Running across the avenue,
she felt the weight of the money in her pocket. With it she
would buy a plump chicken for the next day, shoes for the
children, and then would put the remainder aside. Next time
she would not permit Rachael to overpay her. Less than five
dollars could have been earned from the advice seekers. And
what about the pessary? Had the cost of the appliance been
deducted? From now on Hannah would accept only what she
had actually earned, not a penny more. The windows of the
house on Tompkins Square winked as though they were on
fire as they reflected the pink sky. The wet street shimmered
like a wide satin ribbon. The air was fresh. The world had
been washed clean. The unexpected evening off felt like a
blessing. Hannah mounted the stairs rapidly, anticipating her
children's bright faces.

"Who's this?" cried Benny teasingly.

"Let me introduce myself. I am your mother," Hannah
said, bending for a hug.

"Where have you been?" Lazar asked. His voice was not
welcoming.

"At Rachael's office."

"For so long?" Now he sounded accusatory. For a moment Hannah was tempted to toss her packet of money on
the table, as if that would explain everything, but she caught
herself. This was not like Lazar. Something was wrong.

She went into their bedroom and took off her skirt, which
had tightened after becoming wet in the afternoon showers,
and put on a loose garment. In the mirror she decided she
looked too untidy, so she secured the gown with a sash. Letting down her hair was another release. Even so, her face
appeared tired and tense. Little worry lines had begun to
form at the edges of her eyes and lips. Smoothing them with
her finger, Hannah could recall the young girl she had been
when she met Lazar. How did he see her, as she was now,
or did he retain the memory of the person he first loved?
The problem was that she was no longer that person. Years
of suffering, fear, and hard work had taken their toll. But
still, despite everything, she cared for Lazar. Maybe their
difficulties were her fault as much as his. Maybe if she paid
more attention to him he would feel better about his situation. At this revelation she smiled at herself in the mirror,
and the image that stared back at her was more desirable.

Still feeling restricted, she unbuttoned the top two buttons. She came back into the parlor smiling in anticipation of her husband's appreciative glance.

He didn't look up as she brushed past or as she leaned down, the cleft of her breasts her most obvious feature in that position. She kissed his cheek and rumpled his hair, but he only gave an exasperated sigh. "I'm trying to read."

Emma was sitting on the sofa with a book in her lap, and Benny was munching a crust of bread at the table. Both were trying to fathom the reason for their father's mood. Hannah tried to break the tense barrier. "How was school today?" Neither spoke up. "Is Mrs. Lansky better?" she asked after Emma's teacher, who had been out for several weeks.

"She isn't coming back," Emma replied softly.

"Why?"

"You know, Mama."

"Do I?" Sometimes she did forget what her children said.

"She's having a baby," Benny added. "Maybe you'll see her at the hospital."

"And you? How did your recitation go?"

"Okay."

Hannah loathed her children's brief replies, but knew she could never force them to tell her much more about school. Cut off from her husband and children, Hannah went into the kitchen to prepare a casserole from some leftover liver and vegetables. When it was in the oven, she took a moist rag and wiped the counter free of crumbs, then counted out the plates and forks. As usual Lazar and the children had stacked up their books and papers on the kitchen table. She sorted them out into piles on the sideboard. Under a stack of newspapers in three languages, Hannah saw the story Lazar had submitted to *The Masses*. "What's this?" She held up "The Landlord." "Did Mr. Eastman like it?"

"If he did, it wouldn't be here, would it?"

"I'm sorry, Lazar."

"Why should you be sorry?"

Hannah was not going to argue with him. "What did he say?"

"Do you really want to know?"

Hannah fixed her husband with a sympathetic gaze. "Yes, Lazar."

"Let me see if I can remember everything. Eastman said that I rambled on with little direction. He sensed I was too close to it, that it needed distance, as in the prostitute story. He said, 'You must strive for that tender balance between knowledge and subjectivity,' whatever the hell that means!"

"Did he know it was about Minna?" Hannah asked, thinking Mr. Eastman might have met her sister-in-law at Mrs. Dodge's.

"I *did* change the names."

That didn't answer the question, but Hannah was not going to press the point. As she set the table, the thirty dollars from Rachael suddenly seemed more valuable. She was sorry she had bought the chicken. She dropped a fork.

Lazar started. "Now don't start whining about needing more money," he said defensively.

"Pa, show her the money now!" Emma interceded.

"What do you mean?" Hannah asked slowly.

"Do you think you are the only one who can bring home a dollar?"

Hannah had a queer feeling at the pit of her stomach, which she dismissed as hunger. "What did you sell?"

"I have a new job."

"Writing or teaching?" Her voice was too strident, but she couldn't hide her anxiety.

"Don't you think I can do anything else?"

Hannah had had her fill of these vexing questions. Lacking any calm replies, she turned back to the stove. Lazar soon grew impatient with her silence. He stood up and came up behind her. With one hand he rubbed her shoulder, with the other he slipped an envelope into her pocket. It was heavy with coins. "I'm working as a consultant."

What was a consultant? Hannah wanted to ask, but she preferred this more docile mood and she wanted it to last at least until the children were in bed. She gave a grunt and turned back to stirring the rice in the pot so it would not stick. Lazar went to wash up. When he returned, they ate without any quarrels about anything except where Benny and Emma would sit.

Later, when Hannah undressed to take her bath, she counted the contribution. There were three bills and almost seventeen dollars in quarters. Why so many coins? she mused briefly, until she realized that combining this with her thirty, they had enough to live on for several months and still pay Napthali some of the back rent. Even if she worked out a fairer settlement of Dr. Jaffe's accounts, if this kept up, she soon could work only weekdays. But the nagging question remained: who in the world had decided to consult Lazar? And why?

ᘓᕫᘓ **8** ᘓᕫᘓ

Dorothea Wylie caught up with Hannah as soon as she arrived for her shift the following night. "Did you hear about the lady from Texas?"

"No." Hannah's pulse began to race. She had meant to check in with Dr. Dowd.

"She died."

"Died! How?"

"She must have gotten worse after they moved her. Apparently there was nothing they could do."

"But how—?"

"Don't know."

"I'll have to see Dr. Dowd."

"Mrs. Sokolow, may I speak with you?" The clipped voice belonged to Mrs. Hemming, who must have been waiting for her to come on duty.

For a moment Hannah thought this had something to do with the mortality and her mind rushed to cover her decisions in the case, but Mrs. Hemming was tapping a folder of Hannah's weekly reports. Without a word she flicked it open and pointed to a paragraph. "What is the meaning of this?"

Hannah was confused. She was certain her notes were current and complete. "Yes?" she asked with a pleasant intonation.

"Well, if you don't read it, you won't be able to translate it, will you?" She thrust the paper closer.

Hannah could see several words underlined. She sucked in her breath. How stupid of her! She had written a few Russian words instead of English ones. In the early dawn hours, when she usually worked on these papers, her mind was too relaxed. She had first learned medical terminology in Moscow, so the slips were natural, but to Mrs. Hemming they were unforgivable.

"It's not as though you just stepped off the boat, is it?"

Excuses were never accepted by this woman. Even the doctors preferred to acquiesce to her rather than arouse her wrath. "She's an institution," Dr. Dowd had said at one staff meeting by way of both a compliment and a justification for the tyrannical way she ran her service.

"Yeah, an institution, like a brick wall," Norma Marsh-anck had added under her breath, giving Hannah an inward chuckle. But now as she stared up into the formidable face, Hannah was not laughing.

"I'll fix it at once," she said with as much deference as she could muster, although she wanted to add that considering a patient who had been on the service had recently died, this matter seemed inconsequential. "Is Dr. Dowd in the house?" she asked to change the subject.

"No. And why should he concern himself with this matter?"

Again Mrs. Hemming was focused too narrowly on her little administrative problem, but bringing up Mrs. Weed would only fuel some other procedural nightmare. "I had some information he requested."

"Surely it can wait until tomorrow." The woman's jowls sagged and Hannah could not help but see a resemblance to an aging horse.

"Of course it can, Mrs. Hemming," she said briskly to cover her stifled giggle at the image. Without another word she took the paper over to the nearest table and began copying it over with the corrections. Simply crossing the Russian words out and inserting the English translation would never have satisfied. But before beginning she made a mental note to ask Dr. Dowd about the Weed case the next time she saw him.

Their paths did not cross that week or most of the next. Routine conferences between midwives and the obstetrical staff were usually held directly after morning rounds so either shift could attend on a rotating basis, but Hannah sometimes missed them because they often coincided with the Board of Managers sessions. As head midwife, she reported directly to the board, which controlled the nursing aspects of the hospital, under which midwifery had been pigeonholed. This group of affluent women undertook their volunteer service with a fervent dedication sometimes lacking in salaried employees. Yet they did not make clinical decisions. Midwives did. A constant task was to gently remind the well-meaning ladies of these differences, without seeming to overstep her bounds.

More complicated was the midwives' relationship to the medical staff. To them the midwives were an odious necessity. All births were better handled by doctors, or so they believed, but as medicine moved into the twentieth century, some medieval appendages—like midwives—lingered because there were not enough obstetrical specialists to handle the needs of the bursting population. Reluctantly the doctors admitted that they had to save themselves for the most complicated conditions, if not the most corpulent bank accounts. Ordinary women, normal cases, and the poor would have to manage with what they believed was second-best care until more doctors would be trained. Movements to eradicate the "blight of the midwife" were succeeding in some areas, but there would never be enough physicians to handle the relentless press of maternity cases. Then, of course, some doctors could be more troublesome than others. She would rather face five Dr. Dowds for one Dr. Mariceau any day.

Just as Hannah was going off duty one morning, she was asked to stop by the emergency room to check the heartbeat of a fetus whose mother had fallen down a flight of stairs. Fortunately, the baby seemed fine. In the next bed, however, was a familiar face. The woman was febrile and hallucinating. Hannah studied the chart. The name, Mrs. Hilgerman, was also one she had seen before, but where?

"Who has accompanied this woman?" she asked the nurse.

"Her husband brought her in." The nurse pointed to a man who looked no older than twenty.

"Mr. Hilgerman?" Hannah asked.

"Yes?" He jumped up. "Is she going to be all right?"

Hannah had no answer, so she continued, "Did your wife have a baby recently?"

"Yes. Two weeks ago. A boy."

Could the woman have a puerperal infection? she worried as she gave the woman a cursory examination. If so, she had to review the procedures used in that ward. Hannah prided herself on the low rate of sepsis due to the strict hygienic rules she herself had helped to institute. She would discover who had delivered her, as well as who had attended her postpartum. Every record would be searched. Hannah did not require many skills to realize the woman was dangerously ill. Her pulse was extremely rapid. Her skin was hot and dry. There was such a severe swelling of the face, eyelids, and extremities she looked more like a preeclampsia patient than a postpartum one. Eclampsia! Hannah moved forward in a rush of excitement. She lifted the woman's gown and was rewarded with a blush of a rash that was not unlike Mrs. Weed's. Another case of tick fever? She checked the chart. This woman wasn't from Texas.

She rushed to find Dr. Dowd.

He was in his office with two young assistants when she burst in. "Sorry, Doctor, but I had to ask you something without delay."

The man's thick black hair hung like a curtain in front of his face as he pointed to some numbers on a chart. As he looked up benevolently, he pushed the errant strands behind his ears, then tilted his head toward the men as if to ask: Isn't it charming how women get excited so easily? "Yes, Mrs. Sokolow. Please, do come in."

She did not wait for introductions. "Is the fever one contracts from the Rocky Mountain tick contagious?"

"The insect is the vector, not another person."

"But you sent Mrs. Weed to the contagious-disease ward."

"Just a precaution until we had a confirmed diagnosis."

"And she died."

"Yes, a sad case. It was much too late for a successful intervention."

"Could you have been wrong?"

His assistants glanced at each other tensely.

"Why do you ask?" Dr. Dowd responded, his usual geniality taking on a taut edge.

"I've just come from a very similar case, only this one delivered here two weeks ago. I haven't had time to check her records, but she could have come into contact with Mrs. Weed."

Dr. Dowd's mouth turned down at the edges. His shrewd eyes moved rapidly from side to side as though he was quickly reading from left to right. "Is there a rash?"

"Yes, only worse. The dots are harder and more elevated, and they are also on the lower extremities."

"Have you ever seen a rash like it before?"

Hannah had not thought this through. Many women had diverse skin eruptions, from allergies to scabs from poor nutrition or hygiene, but this was more like an outbreak of a childhood disease, not exactly measles ... more like a pox. "Varicella, perhaps ..." she said cautiously. Her shoulders were racked with an involuntary shudder. No! She hadn't seen a rash like this since her training in Moscow. She gripped the back of a nearby chair as she recalled a lecture at the medical college that all the midwives in training had been forced to attend when that city had suffered an outbreak of the most contagious of plagues. Coffins had lined the corridor, and for the sake of their education, they were made to look at a few corpses. It had been more than a course in the recognition of lesions; it had also been a lesson in the need for vaccination. Her hand went to the circular scar on her left forearm. Everyone who worked in a hospital was protected, as were her children, and all those who immigrated to the United States. But what about a woman from Texas? Or Mrs. Hilgerman, who probably had been born in a poor district of the city? "Not varicella ..."

"Variola!" Dr. Dowd thundered. "I dismissed it myself. There hasn't been a smallpox epidemic in fifteen years." He held his temples with his hands as the enormity of the crisis became clear.

"What can we do, sir?" the shorter of the young doctors asked, at full alert.

"Carlton, you go with this midwife and isolate the patient at once. I'll call an emergency meeting of the division heads. Haas," he said to the remaining man, "get to the pharmacy and see how many doses are available for vaccination." Dr. Haas was halfway out the door when Dr. Dowd called him back. "Wait! Before you do that, try to get an address for the husband of the first one. What was her name?"

"Mrs. Weed," Hannah said. "I can do that."

"Yes, take care of that at once. We've got to find the husband and see where else they've been."

The smallpox alert was the most astonishing rallying of the hospital's forces that Hannah had ever witnessed. Bellevue was closed to visitors if they did not have the telltale mark of a previous vaccination. Everyone else who entered or departed was vaccinated. Even newborns received a partial dose. Everyone with whom Mrs. Weed might have come into contact was tracked down. Most, but not all, were located. Mr. Weed was placed in isolation, but he never contracted the disease, considered by some to be the most con-

tagious of communicable diseases. The best outcome of a
minor case of smallpox is disfigurement, and the worst form,
known as the black, or hemorrhagic, smallpox is almost always fatal.

A ferry boat on the riverfront, which was sometimes used
as a dayroom for the tubercular patients, was turned into
a floating ward for the cases of smallpox that did break
out. By the end of the siege, more than two hundred and
fifty would contract the disease—almost all of whom could
be traced to some proximity with Mrs. Weed or Mrs.
Hilgerman—but with the advanced treatments, only forty
would die, including two Bellevue kitchen workers who
somehow had eluded the vaccination squad.

Before the epidemic had run its full course, Hannah delivered the last of the contagious-disease reports to Dr. Dowd,
giving all the names of maternity staff and patients who had
been in contact with Mrs. Weed, with those who had been
checked underlined. His door was closed. This time Hannah
did not burst in. While she waited, she scanned the board
outside the obstetrical offices. A notice caught her eye.

A Lecture
on
Disorders of the Sexual Function in the Female
to be given by
Fritz Blühner, M.D.
Chief of Clinic, Genitourinary Department
Mount Sinai Hospital Dispensary
Formerly Attending Genitourinary Surgeon,
Bellevue Hospital
Out-Patient Department
Author, *Sterility and Its Treatment*
Monday, April 24, 1915
7:00 p.m. Old Amphitheater

The door opened. Dr. Haas came out and smiled warmly
at Hannah. "Good morning, Mrs. Sokolow." He gave a modest bow and waved her in. "His lordship will see you now."

Not at ease with this sort of banter, Hannah tried to seem
distant but friendly. She knew, though, she had earned the

young doctor's respect. Later, if she ever needed to consult him on a case, this would be useful.

"Good to see you!" Dr. Dowd was also more effusive than usual. Even though the smallpox had created a public health crisis, this up-and-coming gynecologist had been credited for warning everyone about the disaster. "I want to thank you again for your fine work on the Weed case."

"You're the one who deserves the gratitude."

"Really?" he said to prompt her to continue her praise.

"What inspired me to take notice initially was your lecture on looking beyond the obvious diseased organ to the person as a whole."

"Well, I told Mrs. Hemming that your keen eyes deserve the credit. I hope you don't mind."

Hannah laughed uneasily. "All the credit in the world won't keep Mrs. Hemming from her usual . . ." Hannah fumbled for the right word, then shrugged in confusion.

Dr. Dowd pretended not to notice her chagrin. "Now, what can I do for you today?"

"I've brought the final reports for contagious-disease control."

"Good, good," he said absently, then he brightened. "I hope someday I will be able to assist you as ably as you have me."

Hannah turned to leave. Then on an impulse she moved a few feet toward the doctor's desk. "Dr. Dowd, may midwives attend Dr. Blühner's lecture next week?"

"As you know, Mrs. Sokolow, midwives have been welcomed at most obstetrically related functions, but few attend due to the technical nature of the presentations." He stroked his chin, which Hannah noted for the first time had a cleft that looked like a child's thumbprint. "Anyhow, this topic would hardly concern those who manage parturition."

"It interests me, Doctor."

The doctor did not register any emotion, yet a distinct pause indicated he had made a mental note of some sort. "I don't think there will be any other women present."

"Why not?"

"No female physicians have staff privileges in this department."

"My point concerns my midwives."

"Then permit me to be frank. The topic will be a sensitive one. Medical professionals who routinely see the torment suffered by men and women with sexual debilities must have the information to assist them in treatment. Some of the material might be a bit indelicate for the uninitiated."

Although Hannah was irritated by Dr. Dowd's protective stance, she would not allow him to see this. "You are absolutely right, Doctor. However, what you may not have realized is that, for obvious reasons, many women with such conditions find it impossible to speak their concerns to a man. Since, as you say, there are so few female practitioners, these poor souls are reduced to trusting their secrets to some who may seem to possess a certain sphere of knowledge—at least to the outsider—but who are inadequate to help."

Dr. Dowd's prussian blue eyes bored into Hannah as keenly as the lens of a microscope. "I see."

"I myself have at least one such case I have been unable to help, though it is my dearest wish to do so."

"Why not refer her to Dr. Blühner, or to me?"

"I doubt she would come."

"Even if you told her we might alleviate her suffering?"

"This is a modest woman, a Jewish woman," Hannah added, then wished she hadn't.

The doctor swallowed so hard the knot in his tie bulged. "That is most interesting. Well, so long as you will feel comfortable among the doctors, I have no objection. In fact, I would be pleased if you would come as my guest," he said with such a warm reversal of his earlier stance, she felt as though she had been welcomed into an inner circle.

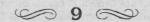

9

Hannah had been the only woman in the huge amphitheater, where the medical staff gathered for everything from the observation of new operative techniques to dissections of curious cases to listening to their colleagues present academic papers. When she arrived, Dr. Dowd already had been in the third row, two seats in from the aisle. There had been one empty place to his right, but since she had been one of the last to appear, she thought it more prudent to take a seat in the rear rather than walk down the long aisle with everyone's eyes boring into her back.

As she went about her rounds after the lecture ended, her mind reeled with the material that had been presented. Since there were no situations her staff could not handle, her thoughts drifted from the maternity routines to what she had learned about female sexual disorders.

Without any preliminaries the bearded doctor, who while short in stature had a domineering air, had taken the podium in the center of the amphitheater, adjusted his glasses, and began to read from his notes with clipped Germanic precision. "In my last lecture I thoroughly discussed the etiology and pathology of masturbation in the female. In my next appearance I will cover vaginismus, dyspareunia, enuresis, nymphomania, and incontinence; and in my final presentation will review some unusual forms of sexual neuroses. Tonight I will limit my discussion to frigidity and the absence of orgasm in the female during coitus."

Excited that this might pertain to Rachael's case, Hannah tried to apply everything he said to her situation. Dr. Blühner removed his glasses, squinted into the audience, and defined a frigid woman as one with the lack of any inclination to sexual intercourse. Rachael desired relations, so this was not the correct diagnosis for her. When he said, "let us turn to the most common of maladies: the absence of orgasm in the female during coitus," Hannah became more alert. "Under this heading will be described that condition in which the female retains normal sexual desire, but fails to experience any orgasm or other satisfied sensations during coitus." He then went into a complicated definition of female orgasm. Hannah had strained to catch every word, but the man's thick accent was a hindrance, so perhaps she had misunderstood him when he defined it as the violent ejaculation of fluid from the female sexual glands.

"Mrs. Sokolow?" a student midwife was calling.

Hannah snapped back to the present. She was standing in the doorway of Ward D supposedly waiting to see if a delayed placenta would be forthcoming naturally. "Yes?"

"Mrs. Brink has just admitted a woman and confirmed twins."

"How far along?"

"Four centimeters only, but she wanted you to know. She's para two."

"Thank you. Tell her I'll be there as soon as the third stage is complete here."

She focused on the woman who had just delivered a son, but once it was clear that the placenta was indeed going to be expelled without a manual extraction being required, she returned to her musings about the intriguing lecture. When she had examined Mrs. Czachorwski, the perineum had been moist, but no fluid had spurted forth. Had she missed this response? Was this another anomaly possessed by her patient? Or—the thought formed awkwardly—could Dr. Blühner be mistaken? Was his theory based on direct knowledge or supposition? Had he ever witnessed anything like Christina Czachorwski's responses? Yet nobody had questioned his supposition. He had gone into a detailed explanation of the transmission of vaginal sensations to the cerebral cortex. A curious metaphor of his kept coming to mind: "If the woman does not experience the natural culmination, her nervous system may be likened to that of a mouse dangling before a cat, which the latter is not permitted to reach."

How did this relate to the emotions of an unfulfilled woman? she wondered as the expert had gone on to explain, "The vice of masturbation may be implicated in the causation of this condition because the sexual centers have been dulled so that the ordinary act of coitus is not enough to arouse sufficiently."

Once again Hannah demurred. Boys and men were known to masturbate far more than women, and she doubted this dulled their senses. More useful was his discussion about abnormalities. She listened carefully as the doctor described cases in which some structures—especially the clitoris—were too small, bound by adhesions, or placed oddly. "These states demonstrate why some women achieve orgasm only when in unusual positions, such as lateral, or even the reverse positions of the parties."

Lateral was the side . . . but what did he mean by reverse? Was the man approaching the woman from behind or was the woman on top? And even if he meant either one, why was that so unusual? She assumed most married people tried variations, much as she altered recipes. Were these doctors so obstinate that they believed there was only one correct position? She gave an inward chuckle. Midwives understood that every birth was different, and while few general rules could apply, flexibility was more useful than rigidity. Might not the same concept be useful in the privacy of one's bedroom?

Ending on a positive note, Dr. Blühner had stated that while some frigidity was incurable, this absence of orgasm was marked by its reversibility. Then the doctor had stepped aside from the podium, accepted the polite applause, and asked for questions. Questions! Hannah had felt like that dangling mouse or unfulfilled woman. What was the prognosis? What was the treatment? How much of this applied to Rachael?

The same young midwife reappeared, giving Hannah the signal to step into the corridor. Her grave expression warned Hannah that her work was about to begin. "How bad is it?" she said without preliminaries.

"One twin is definitely transverse, the other's breech."

"A version," Hannah stated, knowing this is what the midwife in charge would want to try, but not without her approval.

The next three hours were the sort of grueling work that made her forget everything except the matter at hand. Not every baby in the womb responded well to the techniques of being rotated into a better position for delivery, but these two were exceptionally pliable. Mrs. Brink and Hannah were pleased to congratulate each other upon successfully bringing two sturdy boys into the world. The midwife on duty stitched up the exhausted mother, while Hannah made final rounds. By the time she went home, it seemed like days—instead of hours—had passed since the end of the lecture, but her quandaries were as fresh as ever.

Most of the questions posed to Dr. Blühner had seemed rather obscure until Dr. Dowd asked, "You mention that a cure can be effected for this condition. What are some of your recommendations?"

"I use a three-stage method," Dr. Blühner responded with a tinge of reluctance at giving out his formula. "First, the woman must refrain from masturbation entirely. Second, I recommend experimentation with unusual postures, but only for the purpose of bringing the clitoris into better contact with the penis. If that is unproductive, I will allow Rohleder's suggestion that the husband may resort to manual stimulation of the clitoris." He paused dramatically at this suggestion. "No matter what attitude we may take toward this disagreeable procedure, we must weigh it against far more serious alternatives. I have known unhappy women to be tempted to try their luck elsewhere, even consider divorce. These are not idle theories, mind you, but actual case histories." There was a murmur in the audience and several hands shot up, but the lecturer slipped his glasses into his breast pocket, said a curt "Thank you, gentlemen," and walked away from the podium.

Even now as she hurried along a bustling First Avenue, Hannah became so incensed with that reply that she found herself elbowing the shoppers crossly. So, he thought the husband could deign to actually touch his wife! What pomposity! She felt sorry for the woman who was married to him.

Hannah had been fuming about the same point when she saw Dr. Dowd as she was leaving the amphitheater. "I trust the lecture was useful to you?" he asked solicitously.

"Only to guide me to more study."

"If you could have asked Dr. Blühner a question, what might it have been?"

Hannah did not hesitate. "I would have asked him why he focused on the clitoris as the seat of sexual satisfaction when others believe that mature women experience purely vaginal responses."

Dr. Dowd flushed. "Remember he is a genitourinary surgeon, who has not been trained to sexuality in the psychological context." The doctor had given her a polite bow before turning down the corridor toward his department.

Anatomy. Adam out of Eve. Analogous structures. And what was it that triggered Mrs. Czachorwski's reactions? Would Dr. Dowd have any idea what nervous condition she suffered and whether it had a physical or mental basis? Hannah smiled to herself as she imagined trying to describe it to him. In any case, Hannah realized she would have to exploit Dr. Dowd's kindness while she could, for she knew that as far as midwives were concerned, even the best of doctors had short memories.

∽ **10** ∾

A week later Hannah returned from the hospital with a volume she had borrowed from the medical library: Havelock Ellis's *The Sexual Impulse in Women*. She had been looking for the works by Kisch and Rohleder, which Dr. Blühner had suggested, but had not located them on the shelves. She supposed that others at the lecture had gotten to them first.

Usually she would go to sleep as soon as she got home from the hospital, but that morning she decided to skim the volume quickly for some clue for how to help Rachael, then plod through it page by page later. There were the usual difficult references in Latin, German, and French, the smaller type discussing case histories and comparing authorities, plus footnotes with more explanation and detail, then one case caught her attention. Ellis was referring to the work of a Dr. Douglas Bryan, of Leicester, who "succeeded in removing sexual coldness and physical aversion in the wife by hypnotic suggestion." She was told that "her womanly natural feelings would be quickly and satisfactorily developed during coitus; and that she would experience no feeling of disgust and nausea, would have no fear of the orgasm not developing; that there would be no involuntary resistance on her part." Hannah reread the sentence three times. "Fear of the orgasm not developing . . . no involuntary resistance on her part . . ."

This sounded closer to Rachael than anything she had heard before. Her friend wanted desperately to feel what other women experienced. She craved for resolution to the voluptuous feeling, but was afraid it would not happen. Fear was one of the most potent forms of restraint. Fear of retribution controlled much of society. Fear of authority caused children to behave. Fear of hunger kept men working at unpleasant tasks. Fear of the pains of birth prompted some women to become so tense their labor became protracted. Part of being a good midwife was finding ways for each woman to relax as much as possible so her body could do the work for which it was intended. Instead of using direct means to stimulate Rachael, some subtler method of eliminating her apprehensions might be employed. The idea was easier than the solution, but Hannah sensed she was on the right track when Lazar came into the room waving a newspaper.

"The bastards torpedoed the *Lusitania.*"

Hannah startled. "The what?"

"The largest passenger ship in the world."

"One of ours?"

"No, it's British, but it says that there were probably a hundred or two Americans on board. More than twelve hundred are feared lost." When Hannah did not respond, stunned by the thought of so many innocent people dead, Lazar cried, "Don't you see? This is the beginning of the end. Everyone will be screaming to get the Hun after this."

Hannah's head began to pound. She was too exhausted to sort this out. "I'm going to bed. What are you going to do?"

"I'm going to the cafés after I run a few errands. Here, do you need any money?" He reached into his pocket and spilled quarters on the table. They must have totaled close to ten dollars.

Hannah left them where they lay. "No, I'll put them away for later." She was thinking that Lazar was usually right about these matters, and if war did come, extra money was going to be required.

That night, when she emerged from the subway on her way to work, a hurdy-gurdy was playing the lament "In the Sweet Bye-and-Bye." Women were sobbing over the tragedy. Men were arguing, some even raving about the act of piracy. Everyone at the hospital was talking about it, and most were ready to muster guns for the cause. Hannah had the eerie sense two continents had moved closer together.

⤜⤐ **11** ⤐⤜

President Wilson responded to the German aggression by saying: "There is such a thing as a man being too proud to fight; there is such a thing as a nation being so right that it does not need to convince others by force that it is right." A few weeks later, the kaiser seemed to bow to pressure and declared that passenger liners would be given safe passage. All that was proven a ruse at the end of June, when the liner *Armenian* was sunk with twenty more American lives lost.

While many suffered from the effects of the war, Hannah's fortunes had brightened. Lazar's consulting was bringing in far more than she had expected. By the first week in July, she felt secure enough to turn down weekends for the rest of the summer. How delightful was the prospect of having three days a week to spend with her children while they were out of school!

To find fodder for his pen, Lazar eagerly awaited reports from the radical conference being held in Zimmerwald, Switzerland. Everyone was supposed to be there: Lenin, Zinoviev, Karl Radek of the Polish Leftists, Julius Martov of the Menshiviki, and most important, his personal hero and old friend from his university days in Odessa—Leon Trotsky. As communiqués filtered back, he was elated that the delegates had distributed a manifesto against the war, yet he was also frustrated they had not advanced any program with concrete actions. But Lazar stood alone. Most of his friends disagreed.

One evening at the Café Boulevard, with Hannah and Rachael in tow, Herzog and Lazar argued that Zimmerwald was "a ray of light dawning on the blood-drenched earth."

Lazar contradicted with so much vehemence that those not in the know would have thought the men were long-time enemies. At the end, Lazar thundered, "The manifesto would be no more effective than reciting a chapter of the psalms of King David."

Someone across the room was puffing on a particularly fetid cigar. "How can people speak of pacifism with so much animosity?" Rachael asked between coughs.

"A masculine tendency," Hannah replied with a smirk.

"Let's talk of something of more immediate importance," Rachael announced loudly. "Or have you forgotten that Minna's trial starts tomorrow?"

"She claims she won't plead guilty to anything," Lazar began.

"Wouldn't it be easier if she did?" Hannah entreated urgently. At first she had taken Minna's arrest lightly, thinking that, like Lazar's troubles at the university and at the suffrage parade, her case would be dismissed, but it was clear that Mr. Comstock's charges were not going to be dropped.

"That's what they say, but we're advising her not to capitulate," Lazar continued, surprising Hannah with the news that he was so involved in the case.

"Mrs. Sanger, has anyone heard from her?" Herzog interjected.

"They say she'll be back sometime in late September," Lazar explained.

"By then it will all be over," Hannah stated, then felt a rush of annoyance at Minna being left to face this on her own.

The next afternoon, Minna's trial for the distribution of obscene literature was heard before Justices McDonald, Rupert, and Hellman. Lazar took notes on Minna's testimony, and that evening gave Hannah a detailed report. "Everyone thinks Minna is so frail, so naturally innocent, and then she speaks eloquently with that charming accent of hers. The judges tried to remain dispassionate, but I think they were impressed."

Although Hannah found her husband's superlatives disconcerting, she only asked, "What did she say for herself?"

Lazar reviewed his notes. "In her opening statement she began: 'This pamphlet written by Mrs. Sanger is nothing more than a clean, honest statement of the truth, and the truth is never obscene.' Isn't that marvelous? Then she went on even more intensely, 'I admit that I broke the law, and yet I claim it is the law, and not I, that is on trial here today.' "

"Was that wise?"

"The first justice was annoyed. He said, 'You admit you are guilty and this statement of yours is merely your opinion. In my view, the publication is not only indecent but immoral. It is not only contrary to the laws of the state, but contrary to the laws of God. Any man or woman who would circulate literature of this kind is a menace to the community.' "

"How did Minna respond to that?"

"She didn't. From then on she did as she was told and allowed her counsellor to argue for her, but finally Justice McDonald interrupted her lawyer by pounding his gavel. He spoke in a low, almost cruel voice and said, 'The law allows the choice of a fine or a prison sentence.' And then he ordered her to pay one hundred and fifty dollars or to serve thirty days in jail."

"That's too harsh! Where will she get the money?"

"She refused the fine. Minna stood up slowly and spoke so all could hear. 'I would rather be in jail with my self-respect, than be free without it.' That's when the people rallied. It was as if a force had been gathering in the crowded courtroom as injustice after injustice formed into a united storm cloud." Though Hannah became impatient with his flowery language, he was enjoying himself, so she let him ramble on. ". . . A long volley of hand clapping ended in a medley of shouts and cries. People stood on the benches and waved their hats and handkerchiefs. The justice was furious. He shouted and pounded his gavel, 'Clear the courtroom! Clear the courtroom!' But nobody listened."

"Was anyone hurt?"

"Policemen charged into the crowd, but I think they had been warned to be gentle. Even so, it took twenty minutes to empty the room."

"Mrs. Sanger should have been there."

"She'll come home now," Lazar predicted.

"Why?"

"Because public support will have turned to her side," he said smugly.

The following week, Lazar came all the way to Bellevue to walk Hannah home. "I've got wonderful news!"

"What is it?" Hannah said, ready to hug him if he had sold his book or found a job.

"Anthony Comstock is dead."

"Dead? Was he assassinated?"

"Apparently he caught a chill during Minna's trial." He grinned triumphantly. "Isn't that justice at its best?"

∽ **12** ∼

Mrs. Czachorwski had avoided several of her routine examinations scheduled for the second Wednesday of each month. Knowing how modest she was, Hannah had advised her to douche with warm vinegar water morning and evening. For the first few months she had seemed to comply, then her hygiene had deteriorated. On one spring visit Hannah had noticed an unpleasant odor and chastised her patient. The sensitive Mrs. Czachorwski had wept and admitted that she hated touching herself so often.

Hannah had spoken to her sternly. "If you don't cleanse this area better, you might develop a serious infection."

"I do it," Christina responded, pouting.

"How often?"

"Almost every day."

"You must do it twice a day."

Then she skipped a month in August and again in October. Fortunately, Hannah's dire predictions had not come true. The day of the November appointment was particularly miserable for Hannah. A few weeks earlier Margaret Sanger had returned to America. Anthony Comstock had not been on the dock to greet her—as he had sworn to be—and she had been overjoyed with the news of his demise. Her ebullience soon diminished as her daughter, Peggy, became desperately ill with pneumonia. Minna brought messages from the office to Mrs. Sanger, who never left the child's bedside. Peggy responded to the initial treatments, but then began to fail rapidly. She died on the sixth of November. For the next week Margaret would see no one. The night before Mrs. Czachorwski's appointment, Minna said that Margaret was ready to receive a few visitors, and suggested that Hannah stop by the next morning.

The door was opened by a somber maid, who led Hannah into Margaret's bedroom. Pain, unimaginable suffering, infused the room like a fetid miasma. Margaret moved her lips in acknowledgment of her presence, but the words were inaudible. Hannah could sense the unspoken thoughts of a mother who had been away so long and who had returned to confront her worst fear. What had she been doing in Europe? She had seen the experts in several countries, but what else? What was Havelock Ellis like? Were there new devices for women? Sometimes people in mourning welcomed the distraction of routine matters, but Margaret was no more able to respond than a woman racked by the last excruciating stage of birth. Her questions would have to wait.

After a long while Margaret spoke in a hollow tone. "When I was in London I heard her voice calling, 'Mother,

Mother, are you coming back?' " A sob caught in her throat. "And now I'm back!"

Hannah decided it was best to say nothing. The room was filled with a painful silence. Margaret lowered her head like a guilty prisoner. A child's death was a cruel punishment, but one she seemed to think she deserved because she had been a mother who cared more about the tragedies of the children of the world than her own. Hannah thought about her own situation. If she counted the hours she spent caring for others and not her family, she was as culpable as Margaret. Would she have to pay a similar price someday? Lately Lazar was supporting the family more successfully, so why didn't she quit Bellevue altogether? She should stay at home. She should be there any time Emma or Benny needed her . . .

The two women sat facing each other, each bound by their miseries as if they had been swathed in a piece of the same bloody bandage. There was also the unspoken words that hovered like an electric storm crackling in the air. For each knew the other's most fervent thoughts. Hannah's was: Thank God it was not my child! Margaret's was: Why wasn't it her child?

When Hannah thought she could control her feelings no longer, she said good-bye to Margaret, and her husband, who had remained in the parlor. The whole way to Dr. Jaffe's office she sobbed. She managed to wipe her puffy eyes and compose herself before going in to see Mrs. Czachorwski.

The odor was horrible. Hannah stiffened at the assault of spoiled fish. With no concern for the woman's delicate sensibilities this time, she held her breath, plunged in, and removed the pessary. Immediately she took the offending object out of the room, placed it in the dispensary sink, and covered it with a disinfectant solution. She carried a steaming basin and several towels to wash the perineum. On her return, however, she was even more dismayed to find that Mrs. Czachorwski's prolapse had become almost completely relaxed, with most of the uterus being expelled from the vagina. This condition, combined with the virulent infection, was no longer within her sphere of expertise.

"You must go to the hospital at once," Hannah said firmly.

"I can't," Mrs. Czachorwski protested weakly.

"There is no choice. The pessary won't work any longer. Your uterus must be removed."

Christina started to object again, but Hannah ignored her. "If Dr. Jaffe were available, I'd have her confirm the seriousness of this infection with you. In any case, you require a gynecological surgeon immediately. The best one I know is at Bellevue, and either you will go yourself or I will escort you there."

"Would you?" came the tinny reply.

Hannah realized that this would be the best way to expedite the matter. Though it was not her fault that Mrs. Czachorwski had neglected her hygiene and avoided visits, she continued to feel responsible for the case. She went out and had Carrie find transportation for the woman, then updated her chart for Dr. Dowd.

He was in-house when they arrived, a fact confirmed by the chalkboard roster at the emergency room desk. Hannah would let nobody else examine her patient.

When the doctor was finished, he met her in the corridor. "A very bad case," he said, shaking his head. "A prodidentia with infectious complications."

"Will you operate?"

"As soon as I can assemble a team."

"May I observe?"

Dr. Dowd studied Hannah curiously. "Any special reason?"

"This is a peculiar case . . ." she began hesitantly, then launched into an intimate history of the situation.

As she spoke, the doctor's thick black eyebrows twitched from time to time. At some of her more incredible comments, his small blue eyes darted from side to side. "I don't see where this is leading . . ."

"I was wondering," Hannah continued quickly, "if she was anesthetized and continued to have the same singular reaction, we might conclude that she was neurologically different from other women. Does this only happen if the mind is aware of the action, or is it purely a physiological response?"

For a few moments he was thoughtful. "And if she showed no reaction during surgery?" the doctor asked in a low, speculative voice.

Hannah shrugged. "There could be no firm conclusions, of course, but might it not point to the fact that her conscious mind contributed to her condition? From my experience, she is a highly excitable and emotional woman."

"Most unusual," he muttered, then spoke more forcefully. "I would be pleased to have you accompany me into the operating theater and assist at the foot of the table," he said as cordially as if he were inviting her to have tea with his mother. "Besides, since this is your case, I'd like you to explain it to my assistants."

"I couldn't do that!"

Dr. Dowd stroked his chin. "I supposed that might be the case. Nevertheless, why don't you come along anyway to check matters as discreetly as possible?"

∽ **13** ∽

Nothing. Not a flush of color. No change in the genital organs whatsoever. Mrs. Czachorwski's heartbeat and respiration responses were in the average range for someone under the influence of ether. Hannah was especially impressed with the doctor's ability to perform the hysterectomy vaginally.

"A more complicated operation, actually," he said as he lectured on his technique, "but safer due to the infection, which could spread to the peritoneum." Through everything Dr. Dowd had never once intimated that she might have been negligent, and for this Hannah was grateful. As he finished he said, "The vaginal wound should be left open to favor drainage."

He allowed Hannah to feel where he had ligated the broad ligament. Discreetly she used the maneuvers that had aroused Mrs. Czachorwski previously, yet there was no change after the surgery either. Hannah was heartened by this. The idea that a woman might have a sexual response while she was unconscious made her seem depersonalized. Certainly men had involuntary erections, boys had seminal emissions, and many women—even Rachael—derived sexual stimulation from their dreams, but this was the mind engaged with the body at some private level, which to Hannah was more acceptable than a strange touch in an operating theater with medical men standing about gaping.

As Mrs. Czachorwski was wheeled to the ward, Hannah met with the doctor in the small surgery office. He removed his bloody apron, folding it neatly. "What are your conclusions, Mrs. Sokolow?"

Hannah was not ready to share her speculations with him, so she was circumspect. "She did not react as she did previously."

"And do you think her former—shall we say 'sensitivities'—will reappear when she recuperates?"

"I don't know."

"How will she feel if they don't?"

"She was dreadfully ashamed of her condition. With no husband it might be better for her to be more 'normal,' if anyone knows what that is."

"Indeed." The doctor went to the sink and began lathering his hands. Hannah had to follow him to catch his last words. "Would you mind if I shared this most unusual patient with Dr. Blühner? He's going to give another lecture series over here early in the year, and he is always inquiring after our cases."

For some unknown reason Hannah did mind, but dared not admit this. "You are in charge of her now." Her voice was respectful, but she hoped he caught a tinge of caution in her tone.

"Indeed," he repeated as he departed for the doctors' dressing room.

Problem 4:
Stella Applebaum's Distress

◆

1916

Your deeds will bring you near, or your deeds
will put you off from others
—THE MISHNAH, EDUYYOT 5:7

&⁓ 1 ⁓&

WAS it a coincidence that Mrs. Church met Hannah in the training school's lunchroom? By the manner in which the woman, who was wearing a royal blue suit with thick black-braided trim and a hat with three peacock feathers, stood in the doorway searching her out, then made her way directly toward the head midwife, Hannah thought not.

"Hello, Mrs. Sokolow," she greeted brightly and extended her hand as though this were a social encounter.

Hannah, who had been carrying her tea to the table, had to put down the cup and saucer clumsily before she could shake the member of the Board of Managers' hand.

"I haven't seen you for the longest time," she said with a breathy sincerity.

"You usually attend the monthly meetings," Hannah pointed out.

"That's not what I meant!" she replied with a teasing chastisement in her tone. "I do so enjoy our little chats. You had so many good ideas when we discussed the planning of the new maternity pavilion last year. Now everything is in working order. Isn't it amazing how time flies?"

"I admit I was not looking forward to the transfer, but it

went more smoothly than expected, thanks to the board's good planning."

"Let's not forget how hard Mrs. Hemming worked to make the transition easy on everyone."

Hannah nodded and waited. What was this about?

Mrs. Church tossed her head and sighed. "That woman does take on more than her share of burdens, and I don't know how we'd manage without her."

Thinking quickly of something positive to add, Hannah recalled her conversation with Midwife Harvey. "To her it's more than a job, it's her whole life."

"Yes." Mrs. Church lowered her voice as though she were speaking of a religious matter. "She thinks nothing of herself, but perhaps it would be easier if she did not care quite so much."

"In what way?"

"Well . . ." The woman looked down and picked a broken piece of feather from her sleeve. "Her main concern is that every patient receive optimal treatment."

"What does she suggest?" Hannah asked archly.

"Now, please don't take this personally . . ." Her eyes shifted to be certain nobody could overhear them. The two students who had been at the nearest table were just leaving, and the others were at the far side of the room. "At the medical meeting last month Dr. Dowd submitted for review the case you brought to him for emergency operative intervention."

"Yes?"

"Could that not have been avoided by an earlier referral to a gynecological surgeon?"

"Is that what the doctor said?"

"Not exactly. He only stated the facts of the case. But others were speculating whether . . ."

"You mean Mrs. Hemming . . ."

"And the ladies on the Board of Managers," she added firmly. "In any case, we would prefer that our staff restrict their clinical-care duties to their shifts so that each patient receives the maximum benefit of the medical and supervisory staff."

Hannah's first reaction was to defend her position, but she stepped back and thought about the case without the complication of Mrs. Czachorwski's peculiar response. Could she have benefited by seeing a doctor earlier? Might he have prescribed surgery instead of a pessary? No. Her first presenting problems had in no way indicated the removal of her organ. The infection had been caused by her modesty problem. In any case, restricting her private practice would have not affected the outcome of this case. "Why don't you ask Dr. Dowd what he might have done earlier?"

"He claims you acted with excellent judgment." Hannah folded her hands and waited. Mrs. Church cleared her throat. "Nevertheless, we feel that considering your heavy responsibilities here, Bellevue should command your full attention."

"I agree absolutely. I further agree with my landlord, who wants his rent by the first of the month, and the shopkeeper, who wants payment in full with each order. Given the necessities, I do the best I can."

"I'm sure you do," Mrs. Church said with resignation. "I consented to speak with you, and now I have done that." She stood and fumbled in the pocketbook that dangled from her elbow, and then handed Hannah two sheets of folded paper. "This might interest you." Hannah also rose to her feet. "No, please . . . you haven't finished your tea. I just wanted to take a peek at the nursery before I left."

"There are two sets of twins," Hannah said as if she were offering a treat.

"How delightful!" Mrs. Church smiled pleasantly and left.

Hannah opened the papers immediately. The first list was typical of Mrs. Hemming. "Tincture of green soap will be changed from a 4 ounce allotment at bedside to 3 ounces, since there is usually 1 ounce wasted after each confinement. Soaps used for pincushions in the nursery will be cut in half. New mothers will be permitted to take air in the loggias between pavilions only until 4:00 p.m., except on Sundays." Then an item on the second page caught Hannah's eye. "Midwives will require written permission from the Board of Managers before attending any lectures other than scheduled meetings."

Hannah flushed. The Blühner lecture had been more than six months earlier, and as far as she knew, no other midwife had ever attended any in the amphitheater. Then she recalled that Dr. Blühner was to do another series. What harm could come from her—or any other midwife—increasing her knowledge? Hannah raged as she looked in the direction of the nursery in time to see Mrs. Church's feathers gliding through the doorway.

That afternoon, Lazar and Hannah sat side by side on the sofa, both reading. Lazar seemed engrossed in the socialist paper, the *New Yorker Volkszeitung,* but Hannah could not concentrate, since she was finding the writings of Krafft-Ebing more startling than she expected.

"What's bothering you, *neshomeleh?*" he said, using an endearment that meant "little soul."

"Nothing." She nuzzled closer to him and stroked his muscular shoulders, which made her feel warm and protected. Sounds of the children's shrieks filtered through the windows. Hannah listened attentively for the nuance that a mother knows means the difference between gleeful pleasure and the shock of pain, but there was nothing worrisome in the calls and shouts. Then she spoke in a resigned tone. "Maybe Mrs. Church was right."

He raised his brows provocatively. "About what?" After Hannah relayed the conversation, he asked, "What business is it of hers?"

"A midwife's reputation must be beyond reproach."

"And yours is, as much as anyone's can be. Don't tell me those doctors are so holy they don't make mistakes! What about those fellows who missed the smallpox the first time around?"

"That's not the point." She jumped up and went to the window to see if she could locate the children. They were nowhere in sight.

"Then what is it?" Lazar cajoled.

"I don't want to give up my work at Rachael's clinic."

"You think delivering babies is almost too easy."

"How did you know?" Suddenly she felt an immense relief at his sympathy. Here was the one person who knew exactly how she felt.

"I know you thrive on the complications and are bored with the routine. After a while the faces—as well as the bottoms!—must blur together."

"That's true. But what should I do about it?"

"Keep your mind occupied with the questions the other women have been asking, just as you have been, and don't worry about the busybodies at Bellevue."

"In the end I probably have no true influence on their lives, anyway, so why bother?" Hannah sighed deeply. "There's so little science, and no way to really know if I have made a difference, that I feel I shouldn't take the money."

"Nonsense!" Now he was the one who stood and went to the window. "Anyway, the experts do not agree with one another, so why should you worry that you are giving out the absolute truth?"

"You just don't want to do without the extra income," she burst out, then regretted the words.

"Between my writing and consulting I'm taking in more than I did at the university," he boasted. If they averaged his contribution, this was stretching the truth, but in recent weeks he had been bringing home large pocketfuls of change. So much, in fact, that they had caught up on the rent for the first time in more than a year.

"You have been getting so many assignments . . ." she began, for she had been meaning to find out exactly who had been paying him what in order to estimate how much she could count on in the future.

"Things could be worse," he said in a deliberately offhand manner.

"You are doing so much better than I expected."

"And so are you." He gave her a squeeze. "Everybody has doubts now and then, but I know you would never suggest anything that you did not believe had a chance of being useful. Besides, you have done more good than you realize."

Some lingering question started to form, but then, as if on cue, she heard the rumble of footsteps running up the stairs. The door burst open and two children with pink faces and purple lips shattered the moment with their cries and demands.

∽∾ 2 ∾∽

The next day Hannah arrived at Dr. Jaffe's office only to be met with a surprise. A new plaque by the door read:

R. JAFFE, DOCTOR, GENERAL MEDICINE
H. SOKOLOW, MIDWIFE, WOMEN'S PROBLEMS

Carrie was smiling as Hannah came in. "What do you think?"

"I don't know what to say."

Rachael was standing in the doorway to one of the examining rooms. "Don't you like it?"

"Well, isn't it too broad?" Hannah protested. "After all, I can't handle every woman's problem."

"Nor can I cure everyone."

"Well, then," Hannah retorted brightly, "if my name is on the door, I must pay for the space."

Rachael started to protest but caught herself. In her rapidly shifting eyes Hannah could almost hear her analyzing that the Sokolows were faring better now. "We'll work something out."

Hannah realized she had better start seeing patients. By noon she had seen three maternity cases, a vaginal infection, and a woman who wanted a menstrual chart.

"Anyone else?" she called out to Carrie, who must have stepped out. She looked around the waiting room. It was empty except for a bandaged child. Hannah knew this was a boy who had been badly scalded when he had overturned a pot of soup. Every few days he had an appointment with the doctor to have his wounds cleaned, an excruciating process. He always came at the end of the day when nobody else would be subjected to his piteous howling.

"That's it, then?" she asked Carrie, who was in the medicine closet preparing the bandages and basins for the boy.

Hannah was reaching for her overcoat when a clatter outside startled them. Hannah stared out the window. A metal lid was being whirled down the street by a stiff wind blowing off the East River. With the sun beating down the day looked deceptively warm, but she knew that after a few blocks she would be chilled to the bone. She wrapped the babushka around her head and tied it tightly behind her neck, drawing up the fold so it covered her chin. She stuffed her hands into her pockets, feeling for her gloves, which were missing. Probably Emma had left hers in school and had taken them.

Before she reached the vestibule door, a woman in a long fur coat brushed past her. The face was familiar, but since Hannah wasn't expecting anyone, she kept going. The woman turned before the door had shut after Hannah.

"Mrs. Sokolow?" she called loudly.

Hannah stepped back inside and closed the door against the frigid assault. "Yes?"

"Do you have a minute?"

Hannah tried to remember who this was, but all she could do was admire the lush brown fur that insulated the lady far better than her own wool coat.

"Maxine Starr, from Rivington Street, remember?" Her mind was blank. She recalled nobody by that name. "They called me Malka then," the woman prompted.

The wife of the tailor! "Malka Starretzky?" she queried uncertainly. As the woman nodded, her neck seemed to disappear in a sea of fur. Wasn't Starretzky the man who had said for the same amount of work he could either make a coat of cloth or one of fur, the only difference being he would have five times as much for his labors with the latter? Obviously he had succeeded.

"You remembered," she gushed. "I was passing by and saw your sign. How well you must be doing! I didn't know you were a doctor."

"I'm not, but I work with Rachael Jaffe."

"Well, doctor or not, you look wonderful. How are the children?"

"Both are doing fine, and yours?" Hannah asked, wondering how long they would have to stand in the drafty hallway before the tailor's wife would be on her way.

"The oldest of my boys is working with his father already. The next one is finishing high school next year. And you remember Sarah, don't you?"

Sarah Starretzky . . . the last time Hannah had seen her she must not have been more than ten. She had huge eyes set into a delicate face and long tendrils of curly hair that had seemed in a disarray as the active girl bounded down the street—always running, never walking. She was the kind of girl that Mama Blau called a *hitskop,* an excitable person, and someone who required "a mother with eyes in the back of her head."

"How is Sarah?" Hannah asked politely.

"We call her Stella now. She married a few weeks ago. Bernard Applebaum, the son of Cantor Applebaum, you've heard of him?"

Hannah had not, but she nodded anyway. "Mazel tov!"

"He's going to be a doctor. He's at the college at Columbia. Do you know it?" She didn't wait for Hannah to acknowledge but rushed ahead. "The children are living in our building until he finishes. We're on Riverside Drive, near Seventy-first, you should come up to see us. Doesn't your sister live nearby?"

Now Hannah was certain that Malka—ah, Maxine—had not just been passing, and that there was something specific on her mind. She was about to suggest they go into the waiting room to talk when a distant sound, not unlike the groan of an animal, could be heard through the walls. Mrs. Starretzky—ah, Starr—might have taken it for a dog, but Hannah knew the burned boy was being treated and the cries would worsen when the debriding began in earnest.

"I'm on my way to the hospital," she said decisively. "Would you like to walk with me for a few blocks?" Hannah opened the door and gritted her teeth as the wind whipped the hem of her coat, exposing her legs.

Mrs. Starr followed on her heels. "Well, I am lucky to have caught you in, aren't I?"

Hannah had moved ahead, for only by walking fast could she stay warm. Maxine stumbled after her. "Tell me, do you still deliver babies?"

"Yes, mostly at Bellevue." Was this it? Was the daughter pregnant already . . . or pregnant too soon? Did they require a midwife who would deliver a "premature" baby in a few months? "Maybe I'll see Sarah—Stella—there someday in the future," she said, opening the subject.

"Not too soon," the mother replied in a strained voice.

Hannah slowed down so she could catch Maxine's expression. "Not too soon, I hope" would be what a mother of a bride who did not want to rush her young daughter might say. Or another might have said something like she hoped it would be soon, *keyn eyn-hora*. However, this was something else.

"She's quite young, at least by American standards," Hannah said in a deliberately offhand manner.

"Just seventeen, but the boy was such a catch, we couldn't say no."

"Did you arrange the match?"

Maxine waved her hand from side to side. "In a way, yes. We heard about him and thought: what harm could there be to let them talk? So they met and then—" The arms swathed in fur waved around while Hannah shivered. "You need a fur. My Moe could get you one wholesale." Hannah started walking again, and Maxine took the hint and got to the point. "So she liked him, he liked her, we made the *shidech*. Moe could help the boy with his school and she could stay close to us, what could be better?"

"So long as everyone is happy . . ." The words were spoken with the slight lilt of a question meant to provoke a response rather than end the discussion.

Mrs. Starr leapt into the gaping void. "There is one small difficulty . . ."

"Perhaps if I saw her . . ."

"Would you? When?"

"Wednesday afternoon is the next time I am at the clinic. She isn't ill, is she?"

"Not really."

Hannah contemplated the possibilities. An impetuous young husband could have caused an injury. "Bleeding heavily?"

"No."

Maybe he was too frightened to sustain an erection. These studious boys were often the worst, until they caught on, she thought, remembering that once Lazar had been urged to become a rabbi. "Then it could wait."

"Yes, but not too long. There is some pain."

Now, that was a clue. There could have been a tear at the vaginal outlet, and a stitch or two could remedy that. Or, more likely, the girl had a tough membrane which required surgical removal. More than once Hannah had had to excise a hymen to deliver a baby. Midwives had their own theories about virgin births that made Mary's not quite so remarkable.

A Third Avenue trolley was about to stop in front of them. Maxine looked up and realized it would take her uptown. Hannah waved that she should go ahead. "Tell Stella—and her husband—to rest until she sees me."

With an apologetic glance Mrs. Starr smiled at Hannah. "Thank you," she said and stepped up to the platform.

3

"Mrs. Applebaum, come in, please." Hannah tried not to betray how absurd she felt calling this child by her married name.

Even if Hannah had not been told who this was, she would have recognized Stella at once. The honey-colored curls still tumbled down her back, and her wide-set blue eyes retained the mischievous quality that Hannah remembered from Rivington Street. Her stature had remained diminutive, but high, firm breasts and a fullness around the mouth showed that she was not quite as young as she first appeared. Despite her preference for the old country names, Hannah had to admit that Stella suited the child better than the Biblical Sarah.

Nobody else was with her, although Hannah had half expected that her mother would be at her side. It was better this way, Hannah decided, for she did not think the mother knew the whole story anyway. When they were alone in the examining room, Hannah closed the door and sat on the stool. She motioned for Stella to take the chair. "You are married how long?" she asked.

"Five weeks."

"And you are how old now?"

"Seventeen."

"You began your monthly bleeding when?"

"At fifteen, just after my birthday."

This was later than normal, but not too unusual, especially for a slightly immature girl. The parents should not have rushed a marriage. What was the hurry? Then she remembered the spirit in this one and thought she understood something of the mother's fears. "And your husband, what is his name?"

"Bernard Applebaum."

From further questions she learned that he was twenty, somewhat taller than Stella, and studying to be a doctor. "You like him?"

"He's very smart."

The oblique response did not go unnoticed. "Your mother must be pleased." Hannah kept her voice flat. "Does his mother like you as much?"

Stella fluttered her eyes. These questions bewildered her. "I don't know. I guess so."

Hannah explained. "Mothers of girls want to see them secure; mothers of boys want them to wait until they can support a family on their own. Of course, when a boy has many years of school ahead of him, a father-in-law who will help is a blessing."

Now Stella's eyes were darting. Hannah had touched a nerve. She sensed the girl had doubts whether Bernard had married her or her dowry. What this had to do with the physical side of her difficulty remained to be seen. With the preliminaries over, she said perfunctorily, "Tell me about your pains."

"I can't do it."

"It hurts when you try to have relations with Bernard?"

"Yes."

"All the time, or just in the beginning?"

"We can't even begin."

"What does your husband do then?"

"He tries for a while, then he stops."

"How often does he try?"

"At first every night. Now he is waiting to see what is wrong with me."

"Many girls have troubles in the beginning. You have to stretch slowly to be ready for a man. After I examine you, I will give you some ideas of what might help you. There even may be something I can do to make it easier." Stella's face had taken on a rigid set. "I'll send Carrie in to help you undress."

"No! Not her. If you'll just undo my buttons . . ."

Hannah bristled. There were some patients who did not care for Carrie's colored skin and she resented their attitude, but in this case she decided that the girl was so distraught by her circumstances she would not hold it against her.

Once Stella had removed everything but an underslip, Hannah had her climb onto the examining table. She placed a sheet across her chest to keep her warm and preserve an illusion of privacy, then Hannah went to wash her hands. When she turned around, Stella had managed to scurry to the top of the table, her bottom as far from the end as possible. She was sitting up clutching the sheet with her arms clasped around her knees. Most women did not like gynecological exams, and young girls were bound to be more frightened than mature women, but even so, Stella's reaction was peculiar. Where had that exuberant, sprightly person gone? What had made her so afraid?

"I promise I will not hurt you, Stella. What I want you to do is to lie down on your back and place your tush here." She pointed to a pad at the end of the table. "Then I want you to hold up your right hand. If you feel anything you don't like, just point one finger and I will stop."

Stella slid down reluctantly. She stuck her legs out rigidly and her thighs contracted to form a stiff barrier. As her teeth rattled, the examining table quivered.

"Are you cold?" Hannah asked.

"N-no."

"I will warn you before I touch, all right?"

Stella gave a pathetic sigh.

Hannah did not raise the girl's legs to the usual position, nor did she place her feet in stirrups, for that gaping position was far too exposed. Even so, Hannah could see at once the remnants of bruises on Stella's inner thighs. Her heart went out to the little girl, whose husband had not known any approach other than that of a battering ram. While the entrance to the fortress had been dented, the king had not gained this prize yet. Hannah parted her legs gently, then opened her outer lips as though she were reading a book. The tissues were normal and there was no unusual discharge.

"That's good, very good. You are a healthy young woman." Hannah was not certain why she gave that pronouncement when she had barely begun the examination, yet she was convinced there would be no abnormal structures here.

Avoiding the vaginal opening for a moment, Hannah lightly touched the top of her pubis and pressed on the bones gently. Then she moved up the abdomen and felt for the uterus and ovaries. "Just a little pressure, that's all. Does that hurt?"

"No," Stella admitted in a hoarse whisper.

"Good, very good." Hannah withdrew her hand and walked to the head of the table. "That wasn't so bad, was it?"

"Is it over?"

It wasn't, but Hannah had sensed that the girl's tension had been mounting and it might be wise to pause. "I can stop now or go on, but only if you wish."

"Do you know what is wrong with me?" she pleaded in a squeaky voice.

"No, but so far there is nothing unusual."

"I have to tell Bernard something."

"And your mother," Hannah added.

"Yes." A sob caught in her throat. Hannah said nothing. "Go on, then" came as an order.

Hannah walked to the dressing tray and poured some boiling water from the kettle into a pan. Then she measured out a half cup of mineral oil into a metal bowl and set the bowl into the steaming water. This was a trick she had learned from Bubbe Schtern, the old Odessa midwife with whom she had first apprenticed. Bubbe believed that warm oil had many uses, from massaging a baby to managing the second stage of labor. Hannah heated her hands on the side of the bowl, then dipped two fingers of her right hand into the smooth, warm liquid. "Now I will check you, but it won't hurt."

Stella didn't flinch at her approach. She even parted her legs slightly without being asked. Hannah's left hand repeated the earlier maneuvers and there was no tightening response. "Good, good," Hannah encouraged as she slipped her oiled finger along the smooth space between her rectum and vagina. "It's warm, isn't it? And slippery. So I can touch you and it won't bother you." All she did was move her finger to the right and left. "Can you feel that?"

"Yes." The tone was tense.

"Does it hurt?"

"No."

"Good, good." Now she glided upward toward the introitus, the vaginal opening. The flicker of her finger at the very edge should barely have been felt—and if it was, Stella did not react. "Now I will detect where the problem is. You tell me when to stop." Hannah made no attempt to penetrate. All she did was to put different degrees of pressure on the muscles surrounding the entrance. The sphincter vaginae and levator ani muscles were harder than normal. She did not want to force her way in, so she used the other hand to rub Stella's legs in the hope of achieving more relaxation. The thighs trembled and the tension increased. At the rate this was going, Hannah was unlikely to get a proper view of the vaginal barrel and would be unable to see if there had been any external or internal lacerations, let alone appraise the state of her hymen.

"Now I must look inside, just a little," she said, parting the inner lips carefully. For a moment it seemed as if she viewed a narrow portion of the vagina, but then it was as if a door snapped shut. When Hannah's finger poked slightly inside, the muscles at the entrance clamped down. "Does this always happen?"

"Yes, whenever anyone touches me there."

"Shall I stop?"

"You aren't hurting me."

"But if Bernard was trying?"

"I'd cry out."

"Now, if I move away, can you relax it? I won't touch you, I just want to watch."

"No. It doesn't disappear for a long time."

Hannah removed her fingers, dipped them again in the oil, then smeared the oil around the exterior folds. "If I do this, how does it feel?"

"Warm, wet."

"That's all?"

"Ah-huh," she said, turning her head to the wall.

"Good, good." Now Hannah made certain her smallest finger was slick. The nail had been trimmed to below the fleshy tip, but even so, Hannah felt it with the other hand to be certain there were no sharp edges. She pressed the digit into the slight gap between the clenched muscles. "You feel this?"

"A little."

"I will move it around. Tell me when to stop." She made a few circular motions that, without Stella realizing, dilated the orifice enough to allow entrance to the first knuckle. "Does this hurt?"

"Well . . ."

"You feel it?"

"Yes." A sob caught in her throat. "Ow!"

The sound was so pathetic, Hannah withdrew her finger. "Look at me," she said a bit more authoritatively so that Stella could see her wiping her hands on a towel. "All you have is a muscle problem."

"It hurts," she whimpered.

"Even now, with nothing touching you?"

"Yes. It gets tight and doesn't go away for a long time."

"But it does get better, doesn't it?"

"Eventually, but I still can't . . ." she lamented. "What's wrong with me?"

What could she say? Hannah had heard about this condition and thought it was called vaginismus, but she had never encountered a case and would have to look it up before she could be certain. "There are many causes of the condition," she began slowly as she tried to think of something that was truthful, but unspecific.

Hannah helped Stella sit up. She took the girl's shaking hand in hers. It was icy. She rubbed it between both of hers.

"Do many people have it?"

"That is difficult to say. Many suffer in private."

"I'm not the only one?"

"Of course you aren't. Many new brides have one sort of difficulty or another."

Stella's trembling increased. Hannah had no idea why the child was so frightened. Probably Mr. Freud and his friends would have a ready answer. Maybe someone had done something terrible to her when she was younger, or she had seen or heard something that made her fear penetration. Since Hannah doubted any permanent anatomical problem, she saw this as a muscular spasm that could be fixed, even if she had no idea exactly how the cure would come. The studious, inept husband had not helped matters. Until the bruises healed, it would be foolish for him to try again. For a moment Hannah had an image of Bernard anointing his penis with warm mineral oil, but dismissed it. If her fingertip had found the space hostile, surely his organ—no matter how modest—was the wrong implement, at least for a while. Nevertheless, these two young people were wed and the boy had certain rights, certain needs.

"Tell me, Stella, do you like it when your husband kisses you?"

"I don't mind it, unless . . ."

"Forget the other for now. Can you let him kiss you?"

"Yes, I suppose."

"Does he know how to kiss a girl properly?"

Stella smiled. "I didn't know there was a proper way."

"There isn't one proper way, but it must be done so that

both enjoy it. Do you think you could show him what you like?"

She giggled. "About kissing?"

"Yes, kissing. Tell him that I have examined you and you have a problem that requires several weeks to cure."

Her eyes blinked rapidly. "Can it be cured in a few weeks?"

"It's different for everyone, but that's my guess," Hannah said with a flimsy veneer of confidence.

"What shall I do?"

"Every day, when nobody else is around, you must take a bath, as hot as you can tolerate. Then you must get out of the water and rub yourself with this oil for . . ." Hannah was inventing as she spoke, but sensed she was on the right track ". . . for five minutes. Rub everywhere between your legs, especially around the top, and not so much around the bottom."

"But that's where it hurts."

This was the Stella Hannah remembered: complaining, contentious. Was her spasm a way of contradicting her husband—or someone else? Hannah took a breath and continued evenly. "The warm water will help there for now. Just move the oil around. And . . ." She searched for the right phrase. "If it feels nice, don't stop. Many women enjoy that sensation."

"Do I have to see you again?"

"Yes. In one week." She waited a beat. "And tell Bernard, kissing is fine, but nothing below the waist."

$$\backsim\hspace-4pt\backsim 4 \backsim\hspace-4pt\backsim$$

After supper a few evenings later, the children took over the kitchen table with their night work. Benny had a poem to memorize and Emma was prompting him.

"Oh Captain! My Captain! our fearful trip is done,
"The ship has weathered every rack, the prize we sought is won.
"The port is here . . ."

"No, that's wrong," Emma said, a bit too pleased he had slipped so soon. "The port is *near*, the bells I *hear* . . ."

"I know!" he complained. "Now I lost my place."

Benny began again and stumbled only a few more times.

"Very nice!" Hannah applauded.

"Do you know what the poem is about?" Lazar asked as he glanced through a stack of Yiddish newspapers.

"The death of President Lincoln," Benny replied.

"I didn't know he was a captain of a ship," Hannah said.

"He wasn't, Ma."

"But you said something about a ship being anchored safe and sound."

"That refers to the country coming through the Civil War."

Hannah shook her head.

"Doesn't it, Pops?"

"Pops!" Lazar laughed. "Where'd you get that? But yes, Benny, you have it right. The ship is the symbol for the state." He put down the paper and rubbed his neck.

This was something Hannah understood better than poetry. "Is your back hurting again?"

"A little."

"You've had another argument at Sach's, haven't you?" Hannah moved across the room and perched on the arm of his chair. She began to massage the place she knew tensed first. "Every time you try to fight the war in the cafés, you come back wounded."

"You're so good at this," Lazar said with a contented groan as his shoulders relaxed.

She gave an exasperated sigh. "I can get your back feeling better, but if you submit yourself to more punishment, I can't prevent another spasm from occurring."

He shifted around to give her more room to work. "You could make money doing this."

"I did, remember?" she said, kissing his neck. There had been times when they first arrived in America when she had more regular work as a masseuse than as a midwife. "Probably one massage is worth more than all my advice."

As she pummeled her husband's back harder, her thoughts turned to Stella Applebaum. She too had painful spasms, not unlike Lazar's. While there was something more ordinary about one in the back, a muscle was a muscle. When Lazar became angry, his reflexive tensing caused his muscles to contract, just like Stella's reflexive tensing to her husband's approach. Hannah's first instinct had been to recommend heat and a sort of massage, but had that been too simplistic? She had not been particularly successful in preventing Lazar's recurrences, so why did she think she would be with Stella's?

"Why are you stopping? It feels so good."

Hannah hadn't realized her hands had stilled. She began the final rubdown while she contemplated the quandary. What was interesting was that both cases had mental factors. Lazar's problem was a physical manifestation of his emotions, and so was Stella's. Both of them needed to relax, which every midwife knew was easier to suggest than accomplish. Her advice to Stella had been preliminary. She had no idea if it would succeed, but at least it would cause no harm. The real question was: what had caused Stella to be so afraid that the crucial muscle contracted violently and caused her pain? Perhaps Mr. Freud was on the right track when he talked about the transition from girlhood to maturity. If a girl had to proceed from childish clitoral sensations to adult vaginal ones—and she had a reason to rebel against this—didn't it make sense for her to contract her vagina to make that passage impossible?

"What are you smiling about?" Lazar asked.

"You feel better now?"

"Yes." He patted her hand. "Thank you."

"Then I'm happy." She moved over to the sofa, picked up her mending basket, and threaded a darning needle, but after a few stitches she was back reflecting on the question.

Something had caused the vaginismus. But what? Stella was a young girl, no matter what her mother said. Yes, some her age were ready for marriage, but Hannah sensed that this child was not. She didn't blame the parents. In the old country girls were married even earlier. In America, though, families were caught in the bind between what they or their parents had done and the new ways, not trusting either. There was always a risk if you waited too long. The girl could become undesirable because of her age, she could lose her chastity, or worse, become pregnant. Now Hannah felt she was on the right track, for impetuous little Stella must have worried the mother into this decision. If Stella had not felt ready to marry, but lacked the power to convince her parents otherwise, she could have sabotaged their plans—

albeit unconsciously—by rejecting her husband physically. Her head pounded with the possibilities. Tomorrow I'll read more about it, Hannah said, then turned back to her sewing with full concentration.

❦ 5 ❦

"The point is I don't have any idea whether I have helped anyone or not," Hannah said to Dr. Herzog at Sach's Café, where they waited for Lazar and Rachael to arrive.

"The point is you will never know, and you must be satisfied with that."

"I can't be. When I deliver a baby, do you think I can leave the room before it is examined? No. I must know both the mother and child are doing fine."

"Ah, but do you ever know? A hemorrhage could begin five minutes or five days afterward. You look at a baby, it is breathing, it is crying, and then it becomes sick due to a weak heart or dies mysteriously in the night. All you are doing is satisfying yourself by checking off a mental list."

Hannah could rarely win a point with Herzog, so she merely shrugged.

He tilted back his chair and smiled, not smugly but warmly. "Now, Hannah, the important part of what you told me is that you don't *feel* as though you have helped. Here is where I know you are wrong. Just listening to the problem was your first contribution. When someone voices their misery, a certain edge of their complaint is minimized. Then, knowing someone they can trust is taking them seriously is the second assistance. After that, anything else they get is a bonus." As he leaned forward, the chair clanked into the marble tabletop. "I am certain you always offer something from your repertoire of sensible solutions. Maybe they try what you suggest, maybe they do not; in any case they will take a portion—maybe only a fraction—of what they need. The part they use may not be your main concept either, and they may not do exactly as you say, but even so you have helped."

"I don't see how. If they wanted a boy and get a girl—"

"Do they come asking for their money back? No! If the result is not what they wanted, they assume they made a mistake. Why? I don't know the answer to that one, but people tend to blame themselves first—at least on intimate matters."

Hannah's mind took off with his last point. Ever since Rachael had confided in her, she had not felt quite the same toward Ezekicl. Herzog was staring at Hannah with wide, questioning eyes. She felt as if she had to speak or he might guess her thoughts.

"I don't understand it, Ezekiel, but at first the women came to me with the most basic of concerns about having babies. Now they think I know about everything from the navel down."

"Don't you?"

She gave a modest laugh. "Not everything. In fact, I am very perplexed about something."

"Nu?"

"One young woman has terrible fears about her marital duties. I knew this girl as a child. She was always bright, lively—even daring—not the shy, frightened type you might imagine. So what may have caused it?"

"Of course I am no seer, but already you have given me several hints." He paused to allow Hannah to mull over what she had said. "A daring young girl may have found herself in water above her head. She may have gone somewhere or done something that has caused great shame. Or worse, she was assaulted and carries that burden."

"Yes, that could be it," Hannah replied slowly, thinking that pretty little Sarah Starretzky could have attracted a lustful older man. Her mind wandered to the pelvic examination. There had been no evidence of penetration, so any attack had not injured her in that way, but there might have been some other youthful exploration which led to tremendous guilt. How could anyone ever know the origins of fears? Maybe after years of analysis with someone like Mr. Freud, but who had time for that? Certainly not Stella.

"What's going on? Are you two so enthralled with each other you don't notice what's around you?"

Hannah jumped at the sound of Lazar's indignant voice. Had he misinterpreted the way Herzog and she were whispering together? She looked up at her husband with a wan smile. "You're late," she said to gain a momentary advantage.

"Don't you realize who's here?" Lazar continued in a hushed, almost reverential voice. He hissed under his breath and tilted his chin toward a corner table. "There's Alexandra Kollontai sitting with Bukharin."

"Who's he?" Hannah asked naively.

"One of the greatest strategists of the new social order."

"He's very young."

"Not too young to have been arrested at least three times in Russia." Hannah did not miss the admiration in his tone. "Did you know they're publishing a controversial paper together?"

"Which?" There were so many, it was difficult to keep track.

"Novy Mir."

"Oh, that one," Hannah said with a mock yawn. "The offices of *Novy Mir* are just down the street from Rachael's office."

"Then you've met Kollontai?" Herzog asked Hannah.

The woman was directly in her line of vision. And Hannah could not help noticing her beautifully coiffed thick black hair and flashing eyes as she spoke animatedly with her companion. "No, I haven't."

"She's a brilliant woman," Lazar interjected, "even if, in my opinion, her writings on the class struggle are too orthodox an interpretation of Marxism."

As if she had overheard that remark, Alexandra Kollontai caught Lazar's eye. It was hardly a summons to her table, but Lazar strode forward as if he had been welcomed with open arms. Then Kollontai did something unusual. She stood for Lazar. Bukharin did not. For a moment Hannah thought she was offering Lazar her seat, or that she was going to the toilet, but no, it was the same as if a man were greeting a woman. The gesture impressed Hannah mightily, for in one swoop Comrade Kollontai had done more for equality than she could have with a hundred words.

Someone nudged Hannah. She turned to see that Rachael had arrived and was propelling her toward the other table. Herzog already was on Lazar's heels. Nobody wanted to miss an opportunity to visit with these stars of the socialist firmament. Frankly Hannah found it amusing that the socalled Russian revolution was being waged in the cafés of

New York when the czar was as firmly implanted on the imperial throne as ever.

Lazar pushed her forward, saying, "This is my wife, Hannah."

Hannah rankled, thinking that such an introduction would demean her in Kollontai's mind. Herzog was the one who added, "A talented midwife."

"And women's consultant," contributed Rachael.

"What does this mean?" Kollontai queried in Russian.

"She helps women who have difficulties with their reproductive functions."

Alexandra Kollontai arched her velvety eyebrows. "I must say I have never understood the tumult about ordinary relations between men and women. To me, sex should be as easy and uncomplicated as drinking a glass of water." Slowly she lifted up her glass of beer and took a sip, and that simple act was imbued with such immense symbolism that Lazar and Ezekiel seemed as transfixed as if she had taken off her shirtwaist.

Chairs were drawn up to the table. Kollontai made Hannah take the one beside her. "So you are also a doctor?"

"No"—she indicated her friends—"Rachael Jaffe and Ezekiel Herzog have the medical degrees."

"So, *ptu,*" Kollontai made a spitting noise, "what you do is more important." She gave the others a slightly apologetic glance. "I am working on a pamphlet to be called *'Obshchestvo i materinstvo,'* on society and maternity, in which I will show how several women, each named Mashenka, each expecting a child, is treated by society. The first Mashenka is a factory director's wife, the second is a laundress, the third a maid, the last a dye worker. For only the first is motherhood a joyful occasion. The other working women find having children just one more cross to bear. When women see that there is strength in unity and the goal is the better future of our children, they will organize to create a better society."

Fascinated with the woman's face—which seemed like the shell of an egg lit from behind by a candle—rather than her stilted words, Hannah could understand why Kollontai drew crowds to her speeches. In the pause, though, she had no idea how to respond.

No matter, Lazar leapt into the breach. "The reason that women will be more difficult to organize is that no matter their tribulation, they do not experience the alienation of the worker, for motherhood contains satisfactions that counter alienation."

"Perhaps that is true of the woman who is privileged enough to stay at home, comrade, but I am speaking of those who carry the double burden of maternity and the necessity of earning money."

"As I recall, you have not lacked certain privileges throughout your life," Lazar indicated with a tinge of a challenge.

"One need not have been pregnant to be able to deliver a baby," Kollontai said, with a side smile to Hannah. "Now tell me, what do women ask you most frequently?" she quizzed Hannah while ignoring the others.

"I do not think you will be pleased with my response," Hannah began with some hesitation.

"I am here to learn, not to lecture," she demurred.

"Most want instructions on how to have a male child."

Kollontai's lips tightened into a thin line. "I thought you were going to say they wanted to know how to prevent a child. However, I am not distressed. The first step is for women to take control of their bodies, to have choices. If they want a boy—though I doubt you can change the percentages by very much—and they get a boy, they have achieved one of their goals. After the revolution, when men and women work side by side for the good of everyone, the value of the male will be no more than the female." Out of the corner of her eye she noticed Bukharin shifting in his seat. "Don't you agree?" she asked him.

Bukharin, a slender man who clearly had lost the seat of power to his female companion, sniffed, "Where the hell is the waiter?" then cupped his hand over his eyes in an exaggerated gesture as though he were searching for someone over the horizon. "Ah, look who's come in!" He waved to a group by the door. Lazar and Herzog drifted with him to another table, and in the end it was Rachael and Hannah who debated the problems of birth control with Comrade Kollontai.

6

The next afternoon Stella Applebaum was scheduled to return. At first Hannah thought she would do another examination to see if the muscle had relaxed even slightly. Then
if it had, she would comment effusively on how much progress had been made. But if it had not . . . This is where she
hesitated, for she did not want Stella to become discouraged
too soon. Then she remembered how much stock Dr. Herzog
placed on talking. What harm could come from gathering as
much information as possible? Mostly she had come away
from the last visit with questions as to why this was happening. If she listened carefully, she might get some clues on
how to advise her next.

She told Carrie to show Stella into the small office, where
she was able to keep her papers and equipment without min-
gling them with the doctor's. "Let's just talk today," Hannah
began.

"You won't be looking at me?"

"Not unless we decide it is necessary."

The edges of Stella's mouth drooped and her chin lowered, even her shoulders seemed inches lower. Good, Hannah thought, let her unwind. "Did you experience any
difficulties last week?" Stella's eyes fluttered, but she did
not respond. "You took a bath every night?"

"No." Now Hannah was disappointed. Was she going to
get no cooperation? "I did it during the day when nobody
was around." Stella was almost smirking. "Like you suggested."

Hannah had forgotten her exact words, but was not miffed
at Stella's retort. On the contrary, her chutzpah was a welcome reminder of the spirited child of the past. At first Hannah had supposed the best way to help her was through
kindness, a maternal understanding of how difficult the first
months of marriage might be. Now, however, she saw that
Stella might respond better to some sort of challenge, which

would result in a victory for her. And why not? Whatever worked!

"And your husband? Did he behave himself?"

Stella lowered her eyes. "Mostly."

Hannah decided not to pursue this for the moment. "When you touched yourself, did you have any pain?"

"No."

"Good. I never want you to do anything that hurts." Stella cocked her head as if she did not quite believe Hannah. "If we do everything very slowly, there won't be any discomfort." If Stella had any soreness, the muscle would surely contract. Only if she felt confident that pain would not be inflicted might the spasm subside. "You see, you are going to trick that muscle into realizing it will not be hurt."

"How?" she asked with a disbelieving voice.

"Next week you should continue what you have been doing, but this time—and only if you feel ready—take your smallest finger and touch the hard part of the muscle very, very gently, as though you were—" she fumbled for the precise word—"stroking a frightened cat." She held up her hand and pointed at her pinkie. "And cut off the nail beforehand," she said with a soft laugh.

"Is that all?"

Should she add another step if that went well? Why rush? Let's see what happens with this. "Yes, Mrs. Applebaum. But I did want to ask you a few more questions, if you have the time."

Stella uncrossed her legs, as though she realized the hard part was over. "Go ahead."

"I need a more complete medical history. When you were young, were you ever ill?" Stella listed childhood diseases, including a long winter in which she had remained in bed much of the time. "Anything else? Accidents? Trips to the hospital? Visits to the doctor . . ." Hannah didn't know what she was searching for, but she had an image of the active girl being wounded in some way.

There was a long silence. "I was in restraints for a while." Seeing Hannah's puzzlement, she added, "You know, restraints for girls."

"Why would you need a restraint?"

"My mother said it was necessary to prevent me from becoming insane," she answered dully.

"I do not see why anyone would have thought that a

healthy girl might go insane," Hannah said, wondering at the mother's mental state. "Did she take you to a doctor?"

"Yes."

"How old were you?"

"Twelve."

"And what problems did you have before you saw the doctor?"

"There was pain when I went to the toilet. My water burned."

"Many women, even young girls have that symptom, and while uncomfortable, it would hardly have made you crazy." Was this an indication that someone had molested her? "What made it occur?"

"They said I caused it myself."

"How?" Hannah inquired, still ignorant.

"By touching myself." She flushed. "You know, rubbing too hard."

Gotteniu! Hannah swore under her breath. Was all this nonsense about masturbation?

Stella lowered her head. "I was very young. I did not know what I was doing."

For a moment Hannah almost jumped to defend the girl from herself, but held back. She needed to hear more. What was this about restraints? Somewhere she had read of this mania, but she did not think any modern doctor would prescribe them. "So, tell me, what did these restraints look like?"

"It was a special one-piece sleeping garment that could only be fastened in the back. There were straps at the feet that attached them to the footboard and my hands were tied to a collar around my neck. I could choose to lie on my front or back, so it wasn't too bad."

"How long did you sleep like that?"

"A few years, but not every night after the first months. If I promised to be good, sometimes they only bound my hands."

Hannah could no longer control her tongue. "That's ridiculous!"

"No, really, it did work." Stella leaned forward earnestly. "I was better after that. And unlike some other difficult girls, I did not have to go through the next step."

"What next step?" Hannah seethed.

"The surgery . . ."

Livid, Hannah stood and went to the girl. She bent down and took her shuddering shoulders in her strong hands. "Stella, that doctor was a barbarian. Nobody should have done that to you." Hannah rubbed Stella's neck and back as she spoke softly. "There is nothing wrong with what you did."

Tears fell silently down her checks. "But—"

"Most girls touch themselves. We touch our faces, our feet. We suck our fingers as babies. We wipe our bottoms. We scratch when it itches. We press where it hurts. Most of the time we try to avoid movements that will be painful and look to repeat activities that give us pleasure. If you found it felt good and touched yourself again, you were only doing what many normal young women do."

"How can that be true when most of the women in mental asylums have done it?"

Hannah gave a hearty chuckle. "Most people in asylums have eaten bread and all will someday die. Does that mean that bread or the fear of death has driven them crazy?"

"But the doctor said—"

"Listen to me, Stella, I am not saying that a girl should spend the whole night rubbing herself. Maybe you rubbed too hard or used a dirty finger and started an infection, or maybe the problem came from some other source. Who knows? But let us say that you brought on the problem yourself. Even then, you should have been told not to do it so hard or so often. Lots of married women have the same difficulty, and they must be warned to have relations with their husbands less frequently or with more gentleness."

Pausing as an idea formed, Hannah walked around so that she could watch Stella's reaction to her next words. "The body has a wonderful way of trying to do what the brain wants it to do. For a long time you required a mechanical restraint to prevent you from touching yourself, and then you found you did not do it any longer. You convinced yourself that sort of satisfaction was harmful. Then, all of a sudden, bang!" Hannah clapped her hands for emphasis, causing Stella to startle. "You are grown, you are married, and suddenly everything that was considered evil is a blessing. You are not allowed to let your own finger touch your hidden parts, but you are supposed to welcome a man's large organ and let him do whatever he wants to you. Does that make sense?" She tilted her head. Stella's eyes were wide and wondering at Hannah's bold speech. "No matter what you think you are supposed to do as a bride, your brain has already learned the message not to allow anything down there, so your body defends the attack. Your muscle contracts to prevent you from being violated." Perhaps she had gone too far with this theory—for that is all it was—and perhaps she should not have spoken about it before she had given the matter considerable thought, but it did make sense to her, and from observing Stella, it seemed to enlighten her as well.

"Everyone else was wrong?" Her face was flushing with a combination of confusion and fury. "How could that be?"

"Last week I was reading a book by a man named Mr. Ellis. He suggests that masturbation—which means boys or girls touching themselves—may not be as terrible as it once seemed, and may even be beneficial in relaxing the body."

This steadied the girl. "Do you think everyone does it?"

"Nobody knows exactly . . ." she began as she strained to recall the chapter in Havelock Ellis on autoerotism, "but I have read that women throughout the world have been known to practice it in different ways. Of course, most boys try it, and even some animals do it."

"What about you?" she asked eagerly.

The question took Hannah aback. What should she answer? Some version of the truth was required. She was thoughtful for a moment. "I cannot remember when I first tried it, but around twelve might be right, although now that I have a good husband, I find him far more satisfying, as many married women might agree."

"You enjoy being with your husband?" she asked in a throaty voice.

"Yes, as you will with yours when you learn how to please yourself."

"My mother said that a good woman lets her husband do what he wants. She said that if I satisfied him, he would make me happy by giving me a nice place to live and buying me pretty things. She did not say it was going to be agreeable."

"Then I feel sorry for your mother," Hannah responded curtly. "But let us forget about her. You go home and do what I told you. Also . . ." Because she now understood so much more about the problem, she decided to offer another approach. "If your husband would like, tell him that he may rub you—on the outside only—and just with his hands, if it feels good to you. If it feels painful, he must stop. Also, to be fair, you should offer to do the same to him. Would that bother you?"

"I guess not. He's been very kind all week, but he is worried I'll never be any good to him."

"Remind him that this is a temporary condition."

"Are you sure?"

Hannah smiled at Stella, then replied with assurance. "Yes, now I am certain it is."

∾ 7 ∾

More than anything Hannah wanted to talk to someone about Stella, but who? Rachael would have been perfect if not for her problem. While Rachael's case was entirely different, Hannah believed there were subtle connections which she had to sort out. Stella managed to bar intercourse altogether with her spasm, while Rachael prevented pleasure with some other kind of blockage. The roots of Stella's barrier may have been found, but Hannah was a long way from discovering the key to Rachael's. Herzog might be useful for theoretical discussions, but Hannah preferred conferring with a woman about this. The best would have been Margaret Sanger, but upon resuming her birth-control activities after her daughter's death, she had been promptly arrested.

Hannah was beginning to feel that she was the odd one out because she had not been jailed for her beliefs. First there had been Minna, then others who worked for Margaret Sanger—including Margaret's husband. Lazar had managed two minor arrests, once at the university and then at the suffrage parade. And then, only last week, Emma Goldman had joined those privileged ranks. While Mrs. Sanger had been in Europe, Emma Goldman had been giving fiery speeches on birth control across the continent. The authorities played into her hands by arresting her, not quietly at her home, but as she was entering a hall where more than a thousand were waiting to hear her. What was even more senseless, the police did not bother to check her topic for the evening! Charging her with holding a meeting on a medical question in defiance of Section 1142 of the Penal Code, they had not known she had been about to expound on atheism.

While one would have thought the arrests would unite Sanger and Goldman, Hannah saw as much conflict between the forceful leaders of this movement as within the ranks of the Socialists. The clashes were something Hannah and Minna talked about when they met, as they were doing more often because Hannah had been less reluctant to frequent the cafés with her husband when she had time off from Bellevue. Even though Lazar had never given Hannah any reason to distrust him, she did have a twinge of concern that Comrade Kollontai's allure might extend beyond her political opinions, but she would never dare voice her suspicion to anyone, least of all to Minna.

On this occasion, though, her brother and his wife had come by for a dutiful visit with Mama, but had hurried upstairs with excuses to see their niece and nephew as soon as Mama started questioning Chaim on how his printing business was going. For a long time it had appeared that he and his wife were slaves to the printing press owned by a one-legged radical to whom Chaim had shown exceptional devotion. He called old Tobias "a brilliant man, a linguistic scholar, a political genius," but Mama believed the elderly man used his lofty ideals to exploit her son economically. A few months earlier Tobias had fallen prostrate across the press, and either died at once from a heart attack, or quite soon after he became entangled in the machinery. Tobias had outfoxed Mama, for he had left the business to Chaim. Although the Chrystie Street building's exterior was grimy and the presses blackened by layers of ink and sweat, Lazar told his wife that her brother was "making a bundle by printing by the paid page rather than the dictates of his conscience," but would never admit it, not even to his mother.

The children had long since gone to bed. Hannah served coffee while Minna expounded on the last legal maneuvers in the Sanger case, which confounded Hannah.

"Then the judge issued a *nolle prosequi.*"

"Another postponement?" Hannah asked.

"No, the order that says the case is dropped. The judge was afraid to let Margaret become a martyr, but he was also frightened to find himself in the position of having to moderate a public debate on a sexual issue."

"Why is it that people are willing to discuss the vilest crimes, but not the permutations of love?" Hannah began.

"That's hardly the point!" Minna answered tensely. "This way we'll never win the battle for women's biological rights."

Hannah recoiled. "Why do you dismiss my thoughts so quickly? You and Chaim, even Lazar, think me ignorant, and perhaps I do know less than you when it comes to political intrigue, but I see women every day and I have a good idea what they are thinking and worrying about."

"You are forgetting I went to jail for the cause, so did Margaret's husband."

"Where did it get you? The law has remained the same. Have you considered that there may be more than one way to fight a battle?" Hannah recalled her own one brush with the law just after her arrival in America. She had been accused of practicing midwifery without a license and then had been considered negligent in the death of a patient. She had arranged for the charges to be dropped, which she continued to believe was far better than having to stand trial. "You always want complete vindication, but if you don't win, that could lead to a disaster. Isn't it better to have the case dismissed and forgotten so people can get back to the real business of life?"

"If the laws are never changed, women will always be vulnerable to persecution," Minna barked back at her.

"That won't happen until everyone, including Margaret and Emma, bands together. Unless you have peace within your ranks, you will never proceed to victory."

"Why is that when men argue, it is considered a part of the political process," Minna snapped, "but when women do they are 'quibbling' or 'complaining'? There are reasons for dissenting opinions. Both Emma and Margaret are serving the cause, each in her own way. When Margaret opens the new clinic, there will be devices that will offer dependable protection for the first time. Soon women will demand this as a right and no government will be able to wage war on half its citizenry."

"I would very much like to speak to Margaret about what she learned in Europe," Hannah said to defuse Minna's diatribe.

"I am certain she would be pleased to spend some time with you. However, there are so many pressing demands," Minna said, putting her off.

Hannah diverted slightly. "Do you think Emma will go to jail?"

"If the judge gives her a choice, she will. And if her case is dismissed, be certain she will create another commotion until she is incarcerated. Last time E. G. was in court she said that 'women need not always keep their mouths shut and their wombs open.' What do you think of that?"

Hannah was quiet for a few moments, then voiced what was on her mind. "We should be grateful to women like Margaret and Emma who will fight the battle on the front lines, much like the men who carry guns, yet you and I know that wars are won in the back rooms as much as in the trenches. You need the loud noise of bombs to get everyone's attention, but the world changes day by day in other ways."

This volley of philosophy startled Minna. "How is that?"

"What I mean is that there is a place for women who are willing to keep their mouths closed while also finding practical ways to keep those wombs closed as well. I don't have to open a clinic or advertise or write books to explain to hundreds of women how they can prevent conception."

"I disagree!" Minna's neck began to redden as she rallied. "For every woman you assist, thousands suffer in ignorance. If one woman is chained, the rest of us are not free."

"Perhaps your decision not to have children has been for the best, then. However, you must be careful not to allow your privileged situation to place you on a higher plane than those more shackled by their biology. Also, you would be wise not to gloat too quickly, because no family-limitation method is perfect."

"We're not worried," she sputtered tensely.

Hannah's response was a gracious smile. For the first time in many months she felt she had bested Minna, and although this was not a laudable achievement, she felt a sense of satisfaction.

8

As much as Hannah yearned to discuss Stella's case, she would never mention names or revert to the level of gossip. As soon as Eva arrived to have lunch with Mama and Aunt Sonia on Sunday, Hannah was on guard, since she was convinced that Eva had referred the case.

Aunt Sonia had come into the city from New Rochelle, a country town north of the city, where her husband had a prosperous fabric store.

"A pity Leyb had to work," Mama said out of politeness, although all the ladies had excluded their husbands. Everyone knew that Napthali and Lazar clashed, but while devout Uncle Leyb was less abrasive, he could not understand why none of the younger men attended to their religious duties, and he did not hesitate to berate them for their sacrilege.

"You know how he is," Sonia replied with the expected excuse. "Saturdays he goes to shul; Sundays he does the inventory. Coming here is a nice reason to have a day on my own."

"You're working too hard," Mama commented.

"Mama's right, Aunt Sonia, you look tired." Hannah handed her a glass of tea. "It must be that long train ride."

"It can't be any worse than the trolley downtown with two transfers," Eva sniffed.

Mama Blau passed out slices of cake. "Here, this will give you energy." She had splurged to make a sour cream coffee cake dense with nuts and brown sugar.

To change the topic, Aunt Sonia picked up the newspaper and pointed to the picture on the first page. It was President Wilson standing beside his new bride, Edith Galt. "Don't they look happy," she said.

"How long have they been married?" Eva asked.

"Not two months," Aunt Sonia replied.

"Do you really believe that the president met her last March and fell in love so quickly?" Eva wondered in a disagreeable voice.

Mama shrugged. "It happens."

"How long has his wife been gone?" asked Sonia.

"Let's see, she died close to my Doreen's birthday. I think it was in early August of last year."

"So, it was time already," Mama said.

"Only seven months after she's cold in her grave and he's warming to something new," Eva answered as she counted on her fingers. "If you ask me, they must have known each other before." Hannah shot her sister a warning glance, but she was oblivious. *"Az men fregt a sgayle iz trayf,"* Eva sniffed. If there is room for question, something is wrong.

"Nobody should ever speak unless they know the truth," Aunt Sonia reminded in a fluttering voice.

Eva opened her mouth, but a glimpse of her mother's accusing stare closed it fast. At last Eva figured out what was going on. Her pious expression crumbled. She had ruined her aunt's visit with her stupidity. But how was she supposed to remember everything? It seemed so long ago ... the pogrom in Odessa that had killed Uncle Leyb's wife, son-in-law, and pregnant daughter. Hannah had delivered the grandchild, Abraham, by performing a cesarean on the dying girl. Sonia, who was the sister of Hannah's father, had been the widow of Simon Meyerov, Leyb's brother. The two had married within weeks of the pogrom to give Abraham parents. Shortly after the gruesome incident the whole family had come to America. Even today, the eleven-year-old child did not know that his parents were really his grandparents.

In the awful silence, Hannah decided it was fortunate that Lazar wasn't there, for he would not have hesitated to stick in a barb with a double meaning about Eva's own sullied past. However, Eva recovered quickly when she thought of a new line of conversation. "Did you know that Hannah is taking care of Maxine Starr's daughter?"

Hannah twitched as the question she had expected now took her by surprise.

"Who?" Mama asked.

"She used to be Malka Starretzky. You remember her daughter, the wild one?"

"Such a *shaineh maidel!* Is she still a pretty girl?"

"Yes, she's lovely," Hannah replied slowly.

"She's married now," Eva added.

"So young!" Mama gasped. "How old could she be?"

"Seventeen," Eva said.

Mama shook her head with disbelief. "A good catch?"

Eva grinned. "A boy who is going to be a doctor. The mother has told everyone from one end of Riverside Drive to the other."

"I'm happy for the family," Mama said with sincerity, for she liked nothing better than to hear that all her friends' children were doing well. "That one could have driven her mother to an early grave. She was always running after the boys."

"So, why does Stella see you?" Eva asked with a syrupy voice. "Is she anxious to have a boy baby the first time?" To break Hannah's stony silence, she prompted, "Come on, after all I was the one who recommended you to Maxine in the first place."

"Then you must know all about it," Hannah replied curtly.

Suddenly a loud argument erupted in the foyer, where the children had been playing a raucous game. Rising, Mama clapped her hands and strode forward. "Children, children . . ."

"Hannah, may I speak to you for a minute?" Eva asked as she gathered up some dishes.

Hannah carried a platter into the kitchen, following her sister's beckoning gesture. Eva put down the dishes and turned on the faucet. Before Eva could speak, she warned in her most inflexible voice. "I will not discuss my patients with you."

"No, this is about the children . . ." her sister began.

"Is something wrong?" Hannah asked.

"Not exactly." Eva twisted a dish towel in her hands. "I mean, I am grateful for my two girls, you know that," she began in a quavering voice. "But, well . . ." A tear slipped down her cheek. "A man wants a son, doesn't he?"

Hannah bristled at the words. Oh, she had heard them hundreds of times from the women who wanted her services, but to have her own sister say them was worse. "I don't wonder if that's just the excuse women give for what *they* want," she snapped. Usually Hannah would have been more sympathetic, but Eva had put her off all afternoon. Besides, she was tired of Eva's complaints that neither of her children was perfect. Whose were? Isabel was a pretty girl of nine, with big brown eyes and an adorable dimpled chin, but nowhere near as bright as her younger sister, Doreen, who was plumper and more sallow—not unlike her namesake, Eva and Hannah's sister, Dora, who had died in a fire—but she was extremely intelligent. "The smartest of them all," Lazar had said as a backhanded compliment. This had been a relief to Eva, who had been reluctant at first to name a child after her retarded sister, until Hannah assured her that Dora's disability had come from the trauma of her breech birth, and had not been an inherent defect.

Her sister continued to weep, so Hannah softened her words. "Frankly, Eva, I have no confidence that anything anyone does makes a difference."

"That's not what I m-meant . . ." she stammered. "What's the matter with me? Why do I get everything wrong?"

This self-pity did not move Hannah either, for she didn't think Eva was genuinely sorry for the pain she had caused their aunt.

"You can help me, I know you can!"

"All right," Hannah said with resignation. Giving in to her sister was probably the easiest way to be finished with her. "What can I do for you?"

"Doreen is six already and still no more babies."

"You've wanted more since then?" Hannah was surprised, for her sister had never seemed especially maternal.

"Yes, and nothing happens. I mean, Napthali cooperates," she added quickly, so Hannah would not think less of her husband.

"I could give you a chart showing the best days, if you don't know them already. How often does your monthly come?"

"Once a month!" Eva sniffed back her tears and forced a slight smile. "Actually, I am lucky, it's only every thirty-five or thirty-six days."

Hannah felt this might be a simple case. "So, when do you think you would have the best chance?"

"Everyone knows that you tell women to follow the Orthodox rules, so somewhere around the twelfth to fourteenth day."

"Counting from when?"

"From the first bleeding?"

"Yes, that would be true for a woman who has a typical twenty-eight-day cycle, but actually you must count backward."

"I don't understand," Eva said, straining to follow.

"Look, if a woman's menstruation begins twenty-eight

days after the last one and you subtract fourteen, the four-teenth day is best. However, if you subtract fourteen from say, thirty-six, you get the twenty-second day."

Astonishment lit Eva's face. "I've been more than a week off!"

"In your case I would concentrate the effort between the twentieth and twenty-fourth days."

"Do you think it will work?"

"Try it, and if it doesn't, come see me in . . . six months."

Eva's relief was so obvious, Hannah was chagrined by her reluctance to help her. Why would she give advice to anyone who walked in off the street with more generosity than her own sister? She reached out and gave Eva a consoling pat. Her sister smiled in gratitude.

Mama came in carrying a tray of glasses. She looked at her daughters. No, they had not been quarreling. Her face relaxed. "Doreen had two pieces of cake and she wants more milk."

"Mama, you know she shouldn't . . ." Eva admonished, but her voice was softer, less complaining than usual.

↝ 9 ↜

Babies. Either you wanted them desperately or you were desperate not to have them! Hannah thought about how different Eva was from Minna, then about Mrs. Tartaglia and the women who wanted male children, as well as those like Mrs. Sachs, who were willing to maim themselves before having another. Was there not some way to bring balance into this chaotic world?

In early April a meeting of all Bellevue midwives was called by order of the head of the hospital and the Board of Managers. Hannah had been asked to take the day shift, with two nights off in exchange, and the students were to attend the patients, with several midwives stationed by the door of the lecture hall, to be summoned only in case of emergencies. In all her time on the staff or in training Hannah had never heard of such contingencies, and so she, like the others, expected disturbing news.

The meeting was opened by Mrs. Hemming, but after a few curt announcements she turned the floor over to Dr. George Madden, Medical Superintendent.

"As we speak in the comparable quiet of this meeting room, the German onslaught continues. While our noble leaders make every attempt to steer a course toward peace, those of us who must prepare for the worst foresee the tragic day coming ever closer when America must join hands across the sea. To be prudent, we are forming the Bellevue unit. Mrs. Hemming is calling in the finest nurses among alumnae of the Bellevue Training School from as far away as Boston, Pittsburgh, Philadelphia, and of course from our own community. Experience, endurance, judgment, and the ability to cooperate are the main qualities we are seeking. While Mrs. Hemming has valiantly agreed to head the unit herself, we have made the decision that we will need her talents at home, first to organize the unit, and second to assist the overworked staff in getting through the worst epidemic of infantile paralysis the country has ever seen. In her stead, the worthy Miss Beatrice Stamber, formerly superintendent of nurses at Harlem Hospital, has been assigned the job."

Hannah took a long inward breath. Hopefully Mrs. Hemming would be too busy to fuss about insignificant details and even the infraction list might have to be abandoned. Not that she would let up her guard entirely, but this almost made up for the trials of being short-staffed.

The doctor droned on solemnly. "Training-school nurses will be borrowed from every division of the hospital, and the maternity pavilion is no exception. Because of our confidence in the abilities of our midwives, we know you will pitch in to assist one another, even if some of the duties formally relegated to the nursing students must become your added burden during these trying times. Your goodwill and forbearance will be appreciated until a peaceful solution to the tragic conflagration has been found. Dr. Dowd . . ."

A flurry of applause followed the seconds of silence as the midwives realized the sacrifice they were supposed to make.

"Ladies, be assured that the physicians on the obstetrics and gynecological staff of the hospital are in full sympathy for your plight," Dr. Dowd began. "Fortunately, few of us in this department have been asked to respond to be trained for Europe, but we will be doing double duty to cover general medicine. However, we have pledged more time to assist in the midwifery pavilion, so do not hesitate to call on us for consultation, or if the census is unusually high, to ask us to manage a ward if you are shorthanded." He smiled benevolently at the group of nodding heads. Dr. Madden had picked the right man to administer the bitter pill, for the raven-haired doctor with the smooth cheeks and piercing eyes knew how to modulate his bass voice to induce women to do what he wanted.

"Another matter must be addressed today." Dr. Dowd cleared his throat. "Those of us who daily face the miseries that follow as the result of human frailty may not always agree with the wisdom of our spiritual and political leaders. Nevertheless, while we may rule our little kingdoms in the wards and surgical theaters, we are not immune to the laws of society."

Hannah looked around. Others were as puzzled as she.

Mrs. Hemming handed some papers to the doctor. He held them up to the group. "These have been making an appearance in the postpartum ward."

Hannah recognized them at once. In fact, she had brought in a sheaf herself. They were the handbills promoting Margaret Sanger's clinic. Minna had done the translation for the one in Yiddish. They had also been printed in English and Italian and read:

MOTHERS!
Can you afford to have a large family?
Do you want any more children?
If not, why do you have them?
DO NOT KILL, DO NOT TAKE LIFE, BUT PREVENT.
Safe, Harmless Information can
be obtained of trained Nurses
at
46 AMBOY STREET
Near Pitkin Avenue—Brooklyn
Tell Your Friends and Neighbors. All Mothers Welcome.
A registration fee of 10 cents entitles any mother
to this information.

"No matter what I may think about this subject, no matter your personal belief, information on the prevention of conception may not be distributed within the walls of Bellevue Hospital and Allied Hospitals of the City of New York or by any employee on the outside either, since these actions would reflect on the hospital."

Rumblings in the audience visibly disturbed Dr. Madden, who glowered down from the platform. Dr. Dowd did not seem ruffled. Something in his demeanor, which was humbler than his words, heartened Hannah. Almost apologetically he held up his hand. "Let me explain even further. Just this week, Dr. Mary Halton, a staff doctor at Gouverneur's Hospital, was forced to resign her post after she prescribed a diaphragm to a woman with severe tuberculosis. Now, I will admit that in that particular case, even I might have been convinced that such a clear indication that the woman's life would have been endangered by pregnancy might have been the exception to the law, but obviously the authorities disagreed. As on the frontlines in Europe, where valiant soldiers risk their all for world peace, others will wage the battles for reproductive rights. Here in the field hospital, we must manage the wounds as best as we can given the commands, which come from the leaders we have selected to follow." There was a hollowness to his grandiose words. He looked around at the disappointed faces of his staff. Dr. Dowd's voice deepened to add authority. "So there will be no misunderstanding, any information on the prevention of conception, whether direct or indirect, or any referral to a clinic, doctor, midwife, or nurse who may provide it, is expressly forbidden by the Board of Bellevue Hospital. Any staff member who willfully disobeys this injunction will be dismissed without recourse. In the future, when or if the legal aspects of reproductive laws are altered, a new policy will be forthcoming. Until then we will respect the wishes of the state of New York, as well as the Hippocratic oath, and do our best to preserve and promote health and life." When he sat down, there was no applause. In the silence Dr. Madden stood and mumbled a few closing words before the midwives trooped out in silence.

Hannah should have expected this, but somehow Dr. Dowd's pronouncement came as a shock. In her mind there was no argument but that birth control should be completely legal. It harmed nobody. Family limitation was the only sensible solution to myriad social and health issues. Everyone thought that with a lunatic like Comstock out of the way, the

laws would either be changed or ignored, certainly not en-
forced with such vehemence. But they had been wrong. In
the last few weeks not only Emma Goldman but her companion, Ben Reitman, had been arrested for distributing birth
control pamphlets; and he had been given sixty days in the
workhouse. More and more of their friends joined this exclusive club. May Jessie Ashley, Ida Rauh Eastman, and
Bolton Hall also had been arrested for offering one of Emma
Goldman's publications. Margaret Sanger's camp eclipsed
them when one of their intellectual supporters, Van Kleeck
Allison, was arrested for distributing one of her booklets to
a group of factory workers and was given the worst sentence
yet: three years in the house of correction. Until women had
an equal vote with men, none of this would change, Hannah
decided.

On the wards the grumblings of her staff were disheart-
ening. "This is not Dr. Dowd's doing," Norma Marshanck
whispered. "Mrs. You-know-who is behind this, mark my
words!"

Surprisingly, the oldest midwives were the most vocal.
Sarah Brink said, "Women have begged me for years to help
them prevent a baby, and until recently I have not had anything useful to offer. Now that there are devices that women
can use safely and reliably, they are forbidden."

Mrs. Marshanck was even more vitriolic. "Those who
have will always be in control. Don't tell me that those rich
politicians have managed to keep the size of their families
down by merely employing admirable restraint! They have
used French letters for years, while forcing their concept of
virtue on the poor."

The soothing voice was heard from Millicent Toomey.
"Can't you see that because of what happened at
Gouverneur's, the doctors have to make a public show of
disapproval? A quiet word here and there won't ever be discovered."

"I think we should be very careful," Alice Brody, the
youngest midwife, replied anxiously. "With the war and everything, we cannot afford to lose any more midwives."

Norma Marshanck glowered at the girl, but Sarah Brink
stepped between them. "I've two patients about to pop, so I
could use some assistance." Alice stood up, relieved to escape.

With that the group dispersed, leaving Hannah perplexed

about what she could do to improve morale. Instead she decided to tackle some overdue paperwork—her perpetual nemesis—and let the midwives cool off by becoming immersed in the daily routine.

Later that morning, Dr. Dowd sent word he wanted to see Hannah. He probably knew that she had been responsible for some of the leaflets and perhaps knew of her ties to Margaret Sanger. For a moment she was tempted to take a stand and refuse to comply with the new regulations, but where would that get her? Out on the street, that's where! These days Lazar's income was better, but she never knew when he would get paid, and the source of his consulting was still mysterious. He was getting published more often, but that did not account for the bills and coins that he handed over at intervals not concurrent with his publication. When she alluded to this, he had put her off by saying, "Collecting the fee is the hardest part of writing." As it was, she dared not jeopardize her hospital position. The base that Bellevue offered was too valuable. However, since what she did in Dr. Jaffe's office could not be traced, she could continue to tell her private patients they could go to Brownsville.

"Thank you for coming so quickly," Dr. Dowd said as she appeared by his door, which had been opened in advance. "How is the census this afternoon?"

"Average, about four to a ward and nothing particularly interesting except a girl who may not even be twelve."

"Children having children." He shook his head sadly. "Now, that's a case that would never have benefited from birth control, even if it had been available. The man would never have employed it, and she would not have known to search for it." Deciding it was best not to take the role of a sympathizer, Hannah did not respond. Dr. Dowd shuffled some papers. "By the way, I had a case not unlike the one you brought to me last year."

Hannah perked up. "What did you discover?" she asked, barely controlling her excitement that there had been another highly orgasmic woman.

"That the pessary also caused a raging infection. I am compiling data that may point to surgical intervention much earlier, as well as doing away with pessaries altogether."

This was only another prolapse, Hannah realized with a sinking feeling. "But Mrs. Czachorwski had a reason for her poor hygiene. If douching is done daily . . ."

"You forget that the sanitary conditions in many homes makes cleansing the area as often as necessary an impossibility." Dr. Dowd threw up his hands. "Unfortunately, we cannot cure the ills of the world. That's why I have limited my practice to below the waist." He grinned up at Hannah, who had not taken a seat.

There was nothing malicious in his expression, but she did not accept it well. Another day perhaps, when he had not stood against the rights of women, but at this moment she found his words offensive. He gestured for her to sit. She remained standing. "I'll have to go back in a few minutes."

"No, there is another matter," he insisted forcefully.

Hannah knew an order when she heard one. As she sat down, she took her time arranging her skirts, then folded her hands in her lap like an obedient servant.

The doctor saw through her act. "Come now, Mrs. Sokolow, there is no need for us to be in opposition. I admire you greatly. You can't be angry at me because I have my job to do." He gave a musical sigh. "Women always are complaining they are downtrodden, but they do not realize that men must respond to a hierarchy as well. We all have superiors, and I certainly have my share of difficult ones. Also, we must bow to many masters: money, the law, expedience, our parents, wives, and children, family expectations, our roles in society, the tenets of our religion, not to mention the forces of nature, the laws of chemistry. We men, as much as women, are prisoners of our bodies, our age . . ." Where was all this leading? Why did he want her sympathy? She had always liked the man. He was the best sort of doctor for a midwife: concerned, but not interfering. When he was needed, he stepped in and offered his expertise without condescension. That is why the midwives sought him out, and why—after they had checked who else was on duty—they sometimes tried to handle complications that were beyond them rather than subject themselves to the ridicule of the more arrogant members of the medical staff.

"I should be going back . . ." Hannah said when he did not continue. His penetrating eyes, the color of Benny's deepest blue marble, bore into her, keeping her riveted to her chair.

"Do you continue to see private patients?" he asked in an offhand manner.

"Yes, Doctor." Was this it? Could Mrs. Church or Mrs. Hemming have discussed their questions about her outside activities with him? Was he going to give her an ultimatum, or had he already supposed she would defy him when she was away from the hospital?

"Do you have many interesting cases?"

"What do you mean?" she asked cautiously.

"Like that Polish woman."

"She was unique."

"Indeed. The difficulty with my speciality is that I get only those who are *in extremis*—those who require a highly trained surgeon. I regret that I was never able to witness the intriguing aspects of that situation."

Hannah relaxed. Why had she been so suspicious of the doctor when all he wanted was some collegial discussion on gynecological matters? "I do have another curious case . . ."

"Yes?" His bushy brows, so thick yet so tidy she speculated whether he combed them, lifted expectantly.

"A girl of seventeen, recently married, with a severe case of vaginismus."

"Are you certain?"

"Well, it is the first one I have encountered." She gave a modest laugh. "I usually am called a little later in the game."

"Does she have the classic symptoms with the musculature of the vaginal entrance locked in a violent, involuntary spasm, which prevents the entrance of the male organ?"

"Yes, she has that."

"And you have ruled out a urethral caruncle or a hyperesthesia of the mucous membrane?"

"Certainly," Hannah replied defensively. "Also, there are no signs of varicose veins or prolapse of the urethral mucous membrane, fissures of the fourchette, or neuroma of the fossa navicularis."

The doctor gave his head a deferential tilt. "Then you have eliminated a general irritability due to masturbation."

His use of the word, especially the manner in which he drew out the syllables, made her so uncomfortable that she wished she had not mentioned Stella in the first place. "Actually, she does have such a history, including punishment for that activity, which may have had a psychological effect on the problem."

"How did you discover that?"

"She told me."

"That is where you women have an advantage," the doctor said with a shake of his head. Hannah watched as each strand of hair fell back smoothly into place. The doctor was extraordinarily handsome, something he used to his advantage, even in the midst of this discussion. His voice softened purposefully. "Tell me, does her spasm include the entire musculature of the perineum, anus, and bladder?"

"No. Does it usually?" she asked, while thinking that she was one woman at least who would not be swayed by his charms.

"Only in severe cases." He was thoughtful for a few moments. "When I was in school, my instructor lectured about one peculiar case." He leaned back in his chair and stared off into the distance. "While the spasm usually comes on with the first approach of the male organ, in this instance the woman was able to relax sufficiently to permit penetration, but then her muscle clamped down, creating *penis captivus.*" He gave an exaggerated wince. "The greater the husband's attempt to withdraw, the more severe the spasm became. While one would think that this would cause his organ to shrink, the opposite occurred because the interference with the return of blood to the male organ caused it to continue to enlarge." He waited to see if Hannah was sufficiently alarmed, then his eyes twinkled mischievously. "Fortunately for this terrified couple, a servant was called and she summoned a doctor."

"What could be done?"

"It was necessary to chloroform the female in order to release the penis from the spasm. That is a true case," he added to Hannah's incredulous expression. "Now, tell me, what are you doing about a cure?"

For a moment Hannah had forgotten about Stella, but then recovered enough to continue. "As I mentioned, I have talked to her and given her certain exercises to relax the muscle."

Dr. Dowd pursed his lips while mulling over his response. "I agree that there is probably an underlying neurotic aspect and that certain events in her past may have predisposed her to the affliction, but you are dealing with a situation requiring medical attention."

"What would you suggest?"

"The literature is filled with good results from surgical intervention."

"No!" Hannah rose in her chair slightly.

"But she is a young woman. Surely she would want to live a normal life, have a family ..." he said soothingly.

"It's monstrous!"

"The only other way is even more awkward."

"What do you mean?"

"Once or twice a month a physician anesthetizes the wife, since the spasm subsides completely when the woman is relaxed, and her husband can proceed to have ethereal relations with her for the purpose of reproduction or to preserve the marriage."

"What sort of marriage would it be if the man merely uses the woman as a vessel?"

"Not much different from countless others," he replied drolly. Seeing Hannah's opposition, his tone changed. "In any case, I would not put that forward as my first choice. Since surgery would remove the obstacle, it would be foolish to ignore that simple solution to a painful problem." He swiveled in his chair and reached for a book. "Do you read German?"

"A bit," she hedged. Since much of Yiddish was similar, she could usually make out the context.

He handed her the volume by Schmidtmann, *Handbuch der gerichtlichen Medizin, 1905,* opened to the middle. "This technique has been successful for more than twenty years."

"What does the surgery entail?" Hannah asked, even though she suspected that no matter the explanation, she would oppose it.

"Hirst's operation consists of one median perineal incision of ample length and depth to thoroughly divide the attachment of the transverse fibers of the levator ani muscle. This is then sutured in the opposite direction—that is, from side to side—and gives a much enlarged vaginal opening that will not close down as healing takes place."

"How does that affect the contractile action of the bulbocavernosi and levator ani muscles?"

"They are lessened, of course, but that is what is necessary to relieve the condition."

"Then forever after the vulvovaginal orifice will gape open."

"Yes, but once the wounds have mended, there should be no discomfort—and no necessity for an episiotomy later, may I add."

There was a knock on the door. Hannah jumped slightly. Dr. Dowd merely called, "Yes?" in his mellifluous voice.

Norma Marshanck's head poked inside the partially opened door. "Mrs. Sokolow, how soon will you be able to return to the pavilion?"

Hannah glanced at the doctor as she rose in her chair. He nodded that she might leave. "Tell them I'll be there momentarily." The other midwife left at once. "I'll consider your opinion," Hannah responded formally.

"Let me add one more point," the doctor continued thickly. "You may spend weeks or months with dilators or exercises or other palliative measures, but the husband's and wife's anxiety will continue to expand, eating away at any chance of a contented future. A few hours of surgery, a few days in the hospital, the burden is lifted, and they can go on to establish their life together."

"I will discuss this with my patient," Hannah said with one foot out the door.

"That is all I ask." He beamed from behind his desk. "And one more request . . ."

"Yes?"

"I would appreciate the opportunity to examine her. True vaginismus is rare. Even Dr. Blühner has not seen one in many years."

"I'll let you know," Hannah said, shutting the door behind her.

As soon as she rounded the bend in the hall, Norma Marshanck was waiting. "What's wrong?" Hannah asked, concerned.

Norma winked. "You were gone so long, we thought you could use a break from that tyrant."

"He's hardly that."

"Wasn't he reading you the riot act about your associations with the radicals?"

"Not at all. In fact, I think he is sympathetic to the cause, but because of his position, he cannot let his true feelings be known."

"Oh." Mrs. Marshanck gave Hannah a queer look, which she understood immediately. If she was defending the man who was currently out of favor, she must have reasons for protecting him. Many a nurse was quite forward with her appreciation for the doctor, but he had never been linked with any scandal. What did she recall hearing about his wife? Her name was Lulu something—but not Dowd—and she was an actress—no, a singer—and supposedly quite a beauty. Were there children? Hannah's drifting mind snapped back to the immediate issue.

"We were discussing some of my private cases," she said matter-of-factly as they made their way down the hall. "He has been treating a woman for an infection from a pessary and wanted to caution me."

"That's interesting . . ." the other midwife replied without conviction. Then a crash of metal from the ward across the hall caught their attention, and both hurried to see what—or who—had fallen.

10

"I want you to examine me," Stella Applebaum said the moment Hannah closed the door to her small office. "Can we go in the other room?"

Without a word Hannah gestured for Stella to lead the way. The girl was wearing a new outfit in the latest style: the hem of her pea green skirt reached only halfway between knee and ankle and her short coat came up above the shirt. A generous fur trim around the collar and cuffs was an advertisement for her father's profession, and the choice of the rich golden pelt complimented Stella's smooth face and slender arms. For the first time her patient looked—and behaved—like a woman old enough to be married.

Hannah closed the door to the examining room and offered to take the girl's garments and hang them up. Curious as to why the demand, she suppressed the urge to question her. This would be only the second examination. Hannah was interested to see what changes there were. As she watched Stella undressing with so much more confidence than on the first occasion, she had the wild hope that a complete cure had been effected. She handed Stella the drape. The girl wrapped herself almost as tightly as before, and when Hannah turned, she was shaking. At Hannah's approach, she flinched, but then seemed to control herself.

Hannah began by pressing on her abdomen lightly, as she might with a woman whose pregnancy she suspected. There was no swelling, although this was not an impossibility if Bernard had managed to ejaculate in the vicinity of her vulva. This time she placed each foot in the stirrups at the end of the table, but did not move them very far apart. Stella's legs shuddered. Hannah was about to insert her fingers, forgetting all about the warm oil, but when she looked up and saw her patient biting her lip and staring at the ceiling, she gave the thigh a pat and went to prepare more carefully.

"Now I will touch you slowly. Tell me if I am to stop." Stella gave an unintelligible murmur. Glancing at the golden pubis and slender legs, Hannah thought of the young husband, who had to be entranced by his fetching bride. Few girls were as lovely from this perspective, or as utterly frustrating in their resistance, she realized. The bruises on her thighs had healed, and only a yellowed patch remained. Her outer lips were moister than in the past, a positive sign. Without thinking, Hannah inserted her first and second fingers—the ones she would normally employ—instead of the smallest one as she had previously. The longer second finger touched the edge of the offending muscle, but found it spongier, somewhat less defiant than before. Thanks to the slippery oil, her first finger was able to stray past the entrance as well. Hannah held the two fingers still inside the vaginal opening for a few seconds, then moved them back and forth a few millimeters. The muscle contracted around them, but then seemed to open more widely. She might have penetrated even farther, but decided against it. Dr. Dowd's caution not to waste time with dilating and kind words echoed in her mind, but this was so much more progress than she had expected, she was more hopeful than ever that he could be wrong. She withdrew, turned around, and went to wipe her hands.

"That's all," she said with her back to Stella. "Meet me in the office when you are ready," she said, closing the door.

Always with Stella she felt she was part of a charade that had to be played correctly or not at all. Thus far that day she had done what seemed right by allowing Stella to display her achievement. She had accepted the results impassively, as though they were the routine, expected responses of a healing patient.

"I can see why you wanted me to observe you today. Your

progress is excellent. Now you must continue the same way." She held out her hand and showed the width of her two fingers. "You experienced no discomfort with this much stretching, so you should do about the same. Unless you have a problem, don't come to see me for two weeks, but try to move the two fingers around. Don't forget the oil to make it easier."

"When my mother first told me to come to you, I did not want to, and even when I did, I was doubtful you could help me." She chuckled. "I liked the part about the cat. If I think of it like something that is not a part of me, it is much easier. Is there anything else I could do?"

For a moment she considered Dr. Dowd's suggestions, then discounted them entirely. "No, you are doing better than most," Hannah exaggerated, thinking that anything that would bolster her confidence could not be wrong.

"My mother said that you might have to cut me . . ."

"When?" Hannah asked with alarm. Had Mrs. Starr been to a doctor who had recommended surgery?

"Before the first visit. She said she knew someone whose husband could not break her virginity."

"That's not your difficulty," Hannah said firmly, since all the mother had been referring to was an obstinate hymen. The concept of any other surgery appalled her because this child had the most beautiful, intact perineum. To carve it up to make her accessible—no! the idea was too repugnant, except maybe as a last resort . . .

An idea began to form. For a while she had thought that this Bernard may have been a bit of a rogue, especially because of the bruising injuries, but Maxine had supplanted the husband as the cause of the anguish. The boy was probably young and inexperienced, but if he was studying medicine, he was not stupid. "I think the time has come to include Bernard," she said adamantly. She watched Stella's expression. Her pink lips parted, but nothing was said. "First, you show him what you are doing, but don't make it like a hospital. Keep the lights dim, lie back on the bed, and relax. He must wash his hands and use the oil. If you are comfortable with two fingers, let him try only one, since his are probably larger. Tell him to go slowly, to be gentle, and to pretend he is taming an animal. Let him know about the cat. Also tell him when you want him to stop. And then—" She observed Stella carefully. The girl's eyes were wide and she was leaning forward. "You ask him what you might do to tame his animal. Do you understand?"

Stella nodded sagely. "I've touched him before."

"You gave him pleasure?"

"I think so."

"It's only fair, since he is waiting for you to be ready."

Her expression changed. "You won't tell my mother I did that, will you?"

"What has any of this got to do with your mother?"

"You are her friend."

"You are the one consulting with me, not her. Besides, now that she's moved uptown, I rarely see her." Hannah looked at Stella with mock annoyance. "The hardest part about being married is realizing that you have left your home forever. That is not to say you must not honor your parents for many years to come, but from now on your husband and your marriage come first. Everything else is in the past, including what your mother said you could and could not do or say . . . or touch."

The sparkle in Stella's eyes was heartening. She stood to conclude the visit. "In two weeks I want you to report to me not only how your muscle is relaxing, but three things that Bernard did to you that felt wonderful and three things that you did to him that he liked."

If Stella was astonished, she tried to hide it with a flurry of words about her gratitude. Hannah waved her off, feeling buoyant herself.

❦ 11 ❦

Stella did not keep her next appointment, but Hannah was too busy to realize she had not been in until several days had passed. Even then she was not alarmed. When a woman was menstruating she would avoid an examination, or she might have been ill, or too busy. Rachael often complained that the problem with her patients was that once they recovered she never saw them again, and in many cases she never had the certainty of a recovery to close the file. Maybe they had worsened and had gone somewhere else, maybe they were dissatisfied with the doctor, maybe they died. Hannah hardly thought Stella would have succumbed from her condition, but by the fourth week she had begun to think she had been too insistent, or had pushed Stella too far too soon. If she had experienced pain again, they would be back where they began. Perhaps Dr. Dowd had been right after all. Why had she responded so vehemently against surgery? Hadn't Mrs. Czachorwski's life been saved by Dr. Dowd, and was he not the preeminent surgeon at the hospital? He had spared dozens of mothers and babies with his cesareans, managed complicated deliveries with the judicious application of forceps, and his work with cancerous tumors was legion. Besides, it had been unfair for her to make a decision without consulting Stella. The next time she came Hannah would explain how surgery could benefit her. The girl was intrepid—or used to be—so she might not find the proposal all that frightening. And wouldn't Maxine be pleased with so swift a solution?

At the end of that week, Hannah arrived at St. Mark's Place to meet Rachael. They had planned to review the monies due Hannah based on a formula that Rachael had devised but Hannah barely understood. When she opened the door, Stella stood up.

"They said you would be here. I hope you don't mind me waiting for you," she said in a rush.

Stella looked adorable in a peach dress with a matching ribbon pulling back her honey curls. It took Hannah a moment to realize a man was by her side. He was much taller than her, and darker, with thick curly hair and a pink protruding lower lip that was appealing. He had taken Stella's arm, and both were beaming.

"Would you like to come into my office?" Hannah asked uneasily, since she was not certain whether the invitation should be extended to one or both.

Stella did not drop Bernard's arm. They entered the room together.

"We just wanted to thank you," Bernard began in a rumbling bass voice that seemed out of place coming from his boyish face.

Before Hannah closed the door, Stella gushed, "I'm sorry I missed my appointment, but it was the wrong time of the month, and then it wasn't really necessary."

"So," Hannah said, folding her hands together as she low-ered herself into her chair. There wasn't room for both of them to sit. Bernard leaned against the wall, while Stella took the other chair. "Everything is better now?"

"Yes, perfect." Stella smiled up at Bernard.

"There is no pain at all?" Hannah asked hesitantly. She wanted to know much more, but did not want to embarrass either of them.

"Well, sometimes in certain ways ..." Stella admitted. "But nothing that can't be eased quickly, by—you know—trying other positions."

"Good, good," Hannah murmured as she tried to think of what to ask next. "What do you think helped the most? I ask so I can pass it on to the next patient."

"The oil!" Stella giggled. "And the part about taming the animals."

For a moment Hannah had a crazy image of Stella and Bernard dressed like circus performers cracking whips at lions in a cage, but it passed, and a picture of Stella strapped to her bed as a child supplanted it. She smiled at Bernard. He was looking down at his wife dreamily. A fine young man, she decided, banishing any ideas that he had been cruel to her. And they are well matched. About that, at least, the mother had been correct.

While it seemed obvious that Stella believed she was cured, Hannah was anxious to know exactly how far the muscle had relaxed. Was Stella's vagina that of a normal woman with only a little sexual experience, or had they es-tablished some compromise that did not include full penetra-tion? The way to find out was to examine Stella, but unless she suggested the procedure, Hannah had no reason to de-mand one. So far Stella was silent, yet Hannah had to know! Why? she asked herself and then was not proud of her an-swer: to report her success to Dr. Dowd in full clinical de-tail.

Hannah admonished herself. For now these children were content. Stella had the adoring expression that did not come spontaneously with the marriage vows, but could only be carned. If matters were not perfect yet, Hannah felt certain they would be someday.

"Is there anything else I can do for you?" she asked as a matter of form.

Bernard cleared his throat. "Well, Mrs. Sokolow, as you

know, I am studying medicine ..." Stella nudged him.
"... And I am interested in gynecology. Maybe someday
you would direct me to some readings ..."

"Start with Havelock Ellis," she suggested, "but don't pay
any attention to Krafft-Ebing," she added as an afterthought.
Even if the boy needed information on those perversions for
his studies, it would be better to discover them later, rather
than too early, in his marriage.

"Do I need to see you again?" Stella asked wistfully.

"Only if you have a difficulty or ..."—her eyes
sparkled—"... you start a baby."

〰 12 〰

If Hannah had wanted to talk to someone to find a way to
help Stella Applebaum, she wanted even more to boast of
her success. In all her reading she had not seen a formula for
curing this predicament so simply, but without the clinical
data from the final internal examination, she could not approach Dr. Dowd. Besides, the changes in the hospital
schedule due to the shortage of personnel left her too weary
to attend to anything more than the routine responsibilities.
In order to manage her flourishing practice at St. Mark's
Place, she accepted one twelve-hour weekend shift, usually
at night to make up for the accommodation of her other assignments to give three nights off a week. Mama had been
having arthritic attacks, so Hannah also was doing her shopping and cleaning after she came home. Eva was too far uptown to be of much help, although she did come by on the
Saturdays when Hannah worked—well, most Saturdays—
and Mama preferred not to ask Minna, even though her
daughter-in-law had offered.

On that Thursday evening in late April, Hannah had
brought a piece of fish downstairs for Mama and asked
Benny to supervise its heating while running back upstairs to
make certain the kugel wouldn't burn in her own oven when
Lazar burst through the door grinning widely.

"We've got to go to Carnegie Hall."

"Ha! The farthest I'm going is from here to the bed."

"But E. G. has just been released from the Queens County Jail. We're gathering to welcome her back."

"Who will be there?"

"That gynecologist friend of Emma's, Ben Reitman. Do you think it's just a coincidence that Emma Goldman, Margaret Sanger, Dr. Lorber, Ben Reitman, and how many others were first trained in women's health?" he prodded to garner her interest.

"I know all about that supposed connection between anarchy and women's rights." She suppressed a yawn as Lazar went into the kitchen, poured her some cold tea.

"This might perk you up." He made certain she took a few sips, then continued, "The same demands for women to sacrifice, abnegate, and submit are what keep the workers in their place. Besides, Kollontai believes that anyone who brings babies into the world must be in harmony with the basic issues of life, and anyone in harmony with the basic issues cares about not only the betterment of some select individuals but about humanity as a whole."

Hannah did not commit herself, but was beginning to feel as if she should attend ... if Lazar and the children could manage to get dinner on the table. "How about a little male sacrifice, like taking the kugel out of the oven, so I can rest for an hour?" she bantered back as she put up her feet.

"At your service," he said with an elaborate bow.

Outside the lecture hall, they met up with the Herzogs and other familiar faces. Ezekiel pointed out Max Eastman arguing with someone. "What do you suppose that's about?"

Lazar glanced in time to see Eastman as he raised his fist, then spun around, and pushed his way to the street. He passed right by them.

"Max?" Herzog called. "Where are you going?"

At that Eastman turned and bumped into Lazar. "Sorry, but I am leaving."

"Aren't you going to preside?" Lazar asked.

"Not if they let Reitman speak. His crude sexual allusions aren't any help to the cause," he explained before storming off.

"But, who is going to do it?" Lazar inquired to his back.

"You are!" Ezekiel Herzog said, with a cuff on Lazar's shoulder.

"Me? Nobody knows me."

"All the better," guffawed Herzog. "Just give the introduction and get off the stage."

Lazar preened at the honor. Hannah went to sit by Rachael and her husband. It took a long time for the audience to settle, and for a while Hannah thought Max Eastman had changed his mind. Then Lazar strode out on the stage, his back slightly bent, his neck gawking out, broadcasting his lack of ease.

"Max Eastman will not be speaking this evening," Lazar said. He had to clear his throat, but did so discreetly. "A few minutes ago he said he would not preside if Ben Reitman should be allowed to speak. In view of Eastman's past insistence on the right of free speech, doesn't that make his act even more incomprehensible?"

Oh no! thought Hannah. Why had Lazar taken this opportunity to lambast Eastman? Didn't he ever want to be published in *The Masses* again? And if he didn't care about that, Eastman knew everyone in the radical press, and could ruin Lazar before his reputation was established.

Seeming not to care about the consequences, Lazar babbled on. "What does this tell us? Does it not show how poorly some of the alleged radicals in America have grasped the true meaning of freedom, and how little they care about its actual application in life?" Lazar took a long breath and seemed to forget what he was to say next. Recovering, he hurried into the first introduction.

Next, Rosa Pastor Stokes talked about how birth control had ceased to be a mere theoretical issue and would take its place as a vital part of the social struggle. "Deeds, not words, will lead to victory!" she concluded to robust applause. Then, direct from the platform, she distributed leaflets on contraception.

At last Reitman came on stage. His flesh had a waxy glaze, which gave him the shiny pallor of an embalmed corpse. His voice was scratchy, but his words made everyone sit up straighter. "I am not here to speak for myself, and certainly I am not here to speak for Emma, for as we all know, she does this quite well herself." He paused for the expected laughter. "At the trial, the prosecutor referred to me as Emma Goldman's advertising man. Perhaps some of you suspected I took offense at this. In fact, I did not, for it is my privilege to think of myself as a sort of advance agent for social revolution. Unfortunately, family limitation is one small cog in the revolutionary wheel, the wheel that has begun turning and will not stop until injustice and tyranny are blotted from this earth."

So far, so good, Hannah thought, pleased that Mr. Eastman's dire predictions had not come true.

Reitman went on to talk about how Emma had the consolation of her principles, and this made it easy to survive the forces designed to crush the prisoner. "A few hours ago, when I clasped her hand once again, her exact words were: 'But having such an ideal, the fifteen days were a lark to me.'" He paused until the clapping subsided. Then he dropped the bombshell. "Although Emma Goldman will continue to lecture on this essential topic—the one she feels is crucial for women—I have suggested she omit detailed instructions about contraceptive methods, which women can better learn from each other in private. Too many other issues require her attention for her to risk further imprisonment for this cause alone . . ." His next words were drowned out by angry shouts, and while he tried to make his summary, the meeting broke up in turmoil.

Exhausted, Hannah had been ready to leave, and this was a welcome relief. If everything had been more congenial, Lazar might have preferred to stay on, basking in his success. Or worse, he might have wanted to go to a café to extend the evening. As it was, he hurried her into a subway, with thoughtful words about her long, tiring day. Once the train pulled out of the station he threw back his head and laughed heartily. "What a turn of events! Only a few weeks ago Ben completed an article for *Mother Earth* on his arrest, saying that if the authorities think we are going like lambs to the slaughter, they are mistaken. He wrote, 'We believe in birth control enough to go to jail, to the gallows, if necessary.' I wish I could send everyone I disagree with to prison, if this is what the workhouse does to a man's principles."

"I think you missed his point." Hannah leaned against her husband's shoulder and closed her eyes. "He thinks Emma and her comrades are more effective out of jail than behind bars."

Lazar did not respond, but she felt his body stiffen. Slowly Hannah sat up again. The subway car was coming into a station, the one where they would transfer. "Stay down," Lazar said, forcefully pushing her back on the bench. He leaned against her, keeping his head below the window line.

"What is—?" He held his hand over her mouth and pretended to be in a drunken stupor until the doors closed.

"Are you crazy? We missed our stop!"

"We'll walk from the next one."

"Across town at this time of night?" She stared at him furiously. "What's going on?" she demanded.

"There was someone I didn't want to see."

Hannah tried to translate the message in her husband's shifting eyes. "What is this about, Lazar?"

"You know, politics."

"No, I don't know!"

"I have been taking some unpopular positions lately."

"Stupid ones, if you ask me. How could you malign Eastman after all he has done for you?"

"What has he done for me? He published one story, then rejected everything else."

"He got you started. Without him you would not be making such good wages."

"He may have harmed me more than helped," Lazar responded lamely.

"I don't see . . ." she trailed off. There was something else, something about money, that was bothering Lazar, but what could seeing someone in the subway have to do with that?

The train slowed again. "You're right," Lazar said apologetically, "it's too far to walk. Let's take the train back uptown one stop and make the connection." Hannah took his arm as he continued in the same conciliatory voice. "And I did get carried away about Eastman. I'll go see him and explain . . ."

It was so rare to hear Lazar agree with her that Hannah was taken aback, although the question of whom Lazar wanted to avoid—and why—was evaded, but not forgotten.

❦ 13 ❦

A few weeks after the Carnegie Hall debacle, Hannah checked the list of patients for the next Wednesday: Nowicki, Levitt, Zimmerman, and Palladino—all were pregnant. Zimmerman had blood pressure problems, and Hannah was worried enough to ask Rachael to consult on this one. The next two, Jacobson and Dykes, were unfamiliar. Then, on the next page there was one more: Applebaum at 3:30. Hannah's heart soared, then plummeted. She was so anxious to see the girl that she forgot that there had to be a pressing reason, or she would not have made the trip downtown.

Hannah called to Carrie. "Why is Mrs. Applebaum coming in?"

"Don't know," responded Carrie, who, due to the private nature of their consultations, never asked about Hannah's patients unless they volunteered. She would have to wait to see for herself.

Several times over the weekend she had been preoccupied by Stella. Had the spasm returned? Had a new problem surfaced? Was the rapid cure too good to be true? But then her speculations were curtailed when the Jewish community was shattered by the news that Sholem Aleichem had died in his Bronx apartment. They had been calling him the "Jewish Mark Twain." His admirers had not only included Eva, Mama, and almost everyone they knew, but every Yiddish writer, Lazar included.

"We have to go. It will be the greatest funeral New York has ever seen," Lazar said.

"Not me, but you do as you wish."

"But I'm going to be in the procession! You must make sure the children get a glimpse of it when we come through the Lower East Side, for they will want to tell their children about it."

"All right," she conceded, doubting that this was as important an event as he claimed. However, on Tuesday, Hannah was amazed as a hundred thousand people lined the sidewalks of Second Avenue, East Houston, Eldridge, and Canal Streets. They surged toward the Educational Alliance, where services were held for the giant of Yiddish letters. Such sadness, so many crying for a man who wrote simple stories! For the first time she felt proud that her husband was also a writer. Benny and Emma were thrilled by the crowds, while Hannah feared them. She gripped their hands tightly as the hearse halted long enough for Rabbi Joseph Rosenblatt, cantor of the Ohab Zedck Synagogue on East 11th Street, to chant a hymn for the dead.

"Where is he?" Benny asked.

"In the box," Hannah explained.

"Pa's in the box?" Emma wailed.

"No, Sholem Aleichem, the man who died, is in the coffin."

"Where's Pa?" Benny insisted.

"Somewhere with all those people," Hannah said, exasperated. "Let's go home."

"No!" Benny scowled. A few minutes later, he slipped away from Hannah and shimmied partway up a pole. "There he is!"

"Benny!" Hannah shouted. "Come down!"

"Pa!" Benny called over the crowd.

Looking where her son pointed, Hannah thought she could pick out her husband walking amid the prominent members of the Yiddish press: Abraham Cahan, editor of *Forverts*, Dr. Melamed, editor of the *Jewish Chronicle*, and Sholem Asch, but knew Lazar would never spot them. "He can't hear you," she said, tugging at her son.

"I want to go to him," Benny insisted.

"No, you cannot," Hannah said firmly. "I never should have brought you here." She started to pull the children through the crowd, but then had to turn around to prompt Emma to keep up with her. Just then she thought she glimpsed Lazar easing his way out of the middle of the entourage, then hurrying down a side street. She clasped her children's hands to keep them beside her, then pushed forward to make certain. Yes, there was the shock of his straw-colored hair and the back of his brown jacket with the black collar. For some reason she had never noticed before that it had a stain the size of a handprint.

No, she had been mistaken. It couldn't have been Lazar after all. These days Lazar yearned to be in the middle of everything, so why, when he had a role to play, would he be running away from the procession? The children had just made her want it to be him. The crowd closed in her view. When a gap opened, the man was disappearing around a corner quickly, as if he were about to be sick. Probably a mourner who had drunk too much wine, she convinced herself as she maneuvered the children to First Avenue, which was almost empty.

The day had been so exhausting the children were too cranky to eat a good supper. She should never have taken them, for they would remember nothing more than the pushing and shoving of the crowd.

Long after they were asleep Lazar returned invigorated with the news that Sholem Aleichem's will left ten percent of his income to struggling writers. "And they have asked me to sit on the committee to determine who might be worthy."

"You should be an applicant, not a judge," she snapped, but he ignored the remark and went to wash up.

Before closing the lights, Hannah picked up the clothes scattered about the parlor. She took her husband's jacket from the sofa arm and hung it on a hook by the door. Why can't any of them hang up their own things? she thought, then studied the jacket. The brown jacket. She placed her palm over the stain. This had been the one she had seen in the crowd! Lazar had been the one running away. But why?

～～ 14 ～～

Hannah's Wednesday appointments were all talking about the funeral. Mrs. Zimmerman's high blood pressure had stabilized. "Good thing I didn't need to go to the hospital yesterday," she said nervously. "You couldn't get out my door."

Mrs. Levitt, who was about to deliver, had a similar litany as she half complained, half bragged about the crowds that had come out to honor one of their own. "If it's a boy, I will call him Sholem, at least for his Yiddish name, and maybe

Sammy or Shelly for his American name. What do you think?"

"I think I can expect to be seeing you tonight or the next," Hannah said as she escorted the heavily laden mother out.

Mrs. Nowicki didn't appear, and the others only wanted charts done, which were so simple to do Hannah could have turned them over to Carrie. She was finished a half hour before Stella was due to arrive, which gave her time to contemplate the possibilities.

And then Stella was late. Hannah feared she had changed her mind, but then a few minutes before four Stella arrived, flushed and gasping. At first Hannah thought the girl was feverish. Her face did appear swollen and her hair was rumpled, but the day was extremely hot, even for late September, and the winds had been blowing off the river.

Carrie showed her into the office, and she fell into her seat with a sigh. "I am late," she said apologetically.

"Don't worry about it," Hannah smiled. "What can I do for you today, Mrs. Applebaum?"

She seemed confused by Hannah's question. "I'm late."

Hannah felt as if she had been hit over the head. "How late?" she asked when the meaning finally dawned.

"I've missed at least twice."

"You are always regular?"

"Yes."

"Would you like me to examine you?"

"Oh, would you? I am so anxious to know!"

"So am I," beamed Hannah. "So am I."

Problem 5:
The Impetuous Malcolm Brody

◆

1917

> On the one hand Nature urges us on to this de-
> sire by associating it with the noblest, most
> useful, and pleasant of all her acts; and on the
> other hand she allows us to condemn it and
> flee from it as from a shameless and immodest
> deed, to blush at it and recommend absti-
> nence. Are we not indeed brutes to call the
> very act that created us, brutish?
>
> —MONTAIGNE

∞ 1 ∞

MESMERIZED by the gauzy world beneath her window, Hannah stared out at the soft falling flakes, her mind vacant. Not
only was everything cleaner, brighter, it also hushed the
city's clamor so that her thoughts could wander without the
insidious interruptions of grating wheels, calling voices,
bleating horns. The snow had fallen through the night for
twelve hours straight. The schools were closed. Hannah had
stayed over at Bellevue, coming home after sleeping in one
of the ward beds, since expectant mothers either had had
their babies elsewhere or had managed to contain their burden for another day. No trolleys or subways were running,
so as she walked the long, hushed blocks back to Tompkins
Square, her footsteps were the first to sully the pure path.

The flat was littered with cups and glasses, bowls and
plates. Lazar had also been kept indoors by the weather and

had spent the day alone with his children, but had anyone picked up after themselves? No. Emma was curled up on the sofa, an afghan tucked around her, and she had fallen asleep with a book slipping from her fingers.

As Hannah bustled about trying to make order from the leavings of their disorganized day, Benny looked up from his reading. "Who was Marx?" he asked his father.

Lazar beamed as though he had been waiting all his life to hear this question from his son. "A man whose ideas will change the world."

"How?"

"Well, when Karl Marx was a boy—not that much older than you—he began to think of the future not so much in terms of how to make his fortune, but what was the meaning of his life and what purpose it should serve. He decided to study philosophy, and soon he discovered Friedrich Hegel. According to Hegel, people advance only through wars and revolutions. Humanity must struggle to succeed because there is always a fight between the oppressed and the oppressors. If we are fat and contented, we don't make any progress."

"Is that true?" Benny asked wide-eyed.

"No," Hannah interjected. "It is what some people—not everybody—believe. Besides"—she checked her husband's mood before she continued—"some think Hegel was referring to religious struggles, which are not the same as fights between workers and bosses."

Lazar stared at his wife. Hannah rarely spoke on political matters, and forgetting that she had listened to hours of similar debates throughout their marriage, he had no idea her grasp was as good as it was. "Let's look at this another way," he said without rancor. "Marx believed that a backward society, such as the one in Russia, would go through the same stages of development as an advanced Western country, like the United States. In other words, a land with a peasant majority, which has been denied democracy or political rights, must pass through the stage of capitalism first." He paused to be certain his son was paying attention. "Then a man named Trotsky—who I once knew in Odessa, by the way—expressed the view that there was no reason a backward society had to take the same path that another one followed."

"Where does Trotter live?"

"Trotsky, not Trotter. Right now he's in exile in France," Lazar corrected with some annoyance at the interruption. "Anyway, he believes that workers and peasants need not become bourgeois to revolt, that the bourgeoisie are too comfortable to want to confront the aristocracy, even if it would be in their best interests. So he is calling for the peasants to emancipate themselves and to elect a constituent assembly. This is what he calls his theory of permanent revolution." Lazar gave his son his most dazzling smile. "What do you have to say about that?"

"I don't understand . . ." Benny said, looking from one parent to the other.

"We'll go over it another time," Lazar responded. "That's enough for tonight."

With a sigh of relief Benny got up from his chair. "May I go downstairs and say good night to Bubbe?"

"Yes, but don't stay too long," his mother replied. When the door slammed, she said, "Why fill the child's head with political nonsense?"

"It is overdue," Lazar said, more forcefully than Hannah had expected. "Your brother has been after me for months to explain our position to the children. With what is coming, they must be prepared."

"And what is coming," Hannah challenged, "besides another cold winter, where we have to scrape to keep food on the table and fuel in the stove?"

"The revolution, what else?" Lazar sounded as though he were still speaking to a child.

"And exactly when is it coming? Next week, next year, next century?"

"This year, in a few months perhaps. A severe winter, combined with a shortage of food, will help push the disgruntled peasants and exhausted soldiers over the edge so they will rebel en masse. The aristocracy has played into our hands since the beginning of the war. If they had instituted some reforms, they might have averted the impending storm. But no, what did they do?" Lazar's eyes flashed with excitement. "The Romanovs were too stupid to realize the gravity of their own situation, even when the seeds of rebellion have been sown right under their noses. Now that Rasputin is out of the way, the door to their inner sanctum is wide open."

There was such pathos in his shining eyes, his fervent expression, that for a moment Hannah wished the damned revolution would come so his dream would be fulfilled. This eternal talking and arguing wasted too much energy. Lazar would never be galvanized into a more productive activity— nor would he even use his literary talents to the fullest— unless the specter of a more perfect future was not banished. Maybe when the great war was over, she mused. Most of the radicals were pacifist in nature and against that war, opposed to conscription, and actively fighting against America's involvement. A few had begun to argue that Wilson should join the fray and end this once and for all. While she hated fighting, a long, bleak night of labor was far better than days or weeks of protracted agony, she thought, liking the obstetrical analogy. But what of the baby? Would it be delivered whole and vital or be stillborn? She shook her head, as if that would clarify her confused thoughts.

Suddenly she heard a thundering on the stairs. Was that Benny? No, too loud. A man. Her heart skipped a beat. Something must be wrong.

"Trotsky is here!" an excited voice called through the half-opened door. Chaim burst into the room.

"No! Could it be true?" Lazar jumped up and hugged his brother-in-law, who was nodding. "I can't believe it! When did he arrive?"

"His boat docked on Sunday."

"Why did he leave Europe?"

"The czar finally exerted enough pressure on the French to curb the activities of the monarchy's enemies in Paris."

"Is he alone?"

"No, he came with his wife, Natalia, and the two boys, Leon and Serge."

"Have you seen him?"

"Yes, and even though it has been more than fifteen years since the days of the Odessa underground, he knew me at once—but by my nom de guerre, of course."

"He called you Illya Swerdlow?"

"Yes! Do you realize how long it has been since I've heard that name? And he asked for you, or rather for that infamous pamphleteer, Mikael Vronsky."

Lazar glowed. "Now it begins!"

As the men huddled to discuss the significance of the arrival of this architect of the revolution, Hannah's mood darkened, for she suspected Trotsky's appearance was going to play havoc with her attempts to stabilize their life.

Lev Davidovich Bronstein, as Leon Trotsky was born, had come from a small hamlet in the Ukraine, not far from Lazar's early home. Chaim and Lazar also were born in the same year as Trotsky. Both Lev and Lazar had been the sons of Jewish farmers and both had gone to Odessa to study. The three boys had known each other at the university briefly. Together they initially had defended the cause of the populist party, the Narodniks, but the three drifted into the more radial movements. Bronstein's clandestine activity in organizing the South Russian Workers Union was truncated swiftly, when he received his first taste of a czarist prison before he was twenty.

"He's destined for greatness," Chaim had predicted after hearing that Bronstein had been released from solitary confinement and sent to Siberia along with his first wife and baby daughter.

"He's destined to freeze," Lazar had retorted, but had swallowed those words ever since. Instead of wasting his exile, Bronstein began to write essays on Herzen, Nietzsche, Ruskin, Darwin, Voltaire, Maupassant, and other great thinkers. After escaping to the West, he took a false name, ironically selecting the name of a warden in the Odessa prison: Trotsky. When he was free, he found his literary reputation had preceded him.

How many times had Hannah heard her husband grumble, "We should have gone to London," because there he might have joined Lenin's inner circle? Indeed, that was where Trotsky had headed, going to work at once on the publication *Iskra,* meaning "the spark," which became the organizational nucleus of the Russian Social-Democrat Labor Party. Hannah refrained from mentioning that when Lazar was content with his leadership of the Jewish defense organization in Odessa, Trotsky was already making a name for himself in Europe.

In December 1905, when Lazar and Hannah were struggling through their second winter in New York, Trotsky was arrested after what some called a "dress rehearsal of a revolution" was curtailed by government troops and the fifty glorious days of the Petersburg Soviet came to an end.

"Here is a mind who can lead the masses," Lazar proclaimed, as though he had made a fresh discovery after reading examples of Trotsky's fiery oratory. Soon Lazar became a devoted proponent of Trotsky's theory of permanent revolution, despite frequent opposition from the coffee house revolutionaries. While Lazar was trying to run a bookstore on the Lower East Side, Trotsky escaped his second sentence in Siberia and moved to Vienna, where he started his newspaper, *Pravda,* and struggled to unify the party. Stirred to a fever pitch by these writings, Lazar went so far as to book passage to join his compatriots across the ocean, secretly left his family, and even boarded the ship. At the last moment some residual sense of duty—or was it merely basic sense?—convinced Lazar to return home. For a time, when the expected revolution of 1908 and 1909 and 1910 and so on never materialized, he felt his impetuous decision to remain in New York had been vindicated.

During that lull, when the flames of dissent dwindled to faintly glowing embers, Trotsky had appeared stagnant in Vienna. At the outbreak of the World War he moved to Switzerland and then to Paris. Lazar had looked on covetously when his idol played a pivotal role at the Zimmerwald Conference in 1915, but had belittled the outcome of that meeting. From long experience Hannah had learned that her husband's sneers were usually shields for envy. Now, though, Lazar was demonstrating unbridled enthusiasm.

"So, what are his plans?" Lazar asked.

"He's taken an apartment in the Bronx." Chaim could see that Lazar was crestfallen. "I tried to tell him it would be more convenient downtown, but already his children seem excited by the building's elevator and garbage chute."

"They'll be capitalists within a month," Lazar roared.

"Anyway, he will start giving lectures next week, and tomorrow he's going over to St. Mark's Place to help with the publication of *Novy Mir.*"

"Has he seen Bukharin and Kollontai?"

"Yes, they were the ones who introduced him to me."

Hannah observed Lazar's clenched teeth grating together. "I've got to go out," he said, catching her penetrating glance.

"So? Go!" Hannah shooed him much as she might a child making too much noise. However, as soon as he left, she felt tears welling in her eyes, although she was not exactly certain why.

∽∾ **2** ∽∾

"Sometimes I feel like Sisyphus," Sarah Brink said as she turned over her head midwifery duties to Hannah one evening.

"Pardon me?" Hannah inserted.

"He was a man in one of those myths whose burden was to push an enormous rock up a hill, but as soon as it reached the top, it rolled down the other side again. Just as I get one baby out, another is always waiting to be born. I wish the whole world would take a few days off from reproduction!"

Comprehending at last, Hannah laughed. "Then you had better declare a suspension of all male and female relations about nine months ahead of time."

"Not a bad idea," Sarah said as she continued to make notations on the charts. "There!" She closed the last folder. "Sixteen babies. Almost a record."

Hannah checked the list of those admitted but who had not yet delivered. "Thank you for being so efficient. You've left me only three."

"And all in Ward C, for some reason. You could send one of the midwives to the clinic tonight."

"Who is on?" Hannah asked aloud, although she was already looking at the duty roster. "Ah, Alice Brody and Millicent Toomey. That's fine."

Mrs. Brink reached for her sweater and handbag, then headed for the changing room. "I hope you have a quiet night, really I do." Sarah turned back with a twinkle. "But I know that they will start to trickle in by dawn and you'll have them raring to go by the time you sign out."

"I'll do my best," Hannah bantered back.

After she made the rounds with her midwives, she suggested that Mrs. Toomey assist in the emergency clinic, where expectant women often dropped in with minor complaints. This was an excellent place to spot developing problems, and it was felt that a few choice words of caution early in pregnancy could head off many disasters. Millicent took the assignment cheerfully, for it meant an easier night with the possibility of short naps. Hannah had a reason for keeping Alice with her. The younger midwife was not looking well, and Hannah wanted to see what the matter was. Two months before she had suffered an early miscarriage and might not have recovered fully.

After Alice had checked on the three holdovers from the night before, she came to Hannah's desk to make a report. "Nobody's going to explode for a while, although there is a new patient in the examining room."

"Have a seat," Hannah offered.

Alice sat on the hard bench to the right of the head midwife's desk.

"How far along is she?"

"Three centimeters, with very little cervical thinning," she said blandly. "Primigravida. Elderly. She's over thirty."

Hannah shook her head, for the phrase *elderly primigravida* referred to a woman having her first child later in life. Since she was thirty-four herself, the term was amusing. She folded her hands and leaned back in her chair. Now was as good a time as ever. "Mrs. Brody, I'm happy to have you back on my shift, but I hope it isn't too much of a hardship on your husband."

She forced a laugh. "He likes the extra money more than a warm bed."

"You have been married less than a year, haven't you?"

"Yes. Since last July."

"The first months are always difficult, but they have been especially hard on you, haven't they?"

"I guess so . . ." Alice said, staring off.

"The loss of the baby is always sad, even one in the earliest months. I suppose people are telling you that you are young and you'll have another, but they don't understand, do they?"

Tears welled up in Alice's eyes so unexpectedly she was not prepared to wipe them away. "I'm sorry," she sniffed as she fumbled for a handkerchief.

Someone with less experience might have backed off, but from her private cases Hannah learned to walk in when the door was open. "And you still have not recovered physically, which must make it worse."

Alice started to protest. "I—"

"Some bleeding?" Hannah probed.

"Yes, mostly staining."

"You could speak with Dr. Dowd about a curettage."

"I've thought of that, but in the last weeks it has cleared up almost completely."

"You may be anemic. Are you taking a supplemental syrup?"

"I was trying Lydia Pinkham's Vegetable Compound."

"You might consider a fortified iron tonic."

"Yes, I'm sure you're right."

A few moments passed without either saying anything. Alice started to rise, but Hannah's hand waved her back. This was the part Hannah enjoyed: watching what bubbled up in the silence. What did Herzog say? "Nature abhors a vacuum. People want to fill in the spaces, and even the most tightly held secrets ooze out if you give them space."

"The war . . ." Alice began tentatively. "I'm so worried for Malcolm. He'll sign up the minute the call goes out, and then what will I do?"

"You would have liked to have had that baby," Hannah offered, thinking that many wives wanted a piece of their husbands, just in case.

"Well, yes, but also—" She turned away.

A nurse came over, but seeing Alice's distress, took a few steps backward. "The new patient. Her water has broken," she offered apologetically. Automatically Alice stood. "That's all right, Mrs. Brody, I thought you'd want to know right off, but everything is fine so far. Nice clear fluid."

"She'll be in in a few minutes," Hannah said, then turned back to Alice. From the trembling of her lips she knew that a raw nerve had been exposed, but since she had ascertained that her midwife's health was satisfactory, she had no right to probe further. "Would you like to tell me about it?" she asked warmly. If Alice bristled at her offer, she would not interfere any further.

"Maybe," Alice said, leaning dejectedly against the wall. "I know you help other people who have had problems."

"I do what I can," Hannah added modestly, then waited.

An orderly pushed a squeaking cart down the corridor. When he had passed, Alice leaned toward Hannah. "My husband, well, he and I—" She gulped, then started again. "I suppose everything is normal because I was able to conceive a baby, but it doesn't work the way I thought it would."

Another sexual problem! Who would have thought this efficient, attractive, and sensitive young woman would be suffering from marital difficulties? Still, nobody was immune. Even someone as sophisticated and as brilliant as Rachael did not enjoy her relations. If that was this girl's problem, Hannah would not know where to begin, since she had not been able to offer Rachael a solution. "What seems to be the most unsatisfactory aspect?"

"He is too quick. I thought it would take more time, but he puts it in and then it is over."

"Sometimes men are impatient at first . . ." Hannah offered while she marshaled her thoughts.

"It's been seven months!" Alice lamented.

"For you there is no pleasure?"

"I love him and I enjoy when he touches me, so I thought I would find some satisfaction—the way other women say they do—but there is not enough time for anything. Have you ever heard of that before?"

Hannah had seen it mentioned, even knew there was a term for the condition. Falling back on her usual first remedy—to allay fears—she said, "This is not uncommon. I have had more experience with women than men, but I have some books that deal with the situation. Why don't I read them over?"

"Is there a cure?"

"Unless the situation is highly unusual, I am certain there is," Hannah said, perhaps too hastily. "Has your husband seen a doctor?"

"Yes, unfortunately he did."

"What was the diagnosis?"

"The doctor explained that the sexual organs are the seat of nervous exhaustion, but that he could be cured with electrical treatments."

Hannah's back stiffened. "Did he submit to them?"

"Yes, and they were horrible." Alice whitened at the memory. "The worst was one called franklinization." She swallowed hard before she could continue. "There were machines attached to electrodes. One was placed in the rectum and another in the urethra, and then he received shocks."

Hannah was aghast, for she had been perusing a book that had suggested various electrical-vibration techniques to awaken dormant sexual feelings, and had ruminated on whether these might be suggested to Rachael. But what Alice was describing sounded so savage she was relieved that she had not pointed her friend in that direction yet, or she might have been further traumatized by the treatment. "Is he still continuing with them?"

"Not since the last time when—" Alice shuddered. "He suffered some burns. Even some hair was singed."

"That's detestable! The man must be a quack!"

"He's very respected and has the latest equipment. Besides, the doctor was right about Malcolm. He does have a nervous temperament."

"Why do you say that?"

"He does not sleep well, has a tender stomach and—"

"Anyone would be nervous. It's a hard time to be a man," Hannah said sympathetically. "Feeding a family is more difficult than ever, and then he must worry about having to enter this terrible war." She gave Alice a comforting smile. "He is lucky to have you. Not many young wives can earn what a midwife can. That should be a help to him."

"But he's not much help to me," she complained, this time displaying an edge of resentment.

"Would he try another doctor?"

"Oh, no," Alice sighed.

"I don't wonder. Shall I see what I can discover?"

"If it would not be too much trouble." Alice glimpsed the nurse coming back down the hall. "I should go," she said, and without waiting for permission, hurried to her duties.

⤸ **3** ⤷

Another interesting challenge! Hannah thought that morning as she pulled out and marked books to read. After waking in the afternoon, she began to coax a soup out of the leavings of several days' meals. As soon as the water began to boil, she opened her book and read a few pages before checking the kettle. The smell was enticing. A handful of barley, a pinch of coarse salt, another onion . . . Then a quick perusal of the table of contents for something that dealt with Mr. Brody's condition. She found a few promising references and tasted the soup. Wrinkling her nose at the thinness of the

broth, she found a bowl covered with a plate ... a small
piece of chicken ... she sniffed it ... all right ... she added
it to the brew, turned down the flame, and went back to
Havelock Ellis.

The first reference was under "The Sexual Impulse in
Women." She saw Alice in his description of a healthy
woman with unsatisfied sexual potential due to "premature
ejaculation by a nervous or neurasthenic husband, who
reaches detumescence before allowing sufficient time for the
tumescence in the wife, who consequently fails to reach the
orgasm." The words *premature ejaculation* had escaped
Hannah that morning with Alice, but they seemed to be what
she had meant, although Hannah would have to pry further
to be certain that this was the correct diagnosis. What if the
terrifying electrical treatments had added to the problem,
making him impotent as well? Hannah read on to discover
that Ferenczi of Budapest was confident of a "prevalent sexual incompetence in men." Could that be true? She had assumed most men were virile like her husband, but then she
had not warmed to Dr. Petrograv's ministrations, but that
had not entirely been his fault. Thinking about her one other
encounter gave her a painful stab. Nathan Delinsky had involved her in a disastrous court case over the death of his
wife, and she preferred to forget that error of judgment.
Now, so many years later, she could see the seeds of her current interests. She had not been seduced by Nathan's charms,
but rather by his needs. He had declared himself impotent
and had begged for her ministrations. Had she rationalized
that indulgence by thinking she was benefiting a wretched
sufferer? She pushed that thought aside. The point was that
at least one out of those three men had a sexual disorder.
Maybe men's problems were more common than she realized.

Herzog came to mind. Did he fit in that category? She dismissed that idea because Rachael would have hinted if her
husband was contributing to her problem. Then why were so
many men experiencing difficulty with something so basic,
so necessary to human existence? Ellis pointed to the influence of masturbation early in life as tending to quicken orgasm in the man. Since Hannah was convinced that most
people practiced some form of masturbation at some point in
their lives, she was unconvinced it alone could contribute to
so many difficulties. On the other hand, if society frowned

on the activity—even if everybody had the same urges—the self-revulsion at surrendering to the base instinct, or punishments meted by a furious parent, might very well have an enduring deleterious effect. Although it could never be proven, Hannah was convinced that Stella's vaginismus had been rooted in the ghastly restraints. Thus might not a boy who was afraid of being discovered train himself to reach orgasm as rapidly as possible?

Benny came into the room juggling a ball from hand to hand. "What's burning, Ma?"

Hannah rushed to the stove. Some vegetables at the bottom of the soup pot had charred and now the flavor would be ruined. As she ladled out the barley and carrots, she chewed over the question of training, both positive and negative. In a sense Stella's muscle had been retrained. Could she have that much success with a man's penis? What if there was something really wrong with his organs or his health? What if he had a truly nervous temperament that could not be cured by anything as simple as Stella's exercises?

Best talk to a man, she decided. But who? She ticked off several possibilities before settling on Dr. Dowd. Even if he was mainly a woman's doctor, he seemed to appreciate her consultations. In fact, when she had told him about her success with Stella Applebaum, he had taken notes on her therapy "for future reference." For the next three days, even though she remained until nine or ten to catch him, she was not able to find him in his office when she had the time to explain the problem. Was she imagining Alice Brody's questioning glances? The poor girl was counting on her, so she decided to leave Dr. Dowd a note to contact her, which took her three tries to compose, and even then she was not satisfied that her English was errorless. "Please see me about a private problem, H. Sokolow." Later, when Hannah realized that he might think *she* had something wrong with *her,* she wished she never had written it. Nevertheless, early the next morning just after the shift change, Dr. Dowd came to the maternity pavilion looking for her.

Hannah was in the midwives' preparation room lecturing to four new students on the maternity-clock system. "Of course, anyone about to deliver must receive your full attention first, even if it means ignoring the pleas of another patient. Always remember a baby in the birth canal is the highest risk." Hannah slowed as she caught the doctor monitoring her words. She hurried through the next part of her lecture, and closed with a reminder, "Remember the numbers on the clock. The higher the number, the more likely the need for your services. When you scan a room to see where you might be of assistance, merely look at number twelve and work your way around counterclockwise." Deliberately she paused, then shook her head. "But never forget the first rule of the midwife: expect the unexpected. The woman in Bed Nine who is almost ready to push may lose the race to the new admission in Bed Three with a surprisingly elastic cervix. The severe problem in Bed Twelve may never manifest itself into anything that harms either mother or infant, while across the room in Bed Six a seemingly textbook case could have a seizure." She looked back at the visitor. "Would you like to add anything, Doctor?"

"I think you have been quite thorough," he replied deferentially.

"Any questions?"

Nobody raised a hand. Probably they were too intimidated in front of the illustrious physician, and so Hannah dismissed them.

"You wanted to see me?" the doctor asked in the hallway.

"Yes," she began nervously, "I should have explained that it involves one of my private patients ..."

"That is what I gathered," he said, defusing her tension. "Where might we talk?"

Since Alice was on duty, Hannah suggested she meet him in his office shortly. A half hour later, she arrived to find he had ordered tea. "I hope you don't mind," he said as though he had taken an improper liberty.

"You are very kind."

"Might as well kill two birds with one stone."

"Pardon?"

He shook his head and laughed. "An old American expression. Most of them are terribly stupid, if you think about it. All I meant was you could have a break before you leave for the day and take care of your problem at the same time. Here ..." He opened a tin on his desk and showed her that it was filled with tiny cakes, which were dusted with fine sugar and centered with a candied violet. "My mother sent these over. During Sunday dinner I was telling her about how we are short-staffed due to the mobilization for the war.

Nobody on the house staff wants to change their schedule, and I have to be the tough guy and force Sundays and holidays down their throats. Anyway, these arrived with the message: 'Try catching flies with sugar.' " He grinned at Hannah, but her face was blank. "Another old saying about catching more flies with sugar than vinegar."

Hannah nodded that she had gotten that one. "In Yiddish we say, *'Az oyf dem hartsn iz biter, helft nit in moyl keyn tsuker.'* If you are bitter in your heart, sugar in your mouth won't help you."

Now the doctor looked perplexed, but he recovered quickly and said, "Anyway, I am curious about your latest case."

"A bride of less than one year reports that she is unable to achieve satisfaction because her husband seems to suffer from what I believe is known as premature ejaculation."

"I see . . ." Dr. Dowd leaned back in his chair and folded his immaculate hands across his chest. "I believe that *ejaculatio praecox* may be a misnomer. Some especially potent men have such a strong sexual desire that the entire process of coitus takes but little time. Their libido, erections, and ejaculations are entirely normal and thus the whole picture represents power, not weakness. One might liken their condition to a swift racehorse which can outrun his competitors. However, this must be differentiated from that of a man with feeble, rapid ejaculation, diminished libido, and lack of satisfaction from the act."

"How would you do that?"

He noticed the cake crumbling in her hands. "Taste it," he urged, then replied. "A few simple answers to a few simple questions should indicate whether the man derives satisfaction from the act. If he reports that he does, he is normal."

Taking a sip of tea to clear the crumbs from her mouth, Hannah did not respond immediately.

"Do you like it?"

"What?" she replied, since her mind was on the sexual act.

He seemed bemused by her discomfort. "The cake?"

"Oh, it's very good," she answered with relief. Now, where was she . . . "What if he is too hasty for his partner?"

"Mismatches are always unfortunate, but many—if not most—marriages survive one hurdle or another. How long did you say they have been married?"

"Less than a year."

"During that interval has either of them been ill, or have they been apart for any length of time?"

"She suffered an early spontaneous abortion."

"Of course!" That confirmed his thoughts. "So he was probably denied his rights for a while. May I ask if the woman is, ah . . . tempting?"

Masking her annoyance at the question, Hannah replied, "She is an intelligent, attractive young woman."

Dr. Dowd nodded distractedly. "Initially you might not concur with my next statements, and let me admit they are based more on worldly experience than medical science. Since these highly potent men are more likely to get into this condition when they are having relations with a new acquaintance, the man might settle down at home with a familiar companion if he has the excitement he craves elsewhere." Even though Hannah resisted displaying any emotion, the doctor sensed her indignation. "Now, Mrs. Sokolow, if we who service the reproductive organs cannot be realistic, who can?" He refolded his hands and waited a few beats.

"What sort of treatment would you recommend?"

"First you must have a clear conception of the pathological state and the causes which produced them. An initial genitourinary examination must be made, including a routine urine test to rule out diabetes."

"I'm not trained to do examinations on men."

"Indeed. That's not my specialty either. Dr. Blühner might oblige."

"Thank you" was all Hannah replied because she doubted if Alice's husband would subject himself to another doctor's scrutiny, no matter how lofty his credentials.

"At the very least you should determine whether he was circumcised or not."

"That makes sense . . ." she allowed. "I've heard that the uncircumcised feel more intense sensations, which would mean they might have more trouble maintaining control."

"That's an unproven theory, but assuming that he isn't, he might consider surgery in an attempt at a cure."

While doubting this would appeal to Mr. Brody, she could not help thinking that here was another instance where the Jewish laws, which ordained that men's foreskins be removed, might have made it possible for a man to last longer and thus more easily satisfy his wife. Like the injunctions about hygiene, these made practical sense in keeping the tribe safe and united. "What else might he try first?"

"If none of these is evident, absolute sexual rest—to give the exhausted centers time to recuperate, as well as to remove every cause of irritation—should be tried."

"He must take to his bed?" she asked with some surprise.

"Hardly!" He guffawed. "I mean just the opposite. The husband should not even sleep in the same room with his wife, if possible, but certainly not in the same bed."

"For how long?"

"Three months should be adequate."

His prescription did not make sense to Hannah. "How could abstention be the solution? I thought you said that in these cases it would help if the man had other women. Should he abstain with her, but go to another's bed?"

"No. He must be celibate."

"Then how will be become bored with his wife?"

"You are confusing two medical issues. In this situation the plan is to heal any irritated tissues, and thus rule out any pathology." Dr. Dowd sounded impatient, but was that because the question had been foolish or because his authority had been challenged?

"Are there medications to assist the healing?"

"Bromides—at least fifteen grains per day well diluted—should be taken after meals for six weeks, then gradually reduced. At the same time the patient should abstain from the usual stimulants to the sexual apparatus."

"The usual?"

"Alcohol, tea, coffee, eggs, and oysters."

The more the doctor prattled on, the more Hannah disagreed with him. Why did he consider premature ejaculation a virtue rather than a shortcoming? Why did he not allude to the psychological aspects of the case the way Havelock Ellis had? Why did he only look for structural diseases or abnormalities? Could there not be a simple alternative, not unlike the slow opening of the vaginal vault in Stella's case? Hannah reminded herself that it was Dr. Dowd who had believed that surgery was the optimum cure for vaginismus. She had worked out that course of treatment by logically applying a practical solution. If she gave the matter some thought, she also might discover an alternative for Mr. Brody's difficulty.

"Thank you for your consultation," she responded formally. She stood up.

Polite as always, Dr. Dowd did as well. This time he crossed the room and opened the door for her. When she stepped forward, though, he took her hand and shook it. Hannah was too surprised to offer more than a limp response. "I do so enjoy our consultations, Mrs. Sokolow, and I admire your desire to move into areas that most women—most physicians as well—fear to tread. We who are willing to investigate the intricacies of sexual functioning are breaking new ground. Controversies will swirl about us, and yet think how much human happiness hangs in the balance!"

"I only wish I knew more . . ." Hannah replied as she took a step backward.

He did not release his grip. Instead he leaned toward her with a benevolent smile on his soft pink lips. "Really, to be entirely effective a man should team with a woman, since neither has perfect perspective on a marital affliction alone." Belatedly he released her hand. "What do you think?"

What was he asking? Hannah could not imagine bringing Stella or even Alice to see him, and certainly not Rachael. But what if he saw Mr. Brody while she counseled the wife, and then together they would confer about the progress from each side? "I don't know," she replied to his inquisitive gaze.

The doctor tossed his head so that a lock of hair, as silky as that on a coddled cat, fell in front of his eyes. Hannah had to resist the urge to brush it back. "Just a thought," he said lightly. "Publication of interesting cases, though, would circulate fresh ideas." The words were flipped out as though they had no import, but Hannah caught the moment of hesitation that meant he was worried about her response.

"I'm afraid writing reports on cases is too difficult for me—just ask Mrs. Hemming. Anyway, with the wartime schedule I would hardly have the time."

"You would not be expected to do the writing. In any case, it should be done by someone with a medical degree."

While he sounded sympathetic, Hannah heard the message: a midwife's authority would hold no weight in the medical community. "I am certain you are right," she said with a forced smile. She stepped halfway out the door.

"One more thing . . ." He reached over and handed her the cake tin. "Take this with you."

"What about the flies?"

"I tried it, and I am sorry to say the bait failed."

Hannah still did not reach for it. "There's not enough to offer both the midwives and the students, so . . ."

"Please," he insisted. "Take them home. They're for you."

"Well . . . the children will be thrilled," Hannah said truthfully.

Dr. Dowd turned away. Had she insulted him? She looked over her shoulder as she closed the door. No, don't be silly. He was just going back to his work.

◈ 4 ◈

Lazar returned early one afternoon in high spirits. He found Hannah sitting in her mother's parlor waiting for the children to return from school. He gave his wife an affectionate hug and kissed Mama Blau on the forehead, pleasing her enormously.

"Have something to eat?" his mother-in-law asked. She scooped a helping of spicy fruit compote before he could respond.

He took it without protest and grinned at the two women.

"What are you so happy about?" Hannah asked.

"Everything is lining up in perfect order."

"Mama, have you ever heard of an orderly revolution?" Hannah jested. "Where were you?"

"In Brooklyn, at Ludwig Lore's house. You know who he is—the editor of the *New Yorker Volkzseitung.*" He took a few bites while waiting to be pumped for more information. Not especially interested, Hannah busied herself clearing the table. "It was a very exclusive meeting," he continued. "Only twenty trusted comrades were invited, including five Russians."

"You must have been as happy as a rooster in a hen-house."

"Could you hear the squawking across the river?" he asked as he followed her into the kitchen. "It turned into a debate between Trotsky and Bukharin."

"What else is new?" She shrugged. "If you're finished with the fruit, let's go upstairs."

He did not protest. As soon as they were at the first landing, he turned to her. "I almost forgot! We're having company tonight."

"For dinner?" she asked, reviewing whether she could feed another with what was on hand. At least this was her night off.

"Possibly."

"How can I prepare if I don't know?"

"The food won't matter." His lips formed a pout. "Why don't you ask me who is coming?"

Hannah turned to face him on the step below her. "All right, who?"

"Trotsky!"

Knowing how much it meant for him to feel accepted by the exalted Russians in exile, Hannah forced herself to suspend her complaints. "Then you had better help me get the house in order."

While she boiled coarse buckwheat groats in one pot and noodles in another for a hearty dish of *kasha-varnishkes,* she deliberated why she had never liked Trotsky. His figure was slight, his height modest, but since he could not stand still in a room, his short legs always seemed to be striding somewhere. Above his high forehead was a shock of wavy black hair that had an unkempt and unwashed appearance. Although up close his eyes were a pale blue, they did not reflect the light, so behind his thick glasses he seemed to be staring with two black opaque orbs. To be fair, though, she had only met him twice, both times at the Monopole Café. Surrounded by followers, Trotsky had given her but the briefest attention before moving on to whatever more interesting was happening nearby.

Hannah also recalled that when Lazar was with Trotsky, he would insert Trotsky's birth name into the conversation, saying: "Lev Davidovich, what do you think of this dialectic or that postulate?" so everyone would know that Lazar had befriended his idol long before he had come to fame. Unfortunately, Trotsky would respond by formally calling Lazar "Comrade Sokolovsky." The only deference to their past association was his recall of Lazar's name before it had been truncated by an immigration official at Ellis Island. Hannah saw this as a slight, but knew Lazar had chosen to take it as a sign of respect. Anyway, she had to remember that Trotsky was important to Lazar, not only because he respected the man, but because the association might bring him more assignments.

Until the "great man" arrived, the children were banished to their bedroom, to be called in time for dinner. The plan was for Lazar to greet him, while Hannah remained in the kitchen. Although this was not how she would normally welcome a guest, she deferred to Lazar about this entirely. The six o'clock time they usually had supper when she was home passed. As did seven.

"The children have to eat," she insisted.

Lazar relented and had them come out of their room, but by then they were cranky. Their petty squabbles irritated their father, and Emma burst into tears. Hannah nibbled on some eggplant appetizer as she cleaned up their dishes. Not until quarter past eight was there a knock on the door. She waited for Lazar to get it. Another knock. She realized he was in the bathroom and went to open it herself.

"Good evening, Mr. Trotsky," she said, her hand outstretched.

Barely acknowledging her greeting, he walked directly to the dining table and sat down.

"Lazar will be here in a moment," she said graciously.

His expression was one of extreme tension. "That would be good," he replied, then his mouth curled sardonically.

Lazar hurried out. "Lev Davidovich!" he said with forced bravado.

Trotsky's response was a barrage of coughing. The man was nowhere near as robust as Lazar.

"Will you have dinner with us?" Hannah asked.

"Can't you see he needs a drink?" Lazar barked.

Grumbling silently, Hannah brought water and Lazar poured a shot glass of whiskey to accompany it. Watching the man swallow painfully, she berated herself. He had come from a confrontational meeting and was also unwell. What was wrong with her? She was supposed to be a healer, wasn't she? Then again, maybe her extremely negative reaction was merely her jealousy over her husband's adoration of the mesmerizing leader, although at the moment she could not fathom his appeal.

"Shall I serve the meal?"

"I don't eat meat," Trotsky replied curtly.

"I made kasha-varnishkes."

"Without schmaltz?"

"There's some chicken fat, for flavor," she admitted.

"What else?"

"Noodles and kasha ..."

"I mean, what else to eat?"

"Some plain kasha, beets ..."

"Yes."

Hannah was about to ask: Yes, what? but was silenced by her husband's warning expression. She merely made the plates for the men. When neither inquired whether she was going to join them, she went to be with the children.

An hour passed before Lazar came for her. "May we have our tea now?" he asked.

Without a word she handed Trotsky a glass of tea. He looked up at her with his piercing eyes, and his mouth moved as if he was saying *"Spasseeba"* but no sound came out. Then he made a big show of being interested in Benny and Emma.

Lazar told them, "Never forget this moment. You will tell your children about the time Trotsky came to your house and talked with you."

Benny's eyes widened, but Emma was too tired to be impressed. In the background Hannah gloated. She was no dummy. This Trotsky might be a big *makher* at the moment, but in twenty years his name would mean nothing.

❧ 5 ☙

Hannah went to sleep long before Trotsky departed, grateful for a normal night's sleep. As usual Lazar got the children off to school, then disappeared. He was probably making the rounds of the cafés to brag about his evening with Trotsky. Hannah spent the day catching up on household chores until her husband returned home after lunch.

"Well ..." he prodded when he saw her, "what did you think?"

"About what?"

"Trotsky of course!"

She did not want to argue. "He's an unusual man. Very much like an"—she groped for a neutral word—"an artist."

"Yes, that's true," Lazar replied thoughtfully. "He has that childlike charm."

"And the self-absorption and vanity," she blurted.

"That is not true. He never brags and has no preoccupation with himself. His mind is filled with ideas for the world," Lazar defended. "Trotsky is like a brilliant chess player who always has the large picture in mind and anticipates moves far in advance."

"That's just his excuse for being rude and thinking only of himself. He says: 'Oh, sorry, I was worrying about the poor, downtrodden masses when I accidentally stepped on your foot, or ate the last piece of meat, or forgot to pay back that loan.' "

"Trotsky is a vegetarian," Lazar reminded.

There was something else on her mind, but there had been no quiet time to discuss it. Since she wanted to avoid conflicts about Trotsky, this seemed as good an opportunity as any. "I need a man's opinion," she began.

"About what?" he asked wearily.

Hannah took the more dilapidated armchair, while Lazar settled into his favorite reading place. "About the way a man feels when he begins to make love to a woman."

Lazar's jaw slackened at the change of subject. "That's hardly a mystery."

"To those who have problems it apparently is."

"What sort of problem are you confronting, neshomeleh?" His mouth relaxed in a mischievous smile.

"The scientific term is 'ejaculatio praecox.' It's the condition where a man cannot control his excitement and spills his seed too early."

Entranced with his wife's words, Lazar leaned forward. "I had no idea you had experienced that sort of difficulty," he teased.

"Not me, of course." She twisted her hands. Lazar was almost as bad as Dr. Dowd—well, not quite. How much easier it was to think about this subject than to verbalize it. She had been speaking in English, so she changed to the more familiar Yiddish. "A patient of mine has a husband with the problem, and as you might imagine, she is not satisfied."

"Why don't you advise her to be more forbearing? Most men have this experience some time in their life."

"Did you?"

Lazar shifted in his seat slightly, but did not flinch from the inquiry. "As a young man. My first experiences were too rushed, and I was already so excited."

"Was this by yourself . . . or with a woman?" Hannah had assumed that since Lazar lived alone as a student, he had come to her with some experience. Of all the women in his circle she could not forget Vera with the surly mouth and coppery hair, and wondered if he had been to bed with her.

"A woman, but nobody you knew," he hastened to add as if he were reading her thoughts. In the pause he made a decision to go on. "You might as well hear, since it might help the poor impetuous lad. There was an older woman who frequented the Café Bessarabia in Odessa. For a few kopecks she would go with you in a room in back of the alley. We all tried her, but there was always someone in the wings, so we had to hurry. Waiting my turn, I got so excited that all I had to do was touch her and . . ." He reddened slightly. "I didn't even get inside, but the price was the same."

"Well, that hardly counts . . ."

"That's where you are wrong. You cannot know how a man feels at a time like that. The embarrassment never leaves you. It's almost as though you've soiled your pants. The worst part is the fear that there is something wrong with you and that it will happen again."

"Did it?"

"Yes, a few times." He swallowed hard. "With girls I wanted to impress." He looked up to see Hannah's reaction. She forced a steady gaze to prove she was unflappable. "Fortunately, it did not happen every time, or I would have been too ashamed to keep trying. Compared to the control I have now, I was quite the impatient fellow, and not much use to the ladies, I fear."

"With me it has always been wonderful," Hannah said with a generous smile. "What was the difference?" Secretly she hoped he would say something about loving her, but his response was even more useful, if a bit disappointing initially.

"I practiced, first with myself, then with a girl."

"What do you mean?"

"I did it to myself, the way boys will, and when I felt myself getting to that dangerous point, I would squeeze until that surging sensation passed, then work up to it again, stop myself, and so on, until I had mastered it."

"And this continued to work when you went with a woman?"

"Well, initially it was not easy. What I would do is pull out if I felt I was going to lose control—by then I had learned to detect what sensations preceded the discharge—and the break from the thrusting usually brought me back to where I wanted to be."

"If it didn't?"

"I would reach down and give myself a little press. I don't think anyone noticed. Of course, I have not needed to do that in years."

"Do you think the technique would work for another man?"

"Maybe. In any case, it couldn't hurt him."

The image of Lazar blurred as Hannah became transported by his statement. Alice's husband had suffered from the electrotherapy and would endure deprivation if she offered him Dr. Dowd's suggestions, but what harm could come from this? Should she tell the man himself? she ruminated, then rejected that idea. If she had been uncomfortable explaining it to Dr. Dowd and Lazar, she would surely fumble with the agitated patient. Could she describe the technique adequately to Alice? Probably, but would he do as she suggested? Also, how would Alice feel sending her husband away to masturbate on his own?

Just then she had another thought: if masturbation had been involved in making him feel ashamed, as Havelock Ellis suggested, he might not find the treatment something he would want to try, or worse, it could have the opposite effect. What if Alice were to participate, as a wife should? Although Hannah would never know what had really happened between Stella and Bernard, she suspected that Bernard's inclusion in the therapy had brought the problem to its swift conclusion. Alice was warm and caring. Surely she would choose to be involved in a plan that would bring more pleasure to their marriage.

"What are you thinking, neshomeleh?"

Hannah stared across at him. How handsome he looked framed in the window. The light from behind outlined his strong jaw and sturdy frame. The attraction she had felt when they first met was as intense as ever. Their eyes locked and each knew what the other was thinking.

Lazar glanced at a clock. "How much time do we have?"

"Not even an hour."

"Time enough," he said, grinning. He walked over, took her arm, and led Hannah to the bedroom.

They undressed themselves hurriedly, and when Hannah turned around, she glimpsed her husband's obvious excitement. They were so complementary and knew each other so well that they did not need to arouse each other before commencing. Yet Lazar always did something first to please her, sometimes licking her nipples, sometimes caressing her vulva in a circular motion with the flat of his hand, sometimes teasing her with his fingers until she insisted he penetrate her. This time she pushed his hand away and reached for his member. "Let me do it to you, and you tell me when to stop."

"Is this a lesson?"

"Yes, and you are the teacher."

"You had better be a good student or I'll punish you," he quipped in a way that only excited her more.

She straddled him and reached between his fuzzy legs. She touched the velvety skin with a fluttery motion that made him tremble. His hands enfolded hers and demanded she pump the slippery flesh up and down, while he reached up and caressed her breasts. This made her yearn to take him inside, but she forced herself to continue. His eyes closed and his jaw set into a grimace. "Is this good?"

"Oh, yes, good, very good . . ."

"Don't forget to tell me when to stop," she whispered urgently.

His fingers tightened on her nipples, drawing her down to him, but she pulled away so she could pay attention to her task. His hips lifted and Hannah loosened her grip. His hand covered hers and urged her on, but after only one more pumping, he tightened his hand above hers. "Now! Hold me now! No, lower and tighter!" he gasped, then took a deep breath and opened his eyes. Hannah looked down. Her fingers were moist and the head of his penis glistened, but she was fairly certain he had not lost control.

"You stopped yourself?"

"Yes."

"Now what?"

He took a deep breath. "We do it some more." Hannah's hand embraced her task. "No." Lazar pushed it away and propelled her hips until she mounted him.

"But—"

He wouldn't allow her to withdraw and began to thrust up into her, and soon she lost the will to protest. "Now!" he said in less than a minute, and pushed her off him.

Hannah reached around and clasped his penis. "Shall I squeeze?"

"Only if you want to practice. By now I don't need that."

"I don't want to practice," she said in a throaty voice. She bent over and kissed him fervently, while moving around and around with the proficiency of an expert who knew exactly what she wanted. In a few seconds she arched her spine and threw back her head. Lazar clutched her buttocks and shuddered, but Hannah was not content to be still and once more attained her goal.

"Feel better?" he asked, kissing her neck.

She rolled over. "Much. Thanks for your help with my problem."

"My pleasure," he said, patting her abdomen lovingly. He looked at his watch. "The children should be home by now."

"Maybe they stopped in to see Mama," she said, leaping from the bed and reaching for her undergarments. They dressed almost as quickly as they had removed their clothes, laughing at their haste.

"What are you going to do about your case?"

"I'll advise them to try the compression technique. You were right when you said it couldn't hurt."

"One more thing," Lazar said thoughtfully. "Most men don't realize how agreeable it can be to have the woman on top, and so they may not have tried that position. Suggest it, because I think it may be easier for the man to inhibit himself that way. He can signal his wife. She can lift herself off and reach down to clasp him until he has controlled himself, then start again. Also—"

A door banged open. "Ma! I'm home!" called Benny. "Ma? Where are you?"

6

For those who inhabited the world of the Lower East Side radicals, Trotsky's appearance was the one luminous spot in the otherwise dreary winter. Hannah's private patients—most of whom paid their fees promptly—kept her busier than ever, which is why the missing money went unnoticed for so long. She realized that Trotsky had captivated Lazar's attention, but had assumed her husband would be writing about his old friend and this would add to the coffers. In the first weeks, though, Lazar had little time to sit down at his desk, for he was too busy accompanying Trotsky to his numerous lectures.

Trotsky seemed to have an engagement every night. In a month he had covered the whole East Side, from the German Labor Lyceum on 81st Street, up to the Harlem River Casino on 107th Street, and down to Forverts Hall on East Broadway. He spoke in Russian or in German, sometimes translating himself from one language to the other. Although Hannah was not particularly interested in what her husband's mentor was espousing, she listened to his reports like a child trying to cheerfully take her medicine.

"He debated with Hillquit today, but won the round," Lazar reported one afternoon. The next day he said, "Trotsky argued with Cahan, right from the platform. You should have seen the two of them!" He rubbed his hands at the delicious memory. "I don't know which of them is more self-righteous or more arrogant, but Abe thrives on fights, whether in print or in person."

"From what I hear, so does Trotsky."

"You're wrong. He may have to be forceful to win his point, but his reasonable—and rational—approach has already converted Ludwig Lore."

Hannah let the matter slide. There was something else she had to mention. "Eva's day to visit Mama is tomorrow."

"Good for her."

"I need to give her the rent for this month as well as last month."

Lazar shuffled through some papers on the table. "So?"

"The money is not in the book." Hannah waited. Their "bank" was in a hollowed-out copy of *Das Kapital,* Lazar's ironic idea of a hiding place.

Lazar's eyes drifted up to the top book shelf. The volume was in its place. "Maybe Benny decided to read Marx after all."

"Are you accusing your son of stealing?" Lazar hung his head. "You took the money! When?"

"I borrowed it."

"For what?" Her voice was icy but even.

"I had certain expenses . . ."

Hannah cut him off. "What about *our* expenses?"

"Your bourgeois sister can wait."

"Don't do this to me again, Lazar!" Her voice rose out of control. "Where is the money you usually bring in? I haven't seen anything in weeks, maybe months."

"There will be some more soon. Times are unsettled. There has been a reorganization with some of the people I do business with."

"And who are they? Tell me, and I'll go collect for myself."

"Don't speak foolishly," he said, his eyes taking on a fierce feline luster. He walked over to a small cabinet where he kept a bottle of slivovitz for special occasions, carried it to the kitchen, and poured one glass.

"There is something you are not telling me," she began, as months of apprehension bubbled to the surface. Better not give him time to slither out of this, better to bring it out into the open, like a pustule that had to be lanced. "That time after you introduced Reitman at Carnegie Hall and again during Sholem Aleichem's funeral, who were you hiding from?"

Lazar sipped his plum brandy slowly. "I never hid from anyone. Who has been telling you these crazy things?"

Hannah had bundled her suspicion about the funeral along with the subway incident to see his reaction. When he did not leap to refute the former, she knew he had been lying to her. "At the funeral, I saw you running away from the procession. And you were hiding from someone on the subway. The question is who is after you—and why?"

"Don't be ridiculous—" he denied unconvincingly.

"Then what the hell is it?" she thundered.

"It's a business problem, that's all."

"Business? The ones who owe you money should be running from you. Those gonifs who call themselves publishers have been stealing from you for years. Socialists? Ha! They are getting fat off the idiots who write for them and the dullards who read them."

"I almost never get paid for my writing," Lazar mumbled so softly Hannah almost did not hear him. She waited for him to explain. "There's no money for ideas, but ideas will change the world. I had to find a way to make my voice heard and at the same time to satisfy you."

"Me? What about our children? What about you? We all have to eat; we need a roof over our heads."

"I knew you would not understand."

"Why do you always have to find fault with me?"

Ignoring that jibe, he continued on the same track. "I thought you might notice the coins, the one-dollar bills. If you had only asked the right questions—"

Hannah ran her hands through her hair as if that movement would soothe her disordered thoughts. "The money is illegal?"

Lazar put out his palms in supplication. "Technically, but the authorities never bother about it because nobody is harmed."

Hannah slumped in the nearest chair and covered her face with her hands. "I should have known . . ." she sobbed.

"Listen, it's not so terrible. Lots of people can't resist playing the numbers —from Sophie Feigenbaum to that baker on Eldridge Street to the schmucks on Allen Street."

"You take in money from gambling?"

"I don't write the bets or pay anyone off. I was just a helper."

"What sort of helper?"

"I collected the money from the 'writers,' the guys who take the bets from the customer, and delivered it to what they call the 'bank.' "

"You mean the gangsters who run the racket?"

"It's not what you think. They are legitimate businessmen with this on the side. Everybody knows about it."

"Everybody except me!" she spat.

"I meant the government. It's a nice clean business and

nobody gets hurt. Gambling gives a man hope. It helps him rise above his miseries."

"Well, what would the great Karl Marx or your beloved Mr. Trotsky say about your new doctrine?"

This stung Lazar far more than anything else she had said, but he tried to pass it off with a conciliatory smile, the sort that usually melted his wife. "When the revolution comes, it won't be necessary anymore."

Hannah felt herself hardening into stone.

"Anyway, I am not doing it any longer. That's why there is no money. Are you happy now?"

"What made you stop?" Hannah asked, her voice as cold as steel.

"There were some problems . . ."

"In a nice clean business?"

"Look, Hannah, it had nothing to do with me. I was caught in the middle, that's all. Some *schmegegi* got too greedy and was not giving me his whole take. Then, when he was confronted, he blamed the shortage on me. I tried to explain, but decided the best way to prove it was to avoid everyone for several months until he pulled it again with another runner."

"What if he learned his lesson?" Hannah said as she poked holes in his argument.

"It doesn't matter. I'm not going back."

"What about the missing money?"

"I've covered most of that."

"With our rent money. Now what are we supposed to do?" Hannah tried to force her husband to look at her, but he went back to the kitchen and poured himself another drink. This time he took down a second glass. "I don't want any!"

"You'll feel better," he urged. Despite everything, Lazar was calm. His eyes were joyless, but he had not lost his resolve. She had never been able to force him to do her bidding, even if what she desired was the most ordinary request of a wife to a husband. No, that was not true. Once she had gotten her way: when she had been pregnant and wanted him to marry her and join her family's flight to America. Now, with the world turned upside down and Trotsky nearby, she had no chance.

At last the problem crystallized: he would do whatever he wanted, but he still needed to help support them. "I want the money to pay the rent. I don't care where you get it: from the crooks, from Trotsky, or from hell. Just bring back the money you took and we will start again from there. Then we will make a budget and try to live on my income for a while. If we cannot, you will have to get a job."

Lazar's relief at being let off the hook—at least temporarily—lit up the room. "I'll see what I can do," he said, then rushed for his coat.

He closed the door without saying where he was going or when he was coming back. And for the first time in many a year, Hannah did not care.

࿇ **7** ࿇

There was little time to agonize over Lazar's predicament. The next morning Minna was sentenced to thirty days in the workhouse on Blackwell's Island in the East River for again distributing birth-control information. The sentence was shocking, but Minna had been prepared. She issued a proclamation of defiance, which Lazar was asked to distribute to the newspapers. It read:

> While I am in prison I vow I shall not eat a bite of food, drink a drop of any beverage, or do one article of work. If required, I will die for the cause and for my sex.

As soon as Hannah heard, she went to see Margaret Sanger, for she was the only one who could talk any sense into Minna.

"There's nothing I can do," Margaret said as though she were annoyed by Hannah's concerns.

"She could die!"

"That is the decision of her conscience."

"Would you do it?"

"Everyone faces a time in their life when they must make crucial decisions. I cannot say what mine would be when that moment arrives."

"She's doing this for you," Hannah challenged.

"No, I made certain of that," Margaret replied a bit too quickly for Hannah to believe her. "You know better than I the trials your sister-in-law has already endured. When she wants something, she makes up her own mind, then sticks with her convictions. A few weeks ago when the possibility of prison was discussed, she told me she had decided to die for the cause. Then yesterday, as she ate a farewell dinner of turkey and ice cream, I again tried to dissuade her. I warned her that once she started the strike, she would have to stay with it to the end."

"Why did you do that? You are promoting this madness."

Margaret shook her head. "You are giving me too much credit. Even her husband has not been able to discourage her. Did you know that as they were transporting her to Blackwell's Island, she gave a lecture on contraception to the other women prisoners? She so impressed the warden, he offered to get her food secretly, but Minna refused, saying her conscience would not permit it."

In a fury Hannah left Margaret's and went directly to find Rachael. Carrie reported that the doctor had gone home early to nurse Nora, who had the measles, but this did not deter Hannah, who hurried to the Herzogs' house.

Patiently, Rachael listened to Hannah's diatribe against Margaret Sanger and Emma Goldman. "Are they risking their lives? No! They are using Minna to get publicity without hazarding anything of their own." Hannah stormed around the room shaking her fist. "Do you know what I think? Her death would be welcomed by them. Can't you see the headlines now? 'Woman dies in birth-control protest.' Will that make any difference?"

"It could," Rachael replied in a whisper.

Tears flooded Hannah's eyes. "Are you agreeing with what she is doing?"

"No, but I understand it."

"Good, because I don't. Would you care to explain it to me?"

"Well . . ." Rachael ran her fingers through her unruly hair, trying to find the pins to tame it back. "People have certain traits that make up the main seat of their personalities, and each of these traits has a positive and negative side, like a coin. For instance, we might admire a person because he is very friendly, always has a kind word, is amusing to be with. However, that same person can be the one we avoid if we are in a hurry because they are too talkative, their tales are boring, and they don't know when to leave us alone. Do you see what I mean?"

"Not as it applies to Chaim's wife," Hannah snapped.

"What is laudable about Minna is her courage, her determination to see something through to the end, even if the task is unpleasant."

"On the other hand, she can be uncompromising, difficult, stubborn," Hannah interjected. "I know from experience that she won't bend. She doesn't see two sides to a question."

"Which, I might add, may be why you both have clashed over the years."

Hannah sucked in her breath at the comment. Was Rachael accusing her of being obstinate as well? Stunned by the realization that she might have been a contributing cause of their disagreements, Hannah merely nodded.

"This particular problem creates a paradox for her," Rachael continued more benignly. "If she gives in, she loses; if she doesn't, she dies."

"Do you think she will go through with it?" Hannah asked with renewed alarm.

"It's more complicated than that. The first days of starvation are the hardest, but someone with a clear mind and enormous willpower will overcome the pangs and discomfort. After that, a certain numbness sets in and the person thinks that they will bear the burden successfully." Rachael sighed and closed her eyes momentarily. "At last, when the body is about to undergo the agony that starvation inflicts, the brain—which already has suffered the effects of the loss of sustenance—mercifully dims, and she will no longer be able to make rational decisions to take nourishment, even if she changes her mind."

"If she knew about this . . ." Hannah said, groping.

"Would you like me to write her a letter telling her what she might expect?"

"Oh, yes!" At last Hannah felt she had done something constructive for Minna. When her sister-in-law discovered that she would no longer be in control of the situation, she might reverse her ill-advised decision.

"Mother! Mother, I need you," Nora cried imperiously from where she lay in a nearby darkened room.

Rachael went to tend to her sick daughter, while Hannah

waited. When she returned, she asked, "What else is bothering you?"

At first Hannah was not going to let anything supersede her concerns about Minna, but then all her frustrations bubbled out as she told Rachael about Lazar's problems with the numbers racket, her fears for his safety, and their economic insecurity. "And that *groisser gornisht,* that good-for-nothing Trotsky, is making matters worse. All I hear is Trotsky this, Trotsky that, as if the messiah himself had come to New York. I even think Chaim has put Trotsky above his own wife's welfare."

Rachael shot Hannah a glance that meant: you are being unfair. Hannah backpedaled. "Well, Chaim may not be as captivated as my husband, but don't tell me Lazar has put me and the children before that Ukrainian windbag!"

Rachael was amused at Hannah's explosion. "You know what they say, *'Azoy vi di tseytn azoy di leytn.'* Like times, like men." She shook her head sadly. "The whole world is *meshugeh.* Russia is on the verge of revolution; America is about to go to war."

"You too? Doesn't anyone believe that peace will come?"

"Not this year, no. I see it like an infection that has been dormant and will have to develop into a full-blown disease before it can be cured."

Hannah felt defeated. "What can I do?"

"We cannot all be out on the front lines. Both of us are needed right where we are. Every day something good comes from our ministrations. Do you know how I cope?" Hannah looked up as though she were to be offered a blessing. "Since I cannot create peace in the world, I try to put the reports out of my head entirely. I've stopped reading the papers. I won't talk about it with Herzog. At first he thought I was wrong, but now he sees my point. Now he too has decided his task will be to help put the minds and bodies of the victims back together again."

There was much wisdom in the words, even if Hannah could not assimilate them entirely. After a few moments Rachael thought it advisable to change the subject entirely. "It's been so long since we have been able to talk. Had any interesting cases lately?"

"Obstetrical?"

"No, the other sort."

"Well . . ." Hannah debated her answer, then took the

chance. "Yes. There is a woman whose husband complains of ejaculatio praecox . . . and then there is you."

Rachael took a long inward breath, as though something had struck her, but recovered quickly. "I'm afraid this is another one of those dormant cases."

"Let's wake it up, then," Hannah began tentatively. "Although I don't think it has to become a raging infection," she added to defuse the tension. She had neglected her friend for a long time, not because she wanted to, but because she had no solutions to offer. Yet as she gained knowledge from her reading and her cases, Rachael's longings had loomed in the back of her mind. After her "training session" with Lazar, Hannah had spent an hour with Alice Brody, frankly advising her on the normal problems an uncircumcised man might experience as well as the compression technique. So far she did not have a report back from her, but expected to meet with her at the end of the week. However, while talking with Alice, some ideas about Rachael had begun to form.

"What do you suggest?" Rachael inquired, her usually resolute voice wavering slightly.

"May I ask you some more questions?" Rachael nodded, then glanced in the direction of Nora's room as though she were looking for an excuse to escape. Hannah hurried to fill the gap. "Are there any changes from when you first told me?"

"Not really."

"Something slightly different? Anything better or worse? Do you ever feel any pleasure, a mounting sensation, a welcome twinge?"

Rachael shrugged, then sucked in her breath. "All right, then, when Herzog approaches me he usually touches me with his fingers first and this warms me up, otherwise I wouldn't be interested." Her voice was tense, mechanical. "As he rubs me, I feel some urgent sensations and I often think: this time it will work, but then as soon as he starts moving inside me, nothing further happens. I've learned that if I get my hopes up, I feel so aroused I cannot sleep afterward, so sometimes I will myself not to let the tension mount, so I won't be as disappointed."

"How long does Herzog take once he has penetrated?" Hannah asked, thinking that he might be too quick for her.

"As long as necessary."

"Necessary for whom?"

"I don't know. He would like me to respond more and sometimes I pretend to, for his sake."

"Do you mean he does not realize that you have never reached a climax?"

"No, he doesn't. Oh, he knows that I don't do it often, but sometimes, to get it over with, I lie to him."

Hannah controlled her shock at this revelation. "Can he last ten minutes?"

"I suppose."

"Twenty?"

"There's nothing wrong with him!"

"Mother!" Rachael rose and went to the bedroom door.

"Yes, Nora?"

"How can I rest with you talking so loud?"

"If we are bothering you, I'll close the door." She wheeled around with a distraught expression. "Do you think she heard us?"

"No, only the tone of the last words. Don't worry so much," Hannah consoled. "Let's continue over here." She got up to move away from the card table, where they had been sitting, and went to the far side of the room. She took the less comfortable settee and motioned for Rachael to sit in Herzog's wing chair.

"What else?" Rachael asked brusquely.

Rachael's attitude was beginning to irk Hannah. Then Dr. Dowd's caution about treating friends loomed up. She could manage if she reminded herself to keep her own feelings out of the matter, as she would with a stranger. "When you begin to have relations with Herz—ah—" She stopped herself from using the familiar "Herzog" and corrected it to "your husband, what thoughts go through your mind?"

"Doesn't everyone think about the same things at a time like that?"

"I doubt you think about what I do."

"Well then, what do you think about?"

This reversal made Hannah reflect whether she should divulge her own experiences, but as she contemplated how she would reply, her self-mocking laugh provoked Rachael.

"Why don't you want to tell me?"

"It's not that—" Hannah burst into giggles. "It's not what you would imagine. I think about ... buildings."

Rachael's eyes widened and she shook her head at Hannah's ridiculous retort. "Oh, really?"

"No, it's true. I think about staircases spiraling up and down. The steps are made of a shimmering metallic, and I am climbing up and up and up. Well, it makes sense if you think about the increasing suspense."

"And that's it?"

"Sometimes I fall backward, everything swirls around me—" She stopped herself. "Anyway, they are fragmentary images, but you see what I mean."

"You don't think about Lazar?"

"I suppose I do, at least with part of my mind. I kiss him, touch him, as he does me, but my brain goes off on its own. I don't know why. Reading Havelock Ellis has given me a few insights into sexual psychology, but I don't understand most of it."

"So you think I should start concentrating on architecture instead of Herzog?"

"You think about him?"

"Yes, since that is the man in my bed."

"What about him? His body? His penis?"

"Yes." Hannah waited for a more complete answer. "Let me see." Now Rachael seemed to be concentrating, the way she did when she was trying to diagnose a problem. Her eyes were unfocused and her mouth was set into a tight line. If Hannah had not known Rachael so well, she might have thought she had annoyed her. "When he is touching me, I consider the sensations and how to improve upon them. When he enters me, I think about the structure of his organ, how it is working, and my genitalia as well. I contemplate the blood flow to the various regions in my pelvis. I consider glandular function and what I might do to improve my effort on his behalf. I know where he likes to be fondled and when." She gave a little chuckle under her breath. "I wonder if he realizes how much I understand about his secret places."

"Does he know as much about yours?"

"Why should he? Nothing he has ever done has made a difference."

"But, as you said before, he doesn't know that." Rachael's eyes darted as if she had been trapped. "Why don't you tell him?" Hannah suggested gently.

"I couldn't!"

"You don't want to tell him you have been faking."

"How could I after all these years?"

"I think that must be done," Hannah said emphatically. Deception between partners would never help matters. Besides, she had a feeling that Herzog was far too clever to have been duped all this time. Maybe he would not openly admit that he had not satisfied his wife, and preferred to believe in her falsehood because it justified his actions of always gratifying himself at her expense . . . Hannah reflected. Even as she thought this part through, another, more insistent worry crowded in. Rachael had trained herself to view her sexual encounters as a physical phenomenon to be analyzed as a scientist studies a cell under a microscope. Perhaps she had chosen this distance to protect herself from becoming devastated by her inability to reach an orgasm or . . . maybe this impartial angle—as though she were looking down at herself from above—suppressed her ability to relax, to let go, to surrender to the sensations. Yet what could Hannah do to help her? Telling Rachael to think about staircases would not work. There had to be something, some clue, some key to unlock her passion, yet Hannah could not supply it.

In the silence Rachael had been grappling with the import of Hannah's comments. She stood and went to the window. A light, cold rain was falling and her reflection in the gloom was cast back at her. Hannah could see her inward struggle and remained silent. She would do more reading, more thinking about how to get Rachael to relax, but the doctor's first task would be to discuss her situation openly. In the end Herzog's full cooperation would be required. Besides, if she and Lazar could manage to make love successfully— and nothing much else—Ezekiel and Rachael certainly could.

Rachael turned partway around, but did not completely face Hannah. "I'll speak to Herzog," she said faintly.

"Good. And then we'll talk again," Hannah replied in as professional a tone as she could muster.

8

Within a few days Minna's hunger strike was competing with the war news from Europe for the most prominent headlines. On January 26, the right-hand columns of the first page of the *New York Times* announced: TISZA HINTS OF NEW TEUTON MOVE FOR PEACE WITH "ACCEPTABLE" TERMS. The next column was headlined: MRS. BLAU WEAKER, STILL FASTS IN CELL. The United Press story reported, "As Mrs. Blau launched into the fifth day of her hunger strike, it was apparent that the advocate of birth control is rapidly drawing toward the climax of her struggle against imprisonment."

"Look at this!" Hannah thrust the paper in front of her husband.

"Every sign points to the genesis of the revolution," he predicted with enthusiasm.

"Is that all you can think about?"

"This is what we've been waiting for, isn't it?"

"What about Minna?"

"Magnificent propaganda effort. You have to admire her."

"Lazar, how can you be so calm when her life is at stake?"

"She won't go through with it."

Hannah's voice became more strident. "You know Minna never gives in."

"She has both the instinct as well as the will to survive. When those Cossacks drove her into a flooding river, shooting those who resisted, she jumped into the icy water, grasped a log, and floated to safety. She was the only Jew in her village not to perish."

"This is different. Can't you see that this time she's using her will against herself?"

"Give her some credit. She knows they won't let her die."

"Why are you so sure?"

"It would be bad publicity."

Hannah hoped fervently that he was right, for despite their

differences—which now seemed petty—she did not want to see anything happen to her sister-in-law.

On Sunday, January 28, next to the front-page story, PEACE BY SWORD, KAISER REPEATS, the *Times* announced: MRS. BLAU NOW BEING FED BY FORCE.

"She has gone more than a hundred hours without food or water," Hannah said in amazement.

"I told you they would not allow it to go much further," Lazar reminded. "Now we must begin a letter-writing campaign to the newspapers to let them know of Prison Commissioner Lewis's cruelty."

Hannah was incredulous. "You want to stop her being fed?"

"Of course not! But if people are outraged by her treatment, they will sympathize with her even more, and thus with her cause."

"What if they stop feeding her and she gets worse?"

"There is a fine balance . . ." he said as he slipped on his jacket.

"Where are you going?"

"To the press," he said, which is what they called the dingy rooms behind the Chrystie Street print shop, where Chaim and Minna lived. "We're meeting there for the latest news. Do you want to come?"

"Of course," she said, even though she would be late for work at Bellevue.

A crowd of their friends had gathered and spilled out on to the street. Rachael was sitting on the doorstep. "I'm so glad to see you!" Tearfully Hannah embraced her. "I thought Margaret Sanger said they would never force feed her!"

"She was wrong," the doctor replied sadly.

"I don't know if I am happy she is getting fed or angry at the violation of her body." Hannah shook her head. "Do you think it is painful?"

"Probably, and more so if she resists. Did you know that she is the first woman in America to suffer such an ordeal?"

"I'm sorry she did not see the sense in your letter," Hannah sighed.

"If she even received it," Lazar added, then guided the desolate group indoors.

"What are they feeding her?" Hannah asked her brother.

"Her attorney reported to Margaret that they rolled her into a blanket and then—" Chaim began to answer, then choked. Swallowing hard, he continued, "And then they poured a concoction of milk, eggs, and brandy through a tube in her throat." The last words made him gag.

Rachael put her arms around him. "That will bring back her strength."

Chaim stumbled back. "She'll hate everyone for allowing this to happen, but she's gone too far . . . too far . . ." His voice drifted off. He bowed his head and his unruly hair masked his eyes.

"When she realizes it was done in her best interests, she'll forgive you," Rachael said with more conviction than she felt.

"You don't know her as well as I do." Chaim's body heaved with unspent sobs. "She won't be able to live with herself if she returns home defeated."

"Better defeated than in a coffin!" Hannah's vehemence surprised them. "Spend a day at Bellevue and see what life is about!"

"Hannah"—Rachael held up her hand—"this is not helping. Nobody here wants her to starve to death—do they?"

"No." Chaim forced a tiny smile. "At least we have agreed about something for a change." Then his voice became gravelly. "Yesterday Mrs. Pinchot from the Committee of One Hundred came to me and said that Minna's life was too valuable to the cause to be wasted. She told me they were sending Minna a telegram begging her to abandon her strike."

"Did she receive it?" Lazar asked Chaim.

Chaim could barely utter the words. "She responded, 'Tell them that I care not whether I starve so long as this unconscionable arrest calls attention to the archaic laws that prevent telling the truth about the basic facts of human life.' "

"She doesn't know what she is saying!" Hannah shouted. "Her reason is failing. Rachael, tell them what you told me. Minna cannot decide for herself."

"We don't know that for sure," Rachael replied forlornly.

"Couldn't you visit her—as her doctor?"

"Would you?" Chaim implored. "I can't see her, but maybe her physician could!"

The next morning, Dr. Jaffe was permitted a brief medical visit on Blackwell's Island. Hannah remained home from Bellevue, one of the few times she had stayed away from work except when she was ill, but this was a life-or-death matter. She met the ferry as it came into the dock. When she caught sight of Rachael, the doctor was shaking her head somberly.

Hannah rushed down the pier. "Is she gone?"

"No, not yet."

"Danken Got!"

"But her vision is affected and her heart is beginning to miss beats due to a lack of fluids."

"Can she recover?"

"I don't know. The prison nurse reported that yesterday she was unconscious for almost twenty-four hours, but Minna swears she was awake. I also heard that she was expectorating blood, a dangerous sign if it's from the lungs."

"Would she listen to reason?"

"Not to me."

"Is she fit to decide for herself?"

"I would have to say that as of this morning she is."

"Does she know about tonight?" Hannah asked, recalling that Margaret Sanger had scheduled a meeting to support Minna at Carnegie Hall.

"Yes. She said to tell them not to grieve but to cheer, for she will win them a victory."

That evening, Hannah and Rachael sat on either side of Chaim in the front row of Carnegie Hall. Twenty poor mothers from Brownsville Clinic lined the stage, and the boxes were filled with celebrities including Isadora Duncan, the writer Rupert Hughes, and the painter John Sloan. First the Reverend John Haynes Holmes, the socialist pastor, spoke and then was followed by Dr. Mary Halton. When Margaret Sanger came on stage, the audience greeted her with a long exhalation of approval. With a straight back and dignified expression she stood in front of them and waited for the audience to settle before speaking. "I come not from the stake at Salem, where women were once burned for blasphemy, but from the shadow of Blackwell's Island, where women are tortured for so-called obscenity."

Lazar leaned over and whispered, "She's wonderful." He was awestruck more by the forceful delivery of her ardent words than the message itself. Later, in the lobby with their friends, he said reverently, "Mrs. Sanger has vast reserves of strength. You can feel it. She is one of the great women of our times. Don't you agree, Chaim?"

His brother-in-law had not heard a word. He was staring

off into space. Hannah took her brother's icy hands in hers and rubbed them. "She'll be fine. I know she will!" she murmured to console him. What would he do without Minna? He was as tied to her as she was to Lazar, maybe more so. How could she have resented Minna all this time when she had made him so happy? "I haven't been fair to Minna," she offered. "She's been wonderful for you and to you, and I suppose I've felt left out."

"Please, you don't have to—"

"I've wanted to say it for a long time."

Chaim's nod was a wordless acceptance of her apology. Just then Rachael clasped him by the elbow. "Margaret needs to speak with you."

Chaim blinked and looked around. The crowd had dispersed. Margaret Sanger, flanked by several of her wealthy friends, was standing in front of him. "Mr. Blau," she began almost reverentially, "may I introduce you to Mrs. Ashley? And this is Mrs. Pinchot, a personal friend to Governor Whitman." She turned to Rachael. "Dr. Jaffe, might you be so kind to tell these ladies exactly what you witnessed when you examined Mrs. Blau?"

The women paled at Rachael's grim portrait.

Margaret wiped away fresh tears. "How much more time does she have?"

"That I cannot say. We don't starve people to gather statistics."

"Are we talking about hours or days or weeks?" she pressed.

"Her heart is already affected. I don't know how long it could last. A crisis could come at any time, or she might hold out for another week."

"But if she started to take nourishment on her own today, would she recover?" Mrs. Ashley probed.

"She would have a chance."

"Margaret?" the elegant woman queried in a shaking voice.

Mrs. Sanger gave Mrs. Pinchot a penetrating stare. "Would the governor listen to me?"

"He reads the newspapers," she replied with a sly smile. "He cannot afford her blood on his hands."

"Nobody can," Margaret said, meaning no politician, but Hannah also realized she had meant herself as well.

"We have to do something!" Mrs. Ashley insisted. "Don't we, Mr. Blau?"

"If anything happened to Minna, I could not live with myself."

"My thoughts exactly." Margaret's words were directed to the family. Then she turned to her prominent friends. "Would you both accompany me to Albany at once?"

∽∽∽ 9 ∽∽∽

Chaim came rushing back that evening with the news. "They saw the governor!"

Mama jumped up and clasped her hands over her heart. "*Gotteniu!* Will he save her?"

"The governor was sympathetic, but he said he was afraid Minna would violate the law again."

"You could stop her," Mama insisted.

"I wish that I could, but I can't control her, and the governor won't do anything without her promise that she will obey the statutes."

"Is there a chance she'll agree?" Hannah asked.

"I don't know. Margaret's taking his message to the prison in an hour. A doctor may accompany her, but there isn't time to find Rachael or Ezekiel. Will you go?"

"Me?" Hannah asked. "I'm not a doctor."

"Wear your white dress and take your stethoscope. Nobody will know the difference. Maybe you can convince her."

Hannah looked into her brother's desolate eyes and was filled with renewed resolve. Here was her chance to redeem herself for her unfairness to Minna. But what if it was too late?

On the ferry, the glacial wind off the river smarted Hannah's face, yet did not penetrate to her bones because a blazing heat burned under her flesh as she tried to think of what words would melt Minna's iron resolve. Margaret's face was carved in granite. Each of them carried a piece of the burden for one woman's life; nevertheless, in that dark moment the two women had nothing to say to each other.

Minna lay on her cot in the small, dismal infirmary room. Her eyes were sunken, her tongue swollen. Her skin was as gray as the concrete of the floors and walls.

"Minna?" She did not stir at the sound of her name. "It's Hannah, Chaim's sister," she added more loudly in case her hearing was as diminished as her vision.

Minna's bony fingers waved her closer. There was a rash on her face. She opened her mouth, but her voice was a hoarse whisper "I must go away."

Did that mean she wanted to die or wanted out of prison?

Margaret bent close and spoke crisply. "The governor will pardon you if you agree to stop your activities. What shall we tell him?"

"Away . . ."

"She's in no condition to decide," Margaret said. "We'll have to take this on our own shoulders."

"She might hate us for it," Hannah warned.

"What does your brother want us to do?"

Of course Chaim did not want to lose Minna, but he did not want to take the blame for saving her either. No matter what the outcome, Minna could not fault Margaret, who she knew would do what was best for the cause, but she would resent Hannah's interference. Let her hate me forever, Hannah resolved. Let her despise me, as long as she lives. Warm tears spilled down her cheeks, stinging her chapped skin. "My brother loves Minna. He wants his wife back," she replied.

"Then I will guarantee that Minna Blau will no longer work for the abolishment of the laws against birth control, nor will she break any statutes, no matter how unfair they may be," Margaret said to the warden.

"Will you put that in writing and sign it?" the warden asked more gently than Margaret would have expected.

"If it is required," Margaret replied more haughtily than necessary.

Minna, who had been unaware of what was said on her behalf, was carried by stretcher to the ferry.

"She's coming home with me," Margaret announced to the crowd of supporters and reporters. "Do you want to ride with her?" she asked Hannah.

"Yes, thank you."

"We'll stop by the press and pick up Mr. Blau," Margaret announced in a loud voice so everyone standing around could hear.

⤳ 10 ⤳

Hannah was amazed to discover that Margaret already had set aside a room—had it been Peggy's?—to care for Minna. A hospital bed and supplies were on hand. Hannah half expected a nurse to be on duty, until she remembered that was Margaret's profession.

"I did this to her, and I'll bring her back to health," Margaret vowed to Chaim.

"She'll need around-the-clock care for the first few days," Rachael said after she had examined her thoroughly. "She must receive fluids every hour, but only in small quantities. I want her urine measured, her blood pressure taken every thirty minutes. If anything unusual occurs, don't send for me, bring her directly to Gouverneur's Hospital." She turned to Chaim, who was bent and haggard after the long ordeal. "Margaret cannot manage that on her own."

"I can stay," he volunteered.

"You have suffered almost as much as she has. When was the last time you ate or slept?"

"I don't want to leave her!" he protested.

"She's too exhausted to know what's happening. Leave it to us experts, if only for tonight," Hannah interjected, "because she'll be needing special care from you for many months, won't she, Rachael?"

The doctor nodded. "Come back in the morning and you'll see a new woman."

"I don't know . . ." he said in a daze, but she led him away.

"I'll remain at least through the first night," Hannah said to Rachael. "Could you stop in and tell Mama what is happening? She'll have the children stay downstairs if Lazar won't be home."

Chaim embraced his sister. "Thank you for everything!"

For the first few hours, Hannah and Margaret spoke little, except as to what had to be done. Minna was so weak she could not raise an arm or control the muscles in her neck. Twice Hannah became alarmed by the drop in blood pressure when she sat up too far. Each time cold compresses brought her out of the faint, but Hannah decided that if there was one more occurrence, she would take her to the hospital.

After midnight, the dehydration was less noticeable. An hour later, when Minna was able to take the tepid broth on her own, they felt they had passed a milestone. The two of them, each on one side of the bed, lowered her and straightened the covers.

"She's going to make it," Margaret said as though she needed to hear the words to believe them.

"So far, so good" was the best Hannah would allow. They were not out of the woods yet, and even when the dangerous hours had passed, there was the concern that Minna might be debilitated for the rest of her life.

"Why don't you get some rest? I will wake you in a couple of hours."

"I'm not tired yet," Hannah lied. She remembered Rachael's fears for Minna's heart. If only one of them was awake, it was easier to be inattentive. It would take but a few minutes for a crisis to occur.

"Then we had better keep talking to stay alert," Margaret said.

She gestured for Hannah to sit on a small sofa on the far side of the room where they had the best view of the bed, then poured large cups of coffee for them both. So that Minna could sleep, they left the light dimmed.

"Thank you for what you did."

"Even I know when something has gone too far," Margaret said with a self-deprecating laugh.

"My mother has a saying, *'Shvaygn iz a tsoym far khokhme, ober nor shvaygn iz keyn khokhme nit.'* "

"And what does that mean?"

"Silence is the fence of wisdom, but mere silence is not wisdom."

"I must write that down and send it to one of my English friends."

"Might that be Mr. Ellis?" Hannah was thrilled that she finally had an opening to ask about him.

"How did you know?"

"I've read as much of his work as I can find. I thought it was the sort of thing he sometimes quotes."

"You are right about that." Margaret did not elaborate. Then, after a thoughtful pause, she asked, "What do you think of his theories?"

"I don't always understand them, but some of his ideas have been helping me with my patients—my private ones, that is."

"That would please him enormously."

"May I ask what he is like?"

Margaret gave a long sigh. "He's extraordinary!"

"In what way?"

"In every way. His head is powerful, and he has a charming smile. His hair is pure white and he has a long beard, a bit shaggy, although well tended. And his mouth ... very sensitive, very expressive." She halted for a second, then turned to reveal eyes luminous with exhilaration. "After those first few awkward moments, when I realized I was in the presence of a great man, I was at peace, and content as I had never been before. It was a bounteous privilege to know him."

"He might have felt the same way about you," Hannah said, recalling Lazar's remarks at Carnegie Hall.

"Oh, no! The first time we met I made a fool of myself. I tried a few aimless remarks and ended up stuttering with embarrassment. He let me go on while he was perfectly still. Then I saw that small talk was not possible with him. You had to utter only the deepest truths within you." She paused as the memory washed over her. "I cannot explain how I felt when I left him to go back to my own dull little room. It was as if I had been raised up into a hitherto undreamed-of world."

With some shock Hannah realized these were the gushing recollections of a smitten woman. "He is married, isn't he?"

"In a fashion ..." came the chilly reply. "Edith preferred the country and stayed on her farm in Cornwall."

"That doesn't sound very convenient."

"For them it was. You see, his wife was a homosexual leading an independent life."

Hannah was even more astounded. How could a man with his sensitivities have made such a drastic mistake?

Margaret knew she would have to explain. "I think he

thought he could learn from her, and some of his theories on sexual inversion must have come from that relationship."

This did not satisfy Hannah. "I cannot believe he married simply to continue his research."

"That may have sounded harsh, but he was also her protector. They married in the days of the Oscar Wilde scandal, so I suppose he wanted to shield her from the public."

Was this merely Margaret's way of explaining—or justifying—her relationship with the illustrious man? What had transpired between them? Hannah recalled Peggy's death so soon after her mother's return and considered whether Margaret had felt a terrible guilt that she had been with this man when her daughter needed her. "You were lovers," she stated rather than asked.

"Honi soit qui mal y pense," Margaret said. "Evil to him who thinks evil of others." She gave Hannah a self-satisfied glance. "Besides, the unfortunate woman died suddenly of a chill last September."

A long silence. Then: "Our minds and our bodies unfolded to each other in the most natural way. It happened slowly and not in the passionate manner in which most people suppose affairs are begun. We were talking, and then he stood up—this tall, magnificent figure—and approached me. The next thing I knew was the feel of his cool kisses, like the rich petals of some tea rose, falling softly on my face. From that moment he awakened in me feelings I had never known existed."

Hannah's breath stopped. In the silence only Minna's harsh respiration resounded.

"But it is not what you are thinking. Since the average woman or man usually only experiences passion—and not very often at that—he was striving to secure the peaceful and joyous, the consoling and inspiring, aspects of true love."

"You made love with Havelock Ellis?"

Margaret's voice was barely a whisper. "He did not make love to me in the usual way. He did not have those capabilities, or maybe he chose not to exercise them."

What was this all about? Why was she talking in riddles? Although Hannah's curiosity mounted, she knew better than to ask specific questions. She waited.

"He said that it was only by intimate contact that one divines the scent and the taste of the mysterious essences that are distilled from the guarded places of a woman. And thus that is how he came to me, and how he brought me more pleasure than I have ever known."

There was nothing Hannah could say. Havelock Ellis and Margaret Sanger . . . making love, yet not making love . . . did not have those capabilities . . . Had she meant that Ellis was impotent? Intimate contact . . . taste of the mysterious essences distilled from the guarded places . . . Had he excited her by tasting her genitals? The idea was not foreign to Hannah, although she and Lazar had never found it their preference. The last time, she recalled, probably was at the end of her pregnancy with Emma.

A few minutes passed. Margaret struck a match to look at her wristwatch. "Time for a feeding." She crossed the room and poured out a portion of broth, leaving Hannah to mull over what she had divulged.

Minna sputtered as the broth irritated her damaged throat. "Hannah!" Margaret called for help.

Hannah rushed over to support the patient while Margaret held the cup, abandoning her reveries for another time.

✑ 11 ✑

In the next month, while Minna retired to the room behind the press to recuperate, Margaret Sanger carried the torch for the birth-control movement. Sanger's own trial was forthcoming and reporters hounded her with the incessant question: if convicted, would she go on a hunger strike?

"It depends . . ." she hedged.

"On what?" they badgered.

"How long a sentence I get," she tossed off, not realizing this would only fuel them further.

Lazar was displeased with her reply. "Women must learn not to vacillate. It hurts their cause."

"She's been warned that if she starves herself, her tubercular glands might start acting up," Hannah defended. "Besides, there is no point of a hunger strike unless the press follows it, and with the war news crowding the headlines, she'd be relegated to a back page."

"Minna made the front page, and before that nobody knew her name. Sanger will receive far more publicity."

Of course Lazar was right. The mothers of Brownsville packed the courtroom, many with babies, diapers, baskets of food. Nearby sat a group of elegantly attired women from the Committee of One Hundred. As Margaret entered the courtroom she was handed a bouquet of roses. Despite the judge's attempt to get Mrs. Sanger to promise not to violate the law again, she responded, "I cannot promise to obey a law I do not respect."

The judge pounded his gavel and sentenced her to the workhouse for thirty days. Everyone was relieved. They had been afraid she would get a year and a large fine.

"We've won," Minna explained. "They could not give her less of a sentence than mine. This proves they are losing interest in hounding us."

"I hope that is true," Hannah said with relief.

As long as Margaret was not trying to kill herself for the cause and Minna was out of it, Hannah could concentrate on the numerous problems that faced her at home. She continued to see her private patients, but they blurred together with the sameness of their questions, their complaints. There were itches and drips, menstrual irregularities, the pains that were often mittelschmerz, the mothers who wanted the next to be a boy, all the usual. Sometimes they were more amusing than serious. One woman, who was weeks away from delivering, wanted to know how to have a boy. And even after Hannah explained she was too late, the dim-witted patient continued to ask what to eat to change the course of events. "Hot peppers," Hannah finally said to get rid of her.

As it turned out, the woman had a boy and for months Hannah heard rumors that others were trying peppers.

"What can I do to stop it?" she asked Rachael half seriously.

"Sell peppers!" the doctor replied. "I have a good recipe."

The women laughed about it, but Hannah had learned a lesson: never give anyone advice unless you truly believe it might help them.

At Bellevue there seemed to be more and more disagreements between the midwives and the doctors, and the ladies on the Board of Managers were always changing one rule or another in the name of progress—or was it boredom? At least Mrs. Hemming, her most direct supervisor, had been asked to serve on several war-readiness committees, which kept her out of Hannah's hair. The one bright moment during those dreary winter weeks came when Alice Brody offered her report.

"I think it is working," she began when she had Hannah alone.

"Your husband is able to control himself better," Hannah stated flatly, stifling her excitement.

"If I use my hand, he can last as long as he wants. We do get tired, so . . ."

"That's excellent." Hannah tried to think ahead about what she might try next. "Have you attempted penetration?"

"Well . . ."

"You're married, so it's not illegal!" Hannah lightened the moment with a laugh.

"We did it a few times."

"And?"

"It's better, but not perfect."

"These matters take time."

"I know. We are both encouraged. I wanted to thank you for your help."

Hannah waved her hand to show it was nothing. "What about you? Are you finding more satisfaction?"

Alice hesitated before saying, "A little."

Better, but not perfect. But what did Hannah expect? She was groping blindly, but already her advice had brought Malcolm Brody control he had not had before. "Here's what I suggest . . ." she began, and launched into a variation of the hand technique, which instructed either husband or wife to use their fingers to stop the ejaculation when the sensation mounted precipitously. "Work to establish the best position so that you can grab him. If you are on top of him, it might be easiest. Then, if that works for—say, a week—try to see if you can stop him by merely lifting your body off him, either all the way or partway, whatever is required."

"What if he makes a mistake?"

"He will, like any student, but look how far you have come already!" She patted Alice's hand. "Now he must pay more attention to you. Before you begin, ask him to touch you in places that you like, and don't forget to tell him what feels good, what feels even better, and what you don't care for. He has to learn as much about you as you did about him."

"I can wait ..."

Hannah knew that Alice was one of the most selfless of her staff members. She could imagine her doing everything and expecting nothing in return. Tailoring her next prescription to her client's personality, she said firmly, "No. This will benefit him because it will direct his mind away from his own performance." She stopped to see if Alice was following her. The girl's wide brown eyes fluttered as she considered the fresh idea. "Then, after he has finished, he should go back to fondling you if you have not been satisfied. Do you know what I am referring to?"

Alice's cheeks brightened with a rosy flush. "Yes."

"You have reached a climax?"

"Yes."

"With him?"

"A few times in the last week. We did a lot of playing around while he was trying to hold back ..."

"Was he inside you?"

Alice averted her eyes. "No, it was with his hand, but—"

"There is nothing wrong with that. The important thing is that he now knows how to stimulate you. You must tell him what you want him to do. Some women think it is more ladylike to be silent, but the opposite is true." Hannah beamed at her pupil. "Don't forget: two people must be content, not one. Even if you would forgo your pleasure, you must not deny him the victory of knowing he can make you happy."

She knew Alice had accepted her counsel and was not surprised when only a few days later Alice stopped her outside of Ward D to say, "Everything is fine. Thank you."

There were students in the corridor and a patient walking the halls, but it was obvious Alice was in no need of a private consultation. "Keep up the good work," Hannah replied with a wink.

Hannah walked away from Alice with only a momentary sense of elation. How could she be so helpful to other people and so foolish with her own family? That morning she had fought with Lazar. He must have been going to spend the day with Trotsky because he had been acting impatient with her, which was the way he protected himself from criticism. Hannah recognized that the attack was really a defense, but these days her tolerance for his methods was the lowest it had ever been.

"You should quit your job at the hospital," he had started as she was rushing about.

Trying to ignore him, Hannah had continued to put the farina on the table.

"The hours are terrible and the pay is exploitative," he continued while she ladled out small portions of milk.

To save money she was purchasing the cheapest ingredients and regulating the quantities to make everything stretch further. Already merchants averted their eyes when she mumbled something about paying the next day.

"Can't do it anymore," they'd said, or "New policy." Hannah understood that she had asked once too often. Then Chaye, the fishmonger, gave her an idea when she whined in an irritating voice, "Don't you expect to be paid promptly for your advice? And it doesn't spoil like my carp."

"Very true." Hannah fumbled to see if the few extra coins in her coat pocket would make up the difference. "Remember, though, today I need your fish, tomorrow you might need my recipe for a spicier marriage." Hannah forced herself to give the dubious woman a cagey smile.

A few days later, Chaye waved Hannah over when she saw her pass. "I have some extra herring I could let you have."

Hannah shook her head. "Not today, thanks."

"No charge," Chaye blurted before Hannah moved away.

The midwife did not miss the merchant's twisting hands. "What seems to be the problem?"

"Morrie is having troubles, you know, getting hard enough."

"Does he drink schnapps in the evening?"

"Only a little glass."

"But how many?"

She shrugged. "Who knows?"

"Count. If it's more than three or four, that's the problem."

"What should I do?"

Hannah thought quickly. She was on her way home after a busy night shift and too tired to talk all day for a few pieces of herring. "Add some water to the bottle and go to bed earlier."

Chaye wrapped the herring. "Come back next week, I might have more."

The fishmonger was pleased enough with Hannah's prescription to give her two smoked whitefish, as well as to tell several of the other women merchants for whom Hannah was willing to barter advice for food. If they wanted to ask her a personal question, they would begin, "I hear you have a good recipe . . ." and any bystanders would not be the wiser.

Even though a few delicacies were garnered in this way, nobody was allowed to poke about in her kitchen anymore, something the children openly resented. Not that Lazar had tried to explain the situation. If anything, he behaved like one of them.

"If you spent all your time at St. Mark's Place you could make the same amount or more. That way you could set your own hours, pick and choose who you would care for—"

He was being so shortsighted she broke her resolution not to respond to his provocations. "I don't turn anyone away now. What makes you think I could fill a whole day, let alone a whole week with appointments?"

"Once they knew you were going to be there—"

"Don't talk nonsense!" she interrupted. "I'm not a doctor. How many women have the sort of problems I can help with?"

"More than you might think," he said, using his most winsome grin to warm her. He failed. She turned away in disgust. "Hey, I thought I had helped with that last case. You said you passed on my method. It worked, didn't it?"

"Why do you think it did?" she challenged.

"Because if it didn't, you would have rubbed it in," he parried smoothly.

Hannah groaned as she brought out the sugar jar from her hiding place. He was impossible!

"Benny! Give it back!" Emma shouted. "Ma! Benny's got my other ribbon."

"Benny! Leave your sister alone and come to the table before your breakfast gets cold."

Her son ran into the room and pulled out the chair with a scraping sound. "Ugh! Farina! Is that all there is?"

"Yes. Eat it or go hungry."

He reached for the sugar bowl, dipped in his spoon, and

pulled out a heaping load. Hannah slapped his hand. "Too much. None for you."

"Pa?" Benny whined at the unfairness.

"Let him be," Lazar defended.

Incensed by both of them, Hannah took the bowl and put it away.

"Where's the sugar?" Emma asked as she sat down.

"She won't let us have any!" Benny pouted.

"Why?" Emma asked in the slippery-sweet voice she affected when she wanted her way.

"Because we can't afford it," Hannah retorted. "Now eat or you'll be late."

"But why?" Emma groaned.

"Ask your father."

Emma looked for a more satisfactory response from the other side of the table, but all Lazar did was glare at his wife. Hannah answered for him. "Because your father is not bringing in any money, that's why."

With that Lazar stood up. He patted each of the children on their heads, made a show of putting on his coat and buttoning each button carefully before he turned on his heel and slammed the door.

How had it come to this? Why did it seem she was the villain and the three other members of her family were against her? Who had to explain to Mama Blau why there was not enough money to pay the month's rent? Who had to ask Rachael for an advance on the patients who had not yet paid so she could buy food last week? And there was more to worry about.

Twice she had seen the same strange man with a black hat and silver-tipped cane lurking outside the next building. What did he want with them? Was he connected with Trotsky? The police? Or was he after the money that had been lost in the numbers racket? Now wherever she went, she watched for the man and any other shady characters. There were so many odd people, so many sick and broken and desperate ones. There were young boys hanging out with no work. What if Benny started to go with those types? There were men who looked at women dangerously. What if Emma were to be accosted? She should talk to the children about the menaces around them, but she did not want to alarm them. Yet she was frightened. Why shouldn't she be? The world was a frightening place.

❦ **12** ❦

There had to be a way to make peace, if only at home. All she needed was some quiet time to work things out. All she needed was a bit more money each month so she could start with a clean slate and no debts. All she needed was more hours in the day, more sleep, more food, more money . . . In the past she and Lazar had surmounted their difficulties, and somehow she expected they would find a way to survive this confusing time. Then word came that something prophetic had happened in Russia.

On that crucial morning Mama greeted her in the foyer as she staggered in from work. "Lazar said you should go to meet him at *Novy Mir.* Everybody's going to be there."

"What is it?"

"He said it is the revolution, but you know Lazar." Her mother held her hands out palms up. For a moment Hannah was going to ignore his summons, but something in Mama's eyes sent her back out the door.

When she reached the corner of First Avenue and St. Mark's Place, two boys were pointing up at the street sign and laughing. Someone had climbed the pole and painted over the word "St." and changed "Mark's" to "Marx." By the time she reached the offices of the radical Russian daily, which meant "New World," her mood became more hopeful. If there truly was news of a Russian revolution, it might be for the best. As with a medical condition, sometimes the conservative treatment failed and only surgery would suffice to cure. Maybe Marx's ideas would have a place in modern society. Maybe this was the start of a whole new world.

"What's going on?" she asked the first person she met on the stoop of 177 St. Mark's Place.

"We're waiting for Trotsky. He's bringing big news."

Bristling again at the power this impudent man wielded, she was buoyed by the chance his days in New York might be about to end. More and more people crowded the barren offices of the newspaper, which Trotsky had dubbed "the

headquarters for internationalist revolutionary propaganda."
It was as if the cafés had been emptied into this squalid
room. There were Moisei Volodarsky, Grigorii Isakovich
Chudnovsky, Nikolai Bukharin, Alexandra Kollontai, Louis
Fraina, and the others who dubbed themselves anarchists,
revolutionaries, and radicals. While they waited for
Trotsky's report, rumors about what had been happening in
Russia were rife, but the various versions were contradic-
tory. The smell of musty wool and unwashed bodies that
permeated the room became especially strong near the iron
stove, where many tried to dry their damp clothes. Deciding
she would rather be chilly than congregate with the odorif-
erous throng, Hannah kept to the far end of the room.

"Here he comes!" Volodarsky cried.

Lazar, who thus far had done his best to ignore his wife,
moved to her side. Trotsky stood on a desk. With a swift
gesture he brushed his hair back. "The best we can determine is that the czar left Petrograd for General Headquarters
on the seventh. Nothing was especially unusual, except the
frost was severe. There had been a lull along the whole front
and army life was proceeding sluggishly due to the heavy
cover of snow. That was what deceived everybody." Trotsky
folded his hands and sucked in his breath. "The very next
day, strikes began in several factories here and there, like
spontaneous combustion. Workers poured into the streets demanding food. Shortages of bread caused the women to lose
their patience."

During the excited outburst Lazar caught Hannah's eye.
His expression was that of a satisfied cat, and she could hear
his inward exclamation as clearly as if he had spoken: I
knew it! I knew it all along!

"What are the estimates?" Chaim called out.

"Ninety thousand on strike on the eighth, perhaps two
hundred thousand on the ninth, a quarter of a million on the
tenth," Trotsky shouted above the din.

Minna, who was seated because she was still weak, appeared skeptical. "Could that be accurate?"

Her brother-in-law shot a warning glance. Nobody was to
question Trotsky. Disgusted by Lazar's venerating demeanor,
Hannah inched closer to Minna. She reached for her sister-
in-law's hand.

"Here is the best part," Trotsky continued slowly. "The

strikes were not organized. They burst out of the hearts of the people." The crowd cheered, tossing their caps in the air.

More nonsense! Hannah had heard enough. She headed for the door, but Lazar blocked her way. Not wanting to make a scene, she propped herself against a post. Let them talk, it's only talk, she said in a litany to console herself. Then the words, which had been matter-of-factly relating the details of the strike, changed in pitch. Trotsky leaned into the assemblage. Hannah could see Lazar's enraptured face as Trotsky reached the climax of his tale.

"Only a few were injured in Znamensky Square. The Volynsky Regiment mainly shot over their heads, but a few became overexcited. Then, instead of feeling victorious, the regiment itself was infected with the revolutionary fervor that the people had manifested. They shot their own commanding officer and subaltern, to shouts of 'Hurrah!' And thus the Volynsky Regiment went over to the people. It left the barracks in full battle dress and marched to Liteyny Bridge and relieved the Moscow Regiment. Other regiments joined them: the Preobrazhensky, the Litovsky. Soon workers fell in step behind the military and then . . ." Trotsky's voice rose to a fever pitch. "At last, after a dispute with the officers, even the Moscow Regiment was won over to the people!"

"The time has come to go home!" Bukharin shouted.

"Yes, my comrades," Trotsky replied, "but just as a blacksmith cannot seize the red-hot iron in his naked hand, so the proletariat cannot directly seize the power. We must create an organization to accommodate our formidable task."

Chaim leapt up on his chair and raised his arms in salute. "We had better prepare to take over, for surely the czar will fall in a matter of days."

"Hours, my comrades, hours," Trotsky predicted in a purposefully lowered voice out of respect for the impact of the moment, yet his eyes gleamed with a luminous inner light of triumph.

∽ **13** ∽

They were dreaming. The czar was firmly in place. He was in control of the vast Russian armies. Because of the war, because of the frigid winter, because of the mass starvations, he was holding back on releasing his might. Why didn't the others see that while there had always been dissension and strikes, in the end the imperialists stayed in command? Why should it be different this time? If Hannah and her family had not believed that Russia forever would be a terrible place to live, they would not have gone through the upheaval of immigration. Their first years in New York had been rugged, and even now it was not easy to make ends meet, but if you were clever and worked hard—as Napthali and Eva had proven—a better life was attainable. Her situation, though hardly luxurious, was more comfortable than most in Russia. But even comfort was not everything. As a child in Odessa, Hannah had loved their modest home on Melnitzky Square, but there most Jews had been denied an equal chance. The prohibitions began with the denial of educational opportunities. She first had been rejected at the Odessa Technical Institute and had to fight for a place to study midwifery. She, Lazar, and Rachael were among the fortunate few who had been able to gain professional training, while in America, if they were industrious, their children had unlimited choices. Why couldn't Lazar see how far they had come and how much more they could accomplish here? As soon as their family was financially secure he would have more time for his causes. Better to work from a stable platform than the roiling sea of an embattled Europe. But who listened to her? Certainly, with the likes of Mr. Trotsky around, she had lost her clout with Lazar.

Two days after the meeting at *Novy Mir,* Lazar came home excited that Trotsky had asked him to collaborate on a political drama of the American Civil War. "He said we would each be bringing something to the project that the other lacks," Lazar boasted.

"Is that so?" Hannah replied, forgetting to control her sharp tongue. "And what does Mr. Trotsky suggest that he lacks?"

"He said that I had the literary gift and he had the ability to analyze the nature of a civil struggle."

An involuntary shiver coursed through Hannah. "I thought there was talk about him returning to Russia . . ." she began hesitantly.

"He'll probably leave at the end of the month."

"So why are you dreaming of a collaboration?"

If there was a pause before he replied, it was too brief for him to have considered the devastation his words would have. "I might go with him."

Blackness swirled around Hannah. She was not aware of any particular physical sensations, not heat or coldness, not an increase in respiration or heartbeat. All feelings vanished as a cruel numbness enveloped her.

14

The unbelievable, the unthinkable, happened. On March 16, Nicholas II, Czar of all the Russias, signed his abdication papers before officers at the army headquarters in Pskov. "May God help Russia," he said.

"God has nothing to do with it," Lazar commented with glee.

Hannah had been wrong, wrong about everything! What did this mean? Would Lazar keep his vow to return to his homeland? Once before he had said he was leaving, yet he had come back to her. This time, though, she knew he might do it. Why?

Because of her. That was why.

She had made every mistake. She had fought him when she should have supported him. She had belittled his friends. She had disagreed with his predictions. Why had she been so certain? What did she know about politics? Isn't that what Lazar always said, and he had been right about that as well. He was the one on the front lines of the cafés. All along he

had been the one who had known which way the wind was
blowing. The narrow focus of her family and jobs had prevented her from seeing the larger view, and now she would
pay the price for her myopia.

Everything Lazar had expected was coming true. Already
the United States had recognized the Kerensky government.
The fall of the czar brought a collective sigh of relief to the
Jewish community because this meant no more pogroms.
The *Forverts* headlines were euphoric: JEWISH TROUBLES AT
AN END, FULL RIGHTS FOR ALL OPPRESSED NATIONALITIES, NEW
LIGHT RISES OVER RUSSIA. Their editorials were also effusive.
"Mazel Tov to Our Jewish People; Mazel Tov to the Entire
World," one began. The Café Boulevard was filled with
boasting radicals. Those, like Ezekiel Herzog and Chaim
Blau, who had been jailed by the czar's repressive policies,
were the heroes of the day. Even though Lazar had put in his
time in the underground, he had never been caught, so his
contributions were hidden. Hannah knew how excluded he
felt and tried to celebrate with him to make up—albeit
tardily—for her errors, for now she had to demonstrate there
was some reason to remain home.

For support she looked to Chaim, who displayed no interest in returning to Russia. A few months in her prisons had
left him with an enduring revulsion for his homeland.

"A pity Lazar has no such memories," she complained as
she sat on the bed in the room behind the press while her
brother was cleaning a piece of machinery with a foul-
smelling liquid.

"It might have had the opposite effect on him. After all,
look at Trotsky."

Hannah grimaced. "What can I do?" she pleaded. "Why
won't he see that he's better off here?"

"Trotsky is leaving soon," Chaim reminded.

Hannah startled. "Do you know when?"

"I heard he has booked passage at the end of the month."
Chaim glanced warily at his wife. She gave him a signal that
he might as well continue. "Lazar has asked to go with
him."

"I suspected that was coming." Hannah leaned against the
wall and slumped like a deflated balloon.

"Trosky refused him," her brother reported steadily.

"Are you certain?" Hannah's heart beat furiously.
"Why?"

"Because Lazar has no money," Minna filled in as she looked up from her task. She had kept the promise Margaret Sanger had made to the judge, at least on the surface, but in the privacy of her home she was binding birth-control literature.

For a moment Hannah commiserated with her husband, who must have felt rejected by his mentor, but then she was infused with gratitude that he had been so negligent about money. With her greatest fear allayed for the moment, Hannah focused on Minna, who did not look well. Her skin, often the color of a peeled pear, was even more pasty than usual. She had not gained back enough weight, and she had a dry cough. "How have you been feeling?" she asked solicitously.

"Better every day," Minna replied with a wan smile.

"You should take supplemental syrups. I'll bring you some from Bellevue in a few days. How is Mrs. Sanger?"

"She's busier than ever," Minna said with a laugh. "Prison hardly slowed her down. The same day she was released she attended a luncheon at the Hotel Lafayette given by the Committee of One Hundred and in the evening went to see Isadora Duncan dance. Oh, and she's opening a new office near Union Square."

"I don't know how she does it," Hannah said, shaking her head with admiration.

"Her rich friends are very generous, especially a certain gentleman . . ." Minna arched her thick black brows.

"She's living on West Fourteenth Street with Jonah Goldstein, the attorney who defended Minna and Margaret," Chaim explained.

Minna handed Hannah a copy of the newly revised pamphlet, *Family Limitation.* "Open it." The words were in Yiddish. "Chaim helped me translate it. He's taking it around to pushcart vendors and selling it to them for a quarter, and they are offering it for thirty cents. Already he's sold several hundred. We're also getting the contract to print her newest venture. She's calling it the *Birth Control Review.*" Minna babbled on excitedly about the latest on that front until Hannah could politely take her leave.

Everyone was doing well. Everyone was settled. Eva and Napthali. Chaim and Minna. Rachael and Ezekiel. Even Margaret Sanger and Mr. Goldstein. Her resentment at everyone else's good fortune compared to the upheaval of her own life threatened to overwhelm her. Everything she had done had turned to garbage! No, think of the good things, she admonished herself, or you'll poison yourself with envy. Think about how happy Alice Brody is with her husband, and Stella Applebaum with her young doctor and new baby. What about Benny's excellent school report and how beautifully Emma sings her American songs in that high, sweet voice? What was that new tune about the war? "Keep the Home Fires Burning" echoed in her mind, each word imprinting like a searing brand. And there, right in the middle of crossing Avenue A, Hannah burst into sobs. Blinded by her tears, she somehow managed to get to the other side without getting killed. Nobody seemed to notice. With the world at war, with Russia in flux, with Wilson calling a special session of Congress to decide whether America would enter the fray, with so much tragedy and poverty, a woman crying in the streets was nothing special.

ᗪᔆ 15 ᔆᗰ

At last the moment Hannah had wished for arrived. The next day Trotsky was leaving America on a Norwegian ship. He was departing without Lazar. Only a few more hours and he would be gone. Maybe then she could reclaim her husband's heart. To show her good faith, she willingly attended his farewell address at the Harlem River Park Casino.

The first speaker, a man of medium height with pinched cheeks and an unkempt flaming beard, stepped forward energetically. His words, first in Russian, and then in German, were forceful and inspiring.

"Damn Menshevik!" Lazar cursed under his breath.

Hannah strained to pay attention as the unknown orator denunciated the provisional government. He received modest applause from the crowd, but as soon as Trotsky took the podium, cheers rang out.

"This is surely the last moment in my life I shall address my comrades in the land of the plutocrats," he began. After an expressive tribute to the working masses of his native land, he talked for more than an hour, then raised his voice fervently. "Our time has come! The hour is here. I go to my destiny, but our work in this place has just begun. I want you people to overthrow the damned, rotten, capitalistic government of this country." The audience was aroused to a high pitch of enthusiasm, and ovation after ovation was given the speaker. When the cheers subsided, Lazar clasped her arm. "Come, let us say good-bye to Trotsky."

Hannah tried not to show her reluctance as she followed her husband through the crowd. Trotsky waved his arms to include his old friends within the inner circle. When Lazar stepped forward, Trotsky placed his arm around his shoulders, a gesture that Lazar took as humbly as a just-knighted lad.

"I should be going with you," Lazar said with a slight petulance that maybe only Hannah noticed.

"There is work to be done here. Don't forget the permanent revolution," Trotsky offered paternally. Then this man who rarely noticed anyone's feelings sensed Lazar's dejection. He raised his gaze to meet Lazar's eyes, and Lazar seemed to be illuminated by his attention. "Next year we will be together in Petrograd, Comrade Sokolovsky!"

Hannah blanched. "Next year in Jerusalem!" was the ages-old toast at the Passover seder. To hear it twisted this way was like a knife in the heart. She did not look at her husband to see his response. If he spoke, she did not hear him. A roar—whether from the crowd or from the tumult inside her head—threatened to crush her skull. Her knees buckled as Chaim and Minna brought her outside for some fresh air.

∽ 16 ∾

If Hannah were to list the worst days of her life, April 7, 1917, would have come close to the top. The day before President Wilson had signed the declaration of war, proclaiming, "The world must be made safe for democracy." What difference did it make? A war was a war. Russian workers were fighting against capitalism, America was protecting its system, and everyone else was championing some ideal, but Hannah suspected each had a more self-serving end. Millions had already died. How many more would now be added? How many people that she knew would be touched by the horror? Already the Bellevue unit had been mobilized. Soon more doctors and nurses would leave for the front, and who would take over at home? She read that after his return to the White House from his speech before Congress, the president was heard to have said, "My message was one of death for young men. How odd it seems to applaud that." They wrote that he had placed his head in his hands and wept. What use were his tears? If the mighty president of the United States was impotent, the world had no chance.

Nothing else was going right either. Lazar had begun to wage his own war on the home front by rallying the children to his side. Soon everything was like the sugar bowl issue. She was the one denying them; Lazar was protecting them against their mother. Ever since Trotsky left, she had kept tight control on their money, doling out exactly what anyone needed and not a penny more. One afternoon when Lazar asked Hannah for some cash, she said there wasn't any.

"Why do you keep it to yourself?" Benny asked in his father's defense.

Though tempted to tell him about the numbers-running activities, she said only, *"Aroysgevorfeneh gelt."* That's money thrown away.

"You're just stingy," Benny taunted.

"I have three children, not two," she said, groaning under her breath. "Just do as I say," she retorted, then left for the hospital without giving in. After all, what did Lazar need money for? was her silent defense as she pounded the pavement in her hurry to be away. He could become a shnorrer and beg off his friends for a glass of tea, a piece of strudel. He could borrow newspapers. And if he wanted something more, he could do like everyone else in the world: work for it! When her pace slowed, she admitted that there was another reason: if she did not give him any money, if she hid anything extra—even the rent—he would never amass enough to buy a ticket to Russia. Trotsky did not want a penniless moocher. Nobody did. This was the only way she could keep the family together, everything else had failed.

This was her one day on the regular shift when she was expected to complete administrative tasks. But because she was so adjusted to nights, she always felt unbalanced by the middle of the day. Arriving at Bellevue, she learned that Alice Brody had not yet signed in for her shift, so she took over Ward B from the student midwife who had tried valiantly to cope, but as usually was the case when things started to go wrong, every bed was filled. Within the hour she had delivered two babies and talked the trainee through a third, while she dealt with a delayed placenta. The blood pressure in Bed Twelve was unstable, so—just in case—she had a call in for the doctor on duty, who she hoped was Dr. Dowd. As the cries and supplications rang out in Polish, Italian, Serbo Croatian, and Greek, she muttered, "Oder gor, oder gornit."

Then, in the *mitten derinnen*—the middle of everything—Dorothea Wylie came up behind her. "Mrs. Sokolow, there is someone you must see." Hannah shot her a furious glance. "Please . . ."

"What are you, crazy?" Hannah chastised under her breath. "This placenta is almost an hour late." She was clasping the slippery, twisted umbilical cord, while massaging the Greek woman's abdomen.

"But they've brought in Alice Brody."

"Where is she?"

"Outside Ward D."

"What happened?"

"She's aborting again. It looks bad."

Hannah wiped her hands as Dorothea took over the traction on the cord. "Dr. Dowd should be up to see Bed Twelve shortly. If this one isn't finished, have him take a look."

"I think it's coming," Dorothea Wylie said with a touch of surprise—or was it pride?—in her voice.

Hannah turned back to the patient. Indeed, the placenta was finally presenting. "Good, good. Check to make certain there are no pieces left behind." With that she rushed out to see Alice.

The young midwife lay on the stretcher. Her skin was ashen, her arms fell limp at her sides. Hannah brushed the damp hair from her brow. "I'm here, Alice. When did this start?"

"Two days ago . . . while I was off duty. I thought it was over, then the pains . . ." She gasped for breath.

"I need to check you." She glanced up and down the corridor. "Not here." Hannah started to move the gurney, but one of the wheels would not cooperate with the others. She went around and yanked from the front until it did her bidding, then directed the cart to a small procedure room and closed the door. She lifted the sheet. Alice was lying in a puddle of fresh blood. The most vital problem was to discover whether the uterus had been emptied of fetal material during her miscarriage.

"How far along were you?"

"I had just missed my second cycle."

Hannah rubbed Alice's icy hands to warm them. "When do you think you passed this sac?"

"About two days ago."

"Thursday?"

"Yes, in the middle of the night."

"Did you actually see it?"

"It was dark and I was ill. I think I flushed most of it away. I know that was stupid but . . ."

Although Hannah would not trust the word of a typical patient, Alice must have had a good idea of when she had miscarried the fetus, even if she had not seen the small clump of tissue. Her uterus was large, soft, and subinvoluted. Blood pooled in the vagina, and the cervix was blue and succulent. Both the inner and outer os were open to at least a fingertip. Her reaching fingers felt shreds of decidua and meaty pieces of clots. There was no question that she had retained parts of the fetus, and thus suffered an incomplete abortion. She required immediate surgery to scrape her uterus before infection set in or the hemorrhage worsened. Only last summer a woman under similar circumstances—but with even less bleeding—had died before surgery could be accomplished.

Hannah stuck her head out the door. "Get me Dr. Dowd! Now!"

Within the hour, she had Alice in the operating theater, but it was close, too close. If she had not been on duty, if she had not already summoned the doctor, if Alice had not known enough to come in when she had . . . Now Alice was at risk if she conceived again. From now on she would have to take precautions or chance her life. Yet those precautions were technically illegal. Hannah could go to jail for even suggesting the idea to her patient. The world was crazy!

Sending boys to be slaughtered was the righteous path, but preventing a fine woman's death with some information on family limitation was a crime. Alice probably knew most everything anyway, but Hannah vowed to discuss the subject with her after her convalescence.

Once the surgery was finished, Dr. Dowd came to report on Alice's improved condition. "She'll be fine. I am certain her uterus is clean." Hannah felt herself relax for the first time that day. "I thought you would be interested in this." His casual manner caught her off guard.

"What is it?" she asked as he handed her the *New York Medical Journal.* Hannah stared at the cover, which was a detailed table of contents, but did not immediately see why he had shown it to her until he reached over and pointed to the third article: "A Practical Treatise on Vaginismus" by Wendell Q. Dowd, M.D., Obstetrical Chairman, Bellevue Hospital and Dr. Fritz Blühner, M.D., Chief of Clinic, Genitourinary Department, Mount Sinai Hospital Dispensary.

The doctor opened to page seventy-two. "Here it is. Let me know what you think of how we described it."

"Described what?"

"Your interesting case."

"My case?"

"What other one? We consulted together, didn't we? And you did stumble on an effective, although unusual cure." He mistook Hannah's slowness for annoyance, so he persisted. "Well, you did want others to know about your non-invasive solution. We could not imagine any harm in suggesting this be employed before surgery was contemplated—"

"Stella!" Hannah said with a choking sound as realization finally dawned. She had never used the woman's name before, but what did it matter now? "This is about my Stella?"

"Well, ah . . ." He shuffled his feet.

"What did Dr. Blühner have to do with it?"

"The editors were reluctant to publish such a unique case without an endorsement from someone already respected in the field."

Hannah began to read and quickly surmised that Dr. Dowd had pretended that the patient had come to him, and he had been the one to suggest her various massages and treatments. Even the warmed mineral oil was mentioned! She scanned the pages for her name. "I suppose they would not publish the word of a midwife."

"Exactly," he said with some relief that she had seen the point without him having to make it.

She handed back the journal. It took every ounce of professional control not to lash out. He was the one who had proposed a surgical cure, but now had appropriated hers as his own. That was always the way—always!—and the world would never change.

"Thank you for your help with Mrs. Brody," she said formally, thinking: I will never tell him about her connection with the—what did he call it?—ejaculatio praecox, let alone our success on that matter.

Besides, considering her present condition, success was a matter of opinion, wasn't it?

⁓ 17 ⁓

That was the morning of April 7. By the time she arrived at St. Mark's Place late that afternoon she was ready for Carrie's brilliant smile and Rachael's abstracted charm. Neither was offered. Carrie's brother was enlisting, and she was in tears. Rachael was deluged with mothers who implored her to prove their sons were medically unfit to serve. In the end the doctor had to check to see if anyone waiting was suffering a real medical problem. When she was satisfied she had seen anyone who needed her, she locked the door to the office.

"Terrible times . . ." Rachael began as she launched into one tale of woe after another. Most of these women had left another country expecting to find peace here, and now they were plunged into war. Rachael must have noticed Hannah's spiritless expression, and after she had disgorged the worst of her spleen, inquired, "How are you?"

"Don't ask!" Hannah made light of her problems as though they were nothing compared to the lunacy around them. "How are you?"

"Don't ask!" Rachael retorted, then her face crumbled.

"What's wrong? You look worse than I feel."

"What's right? would be a better question."

Now was not the time—but when was there ever time?—so Hannah decided to ask if any of her suggestions had been successful. Her previous cases had brought rapid victories, and so she half expected that once two intelligent people like Rachael and Herzog started talking, improvements would have followed swiftly.

Rachael was terse. "I told him."

"And?"

"And nothing. Worse than nothing. Ever since he seems to have lost interest in me. Oh, he has lots of excuses. This lunacy keeps him out late and he's always tired. Also, he drinks more than usual when he's at the cafés too long, and when he drinks he goes to sleep below the waist. I used to be grateful when he was not in the mood, but now when I am interested in trying some different . . ."

"It will happen." Hannah tried the optimistic consolation that had helped her other patients.

"Since when did you become a *balnes?*" Rachael responded bitterly.

A balnes, a worker of miracles? Is that what she thought she was? A few lucky guesses was all she had delivered, but to what end? Alice was still not free of complications. An infection could be deadly, but she hoped they had gotten the uterus scraped in time. Stella probably would be alone with her new baby—whom she had named Isadora Applebaum after the dancer—for the duration of the war, if not forever. And what had she done by assisting more boys into the world? Fortunately, all were too young to fight this time . . . but when would it be over?

"I'd better go home," she said. "Shall I help you close up?"

"No, I'm staying to finish up the paperwork for the mothers. I have just decided that all their sons are unfit to serve."

❦ 18 ❦

The next week when Lazar read out the headlines that Vladimir Ilyich Lenin, the vitriolic Marxist leader, had arrived in Petrograd after an eleven-year exile in Switzerland, Hannah pretended to be enthused. Ignoring the revolution had been her mistake. She wanted Russia to move out from under oppression as much as her husband, so why not humor him by paying attention to his interests? Then he won't leave . . . was the undercurrent of everything she did.

"How did he get into the country?"

"The Germans sealed him in a railroad car and guided it through the battlefields of Europe."

"Why would the Germans assist him?"

"Because they think Lenin will further destabilize Russia, making the nation easier prey. But they're wrong. The Bolsheviks will unite around Lenin and Zinoviev, Kamenev and Trotsky." The last name was breathed like a prayer. "Bukharin's leaving at the end of the week," he tossed out ruefully.

"Is Trotsky there yet?"

"No. He hasn't been heard from," Lazar responded darkly, then returned to his reading.

Maybe something had happened to Trotsky. Many people would have reason to assassinate the persuasive agitator. If Lazar had gone with him . . . For once his poverty might have saved his skin.

Hannah soon found she had another accomplice in keeping Lazar home: Minna. Bringing a kettle filled with kreplach, she came by with Chaim to visit Mama, whose rheumatism had confined her to bed. Where had the meat-filled dumplings come from? The single burner in back of the print shop was barely adequate to make coffee or heat soup. The joke was that Minna had rejected a stove because she didn't want to learn to cook. "They live on ideas," Lazar had claimed. Both were so skinny it was easy to believe.

"Ask me who made these," Minna said, laughing at herself.

Hannah went along with her. "Who made the kreplach?"

"E. G. She's an excellent cook."

"Emma Goldman?" Hannah was skeptical. "In the middle of everything?"

"Ever since she returned from her latest lecture tour she's been trying to fatten me up. If I see another dumpling, I'll be sick to my stomach! Better that Mama should have them."

"You are looking much healthier," Hannah commented honestly. A newcomer might have disagreed with that statement, but they had not seen her on Blackwell's Island.

"I never thanked you," Minna added serenely.

"For what?"

"For opposing me for my own good."

"It was Margaret's decision."

"She said it was yours."

"Hmph!" Hannah said. "We're both afraid to take the credit."

"Afraid of what?" Minna's eyes gleamed with mischief. "Afraid of me?"

"You aren't angry any longer?" Hannah's concern was palpable.

"I never was. In these complicated times one always must keep the true enemy in sight." A dreamy expression crossed her normally taut face. "Chaim is grateful too. But you knew that . . ."

"I'm glad you married him," Hannah offered for the first time.

A profound relief passed between the women as each speculated why they had resented each other for so long. Maybe it took a world revolving too fast to clarify what was important.

"I am sorry about your troubles, and I will do everything I can to help," Minna continued quickly in case her nerve failed her. "Chaim also thinks it would be a big mistake for Lazar to leave because the people he thinks are his friends will wipe their hands on him, then throw him away when he's soiled. Besides, he's needed here. With the war news the papers are printing extra pages, and Chaim has more work than he can handle. If Lazar would agree to assist him, he could make money and do the cause a favor at the same time. What do you think?"

"Lazar does what he wants, not what I want."

"We'll be the ones to talk with him, if it is satisfactory with you."

Hannah did not reply. For once the sisters-in-law did not require words. They glimpsed into each other's hearts. And they liked what they found.

～ 19 ～

On May 18, President Wilson signed the Selective Draft Act. Ten million men were subject to registration, and a half million recruits were to be called. Already the patriotic were rushing to volunteer. Among the first to enlist was Bernard Applebaum, who thought his rudimentary knowledge would suffice for the medical corps, and Malcolm Brody, who believed he was doing his wife a favor so she could be freed of the anxiety of carrying another baby so soon. In her head Hannah kept a tally of others she was concerned about: the sons of Norma Marshanck and two grandsons of Sarah Brink, the fruit man's gawky assistant, Emma's geography teacher, Dr. Dowd's son . . . the list continued to grow.

"Why do the young men embrace the war with open arms?" Hannah asked Rachael one afternoon during a quiet spell. "And don't tell me they are merely doing their duty. If that were true, they'd wait to be summoned."

"It's a rite of passage . . ." Rachael began slowly as the idea formed. "Men who have served in the military never stop talking about the experience. Somehow it defines them as masculine, but I don't quite know why."

"Then what defines a woman as feminine?" Hannah inquired sharply. "And don't tell me it's something to do with puberty or marriage, since both sexes suffer equally in that department."

"No . . . but what is it that women *hak a chainik,* yammer about over and over?" Rachael asked with a provocative lilt.

"I don't know what you are getting at!" Hannah snapped irritably.

"Giving birth is to a woman what going to war is to a man."

For a second Hannah wanted to correct the doctor, but the words echoed so prophetically she was silenced.

A few days later, Lazar reacted to the headlines with a satisfied exhalation. "At last Trotsky has arrived in Petrograd! With him in place the last vestiges of czarist reaction will expire, as did General Kornilov's counterrevolution. Now the stage is set to establish a new form of human society."

Hannah took a seat on a kitchen stool and began to chop onions for her eggplant *patlajana* in a wooden bowl. As the large hunks decreased in size and turned into a pleasing uniform texture, some of her misgivings abated. This was the old Lazar: the critic, the interpreter, the philosopher. Even though he could never admit it, he was more content on the sidelines. Ever since he had been helping Chaim in the print shop, he had curbed his nonsense about reimmigration. Her sister-in-law had handled him adroitly by begging Lazar for his assistance "during these hectic times" as a personal favor to her because her husband was "working himself to death." Knowing that Minna's full strength had not yet returned, Lazar agreed that it would be churlish of him to refuse.

". . . Those who criticized the overthrow of czarism as a bourgeois imitation of Western democracy will now see the real thing: the long-thwarted rise of the Russian masses," Lazar rambled on as Hannah added the roasted eggplant and peppers to the bowl. "What do you think?"

"A good point," she said to be safe.

He came around to taste the eggplant. When he dipped his finger into the bowl, she did not push it away. Another time she might not have permitted those ink-stained fingers to touch her food, but she did not dare give him an excuse to be irritated by her. He licked his finger. "Needs more salt."

"I haven't put any in yet." She lifted the salt cellar and sprinkled in some. "Is that better?" She offered him a taste from her wooden spoon.

He smacked his lips in reply. "On Sunday there's a meeting to unite socialists in the revolution. Will you come with me?"

"If you like."

Together they attended the conference at Madison Square Garden on May 20. In order not to waste time in meetings and cafés Hannah carried a knitting bag. Sometimes she would look at a sweater and recall who was speaking when she did a particular sleeve or side. The pieces that she had worked on while Trotsky was on the platform were her least uniform work.

This gathering began with rousing renditions of "I. W. W. Unite" and "I Didn't Raise My Boy to Be a Soldier." All

through the speeches by Abraham Cahan, Baruch Charney-
Vladek, and Dr. Anna Ingerman, Lazar became more and
more agitated. At one point he left Hannah and moved down
the aisle toward the stage. In a lull he called out, "Where are
the socialist parties?" The crowd roared with approval.
"Where is the backbone of the Russian Revolution?" he
shouted even more fervently.

More cheers and a bellow from the front row. "Why
aren't we occupying a prominent place in the provisional
government?"

Morris Hillquit raised his hands for silence, but the discord escalated. A few fist fights had to be broken up. Disgusted by their childishness, Hannah barely looked up from
her knitting.

"We cannot expect to have our voices heard from across
the Atlantic," she heard Lazar say above the bickering.

Suddenly Hannah became more attentive.

"What can be done?" a tall, emaciated man demanded.

"We should form a committee to represent all political
factions," Lazar called out forcefully. "Then those confirmed by it as true political immigrants should be sent to
Russia in a delegation."

Once again the monster rose to leer at her. Lazar had
never given up his dream of returning to Russia. If he
formed a committee, he could raise funds; and if he raised
funds, he would have the money for passage—and also add
legitimacy to his mission. Now there was nothing she could
do, nothing at all.

      ᡠᢌ **20** ᡠᢌ

Everybody was ready to support the reimmigration to Russia. *Novy Mir,* the newspaper which had been started by
Bakhunin and Kollantai and given Trotsky his voice in New
York, offered to assist "Russian-born American citizens who
desire to join the revolution and help bring about a republican form of government based on socialistic principles."
Next, in early June, the Russian embassy in New York began

offering financial aid to those "serious comrades who are unable to afford their passage." Just when it seemed there would be no way to halt the outflow, the State Department warned that applications for exit passports were being processed slowly.

"I would have thought they'd be pleased to see us leave!" Lazar complained.

"They probably can't handle the volume," Hannah suggested.

"No matter the excuse, the doors are closing on me," Lazar added angrily. "It's as if I am being squeezed in a vise."

Hannah's disdainful expression, meaning stop sounding so melodramatic, aggravated him further. "Why can't you understand how I feel?" he railed. "My body is in America, but my heart, my mind, and my soul have remained in that land. Don't you have dreams of Odessa, of Moscow?"

"Dreams? I call them nightmares."

"I know you think I am crazy, but the whole of Rutgers Square is ready to leave for Russia. Moscow will soon be to socialism what Rome has been to Christianity."

"But this is your home now—our home," Hannah said as if to a ghost.

"I have been but an exile here," he went on without acknowledging her. "Did Turgenev become French? Was Kropotkin's viewpoint English? Look at Herzen, who lived and died with his soul withdrawn from his London surroundings; and even Dostoyevsky abhorred his German hosts. In fact, no Russian—not Lenin, not Trotsky—of any importance has ever become consumed with the spirit of the country that sheltered him."

What was Hannah to retort? That Lazar was being ridiculous to try to link his name and situation with that illustrious list? No matter, for he did not wait for a response. "So, you see that one's Russian essence is not mere dye on the garment of a man's soul. It is a fast color that cannot be washed away when it might be convenient," he said with emotion cracking his voice.

"Nor can a father ignore his progeny, or a husband his wife and home."

"Why can't you see that a better life for all of us is just over the horizon? If I were one of the lamentable millions about to be conscripted into an unjust war, you would support me."

"That's different because they will return to their homes—or at least hope to."

"And we will be reunited as well. As soon as the initial organization is firmly in place—and the war in Europe is calmer—you and the children will join me."

"I have no plans to leave New York."

"Of course you don't," he said in a conciliatory tone. "But when you see what freedoms a true Marxist state will bring, you will rush to embrace it. And"—he gave her one of his most endearing expressions—"I hope you will want to embrace me again as well."

Talking to Lazar was fruitless. Because his fingernails were almost bone white, she knew he had been working less and less at the print shop, which meant more and more of his time had been dedicated to the reimmigration scheme. Chaim and Minna had failed to make him see reason, and even Herzog could not convince him to look at the situation realistically.

Without giving his friend a chance, Lazar had railed back at Ezekiel. "Prosperity has blinded you," he shouted so loudly half the tables in the Monopole heard every word. "The real world is not here! It is in the squares of Petrograd, the fields of the Ukraine, the alleys of Moscow, the factories of Tula, the oil fields of Baku, the wharves of Odessa!"

Instead of debating the issue, Herzog nodded sympathetically. "What are your plans when you get there?"

"I will work with Trotsky, of course."

"You know, Lazar, I must tell you that many others are saying the same thing."

"Of course I am not the only one to want to go back to Mother Russia."

"No, I meant about Trotsky. I realize that you two go back to your days at the university, but since he was in New York, everyone he met is expecting to become an ambassador, a counselor, an embassy attaché."

Lazar's cheeks reddened. "I am not interested in his patronage! I want to serve the party."

Herzog waved his arms in a calming gesture. "I know that, my friend." He glanced at Hannah and gave her an apologetic smile.

She nodded back. She had assumed that there was nothing anyone could do.

Hannah had one more unexpected ally: Emma Goldman. In May, the famous fanatic had established the No-Conscription League to counsel those who refused the draft and organized meetings to spread the league's view. As patriotic fervor mounted against her, she and Berkman were arrested on charges of conspiring against the draft. After she was freed on bail, Lazar went to see her.

"Put off leaving America, at least for now," she counseled him. "With the most visible of the radicals being jailed to fuel sympathy for the war, you are needed on this side of the Atlantic more than ever."

For a few days after that, Hannah thought her husband was wavering. Then, the following week there was a demonstration in front of the Henry Street Settlement. One of the main speakers was Mr. Bachmatiev, the new Russian ambassador. "I salute you in the name of my sisters who languished in Russia; of my brothers who were tortured in Siberia; and of my dead father, whose eyes were burned out in a pogrom." Hannah's heart stopped as she knew the effect those words would have on Lazar, whose own parents had been killed in the ghastly pogrom at Kishinev. "All you exiled sons and daughters, all you former prisoners of your conscience, we are here to help you realize that dream of returning to a motherland free from oppression. For those who cannot afford passage, monies are being collected into a fund. Let no true partisan feel that he or she will not be welcomed with open arms. Come home! Come home to *Matushka Rossiya.*"

And so the stage was set. Lazar became the organizer as hundreds of fools, who believed that Russian Jews were on the footpath to Utopia, signed up for free passage. Nobody could dissuade them: not their families, not the Zionists who believed they were emigrating to the wrong land, not the voices of reason who tried to convince them that their adopted country needed them too.

On the last day of school before summer recess, Benny came home with his prizes for public speaking and mathematics. Emma was sulking because all she had were the posture and singing awards and "everybody got those."

Benny dumped his papers on the bookshelf. Next to the

one empty space was a pile of papers Lazar had placed there. "What's this?" He held up a certificate.

"How should I know?" Hannah said.

"Is this Yiddish?"

Even from a distance she could see that it was written in Cyrillic letters. "No, Russian." She felt a pang as she realized that Benny could read in only one language. Most of the boys his age were learning Hebrew, but Lazar did not want the rabbis to influence him. He had been planning to teach him Yiddish, but never had the time. And now that time might never arrive.

Benny brought it to his mother. "What does this mean?

"Let me see ..." Hannah perused the official document warily. "It says, 'The representative of the Provisional Government of Russia, residing at the consulate in New York, and issued in accordance with the orders of the Provisional Government, records that the said bearer, Lazar Sokolovsky, formerly of Odessa, and presently domiciled in New York, United States of America, has been paid the sum of one hundred fifty-seven dollars and twenty-five cents plus steamship passage, via the Atlantic Ocean, and land transportation to Petrograd." She gulped, but continued, this time more haltingly. "Upon arrival at the port, the bearer will be entitled to more money and a railway ticket, and on arrival in Petrograd he will be eligible for the people's lodging, and a weekly stipend and ...' " The words blurred.

In the background she heard Emma crying. "Is Pa really leaving us?"

"Yes, stupid. Isn't that what I've been saying all along?" Benny explained crassly.

"But why?" she whined, echoing the shrillness locked in her mother's throbbing chest.

"Because he wants to, that's why!" Benny's words held a tinge of pride that mingled with his resentment like orbs of oil dropped in a glass of water.

Hannah could have comforted the children by saying that other fathers were going off to war and this was no different, except it was safer since Lazar would not be at the front, but maybe that was not true. Conflicts could break out at any time. More blood was certain to be shed before the revolutionaries were satisfied. Let them cry, let me cry ... she thought before she gave in to the grief that overwhelmed her and had to leave the room.

❦ 21 ❧

Lazar had picked the date he would sail: August 1. Hannah did not pretend he had delayed his trip one hour for her sake. He merely had wanted to see the outcome of E. G. and Berkman's trial on their conspiracy to obstruct the draft. Lazar felt he had to attend every session. With so little time remaining—and the children out of school—Hannah was furious that he did not give those precious hours to them. On July 9, the verdict came in: guilty. The sentence was harsh: two years in prison and a fine of ten thousand dollars each. The judge also recommended deportation after their sentences had been served. Emma was sent to Missouri State Prison in Jefferson City, while Berkman was ordered to Atlanta.

Lazar met Hannah at the end of her night shift at Bellevue to give her the news. "That's what would happen to me if I remained in this industrialist, war-mongering hell," he bellowed. "How can they call this a free country? All our friends have been jailed: Minna, Margaret and her husband, Sasha, E. G., and how many others? And for what? What?" he shouted.

The early morning already was dry and hot. Dust swirled in the streets. Hannah licked her lips to moisten them as they walked home in silence. There was something left unsaid. Hannah had missed her period. It was only a week overdue, but that was unusual. Hannah knew how to take precautions, and this she had done for many years . . . until a few weeks earlier. Relations between them had been so strained since he had announced his plans to leave that the one time they had mutually desired each other was in the middle of the night. A thunderstorm had awakened them. Lazar rubbed his hardness against her belly and she did not resist, or go into the bathroom for the device that would have prevented a mistake. Not a word was said. The flashing light illuminated their entwined bodies, the crashing booms echoed their inner turmoil. When they finished, they stayed joined, with Lazar's body curved around her back. Sometime during their sleep he had disengaged, but neither had dressed again. That had been the last time. Since then they had gone to bed too tense to consider lovemaking.

Could that have done it? Of course Hannah knew it could. She counted the days. Not one of the best, but not one of the worst either. After all these years! Emma was already ten, Benny, twelve. If Lazar did not stay to take care of them, who would nurture the baby while she worked her long shifts? These days Mama tired more easily. Minding an infant was an impossibility.

Even worse was the question of whether Hannah should tell her husband. Another woman would. Another woman could. But not Hannah, for Lazar would be certain she had entrapped him.

Both of them knew the reason they had married when they had—the night before leaving for America—was because she had been expecting Benny. Lazar had done the noblest thing: he had given up his political allegiance for a paternal one by marrying Hannah and emigrating with her family. So how could she tell him a few hours before he sailed that she faced the same predicament again? Would he stay if he knew? No. The magnetism of a chance to change the world was a far greater lure than the most loving wife and family. But if he suspected her of subterfuge to hold him, whatever spark remained would be snuffed by his fury.

Anyway, she told herself, she was only a week late. There could be any number of reasons: an infection, a change of cycles, a hormonal imbalance caused by the anxiety of the war, not to mention Lazar's plans. To tell him would be self-defeating. This was one burden she would have to carry alone. One burden of many.

The next day Lazar was set to sail aboard the Danish steamer *United States*. In bed that night he made a joke about the irony in the name of the ship, but she did not laugh. He swooped down and kissed her face gently. She lay like a stone on the pillow, staring at him as if to memorize the face forever. She did not kiss him back. Her lips would not open. He brushed his fingers across her breasts. Even the nipples would not respond. And when his hand drifted between her legs, she placed hers on top of his and removed it insistently.

"Hannah ... neshomeleh ... I have not stopped loving you ... I never will ... someday ..."

That day will never come ... was her unspoken thought. From that moment onward she would be a wife without a husband, married in name only. At least a widow had another chance. Would she have preferred him dead? No! Never! She turned away so her tears would be blotted by the pillow. What would it be like to live alone, to never have another man? Another man? The idea seemed impossible. Would he find himself another woman—perhaps one like Alexandra Kollontai? Yes, this was more imaginable.

"Hannah, speak to me ..." he begged.

"What is there to say?"

"Won't you say good-bye to me?"

"I have tried every way I've known to prevent saying those words. I will not say them now."

"But I am leaving tomorrow." His voice was breaking. "Can you be so cruel to send me off without a kind word?"

"In your heart you left a long time ago." She turned all the way on her side. She pretended to sleep. He managed to doze off, but she did not.

In the morning she did not budge. She had already told him not to wake the children, who had been hysterical the night before. She followed his progress by the sounds: the whistle of the teakettle, the grate of the bread knife on the stale loaf, the plop of sugar cubes, the clink of the spoon stirring, the ping of the empty glass in the sink, the scrape of his heavy satchel against the wooden floor. And then the door. The click of the latch opening. The squeak of the handle. Then footsteps back into the bedroom. He was standing there. She turned over and looked at him. Tears poured down his cheeks. He started toward her. He changed his mind. He turned on his heel.

The doorknob again.

The door creaking.

The door closed.

Problem 6:
Clementine Hardcastle Has
Too Many Children

1918

Every night and every morn
Some to misery are born.
Every morn and every night
Some are born to sweet delight.
Some are born to sweet delight,
Some are born to endless night.
　　　　　　　　　—BLAKE

∽ 1 ∽

A FILM of tears formed a semi-permanent cataract obstructing the flow of light and blurring the world for a time. And so Hannah moved in a daze, following the routines without engaging herself fully. If anyone noticed, they were thankfully silent. Even Mama held her tongue, just as she would for any other true disability. Nevertheless, the days were no shorter, the family still had to eat, and those around her at home and at the hospital continued to require supervision.

Mama had one respiratory infection after another. At least the children were old enough to be a help. Benny ran errands, Emma cleaned house, while Hannah made certain she took her medication. Perhaps it was the war effort that rallied them, but the children accepted their many new responsibilities with little bickering. Benny devised a system: since he had been born on an even day of the month, he did all the chores that day, while Emma, born on an odd day, alternated with him.

"What shall we do about the thirty-first?" she complained. "I don't want to have to work two days in a row!"

"It only happens seven days of the year."

"So, you do it, then!"

"We'll share them," Benny suggested, causing Hannah to be heartened by his good sense.

With matters at home going better than she might have assumed, Hannah gave most of her energies to the hospital, where babies continued to be born, and they seemed to be coming in record numbers. By the first of the year the volume of births were beyond anyone's predictions. The administrators were puzzled at first. Not Hannah, who observed that the first bulge began nine months after President Wilson entered the war.

Then there was the other life, the insistent seed that continued to grow. By October Hannah had confirmed her own pregnancy. So far it was her secret. It grew slowly and did not show. In the past she had tried to visualize what the baby might be like: girl or boy? active or quiet? dark or light? This baby remained faceless, enigmatic. Maybe later, when she felt the quickening sensations, she would begin to believe in it.

Hannah heard from Lazar, irregularly, but she had news, which was more than some wives of soldiers or families of other reimmigrants. Since Lazar had gone off with press credentials from the *Forverts*, his messages came via the office of its editor, Abe Cahan.

The first word was that Lazar had been held up in Halifax for a week. Some of the returning Russians had roused suspicion. In the old days every immigrant's greatest fear was being turned back by the inspectors on Ellis Island. Now, ironically, being denied entrance to Russia was what alarmed these vacillating travelers. By the time they reached the Finnish border on September 3, only seventy-two of the original band boarded the train for Petrograd.

"At sea we existed in a vacuum, nourished by our ideals and not much else," Lazar wrote in an article for the Yiddish newspaper. "News of the happenings inside Russia, or of the war itself, had not penetrated into Sweden since the rumored German advance on Riga."

A personal note accompanying the story was forwarded to

her. "Here I am on a small ferry gliding over the obscure, murky waters between Haparanda and Tornea, the names of two towns I never knew before and am likely to forget shortly, yet they are links from one side of the world to another. As the faint lights of Sweden fade into the mist, I see images of you slipping farther into the distance. The wind is cold and yet while I have you in my mind, my body is warm."

She hurried through the honey-coated prose, mulled over the signature. "Your *Luftmentsh.*" The Yiddish word cut like a knife. He had not used his own name, probably for security. But Luftmentsh! "Luft" for air. "Mentsh" for man. The term referred to a dreamer, the perfect description for the likes of Lazar. If anyone else had called her husband a luftmentsh, she would have taken it as an insult, yet when he did, she knew he saw himself with a fresh clarity. So what? Did that alter the fact that while he was off with his head in the clouds, she had to plod along with her feet on the ground? At that thought the tears just held at bay burst forth from their dam and flowed freely. Anger always released them, but then there would be a small respite of relief while the store was replenished.

As the deluge abated, Hannah considered that this initial message had been written during the first week in September. She had received it in October, just before the revolution. The next one, a letter to her alone, came weeks after the revolution, even though it had been written prior to the outbreak. Before the revolution . . . after the revolution . . . before Lazar went away . . . after . . . Now there was a whole new way to date her life—and that of the world.

"The new Russian army greeted us on the margin of Finland," he began in another attempt to inform his wife. "Robust peasants, who filled out their tattered uniforms with pride, strutted along the shore. When I came closer, I saw there was another difference: every emblem of imperialism had been removed. There was not a brass button with the czar's insignia, or any other superfluous decorations. A simple red cloth armband was the sole adornment. Even more astonishing was the fact that the sentries were seated and did not salute. Did this mean that the facade of militarism had disappeared? Or would we find it otherwise in the heart of Matushka Rossiya?"

Mother Russia. Hannah shook her head at the sentiment

that was the antithesis of her own, then read on: "Upon our arrival in the country we heard that Premier Kerensky had placed Petrograd under martial law. A counterrevolution was under way and the city was in a state of siege. At the border we were required to undress in a cold, dark room, then dress again immediately without any explanation." For a moment Hannah felt a pang of sympathy as she imagined her husband naked, shivering, stripped of his dignity. Then she hardened herself, mumbling, "He made his choice."

The letter contained nothing about what had happened once he reached the city. Since it was posted from there, she thought he probably had arrived . . . or at least the letter had. Who knew anything? When the days of the Bolshevik siege of power began, communications were halted. Like everyone else, Hannah had to rely on a combination of news reports and rumors. They were calling it the October Revolution, even though by Western calendars it did not begin until the end of the first week of November. Wasn't it just like the Russians to confuse everyone? Nevertheless, as she followed the progress of the uprising, she was astonished that her feelings were more of elation than distress. A few days later Cahan received a telegraph message from Lazar. He had reached Petrograd, but discovered Trotsky was in prison. Hadn't she predicted that man would never get anywhere? She might not know politics, but she did know people. If his mentor was out of favor, Lazar had better align himself with new forces swiftly, or he himself would be in jeopardy. Yet she suspected his sense of loyalty—no matter how misguided—might lead him to make shortsighted moves.

For the first months after her husband's departure, Hannah had vacillated between furious anger and crushing sadness. Now she feared for his safety. In another week, when the news came that the Bolsheviks had prevailed, Hannah felt an enormous sense of relief. This time, thank goodness, Lazar had sided with the winners. At last he was exactly where he wanted to be—in the midst of the action. If he had remained by her side, his resentment would have been fomented, and he would have been impossible to live with. Maybe if he was at the center he would be satisfied and would return feeling a victor instead of an expatriate—a real possibility because the provisional government of Premier Alexander Kerensky, which had come to power in March in the wake of the czar's abdication, was supported by the Red Guards and headed by Leon Trotsky.

Trotsky! Who would have thought the insolent man who had sat at her kitchen table a few months earlier would be running Russia? Once again Lazar had been right. And Trotsky would need men like Lazar, a man who understood political matters and who could predict the winds of change so accurately, even when all signs pointed to a different forecast. Trotsky trusted her husband because Lazar had known him in the old days when he was merely Lev Bronstein, another poor Jewish student at the university in Odessa. They had broken bread together in cafés from the Bessarabia to the Monopole, and never once had Lazar curried a favor. His one wish had been to serve the revolution. On his own, and at great personal sacrifice, he had found his way to Petrograd. Surely he would win respect—and the position he deserved.

Now the nuances of who was in control in Russia took on special significance for Hannah, since she believed her husband's fate was intertwined with Trotsky's. The new government proclaimed its intentions of negotiating peace, redistributing land to the peasants, and calling elections for the constituent assembly, but it was rumored that Lenin would be moving into power and that Trotsky would sink into the background. How would that affect Lazar? Lazar admired Lenin, but matters might be complicated if he was closely aligned with Trotsky. Would he be prudent enough not to put all his eggs in one basket? That was doubtful. Lazar never had been ambiguous, even if that might have been to his benefit.

Once the tumult of the revolution had passed, Hannah paid closer attention to her calendar. More than eighteen weeks had passed since her last menstrual date. By then she should have felt quickening, the first fluttery movements of a fetus—"like the wings of a bird" is what she told her patients who inquired what to expect. But there was nothing, not even when she was lying quietly in bed. Had her negative feelings afflicted the child? That was unlikely since, if that were possible, half the babies on earth would not achieve full gestation. Nothing had been quite right from the first, she realized. Maybe she had never been pregnant. Maybe it was a tumor or other abnormality. Hannah made a decision. If after the new year everything had not normal-ized, she would consult a doctor. A few days later she noticed some intermittent bleeding, not red and bright, but brownish and dull. Anyone else might have found this distressing, but the midwife understood this was an affirmation of a pregnancy—albeit a troubled one. Now the choices went from "not too bad" to "worse" to "disastrous." Better to be pregnant than to have a disease. Better to lose an unhealthy baby than to give birth to a damaged one. Then the bleeding abated, and she did not know where she stood. At least she had not told Lazar. To have had him remain because of the baby, and then to lose it, would have been a double blow.

Lazar. Where is he right at this moment? was Hannah's constant thought. Was he a Red Guard on the front lines, perhaps protecting the Winter Palace? Or might he be in some drafty room arguing how a new government might be organized? Where was he living, sleeping? What was he eating? Was he ill or wounded or . . . ?

Enough. If she thought too long and hard, she would go crazy. Even the children did not ask. Thinking about their father was too painful. Not that she wanted them to forget him, but she understood. She was glad she had not hinted anything about the baby to them. They did not need to worry about this too. Hannah was relieved her figure had not expanded enough to elicit their questions. Because it was winter, everyone looked bulky. If she did not lose the baby, they would have to be told. Hannah dreaded their pitiful sighs at her predicament. If it came to that, somehow she would have to maintain a brave front.

As the end of 1917 approached, Emma Goldman and Alexander Berkman were out of jail on bond temporarily. E. G. sent out New Year's cards which read: "Wishes for any personal joy in the world's madness seem so commonplace that I can't gather up the courage to wish such things for the New Year, except that the world may come to its senses. I know that will bring us all joy." This message so echoed Hannah's feelings, she decided to attend the party they were giving on New Year's Eve. It was also to be the first time she would go out without her husband.

Expecting more of Mabel Dodge's set, Hannah was dejected to find she was but a passing acquaintance to most of the people at the party, which was held at the home of Emma's niece, Stella Ballantine. The guests were either family members or belonged to their Provincetown crowd. The few she recognized showed little interest in her after they inquired as to Lazar's whereabouts. "He's in Russia" brought such a weak response, she began adding, "working with Trotsky." This evoked only a slightly more animated reaction before they excused themselves.

The only person Hannah knew well was Herzog, who arrived late and without his wife. Rachael had been battling a bladder infection for several weeks, but Hannah had thought she had recovered. Too preoccupied with her own problems, Hannah had not even visited Rachael during her confinement. "Is she worse?"

"The fever's returned, but don't worry, the best medicine is rest," Herzog said, scratching behind his ear. "Over the holiday weekend her clinic is closed, so she can catch up on her sleep."

"I'll stop by tomorrow."

"Good, good . . ." he muttered, but his eyes were focused on a distant point. Then they riveted on her. "Tell me, Hannah, what are your plans?"

Was he staring at her abdomen? She had worn a loose dress and covered it with a flowered shawl, but he was a doctor. By her calculations she was more than five months along, although her uterus measured less than four. Even her breasts, which were usually much larger during pregnancy, had swelled initially, then returned to their normal size. She was certain that something had gone wrong, nevertheless she kept pushing her worries into a dark corner. "Plans? Who can plan?"

"You can."

"Well, if you will provide me with the outcome of the World War and the Russian revolution, I'll begin" is what she said, but she was thinking she had to factor in a new baby as well.

"The start of a new year is a good time to prepare, if not for the long term, at least for tomorrow. How long have you been worrying about others: the children, the mothers having babies, the women who come to Rachael's clinic, and what Lazar was going to do? Now is the time to start thinking about yourself."

"What's there to think?"

"About what would make you happy."

"How can I be happy?" she asked with vexation, as if he

had coaxed her to spend more than she could afford on a luxury.

"Look, my dear friend, I don't think if you asked anyone in this room if they were happy, they would respond in the affirmative. How could they be with Emma and Sasha going to prison, the war, the situation in Russia, the plight of the masses, and so on? Yet to me, there is happiness in the smallest of pleasures: a perfect piece of pickled herring, a warm slice of fresh bread, a kiss on the cheek by sweet little Nora, a blazing fire, a sonata by Mozart, a good book. It is by allowing ourselves to partake of these tiny delights that we store up an account of happiness to see us through the grim days."

Leaning against the wall in the corridor, Hannah listened intently. She liked Herzog enormously. His voice was mellow, his dark eyes warm and accepting, and his words made sense—intellectually, but what could he know of the hollowness of her heart? He would not understand when she told him that herring or bread tasted the same to her: flat and dull. Music did not move her. She had no interest in reading. Even the kisses of her children could not ignite her extinguished spirit.

"So, Hannah, tell me, now that you have the freedom to make some changes in your life, what would they be?" He stroked his wiry beard waiting for her response.

Even though Hannah's first instinct was to protest this line of thinking, something she had long been mulling—but had never verbalized—popped out unexpectedly. "No more lectures! I've sat in enough drafty halls. I don't want to hear any more about family limitation or revolutions, or any 'isms' for that matter, and that includes communism, socialism, Fabianism, imperialism, Zionism, or bundism. Also, I am sick and tired of all the 'ists'—and that means Veblenists, Marxists, revisionists, Kropotkinists, syndicalists, even pacifists."

"That's a fine start," Herzog said with a wide grin that revealed his tobacco-stained teeth. "What else?"

Hannah closed her eyes. In the darkness it was easier to think. The champagne had eased her aches, and she felt lighter and freer than in many weeks. Herzog was a beacon of reason illuminating these dismal times. She should think more about herself. If she were more content, she would be kinder to the children. She would have more to give to her patients too. Coming tonight had been a sensible choice. She should not be alone so much. Opening her eyes, she squinted in the light. "I will go to the places I like, and with the people I prefer."

"I hope we'll stay on your list," he added just as someone dimmed the lights. Then came a large bang. Hannah's heart lurched. A bomb? No! They were shouting, "Happy New Year!"

Hannah and Herzog were alone. The lights blinked on. "Happy New Year, Hannah," he said with a lustrous smile that, for the briefest moment, allowed her to believe that a dose of happiness might be possible, even in this tumultuous world.

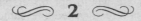 **2**

The cramps came early on the morning of New Year's Day. The pains were mild at first, but since Hannah had experienced miscarriages twice before, she knew what was coming. She had a perfect excuse. She told the children she had overindulged and had a stomach ache. This would explain the amount of time she might spend on the toilet. She filled a hot water bottle and heated a kettle on the stove. She washed rags in the boiling water and hung them to dry along her bedstead. In case there was leakage, she put newspaper under her sheet. She found a small bottle of laudanum she kept at home in case of severe pain. Only twice had she used it: once when Lazar had one of his most brutal headaches, and again when a neighbor's child had fallen down a flight of stairs and broken her leg. In her midwifery kit she had everything else she needed, including ergotomine in case there was an incomplete expulsion from the uterus.

The day wore on much as she expected. When Mama heard Hannah was under the weather, she sent up some soup and kept the children downstairs. What would she ever do without Mama? Later in the day Emma came up and knocked on the bedroom door. "Aunt Minna's downstairs. Do you want her to come up?"

"No, I'm resting."

"That's what Bubbe thought, but she wanted me to ask," Emma said sweetly. "What shall I do?"

"Go back downstairs. I'll be fine."

And she was fine. At least physically. The miscarriage was a routine case, except that the color of the fluid and the degenerated state of the sac indicated that the baby had died weeks before. She knew what to do and she did it. She checked herself to see if the abortion had been complete and found that everything was encapsulated together, so she did not worry about the possibility of retained parts or a nasty infection. To be prudent, Hannah took her temperature every four hours.

Soft footsteps padded by the bed. "Emma?" Hannah asked weakly.

"No, it's me, Minna. How are you doing?" She held up the thermometer. "Do you have a temperature?"

"A bit . . . not serious, but could you send word to Bellevue? I need a few days . . . stomach virus . . ."

"Yes, of course. Let me get you some water." Minna took the empty glass at her bedside to the bathroom. When she saw the number of bloody rags, she paused, then returned to Hannah and pulled her chair up to the bed.

"Not a virus, is it?"

Hannah turned her head weakly and stared into Minna's questioning gaze. "No. I lost a baby. Lazar's . . ." she felt obliged to explain.

"Did he—?"

"No! And he never will," she said vehemently, then fell back on her pillow. "Nobody . . . my secret."

"You can trust me, Hannah. Not even Chaim, if you don't want him to know."

"Better that nobody knows. Everything has worked out for the best, hasn't it? Well, hasn't it?" she asked of nobody in particular. "I'll be fine. I just need extra rest. So many depend on me, I have to take special care" was her sensible pronouncement before the blockage shattered and the tears from some secret reservoir crested and flooded in a tumultuous, unpredictable torrent.

This was a baby! Her baby! And Lazar's baby . . . one he would never know. And she would never see. Never. So many babies . . . she saw them every day. Some welcomed with joy, some rejected, many hardly tolerated. Yet there was nothing like your own. Benny's birth had been a horrendous experience at the hands of callous doctors at the hospital, while Emma had been welcomed into the world with Rachael's assistance at home. Where would she have delivered this one? And what would this baby have been like? A boy or a girl? Either would have been fine, for the other two were so splendid. This one could have been extraordinary as well. But it was not meant to be. No more Emmas or Bennys. Never again. For the best, probably. Who would have wanted a fatherless child? Wouldn't it have been a tragedy when the father did not even know of the child's existence? Yes, these things had a way of sorting themselves out. Such a small misfortune in these troubled times, hardly worth fussing about. If she was crying, she knew it was because of the erratic postpartum hormones, not because she had any regrets. Best to look forward, not backward.

"Don't worry about me," she said to calm Minna's stricken face. "I just have to move on, to forget, to rest."

"Rest . . . yes, that is what you need," Minna agreed, tucking her in.

Hannah didn't protest as she gave into sleep . . . sweet, dreamless sleep.

∽ 3 ∼

And so that calamity passed, and even the crying spells came less frequently, although Hannah never knew when something would set her off and she would have to turn away from a task to restrain herself. Yet the swirling crises continued, although the next one was of a less personal nature. In the middle of January, New York froze up in the worst winter Hannah had ever endured. Contentment came in the times when the water and gas were not frozen in their pipes. The children slept in her bed, one on each side pressing against her for warmth. Coal could not come across the river. They pinned quilts over the windows and tried to burn wood without choking on the smoke. In front of Greenwich House women rioted in the street for coal. Gangs of young men would stop a man with a load and take it by force. One Saturday Hannah and the children lined up across from the mayor's house to collect what coal the city would sell them, then shared half their bounty with Mama.

"The trinity of civilization: light, heat, and water have failed New York, and without them a city is brought to its knees," said Chaim, who had moved in with his mother, since they could not heat the drafty print shop above the freezing point.

"This is but the writing on the wall," Minna continued in the same vein. "A city is an unnatural endeavor. The forces of weather can bring it down because the weak minds of men have not been able to foresee that just as human systems created it, human failures in production and distribution will destroy it."

"But other winters have been as cold, surely," Hannah suggested.

"Yes, but not a winter when the world is also at war, and there are other shortages," her brother added.

"It's probably worse in Russia," Minna added soberly.

Hannah did not respond. The news from Russia was worrisome. Everyone expected the Bolsheviks, who were still a minority party, would have to fight.

"Did you hear about Lenin's speech on the dictatorship of the proletariat?" Chaim began, but he was interrupted by footsteps in the hall. "Oh no, Mama!" Chaim clutched his lapels in a demonstration of mock fear. "They're coming for your secret supply of coal."

"You should have been an actor," replied Mama, then she startled at the knock on her door. "I'll make it easy on myself and confess," she said as she opened it.

The surprise visitors were Eva and her family. Hannah's stomach churned. She had been avoiding her sister. Ever since Lazar left, she had been three months behind in the rent. Eva was aflutter with kisses. Before she even took off her coat, she hugged Hannah twice. Coughing, Minna left the room to put the kettle on.

"Are you all right?" her husband asked. He was still anxious about her health.

"Of course!" she protested, but Chaim followed her anyway.

The little girls went right to their grandmother, who did not disappoint them with her usual greeting. "Close your eyes and think of something sweet," she said, then popped a honey candy in their mouths, which jutted open like those of baby birds.

"Ma, don't spoil them!" Eva complained, without meaning it.

"So, take off your coat and stay awhile," Mama Blau coaxed. "Or is my place not warm enough for an uptown girl like you?"

"She wants to show off her coat," Napthali said. The blue wool with Persian lamb trim had been new the previous year. A half dozen times Hannah had heard about the great price that Eva had gotten from Starr Furs, Stella's father. So what was the big deal?

"Now, darling, you know that they have seen it before," Eva said in a singsong voice. "I want everyone in the room before the unveiling." She moved up and down on her toes like an overanxious child.

"Nu?" Mama said.

"Let's wait for Chaim and Minna," Eva insisted.

To break the suspense Hannah called the others in. When everyone was assembled, Eva dramatically turned her back, unbuttoned the coat, then tossed it to the floor. She was wearing a white wool suit with navy grosgrain edging. It was a stylish shorter length. A new pearl bracelet twinkled on her wrist, but Eva wasted no time directing everyone's eyes to her abdomen. She patted her stomach. "Do you like my new maternity outfit?"

"Mater-nity?" Mama stumbled on the unfamiliar word.

"Can't you see? We're expecting another baby!"

Ten weeks, at the most twelve, Hannah surmised by the small bulge that was not much larger than Eva's usual pudgy stomach. "Mazel tov," she said effusively.

Eva beamed. "It's all thanks to my big sister."

"What about my contribution?" Napthali asked with a teasing pout.

"You've been contributing for many years without delivering the goods," she said in a baby-sweet voice. "Now you'll have the son you've been wanting."

Hannah blanched. There was no guarantee. Her suggestions as to the best days of the month to conceive had not included the instructions for maximizing the odds for a boy. Still, there was a fifty-fifty chance.

"What do you think?" Eva asked Hannah.

Hannah blinked. "I am happy if you are happy."

"How far along do you think I am?"

"I can examine you later, if you want."

"Now!" she said somewhat imperiously, but Hannah attributed it to her excitement and let it pass.

"Let's go into Mama's bedroom." She closed the door. "When was your last bleeding?"

"October twentieth."

Hannah's first thought was: before the revolution, after Lazar had left, but her sister's anxious expression brought her back to the question at hand. "So . . ." Hannah quickly counted back three months and added a week "July the twenty-seventh is your due date and you are about twelve weeks along." She measured the height of her fundus to confirm the date and checked to see what she had been eating before Eva interrupted her.

"Ah, Hannah, Napthali wanted me to speak to you about something." She lowered her voice even though nobody was around. "He wants you to take care of me."

"Sometimes it's not a good idea for a family member to "

Eva sat up, waving her hands. "With us it is different, isn't it?"

"I suppose . . ."

She clasped Hannah's hand. "I don't like the uptown doctors. They treat you like a piece of meat."

Hannah nodded. She had heard similar complaints. "Is that it? We should go back to Mama . . ."

"Yes, but I wanted to talk to you about her too. Napthali and I are grateful you are taking such good care of her. It can't be easy . . ."

"I am happy to do it," Hannah responded. "Besides, I think that because we are both alone, we understand each other better."

Uncomfortable with this turn in the conversation, Eva stood up and straightened her skirt. "One more thing . . ." She cleared her throat, then continued. "Napthali and I don't want you to worry about paying the rent, at least not until after . . ." She tried to pick a date, then settled on the baby's birthday. "At least not until after July."

Hannah was about to argue that one issue had nothing to do with the other, but with a wave of her hand Eva returned to the parlor. As soon as the Margolis family left, Hannah hurried to her own flat. She made certain the children were busy with their nightwork, went into her bedroom, and closed the door. Then she cried. Eva's happiness contrasted with her despair. She had a husband and prosperity. She had two children and a third on the way. She did not have to support her family, and she had help with her house and family. Also, her baby was much desired. But Hannah's husband was gone. Hannah's pregnancy had been a calamity, not a delight. Nobody had wanted the baby, and the baby had ceased to exist. Even though she had no idea what she would have done had the child survived, she still felt its loss acutely. When would this pass? There was too much pain. She needed it to be over! Again fury swept over her in uncontrollable waves. What had she done to deserve such misery? This released a fresh inundation and she gave into the spasms of agony that brought no relief. Down and ever farther down she tumbled into some vast, bottomless black hole. Eventually, though, exhaustion won out and the floodgates closed. Wiping her eyes, Hannah chided herself for her paroxysm of envy. Think of everything Eva has endured, she reminded herself, but it did not help. A fresh stock of tears burst forth as she mourned the loss of Lazar and the baby and the boys dying in the war and in Russia and all the horrors of the world. Mostly though, she felt sorry, terribly sorry for herself.

∾∾ 4 ∾∾

A week later Eva appeared with a large satchel containing dresses and skirts that were too tight for her. "I thought these might fit you now," she said.

Hannah looked away after Eva pulled out the first few outfits. "I don't need any clothes, thank you."

"Of course you do. A woman can always use a change. Anyway, I can't fit into any of these. Should I give them to my sister or leave them to the moths?"

"After the baby, you'll be in them again."

Eva gave a knowing chuckle. "That's what I thought after

Isabel and Doreen, but each time I added another inch. Napthali doesn't mind. He likes me a little *zaftik*. Even now he says I am more pleasing to him." She gave her sister a knowing glance. "Also, this gives me an excuse to get more new things later," she said with a forced laugh. "Just look, there is a wonderful shirtwaist here, and this jacket will be a good color for you."

Eva meant well. "All right, let me try a few things on," Hannah said as though she were being forced to do something for her own good.

Eva handed her the royal blue suit, and Hannah went into the bathroom to try it on. "What is this? You can't undress in front of your own sister!" she chided.

"That time of the month," she called from the door. This was partially true, since she still was wearing pads from the miscarriage. Mostly she did not want Eva to glimpse her figure, which remained slightly swollen from the pregnancy. Even so, the clasp on Eva's skirt had no trouble closing.

Eva clapped when Hannah came out. "See! Isn't that perfect? I don't know why you don't buy anything for yourself."

"Eva, you know I wear uniforms at the hospital and Lazar never cared."

"Too bourgeois, right?" Hannah nodded. "So, now that he's not around you should please yourself."

She sounded as though she'd been conspiring with Herzog. It was well and good to give that sort of advice if you did not have full responsibility for an elderly mother, two children, two jobs. Please herself? Ha!

Eva handed her a dress made of a flowing chestnut silk. "This looks like it has never been worn."

"Try it."

"Where do I begin?" Hannah called from the bathroom again. The piece of flimsy goods had so little shape it seemed to dissolve in her hands.

"How can I help you if you won't let me in?" Hannah opened the door wider. "I won't look!" Eva said as she helped slip it over Hannah's head.

The bodice was tight at the bosom, with a low, round neckline. Long kimono sleeves billowed to the wrist, where roses had been appliqued for a trim. A larger garland of flowers encircled the hips. "Where did you get this crazy thing?"

"It's the latest rage."

Hannah looked down at her legs, which were not covered below the calf. "It's too short."

"No, that is how it is supposed to be." Eva propelled her toward the dresser. "Look in the mirror."

Hannah stared at herself. The color, which in the lamplight rippled from brown to gold, flattered her pale skin. The looseness was gloriously freeing, and when she moved her arms, she felt as if she were gliding. "You could still wear this, it has a lot of room in the waist."

"It looks better on you."

Hannah reached up and tried to rearrange her hair. The toll of the last few months were etched on her face. Her eyes had a pink, swollen appearance and two new matching hollows were carved from her nostrils to her chin, causing her to have a perpetually dejected expression. "I look like a tired woman in a young girl's dress."

"No, you don't," Eva protested.

"Yes, I do. I'm like an old Russian *babushka.*"

Eva stood beside her. "You seem even younger than me. I even have a few gray hairs, and you don't."

In a moment of clarity Hannah saw herself next to her sister. Despite everything her features were finer, her eyes larger and a prettier color. Her brows still had a perfect arch, while Eva's were straggly. Hannah's nose came to a fine, tapered point, but her sister's was broader and had a bump. Eva's plumper face was beginning to sag at the chin, although that could be because of the pregnancy. If it weren't for her frowning face and long, old-fashioned hair . . . "Please yourself" rang through her mind and suddenly she knew what she would do.

∽ 5 ∽

Hannah left a message with Carrie for Rachael to meet her after clinic hours at the Green Gate on 8th Street. The street was really an extension of St. Mark's Place after it crossed Astor Square, but as the name changed, so did the spirit. By the time she crossed Fifth Avenue, Hannah felt she had left the immigrant world of the Lower East Side behind. This was Greenwich Village. The name itself was so American. It sounded snug and safe. Once, at Mrs. Dodge's, Hippolyte Havel had said, "Greenwich Village is a state of mind," and she had not known what he had meant then. Now she did.

While she waited, she ordered tea. She had never been to the Green Gate before, but she had liked the way the outside looked when she walked past, first because it was entirely different than the cafés she had vowed to avoid, and also it seemed like the sort of place a lady could go unescorted. She was not disappointed. The room was quiet and nicely decorated, almost like a living room. On the way to the table she passed through a parlor area, which the hostess called "the reading room," where several people sat on comfortable chairs reading books and magazines, some of which had been provided by the establishment. Hannah wondered if it was permissible just to come inside from the cold to read.

The waitress brought the tea in delicate china cups. A large white teapot decorated with blue flowers matched the cream pitcher and sugar bowl. At the other tables tea was also being served, but each teapot and matching accoutrements were of a different floral pattern. It was probably more expensive than at the Café Boulevard, or even the Copper Kettle, but how much could tea cost?

At one corner table she noticed a woman about the age of Mabel Dodge, but entirely different in appearance. She was sitting with a much younger man with unkempt curly hair. He was leaning toward her and talking earnestly—probably something political, Hannah supposed. An earnest young man, an indulgent older woman—aunt and nephew? mother and son? Hannah dismissed those ideas and saw right through to the physical attraction in the relationship.

"Hannah? Is that you?" came Rachael's astonished voice.

Hannah turned to see her friend's mouth gaping. Her hand flew protectively to her hair.

"You bobbed your hair! I cannot believe it. And that dress . . . where did you get it?"

"Do you like it?" Hannah asked tentatively. "It was Eva's."

"It would look ghastly on her . . ." Rachael made a show of an appraisal. "But it suits you—the softness, the draping, the color. It really does." She reached over and fingered the

embroidery. "Good workmanship too." She raised her eyes
to Hannah's short hair, which fell straight to just below her
ear, where a puff of curl fluffed out prettily but did not reach
her chin. "You look like—like Irene Castle!"

Hannah had seen pictures of the woman, who with her
husband, Vernon, had started a ballroom dancing craze, and
was flattered. "A dancer I'm not."

"It could have been worse. I might have said you looked
like Emma Goldman."

Hannah laughed, for nobody would have considered
Emma a beauty, although she did claim to have invented the
fashion of bobbing hair, since she had done it way back in
1900. "I wonder how she is doing," Hannah commented solemnly. For more than a month Emma had been incarcerated
at a Missouri federal prison, while Berkman was serving his
time in Atlanta.

Seeing Hannah becoming morose, Rachael clucked,
"Enough of that! You didn't invite me here to moan about
the state of the world, did you?"

"No. I wanted your opinion on my transformation."

"Has anyone else seen you?"

"No, I did it today."

"I wonder what your mother will say."

"She's not the one that worries me." Rachael raised her
brows as if to ask: is there something . . . or someone you
have not told me about? Reading her mind, Hannah waved
her hand. "Don't be ridiculous. The children—Benny and
Emma—they might not like it."

"If that is all that concerns you, let's order something to
eat." She picked up the pastel menu. "Do you know what a
Virginia waffle is?"

"They are delicious," Hannah bluffed. "That's what I'm
having too."

After they ordered, Hannah poured Rachael's tea. The
doctor sat smiling at Hannah. "What is it?"

"I was just admiring you. You look better than you have
in months, and I don't mean just the hair and dress."

"I'm feeling stronger."

"You've been through a difficult time, but I must say
you've held up admirably. There are not many women
who—"

Hannah interrupted her. "I was pregnant."

Rachael managed the news with professional aplomb. "Was?"

"I discovered it right after Lazar left," she prevaricated, to avoid one thorny issue. "As you might imagine, I was not happy . . . so I kept quiet."

"I can't believe I never noticed." Unspoken was the question: what had Hannah done about it?

"I never showed much, even though I must have gone twenty weeks, and I tried to hide what there was." She looked at her friend apologetically. "I didn't want everyone fretting about me. Also, I felt something was wrong from the first. I don't know why, but women sometimes have a sense about these things . . ."

"Especially women who also happen to be midwives," she replied gently, then waited as Hannah perfunctorily gave the clinical details of the inevitable abortion.

"How do you feel now?"

"Relieved. I don't know what I would have done with an infant."

"Still, it must have been a disappointment . . ."

"No—" was cut off by a lump in her throat that no amount of willpower would dissolve. Hannah turned her head in anticipation of the grimacing and blinking necessary to bring herself under control. "I-I-I'm so sad, all the time, I don't know why . . ."

"It's all right," Rachael said, reaching for her hand. "Sometimes it must be unendurable, especially to be so alone."

"Yes . . . you know . . . but even so, there has been enough time . . . and . . ."

"There's no set schedule," Rachael said with a rueful chuckle.

There was a long moment of uncomfortable silence. "You can ask," Hannah said slowly.

"Ask what?"

"You want to know whether I have heard from Lazar." Rachael did not blink. "So, what's the big deal?" Her voice rose to a higher and higher pitch. "I either have heard or I have not heard. What does that change? He is there, and I am here," she finished in a seething voice.

The waitress served oval platters with crisp rectangles of a fried bread. "Your waffles," she said. "And here's the syrup and melted butter." She placed two pitchers between them.

"Smells good," Rachael said with a long sniff. "Now what do you do?" She looked at Hannah for directions.

Hannah lifted one pitcher of butter and poured it daintily, but the golden liquid pooled in the square indentations and did not go far. Next she covered the rest of the surface with the syrup. "That's it," she declared. "Then when you cut it, everything runs together." Fortunately, her analysis proved right and she found the unfamiliar tastes pleasing, especially when they mingled with the thin slices of ham on the side. "Mama would faint if she knew I was eating this," she said, but did not stop.

"You were right. They are tasty."

They ate quietly for a few minutes.

"I'm sorry for what I said. It's just that I feel everyone is always looking at me and thinking: poor Hannah. What's the difference between me and millions of others whose husbands are at war? At least I know where he is."

"And that is where?"

"Wherever Trotsky is." She waited a few beats. "That's what he is doing. He's assisting his old friend, Lev Davidovich. So at least I know he's enjoying himself." As if to rid herself of the bitterness in her voice, she tossed her head. At the unfamiliar sensation of hair brushing her ears, she reached up and smoothed it. "And I am enjoying myself," she said as she straightened her back, but the tears that filmed her eyes belied her words.

"But where exactly?" Rachael asked, trying to ignore Hannah's distress.

"He has a cot at the Smolny Institute, which used to be Catherine the Great's school for young ladies and is now Bolshevik headquarters. The big news is that he seems to be Trotsky's personal scribe. Apparently Trotsky is filled with inspirations these days, but does not have the time to record them, so he tells them to Lazar, who dutifully writes them down. Frankly, I don't like the sound of it."

"Why? It sounds like important work."

"Lazar's nothing but a secretary, but at least he's fighting with a pen and not a gun."

"The pen is mightier than the sword," Rachael muttered. Then she cleared her throat. "To change the subject," she began with a wry smile, "I would like to report to my counselor."

Hannah replaced her knife and fork. "Yes?"

"I think I have made some progress."

Hannah waited.

"Now, don't get too excited, it's not what you think, but still . . ." She made a show of cutting off another section of her waffle, but did not taste it. "For several months now Herzog has been much more interested in me. Finally he got over his problem about what I confessed to him. These days—or rather nights—he seems to care more how I am feeling. He asks me if I like this or that, and I tell him. Not that anything remarkable has occurred, but there are signs of improvement, if you know what I mean." Hannah nodded that she did, so Rachael continued. "Also, I am trying not to think about what I am doing. At first I concentrated on what I was thinking about—and it isn't shiny staircases!—but I found that the only thing on my mind was me: what I was feeling, what I was doing, what was wrong with me, and why I couldn't feel what I should."

"And now . . ." Hannah asked to encourage her.

"My thoughts are more—I don't know more diffused . . . I think about as little as possible. I close my eyes and touch Herzog's back and legs and . . ."

"Do you feel more pressure, or anything physically arousing?"

"Yes. I do. But it does not go anywhere."

Hannah understood. More than ever before she felt a kinship with Rachael. Many times during the night she would awaken from a dream in which she and Lazar were making love, but the act would always be incomplete. Her frustration was enough to wake her. She would lie in bed suffused with longing. "I think I may have some ideas . . ." Hannah began, then seeing the tables nearby had been filled, she demurred. "We'll talk in your office in a few days."

"I want you to know that I won't be very disappointed if nothing comes of this," Rachael said, looking away slightly. "I've always known that our marriage is more an intellectual partnership than anything else."

"Come now," Hannah teased, "your Nora is evidence that you two do more than talk."

Rachael's mouth puckered. Hannah was unsure whether her friend was going to cry or complain, so she backpedaled.

"But you are right. Nobody has everything. Lazar might have preferred a woman with whom he could share more of his ideas."

"Wait a minute," Rachael said, forcing a laugh, "you two did your share of talking."

"Maybe we should have talked more," Hannah added ruefully.

Rachael glanced at the watch on the chain around her neck. "I have to pick up Nora at her music teacher's house." She stood.

Hannah reached for the check.

"No, let me—"

"I invited you," Hannah insisted.

"All right, this time." Rachael took a step backward. "I cannot stop admiring the dress, the hair . . . If Lazar could see you now!"

Hannah counted out the money and left it on the table. She followed Rachael through the reading room and waited for their coats. A man with a head of ebony hair was turned away from her, but as she moved toward the manager, who held her coat, she realized it was someone she knew. "Dr. Dowd?"

He looked up, but did not recognize her at first. "Mrs. Sokolow?" he blinked.

"This is my friend, Dr. Jaffe."

Dr. Dowd stood. "My pleasure, Doctor. You are at Gouverneur's, aren't you?"

"Yes, Doctor."

"I've heard about you from your associate, Dr. Kaplan."

"And I've heard about you from your associate, Mrs. Sokolow. She also helps me with my private practice."

"Ah, yes," he said, taking in the two women. His eyes focused on Hannah. "I am sorry I did not recognize you, but the hair and—" It was unusual for Dr. Dowd to be flustered, so Hannah did not miss it. "I'm meeting my wife," he said, as if he was required to explain his presence. "She comes here often, but this is my first time."

The manager came forward and helped Hannah into her coat.

"Try the Virginia waffles," Rachael suggested. "They're Mrs. Sokolow's favorite." She turned toward the door.

"Good afternoon, Doctor," Hannah said and followed her out.

In the narrow corridor they passed someone coming in. She was tall, wore a red velvet coat, a red cloche hat, and carried a matching plaid umbrella. Hannah turned and watched her back. For some reason she supposed this was Mrs. Dowd, and that knowledge made her feel uneasy, although she was uncertain why.

6

For all her reading and thinking about how men and women made love, Hannah realized she knew little about what exactly it was that made a woman climax and feel satisfied during the sexual act. She knew what she liked and what she didn't, but mostly it was tied up with Lazar, who had learned numerous ways to please her. Without him, the urge came upon her less frequently, but when it did, she was overwhelmed by frustration. She had rarely masturbated during her marriage, and not at all since Lazar had left. She had done it when she was a student, not frequently and not terribly successfully. Why was it that women found satisfaction so much more elusive than men? Was it really nature's intention to protect chastity by reducing sexual capacity in immature women? This was logical in the social context of family groups, but Hannah assumed the hymen had been present since prehistoric times. What biological function could that membrane serve? Perhaps it reduced infection by preventing young girls poking themselves. Any other explanation did not make medical sense.

That night she lay in bed and tried to become interested in her experiment. She touched herself but felt nothing. What did Lazar do to stimulate her? He sometimes ran his hand over her nipples. She tried this. There was hardly a difference from washing her body. What next? She used her finger to probe her vagina. If only Lazar were here . . . Where was he? She imagined him in rumpled clothes among papers and books in smoky rooms. Might he be with a woman? Imagining the revolution as being led by men in soiled collars with rolled-up sleeves, she had suppressed the fact that there were women at the forefront of radical thinking. Alexandra Kollontai, for one. She recalled the first time they had met her in the café. Had there been a spark between her and Lazar? Hannah mostly remembered how flattered she had been when Kollontai was more interested in her than the men. Or had that been a ruse? Don't be silly, Hannah castigated herself. They had seen Kollontai many other times and there had been no hint of a flirtation, yet wasn't the Russian woman with the haunting eyes the one who had claimed that "sex should be as easy as a drink of water"?

Despite that line of thinking, Hannah found herself becoming aroused. Her fingers pressed and prodded. She turned over on her belly and arched her back. Soon she was rewarded with the gratifying pulsations. She sighed and rolled on her side. Now what had she learned? Thinking about Lazar had excited her. Or was it thinking about Lazar with another woman? Or . . . not thinking about what she was doing, letting her mind wander. What else? The feelings had been so insistent she had not paid attention to her reactions. Her hand slipped between her legs. An urgency remained, for it had not been as satisfying as being with a man. Also, she often had more than one climax. All right. She would do it again, but this time she would pay more attention to where she was touching and what it was that worked. She would stimulate only her clitoris and surrounding area, avoiding the vagina. Then, later, she would concentrate on the vagina to learn if there was a difference.

After her second, less successful try, Hannah fell asleep. A few evenings later, she went to bed earlier than usual. She placed a chair in front of her door, so she would have a warning if one of the children came in. They rarely did, but she did not want to be caught because this time she was leaving the lamp on.

After discovering how to stimulate herself efficiently, Hannah thought she could learn more if she could visualize what happened during orgasm. Admittedly the sensations were puny compared to what lovemaking with Lazar could evoke, but they were smaller versions of the same ones. Wouldn't it be wonderful to have Mrs. Czachorwski to examine one more time now that she had an idea what to be looking for? Since it was unlikely she—or anyone else with the same presenting symptoms—would reappear, Hannah had only herself. To prepare, she reviewed some anatomy books and made some crude drawings of the perineum. Then, on her pillow, Hannah placed a hand mirror and her chart of the pelvic region. As soon as she climaxed she planned to look at herself in the mirror, then tick off the areas affected, if she could manage the feat. It took a few tries to know when watching herself inhibited the climax, or when she was too far along to stop. As soon as she felt she could hold back no longer, she looked to see what was happening. Finally she was successful in viewing her pulsating perineum. Nothing around the clitoris was obvious, and all she could catch was some light fluttering at the outlet of the vagina.

She tried again with the stimulation limited to her vagina. She would not touch the labia or clitoris. From her experience with gynecological patients she was well aware that many women put objects inside themselves for this purpose. There was a long list of materials that caused embarrassing problems: breakable glass, thin wires, soft bananas, wads of paper. This told her that women not only used poor judgment in what they selected for the purpose, but that many craved something inside them to derive sexual satisfaction. If they needed to stimulate only their clitoris they would not feel compelled to employ whatever object they could find. Hannah selected hers with care. It could not be too small, be breakable, or have any sharp edges. To prevent introducing bacteria it had to be washable, and of course it had to be a welcome size and shape. Her choice had been a small, curved eggplant with a shiny skin, which she scrubbed with soap and water.

She used her vegetable as if it were attached to a man and plunged it in and out. The sensations were familiar, but they did not mount or lead to a climax no matter how long she tried. When at last she permitted herself to apply pressure to her clitoral area, with the vagina still filled with her substitute penis, her orgasm mounted even more strongly than it had with her finger stimulation alone. What did this mean? Was there such a thing as a vaginal orgasm apart by itself or only in conjunction with clitoral stimulation? Hannah knew that women were different and what worked for her might not be the solution for someone else. In her case she had decided that she could be satisfied by the clitoris alone, or the clitoris and vagina together, but not the vagina alone. In normal relations with a man it was impossible to enfold his penis without having some stimulation of the clitoris, unless he approached her from behind. When Lazar had done this— and he had tried this often—Hannah had already satisfied herself on top of him, or he reached around and rubbed her vulva with his hand. So, in most regular relations the parts worked in harmony. Wasn't that how it was supposed to be? If so, why?

Hannah drifted off to sleep contemplating the puzzle. She awoke early in the morning as a dingy dawn broke over the tenements. In her half-awake state the problem reasserted itself, then an answer surfaced. Biologically, women's main function was to produce children. The vagina was sometimes injured during the birth process. In case of vaginal injury during childbirth a woman could continue to enjoy clitoral stimulation. In fact, she could satisfy herself without vaginal involvement. Yet girls who had not yet had a lover found it easier to achieve satisfaction by rubbing the clitoral area, which is why Freud must have thought that a mature woman goes beyond that process as she submits to a man. Parts of his theory made sense, but his conclusions did not.

Hannah sighed with satisfaction at her reasoning, which made such sense to her. She was right, and Mr. Freud was wrong. Wrong! Wrong! Wrong! She doubted that Freud had delivered a single baby. If he had, he might have come down off his high horse and looked at the reality of why women were made the way they were. Nature was not stupid. Look at the penis. A nice, versatile instrument. It served several functions admirably. Usually soft and easy to deal with when it was not needed for a sexual purpose, at the time it was aroused, it became a long, sturdy tool for inserting sperm deep into the safety of a woman's vagina, up close to the door of the womb. In a short while, the sperm could be on their way into the dark interior of a woman's body searching for its match: the egg. Once the penis had performed its task, it deflated and returned to being a dormant organ, its great feat having been accomplished.

Not so with a woman. After intercourse that led to conception, the vagina had performed just one of its more minor functions. The major one, becoming the birth canal, was many months off. And then the trouble would begin. Even in modern times, with centuries of knowledge passed down, the vagina faced numerous traumas. At best it stretched enormously to permit the baby's passage. If the vagina was lined with nerves that sensed pleasure, wouldn't those same pathways provide the mother with excruciating pain during birth? Wasn't it better to have this area fairly numb? Midwives knew that these tissues were not especially sensitive to stimuli such as heat and cold, so why should they respond to the exquisite, delicate perceptions of sexual rapture? Ah, but look at the clitoris. Why else would it have been situated so far away from the critical perineal area, which was subject to the batterings of birth, if not to protect the seat of desire? If the goal of nature was not to encourage reproduction, passion would not play such an important role in human interaction. Wasn't it the urge to achieve satisfaction that drove men and women together, despite all the problems that these relationships caused? One could make a case that only the man needed to experience orgasm to keep the species going. If he felt the urge, was aggressive in corralling his mate and pinning her down, he would not require her cooperation. Her feelings would be of no consequence. Certainly not all sexual encounters were loving interactions.

Why then was it important for a woman to be eager to have a mate? Again, nature not only wanted to reproduce, it wanted its young to survive to reproduce again. Human babies were frail and took at least ten years to become self-sufficient, more than that to be sexually mature. A mother nurturing babies required a man to hunt for her, so she might have stayed with him to be fed, if for no other reason. And yet if a woman felt pleasure, she would willingly return for more sexual activity. If she experienced this satisfaction with a particular man, she would want to find ways to accommodate him so he would volunteer to remain at her side and provide for the family while she nurtured their young. The best way to secure everyone's cooperation for this endeavor was to include enjoyment as part of the package. However, if her vagina was the place where she felt the stimulation—and if this was damaged during childbirth—her subsequent spur to reproduce would be lost.

Hannah recalled a professor in Moscow who had harped on the subject of obstetrical damage. "Once small-headed babies were probably the norm, but somewhere along the line, women mated with men whose heads were less suited to the diameters of their birth canals." This physician had been a proponent of routine episiotomies to both prevent injuries to a woman's bulbar system as well as to tighten the opening to preserve the husband's pleasure. Since Hannah had learned non-surgical techniques for preventing lacerations, she believed these preferable to cutting and stitching. Nevertheless, some accidents were unavoidable, and thus a midwife used every option to minimize injury. So wasn't it clever of nature to have placed the clitoris so far from the battlefield?

Recently Hannah had read that at conception there was no differentiation between male and female. Sometime during the process of fetal development a cue was given and the genitalia of each sex was defined. Most experts claimed that the clitoris was a rudimentary penis, and since it was smaller and performed a much reduced function, this made some sense. Did that mean that all external female genitalia were miniature male structures, and only the internal genitalia were inherently female, as Mr. Freud suggested? Once, several years ago at Mrs. Dodge's, Hannah had felt daring enough to suggest that Adam may have been derived from Eve, and not vice versa. Thus far she had seen no evidence that the penis might not be an enlarged clitoris instead of the other way around.

Nevertheless, theories were one thing, practical advice was another. How could her concept help someone like Rachael? In a few tries Hannah had been able to learn fresh notions about her own body. Maybe Rachael should experiment with herself. Not with a mirror and notes, though, for she was already too self-conscious about her performance in bed. How would she feel if Hannah advocated masturbating? What could Hannah say? Would she hand her friend an eggplant? The idea had Hannah laughing at herself. Then she became more serious and wondered if any harm would come from some clitoral exploration. In her attempts Hannah had discovered that she had particular preferences. For instance, she could not touch the clitoris directly. It was much too sensitive and made her recoil, so movement along both sides was far more effective. Rachael would have her own inclinations. Nobody could tell her or show her. She would have to investigate them for herself.

7

On the first day of spring, Hattie Donovan welcomed Hannah to her ward with a toothy smile. "An interesting day," she said, and since her hands were busy massaging a laboring woman's back, she indicated the women in Beds Ten through Twelve with a tilt of her chin. She was working at Bed Nine. The rest of the ward was empty.

"What's the matter in Twelve?"

"A precaution. She's a para thirteen."

"Thirteen!" Hannah sucked in her breath. "How many living?"

"Six or seven. All have been full-term infants. She lost two to diphtheria, one was deformed at birth and lasted less than a week, two died in the first six years from the usual fevers. You'll have to check the chart for the rest."

Hannah nodded that she would. The more pregnancies, the more complications. Hattie had been wise to single her out for special attention. "The others?"

"No immediate problems. They're racing each other to enter the human race." Hattie chuckled at her own joke, but Hannah was too preoccupied to respond. "Also . . ." she said under her breath, "Mrs. Hemming has been around all morning. She rearranged my cart, refolding the pads to make certain they lined up perfectly." Hannah noted the precision with some irritation. This was a criticism of her, albeit a silent one. The birth rate continued to remain high as the soldiers who came home on leave left something behind to ripen while they were away. With so many nurses doing war duty and the midwives working longer hours, there was hardly time for excessive fastidiousness. The mothers were receiving competent care. Their infant-mortality rate was running less than the previous year. What else did the old battle-ax want?

Reducing her resentment to a slow simmer, Hannah went to check the progress of the women. "Bed Eleven is crowning. Can you handle it?" she asked Mrs. Donovan.

"Yes. Would you do a blood pressure on Bed Twelve?"

Hannah went to the bed which held the most worrisome case. She lifted the chart and read, "CLEMENTINE HARDCASTLE, AGE 35, GRAVIDA 13, PARA 13, 421 E. 15TH STREET." The poor woman! Hannah would be the same age this year. How did she manage? The term *gravida* referred to the number of previous pregnancies she had, while *para* indicated the number of deliveries after the twentieth week. To have had thirteen pregnancies and thirteen deliveries was fairly unusual, because the gravida number was often higher. Since her recent miscarriage, Hannah would be considered a Gravida 5, Para 2. However, out of ignorance or because they were ashamed of their failure, some women did not report pregnancies that had not resulted in live babies. Others wanted to hide an illegal abortion, which Hannah suspected were far more common than anyone admitted, since her staff frequently dealt with the septic reactions from blunders. A few did not want anyone to think that a real abortion—the medical term for a miscarriage—might have been self-induced. Why was honesty so difficult when it came to reproduction? Hannah considered briefly, but had little time to ruminate on the question.

As she checked Mrs. Hardcastle, she asked her about her earlier deliveries. The woman gave brief yes or no responses in a clipped, slightly British accent, but seemed to have good recall. She had successfully given birth to two breech births, had fairly short labors with the previous three, and a minor hemorrhage with the second-to-last birth of an eight-pound girl. Although her skin was an almost deathly white and she showed other signs of anemia, the woman's weight was good, her vital signs excellent. She had a dry cough, but that was typical during this changeable weather. There was a certain docile quality that Hannah found appealing. Even when she was experiencing a hard contraction, Mrs. Hardcastle did not fuss. Midwives appreciated a stalwart patient, but one had to be careful because their sort might complain too late.

Hannah listened to her chest. To assist drainage she suggested, "If you would sit up more, you might feel better." She helped change her position. "Isn't that an improvement? Now I'll be here, so just call me if you need anything."

"Thank you," Mrs. Hardcastle responded gratefully.

Hannah made certain to note that the usual precautions were taken, then was called to do the delivery in Bed Ten, since Hattie was busy on Bed Eleven. By the end of the morning, the four patients had delivered five children. Hattie's case had resulted in surprise twins. Mrs. Hardcastle was cradling her second son. "This is what Herbie has been waiting for. Maybe now I'll have my rest."

"Yes, try to get some sleep," Hannah suggested when she was cleaned up.

"I meant a rest from you know what," the woman said shyly.

Hannah made no comment. There was not a woman in the ward who was anxious to consider marital relations for a while, but she also could predict that a year from now many would be back in the same pavilion.

As the last baby was being readied for the nursery, Mrs. Hemming made an appearance. "Would you like me to take him to the nursery?" she asked Hannah in her most saccharine tone.

"That's not necessary. For a change, everything is calm here."

"I'm going that way."

Hannah faced Mrs. Hemming squarely. She wanted to find a reason to keep the Hardcastle baby away from her supervisor, but why? After all this time, they should have reached some degree of equanimity, but that aspiration was hopeless because Mrs. Hemming was impossible to satisfy. The roots were as complex as their varying backgrounds: Hannah's training in Russia and her fragmented English, Mrs. Hemming's manner of treating even the most senior midwives on a par with the scatterbrained first-year training school nurses. Or was it Mrs. Hemming's ironclad insistence that anyone on staff at Bellevue should—as she had—dedicate their life to the institution, and if they had extra time those hours should be spent on the premises, not in another doctor's clinic? Whatever the cause, Hannah found she cared less and less about Mrs. Hemming's crusades. The important point was that the midwifery staff admired her and she was respected by most of the physicians, especially Dr. Dowd, who since the retirement of the old chairman of the obstetrical service was probably the most influential. The best way to deal with Mrs. Hemming was to humor her, then do what she wanted.

The baby shifted in Hannah's arms. Since there was no

real reason to go along with him to the nursery, she handed him over with the introduction, "Baby boy Hardcastle."

"No name yet?" Mrs. Hemming asked loudly enough for the new mother to hear.

"She has a big family," Hannah said under her breath. "It may take some time."

"Did you ask the mother?" Hannah shook her head. "Hardcastle," Mrs. Hemming repeated and walked over to the bed. "Mrs. Hardcastle, have you chosen a name for your nice little boy?"

"Not yet ..." With spiritless, watery eyes Clementine looked up at the imposing supervisor.

"It's much more efficient to put the name down when we do our nursery intake," she prompted. "Saves so much time, and of course he gets to hear his name right from the first."

"Well, my husband is Herbert and our other son is Harry ..."

"Why not Herbert, Jr.?" Mrs. Hemming suggested.

"No, we used that once."

"Of course." Mrs. Hemming's voice managed to glide over the delicate point. "I suppose you'd be wanting another *H*. Mrs. Sokolow, any ideas?"

This was hardly Hannah's forte. Besides, she resented Mrs. Hemming's meddling, even though she was the one who named the abandoned babies before they were sent to the orphanage. And Hannah knew the reason: because she would never have one of her own.

"No ideas? Then how about Hank? That's a nice sensible name. Hank. I like it. What about you, Mrs. Sokolow? It's almost a male form of your name."

Hannah forced a smile. "What does Mrs. Hardcastle think?"

The new mother lay back on her pillows coughing. With one hand she held her chest, the other her tender abdomen. "That's fine," she said to get off the hook.

"Hank Hardcastle. Shall I write it in?"

"I guess so ..." the mother said, pleasing Mrs. Hemming enormously.

∽ **8** ∾

As much as Hannah hated to admit it, Hank suited the ruddy newborn with the lustiest cry in the postpartum ward. The infant's bellow led her to Mrs. Hardcastle's bed. "You wanted to see me," she asked. Patients tended to attach themselves to the people who worked with them in labor far more than the staff they would meet later in their stay, so she had not found the request to visit her exceptional.

"They said I could talk to you."

"Of course. Is there something the matter?"

"Not now."

Hannah had a peculiar feeling. "How may I help you?"

"I have had thirteen babies. Enough is enough. I don't know how we'll feed them, and Herbie is talking about signing up. He doesn't want to be thought a slacker."

No red-blooded American male wanted to be called a slacker for not doing his part for the war effort. Everyone tried to get into uniform, or at least to obtain some sort of badge to protect themselves from that dreaded epithet. The doctors at Bellevue who were overage, physically defective, or deferred for holding an essential job had paid a dollar each and joined the Volunteer Medical Service Corps. Even Dr. Dowd proudly displayed his small oxidized silver shield with caduceus and wings surmounted by the letters *VMSC*. Hannah, who had always agreed with the pacifist leanings of her socialist friends, said, "We need men at home too."

"Not if your home is filled with screaming children." Mrs. Hardcastle's tone was flat. She seemed defeated.

"Where does he think they came from?" she queried lightly.

Mrs. Hardcastle began to cry. Hannah was not alarmed. Other times a woman might bear up admirably, but during the first weeks after giving birth a new mother's emotions vacillated wildly. In these wards tears flowed over matters as trivial as a spilled pitcher of water or tangles in the hair. A visit from a husband or mother sometimes triggered a terrible sadness that erupted after the caller departed. Mostly these moods passed. Sometimes they did not. A few seemed to go crazy. Quite a few mothers had tried to kill themselves; a couple had succeeded. And then there was the terrible secret of the postpartum ward: mothers murdered their babies. Sometimes it was difficult to tell if it was accidental. *Overlying* was the term on the death certificate, but the staff believed that few mothers—even in heavy slumber—actually suffocated their children accidentally. Every month at least one baby turned up blue and cold in its mother's bed. Other cases were more dramatic—and bloody—as one mother accused another of harming her child. The result was the same: unwanted infants who were dead.

Was little Hank at risk? It did not seem so. Hank was well cared for. His diaper area was clean. He was picked up whenever he fussed, and with his piercing cry everyone would have known if he were being neglected. Was the mother complaining more than usual? No. On the contrary. Was she overly tired? Well, she was sleeping a great deal, but this was probably the first rest she had had in a long time. Hannah decided that this was a borderline situation. To be safe she would sign Hank into the night nursery before she went off duty, although she thought she was being overly conscientious.

"I'm sorry." Mrs. Hardcastle wiped her face with the bed sheet. "I don't know what got into me. It's just that I don't want any more children." Hank stirred in her arms. She bent over and kissed his forehead. "After him, that is."

"I'm sure you are a very good mother," Hannah said, thinking a compliment might help.

"There are seven at home now. Hank makes eight. There are five under the age of nine. Clara will be one next month. I don't know what I shall do if my husband—" A rippling volley of sobs overcame her.

An orderly passing by waved to get Hannah's attention. She was holding up a chart with a green cover: a new admittance to one of the birthing wards. Probably a complication. Hannah indicated she would be along shortly. "I have to go . . ." she said.

Clementine Hardcastle clutched her hand. "Please, just tell me what to do."

"I don't know how to help you."

"But they said you would!"

"How?"

"I've heard there are ways to prevent having a baby. Can't you give me whatever it is before I leave here?"

"I'm sorry." Hannah stood. "I cannot."

"But I'll die if I have to raise another child! You must tell me—"

"Unfortunately, there are laws against what you want. I cannot do something illegal."

"Just tell me where to go. Is there a place—a doctor? I can get the money, if that's it."

The woman was making such a fuss others were listening in. Even if Hannah had wanted to offer her some advice, such as the address of Margaret Sanger's clinic, she could not do it now. For the moment she had to get away, so she said, "I'll talk to you later." The hushed tone of her voice conveyed a promise but offered nothing specific.

Mrs. Hardcastle loosened her grip on Hannah's arm. With wide, sorrowful eyes she stared up at Hannah as she fell back on her pillow in exhaustion.

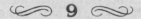

9

Every mother who left Bellevue with a live baby was given a small packet of supplies: absorbent cotton, a small vial of alcohol for drying the stump of the umbilical cord, tincture of green soap for use on the baby's diaper area and mother's perineum, castile soap, a tube of white Vaseline, a dozen sanitary pads, an abdominal binder, two flannel bands, one shirt—cotton and wool for summer, silk and wool for winter. Everything was wrapped in a quilted pad and tied with twine. There were also a list of instructions for the aftercare of both mother and baby. If the mother was illiterate in English, an effort was made to be certain that she understood the basics. Someone had already determined that Mrs. Hardcastle could read, and this had been duly noted on her chart. Although Hannah rarely handled discharges, she made it a point to be there when Clementine Hardcastle was ready to leave. She personally carried Hank from the nursery and placed him in his mother's arms. There was no hesitation as the mother took him, but she did not look directly at the midwife.

Hannah lifted the packet from the cart. "These are for you and the baby. Inside are the written instructions you must follow and the date for the postpartum check-up in six weeks. Until then you must refrain from relations with your husband." The baby began to cry. "You may feed him before you go," Hannah suggested.

"My husband is waiting downstairs."

"I'll walk you down," Hannah offered, since the mother could not handle her satchel, the packet, and the baby. Once they were in the lobby, she spoke softly. "I prepared your packet myself. There is some extra information inside, which we do not give out routinely."

A glimmer of recognition lit Clementine Hardcastle's face. Good, she knows what I mean, Hannah thought, but was disappointed when she realized that the patient merely had spied her husband.

A tall man, so thin he seemed gaunt and sickly, loped over to them. "Here you are, my dear," he said in a voice more aristocratic than his bearing.

She unwrapped the baby so he could see his son's face. "This is Hank" was her curt introduction.

"Well, let's get him home before the rain comes," he said, ignoring Hannah.

The midwife handed him the packet and his wife's suit-case. "Good luck to you," she said, but received only a per-functory nod as a reply.

For a few seconds Hannah was miffed. She had taken a big chance by sneaking one of Margaret Sanger's pamphlets into the bundle. She had even written the clinic address in-side the front cover, as well as that of Dr. Jaffe's office. Then the feeling of annoyance passed, like a brief cramp. Her job was to help people no matter what their ability to pay or reciprocate with gratitude. The Hardcastles had so many problems of their own they could barely think of oth-ers. Maybe Clementine would read the pamphlet and figure out what she might use. Mrs. Sanger described condoms, which many men refused to consider, douches, which—in Hannah's opinion—most women did not employ routinely or quickly enough, and cervical pessaries and diaphragms, which were available at Mrs. Sanger's clinic. Minna had shown Hannah the styles of these protective devices. Of one favored type, the Mensinga, there were fourteen different sizes, varying from fifty to ninety millimeters in diameter. Several years earlier Minna had fitted Hannah with one. Afterward she had offered herself for Hannah to practice measuring and inserting them. Since that time, though, Hannah had never fitted a woman and doubted if she could do so without additional training, but until Lazar's departure, her own rubber dome had been used regularly—well, fairly regularly—and she was certain her unwanted pregnancy had come from a time she had ignored it, not the failure of the dome itself.

Hannah had to return to the obstetrical pavilion. The caged elevator seemed to be stuck on the third floor, so she decided to walk. When the architects McKim, Mead and White had designed the buildings, they had been influenced by Florence Nightingale's ideas of the most sanitary way to construct a hospital. Because the famous nurse had written that fresh air and sunlight were necessary to fight infection, they had allowed for open loggias between the wings that jutted out along the riverfront vistas. Whenever possible, patients were taken outside on these balconies. Also, to isolate diseases so they would not spread, various pavilions for everything from maternity to pediatrics to tuberculosis to surgery were given their own long wings, which met in the center, where staircases and elevators could convey people between floors. However, these distances were vast. If a nurse wanted to go from, say, surgery to maternity, which was right above it, she would have to walk to the middle of the hospital, climb the stairs or take the elevator, then trek back down the long corridor again. Worse, the scarcity of exits made the building a potential firetrap. Currently a building program was adding an external staircase at the far end of each pavilion so that the staff would have another means of exit and communication between the floors. One of the first of these to be completed was the one in the wing where Hannah worked. As she climbed one of these exterior staircases, the wind off the river lifted her skirt and buffeted her ankles. When she reached her floor, she paused to observe a tugboat valiantly hauling a barge against the turbulent, wind-swept water.

"Mrs. Sokolow!" boomed a voice behind her. Hannah

spun around. "Why are you sneaking in this way?" chided Mrs. Hemming.

She was hardly being deceptive, but since it was useless to start an argument with her superior, she only replied, "Good afternoon, Mrs. Hemming."

"Where were you just now?"

"Discharging a patient."

"Isn't that a waste of your time?"

"I had particular concerns about this case."

"And what were those?"

"For a while I suspected a postpartum mental disorder and wanted to be certain the baby was going home in safe hands."

"Mrs. Hardcastle, I presume."

"Yes." Hannah was not surprised Mrs. Hemming knew the name. She read every chart. Hannah's notes about a cautionary nursery stay must have caught her eye.

"I think you exaggerated that one."

"My first worries seem to have been for nothing," Hannah admitted agreeably. "Sometimes it is tricky to tell the difference between the normal melancholy and a severe problem." The wind whipped at Hannah's skirts until she hugged the fabric between her knees.

"In the past I have respected your judgment." The words were not damning, but the tone was ominous. "May I see you in my office?"

∽ 10 ∾

Mrs. Hemming had never looked sharper. Her uniform was so crisp with starch she crackled as she took her seat. Every hair was smoothed into her symmetrical bun. Hannah stood in front of her supervisor like a prisoner before a judge. Mrs. Hemming placed her immaculate tapered fingers on the desk as if she were about to play the piano. "Is this how a discharge packet should be wrapped?" She pointed to a bundle on a cart by her desk.

Hannah stared at the offending object. Was this a matter

of improper corners or the wrong sort of knot on the twine? To her it seemed perfectly done, but then she did not have Mrs. Hemming's eagle's eye. She said nothing.

"What? Don't you see the problem? I was certain you would, since you were the one who wrapped this particular package."

Hannah never wrapped them. That was a job for the student nurses. The only one she had done had been for Mrs. Hardcastle and . . .

Mrs. Hemming was untying the twine. The knot had been false and it fell open at a single tug. She shifted the abdominal binder, which was the top layer of the sandwich, and lifted out the publication. When had the bundles been switched? Hannah mused just before the world tilted on its axis.

"What do you know about this?" The words on the cover, *Family Limitation* by Margaret H. Sanger, rippled as Mrs. Hemming waved the pamphlet between her thumb and forefinger like a foul dressing.

Lying was out of the question. "I put it there."

"Why?"

"The patient requested information on how to avoid another pregnancy."

"And if she had requested information on suicide, would you have packed a gun?"

Hannah heard the question but saw nothing. Her eyes blurred and her knees wobbled. One step back propped her against the wall. What had she done? What would happen to her now? She should have thought about the children. She had been warned . . . even doctors had lost their positions for less.

"I've been watching you. I've suspected you were doing this, but until this moment I had no proof."

"This is the first time—"

"Mrs. Sokolow, let's not make it worse than it is. I know that you have been misled. Your own sister-in-law, whose antics made headlines last year, is one of the best-known of the anarchists who espouse this subversion. I hope she has recovered fully—both her good health and her good sense—I truly do, but for a long time I have worried that she may have contaminated you. Look at this filth!" she spat and randomly opened to a page. " 'Following are some of the solutions to be used for the douche, which when carefully used will kill the male sperm or prevent its entering the womb.' Do you really think genteel women should be reading that? Or this? 'One of the best is the condom or rubber "cot." These are made of soft tissues which envelop the male organ—' " Mrs. Hemming broke off and scanned down the line. " 'In this way sperm does not enter the vagina.' Really, Mrs. Sokolow, what do you have to say for yourself?" She did not, however, give Hannah a chance to reply, for she seemed mesmerized by the publication. Instead of speaking she merely pointed to the diagrams of the French pessary and the anatomical drawings showing how it was inserted. "Do you really think it safe to encourage women to push their foul fingers inside themselves and allow them to contaminate the mouth of their wombs? Don't we have enough infections already?"

"I hardly think—"

"What you think is besides the point!" Mrs. Hemming flung the book aside. "In any case, after our directives about what we expect from our staff and our updates on hospital policy, I had confidence that you would respect the wishes of the institution, at least while you were on the premises. Much harder was to consider your spare-time activities. However, we trusted you would not violate our injunctions there. Yet trust only can go so far. Unfortunately, I must be the guardian of the morals of the staff, and this requires total vigilance. Ever since your husband chose to forsake his adopted country, I have feared that you may have been perverted by his wrong-minded idealism."

Anger galvanized Hannah. Her heart started pumping blood to her brain. "My husband has nothing to do with this. I was thinking only of Mrs. Hardcastle—nobody else! You speak noble words, but what do you know about what it's like for that poor lady? You live comfortably with nobody to care for but yourself. This is a woman my own age who has suffered through thirteen pregnancies. She can barely feed the ones she has. Just because she is cursed with an especially fertile body doesn't mean she should be condemned to poverty and ill health. She hurts nobody if she chooses to limit the size of her family with simple, safe techniques. What would you rather? Should she be one of those who 'overlies' her baby? Or should she find a way to dispose of little Hank that will look like another sad case of a baby who dies by accident? Or, what if she should conceive again in a few months and out of desperation tries to get rid of it? More than likely she will do herself in, and then what? She'll orphan eight babies." Hannah managed a quick inward breath. "I did nothing wrong. But by taking away the book, you have done this woman an injustice." Hannah didn't realize what she was doing until she did it. She walked over to the desk and snatched up the pamphlet. "I'll take it to her myself," she snapped, and without another word she spun around and left Mrs. Hemming sitting there, her fingers tapping out a nervous drill in the midwife's wake.

❦ 11 ❦

"*Dorogiye tovaristchi,*" Dear comrades, was the way Lazar's letter began. It had been carried by Louise Bryant's husband, John Reed, but was several months old.

"I know it's ancient news, but Reed planned to sail from Christiania in late February. For some reason he was detained there by the American consul," Minna explained what she had heard from Louise when she delivered the bundle late one evening.

Hannah began turning the pages to see if she could locate any vital message about her husband's health or welfare. Her eyes blurred at the closing: "Your Luftmentsh." She refolded the pages until she could read them in peace.

"You'll want to read it over slowly," Minna offered finally, and Hannah didn't disagree.

After Minna departed, she tried again. The first part of the letter was difficult to follow because it dealt with some of the behind-the-scenes maneuvers that Lazar was privy to during the treaty negotiations between the Central Powers and Russia. "If L. D. had done as I had recommended and signed the treaty sooner, the Soviet Republic might have obtained less disastrous terms." Hannah chuckled as she read. Lazar was the same as ever. Now Lev Davidovich was "L. D." and her husband was an intimate adviser who should have been followed! Then she reminded herself that Lazar had been astute in predicting the course of the revolution. Also, he had managed to find a niche in the seat of power by becoming ensconced in the Smolny beside Trotsky and down the hall from Lenin. She returned to his words with fresh respect. "Nevertheless, he did a brilliant job of exploiting the propaganda potential of the negotiations. He has convinced the West's working class of the Bolshevik opposition to Austro-German imperialism." Hannah reread the words, but barely understood them. To her husband the world of political ideas was a churning sea into which he dived like an expert swimmer, yet all it took were a few *isms* in a sentence to drown out her comprehension.

Halfway down the page the news became more interesting. "The Council of People's Commissars has moved from Petrograd to Moscow and I, of course, have gone with them. L. D. is giving up his position as the Commissar of Foreign Affairs and is now Commissar of War and of the Navy." Hannah's heart skipped a beat. Did this mean that Lazar was taking on a more dangerous role? "I have a small room across from L. D.'s study in the Kremlin. His room is paneled in Karelian birch with a golden sheen. 'The last time I was the guest of the state in Moscow my quarters were not so nice,' L. D. said when we arrived. (His last domicile was the Butyrsky jail!)"

Hannah's skin felt warm all over. It was almost as though Lazar was talking excitedly, sharing every detail with her. Now that she could picture his surroundings, she read on with enthusiasm. "Lenin is our neighbor, and sometimes we all eat in the Commissars' dining room. Stalin is living in a suite opposite L. D.'s. As you might imagine, the contact between everyone is most intriguing." She knew him well enough to realize this was her husband's way of saying that there were conflicts.

There were more names mentioned, but they did not mean much to Hannah. The minutiae of his existence were what captivated her. "L. D. has decreed that the occupants of the Kremlin must not live better than they did in exile, but there is always a temptation to accept a small privilege when you are in power, and then these mount until one develops a bourgeois attitude as a way of life. Thus we dine frugally. The only meat is tinned corn beef, and the grains have sand in them. One day last week there was some butter on the table, and L. D. angrily asked where it came from. The secretary of the Central Committee had arranged the special treat, but L. D. made a point of not taking any. (I admit to a weakness and accepted a small spread for my dry bread.)" Hannah smiled. She could imagine his chagrined expression as he indulged and knew his winsome smile would diffuse Trotsky's pique. "However, because exports have ceased, there is an abundance of red caviar, and this we enjoy almost daily, probably because the color is politically acceptable!" At this Hannah managed to laugh aloud. "Even the old musical clock on the Spassky tower is being rebuilt. Soon the bells will ring out the 'Internationale' instead of 'God Save the Czar.' " There was more along these lines and Hannah digested every particular. When she had absorbed it all, realizing there was no more, her eyes filmed with disappointment.

Unfortunately, though, there was little about what Lazar actually was doing. She assumed he was continuing to transcribe events from Trotsky's viewpoint, but maybe now that Trotsky was the Commissar of War his role had changed. Better to sit at a desk, she thought as she refolded the letter. Lazar was a good writer. His descriptions were easy to imagine. Maybe someday—as John Reed and Louise Bryant were doing—he would write a book about his experiences in the revolution. Smiling through her tears, she recalled that Trotsky's nickname in exile had been "Pero" for "the pen." Wasn't it curious that her husband had become the pen's pen?

∝ 12 ∝

A few days later the Board of Managers of Bellevue Hospital sent Hannah notice that she was on suspension for "practices contrary to hospital policy."

"It could have been worse," Norma Marshanck said when she delivered the news to Hannah at home. "They could have prosecuted you for violating Section 1142 of the Penal Code, which prohibits the dissemination of contraceptive information."

"Then I could have joined the exclusive jailbird club."

"Oh, Hannah! Think of your children."

"At least I would have been judged guilty or not guilty."

"I don't know what they were thinking!" Mrs. Marshanck drew a long breath and leaned back into Lazar's chair. "There's nobody to take your place."

Hannah asked the necessary question. "Who will have my shift?" Seeing Norma hesitate, she added, "Don't worry about my feelings. I know you are the best one for the position. I would have recommended you myself."

"They haven't chosen me."

"What?" Hannah, who had been sitting on the sofa's edge, bolted up. "There's nobody with as much experience— except perhaps Sarah Brink—but she becomes muddled if there is too much confusion. She's better used in a quiet ward or with long, protracted cases requiring careful monitoring. Of course, there's Hattie Donovan . . ."

Norma was shaking her head. "No. None of those. It's Dorothea Wylie."

Hannah's lips formed an astonished *O*. "But she's one of the youngest on the staff."

"The real story is that Mrs. Hemming believes that Miss Wylie will do whatever she says," Norma replied uncomfortably.

"I don't know. She's a strong girl."

"She didn't defend the maternity-clock system."

Hannah blanched. "What are you saying?"

"Mrs. Hemming has reorganized the wards."

"In less than a week?"

"If she put her mind to it, she could rearrange the whole hospital in a day. I have never seen her eat, and I don't believe she sleeps."

"But it worked so well!"

"You and I know that, but she felt that the circular arrangement wasted space. If she places the beds in lines, she can crowd in three or four more. Also, she claimed that the clock numbers were meaningless because of the idiosyncratic nature of birth. We could not argue with her, since deliveries are always full of surprises."

Hannah opened her mouth to rebut the statement, but closed it without a word. What difference did it make? She would not be working there anyway.

Mrs. Marshanck tried to change the subject. "What are you going to do?"

Hannah shrugged. After another moment she looked up. "You know, I still don't understand how they found out."

"They were watching you. There's an orderly who saw you in the supply room with the postpartum bundles."

"Even so, I had never done it before."

"Haven't other women asked you for birth-control advice?"

"Not many. Since we got into the war, it has been more often, but I usually put them off."

"How much more frequently?"

"I don't know," Hannah said with annoyance, then stopped. The week that Mrs. Hardcastle had come in, she had been one of two or maybe three, but she had been the most insistent. Of course, that may have been because she had the most children, the most acute need. A cloud of suspicion descended. "You don't think . . . ?"

Norma was nodding. "I know."

"Someone told Mrs. Hardcastle to ask me to help her? I don't believe it! Who would do that?" Silently she answered her own question. "It isn't logical. Why would she be trying to catch me? She needed me."

"She was afraid of you."

"That's ridiculous!"

"You knew more than she did, at least about obstetrics. The doctors respected you. Especially Dr. Dowd, and he's the chairman of the department. And that's why I think you could fight to be reinstated. Why don't you go to see him?"

"By now he knows of the situation, doesn't he?" Hannah asked, for she had already pondered why the doctor had not interceded on her behalf.

"He knows Mrs. Hemming's version." Norma bit her lower lip as she contemplated whether she would go further. The unspoken thoughts hung in the air like the rope of a bell. She clasped it, and as she did her face illuminated at the revelation. "Somebody paid Mrs. Hardcastle."

"No!"

Mrs. Marshanck nodded solemnly. "Yes. I went to the records and checked her account. The delivery was free of charge. It was signed for by Mrs. Hemming herself."

"Maybe she couldn't afford to—"

"They always pay something, even a dollar as a token of

services received. Or they pay out over time. Some never make additional deposits, but the account is always open. This one has no balance due."

"How would that help me?"

"I don't know, but they did not discharge you officially. On the records it is just a suspension."

"I'm not coming back," Hannah blurted before considering her response. She could not imagine working under a woman who had paid to get rid of her.

"Don't you need the work?" Norma asked forthrightly.

"Yes, but I'll manage. My husband used to think that if I spent more time in Dr. Jaffe's clinic, I would have more private patients. Now is the time to see whether he was right. Also, I can be available to deliver more babies at home. My sister Eva is on Riverside Drive. If I tell her I am available, I am certain to get clients uptown as well."

"It takes time to build a practice. Months might pass before you are called for many deliveries."

Hannah held out her palms. "What else can I do?"

Mrs. Marshanck seemed overwhelmed. "I wish you well," she responded kindly, and stood to leave.

"Don't worry about me," Hannah said with more confidence than she felt.

∽ 13 ∽

Benny was crying. Moist beads coursed down his soiled cheeks, and he could barely blurt out what was wrong. "He's been killed!"

Hannah, who had just come in the door from the clinic, put down her grocery bag so she would not drop the eggs. Trembling, she ran to her son. "What have you heard?" All she could think of was: Lazar's gone!

"The baron."

"Who?"

"The Red Baron. You know, Manfred von Richthofen. He went down at the Battle of the Somme yesterday."

The realization that her worst fears were unfounded stung Hannah, and she began to laugh.

"Ma! What's wrong with you?"

"I'm sorry." She wiped her eyes and tried to control her floundering emotions. Then she laughed again, this time derisively. "Whose side are you on?"

"He was the greatest flyer who ever lived. I am going to be a pilot just like him."

"No, you won't. Someday you may fly an airplane, but not for the purpose of shooting at an enemy," Hannah said fiercely,

"I did it, Benny. I did it!" shouted Emma from the bedroom. "Come see!"

"What's going on here?" Hannah asked slowly. Benny quailed. "Can't I leave you alone for a few hours after school?" she said as she flung open the door to the children's room.

"Ma! You're home early . . ." came Emma's quaking voice.

The first thing Hannah saw was the scissors. Then she noticed the locks of hair littering the floor. She did not dare look up. "I thought I forbade you to cut your hair."

"You cut yours!" her daughter cried. Then, more meekly: "Do you like it?"

"Oh, my God!" Hannah's hands flew to cover her eyes. "You've butchered it! What did you think you were doing?"

Emma squinted into the small glass on the bureau. "The front's not bad . . ." She reached behind and tentatively felt the uneven areas. "I wanted to be the first girl in my class with bobbed hair."

"I told you not to do it."

"Why?"

"Just because, that's why! And I was right. You look terrible! Now are you happy with yourself?" Emma began to sob. "Sit down and I'll try to even it out," Hannah said gruffly.

As she cut a little here, a little there, she felt both annoyed and confused. How could Benny be crying over a German pilot? How could Emma have done this to herself? A few minutes earlier she had been walking home from St. Mark's Place with a bouncy step. Lazar had been right. She had underestimated her popularity. In the two months of full-time practice she had a full diary of appointments. A few continued to want their menstrual charts done. Many were candidates for home delivery, who were delighted to know that a neighborhood midwife with Hannah's qualifications was available. Thus far Hannah was not quite making the equivalent of her Bellevue salary, but in a few months, when her patients started to give birth, she estimated she might even exceed it. More important, her hours were better. She could be home every evening for the children, and on Wednesdays the clinic closed at noon. Fridays were short days because of the Sabbath. Saturdays and Sundays they were closed, except for emergencies or special appointments. However, more and more she was making "special" appointments.

Some of the people who asked to see her were unwilling to wait in a crowded room because they did not want to be recognized visiting Hannah Sokolow. There were two reasons: sometimes it was because of the problem; sometimes it was because they were men. Where were they all coming from? How had they known to ask for her? Although another practitioner might have investigated who referred them, Hannah realized that confidentiality was a delicate matter. If she did not know how they got her name, she would not know their association with a mutual friend or colleague. No matter how much she explained, they always feared she might discuss their case with that person, and they preferred to have their difficulty kept private.

For the most part Hannah was gratified that she had been able to help the majority of her patients. While dealing with the most obvious part of their predicament, she took the time to reassure each of the normality of their sexual organs and to give them the certainty that they were doing right by getting advice at the first sign of trouble. To herself she admitted that this was the best way to develop customers, a necessity now that she had no regular salary. If people thought it was appropriate to see someone for marital advice, they might refer others to her. Also, she took the time to answer their questions—some abysmally basic—about their bodies. Why, some of the young girls did not even know where their urine, feces, and menstrual blood came from! Few used the correct names for their genitalia.

Hannah began to suppose that there were far more discontented marriages than she would have suspected, and this finding might lead to more business. Now that she was seeing many sorts of patients with myriad complaints, she began to elaborate on the basic questions to elicit information on their marital life, even if their presenting complaint was not of a sexual nature. A simple "Are you satisfied with your husband or wife?" yielded an indicator. Depending on the circumstances, she might pursue a negative response by saying: "Once this matter is cleared up, I might be able to help you with the other." Already several had taken advantage of her offer. In two cases they had simple questions on whether or not some activity was "permissible." One had questioned whether there was anything wrong with "doing it in the morning" because her husband worked most nights. Another enjoyed relations most during her menstrual period, and although she was not Jewish, she thought she was doing something unhealthy. For these answers Hannah did not ask for anything extra. If they required additional time to talk about the problem, or if they had to return, they were charged her advice fee. Curiously, Carrie reported fewer difficulties in collecting on these accounts than any other.

Seven women had hinted—or said outright—that they did not experience much pleasure during lovemaking. One seemed resistant to hearing any counsel, the others were more eager. Hannah regretted not having a prescription to hand out, and to each she offered some suggestions tailored to what she suspected might help. A pang of misgiving accompanied each recommendation since she had never been able to cure Rachael's woes, but what worked for one might not work for the other. In each case she made a future appointment "at no charge" to learn the outcome. One, a corpulent woman named Lena, had returned to say that she was enjoying it more, but did not think she had reached a climax. "I get so excited I cry out, but I don't feel relief. Is that it or not?"

"Any pulsing or spasms?"

"No, I don't think so."

"When it happens, you will know."

The other, Mrs. Krakower, a mousy, timid lady—one who Hannah had bet would never even return—had followed Hannah's instructions to masturbate. The next visit Hannah hardly recognized her. Her head was held higher, her coloring more vivid, and her demeanor more direct. "I am very happy with my husband," she reported simply. "After six years of marriage, I have experienced what everybody talks about." She did not smile, so Hannah did not demonstrate any overt emotion. Inside, though, she was elated. If only she could work the same miracle with Rachael . . .

By late spring the character of her clientele began to change. Initially she had catered to Lower East Side women and their desire to have a male baby. Next she had added Upper West Side ladies, who still preferred the practitioners from their old neighborhoods. Then there were a smattering of women who must have heard about her through some Bellevue connections like Alice Brody and Dr. Dowd. More and more, though, she was seeing addresses from around Greenwich Village, and the sorts of people who used to frequent Mabel Dodge's salon. Who over there knew about her? Emma Goldman was in prison, so she wasn't sending her cases, but Margaret Sanger certainly could. Louise Bryant and John Reed were now living in Croton-on-Hudson, but they had friends in the Village. Whatever the thread, the trend started with Rosy, who cooked for the Provincetown Players; then came Zoe, a poet who won all the prizes at Webster Hall; and Ramona, a middle-aged actress. Unlike the reticent types who seemed ashamed to discuss their sexual questions, these women reveled in telling of their woes. The more detailed the query, the more candid they became. Some of the experiences they had engaged in were so unusual to Hannah she had to consult Havelock Ellis and Krafft-Ebing before she would respond. Best of all, they paid well, and they came back often, even after Hannah had helped them solve their most obvious malady.

Also, they invited her places. Keeping her promise to herself, Hannah did not accept political invitations, not even to the Fifth of May rally honoring the centennial of Karl Marx's birth. On two occasions Hannah had been back to the Green Gate as somebody's guest. She had been to an opening night performance at the Washington Square Players of one of Susan Glaspell's plays, *Suppressed Desires,* which Hannah supposed others saw as an amusing commentary on being psychoanalyzed, but one she found hard to follow. Afterward she was taken to the party for the author, a fragile woman with melancholy eyes. Eugene O'Neill appeared and tried to be more witty than the playwright who was being feted. Even though Hannah recognized many of the guests, including Hippolyte Havel and the Hapgoods, she felt as much the outsider as ever. Then in walked Dr. Dowd with his glamorous wife.

They were with Ramona. So that was the connection in that case! Ramona saw her, but avoided her eye. Hannah did not feel slighted, since she understood why her patient would prefer not to acknowledge that they knew each other. Ramona, who was wearing black, faded into the background while the other woman, whose pearl satin gown shimmered in the lamplight, made certain everyone knew she had arrived.

Dr. Dowd greeted Hannah effusively. "Mrs. Sokolow! What a pleasure to see you here. You are looking well."

Hannah glowed under his warm gaze. "Good to see you, Doctor."

"I've missed you at the hospital." Hannah had no reply. For a moment the doctor seemed flustered, then turned to his wife. "Have you ever met Mrs. Sokolow, a most talented midwife?" The woman, who had been scanning the room, allowed her gaze to alight on Hannah. Hannah peered into her fluttering brown eyes, which were lined with black pencil to make them even more dramatic, but they only took her in for a second. "My dear . . ." Dr. Dowd prompted. She gave him a benevolent smile. When he had her attention, he continued, "Mrs. Sokolow, this is my wife."

"Your talented wife?" the woman replied in a smoky voice.

Dr. Dowd shifted his feet. "Of course, you are both talented, each in your own way."

The woman reached across her husband and offered Hannah her hand. "Hello. I'm Lulu Morse." Hannah's hand was brushed by the many bracelets that dangled from Lulu's arm.

"Hannah, Hannah Sokolow."

"So, Hannah . . ." The *h* warbled at the back of her throat. "Are you at Bellevue?"

"No longer."

In an expression so fluid it must have been rehearsed, Lulu raised her eyebrows and rolled her eyes to the left while lifting her long, sinuous neck. The whole effect was that of an unspoken question.

"A pity for us," her husband interjected, "especially in these urgent times."

"Have you a position elsewhere?" Lulu quizzed in a slippery voice.

"I deliver babies privately, and I also see patients in another doctor's clinic."

"But they need all the help they can get at Bellevue. Why, I hardly see my sweetie anymore." She batted her eyes, but the gesture was not ridiculous. If anything, it was a parody of a silly actress, which made her seem even more sophisticated. "Wouldn't you consider returning until the war is over?"

"They would not have me back," Hannah stated.

Dr. Dowd flinched.

"Oh, and why is that?"

Hannah hesitated a moment. "Do you know Margaret Sanger?"

"Not personally, but I know of her, certainly."

"She wrote a pamphlet on birth control, which, against hospital policy, I gave to a desperate woman who had given birth to thirteen children already."

Lulu tossed back her head and laughed. "That's why you were dismissed?"

"Suspended, actually."

"How utterly ridiculous! Wendell, what do you have to say for yourself?"

Perspiration formed a patina on the doctor's brow. He patted it with his handkerchief. "A long story, my dear."

"Lulu!" came a high-pitched call from across the room.

"Darling, it's Polly," she said to her husband. "Please excuse me." Lulu glided away without a second glance.

"My wife." The doctor's words were a statement and an apology in one breath. "She liked you."

What was Hannah to say? "She's very beautiful" seemed safe enough. She watched the doctor to see if he was annoyed with her before deciding that the petty world of the obstetrical wards seemed far away indeed.

"I do wish you would consider returning," he began softly.

"That's not my choice to make."

"I heard that you walked out, leaving the floor unattended."

"That's partly true, but the circumstances did not permit me to remain."

"I am certain you don't want to discuss this tonight. However, if I can get your case heard, would you be willing to come back?"

"I don't think so," Hannah said with a confident voice. Then, under her breath, "Thank you for the referrals."

He cocked his head as if he did not understand. Hannah's eyes shifted to the corner where Ramona was sitting next to Susan Glaspell, then back to the doctor. There was a wordless acknowledgment before Lulu waved her arms to beckon—no, to command—her husband to her side.

∽ 14 ∽

On Friday, May 24, 1918, Hannah, Rachael, Mama, Minna, and even Eva joined the almost three hundred thousand women who registered to vote in New York. By enrolling with a party, the newly enfranchised women would qualify to participate in the primary elections in September. Ezekiel was there, as was Chaim. Hannah felt a pang when she realized how much Lazar would have enjoyed the day.

"What party did you register under?" Hannah asked Rachael.

"Socialist, of course! Although since I think woman suffrage will be a waste if women merely follow along and repeat their husband's vote, I was tempted to try the Prohibition party."

"I thought the Republicans were more your sort," her husband chuckled. "What's Benny doing this weekend?" Herzog asked Hannah as they headed toward the subway.

"Nothing special, why?"

"I have tickets to a baseball game. The Yankees are playing the Cleveland Indians, but Nora is not interested. It should be an exciting game. Cleveland won by three to two yesterday and the Yanks are out for blood."

With a grateful smile Hannah said, "Benny would love to go." He had not seemed the same since his father left. He angered quickly and cried easily. His reaction to the death of the Red Baron had been just one instance of his volatility. When she told Herzog about that incident, he had stroked his beard and asked, "Perhaps the aviator is symbolic for something else?"

Hannah had stared at him stupidly for a long moment, then realized his psychological reasoning was probably right. "His father?" had been left dangling in the air, since Herzog had not continued. Yet Benny must have remained on his mind, hence this invitation.

"What about me?" Rachael replied with a false pout.

"There's a band concert in Central Park," her husband offered.

"Let's go, Hannah. It will be just for us girls."

Hannah grinned. Rachael knew how much Emma loved everything musical. Then she paused. While they had tried to sound spontaneous, Rachael and Ezekiel must have planned this to cheer her.

Rachael noticed she was lagging behind. "Don't you want to go?"

"Yes, I do. And thanks," Hannah added in a way that let her know that she appreciated her friend's concern.

Sunday was a glorious day. The sun spread its warmth like a benevolent blanket. The sky seemed painted an unvarying blue. Along the margin of the band shell, the trees undulated in an accommodating breeze. They arrived early, carrying a basket between them. Hannah spread out an old tablecloth, and the women filled plates with challah, pickled beets, sliced cucumbers, and cold *lokshen kugel*—a noodle pudding made with raisins and cinnamon.

The children seemed more interested in running than eating. Hannah decided not to scold them unless they interfered with the concert. She put their plates aside. The orchestra began to play, and the clear tones of the brass and the tinny tremors of the strings penetrated to her bones, infusing her with a feeling of exhilaration she had not felt since Lazar had left. Quite content for a moment, she studied the scene. Many had taken seats on the grass or on chairs they had brought. Some strolled arm in arm. A few of the women wore the currently fashionable loose-fitting waistless dresses with flowing kimono sleeves, which Hannah thought were unflattering. Some wore the more drab garb of the ghetto. Most were in outfits not unlike her high-necked, pleated bodice blouse with a practical, round-necked pinafore dress falling to eight inches off the ground. Rachael, however, was as original as usual in a much shorter shirt and a lemon yellow tunic covered with ruffles made from a flimsy material that moved gracefully in the breeze. Why was it that Rachael, without putting her mind to it, always fitted in better than she did? Hannah looked over at her friend admiringly. The doctor's bronzed hair billowed around her face. She kept pushing it back as she made up plates for the two of them.

"You were smart to cut your hair. Mine is always a mess."

"If I had hair as beautiful as yours, I never would have bobbed it." Hannah glanced at Nora and Emma, who were kicking a stone between them. "Emma's looks frightful still." She gave an exaggerated sigh. "It will grow, but not fast enough for me."

"Don't be angry. She did it to please you."

"That's nonsense! She did it to defy me."

"I disagree. After all, who cut whose hair first?"

Hannah wanted to argue, but as she mulled over the idea, she saw the wisdom in it. Rachael was so perceptive when it came to other people. That was what made her a fine physician, but like so many—Hannah included—she was myopic about her own problems.

The music permeated the air like a strong perfume for the soul. After a few bites of her lunch, Hannah lay back on the blanket and closed her eyes.

The announcer introduced the next piece. " 'On the Beautiful Blue Danube,' a waltz by Johann Strauss." There were a few boos. Anti-German feeling was poisoning everyone. Everywhere families of German origin were suspect. Even Mama had been asked if "Blau" was German. Most schools had eliminated the language from their curriculum. Already the food stalls on Second Avenue were calling sauerkraut "liberty cabbage" and hamburger "liberty steak."

Soon the music transported her. The light, lilting refrains did evoke a gliding trip along the water . . . and something more. Her cares floated up and away. The afternoon sun beat down, heating her to the core. Hannah's breathing slowed. The high notes were piercingly sensual. Her back arched slightly as she longed to be touched. And then the music swelled in loudness and intensity. A throbbing took over and she could almost feel her blood coursing through her veins in rhythm with the music. Then the theme began to shimmer, and Hannah felt a tremor from the base of her neck to the end of her spine. Just when she thought the sensation unbearable, the sounds shifted to a mood so delicate it seemed as if a feather were caressing her. But the quiet moment was as deceptive as a lull before a storm, because after the pause, the piece came to its crashing—and satisfying—conclusion.

Hannah lay motionless, not wanting to shatter the perfection, almost as she might have after making love. Then she opened her eyes.

Rachael was sitting with her back to Hannah. Her arms were wrapped around her long legs. Her head was bent and she seemed dazed. Hannah sat up. She touched Rachael on the shoulder. "Music," she said to Rachael's bewildered expression. "Music! Didn't you feel it?"

"What?"

"That waltz. Didn't you get carried away with it? I was thinking of the war and other unpleasant thoughts when I had to give in to the mood. I closed my eyes. I felt a terrible longing . . ." She blinked back tears.

"Hannah, what is wrong?"

"Nothing." She shook her head as if to clear it. "What I meant was . . . well, you and Herzog have that piano that plays music. The one that Emma loves so dearly."

"The reproducing piano?"

"Yes. Tell me, how long does a roll last?"

"Five, maybe ten minutes. Why?"

"That's hardly enough time."

"Enough time for what?" Rachael asked with exasperation.

In the distance, quite close to the band shell, she saw her daughter, who looked like a regular American in her short blue party dress with pink flowers and a wide pink sash. She was holding up her triple-flounced hem and dancing. Light on her feet, arms waving around, she was unconcerned with anything but moving to the music. "Look at Emma. Isn't she lovely? Not a care except for the moment."

"She's going to be a beautiful girl, Hannah."

Hannah brushed aside that comment. "What I am saying is that there is something magical in music that lets us forget the petty problems on our minds. There is also something else—I don't know how to explain it—but it seems to skip over the intellectual parts of the brain—mine, at least—and touches the emotions, and also the body. I cannot tell you when I have felt more of an ache for a man beside me . . ."

"So?" Rachael inquired with some agitation.

"I thought . . . well, that you might try playing music when you are with Ezekiel. Let your mind wander along with the notes and not pay so much attention to what is happening in your bed."

At first Rachael seemed too stunned to reply. Then she gave a crooked smile. "Our piano does have a switch to replay the roll over and over again."

"That's fine, so long as you like the song."

"What shall I play?"

"Anything you like," Hannah answered, "anything you like!"

❦ 15 ❧

They stayed until it was almost dark. In the twilight the vocal part of the program was announced. Two men began by singing patriotic tunes. Nora had fallen asleep on Rachael's lap. Emma was sitting on the cloth with a dreamy expression on her face.

"Shall we wake her and leave?" Rachael asked in a lethargic tone.

"I suppose," Hannah said agreeably, since the air was beginning to become chill.

Then the announcer introduced the next performer. "The one and only . . . Lulu Morse!"

"That's Dr. Dowd's wife!" Hannah gasped. She watched as the woman appeared in the same shimmering dress she had worn to the playwright's party. In the darkened park it took on a more luminous, less preposterous quality. "Rachael, let's just stay a few more minutes."

The soloist had chosen to sing a selection of songs by Victor Herbert, from his operetta *Naughty Marietta,* beginning flirtatiously with the title song. Even more appealing was her rendition of "I'm Falling in Love with Someone." After a long volley of applause, she was beginning the first bars of "The Sweet By and By" when someone blocked Hannah's view. She looked up.

"Mrs. Sokolow, Dr. Jaffe, how nice to see you here this evening."

"Dr. Dowd! We're listening to your wife," Hannah said, then cringed at the obviousness of her remark.

"So am I, so am I," he responded in a loud whisper.

"Would you like to join us?" Rachael asked, even though Hannah wished she had not.

"That is very kind." The doctor took the small section of the cloth nearest to Hannah. He sat so close their arms brushed.

Leaning away, Hannah said, "Your wife has a marvelous voice."

"Thank you. It's quite unusual. For a long time she could not even find a teacher willing to take her on because of its husky quality, but now everyone wishes they could copy her style."

"You must be very proud of her," Hannah said to fill the silence between them.

"Of course, but I must bring her down to earth. When everyone is kissing the hem of your skirt, it is difficult to maintain perspective."

Something in the doctor's tone made Hannah feel sorry for him. Living with someone like Lulu was apt to be difficult, she realized. "Well, she must be an exciting woman to come home to," Hannah blurted, then regretted her impulsive words.

"I've always wished for a more practical wife, but then that's not what attracted me, or what would have made me happy, I suppose." After a brief pause he asked, "Are these your children?"

"One of them is mine." She pointed out Emma. "My son is at a baseball game. You also have a son, don't you?"

"Yes, Wendell Junior is over in France now." The apprehension in those words hovered in the air.

"And a daughter, I believe?"

"Yes. Daphne's still at home."

They both were quieted by the plaintive last line of the song. During the applause Dr. Dowd pointed at the sky. "The moon is rising just in time."

"In time for what?"

"Her next song: ' 'Neath the Southern Moon.' "

Was it her imagination or had the doctor inched closer? To determine at which points their bodies made tenuous contact, she stirred. Keeping her breathing shallow so as not to press into his flesh, Hannah listened to the tune. When it was over she clapped loudly, her elbow acting as a prod to move the doctor over. At least the program was almost finished and she would be able to extricate herself from this discomfiting situation. The last number was the exuberant "Italian Street Song." Soon the entire audience was joining in the chorus, clapping and stamping to the music. Emma leapt up and twirled around. At the finale, as if carried away by the enthusiasm of the moment, the doctor clasped her around the shoulders. "Excellent!" he said. "Don't you agree?"

"Yes ..." she allowed as she made an effort to move away in preparation for standing. To her dismay the applause went on and on. Lulu was returning for an encore. Some of the men in the back were whistling and calling out requests. She held up her arms, which gleamed like waxen tapers in the spotlight. "Yes, yes" was her throaty conciliation. Then, in an impossibly high range, she trilled the melody of the haunting "Ah! Sweet Mystery of Life," filling in but a few of the words and putting in "la la la's" for the rest. The effect was maddeningly teasing, and yet hinted at the enigmatic title. Soldiers whistled and others called out. Lulu bowed her head as if relenting and burst out with the full words of the popular song. "Ah! sweet mystery of life, at last I've found thee/Ah! I know at last the secret of it all ..."

Hannah glanced at Wendell Dowd. His firm chin was uplifted, his eyes riveted forward. What must it be like to see one's wife enthralling a huge crowd of admirers? Just then he turned and met Hannah's gaze. The melody must have disordered her thoughts. Moments earlier she had been anxious to flee, but now she yearned to move closer to him.

After the last lingering note, Rachael roused Nora. In the dark, while they tried to pack their basket, the doctor assisted. A few times he bumped into Hannah, perhaps accidentally, perhaps not. But then once, and only for the briefest of seconds, his hand rested on her hip in a gesture that was more than friendly, less than brazen. Some other time, some other year, Hannah might have been alarmed or angry, distressed or confused. This time it merely made her happy.

❦ 16 ❦

"What's a square root?" Benny asked Hannah one evening. They were sitting around the kitchen table. She was darning the elbow of one of his sweaters. Emma, who was supposed to be doing penmanship exercises, had been doodling on the back of the paper, but Hannah had decided not to comment.

"There's no such thing," Hannah replied, thinking he meant a plant or vegetable.

"Yes, there is. Four is the square root of sixteen because four times four is sixteen."

"Then why are you asking me?"

"I wondered if you knew. Pa would have known."

Would he? Hannah wondered. Mathematics had not been his specialty, but he certainly could have kept up with Benny at this age. She was fairly useless with much of the children's nightwork. Her written English was weak. She knew nothing of American history or literature. She had studied the sciences, but knew few of the English words, and anyway she had forgotten most of the formulae.

"When is Pa coming home?" Emma asked plaintively.

Benny looked at his mother protectively and answered for her. "When the war is over, stupid."

How could she refute that? How could she tell them that their father's battle was far more unpopular, and that the signing of a peace treaty between Germany and America would not bring him back to them? Had Lazar realized how much he was hurting the children when he left? No. He had thought solely of his cause. Better to say nothing. After all, he might return. Maybe it would be tomorrow. Maybe it would be next year. She could disappoint them later as well as sooner.

"What if the war is never over?" Emma whined. Her question was directed at her brother, so Hannah kept her eyes focused on her needlework.

"All wars end sometime," Benny said with the know-it-all confidence he had inherited from his father.

"Why?" his sister asked.

"Why? I don't know why. Because enough people get killed. All right? Now, stop pestering me or I'll never get my nightwork done," Benny groaned.

There was a knock on the door. A driver had come with a message from Eva. "Please come, it might be the baby."

Hannah made some quick calculations. Her baby was not due for at least a month. However, if it was coming early, it could be a rapid delivery. She rushed for her bag and gave the children instructions. "I'll tell your grandmother you'll be down after you've finished your lessons. If I am not home in the morning, she'll get you ready for school. But don't be too much of a bother. Your grandmother hasn't had much strength lately." And with that she was off.

∞ **17** ∞

Eva was not in labor. She was not even in false labor. A woman who had given birth to two children should have known better. "My legs are too swollen, my ankles hurt, my back aches, my nose is always running, my breasts are leaking," Eva had been kvetching for several weeks already. That night she only had cramps from something she had eaten, but Hannah sat with her until she was able to sleep anyway.

"I'm sorry to have called you," Napthali said apologetically. "I didn't want to make a mistake."

"I would have been more upset if you hadn't."

He poured tea into a fragile porcelain cup with a gold rim. No Russian-style glasses in this uptown parlor. "You are certain she is all right?"

"Yes," Hannah responded, then she felt a twinge, the sort that always made her look twice at a case. Had she missed something because this was her sister and she knew that griping was natural to her? Eva's blood pressure was fine— well, slightly elevated, but nothing especially worrisome. Her weight gain was more than average, but she had been indulging in sweets. She had vomited this evening, but that coupled with the diarrhea indicated an abdominal disorder unrelated to the pregnancy. Yet everybody warned about treating people too close to you. What should she do? Rachael might examine Eva, but she did not specialize in obstetrics. She supposed she should send Eva to Dr. Dowd just to be safe.

When she made the suggestion to her brother-in-law, he flushed. "I thought you said—"

"I do believe there are no complications. However, I would prefer if an expert agreed with me. Also . . ." She groped for a way to convince Napthali without alarming him. "Eva knew that the baby was not coming, yet she wanted reassurance. That's why she called for me tonight. If Dr. Dowd examines her and tells her how well she is doing, she may be more persuaded than hearing it from her big, bossy sister."

Seeing the sense in her argument, Napthali told Hannah to make arrangements to take Eva to Bellevue. Hannah asked Carrie to make the appointment as though it was a normal referral. Hannah assumed that Eva would go on her own, but on her way downtown, Eva stopped off at St. Mark's Place because she expected Hannah to accompany her.

Hannah hesitated. No patients waited for her, so that wasn't an excuse. The truth was, she did not want to return to Bellevue. What if she saw Mrs. Hemming? Then she reconsidered. Why should she be worried about that old yenta? Let her see me. Let her worry about what I'm doing there! Hannah decided.

Dr. Dowd's office at the end of the gynecological pavilion was so far from the maternity wards she need not have worried about meeting anyone.

Entering his office, Hannah felt a faint feeling of regret that he was no longer accessible to her. "This is Eva Margolis, my sister. Eva, this is Dr. Dowd."

"My examination room is down the hall. Miss Boyles, my assistant, will show you the way." His smile remained rigid until Eva left. "What seems to be the trouble?" he asked the midwife when they were alone.

"Nothing so far as I can tell, but she has so many petty complaints that I worried I might have discarded them too quickly. This is merely a precaution."

Dr. Dowd gave her a genial smile. "A pity. I thought it was an excuse to see me."

Hannah's pulse quickened. Was that so? There were others who could have examined Eva, yet she had decided immediately on him. It was also true that he had been on her mind since the concert in the park, although these were the idle musings of a lonely woman, nothing more. Some mischievous urge pressed her to tell the truth, while making it seem as though she were teasing him. "What's wrong with that?" Her attempt at lightness failed because her voice had a strangled quality.

The doctor's face became lined with the intensity of his gaze. "Let me see to the patient and we can discuss this later."

Fortunately, Hannah was able to turn away before the color bloomed on her cheeks. What sort of game was she playing? The doctor was a married man. And she was a married woman. For the first time the precariousness of her position irked her. As far as Lazar was concerned, she was his wife, waiting in the wings for world events to settle their future.

The door soon opened. Dr. Dowd entered, more rattled than Hannah at the reunion. He covered his uneasiness with an overlay of medical terminology. "She has many discomforts, but no pathology of concern. While her blood pressure is elevated, there are no signs of eclampsia, and the urinalysis should eliminate nephritic involvement. There is no evidence of a real anasarca, with exudation of serum in the tissues. Otherwise her diet and the hot weather are more to blame for her edema than anything else. I also suspect a baby in the eight-pound range at term, which may be uncomfortable to carry, and this has caused some varicosities. For that reason, and also to mollify her, I suggested partial bedrest with a milk-and-water diet."

Dr. Dowd had not only given Eva a thorough examination, he had understood both Hannah's need to "do something" as well as Eva's to be treated with special care. "An excellent suggestion. I should have paid more attention to the varicosities."

"They can do little harm, so your judgment was sound."

"Thank you. I suppose she is dressed by now," Hannah said as she headed for the door.

"I wish you could stay longer," Dr. Dowd stated. "There is some recent research on infertility I would like to discuss with you."

Hannah indicated the room where her sister was waiting. "I'm sorry, but . . ."

"Of course. This is the wrong time. I was hoping we might meet later." He paused, then brightened as if he were having an original thought. "Might you have dinner with me some evening?"

"I don't think so. My children and—"

"Who looks after them when you are called out for night deliveries?"

"My mother lives downstairs in our building."

"Then this should present no difficulty."

"It would not be simple to explain where I had gone."

"We have consulted many times in the past. Why would this be any different?"

"I suppose something might be arranged," she replied, since if she refuted his argument, she would be admitting her suspicion that some current—other than their professional alliance—was coursing between them.

"What about tonight?"

"No, I wouldn't have time to make plans."

"Tomorrow?"

"What about your wife? Shouldn't you check with her?"

"No, that is not necessary. This week she is on a tour of training camps in New Jersey and Pennsylvania. They are entertaining the troops. So you see you would be doing a lonely war widower a favor."

"I'm certain she is very popular with the young men," Hannah said because she felt she needed to keep Lulu Morse's image in front of them.

"You're right about that," he responded coldly. "Now, what evening would be convenient?"

"I suppose tomorrow is as good as any," she responded with a purposeful flatness.

"Where shall we meet. The Green Gate? No. That's better for luncheon." His fingers parted his perfectly trimmed hair. "What about the Samovar? The menu is Russian . . ." His eyes darted as he realized his gaffe. "No, of course not. Ah, what about the Brevoort Hotel?" Hannah's face betrayed her alarm, and he quickly added, "They have a charming dining room, where it will be quiet enough for us to discuss the papers I would like to show you. Dr. Blühner has been publishing some controversial material lately."

The mention of Dr. Blühner intrigued Hannah enough to make her forget her concerns. "That would be fine."

"Do you know where it is?"

"Not exactly."

"It's on the corner of Seventh Avenue and Eighth Street. Would that be convenient?"

"Yes, if we could meet fairly early. My clinic is over on St. Mark's and I could simply walk crosstown."

"How about six?"

"Yes," Hannah responded. "Six. Tomorrow."

⤜ 18 ⤛

They met at the Brevoort Hotel dining room. Hannah allowed the doctor to order. The evening was warm, so he suggested the raspberry shrub, which turned out to be a fruit juice with sherbet floating in it. While she was enjoying the play of pungent and sweet flavors, Dr. Dowd did not mention anything about Bellevue. Hannah did not bring up any current cases. Both avoided the news of the day. Hannah had barely managed to get past the headline that announced: "Bolsheviks Execute Czar and Family" to the incredible report that "former Czar Nicholas II, the Empress Alexandra, their four daughters, and his son and heir, the child Alexis, are dead, bringing an end to the Romanov dynasty that ruled Russia for three centuries." All day Hannah had felt sick at the horror of the family wiped out by such brutal tactics. The questions she could not shake were: what part had Trotsky played in this decision? And had Lazar known of it? Hannah looked over at the doctor and wondered what he thought of the Russian revolution and the war. She had no idea of where he stood politically, and she rapidly decided that she did not wish to know.

As they ate lamb chops with mint sauce, buttery whipped potatoes, bright green peas the size of lavish pearls, and soft white rolls, she was happy to let him prattle on about the second biggest story of the day: the opening of the Lexington Avenue subway line, which would be a conve-

nience to them both. Then he turned to something of a more
medical nature, talking of his concerns about an influenza
epidemic in France that had killed almost as many troops as
the fighting.

"Is there a cure?"

"I'm afraid not, at least not until they clean up the hideous
battlefield conditions, which are the perfect breeding ground
for disease." He took a long inward breath. "I'm sorry, doctors sometimes forget what is proper dinnertime conversation."

"That's all right. I want to know. Why is it called Spanish
influenza? Did it start in Spain?"

"Actually, it is derived from the Italian word for the disease, which translates to *influence*. They believed that its
cause was a bad alignment, or influence, of the stars, but it
seems the Italians have managed to blame it on the Spanish."

"What if it crosses the Atlantic?"

"Pray that it doesn't." His words hung in the air as the apple pie à la mode and coffee were served. "Dessert already
and I haven't gotten to the matter I wanted to discuss with
you," Dr. Dowd began. "Ah, the ice cream is melting just
the way I like it." With his fork he indicated that she
shouldn't hesitate.

"The work by Dr. Blühner?" she asked before lifting her
utensil.

"No." He seemed flustered. "I did mention that, didn't I?
Well, another time."

"I was curious about the infertility studies." He raised his
eyebrows bewilderedly. "You mentioned them when you examined my sister."

"Oh yes, the German research. Well, there is so much I
would like to share with you."

"But not that," Hannah said, not hiding her amusement
that he had forgotten his pretext to see her.

"No." He smiled at the easy banter. "I hope you'll bear
with me and my latest enthusiasm. I have been reading some
articles on the 'Medicolegal Aspects of Moral Offenses' by
Thoinot, a French physician, which has caused me to examine why some of us who treat the victims of rape are sometimes less sympathetic to the woman than to the perpetrator.
Often a woman's testimony is discounted. This has been particularly problematic when the women are, shall we say,

from rather unsavory background. Does this give the rapist more rights? Some think yes, others disagree. Anyway, I'd be interested in your opinion."

"I'll be happy to consider the cases."

"Good. I hoped you'd say that." He blotted his lips with his napkin. "I have brought along several medical journals with place marks in the essays. They are in the cloakroom. I could give them to you later. Now, what do you think of this pie crust?"

Before she knew it, the meal was over and they were heading out into the summer's night. Little lights winked up and down Seventh Avenue. Men and women strolled along enjoying the cooler evening air. The doctor called her a taxicab and gave instructions to the driver. Hannah saw him slip the driver payment, then he came around and opened the door for her. When she was seated, he handed her the magazines.

"When can we discuss your reactions to those?" Hannah's mouth opened, then closed without a response. "How about next Wednesday, a week from today?"

"All right," Hannah managed coolly, even though she was suffused with gratitude. The door closed. Dr. Dowd stood on the curb, his eyes shining in the lamplight as she was driven away.

∝ 19 ∝

Hannah tried to avoid thinking about it, yet whenever there was a lull she counted the days until Wednesday. She read the journals, which she found almost as shocking as Krafft-Ebing. There were five pieces on rape, three on indecent assaults, others on perversions of the sexual instinct, including exhibitionism, fetishism, sadism, masochism, bestiality, necrophilia, nymphomania, and satyriasis. How the doctor ever expected her to conduct a conversation—even of the most general nature—about this over dinner worried her. Then it intrigued her. Somehow she had always been able to discuss the most intimate of topics with him without mortification—at least those that had related to normal human sexuality. If they could keep to the general moral and legal issues . . . well, it might be possible.

It rained all day Wednesday, cooling off the burning city considerably. By six the streets were flowing with water, but the slate sky merely drizzled intermittently. Hannah walked from St. Mark's Place at a fast clip, both to stay dry and to not keep Dr. Dowd waiting. As she rounded the corner before the Brevoort, she saw him standing under the awning. He was looking in the other direction. His gray summer suit was a superb contrast to his shining hair. She admired his straight back, his polished shoes, and his confident stance. Coming up behind him, she said, "Hello, Doctor." He wheeled around and was clipped by the edge of her umbrella. "Sorry," she said as she folded it quickly. An angry red mark dented his forehead. She touched it and a drop of blood pooled on her finger. "I've cut you." She pressed down to stop the bleeding. He pulled out his handkerchief, blotted his forehead, then checked to see how much. A few dots were all that stained it.

"I'll live," he pronounced. "I'm always amazed how much cuts to the face will bleed. Now, if the sight of me won't make the other ladies in the Brevoort faint, shall we go in?" He offered her his arm. There was a second of resistance. "No succor for the wounded?" She smiled and assented.

This meal began with a Waldorf salad. Hannah was surprised by the combination of apples, nuts, and mayonnaise, but enjoyed it.

"What do you think of Secretary Baker ruling that baseball is an inessential occupation during wartime?"

"Are you asking me or my son, Benny? He thinks it's the worst thing that has happened since the Red Baron was killed." Seeing the doctor's perplexed expression, she worried that she might have offended him, so she quickly explained, "He wants to be a pilot and admired his skills."

Dr. Dowd smiled benevolently. "Anyway, at least Baker is permitting organized baseball to continue until the first of September."

The waiter cleared the plates and brought the chicken pie Hannah had ordered because she remembered the delicious pastry on the last pie she had eaten there.

"Looks tasty," the doctor said. "I should have ordered it myself." He stared down at his baked fish morosely.

"Take mine, Doctor," she offered.

"I won't hear of it, and I won't hear you calling me 'doctor' any longer, Mrs. Sokolow. Now that we are no longer on staff together, and are more friends than colleagues, I hope you will agree that we may be less formal with each other."

"If you like."

"Thank you, Hannah," he said, then ran his tongue along his lower lips as though he were tasting the word.

She busied herself with the dish. When she cut through the crust, steam poured out. It seemed too hot to taste. She broke some bread and waited. He began to eat his fish with an exaggerated gusto to show he was not disappointed by his choice. They looked up at the same time and began to speak in unison. He deferred to her.

"I was wondering how your wife's trip is going."

"I have not heard from her regularly, but then she is on the road a great deal."

"Who looks after your daughter?"

"We have a housekeeper."

"She must miss her mother."

"Actually, Lulu is not her mother. My first wife died from a hemorrhage after giving birth to Daphne."

"I'm sorry . . ." Hannah said as she mulled over the news. Lulu Morse did seem much younger than the doctor, maybe too young to have a boy fighting overseas.

"We never had any children together," he added to answer the unasked question, then offered even more than was required. "She's never wanted any. And I was content with my other two." He paused and cut another bite of fish, which made it to his fork but not his mouth. "Lulu uses birth control with great success." He stared at Hannah with glistening eyes. Nothing else was said for a few seconds, yet inherent in the pause was an explanation, an apology, as well as a recognition of kindred ideals and practices.

Just like the week before, he did not mention the expected topic of discussion until the main course plates were removed. Then he began in a professional tone, "Were you able to find the time to read the pieces I marked for you?"

"Yes, Doctor—I mean . . . Wendell." The word felt unfamiliar on her lips, like the kiss of a stranger. "I think Dr. Thoinot is a very sympathetic man."

"In what way?"

Hannah went on with some prepared replies. The doctor nodded as though he agreed with every point until she mentioned something about not understanding how the legal situation would differ in the United States.

"There was another piece by the district attorney from, I believe, New Orleans, in one of the issues," he replied. "Let me show it to you." He looked at the extra chair, where she had placed her pocketbook. "Did you put them in the cloakroom?"

"Oh, I am sorry! I forgot to bring them." Hannah became unhinged and began to speak too rapidly. "I must have left them at the clinic. It was raining, so I meant to get something to wrap them in, and I must have forgotten at the last moment."

"Don't worry. You can return them to me next time."

"Is this a routine appointment?" Hannah asked a bit superciliously, even though she was hoping he was going to say that it was.

"Well . . ." He turned away slightly. Hannah knew something was wrong. She waited for him to continue. "Lulu does return the middle of next week, Wednesday, actually. She would expect me to be home then."

"Of course. If it has stopped raining, we could walk to the clinic. It's not far. That way I could give them back tonight." She half expected him to say that was not necessary, that they might skip a week, or meet on a different night, but he jumped at the idea.

"Splendid, after this scrumptious-looking dessert, I could use a brisk stroll."

The waiter was just delivering the Charlotte Russe, something Hannah had ordered because she liked the name. The little cakes were dusted with powdered sugar and filled with sweetened cream and a maple flavoring. She finished hers quickly. The doctor ate half of his and did not touch his coffee. He seemed distracted. Hannah sensed she had said something amiss, and searched her mind for where she had gone wrong. Not finding any obvious offense, she decided she may have taken him too seriously. He saw her as a friend, a colleague with a feminine point of view on delicate subjects. Moreover, he was interested in her private cases for other reasons. Hadn't he misappropriated her work with Stella Applebaum by putting his name on the paper without mentioning hers? That slight had been forgiven but not forgotten. All his kindness to her—and these lavish dinners—were merely his way of gathering more information. So far she had no new unique cases or successes to report. Yet he was always hinting that he was interested in her work.

"A cab, sir?" the doorman asked as they stepped out onto the shining pavement.

Dr. Dowd looked up. A few stars dotted the sky. "No, Chester, the storm has passed. We'll walk."

The click of their heels—hers more frequent and softer, his firmer and metallic—echoed off the brick walls. Hannah's heart pounded. She could hear his breathing, which was somewhat labored at the pace he had chosen. Hannah strained to keep up. She supposed this was his idea of a "brisk stroll."

"I do love this part of the city," he said in a thick voice.

"Where do you live?" she asked, surprising herself with her ignorance.

"In a part of the Village called Washington Mews. It's not far from here, just off Fifth Avenue near Eighth Street."

"Oh, then this won't take you too far out of your way."

"Not at all." He paused and rocked back on his heels. "Do you know the Village?"

"Not really. It's so different from the Lower East Side, sometimes I feel I've crossed into another country."

"That's because you have," he said with a gutteral laugh. "The Village has maintained its distinctiveness by refusing to allow its streets to be conformed into rectangles."

"I never thought about it like that."

"What city planners never realized is that regularity, while pleasing on paper, is boring to the eye," he said, warming to his subject. "I am always taken with the curve in Grove Street toward St. Luke's Church, and find a moment of sanity under the bend of trees where Grove meets Christopher."

"I like the old houses . . ." Hannah offered.

"Indeed! How refreshing to see each with a different character, instead of row upon row of modern dwellings cast in the same mold. You would like Washington Mews. The houses there are especially charming."

"I'm sure I would. I prefer individuality. Most people do."

"I don't agree. The Mrs. Hemmings of the world thrive on

the sameness, day after day, ward after ward, street after
street."

Hannah stiffened at the mention of the dreaded name. She
did not want to pick up that line of conversation, so she
prompted, "Tell me more about the Village."

"Did you know that Fourth Street twists around until it
crosses Tenth and Eleventh Streets and that Waverly Place
actually bends back over itself?" He went on with more ge-
ographical facts. "It would be easier to show than tell you.
Next time I'll take you on a tour."

So there will be a next time! Hannah realized with a swell
of relief. She stopped in front of Number 78. "Here we are."

Dr. Dowd saw the plaque and ran his fingers over the
words: H. SOKOLOW, MIDWIFE, WOMEN'S PROBLEMS. Hannah
went ahead to open the door and turn on the lights. She left
the doctor in the waiting room while she looked for his journals in her rear office.

"Here they are!" she called, then was startled when she
realized that he was right behind her.

She handed the books with outstretched arms. He reached
for them, but did not clasp them. His hands went beyond
hers, to her shoulders, and then up along her collarbone until
they caressed her neck, and cupped her face.

"Hannah, my dearest Hannah."

The stack fell from her limp hands. Neither moved to reclaim them. He bent over as though he were about to kiss
her, but his lips merely brushed her cheek. Wrapping his
arms around her, he held on as though she might escape if
he let go. She pulled back, gently, so they were not disengaged. She merely wanted to read what was written in his
eyes.

❧ **20** ❧

This is not going to happen . . . no, not now . . . I don't want
him to break his marriage vows with me . . . not here . . .
was what first ran through her head, then was drowned by
messages too confusing to classify.

As he looked at her with adoration, she felt as though she were being appreciated for the first time. A minute earlier she had been afraid of doing something wrong. Yet what could be wrong about this? Two people out of millions and millions had found each other, and somehow each was more complete. She tried to summon a picture of Lazar, or even Lulu. Neither image would form. There was only Wendell Dowd, his soft, strong hands holding her, his remarkable azure eyes boring into her soul.

Then there was a kiss, like a blessing, weightless on her lips. Her legs seemed waxen and destined to melt if this fire was not quenched. Her hand reached up and stroked the downy hairs on the back of his sinewy neck. "Beautiful," he murmured, nuzzling behind her ear. "You're so beautiful . . ."

She teetered and groped behind her for something stable. There was nothing but the door frame. Which way should they go? Her examining room had but two uncomfortable chairs and a hard table. Rachael's office had softer furniture littered with the usual disarray. Yet they would have to sit. They would have to talk. It took strength of will to push past him and return to the waiting room. Anyone might see in from the street. She closed the lights and soon they were illuminated by the glow from a solitary streetlamp.

Once they were side by side on the double settee, he moved quickly. His hands groped for her and settled on her midriff. His fingers explored her bosom down to her hips and stopped there. Then he took her in his arms and kissed her with his tongue parting her lips until she met his with equal ardor. Somehow her dress hitched higher and his hands reached underneath. Hannah leaned away from him and gave in to the sensations of his fingers exploring her. And then the skillful gynecologist met his mark. Without warning, she convulsed forward, almost slipping to the floor. Shocked, she gave a whimper as though she had been hurt, then cried out as the touch pierced a place that had been dormant too long. He seemed as amazed as she was, and yanked away his hand. She fell on his chest and began to sob. He tried to comfort her, this time rubbing between her legs on the outside of her garments. Later she would reflect whether she should have done something to relieve him. At the moment, though, she was too ashamed to consider anything but what she had allowed to happen.

She drew back from him, but clasped his hands. "I'm sorry. I should never have brought you here."

His face was tortured. Even in the darkness she could see his distress. "You care for me. Tell me you do."

"What more proof do you need?" she responded, turning away.

When he spun her around and kissed her hands, she could smell her private scent on him. "I must be with you again. I must . . ." he choked.

"No, not like this."

"I know. I would never do anything to hurt you. But we can still consult—"

"Is that what you call this?" Hannah said with a forced laugh.

"Call it what you will, just don't deny me." Then he began to cry, incompletely, the way some men did. His sputters were worse because of his shame at losing control.

Somehow—Hannah could never recall the details—they managed to pick up the journals, lock the doors, and return to the street. Somehow they sat side by side in a taxicab the few blocks to Tompkins Square. And somehow Hannah made it to the top floor, to her bed, and through the night, without losing her mind.

21

"Ma! Ma! Didn't you see the message?"

"What message?" Hannah turned over groggily. She felt as if she had slept for weeks instead of only a few hours.

"From Auntie Eva," came Emma's faraway voice. "She's having her baby."

Hannah sat upright, then lay back down as a wave of dizziness knocked her over. "When did she send it?"

"Last night, about an hour after you left. Benny put it on the table. Didn't you see it?"

"I came in late," she said, rubbing her throbbing head.

"Where were you?"

"I told you, at a meeting." She looked around. "Where's your brother?"

"Downstairs at Bubbe's. We slept there because we thought you would be going out again and wouldn't be home this morning. I just came up for my books."

The fog began to lift, and even though Hannah thought she was too late, she knew she would have to go to Eva. She dressed and rushed out, shouting instructions to her daughter.

Eva was not at home. A neighbor was with the children. "She went to the hospital last night when you didn't come," she explained.

"A mixup . . . I did not get the message . . . which hospital?"

"I don't know. They didn't tell me nothin'," she said. "What a mess there was here. Water all over the place. She was leakin', she said."

Hannah was frightened something terrible might have happened while she had been with Dr. Dowd. "Are you sure there was no blood?"

"Nah. I didn't see no blood and I helped clean up."

Oh, God! Hannah prayed. Please let her be safe. And the baby. "Who would know where she went?"

"Mrs. Berger maybe. Downstairs in Seven F. She had a baby a few months ago and was raving about the doctor."

Within an hour Hannah found Eva ensconced in a private room at Mt. Sinai Hospital. She was groggy and looked about as awful as Hannah felt, for she had been administered an anesthetic during the birth of a nine-pound, one-ounce boy. Napthali had already gone to his office. Hannah had missed everything.

She pulled up a chair and sat by her sister. She apologized for not being there. Eva waved her hand like a queen to her court. "It was better this way. No pain. I went to sleep, and when I awoke I had my baby boy. Besides, how can I be angry since you are the one who told me what to do to have him?"

Hannah was about to deny that her system had any merit when she thought: who cares, let her believe what she will. "What are you calling him?"

"There was a name on a book you were reading that I liked."

"I have many books . . . can you recall anything else about it?"

Eva giggled. "Well, it had 'sex' in the title."

"Oh, you must mean Havelock Ellis." She laughed, then became more serious. "Do you really want to name a child Havelock?"

"No, I want to call him Ellis."

"Ellis. That is rather nice. Ellis Margolis."

Eva fluttered her lashes at her sister. "You do like it?" she asked, then closed her eyes and started dozing before she heard the answer.

∽ 22 ∽

From Mt. Sinai, Hannah had to go directly to St. Mark's Place. She was more than an hour late for her appointments. The waiting room was full.

"Mrs. Sokolow," Carrie called as Hannah rushed by. She glanced over and saw the receptionist holding up a medical-society journal. "Do you know where this came from? Dr. Jaffe found it on the waiting-room floor this morning."

"Oh!" Hannah felt her face flushing. "I stopped by last night to get some papers. That must have slipped from my hand."

"Well, that ends the mystery. One of the locks wasn't fastened either and she was worried about a break-in. Nothing was missing, though, and she wondered what kind of a thief leaves medical magazines behind . . ."

Hannah let her trail off while she rushed into her office to check the first few charts. By lunchtime she was already exhausted. Even though she had slept, she had not felt rested. Missing breakfast to rush uptown had depleted her further. Her temples were pounding. She took some headache powders, had some tea, then lay down in Rachael's office instead of eating. The doctor had only afternoon appointments on Thursdays. There was time before she showed up.

"You're here! How wonderful!" came Rachael's gleeful cry when she found Hannah sleeping on the sofa.

For the second time that day she was jolted awake. "What time is it?"

"Quarter after two. Only a few are out there. Don't worry, Carrie will keep them from attacking." She pulled up a chair. "I want to talk to you first. These days we seem to be rushing in opposite directions."

"Did you hear the news?" Hannah asked, thinking Carrie might have mentioned Eva.

"About our mysterious caller last night?"

"No, my sister had a baby. A boy."

"Mazel tov. Was it an easy birth?"

"I missed it. She went to Mt. Sinai."

"How terrible for you. You really should put in for a telephone."

"You know I can't afford it."

"A business expense. Consider it my fee to you."

Hannah rubbed her head. The powders had put her to sleep, but not dulled the squeezing pain. "I don't—"

"Aren't I one of your patients?"

"Well, sort of . . ."

"You've never thought of me as one because you never felt you offered me any useful advice." She paused and shook her tangled curls. "Am I right?"

"I suppose, but—" She struggled to express herself. "We're friends first."

"Not in this case. A friend would not have been so firm with me, or kept at it so long until the cure was found." Hannah's eyes widened. "It worked!"

"What worked?"

"Music! Beethoven's piano sonata. Opus Fifty-Seven in F minor, to be exact." She giggled and clapped her hands. "It's also known as the—" Her laughter stifled her words. She tried again. "The—the 'Appassionata'! Really, that's what it's called. Something about all those trills up and down the keyboard—maybe like staircases of music, I don't know. Anyway, it swept me away."

"When?" Hannah blurted.

"Last night! There was nothing else it could be. I'd never felt anything like it. Never. Even Herzog could tell the difference. And you should see him this morning! Singing, he was. Nora thought we had both gone crazy. I don't know, maybe I have too, but it's a good kind of crazy."

Last night . . . when she had been with Dr. Dowd. With

Wendell. When he had been kissing her, holding her . . . touching her. My God! Who was the crazy one? She was sick over this. She had missed the birth of her sister's baby. She had barely been able to do her work. And now, at her best friend's most triumphant moment, she could think of nothing else but that man . . . that glorious man.

"Look at you!" Rachael grinned. "You are happier about this than I am. Well, why shouldn't you be? You're the one who figured out the hindrance. There was nothing really wrong with me. My problem was that my mind was always on so many things that when I tried to concentrate on the task at hand, I felt as if I were watching myself perform. It was almost as if I were the professor critiquing myself." She gasped for breath, then galloped on. "Once I thought about the music, though, nothing but the hands pounding the keys, and the mounting combinations of the notes, and the dexterous way it was played by the pianist who struck the master for my piano roll, and . . . Well, whatever it was, it was a great success! You'll have to come to the house to see."

The expression on Hannah's face amused her. "Not that! To see the piano roll and hear the piece. I played it this morning after Herzog left. And do you know what? Even at seven in the morning, fully dressed and standing upright in my parlor, I felt some of the same feelings—all right, not exactly the same feelings. But here's the point: have you ever thought how often music is like sex? It starts out slowly, gently, lovingly, and then builds . . . and builds . . ." Her voice rose as an example. "Sometimes there is a feminine part, sometimes a masculine. Then, as the two harmonize and complement each other, there are duets. The first section of the sonata is pleasant enough, but the second one! Ah, that is the one which did it to me because that is where it finally culminates in the same—"

A knock on the door. "Doctor? May I send Mrs. Weintraub into the second examining room?"

"Yes, Carrie. We'll be right out."

Rachael leaned over and hugged Hannah before bolting from the room like a child rushing out to play.

∾ 23 ∾

August was a dreadful month. Because of the new baby, Mama went to stay with Eva for a few weeks. Benny and Emma had some activities at the settlement house, but Hannah worried about them incessantly. Her readings about rape made her frightened for her daughter. Once she thought she saw Benny with the man who had been pestering Lazar, but when she got closer, it had been some other boy in the same blue cap. The clinic was busier than ever, so her hours were long. There were summer fevers and skin rashes and vaginal infections. Minna, whose stamina had never returned completely since her hunger strike, became ill at a rally demanding that labor unions admit women. Rachael, who feared her heart muscle had been weakened, wanted her vital signs monitored. So, while recuperating, Minna was staying downstairs at Mama's and Hannah checked her several times a day.

Hannah went out only to keep clinic appointments, run errands, or deliver babies. Dr. Dowd had not contacted her again, but even if he had, she had vowed not to yield to the temptation to see him. In the meantime, there was no word from Lazar. Nothing. Not a letter. Not a telegram. For Russian news Hannah was dependent on the newspapers, and these brought only distressing reports. Trotsky's Red Army had taken Kazan from the White Russians. Did this mean Lazar was fighting in the civil war? Was he at the front with Trotsky? Or was he back in the Kremlin writing the results for posterity? Then something even worse happened: the United States joined Great Britain, France, and Japan in the conflict against Russia.

Hannah could barely sleep at night. She had nightmares of Lazar being killed by American bullets. In some dreams, Lazar was trying to return but being denied passage; in others, he was being jailed by the anti-Bolsheviks. Awakening in terror, she allowed her mind to drift toward Dr. Dowd. Why hadn't he called? Had his wife found out? Found out

what? That they had had dinner twice. That they had been
alone for an hour and had—what? Had kissed? And more.
But not much more. Yet everything more.

Was he also feeling penitent for what happened? Or was
he angry because of what had not happened? She had done
nothing to satisfy him. At the time she had been too overcome to consider it. If he had wanted to make love to her,
if he had tried to remove her clothes, what would she had
done? The fine line of propriety blurred. Sometimes she saw
herself relenting, and then imagined the man's splendid
hands gliding along her naked flanks and feeling his flesh
pressing next to hers. Was the hair on his chest as silky as
sable? And what about the hair lower down? What did he
look like there? Was he large? Was he circumcised? Would
she have gratified him? Other times she saw herself refusing him, kindly, nobly, but firmly. He would have understood. He would have known she did not want them to
betray his wife, or her husband, despite what Lazar had
done to her.

Nothing good ever came of these illicit alliances, she
chastised herself. Remember what happened the one time
you were unfaithful to Lazar? You were a stupid, a foolish
woman. You must forget Dr. Dowd! Think of the children!
Think of the sacrifices they've already made because of the
incessant demands of your patients, your deliveries, all those
stricken people who pester you for advice. Advice! Ha!
Look who is giving advice: a woman whose husband has left
her, whose children are heaven knows where all day, who
owes money to everyone from the greengrocer on Second
Avenue to her brother-in-law, who almost went to bed with
the first man who showed her any kindness in more than a
year.

Yet her undisciplined mind refused to stop thinking about
Wendell. The name, silly on her lips at first, now seemed
poetic. Now she could not stop wondering about Lulu. What
did he see in her? She was glamorous and mercurial and
talented, but Hannah sensed the woman lacked something
the doctor required, or why else would he look to her?
She laughed at herself again. Men always saw women as a
challenge. What sort of challenge had she presented? Two
dinners and she had parted her legs for him. Worse, she
had shown him how willing, how ready she had been. Even

with Lazar she had never climaxed after only a few caresses.

The last weeks of summer droned on. Rachael was too ebullient to notice Hannah's distress, and Hannah would never intrude on her friend's exhilaration to let her see her agony. So she avoided Rachael and Herzog.

On August 30, Lenin was wounded in the neck by Socialist-Revolutionary Fanya Kaplan. On the same day a young Jewish student named Leonid Kanegiesser assassinated Uritsky, the chief of the Petrograd Cheka, which was the secret internal police. Now they were injuring each other, Hannah thought ruefully. How could the socialists ever offer world peace if they could not settle their internal disputes? Her fears for her husband increased, but that was like saying the pain from a mortal wound had worsened, as if the increments mattered.

September brought school. At least her children were safer during the day. Supposedly the world was safer as well because the Germans were in full retreat across Aisne, with the British in pursuit. Benny was outraged at the outcome of the World Series. For some reason he had wanted the Chicago Cubs to win, not the boys with the red stockings. And Emma, who had hoped her hair would grow out over the summer more than it had, began setting it into pin curls, which took hours every evening. Also, she had suddenly decided she wanted to be a singer—just like Lulu Morse, of all people! In any case Hannah had to listen to high-pitched, stumbling renditions of Victor Herbert's music until she thought she would scream.

Then, in the middle of September there was yet another worrisome bit of news. A hundred new cases of the Spanish influenza, which everyone thought had petered out in the summer, occurred in the same week. The whole matter made headlines when sixty-six men died abruptly on a military base. People became alarmed. Hannah did not. After all, you would expect an epidemic in a crowded, unsanitary army camp to attack its inhabitants—all young soldiers. That did not mean it would spread to the civilian population. Everyone was talking of the war ending soon. The bases would empty out. The disease would die a natural death. She would not think about anything else that would aggrieve her. Not about Lazar. Not about Wendell. Nothing. Nothing except peace.

24

First came the letter from the Board of Managers of Bellevue Hospital reinstating Hannah in her position as head midwife at the same salary. Hannah did not respond. Then, three days later, came a second document offering her a substantial raise. Hannah's attention was piqued, but she was not about to return to Mrs. Hemming's jurisdiction, a drastically changed system, the ghastly night shift, or those rigid schedules. There was another reason: she did not want to be in daily contact with Dr. Dowd. Curiously, she did not connect these inducements with the medical emergency that was brewing. Yes, she had seen the press reports of the flu epidemic but, like most people, believed this was limited to the servicemen and a few others debilitated by chronic problems. She had begun to think about how to keep Mama away from crowds, since her respiration was already strained by an enlarged heart, but Hannah did not fear for the children at school, or for herself. Not a single case of even a suspected flu had come into the clinic. She saw the stories more as a diversion from the war news than anything truly catastrophic.

She was wrong. On September 27, Surgeon General Blue asked for a list of the members of the Volunteer Medical Service Corps, and within two days those selected for active duty were sent telegrams offering them positions as acting assistant surgeons. One of the first to accept was Dr. Dowd. Here was his chance to serve his country with his skills, but before he departed he accepted the task of recruiting Hannah to return to her rightful post.

He appeared in the clinic waiting room unannounced. When he walked through Hannah's consulting-room door, her initial thought was: it used to be that he sat at his desk and I came to him for advice. To see him standing there, hat in hand, was momentarily amusing—even vindicating. His words, however, sobered her.

"My worst fears have been realized. That hideous disease,

incubated on foreign battlefields, is mowing us down on the
home front like some terrible retribution meted out to those
spared by the sword."

"I've read about it, but so far it hasn't affected this area."

"It's much worse than the public thinks. Anyway, my time
has come to serve. I'm taking a leave from Bellevue."

"Won't you be needed there?"

"For now they want to concentrate on New England. The
worst outbreak started at Fort Devens, right near Groton, my
old prep school in Massachusetts, and far more than expected have been succumbing in that region. Most victims
are not the weak or the elderly, as expected, but young people between twenty and forty."

"That's terrible!"

"So you see why we need you at Bellevue more than
ever."

"Yes, but I'm not interested."

"I realize that you have many reasons to feel as you do,
but in this time of national calamity I must appeal to your
generosity of spirit and ask you to forgive people for their
petty mistakes. In a few weeks there are going to be catastrophic numbers to deal with."

"You don't think the stories have been exaggerated?"

"At Bellevue alone we had forty victims during the week
of September the sixth, thirty-six the next, ninety-eight the
week after that. Then last week there were nine hundred and
seventy-two."

"Deaths?" Hannah asked, aghast.

"Yes, fatalities. By the end of this week we estimate we
might have more than two thousand."

"I had no idea." She was reminded of the smallpox alert,
except these cases were ten—no, a hundred—fold more, and
this time no vaccination was available.

The doctor nodded. "To avoid a general panic we've tried
to keep the details out of the newspapers as long as we
could."

"How is it being transmitted so fast?"

"It's like a wildfire out of control. People are dying faster
than we can trace the pattern. And most of them are young
and healthy, that's the crazy part. Please, won't you recon-
sider, at least until this epidemic is over?"

"I don't know . . ." Hannah stared into Wendell's beseeching eyes.

"I'll be gone," he added, as though that might make up her mind.

"Where?"

"Wherever they send me, probably New Hampshire." He appealed to her sense of civic duty. "And I'm not alone. More than six hundred physicians have signed up."

Hannah could see that giving advice on marital woes or treating vaginal itches paled in comparison to his sacrifice. She was not trained to handle people with the sickness, but women would continue to have babies no matter what was going on in the world.

The doctor waited while Hannah gave the matter some thought, then burst out with "Will you ever forgive me?"

"For what?" she asked in a tremulous voice.

"For everything. For selfishly seeking your company, for exploiting your feelings, for not standing by you when you were in trouble . . ."

"I've missed you," Hannah responded simply.

"And I've missed you" came out so softly she was unsure of his words. Then his voice steadied. "You cannot imagine what agony it has been to stay away from you, but when I could not contain my passion, I realized I could only bring you harm."

"And your wife . . ."

"Yes. I suppose I could explain more about that, but she's not the issue. For some reason men can have dalliances without consequences, while women suffer. Already I once failed to defend you, and you were the one hurt." He looked at her sternly. "Don't try to tell me you weren't. I don't understand the situation with your husband, but he also has injured you. I decided that I could not continue unless I could make you happy."

"You did."

He gave a wan smile. "If that is true, and even if it was for the briefest moment, I am grateful. Maybe when this horror is over, maybe when life gets back to normal—whatever that may be—we might resume our . . . our friendship, only that. Do you think that is possible?"

"No." His face fell. He blinked his eyes. "It would be too difficult for me to be alone with you, for I was as much at fault as you. A woman abandoned is sometimes unaware of the extent of her deprivation. That time with you proved something to me. I am the one who could hurt you as well as your marriage. I admit I was disappointed not to hear from you for a few weeks, but now I see your discipline is what we needed. I doubt I could have done the same." She paused to swallow back her tears and managed to continue at an almost even pace. "I will consider coming back to Bellevue, though."

He beamed. "I have talked to the medical staff. They have offered even more pay than the last time they contacted you. Would that help?"

"Well, I can't say things have been easy, but I have a more pressing concern."

"What? You have always been so sensible I am certain they would accede to any reasonable request."

"It's Mrs. Hemming. I won't work under her."

A shadow crossed Dr. Dowd's face, then he recovered rapidly and responded in measured syllables that indicated he was thinking as he spoke. "There has been talk of her heading the epidemic staff. She'd be brilliant at organizing the effort, even with the personnel shortage. In fact, last year she volunteered to run a European field hospital, but her age ruled her out, so I expect she would be keen to undertake this." The muscles in his jaws clenched, then relaxed. "Consider it done. When can you start?"

"It will take me a few days . . ."

"We don't have a few days. At least come in to make the arrangements today."

"Tomorrow," Hannah conceded before she realized what she was doing.

~⤳ **25** ⤶~

On Hannah's second day back on the job a staff meeting was held at Bellevue to train everyone in the symptoms of the latest strain of Spanish influenza, which was being called the most virulent ever recorded in modern times. "Be especially cautious with the twenty-to-forty age group," warned Dr. Madden, the medical superintendent, "because they are responsible for more than half the cases."

By the end of the afternoon, Hannah was tending her first patient. It was almost as if this woman had heard the lecture. Mrs. Jenkins was thirty-five weeks pregnant. She reported that she had suddenly felt terribly ill and thought it might be the baby coming early.

"What else?" queried Hannah, still trying to relate the symptoms to her pregnancy.

"I've had a terrible headache. Nothing helps it."

Now Hannah began to suspect preeclampsia. "Yes?"

"And chills for a few hours, so it might just be a cold."

Hannah checked the chart. The nurse had logged her temperature at just over one hundred. She listened to her chest. "How long have you had that dry cough?"

"A day or so."

"Any muscle aches?"

"Yes, in my back and legs . . . and this morning my joints bothered me, but they often do in rainy weather."

Even as Hannah noted watery and irritated eyes, she had not made the connection. She was so pleased to eliminate nausea, vomiting, as well as diarrhea, it was a while before she accepted that most of the woman's complaints were in her chest.

"Despite the fact that many other symptoms may present," Dr. Madden had counseled, "we must remember that influenza is primarily a respiratory disease." Could it be? Hannah tried to tell herself she was becoming alarmed prematurely. Why, she was as bad as the young medical student who thinks he is suffering from every disease he reads about! Still, the woman was looking more flushed than when she had first seen her. Hannah decided to retake her temperature and was shocked to find it had elevated more than a degree.

"Mrs. Jenkins, for the sake of the baby, I must ask you to remain at Bellevue for observation."

The woman, who was feeling worse by the minute, did not argue. Hannah had her isolated in Ward D, which she ordered remain closed to other cases, and watched as Mrs. Jenkins followed the classical course of the disease. Her fever remained for three days. After the initial rise in temperature had subsided, there was the typical secondary, but lower elevation, resulting in what the doctor had called the diphasic fever curve, which he had claimed also had been noted in the ferrets which had been inoculated with the virus. Hannah warned her nurses not to panic. "Even though this is likely to be the influenza, I want you to remember that many people who contract the infection will not become ill, or may only be slightly indisposed. Right now Dr. Madden believes the number of subclinical infections is probably about the same as the number of clinical cases. Unfortunately, these infections are helping the influenza spread, but at the same time they are producing immunity in those fortunate enough to cope with the virus."

This satisfied them initially, but when Mrs. Jenkins died within forty-eight hours of her arrival at the hospital, the midwives were furious.

"We should not have allowed her to remain on the maternity pavilion!" Norma Marshanck argued.

"She was probably just as infectious when she was first examined," Hannah explained calmly. "Besides, where would we have transferred her? The rest of the hospital has been deluged with patients, and every service has their share."

Norma's anger dissipated, but she did not retreat. "Maternity must be kept a safe haven for mothers and children, which is what Mrs. Hemming intended."

Shocked by this shift in allegiance, Hannah began to regret her return. Then she realized the midwife was speaking more from fear than vindictiveness. "We'll try to transfer suspected cases, if a bed elsewhere can be found" was her way of mollifying Norma.

Among first victims to arrive at Bellevue on the same day as Mrs. Jenkins had been thirty sailors sent over from the Brooklyn Navy Yard. By the end of the week the hospital was jammed as other New York hospitals shipped their contagious cases to Bellevue. Classes at the medical school were halted and the students were assigned to look after flu patients. Ward capacities doubled. Bedside stands were stacked in the corridors to make space for even more beds to be squeezed next to each other. Soon balconies became wards and even the hallways were lined with cots. The children's ward was filled with three to a bed. Even the new tuberculosis boat, successor to the *Southfield* moored at the foot of East 29th Street, had to be converted into a flu hospital. Once the morgue was filled, the alcoholic ward was pressed into service.

While the doctors and nurses struggled with the futility of their endeavors, fear and dismay gripped the city. The mayor's commission warned people to avoid unnecessary exposure, to dress warmly, to refrain from spreading the disease by coughing and sneezing, and to go to bed and call a doctor at the first sign of a respiratory infection. Still the epidemic worsened. Public gatherings were banned, and schools, churches, and some businesses were closed. Anybody with training in nursing, no matter how slight, was pressed into service. The midwifery department was expected to manage with only one fully trained midwife and one assistant on duty through a twelve-hour shift. Everyone did more than that. On one shift in early October Hannah was on duty for forty hours straight. Only after she went home did she realize she had worked through her thirty-fifth birthday.

The shocking death statistics were published every week and circulated to each department head. In New York the numbers of casualties rose exponentially from just over a hundred per week in the middle of September to twenty-one hundred by the middle of October. Then, the very next week, they doubled to more than four thousand; the week after that it was fifty-two hundred! Nationwide the acme of the epidemic came the two weeks ending October 26, when forty thousand deaths were recorded. In New York City alone, on October 23, 851 people died of the flu, the highest daily death rate ever recorded in the city. More than half of those who expired in the city did so on the grounds of Bellevue Hospital.

When this highest part of the wave crashed against Bellevue's walls, the latest victims were having a more sudden onset. Patients collapsed abruptly. More than twenty percent showed signs of pneumonia, and half of those did not recover. Dr. Madden circulated an ominous memo warning: "Be extremely wary if you notice a heliotrope coloration of the lips and face. Because it heralds a massive viral invasion of the lungs, that heliotrope cyanosis nearly always means death within one to two days."

At the peak it seemed that either the birth rate had taken a drastic drop or that women were choosing to deliver at home rather than risk being exposed to infection at the hospital. With so few on her staff, Hannah was relieved. However, she was appalled at the regimentation under Mrs. Hemming's system that had replaced the maternity clock. This could be any surgical or general medicine ward, with no allowances for the special needs of the laboring mother.

Also, even though the quality of care could not be faulted, Hannah sensed a decline in the quality of caring. Maybe this could be attributed to the epidemic, she allowed. In any case, there was hardly time to fret over what could not be changed when chaos—this time in the guise of a malignant disease—prevailed.

Then maternity admissions increased suddenly as expectant mothers with fevers went into labor prematurely. More and more women, and even some babies, were expiring with the flu. Midwives wept in their wards, from exhaustion as much as the emotional strain. Even Hannah broke down one afternoon when she found herself signing more death than birth certificates. Mercifully, though, after the intense October siege, the deaths declined a bit, and by the end of November, had receded to only four hundred a week. However, hospital employees were not immune. Dr. Madden's clerk was one of the first to pass away. Two servers in the cafeteria died the second week. In total, 144 staff members contracted the flu and six died. The Board of Managers called an emergency meeting of the department heads and house physicians. Everyone attending was wearing cheesecloth masks.

Mrs. Hemming, who seemed to be reveling in her role of epidemic coordinator, proposed that the hospital be closed. "We're not saving any lives," she said in a mask-muffled voice, "and we're spreading the contagion to patients who are ill with other diseases as well as to healthy members of the staff."

"Bellevue has a long tradition of being able to meet emergencies," responded Dr. Madden. "We can't run like dogs with our tails between our legs. This is war on another front, and we are trained to fight infection, not ignore it."

"Then close the hospital to new patients" was her second volley. When the board voted down that proposal, Mrs. Hemming offered her last card. "Close the hospital to all visitors, or I shall resign. Besides, the panic-stricken relatives are making it impossible to perform our duties."

This proposal won almost unanimously.

The next day, Hannah worked all through that night and into the next afternoon until Dr. Madden himself came to her ward and checked her time sheet. "You must take two days off."

"How can I?" Her eyes were ringed with the black mask of fatigue.

"That is an order, Midwife Sokolow. We cannot afford staff members who neglect their own health."

She knew he was right, and even accepted his offer to pay her cab fare home. When she got off on the corner of Tompkins Square, she stopped to watch Emma and her friends jumping rope. It took a moment before she comprehended the little ditty they had concocted as a jumping rhyme.

> I had a little bird
> And its name was Enza
> I opened the window
> And in-flew-Enza.

She was about to chastise the girls for their bad taste when she saw Minna gesticulating from the stoop. As she got closer, she saw that Minna's skin looked waxen. For a long time she had feared that the weaknesses from her imprisonment would make her more vulnerable to this disease, especially since her sister-in-law was in the most worrisome age group for this wave of the epidemic. Minna had argued with Hannah. "You won't let Mama out, so if I don't shop and take care of everything, we'll starve." Hannah had not disagreed with her. Who could contradict Minna and survive?

"You look terrible, Minna," she said with more concern than castigation.

"You should look in the mirror," her sister-in-law countered.

Hannah was about to open her mouth with a retort, but closed it when she saw Minna's eyes filled with tears. "What is it?"

"Your mother."

"What are you saying? Mama shouldn't be affected by this flu strain. People her age aren't getting it."

Minna shook her head. "She has it."

"What do you know? Since when did you become a doctor?" Hannah pushed past her and entered the front hall.

Rachael was standing in the doorway. "Gotteniu!" Hannah wailed. "No! Please, no!"

For weeks Hannah had fought the debilitation of overwork, the fears for her family. Her concerns about Lazar and Wendell and her own happiness had seemed petty in this emergency, but at least through this—as well as in so many crises in recent years—Mama had been there quietly making certain everyone was watched, fed, nurtured. Even her criticisms had been grounded in good sense and loving concern. Now it was as if the last plank on the platform that had supported Hannah had been yanked away. She fell through.

_{∽∾} **26** _{∽∾}

Mama may have had the fever for a day or more before Minna was alerted. Then, while Hannah was valiantly coping at the hospital, her condition had worsened. They tried every cure except the ones Rachael thought were ridiculous, which included the inhalation of chloroform and the removal of tonsils and teeth. Scotch was supposed to be the most medicinal of whiskeys, but the price had risen to twenty dollars a quart. Somehow Chaim procured a pint, and Mama was made to drink a shot every two hours. This seemed to relax her, nothing more. By the fourth day of continuing fever, all they could do was wait and see. Her breathing became impaired, and Hannah feared the worst.

The other family members argued with her. Chaim had heard the stories of people dying within hours of diagnosis. "Mama's almost made it through the week," he pointed out.

Minna backed him up. "You said that it was the younger people who succumbed. You've been worried about me, not her."

"She's right. Besides, Mama's a tough one," Eva added bravely. "She's been through much worse than this. Remember Papa's death? The pogrom? Dora? Not to mention what she had to put up with raising us! Now that I have three of my own I can appreciate her so much more."

Hannah said nothing. Mama did not look too sick to revive. Many times she had seen people with a cold—even Mama—who weren't much worse. Why people recovered from other viruses and not this one was a mystery to the medical community. However, unlike the less knowledge-able members of the family, Hannah could not ignore one other sign: her mother's reddish-purplish color, the indication Dr. Madden warned was so ominous. Of course, he could have been wrong. Exceptions were the rule, weren't they?

That night Napthali insisted that Eva return to their home. He was afraid for her, the new mother, to have too much exposure to the disease. Minna agreed. Hannah thought her sister should stay, just in case, but held her tongue. Then after midnight Mama said she was feeling better. She sat up. She drank some sweet tea. She asked to see her grandchildren. Not wanting to tell her it was the middle of the night, Hannah woke Benny and Emma and brought them downstairs. Their grandmother held their hands. The children were too sleepy to know what was happening. Hannah put them back to bed, and since Mama was much improved, she decided to rest herself. Fully dressed, she lay down on her bed. Nobody called her. The next day was Saturday. The children did not go to school. She slept for ten hours. When she awoke Rachael was sitting at her kitchen table. And that's how Hannah knew her mother was dead.

27

Hannah managed to stumble to a chair. Rachael was speaking, but she heard nothing. A roar in the distance blocked everything. Her eyes would not focus. Someone pressed a steaming glass into her hands, and she thought she tasted the hot liquid on her tongue, but could not swallow. Her throat had closed. People fluttered around her, coming in and out of the gloom in slashes and streaks of light. Her head was pounding with a loud, incessant pulse. Cool water was splashed on her face, her feet. Why her feet? She opened her eyes and saw colorful swirls. She closed them and they did not cease. The plug in her chest would not release. She coughed to no avail. And then she shivered. The spasms would rattle up from her feet to her teeth and back down again. She was buried in blankets until the steaming, melting, scalding in her bones threatened to explode, then she lay exposed on the soaking sheets praying to be buried in ice.

People had no names, no faces. She had forgotten what had happened. Sometimes she talked to Lazar, sometimes to Mama. She saw her children beside her as babies and toddlers and grown with children of their own. She conversed with childhood friends, long-dead relatives, and teachers from her days in Moscow and Odessa. How nice of them to come all this way . . .

She neither woke nor slept nor ate nor drank nor dreamed nor had rational thoughts. She drifted along, sometimes on a stormy sea, sometimes on a placid lake, moving whichever way the wind and currents carried her. Sometimes she heard voices calling her, but they were faraway across the widening waters. Eventually, when she arrived alongside the bank she would answer them . . . for now they would just have to wait . . .

Later she would reflect why she survived. She had not fought her way back. She had not tried to get to the shore. Suspended in another sphere, she had not cared about her children, or her husband, or mother. Was that what it was like to be a fetus floating in an amniotic sac? she wondered when she was recovering. For certainly her return to the real world seemed quite like the miracle of birth. The moment itself was the difference between blindness and sight, hearing and deafness, pain and relief. The first sensation was at the tips of her fingers. Pressure. Incessant, demanding, tugging. As she gave into it, her whole body moved upward. The blood drained from her head and a sharp sting shot up her spine. Soft cushions kept her from toppling over. The voice would not stop calling to her.

"Han-nah, Han-nah, pleeeease . . ."

The hovering face shimmered in a golden light. The eyes were the color of a summer sky. There was no body, just the compassionate face urging her to respond. So this is what it is like, she thought . . . and mulled why people were afraid to die when the other side was so pleasant.

"Do you hear me, Han-nah?"

"Yes." The sound of her own voice, deep and echoing, amazed her.

Something was pressed to her lips. She felt the smooth fluid soothe every cell of her parched throat. She leaned back. Her eyes opened farther. Then she saw him. Not as a disembodied, otherworldly head, but as a man, a friend, a doctor. Dr. Dowd.

"You're going to be all right, Han-nah. You're through the crisis now."

Someone was sobbing. She looked around, but turning her neck brought a convulsion of pain. The other person moved into her line of sight. Emma. Her darling little Emma. She managed to reach out her hand, and her daughter clasped it.

"You shouldn't have slept so long, Ma," she chastised. "You scared us."

"How long?"

"Three days," the doctor said, "only three days."

"Emma, sweetheart, go downstairs and tell my mother that I'm going to be fine."

"But—Mama—she isn't there!" Emma wailed.

"Then . . ." Something wasn't quite right, although Hannah didn't know exactly what. "Tell your Aunt Minna. Have something to eat and then come up with your brother in, say, half an hour," she said as her will to take charge asserted itself.

The child's shadow moved across the room, but Hannah could not follow its progress. After the strain of making her wishes known, her eyes had closed of their own volition.

"When did you come?" she managed a few minutes later.

"Last night."

"Were you called back to Bellevue?"

"No. My family needed me—" His voice broke.

Hannah was becoming more alert every minute. His son . . . the war . . . oh, no! "Your son?" she whispered.

"No. He's fine, well, not exactly. He was injured. Just enough to bring him back, not enough to do any permanent damage. Every parent's wish in these insane times."

Hannah felt no relief at the news. Something else was wrong. He couldn't have known about her while he was away. Even if the worst had happened, nobody in the family would have thought to contact him. His daughter? She was under twenty, out of the most dangerous group . . . That did not mean it was impossible, just less of a statistical chance. Then her returning memory stabbed her. Another in a less risky group had died. That's what Emma had meant! Oh, Mama! She forgot about the doctor for a moment and began to cry.

"It's all right. You're going to be fine now," he comforted.

"My mother . . ."

"Yes, I know."

"What happened to her?"

"I heard there was a service while you were ill. Your brother's wife stayed home with you."

"Minna. I worried about her. She's the one with Margaret Sanger and—"

"I know who she is. She's been taking care of you. She said you saved her life."

"Has she been ill?"

"No. Not a single sign."

"Oh," Hannah said, collapsing from the strain of the discussion. Then, after a few minutes of silence, she remembered the doctor's problem. "How is your d-daughter?" she stumbled.

"Well, thank the Lord. She's staying with an aunt in the country for now."

"Good," Hannah said as she recalled that there were fewer cases away from the cities and army bases . . . army bases . . . where Lulu Morse had cheered the troops . . . She could almost hear Lulu Morse singing: "Ah! I know at last the secret of it all . . ." in the park on a summer evening, an evening so long ago.

"Lulu?" Hannah managed.

The raven-haired head bobbed in front of the shaft of light from the window. The glare dimmed. And in that shadow Hannah saw some clarity in her clouded future.

    ♥⌐ **28** ⌐♥

She should have prepared for the worst. Nobody had known her wishes. They had been planning to give her children to Eva to raise, yet Lazar would have hated Emma and Benny being imbued with Eva's bourgeois values. And what of Lazar? If he had been told, might he have come home to them? Or sent for them? She should have left word that she wanted them to remain in America no matter what. Even if it was with Eva.

While she recovered, these and other torments racked Hannah's weary brain. Mama was dead. That's what they said. Yet she did not believe it. How could Mama be gone when she was still needed? Yes, needed! Hannah had never been able to show her gratitude properly. Nor had she told her how much she appreciated the unconditional sympathy her mother had shown since Lazar had left. Now it was too late . . . She had not seen her mother at the end. She had not been to the service. Maybe it was a mistake. Mama could just be downstairs, resting. No, she reminded herself sternly. Minna and Chaim were there. Eva had asked them to remain until Hannah recovered.

She considered the grim statistics. Somehow she had been spared becoming a number in the mortality column while Mama had joined the select ranks of older victims during the second wave. People that age were not supposed to have perished, yet some did. Children too. Statistics don't tell the story. Every death is a tragedy. She had lost her mother, Dr. Dowd his wife. Chaim had brought her the newspaper clipping. Only a few notable obituaries were published each day. Lulu Morse's had included a picture and mentioned her "noble sacrifice to the war effort." Poor Wendell. She knew he had loved her. What man would not have been entranced with her fascinating face, her legendary voice? Maybe—as he had hinted—she had been difficult to live with, although Hannah sensed they had complemented each other: the flamboyant artist balanced by the methodical practitioner.

During her days of recovery, Hannah sometimes allowed herself the luxury of thinking about Wendell Dowd, and how, when she had awoken from her stupor, she had believed he was a messenger from heaven. What had her family thought when he had taken a vigil at her bedside? Had they suspected anything?

Eva had credited him with saving Hannah's life, saying, "If he hadn't returned to New York to bury his wife, he never would have heard of your illness. How lucky for you that an expert in the disease was also the head of your department at Bellevue!"

It was unclear what he had done to turn the tide, so she had asked Rachael why she had survived.

"I can't say for certain. You may have built up some re-sistance from your hospital exposures."

"Did Dr. Dowd do anything ... unusual?"

"Mostly he tried to maintain drainage of your respiratory track. He had you sitting up. He turned you. He brought in steaming pots of water to add humidity to the room and cold basins to sponge you down when your fever crested."

Hannah flushed. "Did *he* do it?"

"No, he was very protective of your modesty."

Hannah replayed that response over and over. What had been Rachael's tone? Direct? Sarcastic? Had she suspected anything? As far as she knew, a doctor had tended a col-league, a much needed head midwife. Once she was on the road to recovery, he had not returned to check on her. No-body expected him to. He had family problems to deal with and had to resume the leadership of his department at Bellevue.

To cheer herself Hannah thought how much she would en-joy working alongside Wendell again, but refused to permit herself to dwell on the future. He may be a widower now, she reminded herself, but you are still a married woman.

She was surprised how long it took to recuperate. For more than a week she could spend no more than an hour out of bed. The children were admirable. They heated soup and made tea. In the other room she could hear Emma bossing Benny to wipe the table and pick up his books. He would snap back at her, but it seemed as though he acceded to her wishes. Because her eyes were blurry, Benny read her the newspapers. He told her how Captain Eddie Rickenbacker, the pride of the American Army Air Service, had added to his brilliant fighting record by scoring fourteen victories in October alone, bringing his wartime destruction total to twenty-two aircraft and four observation balloons. Though she wanted to berate him again for worshiping anyone German or American—who won fame by killing, she re strained herself.

Emma told her that her favorite book, *Little Women,* had been made into a movie. "When you are better, Ma, we'll go see it, won't we?"

Hannah assented. A few weeks earlier she might have put her daughter off, saying she had neither the time nor the money. How meaningless her previous decisions seemed compared to what had almost happened! She vowed to be a better, less critical mother because one could never predict what would happen next.

Even the news from the war front was a series of shocks. Austria-Hungary had surrendered on November 3. Some said the collapse of Germany was certain. Although it seemed that way on November 9, when the kaiser abdicated and fled to the Netherlands, Hannah was leery, because it still didn't mean a cessation of the fighting on all fronts.

The next day she woke to the incessant ringing of church bells, factory whistles, and sirens. The armistice had been signed in Europe! Now that the war was truly over, Hannah was confident everyone would realize how long it had taken and how costly it had been. Four terrible years. The deaths of ten million, including six million civilians. The world had learned its lesson. This would never happen again. Still weak from her illness, Hannah was not about to join the dancing in the streets.

"But, Ma, we have to see what's happening!" Benny grumbled.

"You go, but no farther than Second Avenue, and be back in an hour."

"So soon?" Emma complained, but noting her mother's resolve, reluctantly agreed.

"You should have seen it!" Emma bubbled later. "People were pouring out of shops and parading in the streets. They smashed one another's hats, cheered soldiers in uniforms, even wrapped themselves in flags."

"Yeah," her brother continued. "They had this dummy of the kaiser made of clothes stuffed with rags, and then they burned it in the middle of the street."

"That's enough!" Hannah warned. "I knew it was too dangerous to let you out."

"You shouldn't have told her," Emma griped.

By December 1, Hannah was back at Bellevue part-time. She went in for the first part of the morning shift and tried to make order, develop fair schedules, and make the best use of her decimated staff. Several training-school nurses had not recovered, but thankfully not a single midwife had died. Maybe caring for so many had conferred a degree of protection, or maybe they just were a strong breed. In any case, they would never know why some had been spared. At least the devastation from the epidemic had subsided almost simultaneously with the signing of the armistice. Some were saying it had been God's way of teaching mankind a lesson. Others, like Dr. Dowd, linked the infestation with the dreadful conditions of wartime. In the end the Spanish influenza had killed nearly as many servicemen as the ones who died in battle, ten times that number of American civilians, and twice as many people worldwide as those who died in combat on all fronts during the four frightful years of the war.

Problem 7:
Am I Normal? One Thousand Women Tell All

◆

1919

Sex is a foretaste of the world to come.
—THE TALMUD, TRACTATE BRACHOT

❦ 1 ❦

"I TOLD you, I don't go to lectures anymore," Hannah insisted. She concentrated on slicing onions into her chopping bowl.

"I agree that most are utter bores, but Louise is speaking," Minna said insistently. "Don't you want to know what's going on in Russia?"

"Not particularly." Hannah was not prevaricating. She had decided that she could no longer suffer every fluctuation of a political battle far across the world as if it personally affected her. Yes, Lazar was there, but she had not heard from him in more than six months. She supposed this was mostly due to the obstacle of communications; nevertheless, since she had no idea where he was or how he was faring, she had to focus on the essentials: regaining her health, caring for her family, doing her work competently. Then, with any spare energy, she was going to pay attention to herself. "Go, enjoy," she said, rolling the curved blade of her chopping knife through the large hunks. "Give my best to Louise, and whoever else is speaking."

"It's Albert Rhys Williams. On 'The Truth About Russia.' "

"Right." She had taken down a pot and began to fry the onions. "Let me know what he has to say."

"What will you do?"

"What does it look like I'm doing? I'm making a soup. I have children to feed." For a moment she resented having to account to Minna, but then reminded herself how grateful she was that Minna and Chaim had stayed on in Mama's apartment.

Minna glanced to the bedroom, where she heard Benny provoking Emma about something. "They shouldn't be in the house all day. Why don't you go out?"

"On a freezing Sunday afternoon in February? What do you suggest, a stroll in the park?"

Unaccustomed to her sister-in-law's sarcastic tone, Minna shook her head and waved good-bye.

A walk in the park, Hannah considered. Not a bad idea after all. The sun was shining. Benny and Emma were going stir crazy. They could have tea somewhere, perhaps in the Village. She would show them where Mabel Dodge had lived . . . and the arch at Washington Square. Benny would like the winding streets. She tried to remember what Dr. Dowd had told her about 4th Street crossing 10th and 11th Streets and Waverly Place twisting back over itself. They could locate these unusual places. Yes, they'd like that.

Emma did not want to put down *Little Men*, Benny complained because he had been hoping to visit Izzy, a boy Hannah did not trust, but they both bundled up when they saw she was determined.

The air was sharp, but quickly walking west, they remained warm enough. Hannah did not reprimand the children when they ran ahead. She admired their lively steps, their ringing laughs. Stopping at a corner, she hugged each of them to her in a spontaneous gesture that made both children stare at their mother quizzically.

"What's wrong, Ma?" Emma asked.

"Wrong? Why should anything be wrong? I feel happy." The word surprised her. She reflected on what she had said. Yes, happy. But why? Nothing particular was different. Her husband had left her; her mother was dead. But also the flu epidemic was waning; the war was over. And they had survived.

Hannah pointed out some Village sights and spouted some

of the lore that Dr. Dowd had told her. "Do you know why the streets aren't straight over here?"

"Because the people didn't have a ruler when they planned them," Emma offered.

"Not exactly," Hannah replied. "Benny, what's your guess?"

Benny kicked a tin can. "I dunno, why?"

"Well, about a hundred years ago a yellow fever epidemic broke out, and people moved south to escape the fever-ridden marshes. So, almost overnight, what were merely farms became a full-fledged town. Later, the temporary structures were replaced by those of stone and brick, yet they never got around to changing the curving, twisting streets."

"I like it here," Emma said immediately as she admired the shops on West 4th Street. "Look, this one's called The Mad Hatter." She walked over for a closer look. "Ma, come see!" She pointed to a sign inscribed backward in looking-glass fashion. "What does it say?"

"Down the rabbit hole," Benny translated quickly.

"How did you do that so fast?" his sister demanded.

"You always said I was backward," he teased.

"It's from *Alice in Wonderland*, isn't it, Ma?" Emma asked.

"Don't know," she admitted. Lazar knew about books in English, even the ones for children. "Would you like to go inside?"

"Can we?" Emma hopped from one foot to the other.

"Why not?"

They walked down stone steps which led to a darkened tea room. Candles in holders fashioned from empty cans furnished flickering light. When their eyes became adjusted, they noticed that the walls were covered with quotations from Lewis Carroll, drawings of the Cheshire Cat, and other Wonderland characters. Even though the theme was childish, the room was filled with adults who played backgammon and draughts. Beer was the beverage on most tables, and Hannah suspected that she had taken the children to an inappropriate place. The waiter, however, welcomed them. Hannah ordered tea for herself, hot chocolate for the children. While they waited, Emma prattled on about the story and characters. Hannah did not follow her, for she was thinking how much Lazar, who had first read the book to the children, would have enjoyed listening to his daughter. He probably would have found a political message in the tale, she reminded herself ruefully.

Warmed by their beverages, they returned to their walk. "Where are we going now, Ma?"

"To the park, and then home."

When they reached the edge of Washington Square, Hannah said, "This was once the burial field for impoverished victims of the yellow fever epidemic."

"Who told you that?" Benny challenged.

"Probably Pa," Emma offered.

"No, a friend who lives in this neighborhood," Hannah replied, but when she saw the disappointment in her daughter's expression, she wished she had not disagreed with her. At least the children had not forgotten their father.

As they started north on Fifth Avenue, Hannah noticed a cobbled street to the right. "Doesn't this look like something from a hundred years ago?" she said, pointing. Then she saw the sign: WASHINGTON MEWS. "I know somebody who lives here."

"Who?" Benny's tone was monotonous to demonstrate he did not care.

"Dr. Dowd, the doctor who helped take care of me when I was sick. Do you remember him?"

Despite himself, Benny brightened. "Of course. He brought us apples."

"Really? I don't recall that."

"Which house?" Emma asked.

"I don't know. I have never visited his home."

"Then how do you know he lives here?" her daughter challenged.

"He told me where he lived once, and I remembered it because I'd never heard of a mews before."

Emma skipped down the street. "This is nice. It's like another country."

"Yes. It reminds me of Russia," Hannah said, then regretted her slip. The children did not need to be reminded of their father again. Before she realized where she was going, Emma went up to a door.

"What are you doing?"

"Seeing if there's a name. Maybe we could figure out where the doctor lives."

"Come back!" Hannah insisted.

"He is your friend, isn't he?"

"Yes, but we cannot very well go up and ring the bell and invite ourselves in."

"Why not? We do that where we live."

"That's different."

"Why?"

"Because it is, that's why!"

Just then the door in front of where they were standing opened, and a woman in a long apron came out carrying a sack of garbage tied with twine. She looked at Emma and said, "Hello there," in an Irish accent. "Who might you be looking for?"

"Dr. Dowd," Emma replied.

"Oh, yes, the doctor. He's two doors down. Number fourteen."

"Thanks," Emma said, and then bounded to the door and gave the brass knocker a few fast taps.

Hannah was close on her heels. "What are you doing? Didn't I say—?" But as she caught up, the door opened.

Another woman with an apron answered. "Good afternoon," she said to Emma.

"Is the doctor at home?" Emma replied in her most grown-up voice.

"Who may I say is inquiring?"

"The family of Hannah Sokolow. We have come to thank him for his kindness."

The housekeeper's eyes shifted up to Hannah, who did her best to return a gracious smile. "Please come in," she said, since the woman and children on the doorstep could not be left in the cold.

The hallway, which was painted a rich royal blue on the walls as well as ceiling, filled the entire width of the narrow dwelling. Double doors behind the staircase opened up into another part of the house. Hannah guessed there were probably only one or two rooms on each floor because the servant had gone upstairs to fetch the doctor. Looking around, Hannah felt as if she had just entered an alien world. Although but a mile or so across town from Tompkins Square, she could have just as well arrived in Paris. Everything—from the intricate brass doorknobs to the carved framing around the doors—was so grand, she knew she looked out of place in her drab walking costume. Moisture dotted her brow and palms. Her coat was too warm, but she did not want to unbutton it before she had been properly invited. What would the doctor think of her impertinent visit? What was she disturbing? An afternoon nap? Work on his papers? A visit with family or friends or . . .

"Hannah!" he called down as he descended the steps. Then he glimpsed the children and became more formal. "Mrs. Sokolow! What an unexpected pleasure. Emma, isn't it? And Benjamin." He shook the children's hands, then clasped Hannah's, first one, then the other together. "To what do I owe this delightful visit?"

"To my impetuous daughter," Hannah replied, giving Emma a wilting glance.

Emma bowed her head.

Benny straightened his back and stared at the doctor. "We were out for a walk and Ma—I mean, my mother—remembered you lived on this street. So Emma asked a lady where, and then she ran up and knocked on the door, and—" He faltered as the doctor stared at him with twinkling eyes.

"Is that the truth?" Dr. Dowd asked Hannah.

"I'm afraid it is."

"I disagree. I think my thoughts drew you here, like iron to a magnet. Why, just a few minutes ago, I was reading a new article by Havelock Ellis, which had me thinking about you. Just as I put it down to contemplate how you were getting on, you appeared on my doorstep. Now don't tell me that's a coincidence."

Hannah forced a laugh. "I feel like I've fallen down the rabbit hole!"

"What?" he squinted. "Oh, *Alice in Wonderland!* My daughter has a beautiful edition. Would you like to see it?" He had directed his query to Emma. For once words failed her, and she only nodded yes. "Then follow this black-haired rabbit upstairs." After taking their coats and handing them to his housekeeper, he led the way to his library.

"It's all green," Emma commented as she spun around to take it all in.

Hannah was about to hush her daughter, but then she realized Emma was right. The walls of the book-lined room were papered in a green damask, the ceiling was a lighter shade, and each piece of furniture was upholstered in a variation from emerald to chartreuse. Even the carpet was a pattern of intertwined leaves. Hannah recalled that the entranceway had been totally blue, from the tiles to the seat cushions of the hall chairs.

"Lulu's idea," Dr. Dowd explained, almost apologetically. "She wanted each room to be, in her words, 'an experience in the full range of each color.' Also, she preferred to say, 'Let's go into the yellow room,' instead of the dining room, or 'the pink room,' meaning Daphne's bedroom."

"Really?" Emma asked in awe.

"Would you like to see them?"

"Oh, yes!"

"Doctor, that's very kind but—" her mother interjected.

"I am sorry, I should have inquired whether your mother has other plans."

"She doesn't," Emma answered. "We were just taking a walk."

The doctor caught Hannah's annoyance, but diffused it with a smile. "Let's ask Enid to make us some tea, or would you children prefer hot chocolate? Then we can have a tour and look for the book."

"We've had—" Benny began, but stopped himself when he caught his mother's signal. "Yes, sir, thanks a lot," he managed.

Hannah nodded that he had done well.

"Come along, then," the doctor said as he began his tour.

"I wouldn't mind resting my feet," Hannah said. To make her point, she sat on a jade green velvet loveseat.

The doctor was about to insist, but he sensed her discomfort at seeing his private rooms.

"C'mon, Ma," Benny coaxed.

"Let your mother rest. We'll be right back."

The moment they left, Hannah stood again. She was much too agitated in these foreign surroundings to relax. Even if she had the bank account to afford such quarters, never would she have put the same combinations of furnishings and colors together. Nor would Eva, or anyone she had ever met. She walked around to the desk, where Wendell had probably been working. He had been reading an article in the *Birth Control Review,* Margaret Sanger's journal, entitled "The Love Rights of Woman." She skimmed a few pages, then heard footsteps, and quickly turned it back to his place. When the door opened, she was sitting in a stiff-backed chair. It was not the doctor. The maid had brought the hot beverages.

"Is it all right if I set it here, madam?" she said as she placed the large tray on a small side table.

Hannah was not about to make a suggestion in someone else's home, but the minute the tray was set down she thought it might be in a precarious position should one of her clumsy children bound in and bump it. "Maybe it would be better over there." She pointed to a sideboard near the window.

"Very good, madam," the maid said without any show of displeasure. "Shall I pour you a cup while you wait?"

"Yes, that would be nice," she replied, although she felt she was masquerading as a genteel lady.

The doctor returned and he was beaming. "How intelligent your children are! They ask the most fascinating questions." He paused and stared at her. "Like their mother." His gaze did not linger, for he saw she was discomfited. "You have your tea. Good. Children, how about some chocolate? You know, that's what I am going to have. A nice cup of hot chocolate with extra cream." He licked his lips like a cat as he served the first one. "Not too much. Oops. Much too much. Now what have I done?" Emma giggled as he made an elaborate show of stirring in the cream. "Oh, dear, who will drink this cup? Emma, would you be so kind?" She took it from him and gingerly walked to her seat so as not to spill a drop. "Whoops! I did it again. Benjamin, might you assist me this time?" Benny took the cup and made it to his seat without a mishap. "Now, once more. Ah, just right!" He came and sat across from Hannah.

"How is your son?" she asked.

"Recuperating nicely. He's going to have some surgery on his leg, but after that, he'll come home for a while. The problem is that there are so many stairs in this house. We'll have to turn the parlor into an infirmary."

"And your daughter?"

"She's decided to finish the year at a school near her grandmother's in Poughkeepsie. She's made many friends there. And Vassar College, a fine school for young women, is in the same town. I believe she is thinking about applying for admission." He turned to Emma. "I hope you will consider college when your time comes. These days, if we are going to meet the challenges of a new society, both men and women must be educated."

"I'm going to be an actress, so that won't be necessary," Emma replied forthrightly.

"One doesn't preclude the other," the doctor replied in a more muted voice. He was about to say something to Benny, then changed his mind, and concentrated on Hannah. He asked her routine questions about the hospital; then, as if he had remembered something important, he shot up out of his seat.

"I almost forgot—" He clutched his chest and whitened.

Hannah became alarmed. "Are you all right?"

"Yes. Didn't mean to give you a fright. It's something I should have mentioned when you first arrived, but I had pushed the unpleasantness out of my mind."

"What are you talking about?"

"Mrs. Hemming."

"What about her?" Hannah asked warily.

"Late on Friday evening she came down with the influenza. As she was checking out for the night, she dropped to the floor at the foot of the stairs." He swallowed hard. "She passed away before dawn."

For a full minute Hannah was too stunned to speak. "I thought the epidemic was over."

"She was probably one of the last victims. Wasn't that just like her to hold out to the bitter end?"

"I'm sorry," she said mechanically, and then reflected on how she did feel. She was not elated, but she was relieved. While the supervisor had been the cause of her difficulties, everyone knew that Mrs. Hemming had put in a heroic effort managing the onslaught of influenza cases. If there was a medal for civilian service, she would have been awarded it.

"There's going to be a service at the hospital next Friday. And . . ." He took a long breath. "Mrs. Church on the Board of Managers has proposed renaming the maternity section the Esmerelda Hemming Pavilion in her honor."

"I never knew her first name," Hannah commented somberly.

There was a clink as Emma placed her empty cup and saucer on the side table. "Put it on the tray," her mother instructed. "And take your brother's."

Emma looked as though she might balk, but she restrained herself admirably. They were good children. She was a lucky woman, she reminded herself, then turned to the doctor. He was watching her watching the children. The edges of his mouth curled. What was he thinking? Did he like them? Or were his thoughts more along the lines of hers: wishing they were not present.

The doctor cleared his throat. "Would you like to look at that book now?" Emma nodded. "See if you can find it. My books are in alphabetical order by author, except for the biographies. Do you know the author's name?"

"Lewis Carroll."

"Very good. Now, Benjamin, what sort of book might interest you?"

"Anything about airplanes, sir."

"Do you like them?"

Emma laughed. "That's all he thinks about. He's keeping a list of the aeronautical records."

"Are you? What do you think of that plane that went between Paris and London a few weeks ago?"

"The *Goliath!* Just think, it only took three and a half hours to go between the two countries. Do you know what that means?" Dr. Dowd shook his head. "It means that in the future this will be the way everybody will choose to get around," he said breathlessly. "Soon they'll be building bigger and bigger planes, and by the time I am grown, flying will be as common as taking a train."

"Oh, really!" His sister groaned at his exaggeration.

"Well, it might happen," the doctor allowed. "Anyway, my son had a book on the Wright Brothers. A tall, slender volume under *W*, I believe. Have a look."

With the children occupied, the doctor stood and came to sit on a chair closer to Hannah. He spoke in a voice that was one step above a whisper. "I have been considering how to see you again. I have been so alone."

Hannah's first reaction was to reject him, the second to embrace him. She did neither. At last she managed to say, "I know about loneliness."

"I mean, I want to see you again. To have dinner. At the Brevoort. Might that be possible?"

What was he asking? To have dinner, yes, but his yearning was so palpable she knew it would lead to more. She wanted it to lead to more . . . The doctor cleared his throat. Hannah looked up. The children had found their books and were sitting close by.

"Yes, we must go over some of the recent research," he

was saying to cover himself. "I hope we can do it one evening next week. Would Tuesday be convenient?"

"I think so," Hannah answered uneasily, because she felt a profound distress at acquiescing. Glancing away from him, she made a point of looking out the window. The sky was darkening. Standing, she announced, "We've got to be going."

"Oh, Ma!" Emma complained as she looked up from the book.

"You may borrow the books," the doctor said. Hannah shook her head. "Why not? You can return them when I see you in a few days."

"We'll be careful," Emma promised.

Hannah's shrug was her way of relenting.

In the foyer, the maid brought their coats. When Emma had hers on, she spun around and said, "I do so love it here! When I grow up I want to live in a house just like this one!"

Because Hannah was in the doctor's direct line of vision, she could not escape seeing the expression on his face. It could be read as clearly as if it had been printed on a page: why don't you come live here now? For a moment he closed his eyelids, as if to block out the impossible wish.

Unaware of her mother's acute embarrassment, Emma pointed at the double doors leading into the drawing room, now ajar. "Did you notice the beautiful piano, Mother?"

Grateful for the diversion, Hannah walked closer and peered into the room. It was dark, but she saw a grand piano. The doctor came behind her and switched on the light. The room glittered.

"That's the gold room," Benny explained redundantly.

"It's beautiful," she admitted aloud, then thought: I could never, ever feel at home in a place like this!

"Do you like to play the piano?" the doctor asked Emma.

"Oh, yes."

"She doesn't play," Hannah apologized.

"Yes, I do," Emma insisted.

"Emma!"

"I learned last summer at the settlement house."

"Please," the doctor gestured. "Would you like to try?"

"She's already dressed to go out," Hannah retorted uneasily.

"A quick song. She would like her mother to hear what she has learned, wouldn't you, Emma?"

With her head held high, Emma went to the piano. She unbuttoned her coat and sat down. Placing her fingers precisely on the keys, she tried a few tentative notes. They rang purely in the still room. "What shall I play?" she asked.

" 'Over There,' " said Benny, who was the only one who knew her repertoire.

She banged out the favorite war song a bit pedantically, but did not miss a note. Hannah was pleasantly surprised.

At the end the doctor clapped. "Very good, Emma. How about one more?"

"We've got to be going . . ."

Ignoring her mother, Emma began a few soft notes that Hannah did not recognize at first. What was she playing? What did it remind her of? The day in the park. When Lulu Morse had sung. It was a clumsy version of "Ah! Sweet Mystery of Life." Hannah should have told Emma not to continue, but she did not. With a sideways glance she watched the doctor's reaction. He did not seem to notice Hannah. He was staring off at the far side of the room. Hannah followed his gaze to a portrait over a mantel. This was not Lulu. It must be his first wife. So far Hannah had not seen any signs of Lulu, but then she had not gone on the house tour. Fortunately, Emma did not play more than one chorus of the song. She looked up. The doctor managed to compose himself enough to applaud and praise her again.

Emma realized she had pushed her luck far enough. She stood and closed the keyboard cover. "Thank you for letting me play your piano, Dr. Dowd."

"It is I who thank you," he replied stiffly before he opened the front door himself and showed his unexpected guests out.

∽ **2** ∾

Thank goodness the doctor had suggested Tuesday. Thank goodness Hannah had not been stupid enough to put him off. She had only to wait through Sunday night, the whole of Monday, and Tuesday until six. Hannah doubted if she could

have delayed an hour longer. And thank goodness he had
said they would meet at the hotel. At least there she felt
more at ease than in his exotic surroundings.

The dinner in the hotel dining room went almost by rote.
She did not taste the food, and she could never recall what
passed her lips. There was only Wendell. He was with her
and she was with him. Both of them knew that this time it
was different. There was hardly any talk of Havelock Ellis
or patients, or even of Mrs. Hemming's demise and the
flurry about it at the hospital. They did not mention her children, or his. Or his wife. Or her husband. They must have
spoken, but if they did, she could not have summarized what
it had been about. The first words she did focus on was his
question, "Do you care for coffee?" and when she had said
that she did not, he had added, "Tea?"

"No, thank you. What about you?"

"I think not."

He took up his glass of wine and tried to sip, but the glass
was empty. He replaced the glass. "I have found I cannot
work at home in my study. Too many memories, if you
know what I mean. I stare out the window for hours. And of
course the hospital has too many distractions. The moment
I become immersed in my reading, an emergency develops.
Isn't that always the way?"

"Always."

"So a wise friend suggested a change of scene. He
thought I needed an office, where nobody could bother me
and where I would not be troubled by my thoughts. What do
you think?"

"It sounds like a good idea."

"I delayed acting on his advice until yesterday, when I decided the time had come."

"What are you planning?"

"I've taken a room close enough to my home to walk, yet
far enough that I can be undisturbed." He had been folding
and refolding his napkin. Now he placed it out of reach and
talked with his hands gripping the table edge. "Also, I have
decided to spend more time on research. I have so many
ideas to pursue, not to mention several successes that I have
not yet written up. Really, it is a disservice to my colleagues
not to disseminate them. I plan to tackle them first, but I will
require some assistance with some of my other projects." He
leaned toward her. "Would you consider helping me?"

"I'd like to, but—"

"Of course you would be paid."

Hannah bristled. She did not want his charity. Then she softened. Hadn't he written a paper on Mrs. Applebaum for which she had received no payment or credit? "What do you want to research?"

"We could discuss it later, when I show you my new office."

"Where is it?"

"Upstairs. I have taken a room in this hotel." Though Hannah's eyes registered alarm, he plunged on. "They're usually three-fifty a night, but I made a deal for fifty dollars for the month. Here I think I can do my work without interruption." He paused, then blurted, "Would you care to see it?"

"I suppose . . ." she replied hesitantly.

He stood.

She stood. And followed him.

Without another word they took the elevator to the second floor. He led her to Room 202. There was a desk. There were books and papers in neat stacks, but then he would not have had time to have done more than move in. There were chairs on both sides of the desk, a table with another chair, new notebooks and pens set up for an assistant. And pushed over into the corner was a small bed, large enough for one person. The pillows had been arranged like those on a sofa. An open door led to another room. From the shiny tile she assumed it was a bathroom. She walked around the desk and went inside. She closed the door. She emptied her bladder. She came out and into the doctor's outstretched arms.

When she opened her eyes again she felt the room swirling around her. Her legs could barely support her as he maneuvered her toward the bed. She unbuttoned her skirt while he worked on the tiny clasps of her blouse.

"Oh, my darling, my sweet darling, sweet beautiful darling . . ." he said with a shudder when he saw her breasts, then fell on them with passionate kisses of gratitude. "At last . . ." he exhaled as he unfastened his trousers.

Not every piece of clothing came off, but enough to bare his chest and hers. Enough for his organ to swing out from any encumbrance and her legs to open for him. There was a moment of hesitation when neither knew who should make the next move. Somehow she decided to clasp him with her

hand and offer herself to him. After that he took over with
a long, deep plunge. He flailed for a moment, as if he were
drowning, then his head snapped back for a gasp of air. She
arched upward to bring him into her depths, and he recipro-
cated, this time with slow, deliberate strokes. Soon Hannah
was moaning. He stopped to brace himself on his elbow.
With his free hand he stroked her expertly until she pushed
his hand away to make room for her legs to clasp him
around his waist.

"There! There!" she called triumphantly.

Her hands flew up to his neck and she held on tightly as
he shuddered into her. They collapsed into a tangle of clothing.

Wendell caressed her hand and kissed her fingers reverently. "You're not sorry, are you?"

"No," she whispered. Then, as if she had agreed with
herself, she echoed more forcefully, "No. I wanted you."

"We should have been more careful. I was prepared, but
I forgot . . ."

"I did not."

"What?"

"I did not forget." She turned her head at the confession.
"I wore my Dutch cap."

Wendell looked at her with undisguised admiration.
"You're wonderful, do you know that?"

"You are."

"I have dreamed about this, then I warned myself not to
expect it. I could only hope that someday . . . I did not believe it would be today. Nevertheless, I was willing to take
however long it required."

"I could see no purpose in waiting."

"That's what I love about you, Hannah, you don't shirk
from the truth. Another woman might have found a way to
make it seem it was the man's fault she was led astray."

"I have not strayed. I am where I want to be."

"You put me to shame."

"Why?"

"I have been brought up to believe that everything important must be couched in obscure terms, that an indirect route
is always better than a direct one."

"I don't understand."

"That way, if something does not go the way you planned,

you can always change directions. If you confront the matter head on, you might get your face smashed."

"Or kissed." Hannah leaned toward him and offered her cheek.

Overcome with emotion, he began to tremble. Hannah fumbled with the bed cover, but it was impossible to lift with them on top.

"I'm not cold."

"I know. I wanted to do something."

He looked over at the disarray. "I think we had better either dress or undress."

"What time is it?"

He found his trousers and reached into the pocket for his watch. "Almost ten."

"I need to be going."

"Who's with the children?"

"My sister-in-law. You remember her, don't you?"

"The birth controller?"

"Yes."

"I liked her."

"She thinks you saved my life."

"I didn't."

"Maybe not that night, but tonight you did. I think I was dying inside."

"From my vast medical knowledge I may attest to the fact that you are very much alive." He cupped her naked breast and she quivered. "Very much . . ."

She stirred as if she were about to sit up. He pinned her down and licked the delta of her throat. "We'll be quick," he muttered in her ear.

Hannah did not disagree. Had she ever had such rapidly cresting sensations? Her hand drifted to his penis. He was as ready as she was. This time she mounted him. He kept his hands on her breasts, squeezing, pumping. And when she lowered herself closer, he began to suck on her nipples in the most exquisite rhythm. In minutes—or was it seconds?— she climaxed. He took a bit longer, which was fine with her, since she managed a second, even more voluptuous orgasm that seemed to astonish him.

Then, when she was certain he was content, she hurried to the bathroom to clean herself and dress. In the mirror she saw a woman transformed. The flushed face of a much younger girl smiled back at her. All her worry lines had vanished, and her green eyes had the sparkle of polished emeralds. There was something else, the appearance of a robustness she had not seen in years.

Wendell opened the door gently. "May I?" He kissed her neck and redid her fastenings, kissing her at every opportunity, until she pushed him away in mock annoyance.

"We did not get much work done tonight," he said petulantly.

"I must apologize for my lack of diligence."

"See that it does not happen again, Mrs. Sokolow."

"On the contrary, I hope that it does, Doctor."

"And when would you like to disobey me again?"

"I might be able to get away on Thursday, if we can meet earlier."

"I will see if I can fit you in," he said, his eyes shining like a man suffering from a terrible fever.

∽ 3 ∽

What a glorious year! 1919. Hannah liked the symmetry of the numbers. She liked the world at peace. She liked the hospital's normal routine—without Mrs. Hemming refolding the linen. She liked the early spring, which began the first week of March. Already buds on the trees threatened to open. Carrie brought in branches with fuzzy berries on black stems and placed them in a vase on the reception counter.

Hannah touched the soft gray seeds. "What are those?"

"Pussy willows."

"Do they flower?"

"No, just this."

"Nice." Hannah stroked them again because she was amazed at their animal-like softness. Then she thought: Wendell would like these.

Carrie motioned toward Rachael's office. "The doctor was hoping to see you."

Hannah checked her appointments. Only three. Another day she might have been disappointed to have so few, but now she thought: Good, I can get home and have supper

with the children before meeting Wendell at the Brevoort.
Emma and Benny knew she had another part-time job doing
research with the doctor. They did not seem to mind. A few
days earlier Emma had asked her to invite the doctor to dinner.

"He wouldn't have time," Hannah explained.

"I think he would."

"He doesn't know Jewish food."

"He'll like your cooking, Ma."

"If that is a compliment, thank you, Emma, but the doctor
is too busy to come all the way across town."

"You should invite him anyway," she insisted.

"It's not necessary," she said to end the matter. Selfishly
she was unwilling to relinquish any of their few hours alone
at the hotel, but also she did not want to remind him that
Tompkins Square was so vastly different from Washington
Mews.

"Yes, it is!" Emma was insisting. "We were at his house,
so now it's our turn. That's only good manners."

Hannah looked up at her daughter. Emma was not being
impertinent, but her self-assured expression displeased her
mother. Why? Was it because Emma was making a study of
what was right and wrong by a standard she was learning at
school or the settlement house, a standard that was more
American than their own family's? She knew her children
had a thinly disguised disdain for some of their mother's
old-fashioned, or old-country, notions, but when Hannah
turned to Minna—much as she might have her mother—for
support, Minna defended the children. "Didn't you feel that
your mother didn't know what was happening? I certainly
did. Most children do. That's why they want to change the
world."

Hannah knew Minna had been right, but had said nothing.
It was different when it was your own children and you were
the subject of their criticism. Anyway, at least they approved
of Wendell. If ever there was a chance of staying with him
. . . well, she dared not think about that now.

"Good afternoon, Rachael," Hannah said, grinning
broadly.

The doctor returned the smile with an exaggerated show
of teeth. "The happy midwife."

Rachael knew, or rather suspected, something. Not that
she had been told. Hannah was not ready yet. She had been

"working with Wendell" for only a few weeks, but already Rachael had been informed about the research position as the reason she had to cut back some of her clinic hours. Rachael had not flinched. Nor had she asked any questions. "Are you working tonight?"

"For a few hours. We have some notes to go over."

"On the same subject?"

"Yes. He has been taking observations about vaginal lubrication during routine gynecological examinations. Also, on the same charts is the date of the last menstrual period. We are trying to determine whether there is a pattern of increased or decreased lubrication at different times in the cycle. He's fairly convinced that at ovulation, there is a different chemistry in the secretions, which could aid in conception."

"Where is this leading?" Rachael asked.

If there was a double meaning, Hannah let it slide. "There are several implications. One might be that an alteration in the constitution of the mucus might prevent conception. Wouldn't it be amazing if you could merely take a pill, so when sperm came in contact with the vagina, they would die?"

"It could work the other way around."

"What do you mean?"

"If you found the ideal time of the month, you could aid people who desired to bear a child but were not conceiving."

"That's true, but in my experience more women are worried about the other way around."

"You know what you and your Dr. Dowd should study?" the doctor suggested somewhat distractedly.

"What?" Hannah asked, purposely ignoring the "your Dr. Dowd."

"If there are days of the month that make it easier for a woman to become aroused."

"I'm sure there are, at least in my experience."

"When would it be?"

Hannah thought for a minute. With Wendell it made no difference. Anytime they were together they were both so excited they could not consider working until they had satisfied each other. They had even stopped wasting precious time having supper. Wendell had asked if it was all right if he had a tray sent up, and she readily agreed. But during the years of her marriage, she seemed to have been more receptive from the middle of the month on. Why was that? "I think that pelvic congestion builds up around the time of ovulation, then stays fairly high to the end of the month," she offered as a suggestion. "Once again the Jewish laws make it possible to copulate at the times when a woman is not only most fertile, but also most responsive."

"That's very interesting." Rachael stopped and ran her fingers through her disheveled curls. "I have been paying attention to my own peculiarities and have noticed that too. While I still don't have an orgasm every time, I usually do after the middle of the month. I wonder if other women are like me, and if they are— if they have the same problems— wouldn't it be a good idea to advise them to work on them at a time when they are more likely to succeed?"

"An excellent point, Doctor, but if I recall you aren't supposed to be analyzing everything." She gave a little chuckle to diffuse the admonishment. "You're supposed to be listening to music."

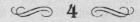

4

That day her cases were an interesting mix. Mrs. Alessandro, whom Hannah had delivered in her home the previous month, came in to complain that when she had an orgasm, milk spurted from her breasts. This she found shameful, and worse, she thought she was wasting the baby's supply. After Hannah assured her the breasts would make up the deficit, and gave her directions to wear a breast binder in bed, the woman seemed relieved.

"I thought there was something wrong with me," she said as she left.

"No, it's perfectly normal," Hannah repeated at the examining room door.

The same phrase was said again twice more that day. Once to Masha Speyer, whose husband had lost interest in her since returning from the war. Hannah counseled that he needed time to recover, even if he did not have any obvious injuries. "Be patient with him, but don't forget to let him know you love him," she added. "It's perfectly normal to take time to readjust."

The last one, Gussie Lansky, was a regular, since she had come for instructions on how to have a boy two years earlier. Subsequently, she had given birth to two boys and was a firm believer in Hannah's advice on everything from the proportions of carp in a gefilte fish recipe to how to toilet-train children. This time she wanted to talk about her husband's insistence that they have sex in various positions, some of which did not appeal to her. "It's not normal," she complained.

"Who says it's not?"

Gussie was silenced. "Then it is?"

"If both of you agree, and nobody is hurt, why not? Everybody needs a change once in a while. Better a change of position than a change of wife."

Gussie got the point.

Later, on the way to the Brevoort Hotel, the phrase "perfectly normal" echoed in Hannah's mind. Who knew what was normal? Who knew what most women did or felt or wanted? Doctors, and practitioners like her, did not see contented people with no problems. What did regular, happily married women experience? How often did they make love? How many had an orgasm? How often? Did they care whether they did or not? What positions were most popular with women, with men?

She met Wendell in the lobby. They had arrived at almost precisely the same time. "Good afternoon, Mrs. Sokolow," he greeted formally.

If the hotel staff suspected there was more to this than doctor and research assistant, they never let on. Certainly a casual guest would never have known. From time to time they had met people they knew in the lobby or restaurant, which was inevitable in the neighborhood where Dr. Dowd lived, and not far from Mrs. Dodge's old apartment. Once Hannah had run into Max Eastman, another time she had seen Floyd Dell. Max had said hello to her, Floyd had not. Later she was sorry she had not introduced the doctor. She had nothing to hide. Her family and associates knew of her work with him. Everybody had been informed—everyone, that is, except the staff at Bellevue. They had decided against that because they were even more afraid of professional envy than rumors.

The moment the door to their room closed, they removed their coats and hung them over their work chairs. Hannah went to the bathroom and came out in her underwear. Wendell lay on the bed, with the covers pulled down. The shades were drawn. Only the lamp on the desk was on. In the soft glow his erect penis demonstrated his readiness. She sat on the bed and he undid her corsets. He would fondle her and remove her panties at the last moment. He said he liked the mystery of it, and she liked what he liked. She would not touch him except with her lips, first on his mouth and then wherever he directed her. Somehow, without a word, they both would decide not to waste any more time, and soon they were joined, and would not release until each was spent. It was always the same. Yet always different.

Then in the flush of the aftermath, they would talk. She answered his questions, and he answered hers. He told her about his first wife, Mary Mathias Dowd. Her father had been an associate of his father, also a Wall Street banker, precisely the sort of capitalist exploiter Lazar had despised. Their marriage had been predetermined by the family. Young Mary and Wendell might have refused, but each had seen the sense in the alliance. Mary was delicate and sweet. Wendell was intelligent and well-bred. They lived in a house her father bought near Gramercy Park, next door to a matching house where her sister, Agnes, had lived. Agnes and Mary were interested in artistic pursuits and did volunteer work for the Metropolitan Museum. Then Agnes's husband, an attorney whose father had been a professor at Princeton when Woodrow Wilson was its president, had moved to Washington to serve in Wilson's justice department. After Mary's death, Wendell had met Lulu through one of Agnes's friends. Her name was really Lucille and she had come from an old Virginia family, but had hidden her traditional past. Lulu refused to live in Mary's old home, insisting on the Village, and Washington Mews in particular. Lulu had many other original ideas, including the one-color-to-a-room concept. Hannah was surprised to hear she had also advocated separate bedrooms—hers was mauve, his the shade of blue that matched his eyes. They would make "appointments" for sex, which Lulu felt kept intrigue in the marriage longer. Wendell had gone along with Lulu. "Well, if you did not, she made your life miserable; if you did, she made you happy, so I picked the obvious choice." Hannah found the description odd, but never reproached him. How could she? Anyone hearing the story of her own marriage would have had plenty of questions.

Wendell refrained from pumping her on that subject because he knew she had so few answers. He could read the newspapers as well as she could. He had told her that his brother-in-law in the government had inside information about the Russian civil war that might be helpful, but Hannah had not asked him for any specifics. Sometimes he probed gently about what she wanted for the future, but he did not press her. Her response would be kisses to remind him of her love for him, nothing more.

After their time in each other's arms, they would dress. Then they would have a bite of supper, and slowly their conversation would turn to their work. Hannah would read from a file while he marked the master chart. Sometimes they would discuss an interesting case or pose a problem. That night Hannah asked the question she had been mulling over.

"What is normal?" she posed.

"This," he said, kissing her cheek. "What could be more normal than this?"

They were sitting on the bed, made up with pillows behind their backs, and the files were strewn in piles around them. So much cozier than working at a desk, even if less was accomplished. She gave him a friendly shove. "Actually, there is probably nothing normal about two sensible people meeting like this."

"I disagree. The reason we meet is to put normalcy in our absurdly abnormal lives. And why do we do so? Because we are constricted by the petty rules that govern supposedly civilized behavior. I would like nothing more than to see you in the comfort of my own home—or yours."

"That's not possible," she said sadly.

"At least not yet."

What did he mean? Hannah wanted to inquire further, but this was one exploration she rejected, since there were more questions about her status than his. She knew he wanted to know what Lazar's plans were, and then, no matter her answer he would ask her what she intended to do about it. What could she do? She knew there was a legal step called divorce. Recently Rachael had mentioned—supposedly in reference to something else—that in the case of abandonment this would be possible. However, was she truly deserted, or was the problem the difficulty of communications during wartime? Wives of men who had gone to war did not consider themselves abandoned, even if they were away for many years . . . even if they were missing in action. Yet her situation was different. Or was it? If she had assumed Lazar was coming back to her, would she have permitted this—she preferred to think of it as an "alliance"—or would she have remained loyal to him? And was he loyal to her? What if when she did hear from him, he refused to return to America and begged her to come to live in Russia? These questions tumbled around in Hannah's mind like tangled yarn until she could not sort the end from the beginning. One thing she did know was she would never go to Russia. Not now during the civil war, not later, even if the people's state were to become the paradise on earth the believers expected. But if he voluntarily returned to her . . .

She smiled at Wendell. He smiled back with the contentment of a man at peace with himself. She knew she made him happy. But did he make her happy? Yes. He did. Did she love him? Yes. She did. As much as Lazar? reverberated in her mind. No, it was different. How different? She had spent many a long night struggling to sort this out.

Lazar was her husband, the father of her children. She had known him as a child, when he had been the friend of her older brother. They were both Russian Jews. They knew Odessa and the tribulations of their friends and family. They had suffered through the emigration—and so much more— together. Love was more than an abstraction, it was shared hours, days, and years. He understood her better than anyone could, even a professional like Dr. Dowd. He had been a friend as well as a lover. Yet despite everything, he had left her for another calling. What kind of love was that?

"Is something wrong?" Wendell asked.

"Why do you ask?"

"I can't read that remote look."

She clasped his hand. "I was far away. Trying to look into the future."

"And did you see me there?"

"I wanted you to be, but I could not focus on how it would work out."

"We could marry," he said, more in the tone of a logical supposition than a question.

"It's hard to believe . . ." she replied to avoid any direct queries about Lazar. If he began, she would turn the tables, for she could not imagine finding acceptance in his world. His first wife had been exactly the sort his family had expected, and although Lulu had been somewhat unconventional, her background had been more than acceptable. The Dowds would never approve of her: the divorced wife of a Red revolutionary who was Trotsky's aide; a Jewess with two children; a lowly midwife with minimal education; an abandoned woman with debts; the sister of an anarchist publisher; the sister-in-law of a convicted criminal; an advocate of birth control; an expert in giving advice to people with sexual problems. Was there ever a less suitable candidate to become Mrs. Wendell Dowd?

"What's so funny?"

She repeated her last thought. "Was there ever a more unsuitable candidate to become Mrs. Wendell Dowd?"

"They didn't approve of Lulu."

"Then 'they' certainly won't approve of me."

"I don't care what they think."

"I would. Even on the job I pretended not to notice the slights about my religion, or the whispers when Minna was in jail, and now I try to ignore the stories about why Lazar left. Someone like you, who has always belonged to a privileged society, cannot know how it feels."

"Together we can work it out."

"We'll see . . ." was all she would allow. To protect against more useless speculation, she picked up a chart and made a show of studying it. "Here's a woman who has been married almost a year, but you noted she had a very small vagina, which measured like that of an unmarried woman. I wonder what is happening in that marriage? Or is there a sexual problem? Do most newlyweds have sex frequently, or are they cautious? What is normal?"

"You'll never know unless you ask those questions."

"To whom?"

"To enough people to give you a statistical sample."

"What's that?"

"Say you wanted to know how frequently married people have sexual intercourse. You might ask one thousand men and women. If one hundred reported once a week, you would know that ten percent have it that often. If three hundred reported twice a week, you would know that thirty percent fit in that category."

"What is normal, though?"

"I suppose you would define it as what the majority of the people do. Let's say that the largest category is the thirty percent who do it twice a week, then that would be normal. Maybe another ten percent do it a bit more or less frequently. That would add up to fifty percent, or a 'normal range' of one to three times a week."

"Once a month or once a day would then be abnormal?"

"Well, I would not go so far as to say that, but it would be out of the normal range. If people were happy with their lot, however, it would be 'normal' for them and of no concern to anyone else. If they were discontented, it might help them to know that a bit more effort to do it more frequently might please their partner, or waiting a night or two to give the woman a rest might mollify her."

"Who says women need a rest?"

"That's the complaint I hear."

"Not from me."

"No, my darling, not from you." He bent over to kiss her and the folder slipped from her lap to the floor.

≋   5   ≋

They had a "work schedule." Mondays, Wednesdays, and Fridays at the Brevoort Hotel. Tuesdays and Thursdays they agreed to have brief meetings—just to see each other—in his office. This alerted nobody, since in the past they had consulted regularly, and without Mrs. Hemming, Hannah became the liaison to the medical staff. There was even talk of Hannah being offered Mrs. Hemming's position.

"It will never happen. No midwife, especially a Jewish one, would be qualified."

"Don't be ridiculous," Wendell responded. "Many of the most respected doctors on staff are Jewish."

"You know as well as I do that the Board of Managers is made up of society ladies."

"Exactly. Women with hearts as big as their bank books.

They care only for the efficient management of the hospital."

"They'll select one of their own," she predicted. "You'll see."

The doctor's comment, a tired sigh, meant he would not argue with her.

Hannah looked forward to Tuesdays and Thursdays almost as much as the rest of the week. She needed to touch him, to hear his voice. Being with him in the same room was enough—well, almost enough. Best of all, he felt the same about her. Both of them were filled with stories they wanted to share about patients, family, even the weather. There was always a rush of words until they were caught up. Weekends were the hardest. Maybe he could stroll over for a few hours' work at the Brevoort, but what could she say to Minna, to her children?

"Monday seems so far away," Wendell said one Friday evening. "Why don't we meet and have lunch with Benjamin and Emma? I would like to see them again."

"And they you. Emma has a song she would like to play for you, and Benny has a new hero."

"Who's that?"

"Some crazy man who said a trip to the moon by rocket may someday be possible."

"Oh, that professor of physics at Clark University, Robert Goddard. He's not crazy."

"Everybody's laughing and calling him the 'moon man.' "

"Benny's not laughing, and I'm not either. Before the armistice, he demonstrated three practical rocket models to the army."

"Anyway, it's impossible."

"Which? Going to the moon or having lunch with me?"

"If you had lunch with us, Benny would suspect, so might Emma, but you may be right about the moon."

"At least I won one point." He offered his most winsome smile. "But I do think you are being too cautious. After all, the children know we work together and are friends, if for no other reason than I supposedly saved your life."

"They're smarter than that. Right after we came to your house they were badgering me to have you to dinner. Emma said you would like my cooking."

"I am sure I would."

"Don't you see why you can't come?"

"No, frankly I don't."

"They want you too much. They miss having a father. They would like a replacement. In fact, I think they would like to select the replacement for me."

"What could be better? I've had it both ways, so I know."

"What do you mean?"

"When I met Lulu, Denny—that's what we call Wendell, Jr., in the family—took to her at once. Daphne despised her. I think she was jealous. I'd been widowed for six years, and of course she never knew her mother. She wasn't willing to share me."

"How did it work out?"

"The first months were difficult, but Lulu was clever. She did not interfere with Daphne's nurse, and acted more like a big sister than a mother. Also, whenever I was around she made certain to stay in the background. Daphne sat next to me at supper, and I tucked her in on the nights I was home. Of course, Lulu was often out with her singing and such, so we came to an equable arrangement."

"You make it seem rather idyllic."

"Do I? Any parent knows both the joys and strains of raising children, but they do better with two parents because each one has his or her foibles. The other parent helps modify the extremes. While I am certain you are a devoted mother, I can see where yours might benefit from some male supervision."

"You don't have to tell me that my children need their father."

"That's not what I am saying."

Hannah regretted her outburst, but did not apologize. "I don't think it is fair to confuse them."

"An outing to the park would not ruin their lives. At least we could be together." His voice rose with longing, which made Hannah even more reluctant to refuse him, yet she put him off by saying maybe another time. And so they suffered through the lonely weekends, knowing that Monday at six they would be in each other's arms.

Nevertheless, the Monday after their "normalcy" discussion, Hannah had to inform the doctor she would not be able to meet him. She caught him after his last surgery of the day, just before she was leaving for the clinic, and told him that Minna and Chaim were going out.

"Aren't the children old enough to stay alone?"

"Not at night, and not with so much agitation going on."

He did not argue with her. Since the end of the war there had been terrible repercussions against pro-Russian sympathizers. Because everyone knew Lazar's unpopular political position, she feared for her children. Maybe all they would hear were a few taunts, but there were stories of rocks tossed through windows, even stray bullets. She dared not expose them to any more than she already had, and certainly she could not be in bed with the doctor, for if anything happened . . .

That night Minna and Chaim went to a meeting on the very subject of political repression. John Reed was speaking. By now Minna knew better than to insist Hannah come along. While she did not understand Hannah's vow to stay away from lectures of any sort, she did sense that political strife reminded her of Lazar.

"There might be some fresh information . . ." was Minna's final salvo before leaving, in case she wanted to change her mind.

"You know I don't want to leave the children alone" was her final excuse. "Come up and tell me when you are home."

Minna coughed lightly. "It might be late."

"I have a lot of reading to do. I'll be awake."

"You've been working too hard. Three jobs. I don't know how you do it."

"I like to stay busy, but I like the money even more. By next week I will be caught up on the rent."

"That's better than we are doing."

Hannah decided this was a good moment to mention what had been worrying her. "Are you going to stay in Mama's flat?"

"Yes. The printing shop is too damp. After a whole day there my bones ache. Also, when Rachael told Chaim that I was at risk for respiratory infections, like the flu, that settled it. We're looking for someone to work part-time in exchange for the Chrystie Street rooms. Chaim thinks he has someone, so that will help with the rent here—if Napthali doesn't raise it."

"He won't."

"No, he's a good mentsh. Do you think Eva knows how lucky she is?"

"She does."

The sisters-in-law were silent as each contemplated the irony of the discussion. Napthali had once been Minna's intended, now he was her landlord. The two of them were in political opposition, yet there was never an ill word between them. Both realized that, in the end, they had made the best possible match.

"Anyway, let me know when you're home safely," Hannah said to break the tension.

"You're worried about us?"

"Yes, and I have reason to be. They say Reed requires guards, or he would be shot down in the street."

"That's ridiculous," Minna replied steadfastly. "You just want to hear the news from Russia."

Hannah shrugged. She could not deny it. Better to know than not to know. She could not go on in the dark forever.

 **6**

Hannah was dozing when she heard the footsteps on the stairs. Her light was still on, so Minna tapped on the door.

"Come in, it's open."

Minna went into the bedroom. "We're back."

"How was it?"

"You were right."

"About what?"

"The meeting was guarded by about a hundred policemen."

"What did he have to say that was so inflammatory?"

"Actually, Reed tried to defuse the audience. He spoke like an American patriot."

Hannah gave a disparaging laugh. "That's a joke!"

"No, not really" came Chaim's whispered voice.

Hannah startled. "I did not hear you come in."

Chaim held up his shoes. "I didn't want to wake the children."

Hannah patted the bed. "So, tell me."

Chaim sat on one side, Minna the other. Hannah smiled at

them. She liked the company, even at that late hour . . . especially at that late hour.

"Well, he tried to argue that the Soviet system was actually more democratic than the American government, at least at this time," Chaim said.

"What nonsense!" Hannah laughed. "Anything else?"

Minna signaled her husband by lifting her eyebrows.

Chaim patted her leg through the blankets. "Also, John asked to speak to me afterward."

"Yes?" Hannah asked loudly to drown out the pounding of her impertinent heart.

"He said, 'Tell your sister that if she wants to know where her husband is, she must first find the train.' "

"What train?"

"The train of the *Predrevoyensoviet,* of the Chairman of the Revolutionary Military Council: Trotsky's train."

"What's he doing on there?"

"Lazar is recording Trotsky's movements. Apparently the new war commissar has gone to the people in an attempt to cement the ideals of the October revolution."

Hannah lay back and closed her eyes.

Minna asked, "Do you want us to leave?"

"No, not yet . . . I was thinking about Lazar living on a train. How long do you think he's been there?"

"Many months probably," Chaim answered softly. "That's why we've lost touch with him."

"How can they live like that?"

"Better than most men at the front, from what I hear. Trotsky has his own coach, which formerly had been used by one of the communications ministers, so I assume it has the required comforts." Chaim took a long breath, then continued, "And they carry every sort of support that a commissar would need—from a telegraph station to an automobile garage."

"The train is so heavy that it requires two engines," Minna interjected. "When they stop at one section of the front, one engine does service as a courier, the other is always under steam, because the front is shifting constantly, and they can't take any chances."

"He's in danger then, isn't he?" Hannah asked slowly.

"Lazar is at the vanguard of the civil war, yes, but most of the train is armored, at least its engines, machine-gun cars, and probably the ones in which Trotsky and his staff reside, and I've been told the crew can all handle arms."

"Do they see much action?"

"Don't worry, Lazar keeps in the background," Minna said in a rush. "He would never be anyone's target."

"Yes, but what if Trotsky was the target and they hit him by mistake?"

"Hannah, you can't think like that," Minna retorted firmly. "You must plan your life independently of him."

"How can I? I am a wife but not a wife! Did he realize what he was doing to me by leaving? No! Does he care even now? No!"

"Even more reason to follow your own mind . . ." Chaim's eyes narrowed. ". . . And your own heart," he added with a knowing edge. "Nobody will think the less of you."

"I don't care what others think," she said with more confidence than she felt.

⤛ 7 ⤜

"I get to be the first to tell you," Dr. Dowd said as they strolled down Fifth Avenue one evening in April. They had both arrived earlier than usual. Wendell had suggested they take advantage of the pleasant evening, and even though Hannah was anxious to go upstairs, she had acquiesced.

"Tell me what?" she said, clasping his arm a degree more tightly.

"The Board of Managers of Bellevue Hospital has voted to ask you to fill Mrs. Hemming's appointment."

Hannah stopped. "I don't believe it."

"I told you this might happen."

"Did you have anything to do with it?"

"Not as much as I would have liked. I was merely consulted."

"And what did you say? Did you threaten to resign if I was not selected?" she teased.

"On the contrary. I told them I had reservations."

"You didn't!"

"I most certainly did, because I *do* have reservations."

"About my abilities?"

"No, about their claim on your valuable time—and mine."
He brushed her cheek with the back of his hand. "You cannot do everything. I know you enjoy your work at the clinic,
and even though the position will about equal that compensation, there you make more—shall we say?—of an original
contribution than you would at the hospital."

"What about my contribution to our research project?"

"My thoughts exactly."

"As I recall, Mrs. Hemming did not work evenings. Hers
was purely a daytime supervisory role, except in periods of
emergency, like the flu epidemic."

"You sound as if you want the job."

"What did you say when you were offered the chairman
of the department? You were reluctant to take on the additional responsibility, but you could not turn down the pres-
tigious offer. It's the same for me."

"And something more . . ."

"Yes, well, it is a vindication, isn't it?"

He beamed at her. "So, you have chosen."

"No, I have some reservations myself. I cannot give the
hospital a full week without giving something up."

"They are prepared to be flexible. Mostly they want a supervisor, not an active midwife. You would have to relinquish most of your hands-on maternity care, and I think that
would include your private home deliveries."

"I have seven women due in the next three months, but I
could refuse to take on new clients after that. With our . . .
project, I had come to that conclusion anyway."

Wendell continued their stroll south toward the Washington Square arch. "Have you thought how the position could
enhance our research?"

"No. What do you mean?"

"Remember your questions about what is normal? Well, I
have been thinking . . . What if you were to make a list of
questions and ask them to hundreds of women who had just
delivered a baby at Bellevue? You would get a splendid
cross-section of women from different backgrounds, then
you could publish the results."

"You mean *you* could publish them," she said in an accusing tone.

"Haven't you forgiven me for that?"

"Not entirely," she said lightly yet truthfully. "I understand why you did it, but you should have conferred with me first."

"You're right. *Mea culpa*. I hardly knew you then, and frankly I was afraid of what you would say."

"You were afraid of me?" She gave a high laugh.

"Most men are afraid of women. It's one of our darkest secrets. And especially women who know as much about men as you do."

They were standing on the corner of 9th Street. Hannah looked up into the windows of Mrs. Dodge's old apartment. She had moved away during the war. "I remember when I first saw you there."

"Me too. I think I knew then there would be something between us. Did you?"

"Of course not!" she said, then wondered if that was the whole truth. To turn the discussion, she added, "Mrs. Dodge certainly liked to have a collection of shabby radicals to amuse her fancy friends, didn't she?"

"Didn't you like her?"

"I guess I did. She was kind to me. Once she had me and Minna to lunch with Margaret Sanger. In fact, that's how Minna met Margaret."

"That's what I love about you! You always amaze me." Then his voice became more husky. "What shall we do now?"

With the sun setting she was acutely aware that their time was running out. "The usual would be fine with me."

He gave an exaggerated sigh. "You are a tough taskmaster. I pity the poor midwives and nurses who will come under your command."

Their pace quickened. They entered the Brevoort with purposeful strides, like two delayed professionals anxious to catch up on work. The door closed to Room 202. And they began in earnest.

8

Hannah accepted the position as Mrs. Hemming's replacement. She had welcomed the few hours' advance notice, as well as the doctor's advice about what she might and might not request. They were eager to have her and had expected her reduced schedule, demanding only that she be available for every board meeting, that she work full days on Mondays to set up the week's schedule, and cover for any head midwife incapacitated due to illness for more than three days. Hannah asked that her title be changed from Supervisor of Midwifery to Supervisor for Obstetrics.

"The doctors might object to that," Mrs. Warren Schyler worried.

"I don't see why," Hannah countered, "when this supervisor reports to the Board of Managers, which does not control the medical departments."

"I have no problem with the change, so long as it is approved by Dr. Dowd," Mrs. Clayborn Church, the new assistant chair, added.

"I certainly would not want to displease Dr. Dowd," Hannah agreed. "Let's have him make that decision."

"Very wise," commented Mrs. Rosenthal, a Jewish woman recently appointed to the board.

"I have an additional appeal," Hannah added after they had come to an agreement about duties and hours. "As you may know, I have been assisting Dr. Dowd in his medical research. He is in need of additional information that is not usually asked during routine examinations, so to amass a large enough sample, he has suggested that I organize a survey of patients. Might I have your permission to interview new mothers?"

"Would you be conducting examinations as well?" Mrs. Rosenthal asked.

"As I understand it, there would merely be a list of questions—some of an intimate nature—and these would be asked during the postpartum period."

"Such a survey would have to be voluntary," the chair reminded.

"Of course."

"And Dr. Dowd would supervise you on this?" Mrs. Schyler inquired, leaning forward.

"He would have to. The results would be published by him."

"What if a woman was willing to participate, but did not wish to answer a particular question?" Mrs. Schyler continued.

Hannah sensed that this woman was opposed to the idea. "We could hardly force anyone to respond. The most important point would be to get truthful answers. So I would assume they would have to be asked in a spirit of trust."

Mrs. Schyler made some notes on her pad. "Who would ask them?"

"I would, or maybe I could train some others, depending on my schedule."

Mrs. Rosenthal turned to Mrs. Schyler. "I have confidence in Mrs. Sokolow's discretion."

"I do too," continued Mrs. Schyler haughtily. "Thus I withdraw my objections, if she is the sole interviewer."

"Does that meet with your approval?" asked the chair.

Hannah had won so many points already, she was not about to push her luck. "Absolutely. I am pleased to be of service to the Board of Managers and Bellevue Hospital in my new capacity."

⋘ 9 ⋙

What first amazed Hannah about her new position was that she did not miss delivering babies. As head midwife she had already taken one step away from routine care, thus this next one was not much of a leap. She saw laboring mothers and newborn babies every day, so that was a comfort, but what she enjoyed was analyzing how to make the experience better for every patient. The maternity-clock plan returned in a modified form with the beds kept in a row so the wards could accommodate fourteen to sixteen beds. More were necessary since record numbers of post-war babies were expected. Also, Hannah developed a new checklist to help ascertain who was at higher risk. Certain characteristics, like bleeding or high blood pressure, carried a high number on a scale of one to five. The admitting midwife added up the numbers, and if the score was high, she placed the problem case in the new high-risk ward, which was staffed with the most senior midwife, a junior assistant, two nurses, and at least one midwifery student. Problems that developed anytime until the actual delivery also were transferred there. Only routine births—which composed the vast majority—were completed in the regular wards.

In a few weeks Hannah reported to the board on the new system. "What we are developing is a standardized treatment for complications. The midwives in Ward A are becoming experts since they are seeing, say, a preeclamptic, every few days instead of every few weeks or months. Also, our supervising physicians, whose time is limited, make the rounds to that ward more regularly to advise us."

"Does that not create two classes of midwives: those trained to handle more difficulties, and those who can only handle the routine?" asked Mrs. Schyler.

"The younger midwives are being rotated through Ward A as assistants. They will pick up the skills from those with more experience. However, I must admit my bias is what's the best care for a particular mother and child, not what enhances the career of the midwife. A woman with a complication requires the finest we can give her."

"Unless we have mortality or morbidity statistics," Mrs. Hubert LaSalle, the eldest member of the board, offered, "we cannot judge how the new system is working. Until proven otherwise, however, it makes sense to me."

The nodding of heads around the table buoyed Hannah.

More informal reports were made to Dr. Dowd on Tuesdays and Thursdays. One afternoon she presented a case of a patient's failure to progress in labor. "You know how I am usually reluctant to call in the troops," she began. "Well, this time I felt it was time to summon a physician to employ forceps, but Norma Marshanck, who was in charge of the case, wanted to wait."

"Always a sensitive problem for an administrator," Wendell commented sympathetically.

"But from the beginning I saw the writing on the handwall."

His expression soured. "The handwriting on the wall!" he boomed. "Why don't you watch what you are saying? You've been in this country long enough!"

Hannah trembled with the affront. She hated it most when he brought up her immigrant deficiencies. It wasn't as though she did not try to use the right word. He should have to practice medicine in a different country from where he trained! The doctor turned away to compose himself. In a moment the cloud passed.

"I am hearing outstanding comments about you," he began again in a smooth, controlled tone. "The doctors are in favor of your new systems because it means less work for them. They are impressed with your efficiency."

"Then why don't they ever smile?" Hannah said, fully conscious that he was due a well-directed barb.

"What do you mean?"

"It's something I have been noticing. They stand out in the corridors talking with one another, often joking, but as soon as they encounter a midwife or a patient, their faces sour." She gave a demonstration of an animated expression forced into solemnity.

He laughed. "Do they really? Where did they get that from?"

"They are afraid of women, remember? They think they must be dignified, or they will betray their fear."

"What shall I say to them?"

"That it is all right to show emotions, so long as they are sincere."

"You're serious about this."

"Indeed I am. If a woman tenses up because a doctor is around, her labor becomes more difficult. Relaxation is the key to an easy delivery."

The doctor shook his head. "I'll see what I can do. Now, how are your survey questions coming along?"

"I think I have far too many."

"Let me see." She handed him the notebook. "Name, address, birth date, height and weight. Do you think you should solicit their names?"

"How else will I know who is who?"

"Might they not give more forthright answers if they

thought that once they left the hospital they would be anonymous?"

"Yes, but if they came in later with a condition we wanted to study, how could we match them up with the charts?"

"Every admission's chart has a number. We could code the surveys with it for future reference."

"Then I'd be lying to the patient."

"Not exactly. For the purpose of the sex survey they would not be identified by anything except a number." Hannah saw the sense in this, so she merely nodded her assent. "Good, then let's proceed. You ask for the date of birth, but why not also the date of marriage? Sexual response might vary if the woman marries at sixteen, twenty, or thirty, don't you agree?"

"I don't see why."

"I don't either, but it might have significance. If it does, we'll find out; likewise if we don't."

Hannah smiled at Wendell. He was so intelligent and his vision was a splendid foil for her practicality.

"Number of pregnancies, good. Number of live born children, good. Number of children who have died, and their ages, good. Now, what about number of abortions?"

"Spontaneous miscarriage or illegal procedure?"

"Both."

"How can I ask that?"

"If they don't feel threatened, they might answer. Don't forget you're going to tell them it is all right to pass on a question. My guess is that if they feel they *may* skip one, they are more likely to answer truthfully. People prevaricate when they feel backed against a wall, at least that's my experience."

"Why ask it in the first place?"

"Well, we've always suspected the numbers who choose to terminate a pregnancy are far greater than those we can extrapolate from the predicaments we see, so it would be interesting to know, especially to match up with gynecological complications later."

"They might think that we will report them."

"At the beginning you must stress the confidentiality and the lack of names. Also, insist that the survey is for scientific, and no other, purposes." He paused and pursed his lips in a gesture Hannah knew meant he was reconsidering his position. "Why not ask the most intimate and worrisome

questions last? That way they won't be put off and stop co-
operating too early. I'd put the abortion question at the end,
and then couch it gently by inquiring, 'Have you ever miscarried before the baby was due?' Then, if they respond in
the affirmative, ask: 'Was that accidental or intentional?' in
an offhand, unthreatening way."

"I like the part about putting the hard ones last. That's
brilliant."

"Hardly," he said, although he glowed at the compliment.
He continued down the list. "Nothing about masturbation?"

"Well . . . I didn't know how to phrase it."

"You'd know better what to ask a woman than I would."

"I guess it ought to be included."

"Don't you want to know?"

"Yes."

"Then that should be your criteria." His finger tapped
each question on the list, then settled on one section. "Ah,
at least I can see you've been forthright about orgasm."

"I find that women are relieved to talk about it."

"I think they're more relieved to have it."

"Wendell!"

"Sorry." He stared down at the page. "So, you also
haven't shrunk from questions about contraception." He
gave a gutteral laugh. "But we have a problem here. Our
sample is composed of women who have just given birth.
One has to assume that those who have used contraception
successfully will not arrive in a postpartum bed."

"Oh, no! What can we do?"

"I'll see if we can add to our sample through the gynecology department."

"What about the limits set by the Board of Managers?"

"Let me worry about them, my dear."

"How many women are we going to need?"

"At least a hundred. A thousand would be perfect."

"I can't interview a thousand!"

"No, that's true. But we could print up a thousand forms,
and the literate could fill them out on their own."

"Let's start with a hundred that I interview and see how
it goes."

"I agree. That will form the basis for our appeal to do a
hospital-wide survey."

Hannah leaned back in her chair contentedly. Wendell
Dowd was always so reasonable. He made thoughtful deci-

sions based on many factors. He weighed his ideas, his words, and never acted on emotions—well, at least not when it came to his work. Even when they were together, she appreciated his levelness. Even though he sometimes had his querulous moments, unlike the volatile, argumentative Lazar, Wendell always sought a compromise. He was willing to listen to Hannah and often agreed she was right, or if he could not concede that much, he at least would admit that she had made a useful point. With him she never felt a loser or a winner, but a piece—a valued piece—of the whole.

Yet there were aspects of Lazar that she missed. Yes, their sexual life was satisfying, but sometimes she wondered whether their passion would be sustained if they woke up together every morning, for it seemed fueled by the forbidden—and limited—aspect of their situation. Wendell was gentle and precise. His professional knowledge of women was beneficial to his task. Yet he lacked the unpredictability, the rawness, the capriciousness of the mercurial Lazar.

In life there were always trades, such as the newness of the doctor compared with the familiarity of a longtime lover. Even now Hannah did not feel completely free with Wendell. She still did not like to undress in front of him, keeping the bathroom door firmly closed. And yet with Lazar sex had never been boring. Was there an innate response to their youthful affair which still triggered Hannah's excitement, or was there some special connection which had made her feel that sex with Lazar was as natural as breathing? In contrast, nothing felt as comfortable with Wendell. She was always on guard, tense, wary, and worried about discovery. If anyone at Bellevue ever became suspicious, the Board of Managers would have to let her go, this time for good. If they knew at home, the children would be injured. If the gossiping neighbors caught wind, it would be the end of her private practice. And yet what could she do about it? She first needed to know Lazar's plans, and this meant she would have to know what Trotsky was organizing, what the Red army was confronting, what the Whites were contemplating . . . Why did her future depend on events on far-off continents? Why could she not have a normal life like everyone else? She grinned absurdly.

"Why do I get the feeling you aren't paying attention to this survey?" Dr. Dowd asked sternly.

"You are not much of a mind reader. I was merely think-ing about normalcy and how it is defined."

"Oh, sorry," he said with a shrug. "Now where are we?"

Where are we, indeed? Hannah thought, and as she did so, she determined to find out.

~ 10 ~

She began by reading John Reed's new book about the Rus-sian revolution. Hannah stared at the title, *Ten Days That Shook the World,* and thought: ten days that shook *my* world. On every page she searched for mention of Lazar. There was none. And yet he was on every page. He had been there. In those rooms. On those streets. She knew he would have cho-sen to be no other place on earth, not even by her side.

The stab of realization passed as she tried to grapple with where he might be at the moment, and what this meant to her. Nobody really knew what was happening inside Russia. The reports in the Yiddish press confused her because they contrasted with the English ones.

She went downstairs with military questions for Chaim. "You don't really care about the maneuverings of Lenin and his troops, do you?" he asked pointedly. "What you want to know is how Lazar is, and I have no information on that." Minna gave her husband a silent plea to be gentler. Chaim ignored her. "Well, I will tell you this much: he's not com-ing home."

Minna was aghast. "How do you know that?"

"I don't. I feel it." He pounded his heart. "Here."

"That's not fair. You're talking about Hannah's life, and her children's too."

"Let's not argue," Hannah said in a hoarse voice. "I'll make my own conjectures. Tell me what's going on over there. What do you know?"

"All right then, you've heard that at last the Bolsheviks control most of the Ukraine. Unfortunately, Makhno and Hryhoryiv have launched their partisan campaign against 'communists, Jews, and Russians' under the slogan, 'Long live the rule of true soviets!' This has put the region into chaos. Do you follow me so far?"

Hannah nodded, even though some of this was confusing, since she had not been following the various leaders and factions closely.

"Anyway, on the other side, there are four White armies. The most important is commanded by Kolchak, but he is fighting a corps of disciplined men scattered throughout the countryside in the form of the Communist party."

Minna was becoming impatient with his explanation. "What's the point?"

"The point is that the Allies have been watching Kolchak's offensive with keen interest. While they are enthusiastic for his cause, they are beginning to be alarmed by our Red successes in the west."

Hannah did not miss his biased "our." Maybe Minna and Chaim thought themselves Bolsheviks, but she did not include herself in that group. "So, are the Reds winning?" she asked.

"Let's just say the Reds are doing far better than expected."

"What about Trotsky?"

Chaim and Minna glanced at each other. They understood that Hannah knew that her husband's fate was linked with this leader. Chaim cleared his throat. "In Moscow they recently held the founding Comintern, and the new organization proclaimed world revolution as its objective, so it would seem that Trotsky's ideals are in the forefront."

"And if they become less fashionable?"

Minna shrugged. "It's a dangerous game. The stakes are high."

"What do you think I should do?"

"Wait for word from Lazar," Chaim offered. "He will contact you when it is possible—or safe—to do so."

"How long?"

"Who knows?" Minna said, getting up from the kitchen table and going over to the stove. She took out a match and lit a burner. "Want some soup?"

"Since when did you learn to cook soup?"

"Minna's little secret is that she really can cook," Chaim said as he shook his locks back and grinned. "Now that it's out, I'm chaining her to the stove."

Minna shot him a look which was inscrutable to Hannah.

She prided herself on understanding human nature, and yet she had never figured these two out. Hannah could not comprehend why Minna had rejected motherhood, or why she supported Chaim's crazy causes. For years she and Minna had been antagonists, but why? It had taken near tragedies—Minna's imprisonment and Hannah's influenza—to unite the women as sisters. Minna had been the only one to share the tragedy of the miscarriage, and although she had never hinted about it again, the sympathy between them had swelled. Even so, Hannah drew the line and did not confide in her about Dr. Dowd, for if Lazar never returned, there would be plenty of time for revelations; if he did, there would be fewer consequences. Yes, it was best that nobody knew for certain about her lover. Not even Rachael.

∽ 11 ∾

"I think we should set a time limit," Wendell said as he stared across the desk in Room 202.

"Why, I think the survey is coming along rather nicely. I managed to interview ten in the last two days. I can't see getting them out faster than that."

"That's not what I meant," he said in a deeper, slower voice that alerted Hannah to a turn of mood. "Your husband. What happens with him?"

Hannah was rankled. This was not something the doctor could determine. "I'd rather continue with our work, if you don't mind."

In reply, Wendell switched off the light on his side of the desk and leaned back in his chair. "You must be fair, to yourself and to me." Fair? What did that word have to do with the situation? He must have guessed her consternation, for he added, "And to the children. Not knowing the future is worse than facing the inevitable disappointment."

"What's inevitable about it?"

"All right, my dearest, I have not brought this up because I wanted to create unpleasantness. You know I prefer to prevent confrontations. Yet that is sometimes a mistake." He spoke gently and deliberately, but there was no mistaking his authority. "On the other side of conflict is resolution. Facing the wall of decision leads to tension. Only resolution brings peace."

Although his words were said softly and in a soothing rhythm, Hannah was becoming more and more agitated. "What am I supposed to do? Am I supposed to say that either Lazar comes home by the first of October, or I will sign papers that I don't want him as a husband anymore? How can I do that on my own? I need to talk to him, to at least write to him. Otherwise, it is . . ." She searched for a word and settled on "deceitful."

"Who is deceiving whom? He is the one who has abandoned you and his children. I want to see you safe, protected, happy. What's so wrong with that?" His voice caught. He cleared his throat. "And also . . . I want to have you for myself. There, I have said it. You've known it, but now I have announced it."

"That might not be possible."

"The legal arrangements are not that difficult. I've already checked."

Why wasn't Hannah astonished? It was just like Wendell, but he had not consulted her. And he had forgotten a few "minor" details. "What about your family? I don't think they will welcome me."

"They will if I say so."

"You cannot threaten them to accept me."

"No, you're right about that. Mothers want their sons to be happy, and as you know, mine has seen me lose two wives. My father has passed on. When everyone else gets to know you, though, you will win them over."

"What about Bellevue? I can't see them approving this match."

"I agree there will be political problems at the hospital. I was hoping that you might choose to resign in favor of our research, as well as your private practice, of course. I thought you might like a consulting room of your own. Then you might use your spare time to concentrate on your duties as Mrs. Dowd."

"What are those?"

"They're not unpleasant, I assure you."

Hannah assumed they were not, and yet she could not envision the life he was offering any more than she could imagine picking up and moving to Russia. "Can't we talk about this another time? I have some preliminary results to discuss with you, Doctor."

In the dim light she could not see his expression, and he did not reply for a half minute. Then he switched on the light. His face was composed. "And what are those?"

"Look at this list of women who report they have intercourse at least once daily, and those more than once daily."

"Are there many of them in those categories?"

"More than I expected. Anyway, I have found a correlation—I think that's the right word—" He nodded that it was. "Good. Well, I have listed these by number of pregnancies. The numbers for more frequent intercourse goes up significantly after the first pregnancy, rises until the third pregnancy, and then falls off after that. But why? I would think the more babies, the less time you would have, but the women with no pregnancies have sex less frequently. Any explanation?"

"I can venture a few wild guesses, that's all. But isn't it exciting? A simple survey and we'll have meat to chew on for the next ten years!"

"Why do you think?" Hannah persisted.

"Pelvic congestion. A woman who has experienced one pregnancy has had the blood vessels in her pelvis dilated. These are apt to engorge with more blood during the arousal state of a sexual encounter, making her more orgasmic and giving her stronger climaxes."

"There could be a connection . . ." she allowed, then flipped to some questions relating to orgasm. "By the way, I have altered these. Most women don't seem to know the word *orgasm,* or even *climax,* and the other terms vary between people of different backgrounds. So now I am asking if they feel a sense of release, and if so, to what degree?"

"How can you quantify it?"

"That is a male question. Did you know that?"

"I plead guilty to the charge."

"I inquire whether their release is entirely complete, fairly complete, moderate, little, none, or if they are nervous and unsatisfied. I also ask them if they are happy with the sexual side of their marriage. I think the tables tell the story of whether or not the responses are accurate." She passed him a piece of paper with a penciled chart. "Of those who report that their release is 'entirely complete,' fifty-seven percent say they are very happy; of those who are 'fairly complete,' only twenty-five percent say they are very happy. Then watch the numbers fall off: eight percent of the very happys say the release is 'moderate,' two percent of the 'littles,' three percent of the 'nones,' and two percent of the 'nervous and unsatisfieds.' What do you make of that?"

"What do you?"

"I think those reporting in the first two categories are experiencing sexual satisfaction, the others are not."

"And?"

"And sexually satisfied women are happier."

"It seems obvious, doesn't it?" the doctor said a bit pompously. "But here's the point: without the survey we could make the assumption, but we could not prove it. There is so much good we can do with this material!" He allowed himself a moment of self-satisfaction, then asked, "By the way, what do your percents add up to?"

"With the decimals it's over ninety-eight percent. The others chose not to acknowledge that question, or their answers didn't make sense."

"Not a bad response, not at all."

〜 12 〜

Throughout the spring and into the summer Hannah concentrated on making her pavilion a model of efficiency and safe childbearing. Her early statistics were significantly better than the previous year, but she did not preen. The last season had been riddled with problems brought on by the flu, and the mortality figures could not distinguish between purely obstetrical problems and epidemic complications. Even so, she knew she had impressed the most doubtful members of the Board of Managers. Then, with Rachael's permission, she had extended the sex survey to their clinic, thus catching women with specific sexual complaints, as well as others with general medical needs from age thirteen up. Hannah had trained Carrie to ask the questions and was pleased at how skillfully the assistant had become at eliciting answers.

By May they had collected almost three hundred question-naires. A thousand no longer seemed impossible.

Unhappily, there was worrisome news for Chaim and his compatriots, who were actively organizing labor movements and other political actions, because these days the very word *radical* carried with it the image of a wild-eyed, bushy-haired Red holding a smoking bomb. As the heroic victors of the war came home, the deportation of anyone who crit-icized American life was being contemplated. Then, in late April, while Wilson was negotiating the peace treaty at Paris, a homemade bomb was sent to the mayor of Seattle. The next day another arrived at the home of a former senator in Atlanta, and an alert New York postal clerk found sixteen similar packages. Marked for death were two immigration commissioners; the senator who led the Bolshevik Investiga-tion Committee; an associate justice of the United States Su-preme Court; the Postmaster General, who had banned radical literature from the mails; the Attorney General; the Secretary of Labor; even John D. Rockefeller and J. P. Mor-gan.

Headlines blazed the news that the Reds had planned a May Day massacre. On the afternoon of May Day the own-ers and staff of the *New York Call,* a socialist paper, were holding a reception to celebrate the opening of their new of-fices. Chaim and Minna planned to be there, and even though Hannah was worried about reprisals for the bombs, they would not change their minds.

"Those of us who have consecrated our lives to interna-tional socialism will not be silenced by the rumors of our sworn enemies," Chaim decreed.

"You don't believe the bombs were real?" she asked.

"They were probably real enough, but who do you think is responsible for them? Don't you think it odd that all were found 'in the nick of time,' as they say? The whole thing is a sham to scare away our supporters."

This line of thinking perplexed Hannah, for she could never determine who was right. Minna also invited Emma and Benny to the party at the Russian People's House, but Hannah would not allow it. "Go if you must, but you cannot take my children."

Minna did not argue, but said softly, "I would take my own children."

"Well, they are *not* yours," Hannah spat, then regretted her burst of temper.

She would not regret it for long, however. The celebrations were stormed by a group of soldiers under orders to disrupt the festivities. They demanded that the Bolshevik posters be torn down. When they were refused, the soldiers destroyed the literature on the tables, smashed up the offices, drove the crowd into the street, and clubbed them so vigorously that seven members of the *Call* staff were hospitalized and many more of the hundreds of men, women, and children in the building were injured.

On the same day riots broke out in Cleveland, Boston, and other cities. The most spectacular action was the dynamiting of Attorney General A. Mitchell Palmer's home in Washington, whose neighbor across the street, Assistant Secretary of the Navy, Franklin D. Roosevelt, alerted the police.

"What do you know about this?" Hannah asked her brother.

"About as much as you do."

"You are not involved?"

"I am involved in socialism, you know that."

"But not this violence."

"No, the sad truth is that this is the work of reactionaries who think they can terrify the ruling classes into destroying the radical labor movement because whenever an explosion occurs, someone shouts, 'Bolsheviks!' in reaction. Why don't they look beyond the obvious to see that it is for the purpose of the shouting that the explosion occurred in the first place?"

Hannah found his circular reasoning bewildering, and while she wanted to believe him, she was not entirely convinced. Years ago he had served time in a Russian prison for his part in a successful attempt on the life of a brutal Russian aristocrat. His contempt for capitalists was not much different. In the meantime she knew that, once again, she was living among suspects.

On one of their Thursday meetings in his hospital office, she confided her fears to Wendell. "What do you think of this?" She showed him a cartoon which depicted a frightened man in a bed labeled "U.S. Senate" with the caption, "Trotsky'll Get You If You Don't Watch Out!"

"Do you know what a backlash is?" the doctor asked.

"It's an overreaction to the aftermath of the war. People fear what they don't know. You must not let it worry you."

"How can I not? Even in the hospital I feel people are whispering about me. Everyone knows my husband is in Russia . . . with Trotsky. Who is more a Red than he is? And what does that make me?"

"They also know he left you, and you remained here, loyal to your new country. Nobody doubts your sincerity."

Hannah stared at him defiantly. "Do you believe that?" He averted his eyes. "Then you have been hearing rumors too."

"Petty gossip, nothing more."

"What can I do about it?"

Wendell was silent for a few moments. "I cannot be neutral in this matter. I have strong feelings, yet I hesitate to express them."

"Go ahead," she prodded.

"Like gathering storms, sometimes these currents of hate become stronger before they dissipate. If you were to take the steps to divorce Lazar . . . if we were to marry . . . you would be safe."

"Safe from what? From being thrown out of Bellevue again? Or out of America?" Her voice had risen so loud that Wendell pressed his finger to his lips as a reminder of where they were. "This is America?" she continued with suppressed rage. "This is the 'land of the free and home of the brave'?" Her face purpled with anger. "Maybe I've been wrong. Maybe the Bolsheviks do offer the best future for me and my family!"

Wendell dropped the subject after saying, "At least you know where I stand better than I know where you do."

Because she kept asking, Chaim made certain she was apprised of the news—both good and bad—from Russia. All through the summer the battle in the south seesawed violently back and forth. When word came that Odessa, the city of her childhood, had fallen to the Whites, she felt an especially painful jolt, for she could not help but root for the Reds. Chaim could offer no word of cheer, for he worried that the more heated the conflict, the worse were the chances of Trotsky surviving the clashes. Also, if the Reds were routed, their leaders—and their staffs—would either escape to exile, be killed, or imprisoned.

"I suppose we should be hoping they'll get out in time,"

Hannah said morosely, "but I doubt that would make a difference for me. Lazar's not about to return with his tail tucked between his legs."

Chaim did not try to dissuade her. "No, I don't think they'd pick New York for their exile. I'd expect Trotsky and Lenin would turn up somewhere in Europe to plot their next move."

Hannah nodded somberly as she faced the fact that none of these maneuverings would include her. However, if she turned her head back to the present, there was Wendell with outstretched arms. He had mounted a campaign of his own to ease her mind, and at this he was doing a fine job, as he did with everything he tackled.

First, he had tried to find a world where they could exist together. Considering the present circumstances, their associates at the hospital were eliminated, as were his immediate family. Hannah had said that she was not yet ready for him to socialize with the Herzogs or the Blaus, although they might have been sympathetic. Even Dr. Dowd's regular social set was out of the question, for it mostly comprised friends from the elite schools he had attended. He had not hesitated to tell her that they had never really accepted Lulu, so she surmised they certainly would never condone his friendship with an immigrant Jew. So Wendell found another, entirely original group—old friends of Lulu's mostly—who did not care who Hannah was, or what the midwife and doctor were doing together.

Even before their marriage, Lulu had introduced Wendell to several Village artists, and over the years they had purchased or had been given a wide range of unusual pieces crafted by their neighbors. For some reason Wendell was attracted to the most somber, realistic of their work. Because Hannah had been to his home only once, and because she had been far too anxious to take in much more than the greenness of the library and the blueness of the foyer, she had not noticed his art collection—except for his first wife's portrait—and so she came to know the painters before the paintings.

Across Fifth Avenue from the mews, in Macdougal Alley, lived a wealthy lady who reminded Hannah of Mrs. Dodge. Gertrude Vanderbilt Whitney had converted an ivy-covered stable into a studio with two-story-high glass windows. Her first call to Wendell had been of a medical nature.

"What a sight I must have been!" she began, retelling the tale for Hannah's benefit. "Clumsily I had tripped over one leg of my easel, taken it down with me, and managed to split open my chin and anoint myself with a full palette of tempera."

"You should have seen her!" Wendell said, chuckling at the recollection. "Blood pouring down her neck like a gruesome scarf, and the rest of her covered with a rainbow of blotches. My housekeeper almost fainted at the sight."

"But, as usual, Wendell was a darling and saved the day!" She tilted her chin to show off his stitchery.

"Ah, my finest work!" he bragged. "At least above the waist."

It was at Mrs. Whitney's that Hannah was first introduced to Stuart Davis, Robert Henri, John French Sloan, Edward Hopper, George Luks, and an old acquaintance from Mrs. Dodge's, the sculptor Jo Davidson. She didn't know what to make of their unusual works of art—especially the geometric shapes in Davis's pieces—what they meant when they talked nostalgically about the Armory Show, or their references to some place called the "Ashcan School," which of them were members of some club called "The Eight," or even where the "Art Student's League" was. And yet she felt a part of them, perhaps because they were so separated from the rest of her worlds. Best of all, the conversations rarely turned either medical or political.

Except once. And that was by accident.

    ∾ **13** ∾

Early on a summer afternoon they met Jo Davidson in the park walking the opposite direction. He greeted them warily, which was in contrast to his usual warmth.

"When did you get back?" Dr. Dowd asked.

"A few days ago."

"He's been over in Europe making busts of our great Allied leaders," Wendell explained.

After a few pleasantries with the doctor, the artist's eyes

flickered, as if he were weighing his words. Hannah wondered if he thought it wrong that they were walking arm in arm in public. She made a point of stepping away from Wendell, but Jo gave a crooked smile and cocked his head as if to say: Don't be silly. "Did you ever meet Lincoln Steffens at Mrs. Dodge's?"

"No, I don't believe so," the doctor answered.

"I didn't mean *you*," Davidson replied sarcastically.

Wendell gave Hannah an abashed grin. "She probably did. She knows everyone who's anyone." The words were tinged with a mixture of pride and playful rivalry.

"I think so," Hannah answered warily. "Why?"

"I know he liked that story your husband wrote for *The Masses.*"

For a moment Hannah thought it rude of the sculptor to mention Lazar in Wendell's company, but let the moment pass with a gracious "Lazar admired Mr. Steffens as well."

"Steffens has been to Russia, did you know that?"

"I thought only spies and armies could get into Russia now," Wendell commented stiffly.

Hannah glanced up at him. She had no idea he knew so much about Russia. He never talked about those things with her, she realized, because he did not want to upset her, and yet all along he must have been following the events as closely as she had.

"How'd you hear that one?" the sculptor asked.

"A little birdie . . ."

"One of your high-placed in-laws?" Davidson replied with a wink.

"Something like that," Wendell muttered.

"Did you know Steffens is an admirer of Trotsky?"

"Did he meet him?" Hannah blurted.

"I'm not certain, but he was quite taken with Russia. In Paris he dropped by the studio while Bernard Baruch was sitting for me. 'So you've been over in Russia?' Baruch asked Steffens. And do you know what he responded?" Davidson paused dramatically. " 'I have been over into the future, and it works.' "

Hannah's knees wobbled. Wendell gripped her arm more tightly. The sculptor didn't seem to want to continue the conversation, and mumbled something about seeing them later. The doctor did not detain him. He steered Hannah to a bench.

They did not speak for some minutes. Wendell broke the silence. "Are you thinking about going there?"

"No. Never! The last time I heard, Odessa was in the hands of the Whites; next week it could be the Reds. They're not finished fighting. Maybe they never will be."

"Then what has upset you so?"

"Do you think Mr. Steffens saw my husband? He knew him. They might have spoken."

"Do you want me to find out?"

"No, I will."

Wendell waited until the color returned to her cheeks, then said, "There is an errand I need to run uptown. I was hoping you would accompany me."

Hannah checked the watch she wore around her neck. It was Saturday, an unlikely time for them to be together, but the children had spent the night at their Aunt Eva's as a special treat. They loved her spacious apartment on Riverside Drive. Hannah did not. She much preferred Dr. Dowd's Village crowd to her sister's friends, even though she should have felt more comfortable in that milieu of former immigrants who had made good than those who had basked in American prosperity for more than a hundred years. "The children will be home at six."

"We've plenty of time!"

Hannah pondered why Wendell was so animated, and thought this was some sort of ruse to cheer her. Not wanting to be alone, however, she agreed.

"Broadway, corner of Fifty-ninth," he told the taxi driver.

They pulled up in front of Maxwell Motor Sales Corporation. He pointed to the automobile in the window. "What do you think?" Without waiting for her response, he ushered her inside.

"Good afternoon, Doctor," a man in a cutaway jacket greeted.

"Is it ready?"

"Absolutely. Follow me." They walked through a back door and into a parking lot. "Have you ever had a self-starting automobile, sir?" Wendell shook his head. "Then allow me to review some fine points."

Hannah stared at Wendell. "This is your car?" He nodded proudly. "Why do you need a car?"

"To drive to Long Island, of course."

"Why do you need to drive to Long Island?"

"To go to the Mineola Flying Field."

Hannah shook her head. "I don't know what you are talking about."

"I have to go there tomorrow. To see the airplanes," he said as though she were extremely dense, but all the while his eyes crinkled mischievously. "Don't you think Benjamin would like to come?"

The salesman waited patiently for the doctor to appease Hannah, as though he had been through a similar scene many times. When there was a lull, he stepped forward gingerly. "Madam, I am certain you will appreciate the sense behind this car. This is a chassis which has withstood a manufacturing run of three hundred thousand over the past five years without a radical change. While some may go in for the latest bells and whistles, we at Maxwell believe that our consistency means perfection in motor car development." He waited to see if he had softened the strain. Still stunned by his acceptance of her as the doctor's "madam," Hannah had not been following his patter. Seeing perspiration beginning to dot the man's high brow, she gave him an encouraging smile. With an exhalation of relief he continued, "You'll soon find that a Maxwell costs no more to run or maintain, while it gives you many extras in comfort and ease of mind. That's why many of the richest men in America drive Maxwells, although you certainly don't have to be rich to own one."

"Whatever makes Wendell happy . . ." she said, joining in the game.

The afternoon sun was broiling, especially when reflected off the highly polished metal of the gleaming car. "Would Madam like to step back inside and have a cool glass of lemonade while we go over the mechanical particulars?" the salesman asked.

Hannah accepted his offer. More than an hour later, Wendell returned for her. "Let's drive it down Fifth Avenue. I think I can manage that."

Without admitting her trepidation, she allowed the salesman to help her into the open automobile. The doctor handled it admirably, and fortunately, that late on a Saturday afternoon there was little traffic.

"Look, I'm doing the limit. Thirty miles an hour and she purrs." He reached over and patted Hannah's hand. Firmly she placed it back on the wheel. Just before they reached the arch, he asked, "Shall I take you all the way to Tompkins Square?"

"No, I don't want to start a riot."

"How about to the corner of First Avenue?"

"All right," she agreed. "But what is this about tomorrow? Since when are we involving the children?"

"What could be wrong with taking Benjamin for a special outing? I've been wanting to see the airplanes myself. Emma would enjoy it too. And Daphne's coming. Can't we all be friends?" His simple request dangled in the air.

They were crossing under the elevated tracks. Hannah looked up and saw the wheels of a train. She thought of Trotsky's train speeding across some barren Russian plain in pursuit of or in retreat from the Whites. Certainly it was not bringing Lazar any closer to her and the children. And here was Wendell making a gesture to encircle her family in his life. One of Mama's sayings popped into her mind: *Rot mir gut, nor rot mir nit op.* Advise me well in this matter, but don't advise me against it. Her heart was telling her to relent. After all, she had hardly heard a word from Lazar in more than a year. How much could he expect from her? Nor could she expect the doctor to wait for her forever. He wanted her companionship now and tomorrow. And she wanted his. She did, didn't she? Her heart twisted in her breast. If she could choose, what would it be? Would it be for Lazar to come home and for life to resume as it had been? He would go to his meetings, perhaps even find some legitimate work. She would continue to struggle with her various jobs. Was that really better than, say, Washington Mews and this splendid car, visits with Village artists, and who knew what else came with the title of Mrs. Dowd? She glanced at the doctor, whose thick hair ruffled in the breeze created by the moving vehicle. He was five years older than Lazar, in many ways harder to comprehend, but easier to be with. They had more in common to talk about, even if his interests in art, aviation, and other subjects were new to her. She could learn about them if she chose to, and if she didn't, he would not care. Emma had liked him, and so would Benny. She was more unsure about the doctor's family, even though he claimed that they would warm to anyone he loved. After hearing about their distrust of Lulu, though, Hannah had her doubts, but their life could proceed without official consent. Then there were his children, whom she had not met, but at least they were grown, with lives of their own. Children. It was not too late for either of them if they wanted one together. Another baby! Who could imagine such a thing?

Wendell was stopped at a crosswalk. He looked over and saw her bewildered expression. "What's wrong? Are you feeling all right?"

"Yes, don't worry about me."

"But I do," he said loudly over the motor. Then he had to concentrate on the mechanical aspects of moving the car forward. When it seemed under his control once again, he stared straight ahead and asked, "What time tomorrow?" The engine did not entirely mask the quaver in his voice.

"Any time that would be convenient for you," she replied, more confident than she had been in many months.

∽ 14 ∽

The drive took much longer than anyone had expected and the weather was threatening. They choked on the dusty farm roads and got lost looking for the airfield, which was hardly more than a dirty swath slashing through a cow pasture.

Benny was the one who saw the rickety sign first. "There it is! Curtiss Aviation. That must be it." The only person around was a man working on a propeller. "Are you a pilot?" Benny called as he ran from the car.

"No, the mechanic. This plane goes back and forth to Atlantic City. Ever been to the shore?"

"Only Coney Island," Benny replied.

"Same ocean," the mechanic answered with a grin that revealed two missing teeth.

Hannah, who went to her son's side, had the feeling the broken propeller and missing teeth had something in common.

At a whirring sound, everyone leaned back in unison, like linked connecting rods of the same machine. "An airplane!" Benny shouted.

The biplane shuddered to a stop. Hannah stayed back

while Wendell went to talk to the pilot of a craft that looked far too flimsy to hold a human life.

"Would you like your boy to have a ride?" the man asked Wendell.

"Bet he would," Wendell replied.

How could he have the audacity to say that without consulting her? Hannah rushed forward. "No, Benny!" she said firmly.

"Ah, Ma!" Benny wailed.

"One of my men living on the edge of danger is enough for me," Hannah said, startling the doctor with her statement.

"What about you, sir?" the pilot inquired.

"Not today, I'm afraid," Wendell answered without even checking for a sign in Hannah's eyes. If she had assented, he might have felt worth less than her son and husband; if she hadn't, he would have felt too much under her control. Instead he focused on Benny's disappointment. "Some other time. Airplanes aren't going to disappear. They're only going to get bigger and better . . . and safer."

After the pilot took off again, they heard thunder and hurried back to the car. "See, it's going to rain," Hannah said, relieved to use the weather as an excuse for her fears.

"We'd better try to beat it back," Wendell said.

Even though the car had a hood that could be raised, as well as flaps to seal the sides, he worried about damaging the leather seats.

"Want to sit up front?" he asked Benny as a consolation.

Benny looked at his mother for permission. She nodded and climbed in the rear with Daphne and Emma. Daphne had barely spoken to Hannah the whole day, but the girl seemed more shy than displeased. Emma fell asleep on her lap.

The whole way back Benny prattled on about flying. "Don't you think that this is the best year there has ever been in aviation?"

"Why?" Wendell asked.

"So many records! Why, in May that hydroplane crossed the Atlantic in less than forty-four hours. Then in June that Brit, Captain Alcock, and his American navigator Lieutenant Brown made it to Europe."

"I thought they crashed in an Irish bog."

"But they landed and walked away."

"So you'll count that?" Benny nodded solemnly. "Then I will too, but you said there was another."

"The Navy NC-4 seaplane."

"Right, but the one I like is the dirigible R-34, which crossed the Atlantic both ways nonstop."

"You know all about this stuff."

"Who took you to the landing field today?"

Hannah enjoyed their banter. She hadn't seen Benny so happy in a long time. Emma also liked the doctor. She was the one who had been entranced by his house. For the first time Hannah began to believe it might work.

"Beat the raindrops back! Shall we go out for dinner?" he asked as they alighted in front of Washington Mews.

"I'm much too dirty, and so are the children."

Wendell could not disagree, for they were all covered with a fine patina of dust that mingled with the dense humidity to stain their clothes. "We could have Enid make sandwiches."

"Dr. Dowd," she said softly, for that is what she called him in front of the children, "thank you for your kindness, but we really must go now." Emma was about to protest, but she saw something in her mother's eyes that warned her off. "If you'll lend us umbrellas, we can take the trolley."

Wendell capitulated, and soon they arrived back at Tompkins Square. Hannah tried to keep the children's spirits up as she ushered them upstairs. "Quite a weekend. First you stay with Aunt Eva and then this surprise."

Hearing their voices in the hall, Minna opened her door. "You're back."

"We saw airplanes! Lots and lots," Emma said, exaggerating a bit.

"And I almost got a ride," Benny said, kicking the newel post.

"That's wonderful. Won't you have some supper with us? I would like to hear more about it, and so would your uncle."

Hannah looked at Minna quizzically. She knew that her sister-in-law was becoming more domestic, but they usually went out on Sunday evenings, a popular night for lectures.

Hannah began to protest, then relented. "All right, let's clean up quickly, and then we'll be down."

"Good," Minna said, then dropped her gaze.

"What's wrong?" Hannah asked at once. Minna did not

look up. "Go wash first," Hannah said to the children. "I'll be there in a minute."

"I don't need to," Benny whined.

"Go!" she ordered in a voice that left no room for negotiation.

Hannah went through the door first. Chaim was sitting in Mama's favorite chair by the window. When Hannah stepped inside, he rotated his body to confront his sister.

There are moments when you know what is coming, Hannah thought. This was one of them. She had been through many shocks in her life, the last being her mother's illness, and she had survived that one. This one was better. This one had been anticipated. In her mind she had already begun to make the transition from Lazar to Wendell, from one life to the next. Wasn't it strange that first step had been taken this very day? Now it would be easier for the children as well. The trip had not been something she had welcomed, and yet she had sensed she should go, and she had. Funny how things fell into place . . . Her heart beat hard, but not alarmingly fast. She folded her hands. "Nu?" she said to Chaim, then turned to Minna. "It's all right. You can tell me."

"Lazar," he began. "We've had news."

"Yes?" Her voice was steady.

"He's been hurt."

"Hurt?" she repeated dully. The word had no meaning when she had been expecting "dead."

Without any preliminaries Chaim launched into his tale. "The train was heading south and they were arriving at Gorki in the middle of the night. Apparently Trotsky was sleeping. Lazar had tried to rest but could not. There were words that needed to be recorded, and he knew he would not sleep until he had done so—"

Hannah cut him off. "Who told you this?"

"He cannot divulge that," Minna whispered.

Chaim plodded on. "So, as I was saying, he made his way from the sleeping carriage to where he had a desk outside the printing press room." He gave a little grin. "Doesn't that sound familiar?" Minna waved at him to get to the point. "Anyway, from the reports of the accident, the train shuddered. Those on board say they had the feeling that the earth was moving, but took it as a bumpy stretch of track. Apparently Lazar wasn't concerned because he continued to open the door between the cars. That's the last thing he remembers."

"What happened?" Hannah asked with rising concern.

"Trotsky says that he awoke clutching the side of the bed. His car was tilted on edge, but didn't either right itself or turn over. In the silence he heard nothing except a single pitiful voice—Lazar's—crying out in pain. When Trotsky realized his car was somewhat stable, he decided he had best escape because he thought he might be held captive by an enemy who had bombed the train. The heavy doors were so bent he could not get out that way, so he leapt from a window. 'Find out where that pathetic sound is coming from,' he ordered the commander of the train. 'What if it is a trick?' the commander retorted, but they say Trotsky shot back, 'What if it is one of our men?' "

Quickly Hannah realized that someone had been feeding Chaim propaganda along with the casualty report, which in her eyes made the whole story suspect.

Oblivious to this line of thinking, Chaim continued the tale. "Apparently the car was standing on a slope, with three wheels buried deep in the embankment and the other three rising high above the rails. The rear and front of Trotsky's sleeping car had crumbled, as had the car in front, the one Lazar had been passing through. He was pinned down by the front grating. Even though Lazar says he has no memory of it, he must have been partially conscious, for he kept calling out in a high, thin voice like a child's. Someone reported he was calling for his mama. Another disagreed, and said it was a name"—Chaim's throat choked—"probably Hannah."

Minna wiped away a tear.

"I assume they released him," Hannah said with surprising coolness.

"Yes, but because they were afraid that with a wrong move he could be crushed worse, it took several hours. Dozens of men wielded iron rails as levers, with Trotsky himself supervising the effort."

"It's a wonder he survived," Minna gasped. "In all, eight cars were destroyed. There were some other minor injuries, but none as serious as Lazar's, and fortunately nobody was killed."

"Was it a bomb?" Hannah asked after a moment to take it all in.

"Trotsky demanded a full investigation, but all that could

be determined was that the accident was due to faulty switching, whether because of negligence or deliberate action, he never found out. Fortunately for Lazar, since they were approaching Gorki, the speed had been reduced to thirty kilometers an hour. Any faster and he would have been cut in half."

Minna shot a glance at her husband that he read as a rebuke. Hannah missed it, for she had heard rumbles on the stairs that indicated the children were on their way down.

"So?" Hannah asked hurriedly. "What is his condition?"

"I don't understand the medical jargon, but I wrote it down." He handed his notes to Hannah.

She stared at the half-Russian, half-English scrawls. "Right side, better place for injury, collapsed lung, minor pneumothorax, broken ribs, possible puncture of lung, possible spleen involvement . . ."

"What do you think?" Minna asked Hannah.

"It could be very serious, or not so terrible. Many people recover from injuries like this if they get proper care. But on a train in the middle of nowhere . . ."

The children came into the room and saw the dour faces. Benny chose to ignore them. "I'm starving!" he announced.

"Help yourself to the kugel in the kitchen," Minna said.

"What's wrong, Ma?" Emma asked.

"We've had news from your father."

"When's he coming home?"

"Well . . ." Minna started.

"He's not," Hannah stated firmly. "He's sick and not going anywhere."

Emma winced. "Not the flu?"

"No."

"Oh!" She seemed relieved. "Then when he gets better?"

"Maybe," Hannah allowed. "Go have some kugel."

"Actually, he's not on the train anymore," Chaim began slowly. "When the accident occurred, the telegraph station on the train made a connection with Moscow by direct wire. Trotsky's deputy there, Sklyansky, was told to have special doctors waiting. They used the extra engine to move Lazar into the city."

"They're doing the most they can, considering the war situation. Trotsky has demanded the best for him, of course. But . . ." Minna waited for Chaim to carry the ball.

"But they think he should come home. He won't be able

to work for at least a year, maybe more. Trotsky is afraid that if Moscow is taken . . ."

"Lazar knows too much," Minna finished the sentence.

"Does he want to?" Hannah asked.

"He has to come home," Chaim said more forcefully.

"Is it possible? They say that only spies and armies can get into Russia. I suppose only the same can get out."

"They don't expect it to be easy, especially now with the civil war so tense. We hear John Reed is still in Finland, hiding out in a country where communists are being hunted down with counterrevolutionary fervor."

"So what am I supposed to do?" Hannah said in a furious tone. "Am I supposed to go over there and carry him out on my back?"

"Don't you want him?" Minna dared.

"Please, Minna," Chaim said in a low, husky tone he hoped the children wouldn't notice, "even John warned Louise not to try to come after him."

Hannah had not heard either of them. She spoke loudly, but meant the words for herself. "Besides, since when did what I want have anything to do with what I got?"

"Let's eat and talk about this later," Minna suggested.

"I'm not hungry. I want my bath," Hannah shouted, then slammed the door behind her.

⤜⤍ 15 ⤜⤍

What Hannah wanted or Lazar required had little to do with the realities of the war. They knew that Lazar hoped to return home to recuperate and that Trotsky supported this plan. How this was to be accomplished was another matter. Also, messages back and forth were few and far between. Months passed before they had further word on his condition.

In New York the summer ended in torrents of rain that kept the Maxwell in the garage and Hannah and Wendell far apart. They continued to meet at the Brevoort on Mondays, Wednesdays, and Fridays, but if the housekeepers there had ever assumed there was something more than a professional liaison, they were now fooled, for every surface, including the bed, was filled with stacks of surveys. Ever since Hannah had heard that Lazar might be leaving Russia, she had not suggested the papers be moved.

"Darling, I want you to know that I understand completely," Dr. Dowd said one evening during a break in their work, "but I also want you to know that this is hard for me, this working beside you and not—"

At that moment Hannah wanted to reach out for him, but her arms felt leaden, her legs numb. "Maybe we shouldn't meet here any longer . . ."

"That's not what I meant!" His voice constricted. "Just being with you is enough."

She knew it wasn't. Not for him. Not for her. But she felt that if she allowed herself to yield to Wendell, she somehow would be wounding Lazar further. At least the survey kept them going. The data was remarkable. After they started, Dr. Dowd had an idea for a new section on sexual complaints. Hannah deliberated whether altering the questionnaire that late in the project would ruin the data, but he convinced her these could be dealt with in an appendix to the main report. Further, they had divided responses by whether the women reported they were mostly happy or unhappy with their mates. The major complaints of women who said they were happy were that the men ejaculated too rapidly, and they desired intercourse too frequently. These responses were somewhat predictable, but Hannah and Wendell both were jolted to note that less than one percent of happy women reported the husband had too little regard for her satisfaction.

"I had thought that most men did not pay enough attention to their partner's needs, which is biased because the men I have known have been considerate indeed." She gave Wendell an appreciative smile and hoped he would not mind the oblique reference to her husband.

"I admit the same prejudice," he said with a rueful laugh. "Why does every man think he is the only one who has ever discovered how to satisfy a woman?"

"That may be something we should study next."

Also they were amazed with the findings that happy women outnumbered the unhappy two to one. "I would have expected it to be the other way around," Wendell admitted, "but that must be because I am accustomed to listening to the complaints of sick women."

"Even healthy women complain, that's perfectly normal, but it doesn't mean they are miserable."

Wendell shook his head in the age-old gesture of men perplexed by the opposite sex. "Do you think it is normal or abnormal to be happy?" he asked.

"Nobody is happy all the time, but everyone is striving toward that goal. I mean, who thinks of ways to be unhappy?"

"Sometimes I wonder about that. I see people sabotaging their happiness all the time."

"What do you mean?" she asked warily.

"I don't know exactly . . ." he hedged, then brightened. "For instance, there are doctors who find excuses to stay at the hospital when they should be home with their families. Surely their wives will protest and their children will not have the benefit of their company. Soon they will find they are less comfortable at home than at their work, and though medicine has its rewards, they don't compare with the pleasures of a contented family."

"I see your point," Hannah said, relieved that he had not involved her in his theory. To bring the subject back to their survey, she added, "Think of how much more satisfied women would be if the squeeze technique for ejaculatio praecox could be more widely taught?" For a moment she was chagrined by her earlier vow not to share the Brody case with him, for when she had, he had been impressed with the technique. "That is the first paper you should write," she told Wendell.

"*We* should write," he allowed graciously.

"Who would publish me?"

"You are now the obstetrical supervisor of Bellevue Hospital. That has some merit, especially if my name comes first. Also, this time we will have numbers to back up our theories."

"Nobody can refute statistics on a thousand women."

"Exactly, and that is why I too believe that happy is normal, and we should work toward that in our own lives as well." He gave her a little self-satisfied grin to prove he had maneuvered them back to what was on his mind.

"I can do only so much . . ." she said in a quavering voice.

In the glare of Hannah's distress, his smile turned a bit sheepish. "There are always two courses of action: one passive, one aggressive. Why do you always take the former?"

"And you the latter?"

"On the contrary, I have been infinitely patient."

She opened her mouth to refute that, but reconsidered. "A long time ago I learned I cannot change the world. It is the great sweep of political events that has chained me, not my own choices."

"That's where we disagree. You can make choices. You can choose me."

"I cannot! Not now. Maybe if I had not heard from Lazar. Maybe if I did not know he was injured. I don't hate the man. I loved him."

"You still do," Wendell offered flatly.

"Yes, part of me does." Her eyes filled with tears as she tried to focus on him. "And part of me loves you. There are no books written with advice for this situation."

"We flatter ourselves if we think we are unique," he commented sadly. "Many women left behind in the last war faced similar confusion. A glance at the hospital birth records in the last year, if matched with the war records of their legal fathers, might give us some interesting statistics on that score."

"That may be true, but I cannot make a decision until I know more."

"And if you never do?"

"Surely a resolution will come by the end of the year."

"The end of the year," he repeated as though he were grasping a lifeline. "The end of the year?" This time it was a question for Hannah to affirm. She nodded. "Now that you have set a time limit, I feel better," he said without asking the question that hovered between them: What if Lazar comes home?

"Until then we'll continue our work," she said firmly.

Wendell seemed calmer than he had in many weeks. "And we'll be together." There was a fresh acceptance in his voice.

⤙ 16 ⤚

The second week of October the White forces made a major thrust. Orel fell to Denikin's troops, and the White advance guards approached Tula, the last city before Moscow, where Lazar lay in some hospital ward inside the Kremlin walls. At the same moment, General Yudenich and his Northwestern Army were making a desperate attempt to take Petrograd with British support; they soon captured Yamburg on the Luga River, less than a hundred miles away. When Gatchina, thirty miles from the former capital, fell on October 16, the world fully expected the Bolsheviks to be routed momentarily. There were even predictions that Petrograd and Moscow might fall simultaneously.

In the wake of these disasters, the Politburo adopted Trotsky's resolution: "Recognizing the existence of an actual military danger, we must take steps to transform Soviet Russia into a military camp. A registration must be carried out listing every member of the party and the trade unions, with a view to using them for military service."

Under Trotsky's zealous command, the Bolsheviks rallied to defend Petrograd to the last ounce of blood, to refuse to yield a foot, and to carry the struggle into the streets of the city. Everyone else expected an early surrender to the Whites, and even Lenin planned an evacuation. Trotsky alone was confident that even if the White army of 25,000 could manage to force its way into a city of a million, it would be doomed by well-organized street resistance. However, he first had to convince Lenin not to continue with his course. As soon as the masses began to feel that Petrograd was not to be sacrificed, the spirit changed, and Trotsky himself took on the role of a regimental commander. In the thick of the decisive battle, his orderly, Kozlov, a Muscovite peasant, ran wildly along the defender's lines, yelling, "Courage, boys, Comrade Trotsky is leading you!"

When Hannah heard the news reports from the field, she was torn by conflicting emotions: how Lazar would have loved to be in the midst of this. But also, how much better it was that he was immobilized in Moscow.

October 21 was a critical day for the siege. At last the Red troops held the Whites at Pulkovo heights along Petrograd's southern border, and by the end of the day the regular Red forces, bolstered by peasant partisans, were harassing the Whites into retreat.

Benny, who was well aware that his father's fate was bound to Trotsky's, clipped the headline: TROTSKY'S ARMY DEFEATS WHITE RUSSIANS, and pasted it over his bed.

"This means it will be easier for Pa to come home, doesn't it?" he asked his Uncle Chaim.

"We think so, if he can get past the British in Halifax."

However, during that same dreary autumn in America, strikes and other Socialist causes widened the chasm between "loyal Americans" and "Red Commies." A few days after a divisive Boston police strike in September came a nationwide steel strike. Next, the United Mine Workers joined them. Soon the public was being drummed with the belief that every union man was under the control of dangerous radicals. Hysteria replaced reason.

Then, in late November, someone placed a newspaper on her hospital desk with the caption underlined with red ink: RAID ON RUSSIANS FINDS BOMB FACTORY. Panic made her too frantic to focus for a few minutes. At last she calmed long enough to scan the story about Department of Justice agents and New York City police who had raided the headquarters of the Union of Russian Workers in lower Manhattan and discovered a large quantity of TNT, chemicals, and acids which could be used to make explosives.

A line caught her eye: "Also found in a search of the room were three ledgers containing names believed by police to be the membership rolls of the Union of Russian Workers and several copies of a Russian newspaper, whose translated name is *Bread and Freedom.*" She began to shake. Chaim was the one who printed that Russian paper! Could his name be in those ledgers? She could not tolerate another loss . . . more jails . . . trials.

Somehow she managed to get through the day at Bellevue, but she left word she would not see the doctor that Wednesday evening, cancelled her clinic appointments, and rushed home.

Minna was lying on the sofa reading. She seemed unconcerned.

"Where's Chaim?"

"He'll be back soon. Why?"

"I heard about the bombs."

"Don't fret about your brother, he's fine."

"He has the contract for that Russian paper. Don't you think—?"

Minna cut her off. "Haven't you heard about freedom of the press? They can't arrest you for what you print, or even write."

"Neither of you were involved?"

"No!" she shouted indignantly. "Look, I know you don't believe me because we are secretive about what we do, and for good reason. If you knew what was going on, you might have to give information if you were questioned. Don't you see it's safer for you this way?"

"You don't sound uninvolved to me."

"We're far in the background. A few years ago we made a decision. Not everyone can—or should—be on the front lines. Chaim is a better theoretician than a foot soldier. Also, keeping the press open is more valuable than standing out in the open and shouting in the wind."

"Like Emma and Sasha—" Hannah said morosely.

"People like us must remain behind to carry on the work."

"By making bombs?"

"That news has been exaggerated. Come to the protest meeting tomorrow night. Listen to the others. You need to hear what's going on."

"I've heard everything I need to hear," Hannah retorted, for in truth she was fed up with both sides of the controversy and did not want to play any part in it.

But she was a part of it, whether willing or not.

❧ 17 ❧

At Bellevue one of the new midwives, Susan Grimm, had been a thorn in Hannah's side. From the beginning the girl had turned in long, detailed reports on her births, but there seemed to be a disparity between her paperwork and her supervisors' accounts of her clinical skills. This was one time Hannah regretted not having more direct contact in the wards. If she tried to observe Miss Grimm too closely, her presence would be resented. If she studied only the written work, she suspected she might be getting a false sense of what had occurred. Until she was more confident, she decided to keep the inexperienced woman in the low-risk wards. Miss Grimm was well aware that she had not had even her junior rotation in the high-risk area. Her first query to Hannah met with a polite agreement to "look into the situation."

Her second was more pointed. "I'm the only one in my class who hasn't been in there yet. What do you have against me?"

"You're not ready yet," Hannah replied smoothly but firmly.

"Haven't you looked at my reports? Or can't you Reds read English?"

Miss Grimm's remarks so astonished Hannah she turned on her heel without responding. She rushed to her office and shut the door before her eyes flooded with tears. The girl was too stupid to know what she was saying, but whom was she mimicking? Benny had complained that kids were calling other kids "radical" and "Russian" as epithets in the schoolyard. Hannah had asked if they were directed toward him, and he had said no, that it was used as a general slur. Now she wasn't so certain. For the first time she feared that Lazar's return might make things worse for them, not better.

She told nobody of Miss Grimm's outburst. Miss Grimm, who must have regretted her words, kept silent as well. Hannah made it a point to treat her like any other member of the staff. She asked Norma Marshanck to keep an eye on her, and when Norma thought she was ready, she began her high-risk rotation under that more experienced midwife's guidance. Yet after that nothing was ever the same. Hannah was always considering what people were saying behind her back.

She was not the only one looking over her shoulder. The word went out that universities and schools were hotbeds of Bolshevism. Hannah saw the names of some of Lazar's former associates at New York University on a list of "pink parlor seminarians." The superintendent of the city's schools said there was no such thing as "nine to three patriotism" and tried to ferret out teachers with suspect convictions. A young woman in Benny's school was forced out in disgrace.

In December, after the Bolsheviks reoccupied the Ukraine, the time had arrived to move Lazar from Moscow to Petrograd, then on to Finland, where he could board a ship to New York. No arrangements had been made, but Chaim's network reported they were almost ready. There was one problem: would he be allowed to enter the United States? Six months earlier nobody would have questioned his rights as an American citizen to return home. Now he was as Red as they came. Even more ironically, many of his former compatriots—whether or not they wanted to—were about to travel the other direction.

The Labor Department had just declared that membership in the Union of Russian Workers was an offense to be punished by deportation. And, while they were at it, they decided to cleanse the country of the Red threat by including a long list of "dangerous radicals." An army transport ship, the *Buford*, was readied for the task. Two hundred and forty-nine deportees were rounded up for this "Soviet Ark" and taken to Ellis Island to await the December 21 sailing. Among the three women was Emma Goldman. Alexander Berkman was at her side. Unlike E. G. and Sasha, however, most of the others had never participated in any terrorist action and did not have any record of criminal activity. They were being deported for their beliefs. So this was freedom? Hannah mused. Which of the rights supposedly protected by the American constitution would collapse next? Freedom of the press? Freedom of religion? While heartened that none of her kin were scheduled for the *Buford*, she assumed there would be other round-ups. Surely Chaim and Minna were already on someone's roster. Or worse, maybe only Chaim would be told to leave. They were not deporting whole families. Some of the wives and children of the *Buford* passengers had attempted to break through the Ellis Island ferry gates in an attempt to join their fathers and husbands, but were turned back.

"All this points to the fact that Lazar won't be coming home, doesn't it?" Hannah asked her brother in a broken voice.

"Not in the near future," Chaim replied with a melancholy

sigh, "and not unless he makes friends with A. Mitchell Palmer and his lot."

⁆ 18 ⁆

At last Hannah had her answer for Dr. Dowd. It was Wednesday and Christmas Eve. He was leaving to spend the holiday with his children at his mother's house in Poughkeepsie. They had agreed to meet for dinner, and only the meal, at the Brevoort. Wendell ordered his favorite traditional dishes for her to taste: oysters in green pepper shells, roast goose, chestnut dressing, warm apple sauce, string beans, potato puff, and plum pudding with foamy sauce. Hannah had no appetite, but she tasted everything to please him.

"It's December," she said over the coffee. Wendell did not comment. "I promised you an answer."

He waved his hand in front of his face. "I don't expect you—"

"No, it's only fair. We can't keep on like this forever. We have to think about others, our children . . ." She swallowed hard. "Benny keeps asking for you. Emma wants to visit you again. Doesn't Daphne wonder . . . ?"

"Yes."

Now she sensed something else in his reticence. "She doesn't approve of your alliance with a Red, does she?"

The doctor's eyes shifted, but he steadied them, and almost convinced Hannah of his sincerity. "My family is not immune to propaganda either, but they will listen to me first—until they get to know you, that is."

"Even if Lazar never returns, we're not home free. What will we do next year?"

"About what?"

"Christmas, for one."

"Why do people always see the obstacles and never the advantages? I think you will be amazed at how well we shall blend our lives. But the point is: will Lazar return?"

"Chaim says he cannot imagine him being allowed into

this country unless he makes a friend of Attorney General Palmer."

"Why? I thought he left the country with the credentials of a journalist."

"Yes, but he hasn't sent any dispatches for more than a year."

"All the better. His name isn't attached to a singular, or damning, point of view."

"His name is connected to Trotsky's."

"Is it? From what I can tell, Trotsky has had no interest in using Lazar's name. Almost everything your husband has written has been under the war commissar's byline. As far as anyone knows, he's an anonymous victim of the revolution lying in some hospital bed in Moscow."

Hannah's heart raced. "What are you saying?"

"I'm saying that I have met Mr. Palmer, and he's not quite the ogre he's painted to be. We've known his family for years. I could meet with them, and they could speak to the attorney general. I think they could arrange safe passage for Lazar on humanitarian grounds."

"You would do that? Why?"

"Because it is what you want, and I want you to be happy."

"But—"

"Love cannot be stolen, Hannah."

"You don't want me."

Wendell started to respond, yet could not muster the requisite control. He made a show of stirring his coffee, but did not lift the cup. Then he spoke. "I am sorry that you are in this terrible position of making a choice. However, you are. If he is here, if he can speak for himself, the stakes will be even. Otherwise you will always have regrets. Regrets poison unions. If after he returns, you see your situation differently, I will be here for you." He fumbled with something in his pocket and stood. Hannah sensed he had lost his composure and was afraid to show his emotions in public. "If you will excuse me—" he gasped.

A waiter came to assist with his chair. "Are you all right, sir?"

Only his head bobbed as he departed the dining room.

The coffee grew cold, but he did not return. At last the headwaiter came by. "The doctor has been called out on an emergency." He handed Hannah an envelope on a silver tray, backing away while she read it.

She unfolded the heavy vellum paper with the hotel crest. A ring set with a sapphire surrounded by small diamonds tumbled onto the stained tablecloth. The message was in Wendell's familiar bold scrawl: *"Merry Christmas, 1919."* Nothing more.

Problem 8:
Minna Blau Changes Her Mind

◆

1920

I am for you, and you are for me,
Not only for your own sake, but for others'
  sakes,
Envelop'd in you sleep greater heroes and
  bards,
They refuse to awake at the touch of any man
  but me.

—WALT WHITMAN

∽ 1 ∽

THE room was painted in three shades of green, each more
hideous than the next. The top of the wall was the lightest,
with the yellow tinge of a patient with liver disease, the bottom the basic issue of the military, and a chair rail of a hue
that went as far as a green could go without matching the
other two and still retain that name. Even so, Hannah preferred concentrating on the wall than on the unctuous man
and his slippery questions.

"So, as you were saying, your husband is a journalist."

"Yes." Chaim had warned her to offer as little information
as possible.

"And you say he was injured during the internal Russian
conflict."

"During that time period, but in a train wreck, not in the
war."

"Why can't he recuperate in Russia?"

"He wants to come home."

"Of course he does." The man's exaggerated show of sympathy was tinged with sarcasm. "Who wouldn't want to come home to a wife as devoted as you, Mrs. Sokolow?"

"I am a nurse," she stated for the second time, since Chaim had suggested that she flaunt her medical expertise, and say whatever it was that they wanted to hear—that is, if she wished Lazar back.

Ambivalence had plagued her right up to this very moment, but she suppressed it as Mr. Gibbons shuffled some documents. "These papers, offering to facilitate Mr. Sokolow's passage, come from an important Soviet ministry. These days, when every contact with that government takes months, your husband's papers have arrived in a timely fashion through diplomatic channels. Why would these people be so helpful about one unfortunate case when there are so many more urgent matters on which they must focus their attention?"

"A courtesy to a journalist perhaps?"

"Your husband may be a writer, my dear madam, but he is hardly Walter Lippmann or Lincoln Steffens."

"Both men are acquaintances of his, by the way," she said with a slight smile. "Perhaps the reason you are unfamiliar with my husband's work is because he does not write in English."

"Oh course, madam." He stopped to clear his throat. "There are, ah, a few, shall we say, other inconsistencies which need to be clarified. For starters, it seems he has been away an inordinate length of time for a journalistic assignment." Glancing through some papers, he added up the time under his breath. "More than two years by my count. Why might that be?"

For this Hannah had come prepared, for the date of his departure—just prior to the revolution—was too damning to be ignored. Chaim had gone over various explanations, but each left gaps that a keen administrator might leap through. In the end, her brother had thrown up his hands. Hannah, whose thoughts had been dwelling on Dr. Dowd, had offered an alternate approach.

"You know, Chaim, in my experience it is sex, not politics, that makes the world go round." With a naughty grin she continued. "If a man is away from a family for several years, might not someone suspect marital difficulty?"

Chaim laughed uproariously. "You're brilliant! What would you say?"

Hannah decided not to rehearse in front of her brother. "I'll come up with something. At least it's in my department because I hear these tales every day."

In the end she had decided to say as little as possible—as a modest wife would prefer—but if she were pressed, she planned to stay within the boundaries of truth, if not the exact circumstances.

The moment had come. "There were difficulties between us." She looked up at her interrogator's shiny brow, then down at her lap. "I think he took the assignment to be as far away from me as possible. Then circumstances intervened."

"And what might those be?" inquired Mr. Gibbons in a more sympathetic tone.

"Well, a few months after he arrived, there was a revolution. Any journalist would have fought to be in that position, especially one who could speak the native language, and who had met some of the leaders."

Here was a delicate point. Hannah hoped she had inserted it at the correct moment. Lazar's links to Trotsky were not immediately apparent, yet some astute investigator might divine a connection. Better to explain it now so it appeared innocent, rather for him to discover the red flag and wave it triumphantly.

"When was that?"

"He did a series of interviews with Mr. Trotsky, when he was in New York for a few months. Mr. Trotsky was most accommodating because my husband had met him many years ago when they were at the same Russian university."

"Did he know Trotsky well as a youth?"

"They moved in different circles, but they had some classes together." Hannah made a purposeful pause. "Actually, I was pleased Mr. Trotsky showed no inclination to renew that association, because I did not like the man one bit." She scowled, and this time she was not acting.

He leaned back in his chair and folded his hands across his bulging belly. Then he moved forward slightly and cocked his head to one side. "You say there was trouble between you and your husband. Then why are you so anxious to have him back?"

Again Hannah was ready. "I was afraid he would not want to return to me. Now that he does, I welcome the chance to

earn his forgiveness. I have so much to make up to him!"
The last came as a strangled cry, which startled the bureau-
crat, who was under the masculine assumption that the husband had been the one who had wronged the wife.

His jaw clenched and unclenched as if he were chewing
on her words. "There was an indiscretion on your part?"
Hannah nodded shyly. "Forgive me for prying," he said in
what he assumed was the properly contrite tone, although
the effect was more cloying, "but let me be frank with you
since you have been so candid with me. As you no doubt are
aware, the government is committed to ferreting out subversive elements who are poisoning our free society. A short
while ago the first shipload of dissidents was sent abroad. At
a time when our policy is to eliminate those who wish to destroy our American way of life, wouldn't it be foolish to
open the doors and allow more agitators in?" He sucked in
a quick breath and continued rapidly, "Now, I have no hard
proof that your husband is indeed one of the troublemakers,
but he has moved in those circles." Hannah opened her
mouth, but he raised his palm. "Let me finish, please. I
could argue—if I were so inclined—that a journalist must be
on the fringes wherever stories that would interest his readers might ripen. On the other hand, I could just as easily
make a case for his profession being a cover for illicit activities. Most men in my position would find it prudent to
make the judgment to deny immigration. Better he should
languish over there than return to wreak havoc here. Who
knows, he might have been especially trained by the communists to incite and infiltrate. And if I do stamp his papers
and he does just that, what do you think will happen to me?"
He gave a little chuckle. "In the end, we think of ourselves
first, don't we?" He winked. "Have you considered that you
might be better off without him? I can't understand all that
medical gobbledegook, but he doesn't sound like he's going
to be the same man who left you." His raised eyebrows were
an unspoken question.

Hannah had no preparation for this turn. Improvising
quickly, her thoughts veered to Dr. Dowd. He was the other
man in her life. If Lazar did not return, he would still want
her. Did she want him? How could she answer that? Only if
the matter of Lazar was settled could she dwell on a different version of her future. Her mind wandered to the children.
That was the crux of this, wasn't it? Men understood a

mother's devotion, so that was where she would lead Mr. Gibbons.

"I have two children who miss their father. They need a man in the house. I must think of them now."

His dark, opaque eyes opened wider, and Hannah had the queer sense that a layer had been peeled off and he was seeing her with a new clarity of vision. "Mrs. Sokolow, if I were you I would not summon him home. You have more to lose than you have to gain." His mouth formed an ugly rictus as he watched her confused reaction. "If you would listen to another man who has been in the same position, he might suggest that his return might be the worst form of revenge."

Revenge? What was this nonsense? What had he said earlier? "In the end, we all think of ourselves first, don't we?" So he was relating some problem of his to her own. But he did not understand, not really. She had been feeding him lies mingled with a few facts so the potion would slide down his throat. His advice was worthless.

"Now what do you say?"

"I could never live with myself if anything happened to him over there." At least this part was the cold truth.

"You don't have to decide today. I could put his file on hold. You could return at your convenience."

"And if I say I want him home?"

"Of course I will have to pass this through my superiors. There are questions that must be answered to their satisfaction. However, if you wish the matter settled another way, just say the word and I will stamp the file 'rejected' and nobody need be the wiser."

"I couldn't do that."

"Think about it, madam. You are a most attractive woman." Mr. Gibbons stood with more grace that Hannah would have suspected possible with his bulky frame. "Surely you could have a better future than with a man who has been crippled in a train wreck." He moved around the desk with simian grace. "Do you need that burden too?" He extended his arms in the most empathic of gestures, but it was all Hannah could do to keep from recoiling openly.

"If you would be so kind . . ." she said in a deliberately slow voice to minimize her trembling at his approach, "could you ask your superior for his approval? With my husband's respiratory problems, the longer he spends in

Petrograd in this foul weather, the worse he might get."
Then she stood, concentrating on where to place her feet, her
hands, her torso, to minimize closeness to his looming form.
Their eyes met. Hannah willed her lips to curl upward. She
offered her hand like a stiff pole, more to ward him off than
to make contact. His palms were moist. He clasped her hand
a moment too long. She forced herself not to turn from his
gaze, which seemed riveted on her shirtwaist. In this harsh
light he might have glimpsed the cleft of her breasts under
the unbuttoned jacket.

"I do wish more women were as fashionable as you,
madam. Bobbed hair and short skirts are so becoming. They
lift the spirits after the long years of war."

Enough. She had to end this. "Yes, I have changed myself
to surprise Mr. Sokolow. I am anxious for him to understand
my desire to begin again."

"A lucky man," mumbled Mr. Gibbons, conceding defeat.
"I will see what I can do to assist you."

"I will never forget your kindness," Hannah offered as a
gratuity, then fled.

∽ 2 ∽

The first shock was his face. His head seemed elongated,
perhaps an illusion created by the hollow pockets of his
cheeks and the pointed edge of his once rounded chin. His
eyes seemed larger, but this was because they had sunk
deeper into the sockets and the flesh around his brow had
disappeared, leaving folds of wrinkled skin. What had she
expected? Hannah considered as she tried to compose herself the moment that she opened the door to find her husband sitting at the kitchen table.

A newspaper was clutched in his hand. Hannah closed the
door and back up against it. A cry had caught in her throat
as the paper was lowered to reveal the man she had married.
Or was it?

Yes, she had supposed he would be tired, possibly even
slightly injured, but basically appear much the same as when

he had left. From this first glance it was obvious he was not the man she remembered. Maybe his wife could recognize him, but even she might have missed him on the quay. And the children, what would they think?

A long time seemed to pass before either of them spoke. "Nu?" he asked with a hint of a smile.

Hannah dropped the bundle of groceries and a uniform she had brought home to launder and moved toward him, aware that she had to force herself to take each step in his direction. Hopefully he was taking her reticence for shock, though the truth was she was reluctant to touch him. She stood across the table from him. "So, you're home" was the best she could manage.

"Either that or I'm the ghost of Karl Marx," he quipped, but the words were constricted.

"Have you eaten?"

"I made some tea and the bread is wonderful. I had forgotten about how good the bread—"

"It's not fresh. I have more in my bag." She started to retrieve it when he reached over and clasped her arm. His hands were icy. "Leave it be, I'm fine. For now. You. Seeing you, that's what I needed."

Hannah could barely bring herself to remain beside him, first because of the physical changes, second because she did not want to spoil the first hour of his homecoming with the bitter words that rose in her throat. Gently she pulled her hand away, indicating she was going to pour herself some tea. She took the glass to the table and sat in the farthest chair. He made a pretense of scanning a column, while she studied him more closely. The first difference was his weight, which had been diminished by at least thirty pounds. Bony protuberances formed the peaks of his shoulders. His hairline had receded as well—whether due to poor nutrition or natural aging she would never know—and the tufts around his ears were flecked with gray. When he stood to go to the bathroom, she was alarmed to see that the once imposing figure bent over in order to favor his badly healed leg injury.

While she had waited for this day, in her heart she had believed it would never come. Even if she was optimistic about Mr. Gibbons's decision, political events of the subsequent weeks led her to believe that his superiors would deny any questionable visa, for the Red Scare had bloomed.

Thousands were arrested as Palmer and Flynn vigorously renewed their search for communist infiltrators.

Chaim had shown his sister a recent issue of the *Liberator* and pointed to a verse:

> Who is it worries all the Feds,
>   And fills the *Times* with scary heads,
>   And murders people in their beds?
>   The Reds.

"They'll never let Lazar in now!" Hannah had moaned with a combination of anger and resignation.

"If he came, he'd turn on his heels and run back—if he could run," Chaim had added morosely. "All along the main intent has not been to stamp out radicalism, but to land Mr. A. Mitchell Palmer in the White House. This is a very dangerous man."

For many weeks after that the radical press ceased its activities. Even Chaim began to be more cautious about what he printed.

"We'd rather have an underground organization in place than no organization at all" was his explanation.

Inwardly pleased that those she cared about had chosen to remove themselves from jeopardy, Hannah had all but given up on ever seeing her husband again. And if that was the way it was, so be it. After an appropriate wait, she would tell Wendell and he would help with the divorce arrangements . . .

At least the children were not expecting their father. Benny was much more interested in the fact that Babe Ruth had been sold by the Red Sox to the New York Yankees for $125,000, the largest sum ever paid for a player. Emma was absorbed by the latest hairstyles and fashions. And the average man was much more outraged about Prohibition, which had taken effect the first month of 1920, than looking for a radical hiding under every bed. At Bellevue the most pressing issue was the alarming news that influenza had returned. On January 28 a bulletin sent to every department head warned that 5,589 new cases had been reported in New York City in only the past twenty-four hours, which exceeded the largest daily total of 5,390 reported during the epidemic of 1918. The hospital prepared for the next siege. Hannah rescheduled her midwives into double shifts, cancelled leaves, and waited for the next calamity to reach her pavilion. A few days later, however, officials announced that since there had been only 118 pneumonia deaths in the past twenty-four hours, this appeared to be a less virulent strain. And so that upheaval dwindled much like the Red panic. Someday the world would stop spinning so fast, Hannah supposed, but probably never in her lifetime.

But for now, it had stopped, at least for her. Lazar was back. Her home was restored. All her worries were over. So why did she feel so dizzy as she contemplated how to get through the next few minutes and hours . . . not to mention days and weeks?

The unmistakable sound of the children clamoring up the stairs two at a time caused her heart to lurch. Minna must have told them. The door burst open. "Pa!" called Emma, who had managed to be in the lead.

"Where is he?" Benny asked as he elbowed his way through the door first. He spun around and saw his father's lean, stooped figure in the darkness of the hall. "Pa?"

"Hello, my children," he said formally.

"Pa?" Emma ran to him with outstretched arms. She hugged him, but then he stepped back from her. "Pa?" she asked as he stumbled. Was he recoiling or had she caused him some physical pain? "You look different."

"So do you."

"We've grown," Benny said matter-of-factly, then blurted, "You've shrunk."

"Benny!" Hannah chastised reflexively.

"No, it's true," Lazar said, coming into the light. "My leg, it is shorter."

"What happened?" Emma asked with a mixture of curiosity and horror in her tone.

"Later," Hannah insisted. "There will be time . . . plenty of time for all that later." She turned to hide her expression, which was contorted by her effort not to cry. Nobody noticed as she went into the kitchen to prepare the meal. As if in a trance, she filled the kettle with water for egg noodles, dished out farmer's cheese, opened a package of smoked fish, and sliced an onion. In the background she heard the children's voices competing to tell their father about school and friends and who had moved where and snatches about what he missed of their lives. He said nothing of his experiences, nor did the children pry. This was but a background din to Hannah, whose mind was muddled by the stark realization that he was back and yet nothing, nothing was the same—or ever would be. So much had been lost! The shining fervor in his eyes had dimmed, his vigor had deteriorated, even his voice was a pathetic echo of his once powerful intonation. And yet he was alive and here, sitting in her parlor—no, *their* parlor—with their children. Maybe when these first awkward hours had passed, maybe when they were alone, maybe after they had talked together ... maybe then she would feel connected with this this stranger, but right now she felt more desolate than she had in months. The Lazar of her youthful love was no more. A different, more fulfilling future with Wendell had vanished as well. Wendell! she thought with a crushing sense of remorse. Her eyes filled with tears. She replaced the salt box and leaned against the cabinet, closed her eyes, and cried.

୬୬ 3 ଡ଼ଚ

Minna and Chaim did not come upstairs that evening. They had seen Lazar briefly before Hannah had come home. Throughout the dinner the children would glance up quizzically, as though they could not believe their father actually was there, or that this man was really their father.

Instead of insisting on staying up late, Benny surprised his mother by saying, "Time for bed."

Taking her cue from him, Emma stretched and headed for the bath, since she always wanted to be the first to wash.

The strain at the reunion had affected them, Hannah knew, so she merely said the usual: "Don't take so long," to her daughter.

"They don't have to keep a schedule, do they?" Lazar asked, a bit miffed that they were hurrying off.

"They have to get up rather early, what with Emma washing her hair every day and—"

"Isn't this a special occasion?" he asked in a thin, anxious tone.

"There's plenty of time now," she said gently.

"Yes, well, I'm tired too."

Hannah sat at her dressing table fussing with her hair while really scrutinizing Lazar in the mirror as he undressed. Although he tried to be discreet, he could not hide the scars, which formed a map of sorrow on his legs, pelvis, and chest. From the myriad welts she could surmise he had received medical attention, but it had been inexpert and delayed. One particular long scar from his groin, down the inside of his thigh, and into the back of his knee cap, made her shudder. Even more alarming was the slow, and obviously agonizing, process of settling into the bed. Once he seemed satisfied with a position, she turned off the light and slipped beside him. In silence she ran her hands along his body. Even though she had seen the scars, her fingers felt them anew. He clasped her other hand but did not speak.

"I hope I won't disturb you."

"Don't worry about me," he responded hoarsely.

"Can I get you another pillow?"

"No. Even one is a luxury."

"You've suffered."

"Less than most."

She groped for something else to say, but when nothing would come, she began to suspect what lay before them. Even with her gentleness and uncritical acceptance he did not touch her body, or respond to her ministrations. Not that she felt sexual toward him, she realized. Maybe he sensed that, nevertheless he did not make any overtures toward her either. Too soon, she thought without any keen disappointment. After all, she had seen him wince when he lay down and tried to settle his broken limbs along the undulations of their uneven mattress. If she had ruminated about resuming their lovemaking, his physical condition precluded it, but it was more than that. Even if he knew nothing about Wendell, he had to have expected her to be wary of him. She was the one he had abandoned. It was up to him to woo her again, but there was no sign of any interest on his part. During the evening's chatter, he had gone through the motions, but it was as if only the shell of the man had returned: the rest was like one of those Russian eggs, with yolk and white sucked out in preparation for Easter decoration—the main case intact, but hollow and precariously fragile.

"Good night," she ventured softly.

"Good night," he muttered into his pillow.

Hannah lay still and listened to his uneven breathing. He did not reach for her; she did not reach for him. Eventually she coiled in on herself, as she had in the lonely nights when he had not been there. Eventually Lazar found a position that hurt less than any other, and at last the two of them slept.

In the morning Chaim and Minna brought up delicacies for breakfast. Before Hannah had bathed, she smelled strong coffee and browning bagels. She came out to find Lazar sitting at the table, his face as pale and drawn as in their initial reunion. Even the liveliness of the children preparing for school did not animate him.

Minna and Chaim, who figured they had given him a whole evening to recuperate, did not hesitate to ask the questions that Hannah had avoided. Lazar did not turn them away, but his answers were slow, modulated, and spoken in a curiously flat tone, utterly devoid of the passionate speech of his past.

"Not many of these in Moscow, are there?" Minna asked as she sliced one of the plump oranges she had brought.

Lazar stared at them as if he had never seen the fruit before. Minna offered him a juicy crescent, which he began to suck as eagerly as a hungry baby at the breast.

"Tell us about your journey," prompted Chaim with a tinge of reverence in his voice.

Lazar seemed reluctant to put down the orange, but when the piece in his mouth was sucked dry, he began with a sigh. "How to get me out was the big question." He spoke in a monotone. "Eventually I received a message from Tchicherin informing me that a thousand new American deportees were to arrive in Libau and needed transportation into Russia at the end of March."

"Palmer threatened to deport that many, but only a few hundred were ever sent against their will," Chaim interjected.

"They must have been reimmigrants," Minna explained. "There are still plenty of those."

Lazar waved his hand as if he were shooing flies. "Whoever they were, they were en route from the United States. Comrade Ravitch, Commissar of Public Safety in the Petrograd District, called a conference at which they decided on a Deportees' Commission. Anyway, it was arranged that I accompany the newly appointed chairman—you'll never guess who that is!—to the Lettish frontier in Sanitary Train Number Eighty-one."

"Who was it?" Minna asked.

"Who better than Alexander Berkman?"

"I should have guessed," she said with delight. "Did you see E. G.?"

Lazar, who had taken another orange slice in hand, nodded as he popped it in his mouth. "Both have been offered positions that would have given them reasonable comfort and access to power, but both have been reluctant to offer unquestioning obedience to the state in return."

"Once an anarchist, always an anarchist, eh?" his sister-in-law quipped.

"I don't know," answered Lazar more solemnly than expected. "These anarchists have a way of transmuting. Take the fight that Emma had with John Reed."

"What happened?" Minna pressed.

"Well, John came to her room to congratulate her on having her dream realized in Russia. After a few minutes he began to talk about what should be done with those who opposed Lenin's programs. Then John—I am not certain whether he was being facetious or not—said, 'I say to the wall with them! The most expressive word I have learned in Russian is *"raztrellyat."* ' Emma asked, 'What does that mean?' Reed replied without a pause, 'Execution by firing squad.' Furious, she cut him off, saying she thought that the revolution would have invented a better method of solving its problems than wholesale slaughter."

There was a long silence and no business with an orange to cover the unspoken thoughts of each of the people sitting around Hannah's kitchen table. What had her husband witnessed? Not only the day-to-day changes wrought by the wars and revolution, but the transformation of a society from an imperialist state run by an omnipotent czar to a people's republic that had to resort to brutality to remain in power. Was this what they had dreamed of for so long?

"I suppose you are speculating what it is like there now," Lazar offered like a prosperous uncle distributing candy. He took a sip of the cooled tea, then stirred in two more lumps of sugar, as though they might help sweeten his words. "I came through Petrograd. The city looks almost deserted. When I arrived there in 1917, the population was almost three million. Today—thanks to pestilence and war—it has been decimated to five hundred thousand. Much of the time the streets are almost deserted. The stores are shuttered closed, and the only fruit and vegetables to be found are painted on those signs still hanging. Even the famous marketplaces are gone. Now the entrance to the Labor Temple has a banner proclaiming, 'Who does not work shall not eat.' "

"What is there in the way of food?" Hannah asked.

"My first day I found a public *stolovaya,* where I was served a thin vegetable soup and kasha. I did not receive any bread because the diners are supposed to bring their own. Since I was passing through, I did not know where the distribution points were. I sat in the large unheated dining room among comrades who had to keep their outer garments on to keep from shivering. What's left of the proletariat is pitiful. If the blockade is not lifted, I don't know how they will survive the winter."

"How did conditions become so terrible?" Chaim probed.

"The civil war took an even greater toll than anyone knows. You wouldn't believe it unless you saw it for yourself. Barricades of sandbags, artillery trained upon the railway station—all remnants of the Yudenich campaign—are everywhere, as are the amazing stories of the victory. Did you know that the Whites were so certain of their superior strength that they had already distributed the ministerial portfolios and appointed their military governor of Petrograd?"

"Now that the conflicts have been settled, won't they be getting back to the routine, at least by spring?" Minna asked encouragingly.

"Trotsky feels the country is just now passing through the most difficult phase of social revolution. Several fronts must continue to be defended, there are counterrevolutionary plots to be guarded against, and the Cheka must be ever vigilant for conspirators."

"You sound like you are reciting a propagandist speech, Lazar," Chaim said with a pleasant, jocular lilt. "You're in America now. You can relax and say not what Trotsky has ordained, but what you think."

Lazar's face darkened, which made his cheeks seem to sink even closer to his bones. "That is what *I* think!"

Chaim backed down. "I misunderstood you."

"I believe what Chaim meant was that we are interested in

your analysis of the situation," Minna burst in a rush. "You were on the inside. What we've been hearing is the regurgitated rhetoric of one proponent or another, as well as the supposedly unbiased news reports. Often we've been confused and have had to make our own assumptions. We were hoping you would clarify matters for us."

For a moment Hannah thought her husband was going to jump on Minna too, but the cloud seemed to lift from his face, with only a few wisps of despair lingering at the downturned corners of his mouth. "I agree that the Bolsheviki have committed some errors. We're all fallible," he offered as an olive branch. "This is a period of transition, which includes the resulting confusion, danger, and anxiety. Now is the time that every sort of socialist must remain true to his ideals, avoid criticism, join to build, not to tear down."

Tears suddenly clouded Chaim's eyes. Minna caught the emotion rising and, as she sometimes did, spoke for her husband. "He's happy to have you home, yet he's wondering if you have any regrets."

Lazar looked from one to the other, avoiding Hannah. He swallowed hard. "My last evening in Petrograd I attended the anniversary celebration of Alexander Herzen, which was held within the walls of the czar's palace. Who would ever have imagined me there? And for what reason? To praise the once forbidden name, to celebrate the feared nihilist and enemy of the Romanovs in their own private sanctum!"

Chaim reached out and clasped Lazar's hand. The two men stared deeply into each other's eyes while their wives looked on without being fully privy to the profundity of their liaison. "And?" Chaim prompted.

"After the speeches the audience proceeded to Herzen's home, which is preserved on the Nevsky. Because of my condition I could not attend, but heard the strains of the revolutionary songs waft up in the bitter cold. Passing under the palace windows, the marchers' silhouettes seemed like ghosts come to life, as if the martyrs of the czar had risen to avenge the injustice of the ages. I could hear a voice in my head, as if Herzen himself was speaking his words from his grave: 'Not in vain have you died. What you have sown will grow.' "

"You must write that down before you forget it," Minna coaxed gently.

"I will never forget it."

"Maybe not the general outlines, but the details will fade, they always do."

"No, I don't think so!" Lazar shook his head morosely.

"Why not?" Hannah inserted. "Everyone coming back is writing their experiences. John Reed's book, *Ten Days That Shook the World,* has been an enormous success, and he was an outsider who did not even speak the language."

"Lenin even wrote the introduction," Minna continued encouragingly. "I would think he might do the same for you, or what about asking Trotsky?"

"That's not possible!" Lazar snapped in a choking voice. "Lenin couldn't have written something for that book."

Hannah went to her bookshelf and pulled down the volume. She handed it to her brother. He read aloud, " 'Unreservedly do I recommend it to the workers of the world. Here is a book which I should like to see published in millions of copies and translated into all languages . . .' See for yourself," he said, handing it over.

As Lazar scanned the page, Minna continued to wax enthusiastic. "There's been a rush to put everyone's reminiscences in print. Rheta Child Dorr wrote her version of the revolution, as did Albert Rhys Williams, Bessie Beatty, and a correspondent with the *Times* named Ackerman. But you know more than any of them, at least about what everyone is panting to know."

"And what might that be?" Lazar asked gruffly.

"You lived at the Smolny. You were in Trotsky's inner sanctum, even Lenin's bedchambers. You knew their wives, families, what they ate for breakfast, how they treated their staff. You rode through Russia on Trotsky's train. You understand the way their minds work, and—"

"Forget it!" Lazar cut her off. "I could never do that."

"Why not?" Hannah dared.

"I was working for Trotsky, writing his version of events. I had to stand outside of myself, purge myself of my own opinions, make myself the statesman's vessel. Can't you understand?"

Hannah could not, but she did not admit this. Even if that had been Lazar's most fervent intent, she knew the man well enough to know he could not have removed himself entirely. Never was there anyone with more opinions of his own, and while he may have made a brave attempt to bury them, he could never had subjugated his ideals to anyone—not even

Mr. Trotsky. "I don't see why you could not write a personal version of events, or even your own analysis . . ."

"Then you do not understand what a pledge of loyalty is about," he snarled.

Chaim felt he had to defend his sister. "What I think Hannah meant was—"

Lazar held up his hand. It was trembling. "Impossible! I refuse to discuss this further!" He made a first attempt to stand, which was a clumsy scraping of the chair and reaching for his cane. When he was upright, he composed himself long enough to conclude the subject once and for all. "Can't you see the consequences? Or will I have to spell them out? Too dangerous. Even now, even here." His eyes searched the room like a cornered animal looking for an escape opening. Then he staggered to the toilet.

∽ **4** ∽

Dr. Herzog's thorough examination of Lazar confirmed Hannah's opinion that with good food, rest, and medical care for his respiratory problems, he might make a significant recovery over time.

"The cold, particularly the dampness, has been terrible for him. If he stays warm, eats heartily, I think you will see a major improvement by the summer," he predicted.

Yet Hannah was more concerned with the changes from determined agitator to apathetic bystander. When he was well enough to be employed, when he found what it was he wanted to pursue, she expected this would lift as well. Yes, she was disappointed that there had been no passionate reunion, but the respite might be what she required to make the transition from Wendell to Lazar, as well as what Lazar may have needed to make the transition back to her from something—or someone—else. Had there been a woman in Russia? Or more than one? She burned to ask the question, but knew that some doors were best remained closed because once the scene behind them had been beheld, it could never be erased from one's memory. This was also her reason for not mentioning Wendell, although she ruminated on the plusses that might come from airing her secret. She wanted Lazar to know that she had had choices. She did not want him to believe that he could leave her for several years, then march back thinking that she had suspended her life to suit his will. Also, if he knew she had decided on him, it might bolster his flagging spirits, or even rekindle his desire for her.

But would the gains from that confession offset the risk of his revulsion? What if he became angry, even though he had no right to? Potent emotions swirled around sexual matters, and she feared that Lazar—no matter how liberal he professed to be—might react from the gut instead of his intellect. Nobody knew better than Hannah, the advice givor, the unpredictability of these situations. Better to remain silent. Better to work on his confidence some other way and show him that she was determined that since they were together again their marriage would flourish anew. Besides, there might indeed be a physical reason for his impotence. The man had been crushed in the train wreck, so who knew what vital parts had been damaged?

Hannah also realized that this was a most delicate situation. From her readings about men's tribulations she knew that the fear of loss of virility could have the same result as a true physical condition. In this case, where there had been trauma leading to a possibly temporary—yet equally possible permanent—debility, she had to approach the issue with supreme tenderness. Thus far she had determined he suffered true pain. His ribs still ached, his leg was troubling him. Her decision was that she would not press the point until some degree of healing was evident. And certainly she would not mention Dr. Dowd, or Russian women, or anything that might widen the fissure looming between them.

She had never expected the rift in their marriage would mend at once. Even if she did everything in her power, there were some situations she could not change by force of will alone. In any case, she had not brought him back for her sake, but for the children's. So what perplexed her was his lack of attachment toward the children. She had expected to see their heads pressed next to their father's over school assignments, to hear them laugh at his jokes, to watch him chuckle at their antics. What had happened? Benny and Emma sometimes walked by their father's chair as though he were an inanimate piece of furniture. Worse, he did not look up, smile, or greet them. No, that was not the worst. What she hated most were the quarrels.

The first one came after Lazar had been home less than two weeks. Emma had asked her father to see the newspapers. She scanned several before alighting on the article about which she had been curious. "Here it is!"

She was reading when her father looked over her shoulder. "What is it about?" he inquired.

"Douglas Fairbanks and Mary Pickford were married in Los Angeles. At last!"

"This is what has you so engrossed!" he shouted. "Is that what fills your mind these days?" He ripped the paper from her hand. "Don't you care about what is going on in the world? Did you know that the American Senate just failed to ratify the Treaty of Versailles? Do you realize what that means?" His daughter had drifted off toward the kitchen and opened a cabinet door. Hearing no response, he spun around and saw she had left the room. Lazar rushed behind her and slammed the cabinet shut. "Don't you dare move away when I am talking to you, Emma! Where did you learn that behavior? Not from me, I'm certain of that."

"Of course not, Pa. How could I, when you deserted us?"

"Is that what your mother called it?"

"No, that's what I call it. You left her and us—and for what? For what?" she repeated, pushing past him.

Lazar grabbed her arm. "Don't you ever speak to me like that again!"

Emma winced, but did not cry out as his fingers dug into her flesh. "Free speech is a *right* in this country, or have you forgotten that too?"

Hannah, who had witnessed the confrontation from the far side of the room, had been too stunned to intervene, but when she saw the impasse, with Emma's grimace proof that Lazar actually was hurting her, she could hold back no longer. "Lazar, let her be!"

"Shut up!" he commanded. "You've let her run wild. If we always give in, she'll never learn."

Hannah leapt up and ran into the kitchen. "You're hurting her. Stop it!"

With reluctance Lazar loosened his grip. Emma and Hannah stared at the bluish marks on her arm: the girl with a sly grin of satisfaction, the mother with horror at the implications of what she had witnessed. If the fight had been between brother and sister, Hannah could have separated the two and given each a suitable punishment. What now? Emma had been wrong to speak back to her father, but Lazar had incited the rebellion. By breaking them apart she had seemed to be against her husband. To repair that damage she said, "Go down and see your Aunt Minna. And don't come back until you are ready to apologize."

Emma stomped out of the flat and down the stairs so that each angry thump echoed up to their floor.

"Lazar . . ." Hannah pleaded, "you must not explode like that over nothing."

"Nothing? Our daughter is ignorant of everything except songs and cinema. What's to become of her?"

"She's no different from the other girls her age. She does well in school. She helps around the house. What more can you expect?"

"People are dying, people are starving, and she fills her head with dreck."

"Thirteen-year-old girls are not supposed to take the world's burdens on their shoulders. There's time enough to worry. Let her enjoy life while she can." Lazar's face remained pinched with fury, so she made another appeal. "She missed you terribly. For months after you left she would cry herself to sleep. During the epidemic her grandmother died, and then she thought she would lose me too."

Lazar was unmoved. "You don't understand. You are like the rest of these silly Americans who think just because the Great War is over, just because their soldiers have returned, that this is the time to think only of frivolities. If you'd read the papers once in a while, you would see the worrisome signs. Right this moment a new political party in Munich is attacking large property owners, capitalists, and Jews."

"Sounds like two-thirds of the time you are in agreement with them."

This halted Lazar for a minute, but then he lowered his voice to a level Hannah knew meant he was truly concerned, not just fighting for the sake of an argument. "I have a sense about this group, and its leader, a disciple of that anti-Semitic mayor of Vienna. Why, everywhere you look there is more trouble brewing."

"All right, Lazar," Hannah said with a long, exasperated sigh. "You can tell me about it. I am interested in what worries you, but please, for my sake, leave the children out of it."

∞ 5 ∞

When Lazar went out, Hannah decided to see how Emma was faring. She knocked on the door to the downstairs front apartment.

Minna called, "Chaim? The door is open."

Hannah walked in, but did not see Minna anywhere about. "It's me," she announced. "Emma?"

"In here!"

Hannah opened the bathroom door slightly and was greeted by a burst of steam. "Where's Emma?"

"Oh, she was so upset Chaim took her out for an egg cream. He forgot his key, so I left the door open."

"Anyone could have come in," Hannah said with alarm as she was able to glimpse her sister-in-law's pink knees protruding from the bath water. "Didn't you hear about those boys who took Mrs. Nadleman's purse while she was hanging the clothes?"

Minna splashed about but did not respond. "Is Lazar calmer now?"

"I guess so. He doesn't understand that the children are different from the little ones he left. They have minds of their own now."

"Like he did at that age, I'm sure," Minna giggled. "Why don't you remind him of that?"

"Not now. He's been through too much."

"Well, as I told Emma, she's welcome down here anytime. The best thing we ever did was move to Tompkins Square. You don't know how much we've enjoyed being with your children."

Hannah, who remained in the doorway, blinked in the foggy air. This comment was totally unlike anything she had ever heard Minna say, but it was gratifying nevertheless. For so long she had felt she had unfairly placed a burden on her brother and his wife to watch out for the children when she was called away. Now that they were older and did not need as much minding, they continued to gravitate downstairs rather than fix themselves a meal. Or sometimes they just preferred the company of someone other than their mother. Once Lazar had returned, she had expected they would be content with him, thus relieving her brother and his wife from this chore. Instead they remained closer to their aunt and uncle, sometimes seeming to avoid their father. But they could be agreeable children—and interesting too, if you stopped to listen to their admittedly Americanized view of the world. Without Emma, Hannah would not have known who Mary Pickford was, let alone the details of her romantic courtship, or the words to the latest tune by Irving Berlin, or the steps to the current dance in vogue. Benny kept her informed about the feats of the aviators and the baseball scores. She much preferred the debates over the World Series to those about the World War. Babe Ruth and Douglas Fairbanks were more uplifting than the latest exploits of Trotsky or Admiral Kolchak. People thought that children learned everything from their parents, but nobody realized how much they brought into the home from the outside.

"I am happy you said that," Hannah replied wearily.

"Sit down, I want to ask you about something." Hannah started to back out to the bedroom. "No, come in, I've nothing you haven't seen a thousand times before."

Hannah was perplexed by the request, but did as asked. She replaced the commode lid and balanced on the edge.

Minna leaned back and closed her eyes. "I do like a nice long soak in the tub. Is that wicked?"

"Hardly, especially after what I am accustomed to hearing."

"Do you ever hear about women who want more than anything to have a baby, but who can't?" Minna burst out.

"What?" Hannah was taken by surprise. "Is this what you wanted to talk to me about?"

"Yes." The only sound was the sloshing of the water as Minna sat up straighter.

Hannah watched as her small breasts popped out of the water, the nipples reacting to the temperature difference by protruding. "I thought you said . . . that you had decided . . ."

"We've changed our minds."

"I see. Then what's the problem?"

"We don't know. We've been trying—or rather not using anything—for more than a year. When the war was ending, when the revolution was over, well, we thought this might be a better time to bring a child into the world. He or she would have more choices than ever before."

"So far you have been disappointed with the results."

"What results? Nothing. Maybe we waited too long."

Hannah did some calculations. They had been married thirteen years. Most of that time they had been experimenting with birth-control devices, at least as far as she knew, but there had to have been times in the beginning, plus the recent attempts, when they had not. Of course, a certain percentage of couples were infertile, but she had not imagined her brother's wife would be. In fact, when they had announced they would never have children, she had been acutely disappointed because she had assumed she would have a special relationship with her brother's children. Eventually that frustration had been supplanted by respect for Minna and the depth of her commitment to choices in family determination. She stared at Minna, who was as slender—actually, after watching her in the bath the word would have to be skinny—as ever. In truth, she did not look like a robust candidate for motherhood. Perhaps she had defective organs, either since birth or due to the two major traumas she had suffered: her near-drowning during the Polish pogrom, and her self-induced starvation in the Blackwell's Island protest. Hannah suspected the latter.

"Didn't you tell me that after you were in jail you did not menstruate for more than a year?" the midwife asked calmly.

"Yes, but since then everything has been absolutely on schedule."

Age might be a factor. Chaim was forty-two and Minna was about five or six years younger. "How old are you now?"

"Thirty-six next month. Is that too ancient?"

"We have many mothers well past that, but not too many first-timers. In any case, that wouldn't rule you out."

"Do you think there is something wrong with me?"

"I don't know. I could examine you, but there isn't much we can tell from the external signs, and we have no satisfactory way to see inside."

"Would you do it now?"

"I'd prefer to see you at the clinic, where I have equipment, a good light—"

The door slammed behind them. "We're back, Minna, and we brought you an egg cream too!" called Emma in her high soprano. "Ma! What are you doing here?"

"I came to see how you were doing," she said, then waved at Minna. "We'll talk more about the other later."

"More about what?" Emma inquired curiously.

"About whether chocolate or vanilla egg creams are best. What else?"

The next afternoon, Minna submitted to an examination. Hannah found that—on the surface at least—she was absolutely normal.

"I see no obvious difficulty," Hannah admitted.

"What could be wrong?"

"The process of conception is so complex I sometimes wonder how any babies are formed, and yet the other paradox is that impregnation can take place under the most unfavorable conditions, and often occurs when both parties have done everything possible to prevent pregnancy. While I am hardly an expert, there is a logical approach to examine the possibilities."

"What is that?"

"All right." Hannah flipped over one of her charts and began a diagram. "The first list is the simplest. The man either can produce spermatozoa that are possibly incapable of conception, or he has an inadequate supply. Since a woman's structure is more complex, the difficulty is usually blamed on her, but we should not rule out his responsibility."

"What does that mean?" asked Minna, who was usually analytical but seemed in a fog.

"Chaim must, if he is willing, make a donation in a jar. Some prefer to wear a condom during a regular sexual activity. Either way the result would then be examined by a laboratory."

"But it's probably me, isn't it?"

"I can't say. Sometimes both contribute to the difficulty. The books state that in order for impregnation to take place, live spermatozoa must be ejaculated from the penis to the cervical os, or opening, of the woman's uterus. However, there are a few documented cases of conception where the spermatozoa have merely landed on the external genitals of the woman, without any intromission, but these must be con-

sidered exceptions and have no bearing on your situation . . .
I would presume."

"I don't understand."

"I must make the assumption that your sexual relations
are normal, involve full penetration, ejaculation deep inside
your vagina, and occur frequently, especially at the time you
would be ovulating."

"Why would you think it would be any other way?"

"Minna, I am not trying to pry into your private life, but
you would not believe the stories I hear!"

"I know. When I worked with Margaret, I was sometimes
shocked by the ignorance. I can assure you that there is
nothing peculiar about what we do."

"Even the frequency?" Hannah pressed.

"I don't know what normal is."

"Neither did I, at least until Dr. Dowd began his study."
Hannah attempted to glide over the man's name as though it
meant nothing. At least Minna was too wrapped in her own
worry to notice the catch in her voice. "For a couple married
ten years or more, once or twice a week seems the average,
although some deviation on both ends might be considered
routine. However, for a couple actively trying to conceive, I
would think that three or four attempts at the most propitious time of the month would be desirable. Do you know
those dates?"

Minna lowered her eyes. "After all these years around you
and Margaret, I should, but I relied on my Dutch cap for so
long that I ignored the charts. Anyway, it's usually twice a
week, unless one of us is ill."

"That should be sufficient," Hannah responded crisply.
"Later, I'll do a chart and point out the best chances."

"If there is something actually wrong with me, what
might it be?"

"The most typical would be a blockage." Hannah began to
draw a diagram of a woman's internal organs. "Although
there are some who suggest more subtle factors are often the
cause."

"What might those be?"

Hannah hesitated. Rachael was a special case, yet she
knew it was worrisome to become involved in the sexual
lives of those close to her, especially Minna, with whom she
had only recently developed a warm friendship.

"You don't have to be restrained with me," Minna prompted.

"There are some doctors who claim that a woman who enjoys her relations is apt to have an easier time conceiving. Personally, I find there are gaps in those theories, since many women who dislike sex seem to have no problem reproducing. However, it might have to do with secretions or spasms encouraging the spermatozoa upward . . ."

Minna moistened her lips. "Don't worry, you can rule that one out too."

Hannah felt an immense release. She tapped her pencil on the chart. "You could look at this like a plumbing diagram. We're just a bunch of tubes and pipes, some very thin and fragile, others more substantial. The woman's ovum makes its journey downward, while the man's spermatozoa travel in the other direction. They must meet here . . ." She pointed to a fallopian tube. "Then the united cells venture back to the uterus, where they multiply into the fetus." Hannah pointed out several tight places. "Either the sperm may be blocked in its passage, or the same might happen to the ovum, or to the fertilized ovum before it safely attaches to the uterine wall."

"How would a blockage occur?"

"A wad of mucus might act like a cork. Infections can cause scars that bind the tubes closed."

"If there is a blockage, might it be repaired?"

"I'm afraid not. The only time we see them are during radical procedures to remove diseased organs. It would be far too dangerous to open up a woman surgically for an examination, and even if this was done, the tubes, for instance, are so slender the additional scarring from the actual repair could worsen the woman's chances."

"What about X rays?"

"They don't give us an outline of the soft tissues. The state of your pelvis might be important in determining how large a baby you might be able to deliver with ease, but not much about your fertility."

"So there is not much we can do," Minna commented dejectedly.

"On the contrary. We can rule out Chaim as the cause, we can increase your chances by pinpointing the days on the chart, there are positions that some believe will help deposit the sperm deeper into the vagina and closer to the os. Also, you might be better off staying in your bed for several hours after relations, so nothing valuable leaks out. I might even recommend a sponge be put in place afterward to drive up any timid spermatozoa as well as to keep them going in the right direction."

Minna laughed aloud. "I feel better knowing there is something I can try."

"Good. We'll start on those prescriptions. I will also consult the recent medical journals. I have heard of many experiments in this field. Who knows? Maybe I'll find something that will apply to your case."

Minna left heartened, but Hannah had the opposite feeling. After a year of frequent unprotected sexual activity, their chances were poor. Besides, maybe they did not really want to be parents. This decision to have children seemed less calculated than their choice not to. Might this impulse pass? Anyway, maybe they were better off without children. Every hour of every day a parent had to worry about them. Even with Benny and Emma so much more self-sufficient, she had more fears for them rather than less. Maybe she should explain to Minna about the trials, the sorrows, the decisions made on a child's behalf that forced a man and a woman to compromise every hour of every day. Why, if it had not been for the children, she might not have fought for Lazar's return, and at this very moment she might be with Wendell.

No, she mustn't permit that line of thinking! She had taken the right course. She could never have lived with herself if she had to contemplate Lazar languishing in some Russian clinic. Wendell had been a lovely diversion, nothing more. Her vows to Lazar were irrevocable, no matter what he had done. And what had he done? He had fought for his principles, won some of the battles, lost others. The whole while he had expected his wife to join him, as a dutiful woman might have. She had been the one who had refused to traipse after him. Then he had returned . . .

Hannah chided herself for allowing her mind to wander. The question was Minna's fertility. Maybe she had been wrong to give her so much hope without mentioning the consequences of her frailty, her illnesses. Also, there was something else. Hannah's intuition warned her that this was, if not a hopeless case, one that would be endlessly frustrating for both patient and adviser. Yet for Minna the plunge had been taken. They were linked until either the goal was achieved or one of them gave up. Knowing Minna, Hannah suspected she would have to be the one to end the process, for Minna never backed down. Never.

On Wednesdays Hannah continued to meet with Dr. Dowd. Not at the Brevoort but at his Bellevue office. Early in the new year he had decided to give up his hotel room. The reason was clear, yet unspoken. If he felt as uncomfortable as she did, he disguised it better. By Tuesday night Hannah was a bundle of nerves in anticipation. One look at her pathetic, broken husband was enough to start the flow of tears, but she had to guard against his sensing anything, which made it more difficult. If it were not for Wendell, Lazar would not be here, she reminded herself, always bitterly aware of the irony. The doctor's motives were either too pure or too clouded for her to fathom. Or maybe, with his inside information on the Red Scare, he had taken a calculated risk—and lost. Or maybe he had wanted to end their relationship because she would have made a most unsuitable Mrs. Dowd and this was the easiest way out. As soon as she had processed that thought, she berated herself. Why was it so difficult for her to imagine that Wendell loved her and his only ambition was to spend his life with her, but only if it would not cost her a penalty? Besides, what did it matter now? It was over. Over! If she had any regrets, she would just have to keep them to herself.

In the morning she would anticipate the moments with the doctor with a curious admixture of desire and fear. Did Wendell hear the hard beating of her heart or notice the quiver in her hands when they were near? Was the quaver in her voice noticeable, or did he realize that her stumbling words were the result of holding in what she really wanted to say to him?

Anyway, an outsider never would have suspected there had been anything between them, especially since he had begun to speak to her more brusquely than he ever had—at least to her—although she had heard that crusty tone with others.

She knocked on the door. "Come in," he called without glancing up. "Mrs. Sokolow, here are the proofs for the first journal article. Check them now, because they are due tomorrow." No welcoming words, no gentlemanly phrases, not even a "please." The words "Mrs. Sokolow" had the sarcastic tinge senior physicians sometimes reserved for doctors in training. Better this way, Hannah thought as she accepted the sheaf of papers without making contact with his azure eyes.

To insure the timely publication of their first attempt at interpreting the statistics from their study, Dr. Dowd had suggested that they tie their work into "a political theme."

"But we didn't ask any political questions" had been her retort.

"Take a look at the one hundred and thirty-seven marriages that began between 1915 and 1919, the stressful years of the war. Before studying the data, what assumptions might you make?"

"Maybe those unions were more hastily made than in other times?"

"Indeed. So would they be happier or more troubled in the long run? Also, while men have always entreated their beloveds to have carnal relations with them, with the specter of never returning again their pleas may have been more successful, leading to more premarital experiences."

"That makes sense."

"Right, but I've broken out their responses and begun to compare them with those married during more stable times, and the preliminary results are not as expected. Right now everyone is interested in the effects of the war on society, so we are certain to get an audience. Once the powers that be are aware of our wealth of data, we should have no trouble publishing further findings for years to come."

While the doctor busied himself with some paperwork, Hannah browsed through the finished article, "A Comparison of Premarital Sexual Experience During Times of War and Peace," which had been set in type. She focused on her name at the top of the page: H. Sokolow, Supervisor for Obstetrics, Bellevue Hospital, coming after W. Q. Dowd, M.D., Chairman, Obstetrics and Gynecology Department, Bellevue Hospital, Consultant to Harlem Hospital, Gouverneur's Hospital, and Allied Institutions, Member American Gynecological Association, American Medical Association, Fellow of the New York Academy of Medicine. Her mind drifted as she mused: If they only knew what really happened between the doctor and the midwife . . .

He looked up and smiled at her. "By the way, I added a new introduction, and put the one we wrote before at the beginning of the conclusions. Do you see any immediate problems?"

Hannah had not read a word of the body of the text, but said, "I think it looks fine, at least to me."

"Good. I must say I enjoyed the editorial responses to our conclusions." He gave a little chuckle. "What surprised them the most was that while in the wartime group, the happiness factor was lower, they were more chaste, suggesting the alleged wildness of our youth is largely mythical."

Idly Hannah flipped to the index. "I see that Dr. Blühner has a piece in the same issue."

"Yes, we'll be in good company. There's also one by another Mt. Sinai man, Dr. Rubin, and I'm afraid his is the one that will receive the most attention."

"Why?"

"Some are saying that his uterotubal insufflation test is the breakthrough of a lifetime. With it we will finally be able to diagnose tubal patency without surgical intervention."

Hannah's pulse began to gallop. If Chaim's spermatozoa were healthy, this was the most likely area of Minna's difficulty. "How is it done?"

"The test is deceptively simple. Rubin has been searching for a way to investigate the causes of female sterility. Since tubes cannot be seen, and manual examination reveals nothing significant about them, most supposed cures have involved dilatations of the cervix, curettage, and the use of stem pessaries, on the theory that obstruction could be found in the cervical canal."

"But that's only a small part of the entire system."

"I know that, but we've been reluctant to even discuss what we cannot see, or attempt to fix. Thus Rubin speculated whether there was some way to visualize the tubes without opening the abdomen. He wanted to outline them with a substance that could be seen on a Roentgen-ray plate. For several years I've heard rumors of his first attempt with a radio-opaque substance called Collargol. This, and the halogen salts he tried thereafter, apparently produced a reasonably good picture of the tubes, but their use carried grave dangers of chemical irritation."

"Has he found something less toxic?" Hannah asked excitedly.

"Why, yes," Dr. Dowd responded with a bemused smile at her unexpected reaction. "He devised a clever way to pass a harmless gas through the tubes. If they are open, the oxygen rises through the abdominal cavity to the diaphragm, producing an artificial pneumoperitoneum. However, if the tubes are closed, the gas is regurgitated through the vagina."

"Is he doing the procedure on a regular basis?"

"Hannah," the doctor said, dropping his formality, "why are you so interested?"

"My sis—I mean, a patient—may be suffering from undiagnosed infertility, and I would like to know the status of her tubes. Would he see her?"

"I don't know. The question is: would she wish to submit to an experimental procedure? I don't think it is dangerous, but it does not sound pleasant."

"She would."

"Don't you think you need to discuss it with her before you jump to that conclusion?"

"I know this woman, and what she would reply."

"Well, I am not going to argue with you," he said diffidently.

"Would you ask Dr. Rubin to see her?"

"I could make the referral, but not unless I examined her."

"That would be no problem," Hannah ventured before she worried she had spoken too soon. Would Minna agree to having several doctors perform intimate examinations? Hannah reminded herself that Minna—with her steely core—would suffer anything to win her aim.

An idea began to form, like a sauce thickening at the bottom of a heated pan. Hannah imagined the chart of a woman's reproductive organs she had drawn for Minna. If there was a blockage and a gush of air was forced through the pipes, might not a plug of mucus or other minor obstruction be removed by the procedure? Of course, permanent scarring, adhesions, or tumors could not be dislodged.

The doctor noticed her face brightening. "What is it?" he asked more affably than before.

She mentioned her concept, and Wendell beamed. "That's the result Rubin is hoping for, but it will take a long series of trials—with women who attain pregnancy after the procedure—to test the validity of that hypothesis."

"I would feel better if I could tell my patient that the test might be more than diagnostically beneficial."

"Don't make promises, but I would not think it unreasonable to suggest the possibility of a remedy."

Hannah watched his mouth as he painstakingly worded his sentence. She loved the pinkness of his lips, the whiteness of his raised cheekbones, the firmness of his chin. Compared to Lazar's wasted body, he looked splendidly robust . . . and virile! There was so much she wanted to say to him, to explain. She wanted him to know that he was the last man she had made love to—and that she longed to do so again—yet to express her regrets would be to sound ungrateful for what he had done, what he had relinquished for her sake. Better that he should believe that she had what she wanted, that his sacrifice had been worthwhile. Better to relieve him of any hope for their reunion. He liked women. He needed a woman. Eventually he would find another, if she gave him the chance. Ah, but there was the paradox: she did not want him to have anyone else because she didn't really have Lazar, did she? Maybe they could resume some part of their friendship. Hadn't he said the survey could keep them occupied for years? After this publication nobody would question their professional association. They would have to see each other more often than Wednesday afternoons.

Hannah was standing. So was Wendell. She was returning his pages. His hand was outstretched. The walls of the room seemed to be receding. The usual hospital noises were wiped out by a whirring in her brain, which became louder and louder, like a thundering train. To prevent her world from tilting, she focused on his mouth . . . his lovely mouth. Then, thankfully, blessedly, it moved closer and met its inevitable mark. Was he moaning, or was it her? They clutched each other as if they were providing a life-saving procedure, although which one was the patient neither could have determined. Any concern that they might be interrupted had been blotted out by incessant need.

For a moment Hannah felt a chill. Wendell had broken the seal between them. Cool air from the window chafed her burning skin, and then the draft was silenced. The window was closed, the shade drawn. A click. The door was latched. The light dimmed. On the floor, in the narrow space behind his desk, was a thick woolen rug with an oriental design. Hannah had never noticed it before. It had been placed there to warm the cold linoleum or to brighten his little bureaucratic corner, but now it was a lifeboat in a hard, cruel sea. As if in a trance, she lay down. He removed her stockings, her underwear, his trousers. What happened next was a series of frenzied movements as they grappled to resume what they could not resume, to steal what they could not give freely. From a distance it might have appeared crude, even ugly. From behind closed eyes, clenched teeth, wild groping arms and grasping legs, it was warm, dark, moist, and familiar. She clasped his buttocks and forced him deeper. One leg found purchase on the seat of his chair, the other on the outside wall. With these firm fulcrums she could move as savagely as the demons demanded. He cradled her head so she would not pound it into the edge of the desk, but after that tender gesture she was oblivious to anything else except the voluptuous sensations that tumbled through her loins again and again and again.

7

According to Wendell, Isidor C. Rubin had received his medical degree from the College of Physicians and Surgeons in 1905, then spent time studying in Germany and Austria before returning to a practice at Mt. Sinai Hospital in New York. The first Rubin test for uterotubal insufflation was performed on October 3, 1919, in that institution's Roentgen-Ray department. Initially the apparatus was not perfected and not enough oxygen was administered to distend the patient's abdomen. Very shortly thereafter, the rate of flow and the amount of gas were regulated so that the absolute minimum necessary for the test was passed in the tubes.

"Will he see her?" Hannah asked after his explanation, which had been given in the most clinical of voices, despite what had occurred the last time they were together. She too had been determined to subdue her conflicting sensations, and so far had been succeeding admirably.

"Rubin is so anxious to evaluate his developing apparatus, he welcomes any candidate for the procedure." The doctor puffed out a bit before adding, "He also said he was 'complimented to have a referral from one whose seminal survey of women's sexual experiences was surely to propel him into the ranks of innovative gynecologists.' "

"Had you met him before?"

"Yes, but Dr. Blühner always seemed to be between us."

"What does Dr. Blühner say about Dr. Rubin?"

"As little as possible. Unfortunately, Dr. Blühner has a bit of a jealous streak, which he thinks he contains masterfully but does not."

"I'm glad Minna won't be needing his services," Hannah said while tidying her hair.

"So is Dr. Rubin, I assure you. Fortunately, I took the precaution of testing Mr. Blau's spermatozoa, which have proven viable, so there is no need for a referral to Dr. Blühner, who is keen on analyzing male secretions in minute detail. If Blühner had become involved, Dr. Rubin said the case might have taken a diversion into studies on everything from gonococci to motility, and most probably including his latest craze: aspiration of spermatozoa from the testicles," he concluded with a wince, which so successfully terminated the conversation, Hannah was able to leave his office without losing her composure once again.

On the appointed morning, Dr. Rubin greeted Mrs. Blau, Dr. Dowd, and Hannah, who was introduced not as a midwife but as Wendell's research assistant. Normally a patient would not have arrived accompanied by these other practitioners, but they were as ardent to see his procedure as Dr. Rubin was to demonstrate it. The doctor was younger than Hannah had expected, with a sleek head of hair that featured a prominent, flattering wave along the edge of his forehead that offset the intense expression in his eyes. Hannah supposed the curl to be natural, even though it had the marcelled look that Emma spent hours trying to perfect.

Dr. Rubin asked his young associate, Dr. Anspach, to review the apparatus with the Bellevue visitors while he spent a few moments perusing the patient's file and conducting a preliminary examination to see if she was fit for the rigors of the test. Although Dr. Rubin did not know exactly what to expect, the Mrs. Blau who sat across from him was not quite the retiring Lower East Side thirty-six-year-old matron he had envisioned from the file. Slender, with almost painfully protruding bones, she did not have the *zaftik* quality that would make an excellent candidate for motherhood, particularly so late in life. Nor did she have the bent and beaten aspect of an immigrant who must have scrabbled hard. There was a nobility in her straight spine, primly folded hands, and direct, questioning stare.

"You are aware that this is an experimental procedure," he stated at the end of his basic explanation.

"Yes," she responded like a witness to a jury.

"I cannot guarantee success, either in a diagnostic or therapeutic sense."

"I realize that, Doctor. My only desire is to be informed of everything that is happening, and to receive a forthright explanation of the result."

"Of course, Mrs. Blau." Dr. Rubin flipped through the pages in her chart.

"Is something the matter?" she asked.

The doctor looked up with consternation. He was accustomed to being the one asking the questions. There was something else. An enigma was unanswered about this woman, yet he could not find a clue among the papers. Minna Blau. Had he treated other members of her family? "I have other Blaus as patients," he offered to see if she would supply the missing link. "Could they be members of your family?"

"The only other Mrs. Blau was my mother-in-law, and she never left the Lower East Side for treatment."

"The name is familiar . . ." Something on the next page caught his eye. "You have been married for thirteen years without success at conception."

"Not exactly. We have been attempting for less than two."

The doctor looked up curiously but did not speak. In his many years in this business he heard about all sorts of various sexual alliances. If she cared to explain, she would.

"I have utilized the latest forms of birth-control devices until we made a commitment to raise a family in this worrisome world."

Birth control . . . Margaret Sanger . . . Minna Blau! This was the woman who had almost died to win her point. How he had admired her stand—privately, of course, since nobody in his profession could have afforded to align themselves against Comstock and his crew. What a paradoxical position! After years of contraception, she had abandoned that notion at the twilight of her fertility. Now he saw her as though a curtain had been lifted. The long line of women who had submitted to his earlier studies had been no more than hopeful candidates for a pilot procedure, but this was someone special. As he ticked off her chances, his spirits deflated. Her age put her in the "elderly" range for a primary conception. A rapid assessment of her pallor, delicacy, and intellectual aspect placed her in another vulnerable category. Even if she were to become impregnated, her pelvis appeared marginal. If he had known all this before Dr. Dowd requested the procedure, he would never have accepted the case. One more subject for the purpose of data collection—which would inevitably help women in the future—was of little consequence, but this was one person he did not want to fail.

"As I have suggested, Mrs. Blau, the most I could hope to accomplish would be to apprise you if, in my best judgment, you seem to have obstructed tubes, or if you do not." Without realizing it, the doctor had lapsed into Yiddish. "In the first case, I will merely be confirming your worst fears; if you do not, then I have given you one less reason to be concerned, but no reason to have more hope."

"I heard that you might be able to unblock the tubes," Minna responded, also in Yiddish. Somehow they both thought it easier to convey their real meaning in this universal language between Jews of any age, distance, class, or profession.

"That is a supposition we are testing, but I have to tell you that not one baby has been born as a result of this procedure. Nor have I been informed of a single pregnancy. That does not mean the data will not be forthcoming. I have every reason to believe—"

"Well, it is consoling to think that no matter my outcome, I will fall into one column or the other, and that should be of assistance to future cases like mine." Minna was standing. "Let's not keep the others waiting."

Dr. Rubin was about to ask her to sit back down, but why? Because he was used to controlling these exchanges, he realized. He followed her lead. Better to get this over with, he decided, as he led her into his laboratory.

Hannah watched Minna's approach. She was wearing a hospital gown tied lightly in the back. Many women gripped these flimsy garments to preserve their last vestige of modesty, but Minna walked as though she were a regular guest at an imperial gathering. Hannah had hoped to have a moment to talk to Minna alone, but she had remained with Dr. Rubin for more than a half hour, then had been prepared by a nurse, while Hannah and Dr. Dowd had been held captive by Dr. Anspach. His explanation of the equipment had done nothing to allay her concerns, and by the time he had finished, Hannah knew she had made a terrible mistake involving Minna in what was clearly an unsafe experiment.

The equipment was a horrifying conglomeration of pumps, tubes, and wires. A large silver tank marked "O_2" dominated the structure on the stand. The dials and graphs on the wall had notations that showed the varied settings they had tried. "What is the usual pressure?" Dr. Dowd had asked.

"We still are in the process of determining that," Dr. Anspach answered without hesitation, "although anything greater than two hundred is still in the experimental stage."

"Have you considered CO_2?" Dr. Dowd queried.

Dr. Anspach shifted his feet. "Actually, we have. We may do trials with it later this year."

Poor Minna was going to be pumped up with an unknown quantity of gas under an unexplored pressure. Even if a certain degree had been suitable for, say, a hundred-and-fifty-pound woman, would that be too much for ninety-nine-pound Minna? From the beginning she had had her doubts whether this would assist Minna's goal of having a baby. Now Hannah was concerned that the test could rupture something, doing irreparable damage to her reproductive organs—or worse, to something more vital.

She looked at Dr. Dowd for support, but he was busily reviewing the techniques with Dr. Rubin.

"Pressure reading?" Dr. Rubin asked his assistant.

"Fifteen pounds, needle valve opened, 60 cc's per excursion," replied Dr. Anspach.

"If you are ready, Mrs. Blau," Dr. Rubin inquired gently, "we are going to begin the procedure." Hannah watched as he came around to the head of the table and spoke close to

Minna's face. He took her hand in his, then whispered something. Hannah caught the phrase: *"Zol zein mit glick."* He was wishing her luck in Yiddish! This was not an unfeeling researcher. He would not do anything to harm Minna, Hannah murmured to console herself as the process commenced.

Automatically she moved to the foot of the table to watch the cannula as it was taken from a sterile tray, shaken to eliminate the water in which it had been boiled, and attached to a metal adapter at the end of the outlet rubber tubing. As Dr. Anspach explained the procedure in scientific terms, Hannah glimpsed Minna's hands, which were tied down to handholds, whiten to the bone of her knuckles. Hannah returned to the head of the table. Bending over, she saw Minna's jaw clenching and unclenching.

"Take a deep breath. Another. Another. Good. Now let it out easy, now in slowly, now out, now in." Minna was soon concentrating on the rhythm. Ignoring the others, Hannah continued assisting Minna in coping with the inevitable cramping.

In the distance she heard Dr. Rubin's whispered voice: "Watch the fluctuations of the mercury column in the manometer. These indicate the tubal contractions as the gas is released. What we have found is the readings depend on ovarian function, and hence vary with phases of the menstrual cycle. To prevent the sad accident of disrupting an early pregnancy, we have restricted testing to the fourth to the seventh day following cessation of the last regular period, and are calibrating from these dates."

"Dr. Rubin, look!" called Dr. Anspach. Hannah turned in that direction in time to see the assistant pointing out a significant reading. "One hundred fifty-five millimeters."

"A stricture reading," mumbled Dr. Rubin. He turned away with disgust as his worst fears for the patient were realized.

"One hundred seventy, eighty, eighty-nine . . ." Dr. Anspach called. "Do you want to stop at two hundred, Dr. Rubin?"

He nodded as he continued to educate his observers. "We're determining norms so we can recognize patterns of contraction that will establish patent, partially blocked, and wholly closed tubes. This reading is consistent with—"

"Wait, it's going down! Dr. Rubin!"

As the eminent researcher looked up at the dial, the fluctuating needle seemed to invigorate his drooping features. "Mrs. Blau, are you feeling discomfort?" Minna mumbled an affirmative reply. "Where?" She tried to lift her hand, but it was bound to the table. The doctor untied it. She indicated a spot on her abdomen. "In which direction does it seem to radiate? Good. Dr. Anspach, take it back up. Hold her down!"

Hannah heard a grinding sound. She glanced toward the machine, then back at Minna. The tight control of her face fell away like an icy sheet breaking loose from a roof line. Her mouth twisted and her eyes bulged as the reason for Minna's bindings became evident. Her pelvis rose from the table at the same time her spine arched toward the ceiling, but her one tied arm and legs snapped her back to the table with a clatter. Her head rolled from side to side, almost as if she were having a seizure. Then she was still. Sputum dripped down the side of her chin, tears ran from her eyes while the machine purred on, ignorant of the horrible shudder that had wracked poor Minna's fragile frame.

Hannah bent close. Minna was breathing softly between low moans. Hannah wanted to scream at the doctors who had made the ghastly error. What had they done? Had her brain been damaged? Had she ruptured anything? Why was Dr. Rubin smiling? Why was Dr. Anspach shaking Wendell's hand? She felt as if she were watching this scene from the wrong end of a telescope.

"Han-nah?"

"I'm here, Minna, I'm here," she said, unable to choke back her tears.

"I'm impressed," boomed Dr. Dowd's most pompous voice.

"That's the most evident purging yet," Dr. Anspach announced. "Watch her diaphragm." Everyone, including Hannah, noticed an artificial pneumoperitoneum forming as the gas rose out of her now open fallopian tubes into her chest cavity. "Gentlemen, if you will look at the fluoroscope screen, you may note the movement of the gas."

Dr. Anspach was trying to assist Minna in sitting upright. "Can't she rest?" Hannah asked.

"This is part of the procedure," he replied with some annoyance. "Do you have any pains?" he asked the patient.

"My stomach hurts."

"Anywhere else?" Minna seemed too stunned to reply. "Take a deep breath and then tell me."

"Oh! There!"

"Where?" queried Dr. Rubin.

"My shoulders."

"Which one?"

"My left . . ." She rotated her shoulder blade as a test. "Ouch! Yes, it really hurts."

"The right does not?"

Minna rolled her other one and grimaced. "Yes, that too, but not as much."

Hannah could contain herself no longer. "What happened?"

Dr. Dowd grinned like a child who has a chance to win a prize. "There was a blockage in each tube, but with a little extra pressure he blew out the plugs, and now both are probably patent. Am I right?"

Dr. Rubin nodded. "The amount of gas allowed to enter the peritoneal cavity and to rise to the subphrenic space determines the intensity of shoulder pains. If no patency had been demonstrated, no shoulder pain would have been present. If they were irrevocably blocked, the worst pain would have accumulated in the lower abdomen. If you will place her in the Trendelenburg posture, the present discomfort will abate in a few short minutes."

Hannah assisted Minna as the table was tilted so her head was lowered about forty-five degrees from the floor. Meanwhile, the men conferred in the corner of the room. Fortunately, they spoke loud enough for Hannah to overhear. "She never could have conceived before, but now she has a fighting chance."

Hannah looked down at her prostrate sister-in-law. For the first time since she had seen her at Blackwell's Island Minna did not seem ready for a fight, but then the midwife realized that on this occasion—as on the last—Minna had achieved her goal.

~~~~ 8 ~~~~

To permit healing from the procedure, Dr. Rubin instructed
Minna not to have intercourse for three weeks. Later she
complained to Hannah, "I'll miss an opportunity this cycle,
won't I?"

"I suppose so, but it is probably for the best. Your organs
have been traumatized, so even if you did fertilize an egg it
might have difficulty being accepted by your uterus."

Minna relented, but kept Hannah apprised of her dates.
"I'm having a normal monthly," she whispered one afternoon as Hannah arrived home from taking Emma to purchase a badly needed pair of shoes.

"What do you think, Auntie?" Emma asked, twirling
around and kicking up her heels to show off the shiny patent
leather.

"*Élégant,*" Minna said in a mock-French accent which
pleased Emma. Then to her mother, "When should we start
again?"

"Start what?" Emma asked. Hannah shot her daughter a
warning glance, but this only piqued her interest more.
"What's the big deal?" Placing her slender fingers on her
hips, she pouted.

"That's enough out of you, Sarah Bernhardt," Hannah
chastised. "Anytime you want," she added over her shoulder, while prodding Emma up the stairs.

Minna's next complaint was: "What am I going to do?
With all this nonsense over May Day, Chaim is almost never
home."

"He must have a few moments to spare," Hannah replied
with a wry grin, knowing that Minna could easily rein
Chaim in any time she wanted.

In recent days he had been furious because Attorney General Palmer had told the Cabinet that the illegal railroad
strike had been fomented by the I.W.W. as part of an international communist conspiracy. "Why can't those thick-
headed stuffed shirts in Washington see that nobody is trying

to overthrow the government or establish a dictatorship on the part of the proletariat?" he had railed the last time he sat at Hannah's table. "They keep warning that the socialists are trying to transport this country into the same chaotic conditions that exist in Russia. Don't you and I wish it were that easy?" He waited for Lazar's comeback.

"It seems that Palmer believes Trotsky's press more than he does himself," Minna interjected to fill the gap.

"Once again the pen is mightier than reality," Chaim laughed, looking over at Lazar. "So, Pero's pero," he continued. "What do you think?"

Lazar was rubbing his chin and staring out the kitchen window. Across Tompkins Square he watched observant families returning from synagogue. Chaim cleared his throat, but Lazar still did not respond. Hannah, who had always wished her husband's intense interest in these debates would lessen, was now alarmed by his lack of concern about everything from politics to his children to his wife's sexual needs. It was as if the train accident had crushed far more than a few bones.

Surely Chaim noticed as well, but he decided to plunge on, even if he could not raise his usual response. "The point is: what are we going to do about the federal agents who think they are going to uncover an insidious nationwide Red plot to kill American officials on May Day?"

"Let's not disappoint them," Lazar replied dully.

"Lazar!" Hannah castigated.

Chaim strained to control his temper. "Don't you realize that nobody is listening to them?" he persisted in a seething voice. "You remember the story of the boy who cried wolf. Already Attorney General Palmer is having to explain his actions to a congressional investigating committee."

"What do you propose?" Lazar challenged abruptly.

Chaim took a deep breath and lowered his register. "What we should do is absolutely nothing. More than that. An organized nothing."

Lazar did not hide his disgust. "You're talking nonsense."

"No, he's not," Minna said as she grasped her husband's logic. "Let's entice the GID to declare that there is another nationwide plot to kill high government officials. Let them imagine this is part of a scheme to overthrow the American government and force recognition of Soviet Russia. Let's give the press a field day so they can print big black headlines screaming that Red Scare is back in full flower," she said gleefully.

Chaim picked up where she left off. "What will happen? On May Day the police will be put on full alert, especially in New York. And what will we do? Secretly we can decide to cancel the parade, hold a few neighborhood picnics, without even the usual inflammatory speeches. Before the night is over, Palmer and his pals will be the laughingstock of the nation."

A glimmer of Lazar's old spark flickered in his eyes. "An original concept, but unworkable. When have radicals ever agreed with each other? What makes you think you can get them to go along with this peaceful celebration, especially on May Day, which is symbolic of the spirit of change?"

"Would it hurt to try?" Minna asked.

"There are only a few weeks left. Hardly enough time," Lazar barked. "How could we get the word out?"

Shaking his head, Chaim muttered, "Lazar, if you would stop drowning in that sea of self-pity for a minute, you might start swimming toward the island of sanity that's right over the horizon."

"Now you've lost me completely," Hannah started to say, until she saw her husband waving his hand.

"The press! We'll print up pamphlets. In Yiddish. In English. We could do it overnight."

Hannah and Chaim stared at each other as Lazar began taking charge. Their wordless communication was clear: let him accept this project. He needs something to do.

"What are we waiting for?" Minna stood up. "I'll help set the type."

∽ 9 ∽

When May 1, 1920, dawned, the entire New York City police force of 11,000 men was placed on twenty-four-hour alert, with the public library, post office, and Pennsylvania Station heavily guarded. Other cities reacted as well. Boston had trucks mounted with machine guns stationed at strategic locations including the city jail and state house. Washington ordered protection of all federal buildings as well as the homes of officials who might be targeted. Chicago went further, placing more than three hundred radicals in jail as a precaution.

In New York, Union Square, a scene of previous May Day congregations, was deserted except for a children's concert, which drew mostly young families. Other socialist and communist groups congregated, but the occasions were militantly social, despite the cordons of police, whom the participants approached with greetings and thanked for their attendance. The results baffled the Justice Department and infuriated the press, who had set aside front-page columns to report the inevitable clashes.

The morning of May 2, Chaim and Minna pored over the headlines with glee. "Listen to this one: 'Mare's Nest Hatched in Attorney General's Brain,' " Chaim read.

"In these they're calling Attorney General Palmer a 'national menace' and 'full of hot air.' There's even a reference to 'Little Red Riding Hood and a cry of "Wolf" ' just like I said!" trilled Minna.

"That's the end of that shlemiel," Lazar crowed. "I knew it all along!"

The others ignored his boast, although he had written the different versions of the "call to disarm" that had intrigued the various factions. Skillfully he had woven in early pacifist arguments, which had never won a popular voice before the Great War; talked about the value of propaganda, which Trotsky had honed to a fine art; and had alluded to the origins of the May Day holiday as a celebration of spring, renewal, and rebirth. There had been something for everyone in Lazar's arguments, but he had not foreseen how widely his words would spread, or the crucial anticlimactic effect that would bury the Red Scare once and for all.

Of course, the Justice Department claimed that its timely warning had headed off an impending revolution, thus saving the country. Nevertheless, the nation was torn between laughter and rage, and this time the attorney general became the butt of the jokes. In a few days Nichola Sacco and Bartolomeo Vanzetti were arrested for murder in a payroll robbery. Finally the papers had a fresh front-page story, and anything about Reds was relegated to the back columns.

Once again Lazar began to retreat. When Hannah prodded

him about what was the matter, he claimed that he was distressed because the Poles and Russians were battling for control of Kiev, a city close to where he had been born. His wife suspected that he was merely deflated because he felt adrift at the end of his successful effort. The following week, Chaim, who sensed his depression as well, tried to cajole Lazar into attending a Socialist party meeting in Madison Square Garden.

"Why bother? There will be no surprises. They'll endorse Debs as the party's presidential candidate. So what?"

"The formal nomination of a man who is serving a sentence in federal prison for violation of the Espionage Act will be a statement in itself," Chaim asserted.

"Then in November he'll be defeated for the fifth time. Where will that get anyone?"

At his tone of bored indifference Hannah looked away sadly. In the days before May Day she had seen such a miraculous change she privately began thinking of him as her Lazarus risen from the dead, although she had been wise enough to keep the phrase to herself. Several times he had even come behind her and touched her back, her shoulder, her hipbone, not in an obviously sexual way, yet it was more than he had done before. For a while she had entertained hopes that he was beginning to thaw. On the evening after the Union Square meeting Lazar had even kissed her with a zeal she only dimly recalled. In response she pressed against him and for a moment thought that she felt his penis lift against her leg. She almost reached down and stroked him, but restrained herself. The next morning he rolled over and fondled her breasts when he thought she was asleep. Keeping her eyes closed, she parted her legs and melted into him, but he did not continue. Still, her hopes had been inflamed. Now he seemed to have a foot back in the grave. If only he became more involved, felt he were needed . . .

"What do you suggest?" Lazar challenged to their silence. "Should I run against Debs for president?"

"All Chaim is proposing is that you let your voice be heard," Hannah filled in impulsively. The words reverberated in her head to form a more complete thought. "They listened to you about the May Day celebration. The idea may not have been yours, nevertheless you made the greatest contribution by convincing the factions to cooperate. Why bury this talent? Why ignore it?"

"I said I would attend!" he replied with a raised voice, even though he had not. "I'll go to listen, not to speak. Is that all right with you?"

Hannah began to back off. "Whatever you think best." Lazar did not even bother to suggest that she accompany him, for he had sensed her distance from the political arena. Then, impulsively she erupted with: "Eventually you will regret hiding your opinions, though." Her voice tapered out, ending on an apologetic lilt.

Lazar did not respond, which was a much more positive sign than if he had argued with her. Agreement was out of the question, Hannah was resigned to that.

After the rally, though, he bounded up the stairs with Chaim and Minna bringing up the rear. "There were dozens of reporters, but they are so predictable you and I could write their reports ahead of time," he said before he sat down to the steaming glasses of tea she had ready.

"Nu? What's the mystery?" Hannah replied sleepily as she shuffled around in her bathrobe passing the sugar cubes.

"Exactly," Chaim took over. "People are bored with the same monotonous viewpoints. What better moment to make a statement?"

"You're talking in riddles," Lazar responded sullenly.

"And you're sounding like an *alte kocker*. When are you going to stop being a cranky old man and do something useful for a change?" Chaim knew he was inciting his brother-in-law, yet he did not ease off even slightly. "That's right. At first we pitied you because of your injuries—not that they were benign—but you obviously have survived and are going to live a good long time, so why don't you stop this self-indulgent act and rejoin the human race?"

Hannah moved forward, standing almost between them. Lazar brushed her away so he could better view his opponent. She took a seat at the table and listened as her brother laid out his plan.

"There needs to be a daily Yiddish paper willing to express a modern, post-war, post-revolution view. The *Tageblatt* has a decidedly Orthodox orientation that has moved further and further into the conservative and Republican camp. *Die Zukunft* acts like an organ of the Yiddish-speaking Socialist Labor Party, but a monthly is not limber enough to react to daily events. The biggest competition would come from the *Forverts.*"

"Abe Cahan has his devoted followers, nobody could touch him."

"However, he's become too secure, too blasé," Chaim continued without sounding contentious, for he was trying to convince, not contradict Lazar. "The trouble is that he espouses circulation over socialism."

Lazar laughed loudly and Hannah joined in spontaneously.

"Besides, everyone knows Cahan can be a tyrant to work for," Minna contributed. "You can't become a member of the Forverts Association unless he approves of you. With a snap of his fingers you are either in or out. This has galled many talented writers and editors."

"Even so, they are putting out almost a quarter of a million copies a day," Chaim said.

Lazar's eyebrows arched with surprise. "Where did you get those numbers?"

"Their regular printers cannot handle special overruns. We've bid on some of the jobs but never gotten one. I don't think we ever will."

"Why? Does he have a problem with you?"

"I suppose I am too independent to win his favor."

"Which means Chaim doesn't care for the taste of his shoe leather," Minna explained.

Chaim gave a wry smile. "I don't think he's ever forgiven me for criticizing his ambiguous positions in public. His defense is that it's pragmatic to be moderate, for that's how he can reach as many as possible, thus permeating the Jewish community with the doctrine of socialism. Yet I feel that a watered-down doctrine is worse than none at all."

"Nu?" Lazar was becoming restless. He stood and stretched. "What are you proposing?"

"Why don't we start a new paper? I'll be the publisher, you'll be the editor. It will be the first Yiddish-language daily with a lucid communist persuasion."

"Don't you think those doomsayers in Washington will try to close us down?"

"If the Red Scare starts up again—and I doubt that it will—our language will be the perfect cloak. Do you really believe they have folks in government offices translating from Yiddish?"

Ignoring the remark, as well as the women's laughter, Lazar said sourly, "It couldn't work."

"Why not?"

"Too much competition."

"No, not for what I have in mind. It would be unique. It would fill a gap." Chaim's voice rose as he tried to convince himself as much as the others. "Why, if I'm right, in a year we should be able to win a quarter to a third of the *Forverts* customers, with maybe more added from the ranks of those who wouldn't be caught dead wrapping their fish in that rag."

"You actually think we could attract more than fifty thousand readers?" Lazar asked with a mixture of disbelief and awe. Chaim stared off into the distance. "Did you hear what I said?"

"I caught the 'we,' if that's what you meant."

Lazar nodded. "Well?"

"Those are my conservative estimates. Our shop is small, our costs are minimal. I expect we could make a profit at less than ten thousand, and if advertising revenues are even a tenth of the *Forverts'*, we would not even need that many."

"If we try to remain independent, nobody will know where we stand. I suggest we accept Communist party disciplines and standards, which would give us instant legitimacy."

"That would be an editorial decision." As Chaim pointed a finger at Lazar, Hannah watched as a healthy flush bloomed on the invalid's gaunt cheeks.

"What would it be called?"

"Do you have any ideas?" Chaim asked.

"You've obviously had a head start on this, so what would you suggest?"

"Well, how about the *Emes?* That's what the Yiddish paper in Moscow is called because it means the same as *Pravda:* the truth."

"Don't you remember that *Emes* was the name of the paper Trotsky edited in exile sometime around 1908?"

"That was one reason I thought you would approve of it."

"Then you were wrong," he cried, seething, and walked over to the kitchen window, opening it forcefully as though fresh air was suddenly a necessity.

Chaim and Hannah both startled at Lazar's vehemence. Why the sudden emotion regarding Trotsky? Hannah had guessed his reticence on the subject of his hero had been based on his distress at having to leave Russia because of ill health. She had supposed he felt as if he had abandoned

Trotsky's ship. Now she suspected that remorse might not be his prevailing sentiment.

"What would you suggest?" was Chaim's gentle response.

Lazar stared out the window for a few seconds, then pivoted around, and spoke in a harsh whisper. *"Freiheit.* Freedom." He licked his lips as though he liked the taste of the words.

"Isn't that an ironic name for a communist paper?" his wife inquired.

"Do you think anyone is truly free in this society? No, everyone is relegated to the expectations of his class, his sex, his economic status, his religion, his country of origin. True freedom will only come in the workers' state. That must be the message of our organ, otherwise it isn't worth doing."

Chaim stood up and went to join Lazar by the window. "You're right." He clasped his shoulders. "I feel as if we have been traveling down a road without knowing our destination. Now that it's in sight, I realize that's where we were headed the whole time."

Lazar seemed stunned for a second. Then he did something uncharacteristic. He hugged his brother-in-law with a fierceness usually reserved for a moment of dramatic reunion. "Yes, Chaim," he said, "that's where we were going the whole time."

∾ **10** ∾

As the weather warmed, more and more people began to assemble in Mama's old parlor, now the office of the gestating periodical. The first discussions revolved around a structure, partly borrowed from the successful organization of the *Forverts,* with a generous dollop of Communist party framework. Next they tackled an editorial policy.

Chaim attempted to moderate Lazar's tendency to make everything a political issue. "Nobody's going to want to read an acerbic diatribe on every page. People are curious about other people. Like Trotsky. We may have a strong reaction to his doctrines, but what do we know about Trotsky the man?"

"I told you I can't violate that trust."

"Nobody's asking you to tell the secrets of the revolution, but there would be no harm in a story about, say, what his office in the Kremlin looks like. Or an anecdote about his wife or—"

Lazar cut him off. "I see what you mean. There were many humorous things that happened." He allowed himself a smile. "For instance, once a reporter from America, a guy named Seldes, was interviewing Trotsky. After he was finished, he asked if Trotsky would pose for a few photographs. Trotsky started to agree when another man stepped forward with a camera and said that since he was the official photographer, photos would have to be purchased from him. Trotsky stared the Russian photographer in the eye and said, 'There are no monopolies in the people's state.'"

"That's perfect." Chaim clapped his hands. "Which gives me an idea. In order to establish you as editor with important connections, I suggest that you have a column on the editorial page titled something like, 'Out of Russia' or 'View from the Kremlin' or 'After the Revolution.'"

"I don't like any of those," Lazar scoffed.

"Only suggestions," replied the conciliatory publisher.

"I have almost as many stories about Lenin." Lazar's eyes flashed with enthusiasm. "I never promised not to write about him."

"For instance?" Chaim's cheeks burned brightly, as though warmed by his friend's change of mood.

"Well, I'm quite a bit taller than him. Once when we were in a narrow hallway talking over an issue for a long while, I looked down and noticed that I had placed my hand on Lenin's shoulders and had been leaning on him the whole time. When I suddenly realized it, I whipped my arm back as though it had been burned. Lenin looked up at me with those twinkling eyes of his and said, 'What else is a leader for if not to lean on? At least it makes me feel useful for a change.'"

"Don't you see how everyone will love these morsels? They'll come begging for more."

Lazar was fueled by the encouragement. "Then there's the time—"

Chaim cut him short. "Save a few to surprise me another time."

From the beginning Minna was brought into the *Freiheit* organization. In her meticulous hand she made notations on everything Lazar and her husband discussed "in case they need to refer to it again." Hannah knew she wisely was avoiding future disagreements regarding what had transpired. Nevertheless, by the middle of June, her attention began to wander. Every day or so she reported to Hannah about her expected menstrual period. "Nothing yet! Nothing." A few days after that it was: "I'm a week late . . . ten days late." Then, just before the Fourth of July, she decided on a celebration. "This must be it! I want to go somewhere and rejoice," she said as she caught Hannah coming through the front door.

"Possibly . . ." Hannah allowed, not wanting to disappoint her.

"I'm never this late."

"The tubal test could have altered your constitution for a while," the midwife warned as she set down her bundles.

"Really? Do you think so?"

Hannah was sorry to see Minna looking so crestfallen. "Could have, but may not have. Give it two more weeks. Anyway, we could still go somewhere for the holiday. Where would you like?"

"How about Central Park for a picnic?"

"I don't like the city crowds," Lazar replied in his grumpiest voice when they went to tell the men what they were planning.

Hannah would have defended Minna's idea except she had not returned to that park since she had heard Lulu Morse sing, and did not want to relive that memory.

"I'd rather not go anywhere" was Chaim's comment as he sorted through a pile of clippings. "I could use the time at the press to set things right while the staff is out. When people are about there's constant confusion, questions, so I never get anything done."

"That's because you are trying to do everything yourself," Minna challenged.

"I won't ask a worker to do something I would not undertake. It's bad for morale."

"I disagree. I think it's worse for morale if you insist on

redoing everything anyway. The men think you believe they are incompetent."

"That's not it . . ." her husband demurred, then threw his hands up in defeat. "All right, I'll go!"

"Let's not go to the park, though," Hannah inserted.

"How about Coney Island?" Minna suggested.

"The children would love it, wouldn't they, Lazar?" Hannah asked hopefully.

Lazar grunted his reluctant assent, and for once the children voiced not a single objection.

∽ **11** ∾

Lazar smiled. From the moment the Broadway–Brighton line subway train arrived at the Coney Avenue terminal his lips turned up to greet the beating sun and never relaxed, at least not until his children annoyed him. Lazar, Hannah, and their children, accompanied by Minna and Chaim, as well as Rachael, Ezekiel, and Nora, followed the crowds down Surf Avenue taking in the rows of hotels, bathing establishments, and amusement parks. Not knowing when to turn toward the beach, they arrived at the midway point along the strip, which was bisected by a network of narrow intersecting alleys and arcades.

"Let's go this way." Benny pointed to a gaudy sign indicating a passage named the Bowery. A whistling sound indicated a shooting gallery. Benny rushed over. "Can I try?" he asked. Lazar handed over a penny before Hannah could complain about her son firing a rifle.

Emma was attracted to a machine with twirling lights and a honking sound. "May I do that?" Lazar handed her a penny too.

"If you keep on like this, we'll go through all our money in the first five minutes," Hannah griped.

"I thought you wanted to come here."

Herzog drew up behind them. He showed them a handful of coins. "Why do you think they're called catch-penny machines? I've been saving these in a jar for a rainy day, but Rachael thought they might be more use on a sunny one."

For a moment Hannah felt the old twinge of resentment at having less money than her friends and yet not wanting them to have to pay for her. Then she caught herself. Chaim was convinced this newspaper venture was going to be lucrative. None of them expected to get rich, but even the initial salary they budgeted for an editor would provide a welcome addition to their pocketbook. Soon they would be the one treating, she vowed.

In the background she saw Lazar, Chaim, and Benny all shooting rifles at cardboard ducks and birds moving across a motorized track.

"This is boring," she overheard Nora confide to Emma as the men finished. "Let's go to the beach."

"Sounds good to me," Rachael agreed and motioned to Hannah to move in that direction. "If we stand around, the men will be shooting all day."

"Which shall we do?" Chaim asked the group. "Luna or Steeplechase Park?"

"Luna!" chorused Emma and Nora.

"Steeplechase is much better," demanded Benny.

"How do you know?" challenged his sister. "You've never been there before."

"Well, neither have you!"

"How shall we settle it?" Herzog asked.

"How about a vote?" Rachael suggested.

"Since when did you become a democrat?" Lazar queried, but without his usual malice.

"Perhaps we could reach a people's consensus," Herzog offered.

"Darling, we'd be broiling in the sun for hours," his wife pleaded.

"You're right. There's only one choice left: the scientific solution."

Benny moved closer. "Whaddaya mean?"

"Benny, stop talking like a bum," his mother reprimanded.

"Leave him be," Chaim whispered.

Ezekiel took out another coin. "The mathematical odds of chance. Heads Luna Park, tails Steeplechase." He tossed the coin high in the air. They all looked up, squinting into the sun. Momentarily blinded, the doctor did not catch it, but they heard it fall on the pavement. Emma ran over and placed her foot over it before Benny could contest it. When Herzog moved closer, she removed her toe to reveal that she had won. "Perfect justice. The lunatics go to Luna Park."

The laughter diffused Benny's pique, and they headed west into the enclosed amusement park containing scores of devices each designed to give a variety of breathless thrills. Chaim walked up to the ticket booth, painted in a garish combination of pinks, greens, and oranges that in any other setting would have seemed abominable. "Let's see, which is the best deal? Benny, come help me decide." The two conferred over the books of tickets, rapidly settling on the forty-five pack. "You're good with numbers, kiddo," his uncle complimented, then tore off ten tickets for each of the children and took the rest back to the adults.

"Aunt Eva never goes to this part of the beach," Emma was saying to Nora. "She told me that Manhattan Beach is much nicer and has less trashy people. They even rent a changing room for the season."

"You aunt is a pompous capitalist," Lazar retorted. Hannah shot him a warning glance. "Well, she is. Why hide the truth from them? Otherwise they'll soon be after us to have private lockers and summer passes."

"What's the matter with that?"

"It's elitist, that's what."

"I don't see what's so wrong about not wanting to fight with the crowds," Benny chimed in defense of his sister. Hannah was so pleased he was not arguing with her, she ignored the irritating whine to his voice. "I mean, I think that everyone should have an equal chance, but the truth is people don't work equally hard. If you can't reward diligence, then nothing is fair."

"Fair?" Lazar snapped. "What do you know from fair? As soon as those who didn't have get, they begin to trample on those below them. Can you help it if you were born male, or short, or a Jew? What about the blind, the deformed? Don't they deserve a reasonable quality of life?"

"You're twisting my words!" his son shouted.

"Don't use that tone with me!"

"Why not?" Benny spat. "It's the one you use with me!"

Chaim stepped in between them. "I thought you were going to see the attractions."

Benny started to protest, but his uncle's firm hand patted

his back in a way which made him feel someone was on his side. He turned on his heel and headed for the Biggest Freak Animal Show in the World. "Are you coming?" he ask the girls.

Nora wrinkled her nose. "Nah, let's go to the Eden Musee Wax Works instead," she said to Emma.

It was a relief to have the children away for a short time. Arm in arm Dr. Jaffe and Dr. Herzog strolled past the thrill rides. Maybe it was Hannah's imagination, but she saw them looking for opportunities to touch and hug. Was the music cure still working? she wondered, but dared not inquire. She decided to assume the obstacles of the past had vanished.

Yet did they ever? Maybe they went into remission, only to rear up when the body's defenses were down, like a cold sore heralding an infectious process. Look at her and Lazar. To others they seemed reconciled. Everyone thought she was overjoyed to have him home—as any decent wife would be—and to have his body healing from what had once been thought to be irreparable wounds. Nobody would have suspected how estranged they were in their bed. And nobody would have guessed that during this happy family outing she was wishing she were walking beside a different man.

Wendell. They had not been alone—not even to confer about a patient or their research—since their impulsive indiscretion behind his desk. Was this on purpose or coincidental? For her part, she had avoided any opportunity. She had hardly been able to face Lazar—or her children—after the last encounter, so she had vowed not to let it happen again. And yet she suspected that given the right circumstance . . . if they were alone, if he approached her, if he desired her . . . she might capitulate.

"What do you think, Hannah?" Ezekiel was saying.

"What?"

"Where have you been?" Rachael smiled.

"Thinking about one of my cases . . ." Hannah offered lamely.

"That's subversive on the Fourth of July," Herzog reprimanded. "Anyway, I was pointing out the Freudian symbolism of the rides. Look how many—like the Canals of Venice and the Tunnel of Love—take their patrons into dark, winding passages. Is this not a perfect representation of an anal experience? And what about the obvious erotic elements of the Cannon Coaster, which shoots people out of a pipe and onto a slide in an imitation of ejaculation?"

"Is that all you think of these days?" was his wife's nonchalant tease, in which Hannah gleaned a boast.

Ignoring the comment, he continued to pontificate. "Just listen to that barker's spiel."

They moved closer to the man in a bright red suit, who waved a cane and shouted, "Will she throw her arms around your neck and yell? Well, I guess the answer to that will be yes!" He fluttered his arms toward the entrance to the coaster. "Come and see for yourself. Come on, you there, what are you waiting for?" The man was pointing his stick toward Lazar.

"Can't, war injury," he said with some embarrassment. Since this had been assumed by everyone who noticed his bent posture and limp, he decided not to disabuse them of the notion, apologizing to those who knew him, "I don't have to say which war, do I?"

"What about the young lady?"

Minna was the one closest, and she did look the youngest of the group. Chaim clasped her arm. "How about it?" he asked.

"Sure," she said and handed the man her ticket without a second thought.

"Which are you going to try?" Ezekiel asked Lazar after the Herzogs had made their choice.

"I suppose that Dragon's Gorge looks tame enough for me."

Before Hannah could protest, she was steered onto a ride that whisked them in a little train from a North Pole, where the wind was blowing, to a bumpy track that took them past a stage set of Havana harbor, on to Port Arthur in winter, back up to the Rocky Mountains, down to the bottom of the sea, and then plunged into a tunnel depicting the lower depths. After an almost certain collision with a great cataract, the train swerved violently, and they emerged into the sunlight with nothing to show for their myriad journeys besides a light spray of water that sprinkled their faces.

Hannah stepped out laughing. She hated to admit it, but she had enjoyed the ride far more than she had expected. She turned to her husband. Instead of some sarcastic remark on the silliness of the adventure, she saw a sparkle in his eyes that meant he too had been charmed. His smile was resolutely back in place. Good. Maybe he and Benny would have the sense to avoid another confrontation.

The first intellectual comment came from Herzog, mumbling something about "the windings of the psyche personified by the experience."

His wife placed a finger to his lips. "Sometimes it's better to feel something rather than analyze it."

Inside, Hannah was applauding, for wasn't this the message she had preached about her friend's sexuality? Before she could catch Rachael's eye, she heard a voice calling, "Hannah!" Then another even closer, "Ma!" Emma was rushing toward her.

"What?" she called out.

"Minna's sick," Emma panted. She tugged on her arm. "She's over there, behind the Eskimo village."

Minna was retching. Chaim was holding her hair away from her face.

"Did she hurt herself?"

"No, she seemed fine until we walked away from the ride," he said. "Then she turned white, her knees buckled, and she hasn't been able to catch her breath since."

"Get some water," Hannah told her daughter, "and a wet rag."

Herzog and Rachael stood in the background. They had not been told of Minna's encounter with Dr. Rubin because Minna had not wanted others to know about her quest to have a baby. "Something she ate?" Herzog inquired.

"Nobody's had anything to eat yet," Rachael prompted. "Maybe you would like to attempt a Freudian explanation," she suggested in a prickly tone, for she placed far less confidence in this new science of the mind than he did.

Hannah wiped Minna's brow and massaged between her shoulder blades. Soon the heaving stopped. She maneuvered Minna to a bench. If she and Chaim had not bolstered her like bookends, she might have crumpled into a heap.

"Gotteniu! I should never have come."

"Don't say that. You'll be better soon. Why don't we get something to eat?" Hannah cajoled.

"Across the way they're featuring a shore dinner at Henderson's. How does that sound?" Chaim offered.

Minna gagged. Chaim leapt back so he would not get splashed with vomit, but only a trickle was expelled. Groaning, Minna lay back. Chaim paled. "She's really sick, isn't she?"

"No," Hannah responded with some confidence, "it's a very normal symptom ... of pregnancy."

Problem 9:
Lillian Neufield's Preference

◆

1921

When a thing ceases to be a subject of controversy, it ceases to be a subject of interest.
—WILLIAM HAZLITT

❧ 1 ❧

BENNY was late. He knew he was supposed to be home for dinner at six. If she had told him once, she had told him a hundred times. The more insistent she became, the more he defied her. How many times had she asked Lazar to talk to the boy? He claimed that he had, but there had been no improvement. Maybe she should not have spurred Lazar's involvement. While Benny avoided his mother, he clashed with his father. If Lazar said black, Benny said white, even if black would have been his first choice. Maybe it was for the best that Lazar was rarely home, not even for supper except on Friday nights. And he only came upstairs that one night at his wife's insistence.

"We must eat together at least one night a week," she had declared, although when was the last time they had sat through a cordial meal? She had been taking special pains with the food, saving up through the week to have a plump chicken, a thick brisket, a firm piece of fish. She made her specialties: sweet potato and apple casserole, creamy spinach ring, honeyed lima beans, kasha-varnischkes, mamaliga, sweet and sour lentils. She even baked cakes, the one with applesauce Emma preferred or the jelly roll that Lazar favored. For Benny it would be tayglach with syrup or anything with poppyseed filling. Not that it mattered. By the last course the only sweetness left was in the desserts.

How did it start? She was always looking for signs, so she might head off a collision. Every time, though, the danger appeared suddenly, as if they had come around the bend to find it looming there, positioned to pounce on its defenseless prey. If she only understood the situation better, she might advise them how to proceed around the obstacles instead of continuing to smash into them. As it was, after the inevitable confrontations the family members retreated to tend their wounds without learning how to avoid another onslaught.

Hannah stared out the window. At least this was not Friday. If Benny arrived late, Lazar never knew. During the day Lazar spent his time at the expanded Chrystie Street pressroom, where Chaim and Minna had once lived. They had taken over the second floor of the building for editorial offices, but in the evenings they came home to Chaim's flat downstairs and continued working on the *Freiheit* long into the night. In the beginning she had sent Lazar's supper down to him; these days she left his plate on the stove. If he wanted to eat, he could come up and get it. He could say hello to her and the children too, while he was at it. Lately, he rarely came up to eat during the time the family was awake. Minna kept a kettle going. They lived on tea, cigarettes, and day-old knishes that one of the staff member's uncles had not sold the previous day.

While Lazar never bothered to come home at any set time, he had the stern conviction that his son should be in before sundown, which he rarely was, if only to defy his father. Not that Lazar would know the difference. Knowing the tumult that would ensue, Hannah was not going to report the boy's infraction. To think she had gone to see that man, the maggoty Mr. Gibbons, and begged for Lazar's visa for the sake of his children!

At least she knew where he was, she consoled herself. Better he should be working on the *Freiheit* than languishing in Petrograd. Better he should be working downstairs than sitting in the chair by the window morosely staring out at the street. Better he should see his children—argue with them even—than not know them at all, she pondered idly without being utterly convinced by her own platitudes. Was it better? Was it really? Was it really better for her?

What if Lazar had not returned? Was it foolish to have believed that the venerable Dowds would have welcomed a Jewish immigrant into the family? Besides, it was easy to forget that Wendell could be charming one moment, aloof the next. In his work he required perfection from himself, and thus demanded the same from others around him. He had rarely shown her his impatient side, but the times he had—especially regarding her mistakes with the English language, in writing or speaking—he had lashed out with caustic criticism. Yet what good did it do to remind herself that she might not have been happy with Wendell either?

Morosely, Hannah faced the fact that the gap between her and her husband had widened to the point that they could sleep in the same bed without hardly touching. For a while she had the notion that his elation about the *Freiheit* would lift his spirits, and eventually his organ would inflate as well. Now she was resigned to the fact that the train wreck had damaged some essential nerve pathway to his genitalia. Nothing could be done about it. Nothing. There had been a time when she thought he was healing. In the early hours of the morning, when she had to rise in the dark to be at Bellevue for the first shift, she thought she had seen his penis slipping out from his underwear. It looked plumper, almost swollen into an erection. Had she been mistaken about his ability? she deliberated, until she realized it was merely engorged by his need to urinate. At least he had those functions. At least he was not a complete cripple. Only she knew of his impotence. Only she suffered from it . . . well, he may have as well, but he probably was so relieved to be alive, to have the pains in his chest and leg diminishing, that he had accepted the cost of his survival.

Every day she was grateful to Chaim for not only putting Lazar to work on the *Freiheit,* but making him the editor. Her brother had known that Lazar needed to be in charge. The only master he had ever respected was Trotsky. To have his own paper, to be able to express his point of view openly, was the assignment of his dreams.

In his first editorial he had taken his stance, firmly and without equivocation.

> Beware. You are not reading the *Forverts.* It has become too dignified, too wealthy to be in touch with the true conflicts of its readers. This periodical will be un-

like it, or any other paper that you know. We are struggling, and thus we can identify with people who are struggling. We are a fighting paper, and will never sway from the side of the worker.

We will also rally along another front to preserve Jewish culture and the Yiddish language. In order to do this we must unite to oppose assimilation, for in assimilation we lose what is unique, what makes us strong. Does this mean we are opposed to progress? On the contrary. We must organize to improve the conditions for all the workers, yet we must do this within the scope of our Yiddish and Eastern European culture. For those who have made the journey thus far, join your companions on these pages, and together let us follow the trail.

His words met their mark. The premiere issue of five thousand copies was sold out within two days. A daily was planned, but they decided to publish weekly until the end of 1920, when they would be properly staffed, organized—and financed. Chaim doubled the next week's circulation, but had overestimated his ability to find that many new readers. He cut back the following week. Then in mid-October, he had a story worth expanding into a memorial issue, so he took the chance and printed twenty thousand papers. The headline, banded in black, proclaimed: JACK REED DIES IN RUSSIA.

The socialist community of New York was in shock. Louise Bryant had returned to be with her husband, and fortunately been at his side when he succumbed to typhus a few days shy of his thirty-third birthday. Three columns were given over to Bukharin's funeral address. Chaim wrote a short biography. The two reporters who were dispatched to gather reminiscences managed to get quotes not only from leading Communist figures, but also from Lincoln Steffens, Gene O'Neill, Max Eastman, Dr. Lorber, Ezekiel Herzog, Hutch Hapgood, and Mabel Dodge. In the center of the second page, surrounded by the eulogies, was a box. Inside was printed the words: JACK REED'S REMAINS WILL REST IN RED SQUARE.

When Hannah saw this, tears stung her eyes. She knew exactly why Lazar had them set off in that manner. He had been thinking that if he had passed on in Russia—and he had indeed come close to death—that would have been his fondest wish. Now when he died, he would be buried among family and friends in some commonplace plot on American soil.

His despondency was somewhat ameliorated by the demand for the next week's issue. Because there was no special topic, Chaim had printed far too few, for they had underestimated that they already had a following. The first week of November Lazar suggested they tackle a story about the rise of anti-Semitism in the United States. Since rabbis were accusing Henry Ford of libeling Jews, Lazar saw an opportunity to attack this flagrant capitalist along several flanks. His aggressive stance sold even more papers.

Best of all, Lazar wrote what he wanted without any apprehension. The Red Scare was dead. The previous September, fears of a rebirth had been roused when an explosion, believed to have been caused by a time bomb, ripped through the financial district, killing thirty people and injuring three hundred others. William J. Flynn, chief of the Justice Department's Bureau of Investigation, theorized the explosion was set off by Reds as part of a Soviet plot to overthrow the government. He and Attorney General Palmer led the investigation, but when they failed to uncover the perpetrators of the crime, Palmer and Flynn were ridiculed again. As Chaim had predicted, Attorney General Palmer had announced his candidacy for the presidency the previous March. Running as the "fighting Quaker," he concentrated on keeping the Red Scare alive, but the May Day and Wall Street bomb fiascoes lost him so much prestige, he became better known as the "Quaking Fighter," "Faking Fighter," and "Quaking Quitter."

Without these men looking over his shoulder, Lazar began searching for a way to turn any news story into a metaphor for his political slant. Though he had never been particularly interested in sports, he overheard Benny discussing the charges that the White Sox had thrown the World Series in October.

"I can't believe that a man like Shoeless Joe could have done such a thing!" Benny protested. "What do you think?"

"Anybody can be corrupted, especially someone who has known so much poverty and has no hope of ever receiving a fair shake from society," Chaim responded.

Lazar became curious and so Chaim explained that Shoeless Joe Jackson, the player who had risen from a Southern cotton-picking family to one of baseball's greatest heroes, was said to have received $5,000 of a promised $20,000 bribe to play poorly in the series. Seizing on this current issue, Lazar's column blared: THE AMERICAN CREED: GREED SAYS IT IS SO, EVEN WITH SHOELESS JOE.

This article brought more letters from readers than any other to date. However, it was hard to match these successes week after week, and soon Lazar began to lament the lack of fodder for his ferocious pen.

"We can't rely on sensational events to keep our readers buying the paper," Chaim offered sympathetically. "We need regular feature articles on subjects they care about."

"You are forgetting that women often control how their husband's hard-earned dollars are spent," Minna chimed in. "Since they must be convinced of the paper's value, we must give them more of what they want."

"What is that?" Lazar inquired, for he had no idea how to appeal to anyone except those burning for his particular political perspective.

"Diversion," his publisher's wife decreed. "Everybody has their own troubles, that's why they like to read about those of others, whether it's starvation in Russia or riots in Germany. The *Forverts* has the "Bintel Brief" giving advice to people who always sound worse off than you are. They also have fictional stories, with nice tidy endings that help a person relax."

"That's brilliant!" Chaim beamed at his wife. "Who knows Yiddish literature better than you, Lazar? We'll find some interesting stories, even longer novels and print them in serial form, the way Dickens did. So if worse comes to worse, and peace blankets the world with nothing but sweetness and light, the Mrs. Goldblatts and Mrs. Silversteins will still want to buy a paper to learn whether Herschel marries Fanna."

Seeing the wisdom in this, Lazar began a quest to find—and lure—the best Yiddish writers into his fold. Soon poets and novelists were attracted to the *Freiheit* because of its editor's appreciation of a higher literary level than his competitor. Eventually Lazar could boast that H. Leivick, Moishe Nadir, Moishe Leib Halperin, David Ignatoff, A. Raboi, Varch Glazman, Mani Leib, and Abraham Raisin were toiling exclusively for him.

Hannah's musings were interrupted by banging in the hall. Benny was pounding mud from his boots. Where had that child been? How had his shoes become so clogged with dirt? She flung the door open.

"Why are you late?"

"I was working, Ma! You know that!" His words were accusatory, just like his father's when he wanted to protect himself.

"Working at what?"

"This and that." He reached into his pocket and pulled out a roll of bills. "Sixteen bucks! Whaddaya think of that?"

"Where did you get them?" she asked in her slowest, deepest voice. The specter of the numbers racket never loomed far from her door.

"Here and there," he said, sliding by her.

Hannah caught his shirttail. "Hold on! That's not good enough for me. You're always late. You always have money. I want to know exactly where you have been."

Her son's mouth turned down into a surly sneer, but there was something artificial about it. Benny's eyes were round and clear. He did not flinch from her gaze, nor did he shake her hand from his back. "Ah, there's no big secret. Nothin' for you to worry yourself about, Ma. Besides, I got you a present." He moved back to the door and she let him pass. Reaching around the corner, he picked up a parcel wrapped in brown paper and tied with twine. "For you. I got a great deal on Orchard Street."

With some reluctance Hannah opened it. Out slipped a long, slouchy sweater knitted of the finest cashmere.

"Feel it, Ma! They said it's wool, but it feels like silk, don't it?"

"Doesn't it!" Emma corrected as she came into the room. "What's that?" She reached for the garment. "Ooh! Nice color. I love blue."

"It's for Ma, not you, creep."

"Oh, stop thinking you're the cat's meow. Where'd you get it?"

"I bought it from a guy on Orchard Street. He said some ritzy lady ordered it, but changed her mind." He gave his sister a toss of his head. "And no, it's not what you're thinking. It's not hot or nothin' like that."

"*Anything* like that," Emma insisted.

"Anyway, it's all on the up and up."

"I didn't say it wasn't!"

"That's what you were thinking!"

"Was not!"

"Emma!" Hannah warned.

"Why is it always me you stop from speaking?"

"You're both tired and hungry. Come to the table and we'll talk about it later." She placed the sweater over the back of the stuffed chair, stroking it one last time for sheer pleasure.

After Benny had cut into his meat, he gave Hannah one of his most cherubic smiles. "You do like it, don't you?"

"Yes, Benny, but I still want to know where you are getting your money."

"Ma, there's millions of ways to make money. Just look around and see what nobody else is willing to do, find a need that is not being filled, or something that has to be done—like taking out the garbage or bringing in the coal. Then the next step is where so many guys fail. You have to make people think they need you, even though they really don't. That's what I've been doing. On my way home from school I have five buildings where I do what the supers don't want to. They know what time I will be along, and they have me lug stuff, or climb up a pipe, or carry something down from the roof. You can't complain about that, can you?"

"I guess not," Hannah said between bites of mashed carrots. She was contemplating how Lazar had spawned such an enterprising son, or maybe he was that way just to be in opposition to his father. At least Lazar wasn't here to quarrel with the boy's capitalistic speech.

"You see, it's actually very simple. In this country anybody who wants to work can. Most people think that the way to get ahead is to work for others, but really I'm working for myself."

"That's not true," his sister interjected.

"Yes, it is!"

"I don't see how," she whined.

"A long time ago I figured out that being paid what I ask and working when I choose makes me the one in charge. First, you must not price yourself too cheap, or they think you are worthless; or too high, so they feel they could get a better deal elsewhere." Benny stopped to dip his bread in the sauce. "Don't think I'm going to be a laborer forever. No, siree! The way to make it really big is find something that is composed of cheap raw materials, but the result is worth more than the sum of the parts. All the *gontser makhers* traffic in something disposable, like coal or food. They know the secrets of how to make their goods look special by the way it is offered or arranged. They are good salesmen too, making people think they are doing them a favor." He took a gulp of milk. "You know something else I've learned, Ma? People have bigger hearts than you would at first suspect. They like a kid with a friendly smile, a kid who says thanks, a kid who isn't out to cheat them . . . even though he's not about to let anyone cheat him either!"

Hannah did not know whether to laugh or cry. Who was this child? At fifteen he was taller than her and fast approaching his father's height. He had the sort of face—open, bright-eyed, with dimpled cheeks—that people liked. From his hard work of lifting and carrying, his chest muscles were beginning to show through his shirt, and his arms were stronger than they looked. For a while she had thought he would always be a bit chubby, but as his legs lengthened, he developed his father's firm, well-proportioned look—at least the way he had been before the accident.

She reached over and tried to fix a lock of hair that perpetually poked out from behind his left ear. "Ah, Ma!" Benny brushed away her hand. His movement was graceful, even soft, as though he could not admit he liked the attention.

For a moment Hannah smiled fondly. Then she winced at the thought of how Lazar would react if he heard his son's philosophy. She could see a disastrous clash as clearly as a runaway horse headed for a brick wall. Even if she could pull the reins in time, even if she could head off the direct blow, she realized that in order to succeed, Benny would still have to break his father's heart.

〆 **2** 〆

As Minna approached the final weeks of her pregnancy, she was never far from Hannah's mind. The months of gestation had gone smoothly. Contrasted to the habitual kvetching of someone like Eva, Minna sailed along the uncharted seas finding each rolling wave, each slight storm, part of the adventure rather than a trial to endure. To her, pains were twinges, an active fetus a minor miracle rather than a personal inconvenience. Questions revolved around how the baby was developing and whether it was healthy and happy rather than her own discomforts. Hannah had always believed that attitude was nine-tenths of the battle. If that was the case with Minna, she should have had a perfect pregnancy. Unfortunately, one concern which had plagued Hannah since Minna's exam to confirm the pregnancy seven months earlier continued to trouble the midwife.

During the initial maternal-assessment examination, pelvic capacity was duly noted. The female pelvis forms a bony canal through which the fetus must pass during the birth process. In the midwife's experience the vast majority of pelvises were more than adequate to deliver safely a larger-than-average full-term baby. While the lay person might try to estimate size by the woman's physique and stature, outward indications were worthless. Even a practitioner required years of experience to accurately take the measurements using digital pelvimetry. On the first try Hannah had merely gone through the motions, doing an estimate so as not to discomfit Minna. The midwife had presumed that Minna, while smaller than the average woman, was well proportioned. Thus, the following month, when she remeasured more carefully, she had been surprised by the narrowness of the diagonal conjugate.

On that occasion Minna was less excited, and also her early nausea had lessened, making it easier for the midwife to poke and probe to be certain she was touching the spots to obtain an accurate measurement from the lower border of the symphysis pubis to the center of the promontory of the sacrum. To allow for the depth of the pubic bone, she subtracted two centimeters, wrote down the answer, then reviewed her result: Ten and a half centimeters. Since twelve to thirteen centimeters was the normal range, this was not exceedingly small, but it was worrisome. After using her fingers to figure the lower border of the symphysis pubis, she calculated the distance between that point and the tip of her middle finger with calipers. Again she was disappointed with the result.

"Is everything all right?" Minna asked.

"I think so," Hannah demurred. "Sorry to take so long. I don't like to do these measurements later in the pregnancy, when it would be even more uncomfortable, so I must get them right during the first trimester." Hannah forced her voice to sound light to put Minna at ease, but she wondered if she was covering her anxiety. "We're almost done," she advised before taking the final measurement: the assessment of the pelvic outlet.

The upper border of this, the passage through which the baby has to navigate, is at the level of the ischial spines. The distance between these is known as the bispinous diameter, which has great obstetrical importance because it is the transverse, or sideways, measurement of the narrow pelvic plane. First Hannah palpated the spines to see if they were unduly prominent, and was relieved to find Minna's were not. Two fingers were then placed in the sacro-sciatic notch to determine if it was sufficient. Not bad. The curve of her sacrum was also decent. Before removing her fingers, she examined Minna's pubic arch to see whether two fingers could be accommodated in its apex. Just barely, but they could fit.

Using her closed fist, she inserted it between the ischial tuberosities. A midwife needed to know how her fist measured in comparison with dozens of pelvic outlets in order to judge whether the intertuberischial diameter was average, small, or large. Here is where Hannah's heart quickened. Not one measurement, antero-posterior, oblique, or transverse, was within the normal range! Each was slightly below a safe number, but only by a centimeter or so. The word to describe Minna was borderline. If the baby's head was small ... if she delivered within the earlier ranges for her dates rather than the later ... if the baby's head molded well ... if its position were the most providential ...

"Is that it?" Minna asked in an optimistic tone.

"For now," Hannah replied somewhat distractedly as she made her notes.

"Am I all right?"

"There is no right or wrong here," Hannah began hesitantly. "These are merely measurements, like shoe sizes. Just as the bones of the feet are different in every woman, there is also a wide range of pelvic forms and sizes."

"How interesting," Minna commented pleasantly. "I don't know why I would have expected everyone to be alike. After all, Margaret used to say that there were as many differences in vulvas as in faces."

At that Hannah spun around and caught Minna's mischievous grin. Together they burst out laughing, further disguising her concern. No need to alarm her, Hannah decided, while making a note to measure the fetus's head at every subsequent visit.

"The fetal head is the best pelvimeter" had been the dictum of Dr. Stepanoff, her anatomy professor in Moscow. "If the pelvis is not large enough to accommodate the head of the very fetus it is carrying, the fact that the bones measure of adequate size by some textbook table is inconsequential." However, it was not until the thirty-sixth week of gestation that a baby's head was sufficiently large to judge for certain whether it could enter the pelvic brim, or whether a true disproportion existed.

Hannah allowed extra time when she scheduled Minna's crucial visit. The day could not have been worse. January had long been her least favorite month, and this one was no exception. The temperature had not been above freezing the whole week. Crusted snow and icy patches formed an obstacle course on streets and sidewalks. Trolleys and subways were invariably running late. Minna was also delayed, but for another reason. Word had come that Prince Kropotkin, the Russian revolutionary and theorist on anarchism, was dying in Moscow. "Lazar wanted to alter the front-page layout of tomorrow's *Freiheit* to accommodate the news," she explained breathlessly, then began to cough.

"Are you getting a cold?"

"I don't think so. It's so hard to breathe with the baby

pushing up here." She pointed to the narrow space between her swollen breasts and barreling abdomen.

"Won't be long now," Hannah said in her standard soothing voice.

"Well, she's certainly ready to come out into the light."

"This week it's a she," Hanna commented. Most patients called their fetus "he," but Minna had taken care to alternate.

"Always a possibility," she murmured as she lay down on the examining table without being asked.

As Hannah warmed the chest piece of her stethoscope, she thought about the baby imprisoned in Minna's pelvis—in her slender pelvis—and gave an involuntary shudder. She willed herself to concentrate on the baby's strong, vital heartbeat before placing her hands in the customary position for estimating its size. After locating the baby's head, Hannah exerted a light but steady pressure on it, moving it slightly downward and backward. She held her breath as she tried to establish that wonderful sense of looseness that she could feel if there was no overlap, proving that the head could slip through the mother's pelvis. Her first try was a disappointment. Moving around so she faced Minna's feet, Hannah's left hand grasped the fetal head once more, making certain her thumb was on Minna's right side. Then she pushed the head in a downward direction. Usually in this position the "give" of the head was more obvious. Unfortunately, the first two fingers of her right hand noted a distressing overlap at the symphysis pubis, an almost certain sign that true cephalo-pelvic disproportion was present. Several other maneuvers, with Minna sitting up and in other positions, failed to disprove her predicament.

Hannah turned her back and pretended to write in the chart, but her vision was blanketed with a crimson film of anger. How could it be worse? Everything that could turn against Minna had. The baby was too big. Its head had grown to an obstinately large size, now on the opposite end of normal from Minna's small pelvis. Even so, Hannah reminded herself, you never could tell whether a head would pass safely through the pelvis until labor had begun. The strength of the uterine contractions, the natural relaxation in the pelvic joints, and the degree of the overriding of the baby's skull bones all could influence the outcome of the labor. That's why minor degrees of contraction were so diffi-

cult to diagnose. That's why a trial of labor was always preferred to a rush to operative delivery with its attendant risks
and complications. Yet there were certain cases when it
might make sense to arrange surgery before labor had even
commenced. A trial of labor took at least twelve hours, unless another obstacle intervened. By then the patient had
been depleted of the energy to face a crisis. Also, what if the
right surgeon and supporting staff were not on hand when
the decision to abandon the vaginal route was made? Certainly she did not want a novice attending Minna. Dr. Dowd
was the sole surgeon she trusted implicitly.

"Not long now?" Minna was asking.

"The baby's a good size, but another two weeks is what
I would estimate," Hannah replied mechanically.

"I can't wait!" Minna said with an enthusiasm that
wrenched Hannah's heart. Had there ever been a more
wanted child? Maybe she had been too ensnared in Minna's
hopes and dreams to have assessed this situation properly.
Minna would be an excellent candidate to weather the
storms of labor. If she ambulated, squatted, used every physiological and gravitational benefit, if she exerted the maximum muscular force to expel the child, if the baby's skull
bones forged their way forward—No! Stop it! she warned
herself. You must consult with someone—with Dr. Dowd—
and let him determine what should be done.

Hannah felt herself resisting this sensible plan. But why?
Hadn't she run to the doctor the minute she had a question
about Eva, only to find that her own assessment had been on
the mark? Yet to do the same with the next relative to become pregnant made her seem foolish for taking on cases of
family members, as well as ignorant of how to handle simple
complications. Besides, to stave off temptation she and
Wendell had been avoiding each other. Might he not think
this an obvious attempt to spend time with him? Recalling
the raging sensations around the time of Eva's pregnancy,
including the reason she had missed her sister's delivery,
Hannah found herself flushing. Wendell would find this excuse for a consultation equally transparent.

What if he did? She wanted to see him. She wanted to
work with him again. She wanted to talk with him. She
wanted to be with him. Yes, be with him, to hold him, to
kiss him. Yes! She wanted him. What was so wrong with
that? Lazar was no more to her than a good friend. Any ex-

pectations that they would become lovers again had long been dashed. They shared the same bed, true, but when was the last time they had done something as simple as fall asleep together? Usually Hannah slipped beneath the quilt hours before her husband and was always long gone before he roused. Just because he had his accident did not mean she was to be denied any physical release with a man for the rest of her life, did it?

Minna's voice broke through Hannah's barrier. "You look tired, Hannah."

"Oh, yes, well . . ." she offered stupidly. "The weather, so cold . . . that's all."

Minna sat up and began to button her shirt, one she had borrowed from Chaim. As she redid the lower fasteners, she gave her stomach a loving pat. "She's hiccoughing, at least that's what it feels like. Could that be it?"

"Yes, they do that a lot," the midwife replied flatly, then somehow found the strength to say what was on her mind. "Minna, the baby is very strong, very healthy. I'm delighted you've avoided some of the difficulties of this phase of pregnancy, but I do have one concern."

"Yes?" Minna fluffed her hair while peering in the glass at the back of the door.

"Well, your pelvis is smaller than many, and the baby seems a trifle larger than I expected . . . probably nothing unusual, but just to be sure . . ." Every attempt at making this sound minor was failing, but for some reason she was not daunting Minna.

"Oh, now don't go treating me like a china doll! When I come in to Bellevue on the big day, I'm hardly expecting it to be a trip to Coney Island." She laughed at her own allusion. "Remember Luna Park?"

"How could I forget it?" Hannah forced a chuckle.

"I'd never been so sick, as well as so happy to be sick before. Is that what delivering a baby is like?"

"In a way . . ." Hannah decided on another tack. "Do you remember Dr. Dowd, the one who suggested Dr. Rubin?"

"The miracle man who cured you of the flu? How could I forget him? He's the fellow with the gorgeous mane of hair. You're crazy about him, aren't you?" Hannah's lips parted to form a silent *O* while Minna prattled on. "You think he's the best doctor in New York. Well, why shouldn't you? He may have saved your life, and he's the one I should be thanking for this gift." She patted her abdomen again, and Hannah relaxed as she was reassured of Minna's ignorance.

"He has been curious about your case. You might not realize it, but the baby's already famous, at least statistically, since it was conceived so recently after the test. When it is born, it will be listed as one of Dr. Rubin's first successes."

"I guess that may be why I am having so much gas!" Minna giggled.

There was no way anything was going to shatter her sister-in-law's good humor, so Hannah decided she might as well tell her the truth. "If you would have no objections, I'd like Dr. Dowd to examine you this week."

"No, of course not, but I don't see why—"

"A precaution. According to my measurements you are on the borderline for having a pelvis large enough to permit the baby's safe passage. While it probably would come through, I don't want to worry that it might suffer some damage along the way. You remember my sister Dora, don't you? Well, the reason her mind was slow was due to a traumatic birth. She was born in the breech position. That means her buttocks arrived before her head—which is not the case here—but she did not get enough oxygen during the crucial final stages. Since there is a slight chance of something similar in your case, and since there now are alternatives that Mama did not have in those days . . ."

"What are you saying?" Minna asked with the first sign of alarm.

"Just that I'd like the doctor to reassure me. I am too close to this case to be objective."

"I agree with you about that," Minna said with some relief. "Let the doctor look all he wants. He's such a handsome devil that I'll lie back and enjoy every minute of it."

A new emotion clutched at Hannah as quickly as if she had been touched with a stranger's icy fingers. She stared at Minna, but saw no malice in her smooth, puffy face. No, Minna could not know how haunted she was by Wendell, or how alienated she was from Lazar. Minna's world revolved around the coming baby. The baby, must concentrate on the baby, Hannah vowed one second, then the image of the shining newborn sliding between Minna's legs was supplanted with that of Wendell standing naked in the sunlight reaching his arms out to her.

3

"Absolutely no other choice," Wendell boomed much louder than necessary. Minna was in the next room, and Hannah did not want her to hear the discussion. She had not begun to prepare her for a surgical delivery, since she had almost convinced herself that Dr. Dowd would minimize the disproportion and recommend a wait-and-see approach.

"There might be some latitude—"

"Why don't you go back and study your De Lee?" he sputtered. "You should have spotted this at the initial assessment."

"I did, but I waited until thirty-six weeks to confirm the baby's circumference and—"

"But any first-year student would have diagnosed a clearly contracted pelvis from the diminution of one and a half to two centimeters variation in any important diameter. You have several very divergent calibrations, which probably indicate malnourishment during her childhood, or even during her own mother's pregnancy, if not some genetic predisposition. I will allow that various authorities might dispute the *degree* of contraction, but not its existence."

"Might there not be a chance?"

Dr. Dowd shot her a long-suffering look, which quickly dampened any romantic notions Hannah might have harbored about their reunion. "My dear, this woman is almost at term, the head is high up, and not about to become engaged. It does not even project into the pelvis, but floats almost out of reach of my finger with marked ballottement. If labor were to begin, the membranes over the os would be exposed to the full force of the uterine contractions. You know as well as I do the evil consequences of early sac rupture. If this baby dies, have you thought about how disappointed Dr. Rubin would be?"

"Dr. Rubin! What does he have to do with this?" Hannah realized she was shouting, but she did not lower her voice. "I am fully aware of the risk. That is why she is here, and to date she has been in no danger whatsoever. The measurements have always been marginal, but only this week could the baby's size be determined with the accuracy required for such a momentous determination."

Dr. Dowd stepped back and tilted his head, a sign that he was listening to her. "And what shall that be, Midwife Sokolow?"

"Induction of premature labor would be useless at this point," she began slowly.

"I agree. Even two or three weeks ago would not have made a significant difference," he allowed to relieve her of the responsibility for not making the judgment earlier. "I know you feel this will be difficult to explain to Mrs. Blau, but let me tell you it is much worse to have to contemplate dismembering a trapped infant."

"I suppose a preplanned cesarean section might be proposed."

"There is less than a two percent mortality in one that is known beforehand," Dr. Dowd added in a silky voice that carried a faint reminder of the lover he had once been. Nevertheless, Hannah was so distressed by the way he had spoken to her initially, she could not bring herself to look into his eyes as he continued, "There are compromises sometimes suggested in these cases, including an operation to enlarge the pelvis . . ." he offered.

"No!" Hannah replied firmly. "That can have a crippling effect on the mother."

"We could explore various forceps manipulations, but the child would fare better without these interventions, wouldn't you agree?"

Even though Hannah knew she was being herded into a corner, where the only solution would be Dr. Dowd's, she felt powerless to stand her ground. Still, she felt she owed Minna the choice. "She does not follow the definition of an absolute contraction."

"We have been endeavoring to define relative indications for cesareans more broadly than merely centimeters for the conjugata vera or grams of fetal tissue. Now we are comfortable if we can say that the abdominal delivery offers a significantly better option for both mother and child than delivery from below. I will admit that without clinical definitions of the chances, the choice is largely subjective. In fact, some of my esteemed colleagues have stretched the definitions of risk to include women whose nervous constitutions and general makeup make them unfit to withstand the strain of labor."

This was too much for Hannah and she burst out, "Sometimes I sense that it is the practitioner himself who may be unfit, because he would prefer to spend the balance of his night under his own blanket instead of riding out the long process at the bedside."

A bemused expression crossed the doctor's face. "Perhaps you are being a bit unfair."

"You are saying that it is not possible to know for certain if the decision is correct," she continued more sedately.

"Exactly. Mrs. Blau could go into spontaneous labor tomorrow, have every force of nature align properly, and expel the baby through that perilous cavity with no consequence greater than an episiotomy for her and a temporarily misshapen skull for the child. Or, you and I could exchange a long list of trials she and the child might endure, giving the statistical odds for each occurrence, as well as the worst and best outcome of each intervention we might employ, but we would still never know if we had been right to take the gamble until *after* the fact. Are you willing to wait that long?"

"I will explain this to Minna. Do you want me to do this now, or would it be better not to occupy your examining room much longer?"

"I think you should tell her here. Then if she has questions, I could answer them. Besides, I hate to have you run off so quickly. You're always running off these days, Hannah." His voice dropped as an opening for her to protest or explain. Seeing the trap, Hannah took diversionary action and kept going through the door to where Minna waited.

4

"Do whatever's required" was Minna's rapid comment.

"But there are risks . . ." the midwife began.

"There are risks crossing Second Avenue, so what else is new?"

"I don't believe you understand . . ."

"On the contrary, I understand far more than you think. I've known about the measurements for some time. Any woman who has to wear children's belts at my age has a fairly good idea that her body is not that of a full-grown woman. Anybody who's carried this hefty baby around for nine months has figured out that bringing him forth is going to be as sorrowful as the Bible warns."

"Why didn't you ask me about it earlier?"

"I knew you were watching out for our well-being, so I knew you would make the right choice."

"As I explained, we'll never know what is right or wrong."

"If I survive, and the baby too, then the choice was correct. Long ago I learned not to speculate on what another turn in the road might have brought. Just think, if things had gone according to plan, I would be married to Napthali! And don't forget already I have survived a pogrom, Blackwell's Island, the Red Scare, Dr. Rubin's machine, even the birth of the *Freiheit*."

"Well, that was probably the most traumatic of them all!" Hannah allowed with a laugh.

"When should we do it?" Minna questioned.

"During the thirty-eighth week. Dr. Dowd doesn't want you going into labor. Pick a date around February third."

"How about the first of the month? Then the baby would have an easy date to remember: two one, two one."

"Sounds like odds at the racetrack!"

"They might be good for a bet, but I'd prefer better ones on my life." Minna's forced good cheer faltered. Her mouth opened to speak, then closed in a thin line.

"What is it?"

"My odds. What are they?"

Hannah recalled Dr. Dowd's two percent mortality rate. It sounded low, unless it related to someone you loved.

"Are they that bad?" Minna asked with a quaver.

"Oh no! They're something like to fifty to one."

Minna brightened at once. "Put your money on this horse!" She clapped her hands with the fighting spirit Hannah had always admired.

5

On the morning of February 1, Hannah accepted baby boy Blau from Dr. Dowd, who had just lifted the child from his mother's gaping abdomen. Using suction equipment, she cleared the child's airway thoroughly, since a baby denied the natural compression of a journey down the vaginal canal requires some assistance to eliminate the excess fluids accumulating in its respiratory system. The moment the tube was removed he yelled loudly enough to cause his etherized mother to stir. The doctor at the table's head had to increase the anesthetic. He claimed it was impossible for her to have heard the child, but later Minna would swear she had been privy to her son's first cry, and Hannah did not dispute that claim.

As it was, though, the father held the child first, exclaiming that his son's size was extraordinary. His weight of almost nine pounds bolstered Hannah's confidence that the cesarean had not been performed in vain. Seeing the perfectly round, unmolded head, the skull unblemished by forceps or other instruments, the face not even slightly tarnished by bruises, she realized—perhaps for the first time—the true beauty of babies who had been spared passage through the pelvis.

"Pyotr Alekseyevich," Chaim mumbled in Russian, "welcome to this meshugeneh world!"

Hannah had known they were considering this name for a boy in honor of the ailing Prince Kropotkin, who would die at the end of that week. In his writings, Kropotkin proposed a society in which all material goods were held in common, with individuals receiving according to their needs. After years in exile he had returned to Russia in June 1917. However, disappointed by the Bolshevik seizure of power, he had withdrawn from public life. Chaim and Minna both regretted the man had not been appreciated in his lifetime, and hence the name for their son. Yet Hannah wished her brother had picked something more neutral, for if the child raised in

America demonstrated even a few of Benny's materialistic traits, the name would be ironic indeed.

"Peter's a beautiful baby." She purposefully Americanized his name. "And that's in the professional opinion of his midwife, not his aunt."

"Peter Blau. Not bad even like that," the new father allowed. "How's Minna?"

"She's been stable throughout. These surgeries are usually done at the last moment when everyone, including the mother, is more frantic. Of course, we must be vigilant for complications, but we don't expect any. The baby is as healthy as any I've ever delivered, and well ... you know Minna!"

Chaim lifted his son's hand, and the child's fingers curled around his. "Look at that!" he said as though the child had performed a miraculous feat. "I didn't know a baby could do that!"

Dr. Dowd appeared at the nursery door. Hannah looked up and a feeling of dread passed through her until she caught the calming sparkle in the eyes above the mask. Just in case, though, she stood to block Chaim's view. The doctor was nodding. She approached him and listened as he gave some final notes about the closure, Minna's aftercare, and his findings. "Couldn't have gone better. How's the child?"

"A wonder. He can hold his father's hand already."

Wendell pulled down his mask to reveal his beaming smile. They had done the correct thing. Together they had made the right decision. Together they had brought Minna to Dr. Rubin, they had managed what could have been a nightmare of a delivery to perfection. What a splendid team they had been—and could be in the future! As Hannah's hopes surged, he seemed to understand without being told, because he mumbled, "We need to talk, alone, later."

"Yes, of course, Doctor," Hannah replied as the operating room nurse passed them. "Where and when?"

"My office, late this afternoon?"

"Can't. Clinic hours. Could we meet after that?"

The doctor's eyes darkened. He must have had the same expectations, the same desires, but had to cloak them. Wasn't it time that they stopped this foolish dance? She had to tell him. They had to make a plan. Lazar would understand. After all, she had allowed him freedom to return to

Russia. She had encouraged the *Freiheit*. Now it was her turn. "Couldn't we meet at the Brevoort?"

"I don't know if that would be a good idea . . ."

"As a favor to me," she dared.

"I suppose," he deferred, in what she saw as an amusing switch of roles. That's what she loved about him. One moment he could be preaching to her about a medical matter, the next he could be asking her to assist in surgery, or offering an opinion on a sexual survey matter, then caressing her more expertly than any man ever.

"Tonight, then," she said as she turned back to harvest strength from the serene scene of her brother falling in love with his first child.

◅◦ **6** ◦▻

At Bellevue most of Hannah's duties were of a supervisory nature, and she felt she was an excellent administrator. That was the problem. Now she was reduced to glancing at babies through a door, if there was even time for that after completing the dreaded paperwork that documented the trail of chaos into order, sorting out of petty squabbles, making equitable schedules, and attending meetings with the Board of Managers, the Committee on Maternal Affairs, the nursing supervisor, even the Architectural Board. How long had it been since she had been bathed in the glow of a new mother's amazed—as well as relieved—smile of deliverance? No wonder she looked forward to her clinic days, for this was the only time she actually worked with patients.

That afternoon, though, her thoughts were not so much directed at the cases as her reunion with Wendell. How careful he had been not to seem as though he were pressuring her! Another man might have taken advantage of the opportunity. As she walked up St. Mark's Place, she tried to imagine how the evening would proceed. At the door to the clinic she paused. Her mind had just encountered the door to Room 202, and soon she was flooded with feelings of acute anticipation.

"Good afternoon, Mrs. Sokolow," chimed Carrie in her singsong voice. "You look very radiant today."

Hannah flushed as though her thoughts had been read. "Yes, well . . . a lovely, mild day, isn't it?" she managed, but one glance around the waiting room curtailed her flight of fancy. A full house . . . Must be some walk-ins . . . Many new faces . . . Not enough time . . . Might be late for Wendell . . . Her enthusiasm at the task began to deflate, but she willed herself to press forward. Reminding herself not to allow the women to prattle on and on, to be efficient during her exams and firm with her advice, she indicated she was ready for the first case.

Mrs. Snadowsky had voluptuous lips, muscular arms, and short, thick legs. Two of the smallest of her five children had remained in the waiting room, but she asked to keep the door slightly ajar in case she heard them moving from their assigned seats. "They know they'll get a *potch in tukhis* if they don't mind," she explained. "If I don't watch Jerry every minute—"

"I'm sure they'll be fine," Hannah cut her off calmly. "Now, what seems to be the difficulty?"

"It burns when I go."

"When you urinate . . . when you make water?" She nodded her head. "Anything else? Itching? Discharge?" Mrs. Snadowsky kept agreeing. "I'll have to examine you, and I could use a urine sample."

While the woman was getting undressed, Hannah directed Carrie to position Mrs. Snadowsky and to check the urine, then hurried across the hall to see the next case so as not to waste time. The name on the next chart seemed familiar, but Hannah could not place it with the scowling, disheveled woman in the chair. Vivian Glanz, Vivian Glanz . . . who was she? Now she recalled the apple-cheeked face on the timid daughter of a baker on Second Avenue. She checked the girl's birth date. She was twenty-one, but looked more than thirty. Her clothes were ragged and greasy, her face was rough from exposure to the cold, but the resemblance was there. Obviously the girl had troubles, but the waiting room was full, and then there was Wendell . . . "What seems to be the difficulty?"

"Der's a baby in d'oven and dis one don't come out," she said so mushily Hannah barely comprehended her.

"You think you are pregnant."

"Sure am."

"How far along?"

"Three, four months without any bleedin', except when I tried to get rid of it."

"You had an abortion?"

"Yeah, lots of them. The first time I got knocked up my mother threw me out in the street. Know why?" Her face became defiant. "Da kid was my old man's, but she wouldn't believe me."

For a moment Hannah was incredulous, but then recalled some scandalous rumors about the baker. "But you didn't try to get rid of this one?"

"Tried, but it didn't take. I used to go down to Allen and Canal, but the lady der is gone."

"Sewer Sue!" Hannah gulped.

"Geez, you's heard of her?"

The Bellevue midwives regularly mopped up the damage from this abortionist's mistakes. The woman had some sense of decency, however, since she gave her victims a list of early warning signs and recommended that they stop in at Bellevue for treatment at the first indication of trouble, knowing that once the aborting process had begun, they would be admitted and cared for. Many emergency cases, which resulted in massive infection and death, never made it to Hannah's pavilion. The better outcomes had resulted in emergency surgeries to remove the rotted uteri. "Where'd she go?" The girl shrugged. "Who did this one?"

"Ah, I just took some powders. They made me real sick at both ends, I even got some bleedin', but then it stayed, so I guess I'm gonna have it, ain't I?"

"Are you married?"

She gave a rueful laugh. "You gotta be kiddin' me!"

"Do you work?"

"How'da think I got this way?"

So the baker's daughter was a pregnant prostitute. That was all she needed to begin the day! She completed the exam, confirmed the pregnancy, and put Vivian on a regular maternity-care schedule. The rest she would handle at subsequent visits. Then, after washing her hands up past the elbows, she returned to Mrs. Snadowsky.

The vaginal discharge was greenish-yellow pus. The urine was filled with blennorrheal filaments. How in the world did Mrs. Snadowsky have the symptoms of gonorrhea? she asked herself, and responded mentally: from her husband . . . or an indiscretion. Again Wendell loomed before her, but she forced herself back to the case at hand. Was it just in her practice, or since the end of the war were others experiencing a rise in venereal cases? Maybe the diseases always had been as rampant, but the victims had been more reluctant to seek help. Fortunately, Mrs. Snadowsky had the earliest symptoms.

"You have a venereal infection," she pronounced matter-of-factly. "That means it was contracted from a man during sexual intercourse."

"That's not possible!" she protested.

"When was the last time you were with a man?" Hannah asked.

"Well, a few days ago . . . but my husband couldn't—" She trembled so hard the metal examining table rattled slightly.

"This is very common. There are many girls who will tempt a man," Hannah said to ease the sting, but she did not verbalize the rest of her thought: that one of those temptresses was in the very next room. For a second she felt the pangs of both women. Vivian Glanz was the victim of her father's perversion; Mrs. Snadowsky was the victim of a girl like Vivian as well as her husband's wanderings. No time for philosophizing, she warned herself, and began to describe the various solutions of acriflavine and silver salts that had to be employed to halt the infection. "Try this course of treatment for two weeks, then stop and see if any symptoms return."

Again she scrubbed her hands, this time pouring a solution of potassium permanganate over her skin. More than an hour had been spent, and she had seen only two patients. Fortunately, the next few were repeat visits, two for pregnancies that were advancing normally, one a postpartum visit with a breast abscess that could be treated with hot compresses and a brief demonstration on how to empty the milk ducts more thoroughly. After rushing through those, she checked with Carrie. Two more to go, although each was unknown to her, which meant a long explanation of the problem and probably a complete examination.

"Who shall I send in next?" Carrie inquired.

"What are the complaints?"

"Lillian Neufield has not been in before and said she

would rather discuss the problem with you. Bella Taub has abdominal pain, but you might want the doctor to see that one, she looks quite ill to me."

"When's Rachael due back?"

"Any time now."

"Better put her in the doctor's first room. I'll do the initial work-up, then send Rachael in."

In a few moments it was clear Mrs. Taub's problems were not gynecological. Hannah suspected an inflamed appendix, which was tentatively confirmed by the doctor's quick examination. "Let's make arrangements to ship her to Gouverneur's," Rachael told Carrie, leaving Hannah free to see her last patient of the day.

❧ 7 ❧

Lillian Neufield strutted into the room, made a quick turn on her high heels, then settled into the chair with a well-rehearsed cluster of gestures, ending with a leg cross that revealed long legs encased in silk stockings.

"So kind of you to take the time to see me," she said with elaborate politeness.

Hannah skimmed the information Carrie had filled out on the new chart. The patient was unmarried, thirty-two years old, five feet, ten inches, and weighed one hundred and fifty pounds. Looking up, the midwife noticed that she did not seem large anywhere except in the shoulders. Also, Miss Neufield's bust was firm and high, probably more the result of a fine corset than a natural shape, for the breasts formed a fashionable cone under the tight bodice outlined with lace ruffles. Her face was elongated as well, with an equine shape that was made even more pronounced by large coal black eyes and an artificial arch of eyebrow, in an imitation of Gloria Swanson. Her dark hair was immaculately coiffed with a center part and freshly brushed sheen. Tight curls fringed the face flirtatiously. The chart listed her occupation as artist, but for some reason it was spelled *artiste* with an *e*. She had given a Greenwich Village address, so Hannah was surprised that she had ventured across town for a routine medical appointment. Here was a place to begin.

"My, what a long way you have come. What seems to be the difficulty?" Hannah inquired for what she prayed would be the last time that day.

"I do prefer confiding in a woman," said Lillian as she leaned closer and spoke in a conspiratorial whisper. "Men just don't understand about some things, do they?"

"I see," Hannah answered neutrally. She had fallen into this trap before, only to have to dig herself out of it when she had to refer a complex complaint to a male specialist.

Miss Neufield crossed her legs to the other side and rearranged the pleats of her skirt. Hannah could tell by the stitchery that she had a talented tailor. The woman cleared her throat but did not continue.

"You have taken a great deal of trouble to come here today, haven't you?" Hannah started again.

"Yes, I don't know why there isn't a direct trolley or subway or anything across town. Something should be done about it."

Controlling her urge to bolt from the room and be off to the Brevoort, Hannah wracked her mind for a way to get Miss Neufield to—as Benny would say—spill the beans. "The first step in ironing out any problem is to seek help," she offered more limply than she might have, but her words seemed to have kindled a spark.

Miss Neufield clutched her handbag, then began to speak. "I've heard you are good with private problems, but I'm afraid you might not be able to help me with mine."

"When you have not felt a pain before, you think it is something quite extraordinary, and that is the most frightening part. A few minutes ago I examined a woman with a potentially serious yet treatable ailment. Even though she is not free of her misery yet, the relief she senses just knowing what is happening has helped her immensely." Hannah had babbled on too long about the appendix case, but there was something about Lillian that made her feel particularly ill at ease.

"Well, that is a relief. Even though you might not have heard of a situation precisely like mine, maybe you have come across something similar."

"That's very possible." Hannah waited too long for a response before continuing, so she had to rush in with a disorganized thought. "Saying it aloud for the first time is the worst part."

Lillian was nodding but not speaking. Impatience mounted like a fluttering bird against the bars of its cage. Hannah was supposed to meet the doctor in less than thirty minutes. He would wait, but she knew how touchy he could be at the end of the day, and did not want to start off with any frayed edges to mend, especially not when they were going to work out a plan to be reunited.

"I assume you are not having any immediate illness," Hannah prompted.

"No, not really."

"Good." Hannah made a note on the chart. "Now, when was the date of your last menstrual period?"

"I haven't had one for some time."

A pregnancy. What a relief! Well, at least for Hannah, if not the single woman. But anyway, after a few minutes of basic advice, she could be given another appointment for a thorough prenatal work-up. "Can you estimate? Three weeks. A month? Two months?"

"Oh, much longer than that. I'm very—how do you say it?—irregular."

Hannah scanned the woman's narrow frame for any hint of a long-standing pregnancy. Her hopes deflated. This might be a hormone problem, which were almost impossible to treat but would take many sessions to evaluate. "May I assume that since you are unmarried, you are not attempting to conceive?"

"Well, naturally, I would like a child someday, but first I must find the right partner."

"That's one problem I'm not equipped to solve," Hannah said with what she hoped was a polite laugh. "As you might know, my primary profession is as a midwife. Somehow this has stretched to include aspects before a baby is conceived to the subsequent care during pregnancy, delivery, and the postpartum period. I also handle miscellaneous gynecological problems in conjunction with Dr. Jaffe. Is there something in that category with which I could assist you today?"

"I've heard people just talk to you and you make helpful suggestions."

"Sometimes . . ." Hannah said warily as she wracked her mind speculating who had made the referral. Probably someone from the Village, someone with a frigidity problem perhaps. This woman seemed progressive. She might have had boyfriends with whom she had experienced some sexual problem, but how long was it going to take to get to the point? "Before I can assist someone in that way, I have found it helpful to get to know them better. Now that we have become acquainted, you could schedule another appointment and we could explore the matter further the next time."

Miss Neufield began to squirm in her seat. Was she indicating her desire to end the interview or her distress at the suggestion? Usually Hannah had a better sense of what was going on, but now she was muddled. Her longing to see Wendell was clouding her vision. This was not fair to the patient. "Of course, I would not charge for this consultation," she offered.

"I was hoping you might examine me."

So there was a physical problem. "What seems to be the difficulty?" slipped out automatically once more.

"I am worried about how I look down there."

Hannah was about to say something consoling and put the matter off, for an exam would surely cause her to be late, but then she remembered the one clue to her condition: the patient was not menstruating. Amenorrhea had many causes and it would take several visits to work on them, but after coming all this way the least she could do was to accommodate the woman. "Very well, I'll send Carric in to prepare you."

"No!" she said so furiously Hannah startled. "I mean, well, I'm shy."

This was one lady who did not seem modest by any manner of her dress or actions, but Hannah was not about to argue. Handing her a gown, she said smoothly, "Just undress yourself then, and place this over your head."

"Do I take everything off?" Lillian asked in a high, tinny voice.

"From the waist down will be sufficient for today," she said with a sigh, then left her alone to prepare.

Rachael was almost ready to go to the hospital with the appendix case. "Surgery is definitely indicated. What are your plans?"

"I have to meet Dr. Dowd," she said in an excited rush, then had to cover her tracks. "We've another idea for an article based on the survey, and there's never enough time to discuss anything at Bellevue."

"I know what you mean. Give my regards to Wendell, will you? He's a fine man, and so sexy, don't you think?" Hannah was speechless, but Rachael didn't seem to notice. "Poor fellow is probably desperate by now," Rachael prattled on without giving Hannah a chance to reply. "It's a good thing I'm not doing any research with him, I'll tell you that."

"Why?" Hannah blurted.

"I could not keep my hands off him! Does that shock you? It should, because it shocks me. Ever since I've learned what love is really about, I've been yearning to discover what it might be like with another man. Not that I don't adore Herzog, you know that I do. But to have had only one man in my entire life . . . well, it does seem a waste. Look at you! You are shocked. Hannah, you sweet thing, if you don't close your mouth something might fly in."

Hannah had barely heard her friend as her mind swirled with confusion. Did Rachael really desire Wendell, or was this a ruse to discover whether her suspicions about them had been true? Rachael knew her so well, she had probably long suspected that Lazar was impotent, and even might have guessed what Hannah was planning. It would be so much easier to confide in her friend. Yes, she would do it. Rachael would understand. After she and Wendell worked out their plan, she would tell Rachael everything.

"What are you thinking?" Rachael continued, oblivious to Hannah's churning inside. "That I'm a naughty girl? Well, I guess I am. But it doesn't hurt to dream, does it?" She looked at her watch. "I've got to dash off." She tossed her vibrant curls before she rushed down the hall.

In her wake Hannah was stunned. How uncharacteristic of Rachael. Something was going on there, but Hannah had no time to sort it out. She turned and stared at the examining room door. Reluctantly she stepped forward, coaxing herself with the promise that she would do a swift check of the pelvic region, then ask Miss Neufield to return to go over the results at another time. Five minutes. After that she'd leave Carrie to close up. Five minutes and she would be on her way.

Without so much as a glance at the body draped with a white sheet across her pelvic region, Hannah went to the bowl and washed her hands, dried them, then said, "Would you please place your feet in those handles?" She arranged the speculum, light, and the few instruments she would be requiring. Knowing the woman was unmarried, she expected a virginal or tight vaginal area, so she spread petroleum jelly on her fingers. She looked down at the bare feet, a bit taken aback by their size. There was even some hair on the toes. More evidence of a hormonal imbalance? The knees were locked tightly. Reluctant to tarry any longer, she spoke more crisply than she might have at the start of the day. "Open your legs a little more, please, this won't hurt. I'll tell you everything I'm going to do."

In a practiced maneuver she adjusted the drape so that she had a good view, but preserved an illusion of privacy, then rotated her examining light. Hannah lifted her speculum and reached her slippery fingers forward.

Then she faced the patient's perineum and saw the strangest sight of her life.

8

Lillian Neufield had a penis. The cry in Hannah's throat could not be stifled entirely. She backed toward the door, placed her hand on the knob while her mind raced to consider whether she was alone with a deranged man. At this distance she caught the expression on his face. She—or rather he—had a bemused smile.

"What kind of joke is this?" Hannah shouted. "What sort of a person do you think I am? How dare you come in here and deceive me! Now get up at once!"

The man obeyed. With one lithe movement he stood at the side of the examining table. The drape formed a puddle on the floor. She kept her eyes firmly on his mischievous eyes as he said, "Like this?"

Her glance followed his and soon she was confronted again with his genitals. One did not have to be in the medical profession to know that he was enjoying the scene he had created. She reached down, grabbed the sheet, and thrust it toward him. "Put this around you at once. Then get dressed and get out!"

"But—" he said in an imploring tone. "Please, I need help."

"Not the sort of help I can give you."

"The sign outside said 'Women's Problems.' "

"Well, you are most certainly not a woman, no matter how many fancy dresses you put on!"

"I should be a woman," he said with a catch in his voice.

"That's ridiculous. You are just caught up in some ridiculous fantasy. In any case, you've come here under false pretenses." She lifted his chart. "I don't know why I have wasted my time with you. In fact, I don't even know your real name."

"Neufield. Lester Neufield, but I feel like Lillian, not Lester. Can't you understand? No? Well, if someone like you can't, how can I? Ever since I was a boy I've enjoyed dressing up in women's clothing."

There was something about her argument—his argument—that captured Hannah's attention. "I don't know what I can do for you," she said with resignation.

"Maybe you could tell me more about why I feel as I do."

"I can't. Not tonight. I'm already late for a meeting."

"Should I make another appointment? I can pay. I have a good job."

"Whatever you wish," she allowed to get away from him. "See Carrie before you leave." She opened the door and stepped out into the sanctuary of the hall, then turned on her heel, and thrust her head back in the room. "If there is a next time, please come as Lester Neufield."

9

Wendell Dowd was waiting in the lounge of the Brevoort Hotel. On her fast walk across town Hannah glanced into the passing windows, wondering if her image would please him. She was quite a bit slimmer than the last time they had been together, and she had recently had her hair trimmed so it moved prettily when she turned her face. From this distance she looked younger than her years, and she had been paying more attention to the cut of her clothes so that they flowed in flattering folds. Her skirt was fashionably short and her legs were slender enough that she could flaunt them without shame. Yes, despite the harrowing day, she looked fine. Then she took a deep breath and practiced what she would say. She would apologize for being late, opening with something like: "You won't believe why I have been delayed!" Then she would launch into a tale of Lester's case. The farther down the road she went, the funnier the vision of Lester's clumsy feet, immaculately shaved legs, and shocking genitalia became. He'll never believe it. Nobody would ever believe it! Maybe I'd better not tell him, or at least not right off. No, not today. Wendell might want to explore the psychological and medical aspects of the case. Best to keep her words as pure as her intentions. Best to look him straight in the eye and tell him how much she needed him.

The doctor stood at her approach. His face was blank, with the slightly perplexed expression of one who has just awoken. His eyes were duller than usual, as if a light had dimmed. He has probably had a day at least as difficult as mine, Hannah reminded herself, for she knew that the morning had begun with the birth of Minna's child. How long ago that seemed! Suddenly she berated herself for not worrying more about her sister-in-law's recovery.

"Hello, Doctor."

"How are you, Hannah?" His voice was smooth but tightly controlled. Obviously he was as nervous about this as she was.

"An impossible day, but I feel better just seeing you," she allowed, feeling a risk taken with each word. "How is Minna? I wasn't able to get back to see her this afternoon."

"A slightly elevated temperature, but that is to be expected. I'm not worried about any serious complications."

"That's a relief. Thank you for everything."

"That's entirely unnecessary. Now, if you wouldn't mind, I am quite hungry. I haven't eaten since this morning."

"Oh, yes . . ." Hannah followed him docilely into the dining room. Food was the last matter on her mind. Her stomach was too jumpy with thoughts of what might yet pass between them, although her head was pounding, often a signal she needed nourishment. At least at the Brevoort you could order the set menu for guests on the meal plan, so she would not have to make a decision.

Dr. Dowd mumbled something to the waiter, and the soup was served at once. Hannah stirred the broth. Kernels of rice, bits of carrots and peas whirled in a little eddy into which she stared while she gathered her wits. Wendell's uncharacteristic silence did not help matters. He must have ordered wine—although Hannah had no idea when—for she heard the sounds of the waiter uncorking the bottle and pouring it into their glasses. Concentrating on the bubbles rising to the surface of the golden fluid calmed her sufficiently that her mind began to make connections again. Wine . . . bubbles . . . champagne . . . why? Minna's safe delivery. Of course! Her brain continued with curious associations from the gas that had bubbled up during Dr. Rubin's test . . . to Minna on the operating table being sliced open . . . to Lester Neufield lying on the table . . . Vivian Glanz . . . and Mrs. Snadowsky and . . .

"What's wrong?" came the doctor's faraway voice.

"I-I—"

"You haven't eaten all day either, have you?"

"I guess not."

"Then have some soup before we do our champagne toast."

"Champagne toast?" she echoed while images of wine poured on bread confused her.

"A celebration."

"Celebration?" she repeated stupidly.

"I have some wonderful news. I was not going to tell you yet, but then you suggested we meet, and I decided there would not be a better time. I want you to be the first to know."

"Know what?" There was a moment—did they call it a "split second"?—when Hannah roved rapidly over the possibility of a promotion in the hospital or some news of his children's successes; and another, the length of the firing of the nerve ending in her brain, when she was certain what he was about to say would not be to her liking. Thus, when he spoke, she thought she had already known—even if she really hadn't—and yet this knowledge did not help her absorb the impact any more than someone who sees the boulder coming down a hill in time to brace for the thundering blow.

"I will be marrying again." There was a long, a terribly

long, agonizing pause. If Hannah had been expected to offer a smile of pleasure or even a polite query, she could manage neither. "Her name is Angela. Angela Rush. My mother said, 'Why the rush?' when she heard, and that has become the big joke. Of course, it is hardly precipitous. Lulu's been gone for more than two years, but I suppose she means that Angela and I have not been together long." Wendell took a quick breath and hurried on with his explanation while twirling the champagne glass so that it caught the light, sending little flashes across the table. The sparkles mesmerized Hannah and made the words seem more remote.

"Actually, we have known each other for ages, or at least our families have. My mother went to school with Angela's Aunt Meredith, and our paths have crossed numerous times at weddings and other events, but she was so young that I barely took notice of her. Well, that's not exactly true. Even as a young adolescent she had a charm that made me remember her. Yes, she is quite a bit younger . . . well, it may seem like a lot now . . . not that much older than Daphne . . . but very bright, very wise in her own way . . . traveled abroad . . . and . . ," His voice faded away. His chin sagged. He waited for Hannah to spur him on with words of encouragement.

The waiter removed the soup bowls without a protest from either diner, neither of whom had taken more than a few spoonfuls. A platter of fish and boiled potatoes sprinkled with something bright green took its place. The smell, the colors, the melting pat of butter oozing along the flanks of the gray flesh gave Hannah's stomach a violent churn. She had to close her eyes and concentrate to hold down her gorge. When she opened them, she saw that Wendell's skin had turned a shade similar to the fish's.

"You must understand how it's been for me. I don't want to be alone anymore." A sob escaped from his throat. "I know I did the right thing for you, but it almost killed me. I've lost two wives already, and I dearly loved them both. I did!" The last came out as an exaggerated attempt to prove his point, then he regretted his defensiveness. His voice modulated to a whisper. "From the beginning you were an impossibility. Even if your husband had not returned, you would have been suspended and unable to commit yourself to me. Then as you yourself have said . . . well, we are from such different backgrounds. You never felt at ease in the

Mews, did you? Why should you? I remember my visits to Tompkins Square when you were ill. Around your family and friends I felt like a—a fish out of water." He stabbed at the fish on his plate and managed a weak smile, which came out more as an apologetic grimace. "No, certainly not. It never would have worked. How stupid of men to think we can all be Pygmalions and transform our women into our own image."

Hannah didn't comprehend half of what he was saying, nor did she care. It was as if she were witnessing the shipwreck of her life being dashed against the rocks by one relentless wave after another.

"You don't think I'm being a silly old fool, do you?"

The time had come when she would have to speak, but this was like being in the middle of a nightmare where you have suddenly lost the inability to speak . . . or scream. She clasped the glass like a life-saving ring and brought it to her lips. She drank. She swallowed. She replaced the glass. Everything in the background had blurred. The chatter in the dining room roared in her ears, but she fought her way up from the bottom as words formed in a massive contraction that could not be held back any more than a baby determined to be born.

"Don't. Don't marry her. It's a mistake. Terrible mistake. A silly young girl has nothing to offer. You need someone to share your life, your whole life, not just your home. You need a partner. Remember what you said? You found the social activities of your first wife strangulating. You resented the time Lulu spent away from you. We always prefer to remember the good times and forget the problems, but don't deceive yourself now. It's not too late. You did not give me enough time. My fault. I didn't tell you sooner . . . couldn't . . . today . . . It's not too late!"

"Hannah, what is this about? I thought you would be pleased. I know you have been worrying about me. Angela's young, but she's not what you think. She will be my partner. We've already spoken about her working on the survey. You don't have to be a doctor or a nurse to ask the questions, to work on correlating the results. I'll train her myself . . . you could help me . . ."

"Help you! What about me? Why do you think I wanted to see you today? You haven't asked. You don't care."

"I cannot imagine what you are talking about. I never

meant to upset you. It's been a difficult day. We were both worried about Mrs. Blau's baby, but I should have kept in mind how important it was to you."

"This has nothing to do with Minna!" Hannah seethed. A spiral of anger had coiled around her and was squeezing her tighter and tighter. Her face reddened and her palms became slippery. If they were not so far apart, if some last vestige of sense had not kept her in her seat, she would be pummeling him as blindly as a contentious street urchin.

"Is something wrong with you? With Lazar?"

"Everything. Everything is wrong . . ." The wave had crashed, cooling her off. In its ebbing moment she saw herself standing alone, drenched and shivering. Alone. Without Wendell. Without Lazar.

"I did not know. He hasn't recovered?"

"No. He never will."

"Yet he works at that paper with Mrs. Blau's husband. I thought it was a successful endeavor."

"Yes, it is."

"You have not rediscovered happiness with him," he added sadly.

"He's not the same man."

"You had to find that out for yourself. If he hadn't returned, you would never have known." The words were spoken slowly, wisely, and with sincerity, but each one irritated Hannah more than the next.

"It's a living death. I cannot go on the way we have been. That's what I wanted to say to you. I thought we could renew our . . . our friendship. I thought we could work out a way to be together eventually."

"That could never have succeeded. Neither of us were made for deception."

"You deceived Lulu!"

"Yes, very briefly. But if you recall, other than that one impetuous moment, we never really were together until after her passing."

"And what makes you think Lulu was so pure?" The doctor twitched. Although Hannah had heard suppositions and rumors, there had been no reason to smudge his tidy memories, and besides, she had no knowledge of any actual infidelities. Before he could speak, she apologized. "I'm sorry. I don't know what made me say that."

"Nobody's judging you, or me. We made mistakes; we

also did some good together, and can continue to . . . if you are able to tolerate me."

Realizing he had not backed down about Angela or followed her lead about their future together, she felt too stunned to continue.

"Is something wrong with the fish, madam?" asked the waiter at her elbow.

"I'm afraid Mrs. Sokolow's had a bit of a shock this evening. Could you bring her some tea?"

"I'm sorry, madam. Certainly, Doctor."

Dead silence. The room had mostly cleared. The tinkling of silver and glasses echoed hauntingly. A shock, he had said. Yes, that was what it was. Like hearing of a death. That same funny unreal feeling that it's a grand mistake. You focus on the little bits around you to make certain you are awake, alive, and when you are sure that you are, you wish you were not. Then the next sensation: trying to summon the power to move past the present and slip back into the past, just a few minutes or hours to prevent that dreadful moment in time from ever occurring. Hannah raised her hand, palm out, pressing it against the nothingness as if that would stop the world from revolving and bring her back to that safe place she wanted to be.

His hand enfolded hers. Warm, thick fingers clasped and squeezed, as if they could pump the blood back to her heart and remove the dreadful clamp that was sealing her off from the rest of her life. "Ah, here's the tea. Something hot is just the thing," he said rapidly.

With his free hand, his left, he clumsily stirred in sugar and offered it to her. Hannah took a quick swallow, allowing the steaming liquid to sear her throat. This pain was easy. This pain could be recognized. She drained the cup.

"We really must eat something. The food's cold, but why not some bread and butter? When I was a boy, I finished off every meal with a soft roll and lots and lots of butter. If I did not take it, Mother would think I was feeling poorly and out would come the castor oil." He let go of her hand, buttered a roll, taking half for himself and offering her the other. She would much rather have retained the hand clasp, but the crust was hard, the inside soft and doughy, and the chewing was satisfying in its own way. At least it prevented any more terrible words from spilling out and soiling the air between them.

The doctor finished his second or third glass of champagne and another roll. His head tilted slightly and his lips curled. He looked very debonair. Of course she was entirely unsuitable to be his life's companion. He had seen that long before she had. His great gesture to help Lazar reenter America had been the perfect diversion away from him. How clever for him to discard her and appear magnanimous simultaneously! Once again she had been artfully outmaneuvered.

He wiped his lips with the yellow linen napkin. "That feels better, doesn't it?"

For a moment she focused on how ghastly the napkin looked next to his skin. He did not look well. He was not the robust man she had loved. Maybe this Angela could breathe some life back into him.

"More tea, madam?"

"Yes, she would," the doctor answered for her when she was silent a beat too long. "And some of your rice pudding." He smiled at Hannah, the corners of his mouth making that boyish bow that she found so winsome. "Just what the doctor ordered."

When the waiter had disappeared entirely, Wendell leaned forward. "I had no idea how unhappy you have been. If I had known—"

"There was nothing you could do, nothing I could do. I never imagined it would be like this . . ."

"Is it your children? Your work? Your husband?"

"All of the above, but mostly the last. He hasn't recovered—"

"Who is he seeing? There might be surgeries, medications—"

"Not for his problem."

"Is it mental?" he asked, then did not wait for a reply when she did not protest. "That surprises me, really it does. From what I've heard, his newspaper is going to be successful. Maybe the strain of the new endeavor—"

"The problem seems to stem from the compression of his spine during the accident. It has affected his sexual performance," she managed in a stiff parody of a professional explanation.

Arching his thick, tangled brows, he stared at Hannah with a mixture of disbelief and concern. When he spoke, his voice was composed. "My dear Hannah! Of all people to have to endure such a hardship! Now I understand so much more ..." As he trailed off, she supposed he was recalling the last time in his office at Bellevue, finally comprehending her wanton hunger. In the calm, the waiter tiptoed forward with the puddings, each topped with a maraschino cherry. The juice formed nasty red rivulets down the mound, making Hannah think of a nursing mother's cracked and bleeding nipple.

Mistaking her scowl, Wendell drew closer. "Maybe it isn't as hopeless as you think." You're saying that because of Angela, Hannah thought, as her fury simmered. She fought to keep her face expressionless but must have failed, for he continued, "Now, don't carry on like that. You understand the cycle of anxiety at not being able to perform and then having that anxiety cause the lack of performance, thus fulfilling the expectation. Maybe this is his situation. Have you considered that?"

"Of course I have!" she said, writhing under his scrutiny. "I'm no fool. I've tried every sort of gentle, unthreatening approach. This is not in his mind, this is a real physical problem. For months after his return it was agony for him merely to find a position he could lie in. Heat, pillow arrangements, mattress positions, everything was done to accommodate him. His scars have made his body look more like a railway map than human skin. It's a wonder he has as much function as he does, but what does that do for me?"

Waving his spoon, the doctor coaxed her to taste the rice pudding. The cherry had slipped down into a puddle of cream. She scooped it up and swallowed. The cream bathed her tender throat with a soothing balm. She tried the pudding, astonishing herself with the pleasure she felt at the sweetness, the spark of cinnamon, and the chewy discovery of the plump raisins.

"It sounds as though he is healing, even if it has taken longer than expected. Tell me, does he have any trouble with incontinence?"

"Of course not."

"Or his bowels?"

"No."

"That's good news, don't you see? The spinal damage must be minimal. His limp could be attributed directly to the trauma to the leg. The part you are concerned with might revive itself if—"

"You are saying that because you don't want any responsibility for me," Hannah retorted before she could contain herself.

Keeping his eyes riveted on her, Wendell rapidly spooned two large helpings of pudding into his mouth, then made a show of scraping the edges of the cut-glass dish to finish the portion. At first she found his reticence infuriating, but then she saw that two waiters were setting up a nearby table for breakfast, and realized he was playing for time.

He patted his mouth with the napkin. "If you are finished, why don't we go into the lounge? There should not be anybody around at this hour." Without waiting for her response, he stood and guided her out of the deserted dining room.

"Sherry or port, Doctor?" asked the waiter when he saw where they were headed.

"Not this evening, Nick."

"You knew his name."

"I come here often enough."

Before she could stop herself, Hannah blurted, "With Angela."

"Angela has nothing to do with this, or with us." He pointed to the most comfortable chair in the lounge and indicated she should take it. He pulled up a ladder-backed chair. "Now, listen to me," he began with the familiar gruffness he reserved for his favorite interns, "you are a married woman with two children. Dissolving that union would fracture your family, and possibly ruin your career and reputation as well. I admit I have been at fault with you, which places me in a position of some responsibility, but I cannot make you happy. Happiness cannot be purchased from the misery of others. There is a myth of greener pastures or pots of gold over the horizon, but I have come to realize that there were too many stumbling blocks along the path between Washington Mews and Tompkins Square. From what I can tell, you had a good marriage for many years, better than most. Yes, there were problems with money, and I admit the world did not cooperate by putting on a war, a revolution, and a monstrous epidemic, but except for your elderly mother, your immediate family has survived, which is better than millions of others." He clasped both her hands between his. "Are you listening to me?"

"Yes, Wendell." His touch brought solace rather than arousal, but even so, this was only a distraction. She wanted him, not Lazar. Hadn't she made that plain enough? Nevertheless, the doctor was blocked with visions of his much younger—probably more beautiful by far—and decidedly more socially appropriate little Angela. This was her last opportunity. She grabbed it.

"I want you, Wendell. I always have. Now that I see it, couldn't you grant me another chance? I'm not asking you to give up Angela. Not yet. But couldn't you put it off for a while, even a month or two, and in the meantime spend more time with me? We could talk about the problems—I know there are many—but together we might find solutions. Lazar is hopeless, I know he is. I don't love him anymore, not sexually, not in any way. We're like old friends—for the children's sake we could stay amicable—but he's only interested in his newspaper—and himself. I thought by bringing him home I was doing the right thing for the children, yet even that was a terrible mistake. He cannot tolerate them. They're too shallow, too American. Benny thinks too much about money; Emma is more interested in singing and dancing and pretty dresses than ideas and politics. They've disappointed him, so he's turned his back on them. And on me. He's never forgiven me for refusing to go to Russia. He feels that he had to relinquish serving at Trotsky's side because of me—even if that isn't true. The trouble is, he won't face the truth. I admit that facing reality hurts. This hurts. Now. Telling you. Yet if I didn't, I would regret it for the rest of my life and . . ." As quickly as the outburst had formed, it dissipated. There was nothing more to add. The tears flowed.

Wendell proffered his handkerchief and wiped her cheeks himself. "I cannot lie to you. Your words please me enormously. I knew I never would have heard them unless your husband returned, and once he did, I backed off. I had to assume that I had done the right thing. All along I wanted you to care for me. You should have heard my thoughts, a regular Sydney Carton I was. You know, in *A Tale of Two Cities,* he goes to the gallows for a friend saying, 'It's a far, far better thing that I do than I have ever done.' And maybe you have a point: if I hurry off with Angela, I might have some regrets. Anyway, we won't be married until May or June. We haven't even announced our engagement. She wants to do that on her birthday in March."

"Then there might be time."

"Yes . . . and no. As hard as I try, I cannot imagine a life with you. I had always hoped we could continue our collaboration and that it would suffice. Angela knows of our work, but not . . . the other." He retrieved his handkerchief to wipe his own eyes. "Well, aren't we both a mess?" He forced a charming smile. "Do you know what I think? I think it is going to work out for us both, just not the way either of us can guess at this moment. Maybe we'll be together, maybe we won't, but we'll always be friends. I refuse to believe otherwise."

Hannah blinked away the last of her tears. For some unexplained reason the throbbing in her chest had lessened. Was it from the exhaustion of her confession, or did she really feel better? She took her mental pulse. Yes. Better. Getting better. There was time. Wendell was not speeding to the altar. At least he now knew exactly how she felt, and she knew that he did care for her still. Yes, she was going to be all right, at least for that night, and maybe the next.

∽ 10 ∽

When Hannah next spied the Neufield name on her list of appointments, she was annoyed. She had hoped he would have thought better of it and never returned. "Which Neufield is this?" she asked Carrie innocently.

"Lester. The brother of the lady who was here last, I believe, since they both gave the same address."

When Hannah was introduced to Lester, a fairly tall, spare young man, impeccable in tweeds and a silk tie, she felt foolish for being ignorant so long the first time. Lillian's hair must have been a wig, for his own black hair was trimmed very short to a precise line that curved around his well-shaped head. Without makeup his dark, deep-set eyes had a hunted rather than flirtatious look. For a man his lashes were long, but as Lillian he must have extended them artificially. Hannah had assumed that his male character would be more retiring, but this was not true.

"What is your profession, Mr. Neufield?"

"I work on Wall Street in a bank. They have no idea of my other identity."

"You know," she said honestly, "I think I prefer you as Lester."

"How can that be?" he protested. "Lillian is my true self."

"When did that happen?" she found herself asking out of curiosity.

"Probably around the first time I dressed in women's clothes, but it wasn't my idea. The whole thing began as a game started by my older sisters."

"Did you like it right away?"

"In a way I did, in another way I didn't."

"How was that?"

"I'd fight them off, then they'd overpower me, so I'd give in."

"How did you feel when they won?"

"Well, I enjoyed looking in the mirror, seeing how pretty I could be, and when they said I could pass as a girl, I was pleased, even stimulated, especially when I fooled strangers. But I will admit that I also felt humiliated."

Hannah wondered why anyone would find humiliation diverting, but then she recalled that some people enjoyed sadistic sexual situations. "Well," she began slowly as she tried to organize her thoughts, "I will admit that I find your history intriguing, but frankly, I doubt I am helping you by listening to your confessions."

"That's not true. I feel so much better just knowing I can talk to someone."

"When you first dressed up to come here, it was something of a game, wasn't it? You wanted to see if you could deceive me, and you did."

"I knew you would understand!" he said, glancing at her with a coy tilt of his head. "That is the part I like best."

"Yes, but maybe now that the joke is known, it won't be so exciting."

"On the contrary, I never tire of dressing up. You women are so fortunate. There are endless decisions: what to wear, what colors, what shoes, stockings, undergarments, fabrics. Men's choices are so limited, so dull. Sometimes just thinking about a pair of panties, merely touching them, causes me to become aroused." He gave an exaggerated sigh of pleasure.

When their time was up, Lester asked if he could set another appointment.

"I suppose so," she allowed, not knowing whether she was taking the right course.

⁓ 11 ⁓

The distraction of Lester Neufield's unusual preference threaded through her thoughts in between the complications of her hectic life and the terrible weight of Wendell Dowd's impending calamity. Hannah knew Angela was a horrendous mistake—for him as well as her, but how could she make him see it? People who were smitten were blind to common sense. But she doubted he had a crush on that youngster. No, this was the opposite affliction. His common sense, combined with his loneliness, had stirred him to form an alliance with this socially suitable partner, and this is what had blinded the doctor to his true feelings. Much of this was her fault. If she had dared to cast her lot with him before Lazar returned, they would still be together. Somehow matters would right themselves. Hannah had just to be alert for every opportunity to insert the wedge to drive Angela and Wendell apart and make a space for herself.

But where was the time . . . or strength? Hannah felt her energy being sapped by the endless petty squabbles between Lazar and his children. More and more her neutrality was ruptured as she had to act as referee. Then, when her husband was not around, the children had started criticizing her ignorance about everything from the proper word in English to the current fashions. If only everyone would be gracious to each other, she could have a much needed respite from confrontations.

She was also ready for a break in the amount of time Lazar spent on the *Freiheit,* as well as the endless debates about the stance the paper would take in relation to every issue: local, domestic, or foreign. So far Chaim had been able to rein in Lazar's tendency to allow the paper to become a full-fledged Communist mouthpiece.

"Our position must never vacillate, never waver," Lazar argued. "Our readers need a bright star to steer their course by."

"I agree that our political position should be clear at all times," Chaim retorted, "but shoving communism down the throats of our readers might cause them to gag, when we want them not only to swallow, but be left with a good taste in their mouths."

That had mollified Lazar for the moment, but Hannah knew the next week would bring another encounter.

She was more than ready for a moment when Minna, who doted on Peter so entirely that she was ruining the child, would be receptive to her wisdom on the one subject in which she truly was an authority.

"Just because you've helped babies into the world doesn't make you the expert on how to raise them," Minna challenged. "Why, you yourself left half the task to your mother, so you can't fault me for doing the opposite" had been one of her rejoinders to a simple comment about not keeping the child in her bed the whole night.

"He'll never sleep alone if you keep it up."

"That's fine with me!" she retorted to end the unwanted advice.

She was also anxious to be alone with Wendell again. They needed time to rekindle what it was that had bound them to each other. If he could only see what he would be losing . . . She allowed that thought to drift just so far, then reeled it in, like a disappointed fisherman. No! she warned herself. Not while she was living with Lazar. The doctor had been right about her reluctance to deceive anyone. Then another idea formed: why deceive him? Why not tell Lazar the truth? The bitter pill might be unpleasant to swallow, but the facts were there. Lazar was not interested in her any longer, and even if he were, he was unable to perform. Now that he was so engrossed with the paper, now that he was so alienated from his children, the loss would be muted. His life would hardly change. There would still be the *Freiheit*. There would still be her friendship. Maybe distance would even improve his relationship with his children. Yes, when the moment came, she would tell him.

More than anything Hannah was ready for a reprieve in the rift she was having with the Board of Managers now that Mrs. Giles had retired as director of the Committee on Ma-

ternity Affairs. Her successor, Mrs. Clayborn Church, had
been selected because they thought she would bring a youthful verve to the task. What she brought, however, was a dangerous unsophistication about obstetrical matters. Because
her father was a prominent doctor, as well as a close friend
of Dr. Jacobs, Bellevue's medical director, she saw little use
for "antiquated midwives in modern society" and had decided that they must "use foresight to prepare for the transition into an obstetrical service managed by doctors." At a
recent meeting she had proclaimed, "Who knows better than
a man, who has far greater years of education, what to do,
especially regarding the great blessing of anesthesia, which
frees women from the suffering of bearing children?"

Although Mrs. Church had listened to Hannah's protests
with a veneer of patience, she had not hidden her disdain for
the immigrant, who not only made mistakes in her expressions but had reason to defend her territory. "Don't think I
am not sympathetic to your ideas," she replied unctuously.
"Don't be afraid you will lose your job either. I expect that
with conditions as crowded as they are during this post-war
baby boom, the midwives will have to take up the slack.
What I am asking is that those on the board—as well as
those who report to it—look more to the future than to the
past." Her words had Hannah contemplating her own future,
one which did not include Bellevue, but she did not dare
consider that yet.

At least she had been successful in keeping the fissure in
her marriage a secret from even her closest friends. "Lazar
is so much improved, don't you think?" Rachael began one
day at the clinic. "His limp can hardly be noticed."

Deciding now was not the time to bare her soul to anyone,
she responded, "He's much better than I could have hoped."

"Herzog says the best medicine is success, and at least in
this case he seems correct," she went on gaily. "The *Freiheit*
is thriving, isn't it?"

"The signs are positive," Hannah admitted.

"Two incomes are better than one," she continued, to be
certain Hannah was indeed reaping some economic benefits.

"Yes, but there is a price for everything, isn't there?"

"I know what you mean. Herzog is totally immersed in
becoming a full-time psychoanalyst. Now he's talking about
going to Switzerland to study with Carl Jung."

"Who's that?"

"A psychologist whose theories on types of personalities make more sense to Herzog than the Freudian explanations for behavior."

"Sounds interesting. I have a case I'd like to discuss with him," she said to move the subject to something more impersonal.

"By all means, but let me forewarn you: once he launches into this topic, he won't be able to resist analyzing everyone and everything according this theory."

"What is it about?

"Mostly it's a way of classifying people. Everyone is either an extrovert or an introvert, and then is subdivided by one of four primary functions of the mind: thinking, feeling, sensing, and intuition. You'll have to ask him more about it."

The opportunity to do just that arose a few weeks later, when Hannah went to the Herzogs' to pick up Emma, who had spent the night with Nora. Hannah had freed that Saturday to take Emma to Wanamaker's on a shopping expedition. Not that they ever purchased more than a scarf or pair of stockings, but Emma loved to try on clothes off the rack. When she found something flattering, she would study its construction, then try to recreate it in the settlement house's sewing room, using fabric given to her by Aunt Sonia. This trip, however, had been instigated by Emma for a different reason. From the moment the elegantly engraved card inviting the Blau family to attend the marriage of Miss Angela Rush to Dr. Wendell Dowd had been delivered, Emma had been imploring her mother to go.

"We have nothing to wear to an occasion like that" had been Hannah's first response.

"Aunt Sonia will have a gown made for me."

"I can't ask her for one for me."

"You can borrow something from Aunt Eva."

"Your father doesn't know these people."

"He doesn't have to come. Neither does Benny, if he doesn't want to. It would be fun, just the two of us. He was such a nice man, Mama, and don't forget he saved your life!"

These days Hannah noticed that Emma called her "Mama" when she wanted to cajole her. Otherwise it was "Ma," short and flat. "I don't know about that . . ."

"You once said he did."

She shooed the idea with her hand. "It will be a small, family affair. He's only invited me as a professional courtesy."

"That's not true. He once said I had a very special mother. And he likes me. I am certain he does!"

"Yes, he likes you Emma, but—"

"But what?"

"We'll see" was the best she could do.

By putting her off, Hannah thought she could sort out her conflicted feelings. Every time she approached Wendell, he said, "Too busy" or "I'm late for a conference" or "Let's go over that later this week." How could he treat her this way? The night in the hotel he had virtually promised to give her another chance, but he was avoiding an opportunity for her to prove to him that her intentions were to be with him at all costs.

Yet that wedding invitation was concrete evidence of what his intentions had been all along. Of course, even after he was married there was a chance that they—but no! Hannah had to chastise herself for even thinking the thought. What they had done in the past had been wrong, but to allow the doctor to make his vows with the full intention of breaking them was outrageous. She had to control herself. She had to let him go. It was over. Over! Over . . .

When he married Angela, she would be forced to accept the fact that he would be lost to her forever. Maybe she should go to the wedding. If she saw it for herself, the issue would be a closed case. So when Emma had suggested they peruse Wanamaker's to see what women were wearing that spring, she had relented like a patient accepting an unpalatable potion that will lead to a cure.

"*Vi gaits?* How goes it with you?" Herzog asked warmly when he greeted her at the door.

"*Nishkosheh.* Not so bad."

"Any interesting cases?" he asked in an offhand manner, which Hannah took as an opening to ask him about Lester Neufield. "I do have a curious patient—a man—but he prefers to dress as a woman," Hannah said without any preliminaries.

"Do you know much about the man's mother or father?"

"The father died during his childhood."

"At what age?"

"Six or seven, I believe."

"Ah, very traumatic in the Oedipal phase!"

Rachael knocked on the door. "Emma's almost ready. Those two must have been up all night talking. Do you want a cup of tea before you go?"

Feeling torn, Hannah looked to Herzog for direction.

"This sounds too complicated to settle in a short interval." He waved his hand as though he were dismissing a student. "Why not bring me your notes? Or better still, refer him—or is it her?—to me."

"Yes, well, maybe I shall . . ." she hedged, since she felt slightly proprietary about Lester.

"There is one other point . . ." he began as he sensed he might be losing his audience as well as his referral.

"Herzog, later!" Rachael demanded, then went into the hall, and called up the stairs. "Nora, Emma, we're waiting for you!" She turned to Hannah with a sigh. "Once you get Herzog started, he's impossible!" Then her expression changed and she eyed Hannah warily. "You really don't want to go to this wedding, do you?"

"Why do you ask that?" Hannah asked, bristling.

"Well . . ." was all she could manage before Emma arrived.

"I'm ready, Ma," she said impatiently.

"One minute more . . ." her mother replied.

"Well, I'll wait outside, Ma."

Hannah did not move. What did Rachael know about Wendell?

"You should go. If only not to disappoint Emma."

"Now look who's giving advice."

"Also, Wendell would appreciate it. After all, your name will always be linked with his."

Hannah's heart hammered wildly. "What do you mean?"

"On the papers that have resulted from your collaboration. Even I've heard about the Dowd–Sokolow Survey."

"That's what it's called?"

"What planet are you living on? How did you think it was referred to?"

"The Bellevue survey . . . or . . . I don't know. I never gave it much thought."

"You're too modest for your own good. If that doctor was not looking out for your interests, your work could have been buried by his credentials. That's another reason you should give him the courtesy of going, even if you don't approve of the marriage."

"Who says I don't approve?"

"Come now, Hannah, I know you better than that. Every time you mention it, you wrinkle your nose in disgust. At our age we cannot help but repudiate the alliance of men the age of our husbands with much younger women. Besides, we both admired Lulu Morse. This one sounds like a piece of fluff compared to her, but who knows, maybe it's what he needs."

"I am not convinced . . ." she dared admit. "I hear about so much unhappiness, he might be better off alone than with the wrong woman."

"He hasn't asked you for your opinion on the matter, so there's nothing you can do about it." She gave Hannah a perceptive look that said more than her guarded words.

"Ma? Aren't you coming?" Emma called from the outside steps.

"Ya, ya," she said, hugging Rachael in farewell harder than either of them expected.

∞ 12 ∞

On Saturday, June 4, Hannah and Emma sat side by side at Grace Church on Broadway and East 10th Street. Emma had been so anxious not to be late that they had arrived too early. She shivered as she found a seat in a rear pew. They had dressed in frocks meant for a summer day, but the thick stones of the church had retained the icy chill of distant winters.

"I've never been in a church before," Emma whispered.

Hannah barely heard her, for as she was taking in the great white limestone edifice, her thoughts had soared to how ridiculous her dreams to be with Wendell really had been. This was his world—as much as Bellevue and Washington Mews and Mrs. Whitney's studio and the ateliers of the painters she had met. They could not have remained in bed or in the hospital forever. Why, she had never even been

introduced to his son and hardly knew Daphne. His
parents—well, they were unthinkable! It was true what they
said about people going crazy when they fall in love. For the
first time she felt the insanity falling off in layers. Her decision to attend the wedding had been right.

"The windows are from the Bible, Ma. Look. That's Na-
omi and Ruth, that's Moses. And there, that's Lazarus. Pa's
namesake, right?"

"Suits him too, doesn't it?" She squeezed her daughter's
hand.

"He did come back to us from the dead. I never thought
of that before."

If only that would be possible in more ways than one . . .
Hannah wished to herself.

"Look over there." Her daughter pointed to a nativity
scene. "It's the sort of idea you would like to believe because there's so much mystery and hope to it."

Hope? Hannah mused ruefully. At this moment her hopes
were being dashed. Mystery? How apt. In a few moments
Wendell would be entering into a mysterious alliance. The
day of one's marriage nobody ever knew what lay down the
road one would travel.

The sanctuary had filled. The organ boomed a long introductory chord, causing her to sit straighter and smooth her
skirt. Emma jumped and Hannah pushed her down. "But,
Ma," she whispered, "listen to what they are playing!"

As comprehension filled every member of the congrega-
tion, a communal gasp rose to the spire of the marble tower.
"Ah! Sweet mystery of life, at last I've found thee . . ."

Emma couldn't repress her thought. "Why are they playing Lulu Morse's song?"

"I suppose he wants to include the ones he has loved as
well as those he does love." Tears filled her eyes at the next
refrain: "Ah! I know at last the secret of it all." She had to
take long, deep breaths to prevent her from disintegrating
in public. "All the longing, seeking, striving, waiting, yearning . . ."

Blessedly, the entire song was not played. The chords on
the organ changed key. The bridal party entered the aisle.
Everyone stood. Hannah had to prop herself up on the pew
to steady herself as she glimpsed Angela walking by on the
arm of her father. A veil covered her face, but her body was
more mature than Hannah had suspected. Then, when

Wendell slipped beside his bride, she noticed that the shade
of blue in the bouquet she carried was a precise match to
Wendell's dazzling eyes. A good choice, she decided, and as
she did so the lump in her throat eased, her pulse slowed.
Turning to the stained glass depiction of Lazarus's resurrec-
tion, Hannah became aware that the light through the azure
and crimson panes pooled across her lap and combined into
a lush violet shield that warmed her from head to toe.

❦ 13 ❦

Lillian Neufield, not Lester, arrived the following week. "I
hope you aren't cross with me about this, but I couldn't resist showing off my latest costume." He rearranged the ruby
red chemise and fingered the silver beads.

Deciding to remain neutral, Hannah said, "It doesn't matter to me."

"Oh, I was certain you would understand." Neufield
puffed out his chest to show off his stuffed corset. "Now,
what do you want to know about me today?"

"What do you want to talk about?" she parried, thinking
how pleased Herzog would be with her.

"My mother, my father?"

"I'm not a psychologist, you know."

"You know far more about women, I'm confident of that."

"You are not a woman," she reminded.

"Nor do I want to be."

For a moment she was taken aback. "On the first visit you
said you should have been a woman."

"You remembered."

"So, you should have been a woman, but now that you are
not, you do not wish to be one. Why is that?"

"I wouldn't have my favorite play toy, that's why." He
gave her the naughty grin that always made Hannah wish to
flee. "How can I explain it?" He twirled the beads that
draped in three strands around his neck. "I know it doesn't
make any sense, but I never feel more like a man than when
I am dressed like a woman."

Hannah barked, "That's nonsense. I think it's hopeless for us to go on because you continue to twist everything into such a paradox I cannot begin to sort it out."

"At least you could try," he spat with more anger than he had expressed before.

All of a sudden the air in the room cleared, and she saw him as a tightly wound ball of yarn, with the end lost somewhere along the exterior edge. If she could find the nib, tug it away from the ball, and begin the unraveling, it would lead to the other side where it originated. "I am trying," she insisted, her voice harsher than she had wished it, "but I don't know where to begin."

"You could examine my body. The last time you were not very thorough."

"Don't be ridiculous. I don't examine men ... no matter who they think they are! Anyway, from what I can tell, you are perfectly normal, at least in the physical respect. There are those who have what are called ambiguous genitalia, which means they have some of the parts of a man and some of a woman. I've seen photographs in medical texts and one infant with the syndrome, but they are very, very rare."

"Couldn't the exterior be normal, but the inside be confused?" he asked sensibly.

"Yes, I suppose. But my guess is that there are no *physical* problems."

"Well, I do have a girlfriend."

Taken aback, Hannah was quiet for a moment, then she asked, "Have you told her?"

"Not yet, but since we've been talking about marriage, I suppose I will have to."

"Marriage! Is that wise?"

"Maybe if I had a wife, I might lose interest in the other. Just seeing her clothing, touching it—the idea intrigues me greatly. That's why I like Mercy—that's her name—so much. She has wonderful taste in clothes."

"I see," Hannah said lamely, since she was more perplexed than ever. If only there were salves or creams to prescribe, she wished as she sent him on his way with platitudes, more convinced than ever she either would have to refer him to Herzog or end the sessions once and for all.

The questions about whether or not she could offer Mr. Neufield anything festered until the fifth visit. For a while she could see no harm in letting the man pay for the privilege of being advised by her, but then she came to the conclusion that her acceptance was promoting his illness. The greatest help she could give him was to kick him out. Did this have something to do with her acceptance of Wendell's marriage? she wondered. Probably a psychoanalyst would find connections between how she perceived people and what was happening in her own sexual life. Nevertheless, whenever she tried to contemplate those connections, she felt as if she were looking into a murky bowl of water that, if stirred, hinted at the bottom but covered it over in frustrating whirls and eddies. Best to finalize it, she concluded, for when all else failed, she had to trust her sixth sense, which had saved her as often as her forays into books for answers.

Determined the next session would be his last, Hannah planned out how the interview would begin as well as how it would conclude. "I think we've gone as far as we can go together," she said as soon as she politely was able. "You've told me your stories, but I have no further advice for you."

"But I want to see you again," he whined.

"There's no point."

"But as I've said, I've been happier since I've met you."

"That's fine, but there's nothing more we can do. I'm not helping you."

"But you are."

"In what way?"

"I've never been able to tell anyone else."

"You should have told Mercy already," she said with more severity than usual.

"I am afraid to. What will she say?"

"I don't know her, so I cannot predict," she began hesitantly. Since she was sailing in uncharted seas, she had no idea where the land masses of truth lay. For the present the only course was to follow her instincts. "From my experience, though, it would not be impossible for her to accept you as you are if by doing so she achieves what she wants," she continued, warming to her subject. "Maybe she is extremely anxious to be married. If she wants a normal husband, to have children of her own . . . well, you would have to tell her whether you would be able to participate."

"I have been to bed with women."

This revelation astonished her. "And?"

"I find it enjoyable, although I admit that touching the

clothing, or even wearing it first, is what gets me aroused the quickest."

Maybe Hannah had heard too many stories, maybe she had grown to like Lester, whatever it was she could not become scandalized. What difference did it make? His requirements were basically harmless. If the lady did not mind, if Lester was satisfied, who should care? And that is what she told him. "Tell Mercy about everything. Then let me know what she says."

"That means you will see me again!" Lester crowed.

Hannah sighed. "It might be better for you to see a doctor. I know one who—"

"I don't want to see one, especially not a man."

"Yet a man might be precisely what you require."

"It's not!" he said so defiantly Hannah did not press the point.

Lillian did not show up for her next appointment. Lester's arrival, however, was a pleasant surprise. "I don't have too much time," he began, "but I promised to tell you what happened when I spoke to Mercy."

"And?"

"She said she would enjoy a man who might be interested in clothing and shopping and the like."

"Did she truly understand what you were saying?"

"I'm not certain."

"Maybe she should be introduced to Lillian."

"She was."

He went on to recount their meeting at a restaurant and Mercy's amused reaction. "She's like my middle sister, Patricia, and wanted to play the game."

"Then you don't have a problem any longer, do you?"

"I suppose I don't," he admitted.

With a wonderful sense of relief, she bid Lester farewell at the end of the session, and yet she had her doubts that the future he envisioned could ever work out quite as well as he wished.

❦ 14 ❦

At last Minna put her foot down. "You must set a deadline. From now on the paper goes to bed every evening at six, no matter what," she told her husband. "If you've left some thing out, the world won't end. You can always include it the next day."

"Six?" Chaim shouted. "Impossible!"

"Not if you tell Lazar, and stick to it. All he does the next five hours is change his mind. I know that in the beginning there were many complications, but now the extra time has just become a bad habit."

Chaim argued further, but Minna won her point when she said, "After everything I went through having Peter, the least you could do is to spend some time with him. And now that I'm expecting again, I need your help at night."

"Why didn't you tell me?" he asked, dumbfounded by the news.

"If you had been paying any attention to me, you would have known," she retorted.

"I must have been paying some attention . . ." he said with a tender pat.

The new plan was instituted the following week. Six o'clock was a reasonable target, but Lazar rarely made it home before eight or nine. Even so, throughout the summer they began to have a semblance of normal family life.

The children responded to having their father around with more cheer than Hannah expected. The second month on the restricted work schedule she had intervened in a fight between Lazar and Benny by asking her son to "humor his father." This he took as a literal challenge, and began telling jokes.

"Hey, Pa," he said, pushing back his patent-leather hair, expertly parted in the center. "I know baseball so well, I can tell you the score of a game before it starts."

Lazar fell for the ruse. "What's this? Have you started gambling?" he grumbled.

"No, Pa, it's easy."

"Okay then, what's the Yankee game going to be tomorrow?"

"Nothing to nothing—before it starts."

Lazar's face melted, and he roared with laughter. Soon she noticed that he had even stopped criticizing his daughter's short skirts, turned-down hose, and powdered knees. He'd call, "Here comes Theda Bara!" in a tone that won a smile instead of a rude retort. And he let her go on with her talk of dance contests, wishful sighs over a raccoon coat, even her groans about everything making her feel "so disenchanted." Nor did he complain when his daughter told him to "go fly a kite" or "go cook a radish," if it was said in a lighthearted way. He even began to join in on the choruses of her songs from the silly "Barney Google" to "Yes Sir! That's My Baby" and "Ain't We Got Fun."

By the end of the summer Hannah began to feel differently than she had in many years. Was it because she was beginning to accept that she would never be with Wendell again or that she and Lazar could have a life together, even if it would never be what it had been before? Or was it merely due to his cheerier attitude?

Another reason Lazar's disposition had improved was because he was basking in the praise pouring in not only for the paper, but for his editorial column "From Red Square to Tompkins Square." Much to his delight the word was out that Editor Sokolow wielded the most vitriolic pen in the immigrant sector. To some this would have been derogatory; to him it was a great compliment, for he delighted in his escalating war of polemics against his peers on the *Forverts*.

Or was her mood better because Emma was enjoying her music lessons at the settlement house or because she was filling out and becoming prettier by the day? Perhaps it was because Benny was up before dawn on his quest to see if by the end of the summer he could put two hundred dollars into his bank account as well as buy a radio. The amount seemed unrealistic, but the boy was busy, and the work kept him out of trouble.

Or was it because Mrs. Church was taking a long vacation on the New Jersey shore, or maybe because her most difficult case, Lester Neufield, sent Hannah a wedding announcement with a note that he doubted he would be seeing her again. Was it because Herzog had gone to see Jung in Switzerland, taking Rachael and Nora along? "What I really wanted was a change, any change," Rachael had admitted. Hannah was confident the two would come back more united than ever before.

Of course, the world did not stop spinning. Sacco and Vanzetti were sentenced to death, even though Lazar was convinced they had been framed. The Russian people were starving as a result of Lenin's foolish policies; then the Soviet leader had the chutzpah to ask the world for aid. Wendell Dowd moved uptown with Angela and was planning to open a practice on Fifth Avenue, continuing on at Bellevue only as a consultant. Work on the survey seemed to have been suspended, which was probably for the best, because Hannah was unsure whether she could trust herself alone with him. But without his presence she thought of him less and less often, and when she did the pangs were not quite as acute as they had been even a month earlier.

Realistically, she suspected this peaceful period was merely the calm before the storm. Lazar was convinced the world was in a lull between wars, but then he saw revolution around every corner. The children were bound to create more of an uproar as soon as they began to discover the opposite sex. Mrs. Church had a new reorganization plan to discuss in September. Even though Lazar had been in better spirits lately, that did not mean that they had renewed any aspect of their marriage. There was never a kiss and hardly any touching; nevertheless, if they could be friends, kind and helpful to each other, perhaps that would be enough.

Maybe because it was summer everything was easier. The sun glittered day after day. The fast, swift rains cleansed the city and renewed the bright flowers that danced in the window boxes set out on fire escapes. Perhaps the world was never going to become settled and organized. Chaos was never going to yield to calm. And yet every now and then as Hannah proceeded through the protracted days at the hospital, managed the confused cases in the clinic, cleaned her cupboards, or shopped the Second Avenue stalls, she found herself humming one of Emma's tunes: "Ain't We Got Fun."

Problem 10:
Dr. Blühner's Bands

◆

1922

Although at every instant a leaf falls from the human tree to revert to dust, at every instant also germinates a new life whom the joys of love await in its turn.

—PAOLO MANTEGAZZA

❧ 1 ❧

BELLEVUE was frigid. The corridor leading down to the maternity pavilion seemed longer and draftier than on other bitter January mornings. As the wind howled along the riverfront, Hannah felt an even icier inner chill that no amount of steaming tea or woolen sweaters could abate. Years ago, when Mrs. Hemming had been her nemesis, she had experienced the same disconcerted feeling, but she thought it had been vanquished by the glow of her success. Even as recently as a year ago, Hannah had the sense that she was in command—not in the imperious manner of a supervisor who frightened her charges, but as a teacher, a friend. Now when she approached a staff member, she thought she saw averted eyes, scurrying feet, and phrases hastily invented to placate her. Was this the fate of all leaders? If so, no wonder those in political power—like Lenin or Trotsky—had to become ruthless to insure their supremacy. Even here, in this minor domain designed to foster benevolent care to childbearing women, she felt she had to protect her territory and her reputation from those who disagreed with her. Why didn't they realize it was precisely when the staff was divided with pettiness that the seeds of chaos—that system of tiny particles of discontent and confusion—began to form in swirling clouds that soon clogged even the most deliberate systems?

For more than a decade Hannah had been battling the whirlwind that accompanied labor and delivery in a supervisory capacity. She had struggled through the lean years by working extra hours, put in valiant service during the war, and had almost succumbed treating patients during the influenza epidemic. With clinical skills superior to most American-trained midwives, she still had to battle to win respect from every quarter: the other midwives, the training school nurses, the ladies on the Board of Managers, the medical staff, the attending physicians, as well as her direct supervisors. Some days it seemed more difficult to maintain favor with subordinates than it had been to mollify superiors. More and more, though, she was tiring of the struggle.

Hannah looked in every doorway that she passed. Once she might have been checking to see if everything seemed orderly. Now she realized her first glance was for Mrs. Church's stiff back and thick-soled shoes. Here was Mrs. Hemming's ghost in a different package. At least Hannah had understood Mrs. Hemming, who had trained in nursing and had been devoted to raising the standards as well as the respectability of that profession.

"Never forget whence we came," Mrs. Hemming would remind her students, then would commence a lecture on how the early Bellevue nurses were poverty-stricken women who stooped to minister to the sickly flesh of those too destitute to be cared for at home. "We are the ones who have made hospitals safe institutions, for no matter the medical treatment, without fastidious nursing management, few patients would have survived."

Hannah thought Mrs. Hemming may have overstated the case, but understood that strong words were required to motivate the young, rather idealistic recruits, who had little conception of the arduous tasks they would have to perform. In any case, Hannah's way was to compliment before criticizing, but she did not fuss about details—like creases in bed sheets—unless they compromised sanitary rules. However, she was especially hard on anyone demonstrating unkindness toward a patient.

A few months earlier a young midwife had rushed from the ward in tears after Hannah corrected her for noisily clanging the metal bowls that were used to transport the placenta and cord. "The newborn is startled by such harsh sounds. Wouldn't you want your first moments in the world to be calm?"

The artless midwife made the mistake of pointing out that the crowded ward, filled with moaning women, was hardly going to accommodate the baby.

"That may be true," Hannah replied archly, "but that is no excuse for your lack of consideration."

Later Hannah wondered what she had accomplished. Had the lesson been absorbed? Would the girl be more sensitive the next time, or had all she done was to alienate her, creating another enemy? The old guard, the ones who really understood what she was trying to achieve, were disappearing. Sarah Brink had retired the previous year. Norma Marshanck had been offered more money to do private duty work at Mt. Sinai and was departing the next month. Hattie Donovan was on medical leave due to an infected foot brought on by diabetes. Alice Brody's husband had returned from the war and—miracle of miracles—they had already had two healthy children and a third was on the way, making it impossible for her to work. Like many of the younger midwives, Lenore Harvey had married and started her family. Few women with small children had outside jobs any longer. Most had husbands able to support their families, since there was little unemployment in these post war years. How the world had changed since she had been an immigrant, grateful for a skill that could bring in more dollars than piecework or selling from a pushcart!

"Good morning, Mrs. Sokolow" came the pleasant soprano of Carlotta Valerio, the new head nurse on the pavilion.

Hannah felt blessed by that wide smile, which transformed the woman's dull face into a momentary beam of beauty. "Has Mrs. Church been around today?"

"No. She never comes downtown on Wednesdays. It's her book club day."

"That's right," Hannah recalled with a mixture of relief at the reprieve and annoyance for not remembering the schedule.

"Are you all right?" Mrs. Valerio inquired with more than routine politeness.

"Yes, why?"

"You seem pale. Why don't you let me get you a cup of coffee—I mean, tea? You never drink coffee, do you?"

"Sometimes."

"You prefer tea, though. That's what you usually drink."

Even though she realized the woman was trying to win her approval, her obsequiousness annoyed Hannah. "It doesn't matter!" came out too harshly. "Sorry," she whispered. "A headache," she lied.

"Let me make you my special coffee, and if you don't like it, I'll have tea in a jiffy." The nurse scurried off before Hannah could protest.

Just then Dr. Starling, Dr. Dowd's new recruit, rounded the corner. Supposedly a brilliant surgeon from Harvard, he was filled with ideas on how to modernize Bellevue's gynecological surgery department. So far he had not taken a keen interest in obstetrical matters, even if he deigned to accept a cesarean or complication when one occurred while he was covering the floor. The problem was that he was so youthful—and aware that he appeared even younger than he was—that he hid his insecurity behind a veil of arrogance. As clearly as Hannah understood this, she wished she could pound some sense into the boy before he estranged himself from every midwife and nurse, but he would not have listened to her. If Dr. Dowd were aware of the problem, he was too preoccupied with his bride to have tackled it.

"Good morning, Mrs. Sokolow," Dr. Starling said with an elaborate politeness that screamed insincerity. "May I have a word with you for a moment?"

"Certainly, Doctor." She waved her arm to indicate her office might be the best place for the meeting.

She took a seat behind her desk, pushing her chair close to the drawer as if to gather strength from the metal rim. "How may I help you?"

"Well . . ." His watery gray eyes, slightly bloodshot from lack of sleep, focused on a painting of a band concert by one of Mrs. Whitney's lesser known protégés. Dr. Dowd had given it to her as a reminder of the night they had met at the park. "As you probably are aware, the obstetrical staff met with Mrs. Clayborn Church and several other ladies on the

Board of Managers on Monday. Dr. Jacobs stopped by as well."

"Yes?" Hannah asked as she forced herself to remain calm. Nobody had informed her of the meeting, one to which she should have been invited, and from which she had obviously been excluded.

"Mrs. Church has made some proposals for you to consider."

Mrs. Church! Although it may have been Wednesday, her glacial presence permeated the room.

"And what might those be?"

Brushing back his wispy strands of straw-colored hair, Dr. Starling gave his thin lips a mechanical lift. "I must begin by saying everyone present was most complimentary about the manner in which you have administered this service, so nothing reflects on you in a personal way. The point is that we require a twentieth-century approach to obstetrical care and dare not attempt to maintain obsolete practices for the sake of tradition. Don't you agree?"

"The only tradition here is one of excellence. We are always studying to update our skills," she replied haltingly as she tried to fathom where this was leading.

"I'm pleased to discover we are of like minds. It will make the transition much easier."

Hannah's heart quickened at this hint of upheaval, but fortunately she was given the opportunity to gather her wits as Carlotta came in with a steaming cup. "Your coffee, Mrs. Sokolow. Italian, with hot milk, the way my mother makes it. I hope you like it," she said with deliberate slowness before turning to the doctor. "Would you care for some, Dr. Starling?"

"No, thank you. I'm certain you have more important things to attend to than whipping up your mother's specialties, as nice as they might be."

Hannah raised her brows to let the nurse know they were on the same team before the woman flushed and hurried out.

"Now, where were we?" the doctor continued.

"The transition . . ." Hannah offered tensely.

"Yes, well, let me outline the problem as it was presented. With the recent advances in the management of obstetrical cases, we are fortunate at having many more options in the arsenal to attack the terrible predicaments that both the transporter and the passenger must endure . . ."

The transporter! The passenger! Hannah's mind reeled as she applied these terms to the mother and baby. As he rambled on, she recoiled at more of his callous terminology. Is this what they were teaching in medical school these days?

"The point is that nowhere else in medicine can the physician accomplish so much, both in the prevention of disease and accidents as well as in treatment and operation. With the establishment of model maternity departments, such as the one this is determined to be, the aggressive use of anesthetics to keep the clients comfortable, and the employment of sufficient assistants, the practice of obstetrics is being divested of most of its objectionable features. Thus we are seeing more and more of the public developing a sentiment toward the employment of specialists and a much reduced requirement for the second-class alternative."

"The what?"

"Even you will admit that a doctor is always preferable, but to date there have not been enough available."

"Preferable to what?"

"Must I spell it out?"

"Yes."

"Given a choice, any modern woman would prefer a physician to a midwife."

"That's not true!"

"Come now, I would have expected a clinician with your level of experience to rise above proprietary concerns. The point is that the field of obstetrics—due to its broader definition and operative opportunities—is becoming more inviting to the ambitious physician. Hence the problem of supply and demand is lessening. We feel we soon will be able to staff Bellevue with a top layer of attending obstetricians, such as myself, who will supervise student doctors to provide the premier service in New York."

"Are you trying to eliminate midwives?"

"Not at all. You misunderstood completely. They will make the most superior assistants."

With a deep breath Hannah launched her attack. "Most women do not require specialists. The vast majority has predictable labors and deliveries. Look at our statistics!"

"Due to the vigilance of the medical staff, we have been fortunate in recent years. However, there continues to be an immense amount of invalidism resulting from childbirth, which you don't see. Long after delivery, hundreds of thousands of women flock to our hospitals for the repair of injuries contracted during labor. The problem is that once a mother leaves this pavilion with her babe in arms, you never have to handle the consequences."

"Doctor, I do think you are exaggerating."

"Do you now? Some researchers have concluded that fifty percent of women who have borne children bear marks of obstetrical affliction, and will, sooner or later, suffer from them. Why don't you ask Mrs. Church about her mother's tragic confinement on account of a ruptured bladder after one of her deliveries?"

"That had to be more than thirty years ago."

"Then ask her about the pain she continues to endure due to her own pelvic floor condition."

"Did a midwife attend her?"

"I-I—" Dr. Starling stammered. "The point is prevention. The training today's physicians are receiving is far superior to any in the past. I, for one, have heard no complaints about my skills."

"Nor I about mine, nor those of my midwives."

"I had hoped you would be sympathetic. I was certain you would agree that as a team we could run the best service in the country."

"I am not following you . . ."

"What the Board of Managers, in consultation with Dr. Jacobs and the Medical Board has determined, is that a doctor must manage every aspect of the obstetrical service. From now on each practitioner must answer to a member of the medical staff. Accountability will be the watch word. A doctor will sign off on every procedure and will supervise every case. This is the way of the future, and Bellevue will not be left in the dust of nineteenth-century attitudes or prejudices."

"Who will be in charge, then?"

"I thought you understood. I will."

"I'm surprised Dr. Dowd, as the senior member of your department, was not given the chore of explaining this to me."

"Due to a previous engagement as a lecturer at the Columbia Medical School, he was unable to attend the meeting."

"But he knows of the decision?"

"In theory. Nothing has been carved in stone yet. However, I don't expect he'd want to lock horns about this with Dr. Jacobs."

With terrible clarity Hannah saw the futility of an argument. Dr. Jacobs was close to Dr. Osborn and Dr. Osborn was Mrs. Church's father. Also, she recalled that Mrs. Church's mother was a cousin of Dr. Dowd's first wife, Mary. The next thing she expected to hear was that Dr. Starling was engaged to be married to Daphne Dowd. Wouldn't that put a tidy knot on the package? Once again she felt excluded from that lofty circle of the doctor's social class, which had hindered not only her liaison with him but now her professional security.

"I can't see why you will need midwives at all. A well-trained nurse should be sufficient," she threw out as bait, expecting to be mollified.

"Mrs. Church was afraid you would react that way, but I assured her that someone with your management background would see the light." He smiled as though he had been vindicated. "There won't be any reason to keep the Training School for Midwives open past this term. Nurses will be given a semester or so in specialized training. Some will prefer to work with patients in labor, some in postpartum, while others will polish skills in operative techniques and anesthesia. Of course, the midwives we do have will be assets because of their experience level, if nothing else, and they will be placed in supervisory positions." He gave a hollow laugh. "Besides, now and then Mother Nature plays her tricks and a physician might not get there in time!"

"Aren't you forgetting how much more comfortable women are when they are attended by other women?"

"Really, Mrs. Sokolow, I did not expect such an antiquated statement from you. Dr. Dowd has told me how . . . ah, enlightened you are about these questions. Don't forget nurses will perform many of the untidy, personal tasks. Also, you know better than most that when a baby is determined to be born, a woman drops modesty like a prisoner his chains. In the future we would expect more women to train in medicine, although that is a long way off."

"And I think you are a long way off. After attending thousands of births on two continents, in hospitals and in the home, the most common denominator is the normalcy of the vast majority." Her tone went from seething to accusatory. "The problem is that you doctors, to justify your calling, must condemn parturition as perilous. Why, if you checked out your holy statistics, I think you would find that crossing Third Avenue is more dangerous to life and limb than giving birth any day. Does that mean that every pedestrian requires an attendant to steer him past trolleys and cars? Of course not! That would be as ridiculous as treating every laboring woman as if she were a pathological case!"

She took a quick breath and continued even more firmly. "I'm not about to resurrect those old arguments about physiologic birth, or whether pregnancy is a disease of nine months' duration, or the explanations about civilization not progressing if birth were so treacherous, for I am certain you are prepared with rebuttals on each point. Nevertheless, I do think your cause is self-serving and goes against the best interests of our typical patient."

"And so?" The doctor tilted his head in a cocky challenge.

What did he expect? Was she to stand up and walk out in a huff? Was that what he wanted? Yes! How much easier it would be for him to hold onto his position. She was a barrier to his goal. For a second Hannah thought she was too exhausted to continue. Gathering her thoughts, she sipped the coffee. It was utterly delicious. As the creamy liquid bathed her tight throat, she thought of Carlotta's kindness. How would a nurse like her fare under this man's brashness? Even worse, his conceit could be dangerous. He was the sort who would not admit a mistake before it was too late. But then he was merely an untutored purebred puppy with big clumsy feet and a loud bark. No, she would not give him the satisfaction of seeing her run the first time he jumped up and pawed her, or he would believe that he was more essential than he was. No, she would stay around and tame him so skillfully he would not know the leash and collar were on until it was too late.

2

"Why don't you fight it?" Rachael probed.

"Why don't you quit?" was Lazar's response.

Hannah's reaction was to analyze their attitudes instead of answering their suggestions. Why didn't Rachael want her to leave Bellevue? In the past she had been in favor of having her at the clinic full-time. Had she overstayed her welcome there? Or was she, like all the doctors, protecting her territory too? And Lazar, the old soldier himself, why didn't he encourage her to go to battle to save midwifery?

Because he was tired. And she was tired. Also, she lacked defenders. Not even Wendell rose to champion the midwives' cause. She had expected his marriage would create a barrier between them, but she had not anticipated that he rarely would be in the hospital. Any hopes that she had entertained about continuing to work on the survey had vanished. Dr. Dowd's reputation as the survey's director had made him a popular lecturer in gynecology. This seemed to suit into his new life better than a rigorous clinical schedule. Rumor was that he would step down as chairman of the department, accepting the designation as a doctor emeritus and a position on the hospital board. Dr. Starling was too young to fill his shoes, but another tier of men in black coats were wriggling to curry favor. From the sidelines their espadrille might have been amusing if the midwifery department was not about to be trampled in their wake. Perhaps the time had come to resign. She was primarily interested in her consulting work anyway. From her experiences she was beginning to formulate a philosophy that sexual health went a long way to promoting individual and family satisfaction.

"Margaret Sanger had the right idea from the beginning," she admitted to Minna, whom she had stopped in to see before going upstairs early one evening. "When a family's size is manageable, when babies arrive when they are expected, they receive more love. When a mother is strong and rested, she gives them the care they require and they feel secure. Children who are loved and cared for respond better and create fewer problems for society. In the same way, adults who receive satisfaction in their sexual relationships feel loved and respond in a more positive way to each other. If you are devoted to someone, you will put up with the difficulties that life imposes. There are so many unexpected events, a united, contented family is the best defense."

"How well you stated that!" Minna said with genuine appreciation. "You should write it down and let Chaim publish it." She cocked her head to listen if Peter was waking from his nap.

"You know that I can't write."

Minna stood and went to the bedroom door and opened it slightly. Sweet gurgling sounds of a contented baby bubbled from the room. "Just put what you said on paper," she whispered.

"It never comes out the way I meant."

"I'll transcribe it for you."

"Don't be silly. It's not newsworthy."

"Even so, our readers would be interested. Chaim keeps complaining that the women are preferring the *Forverts*. Do you know why?"

"No."

"What do you think Mrs. Cohen or Mrs. Levy reads first?"

"Well, Eva reads the 'Bintel Brief' column."

"Exactly. The question is why?"

"Because one's own problems seem smaller when you hear someone else's. I'll admit I read it to see if I agree with the advice given."

"And do you?"

"Sometimes I do, sometimes I don't. Often I think it's a man's solution."

"Could you do better?"

"Who knows? When someone writes a letter, it is but their side of a problem and there is only space for a concise answer. If you investigated, you might discover these responses probably do more harm than good, at least to the person who has written in. The rest is just entertainment for Peeping Toms."

"Or Peeping Thomasinas," Minna giggled. Just then Peter yelled to get her attention. She ducked into the room and came out with him. The minute he glimpsed Hannah, he shyly tucked his face into his mother's neck. Minna suddenly became animated. "Why shouldn't the *Freiheit* have a similar feature to attract women readers?"

Peter began to wail again. Minna raised her voice above his. "Who would give the answers?" Minna asked as she patted her son's pants, then lifted her hand gingerly as she located the source of his distress.

"How about a doctor?" Hannah offered. "Everybody likes free medical advice."

"Who could we get?"

"What about Herzog?" Hannah shook her head and answered her own question. "No, he'd never be satisfied unless he knew about the person's mother, father, and dreams, but Rachael would be wonderful."

Minna wrinkled her nose. "Better tend to this." When she returned with a freshened baby, she asked, "What about you?"

"Ha!" Hannah reached for Peter, who tentatively went to his aunt. "Who respects a midwife these days?"

"The whole world doesn't care what's going on behind those doors at Bellevue."

"Are you suggesting I write a column for the *Freiheit* about women?" She clasped her neck and pretended to squeeze it. "Dr. Starling would choke! Mrs. Church might have apoplexy. The Board of Managers might even dismiss me." At the harshness of her voice, Peter's lower lip trembled. "Sorry, Peter, sorry," Hannah comforted and bounced him on her lap. "He's getting so heavy!"

"Nu? A year. Time flies. Anyway, I thought you were thinking of leaving Bellevue. You've been there more than ten years, haven't you?"

"How can I give up the one reliable paycheck in the family?"

"You would get money for writing the column."

"Not nearly what I receive from Bellevue."

Peter reached out his hands to his mother. "Mama!"

Minna gathered him to her, but he wriggled off her lap. "Lately Lazar had been managing to support you without your income, in case you haven't noticed."

"I've noticed that Benny needs a new coat every six months, that Emma wants private music lessons, that our sofa is falling apart, that Lazar needs to go to the dentist, that Benny should enter the university next year, and that—"

"And I've noticed that Benny is working hard to pay his way. You should be proud of him. And Emma has a perfectly good teacher at the settlement house." She was diverted by some lint Peter was putting in his mouth. "No!" She took it away. He frowned but decided not to fuss. "I'm not arguing with you, but you have more choices than you think you have. We all do."

Hannah stopped herself from an automatic rejoinder. "You're right, I suppose, but I wouldn't know where to begin."

"Let me talk to Chaim. It's his paper—and Lazar's, of course," she added quickly.

~⌒ 3 ⌒~

"So you'll do it?" Chaim asked Hannah that Friday night, the first moment they had taken to have a serious discussion about the women's column.

"I think so," Hannah answered tentatively. "How often would it be in the paper?"

"The 'Bintel Brief' is a daily feature, but we might not get enough letters for that. Why don't we try it once a week, say on Wednesday, which is always a slow day?"

"How are we going to get letters to start it off?"

Chaim scratched his head. "That's a good question."

"We could write them ourselves," Lazar offered from his usual position behind the large rolltop desk in Chaim's parlor, which was his office away from Chrystie Street.

"Is that fair?" Hannah questioned.

"Why not? Just ask yourself the sort of question a regular patient would."

"I couldn't respond to those in print!"

"Why not?" her brother asked. "The writer is anonymous."

"But I wouldn't be."

"Your name doesn't have to be on the column. You could sign it 'Mrs. X.'"

"'Doctor X' might be better," Lazar suggested.

"I'm not a doctor, I'm a midwife!"

"There's nothing wrong with that," Chaim soothed.

"On the contrary, it's an advantage for our readers," Lazar continued with mounting excitement. "Women will trust a midwife, first because she's another woman, and also because they know she treats intimate matters."

"I've got it!" Chaim stood up so fast he tipped over his chair. "We'll call the column 'The Midwife's Advice.' She won't need a byline. That says everything."

Lazar was elated. "Yes!"

Chaim was twisting his hands. "What do you think, Hannahleh? It's good, isn't it?"

"Well ... I don't want to be discussing private parts all the time, nor do I want to start that business of menstrual charts, or telling people how to have a boy."

"You won't have to," said Chaim, waving his arms. "You can set the tone by the initial letters we write. After that, you can pick and choose. This deserves a celebration. Minna, where have you hidden the slivovitz?" he called into the bedroom, where she was changing Peter's diaper.

"Behind *The Idiot.*"

"Where?"

"Dostoyevsky's *The Idiot,* because Prohibition is idiotic."

"Right," he said, reaching high on the bookshelf. "Minna's filing system always makes perfect sense ... to her."

Unable to find enough clean glasses, Chaim rinsed some out in the kitchen. Minna brought Peter in and placed him on the floor, but he pulled himself up and began to toddle about, holding onto the knees of the adults as he made his way across the room. Finally Chaim had poured the four drinks of plum brandy and began to pass them around. He raised his glass, then set it down. "Wait. You should get Benny and Emma in here."

"They're studying, or that's what they are supposed to be doing. Benny's got big exams for the end of the turn."

"End of the term," her husband corrected.

"See, I told you I can't write English."

"The *Freiheit* is in Yiddish," her brother reminded. "Anyway, this is a big moment, this is your *turn,* so get the kids, won't you, Lazar?"

"I'll go," Hannah said since the stairs were hard on his bad leg.

"No, he gets cramps if he sits too long. He needs the exercise," Chaim insisted.

With some reluctance Lazar put his glass down and made his way up the three flights of stairs.

Chaim stood up and took a seat beside Hannah on the sofa. "I did not want to discuss money with Lazar in the room. He's the editor, but I am the publisher, and that means I hold the purse strings."

"Better you than him," Hannah winked, "or the paper would have not lasted this long already."

"What I wanted to offer was five dollars for each column. If you do it once a week, it would not be that much, but it would not interfere with your Bellevue work."

"The way things are going, that might not be lasting much longer."

"Eventually you might write five or six columns a week. What do you get from the hospital? Thirty or forty dollars?"

Hannah knew her brother was exaggerating her pay for politeness. She received twenty-four, only recently qualifying for a raise of two dollars. "It's too much for me to answer a few letters . . ."

"Let me judge that. If it increases our circulation, it will be well worth it. If it doesn't, well . . . we will discuss that when the time comes."

Benny burst into the room. "If what increases the circulation?"

"Your mother's advice column."

"Good for you, Ma! You're going to do it."

"I don't seem to have a choice," she laughed.

Emma's eyes widened expressively. "You won't be using your name, will you?"

"No, we're going to call it 'The Midwife's Advice,' " Chaim explained.

"But everybody will know it's you!" Emma whined. "How will I explain it to my friends?"

"Emma, she will be helping people, not hurting them," Minna reminded tranquilly. "Besides, how many of your friends read Yiddish?"

This seemed to mollify Emma, but she sat with a pout. Only Peter's tugging at her sleeve softened her cross expression.

"Anyway, Ma's going to increase the circulation, isn't that right, Uncle Chaim?"

"We certainly hope so."

"Then Ma should get a percentage of the increase, shouldn't she?"

"What are you talking about, Benny?" Hannah chided. "Your uncle is being more than fair already."

"That's because he thinks he can make money off you."

"Benny!" his father scolded.

"See, Ma, they are upset because I touched on the truth."

"No, your father is right. This is a family, not a big company. We have always helped each other and shared."

"Yeah, but that was when everybody was broke. When fortunes change, greed is the prevailing emotion."

"Where did you learn that?" His father pointed his finger between the boy's eyes.

"Enough!" Chaim shouted and raised his glass. "We're here to celebrate, to toast your mother. Pick up a glass and give one to your sister."

Emma wrinkled her nose at the homemade brandy. "I don't want any."

"Just a taste," Lazar seethed. "It won't kill you to be nice for five minutes."

"Yes, it will," Benny muttered under his breath.

His father shot him a foul glance.

Chaim cleared his throat. "Here's to the midwife and her advice. May she help many people with her wise words and help the *Freiheit* at the same time. *L'chayim!*"

"*L'chayim!*" the others chorused.

Emma put down the glass without a sip. Benny swallowed his in one gulp, hiding the stinging that smarted his eyes. He reached for the bottle and poured himself another. Lazar started to stop him, but when he saw Minna tossing her head to let him be, he shrugged.

"Why not give Ma a percentage of the circulation change from when her column first appears?" Benny offered recklessly.

"I've already made her a generous offer."

"You are sounding more and more like a capitalist boss, darling," Minna said sweetly as she wiped some drool from Peter's chin.

"It already seems like too much money for what I will be doing," Hannah offered meekly.

"Then my idea is better. Ma says she feels guilty about accepting more than she deserves, but she wouldn't disagree if she were bringing in additional money to the paper, as well as getting a piece of the action."

Chaim tossed back his head and roared. "A piece of the action!" He nudged Lazar's arm. "Whose son is this?"

"Wait until Peter can talk back," Lazar countered sarcastically.

With a glance at his son's toothless grin, Chaim said, "I'm looking forward to it."

"Well . . ." Benny pressed.

"It is up to your mother."

"Let me handle this, Ma, okay?"

Shifting her gaze between her husband and her son, Hannah felt torn. Benny was not stupid. He had worked hard through the year, and as amazing as it seemed, he had not only saved his two hundred dollars but bought his radio too. His grades in school were excellent. There had been no hint of any trouble, although a few of his friends had run into problems with the police. He was a good boy, a smart one, and as far as money went, he probably was more knowledgeable than his father—although that was a fairly easy feat. Besides, Chaim's offer was too liberal. "All right, then I'll take the five dollars for the first column a week, then a percentage after that, with the number of how many columns I do a week dependent on the letters I get in. Benny, you and Chaim will work out this percentage business. I'm lost there."

"How about half a cent a paper above the business you do the week before the column appears?"

"You're a meshugeneh kid," Chaim complained without rancor. "We sell them for two cents a day, three on weekends. That's twenty-five percent."

"But not on weekends." He caught the disapproval in his mother's eyes. "Okay, okay. That's too much. How many are you selling now?"

"Between ten and fifteen thousand a day, and more on weekends."

"What does it cost to print and sell?"

"A little less than a penny on the daily edition."

"So you net one hundred dollars a day!" He whistled. "Almost a grand a week. Not half bad!"

"That's before rent and the expenses of the press and salaries, not to mention deducting the cost of the papers that don't sell."

"What about advertising?"

"That's picking up, but not predictable."

"Yeah, but if you double the circulation by attracting lots of ladies, the costs of the press and the rent will be the same, so only your profit picture changes."

Chaim raised his eyebrows. "They teach you this in school?"

"Hey, it isn't exactly Karl Marx High!"

Hannah flushed. "Benny!"

"Anyway, I think it wouldn't hurt you to pay Ma on a sliding scale, say a tenth of a cent for every copy from ten to twenty thousand copies, then a fifth of a cent for the ones over that. That means if you sold twenty thousand copies every day for a week, and she did seven whole columns, she would make her five dollar guarantee, plus she would get seventy dollars extra."

"After subtracting the unsold copies," Chaim reminded.

"Sure," Benny conceded.

"That's more than I get!" Lazar grumbled.

"So? She would have earned it."

"Ma?" Emma brightened for the first time. "What do you think?"

Hannah straightened her back. "I think Benny has a good idea, and we should try it his way." She smiled sweetly at her brother and husband, then beamed at the boy. Behind the impish eyes and apple cheeks Hannah saw her first glimpse of a man. Yes, Benny might be too optimistic about this venture, but he was going to make something of himself. She rotated back to the others.

The men were silent. Minna had turned away. Emma was grinning as though she too had triumphed. The only sound was Peter, who stood in the center of the room clapping his chubby hands.

4

Hannah attempted to compose three letters that she proposed to answer, but they seemed terribly stilted. At last she gave up. "I can't do both sides. Why not ask some members of the *Freiheit* staff to submit questions? I'll respond to one of those."

Chaim was pleased with the idea. One of the men wrote, asking how to get his wife to be more responsive in bed.

"I won't tackle that so early in the game."

"How about this?" Chaim handed her one about stuttering.

"I don't know anything about that. Didn't you explain I'm a midwife? That should have given them some clues."

Biting his lip, Chaim gave her the six remaining. "You choose."

The one she picked had been written by the bookkeeper, but it had exactly the right tone:

> Worthy Midwife,
> My daughter, who is fifteen, is wanting to wear her skirts very short. I know this is the fashion for some, but don't you think that a girl her age is asking for trouble if she wears them so close to the knee? When she sits down you can see even higher, but she thinks I don't know anything. What should I do?
> Your thankful reader,
> A Desperate Mother

"I don't know about this 'worthy midwife' and 'thankful reader' nonsense," she complained.

"So, are you now an editor?" Lazar admonished. "That's to make it sound like a 'Bintel Brief.' "

"Why not be different?"

"We are, but not too different. We want it to seem familiar, at least at first. Besides, how you respond is what will make it distinct."

Chaim rolled his eyes, and Hannah could almost hear him saying to himself: I was worried about those two arguing, and here they go with the very first test letter. "I am interested in Hannah's reply," he offered diplomatically.

"Let me think . . ." she said as she studied the letter.

"You should let the daughter have her way without offending the mother," Minna suggested.

"Who is going to buy papers, the mother or the daughter?" Lazar retorted.

"That's not the point. Controversy is entertaining," Chaim injected reasonably.

"The point is that I will say exactly how I feel without any consideration for selling papers or entertaining anyone!" Hannah announced angrily. "Now leave me in peace!" She stomped out into the foyer and paced back and forth.

After fifteen minutes of brooding, she burst back into the room. Lazar looked up expectantly.

"Now I will give you the reply. Write it down exactly as I speak it, and don't contradict me, or we can forget the whole business here and now!"

Lazar opened his mouth to say something, but his brother-in-law was right behind him with a firm hand pressing on his shoulder. "Yes?" was all her husband dared.

"Dear Desperate Mother,
Every daughter of this age wishes to be different from her mother and more like the young women of her age. Clothes are a simple way to make this transition. If you force her to do as you wish on this matter, she might defy you on another which might cause her more trouble in the end. Together you should look at magazine pictures for examples of dresses on refined women and select a length that these ladies are wearing. This will prove the choice is in tune with the times. But don't let her pick an example of an actress in the films, for these will be too radical for a girl of her age. Also, you must be certain your hems are several inches below hers, so she feels she has won her point, even though you have had the final say in the matter."

"Is that it?"

"Yes. Sign it: 'The Midwife.' No. 'The Midwife's Advice.' She asked for my advice and that's what she received." Hannah crossed her arms on her chest and plopped herself in Minna's most comfortable stuffed chair.

Chaim glanced at Lazar. Lazar looked toward Minna, who dared speak. "It's good. No, it's terrific! Really! You've said it all, and more. There's a whole commentary on mothers and daughters. Even Herzog could find meat to analyze there. Something for everybody. Perfect!"

"Yes! Perfect!" Chaim came around to hug his sister.

Lazar was silent.

"You didn't like it?" his wife challenged.

"No, that's not it."

"Well, what then?"

"It's not what I expected."

"What did you expect?"

"Something lighter, sillier, I suppose."

"What do you think I do all day at the clinic? Tell jokes?"

"No . . . but I didn't know you could be so . . ." He shook his head. "So profound."

"You liked it?" Hannah's voice trembled.

"Yes," he began softly, then more firmly. "I'm afraid we are going to discover that Benny made a very astute deal."

∽⌒∾ 5 ⌒∾⌒

In late March the headline of the *Freiheit* echoed those of the other major dailies with the latest on the six million coal miners who were threatening a national strike. While their reporters dutifully covered every aspect of the story, and Lazar's editorials eloquently defended the workingman's position, there was little doubt that the readers were spending far more time poring over the inquiries to "The Midwife's Advice" than the warnings that an action would lead to violent confrontations with thugs hired by the companies.

After the first three columns appeared, letters poured in. Hannah found it was taking several hours each night just to sort through them. Already Chaim was printing them in every other issue, but daily responses would hardly be more trouble. The problem was what to do with those she did not answer in print.

"I could spend my life on these," she complained.

"Pick the best or the most unusual, and forget the others," Lazar suggested.

"How can I? These people are miserable. I want to help everyone."

"You can't. You have to be professional about it."

"Here's one who says she is having abnormal bleeding.

From what she describes, she might have a tumor. What should I do? Ignore it and let her die?"

"Answer it in the paper."

"No, it's too worrisome, and I can't offer her much hope."

Lazar gestured with his palms to the ceiling. "Do what you want."

"It's not a matter of what I want, it's a matter of time. How can I work at Bellevue, the clinic, and do this too?"

"You'll have to choose."

Even though she knew he was right, there was no easy answer. For all the talk of Dr. Starling taking command at Bellevue, she was the one who did the work while the doctor poked his head in the door, smiling with those expensive white teeth and flicking his wrists to flash his gold cuff links, but not much else. She had expected the role of her midwives to be altered, but so far there were not nearly enough doctors to cover the service, and the few that were about lacked any interest in coaxing a woman through labor, mopping perineums, or waiting for placentas to emerge. They also seemed averse to delivering women in the wards, preferring to select their charges, which they labeled "complications," and move them into one of the tiled delivery rooms for a more medically managed procedure. Ignoring the midwives, they used nurses as their assistants, but these were but a fraction of the cases. The only routine deliveries handled by the doctors were private patients, who had received prenatal care, not those typical poor women who arrived on Bellevue's doorstep in active labor.

Once Mrs. Church and the Board of Managers had set their new proposals in motion—or at least on paper—they seemed content to allow the dust to settle. However, she was certain that if they ever discovered she was the midwife behind "The Midwife's Advice," she would be reprimanded. Not that it was a secret. Anyone who read the *Freiheit* knew that Lazar Sokolow was the editor. The connection was inevitable. Already, as those in the neighborhood put two and two together, her clinic appointments had been increasing. But who at Bellevue read radical newspapers, let alone Yiddish ones? Certainly none of the society ladies or the house medical staff. Yet eventually they would find out. There were many Jewish doctors and nurses connected with the hospital, and a strong contingent of Yiddish-speaking patients. Until then Hannah decided she would not think about it, nor would she censor herself by pondering how the officials would feel about certain topics.

For instance, letters asking for assistance on family planning had been among the first to arrive. From the beginning she had consulted with Minna on how to proceed on this delicate point.

"These days getting arrested won't help," Minna explained. "Mostly they are interpreting the laws more leniently. Only when Margaret taunts the Catholic church with banners screaming 'Birth Control! Is It Moral?' like she did in November at Town Hall is there any publicity worth the bother." Minna chuckled, but then her face darkened. "Basically we're attempting to avoid invoking Section Eleven Forty-two of the Penal Code, and trying to have our endeavors interpreted under Eleven Forty-five."

"I don't understand . . ."

"The first one, which makes it illegal to give contraceptive information to anyone for any reason, is the most sweeping and suppressive of the laws. But for a long while everybody forgot the second law, passed a decade after the first, which declared that an article or instrument used by physicians legally practicing or prescribing could not be considered to have an immoral or indecent nature."

"Does that mean that if contraception is used for medical purposes it is legal?"

"Some think so."

"Then why hasn't that law been used more often?"

"Because its intent was to allow men to use rubber shields for the prevention of venereal disease, but not for women to use them for the prevention of pregnancy —even if it was the very same product!"

"That doesn't make sense."

"Doesn't it?" Minna gave a wry smile. "Who makes the laws? Men."

"So when I answer a letter from a woman wanting to know how to prevent a pregnancy, I should refer her to medical treatment."

"Right. Then, if anything happens, we can point out both the federal protections of free speech and the state protections under the amended section of the law."

Hannah shuffled through a stack, not seeming to read the letters.

"How do you keep them straight?" Minna asked.

"When I first open them, I code them with a letter and a number. For instance an *M* indicates a menstrual question; an *M-1* would be one of a serious nature, and *M-10* would be the most routine. I put a little star by those that might pique the general interest, yet are not so weird as to not help others in a similar situation. Mostly, though, I answer the stars, but I also circle those with serious consequences. I try to respond to those privately—don't tell Chaim or Lazar, they wouldn't approve." She pulled up one with *BC-1* top right hand corner. "Here's a query that might make a fine test case!"

Minna took it from her and read aloud:

"Worthy Midwife,
   I have delivered four children, but after each, the bleeding is worse and worse. I have been advised that if I have another, I might not survive. I try to be a good wife and mother, but now if I am to live to help my children grow, I must deny my husband. What other choice do I have?

> Yours very truly,
> A Frightened Wife."

"An excellent selection!" Minna crowed. "How will you respond?"

Hannah took a few minutes to scribble a response. "What do you think of this?" She handed Minna her answer.

Dear Frightened Wife,
   Your predicament is more common than you might imagine. There is no reason for you to suffer any longer. You must see a specialist who will prescribe methods to safeguard your health. These are easy to employ, inexpensive, and very reliable, if you follow the directions accurately. If you will stop by the *Freiheit* office, we will be happy to supply you with the addresses of trustworthy clinics, or you may ask your doctor for a referral.

> *Zei gezunt,*
> The Midwife's Advice

"Marvelous. I especially like the closing: be well. That reinforces the health issue."

"Do you think it's safe?"

"If it isn't, it would be a test case that could go to the Supreme Court."

"I have no interest in going to court. Maybe we shouldn't print it."

"Hannah! I'm surprised at you! Where's your fighting spirit?"

"It's been pummeled out of me, or maybe it's something you shed with age, like a snake does its skin. Look at us! We're all a pretty sorry lot of revolutionaries, aren't we?"

Minna patted her abdomen. "You couldn't tell by the one inside? She's kicking up a storm of protest night after night."

"They all come out screaming. Eventually, though, the throat becomes too sore."

"Or they get their way."

Hannah shook her head. "No, nobody really does. We just learn to settle for what we have."

"Hannah, that doesn't sound like you!"

Hannah turned away as she was overcome by a wave of emotion. The name "Wendell" crashed inside her brain, and it took all her control not to say the beloved word aloud. To cover the lapse, though, she managed to lift the sheaf of letters and spread them in a fan. "These must be getting to me," she said with a gulp. Then, recovering, she continued, "You would think that working with real live patients would be more demanding, but for some reason I see more *tsuris*, more pain, in these than in the hospital or clinic. At least there you can put it in perspective with how they look, how they are dressed. You can ask questions, receive clarifications." She pulled out a letter with a big red circle over the number and letter in the corner. "But one like this! *Oy vay iz mir!* The husband dies, the house burns down, the brother-in-law takes the money, the child is sick." Hannah shook her head. "There's nothing I can say or do. What she needs is money, not advice."

"So you cannot help her . . ." Minna responded slowly. Her eyes began to sparkle. She jumped up, then clutched her belly.

"Are you all right?"

"Yes, yes, just the baby moving around. But listen, why not do a feature? How about giving me that letter, and others you think are especially worthy, and we'll send a reporter out to do an interview, maybe take a photograph. Once a week we can tell a tragic story, which will make others thankful they have it so good by comparison."

"Isn't that exploiting someone's misery?"

"Not if it brings them help."

"How?"

"We could start an account—the *Freiheit* Fund, the Freedom Fund. Donations would be accepted for these victims."

"Yes, I see."

"Even if a reader sent a few pennies, if they came from a hundred, or a thousand, it might make a difference." A shadow crossed Hannah's face. "What is it?" Minna inquired.

"I hope I won't ever need it."

"What will convince you those times are over?"

"Not for food, for a lawyer. I still am not certain we should publish birth-control advice."

"Don't worry. You're anonymous, remember? Nobody knows who the midwife is, and nobody can force us to reveal it either."

"I hadn't thought of that," Hannah admitted. "Minna, have I told you lately that you are a very smart lady?"

"No. And it's about time!"

∽ 6 ∾

The knock did not wake Hannah. In the first months after Lazar had returned, when she was cautious not to disturb his fragile frame or to press too close for other reasons, she had slept more fitfully. Now, along with their compromises about the children and her column, they had worked out a truce in bed also, allowing her the luxury of a much sounder sleep.

"Ma!" The voice was Emma's coming from the far end of a tunnel.

She forced herself toward the light.

"Ma!" A hand was shaking her shoulder.

"What . . . ?" She saw Emma standing in her nightdress,

her lovely tousled hair glistening in the soft light from the parlor. "What time is it?"

"Four or five, I don't know. Uncle Chaim wants you to come down."

"Why?" She had perched on one elbow and was blinking. "What's wrong?"

"He said it might be the baby."

Alertness gripped Hannah like an electric shock. Her mind snapped on. Too soon . . . three weeks . . . not that it was impossible . . . a cesarean had to be planned . . . it was far too dangerous to permit a woman to go into active labor after she once had given birth through an incision in her uterus , the old scar could rupture . . . Dr. Dowd . . . was he around or on one of his lecture tours? . . . who else . . . Starling? No! Never! She was out of bed, reaching for her robe. No, must dress. If there was any sign of labor, Minna would have to be transported. Good thing she had the sense to wake her at the first twinge.

"Hand me my corset," she called to her daughter, but Emma had drifted back to her bed.

"What's going on?" Lazar asked, turning over.

"Minna might be in labor. Maybe it's a false alarm. Sometimes the first contractions feel like the real thing. Anyway, I'm going to check her."

"You want me to come?" he asked with his eyes closed.

"What could you do? Try to sleep. If I don't come back, it means I've taken her to Bellevue."

He pulled Hannah's pillow to his chest, wrapped his arms around it protectively, and sighed deeply. For a second she was envious, but banished the thought with an image of Minna's next baby entering the world.

Minna was sitting on the sofa, her legs propped on pillows and covered with an afghan. Chaim was holding a cup of tea, and she was taking tentative sips. When Hannah moved closer, she could see Minna was trembling though the room was extremely warm.

"Sorry to wake you," Minna managed between chattering teeth.

Hannah dismissed her with a wave. Her hand landed on Minna's forehead, which was bathed in sweat. "Are you hot?"

"No, cold, terribly cold."

"What has been happening?"

"Last night I spent a long time on the toilet. I emptied my bowels over and over. Indigestion, or so I thought."

"And she didn't even have any of Emma's strudel!" Chaim quipped, but neither woman took notice.

Hannah was thinking that diarrhea was often a prodrome, or early sign of labor. "What else?"

"I kept peeing and peeing, so much I couldn't stop myself. It ran down my leg when I was trying to return to the bathroom. Look!" She pointed to a stain by the door. "Didn't have time to mop it up. I just crawled into bed and fell asleep."

"Your bag of waters must have broken."

"Yes, I thought of that when the pains began."

"When was that?"

"I'm not certain. When did you come to bed?" Minna asked her husband.

"Peter didn't settle down until past eleven. Then I went over the latest on the coal strike for at least an hour. Must have been between one and two."

"When I heard you come in, I was feeling something, enough to keep me on the edge of sleep, but it didn't really hurt. I thought they were cramps from something I ate."

Hannah glanced at her watch. It was almost six. "So, you have had some pain for about four hours. Is that right?"

"Not really. I wasn't right all day yesterday. Just soreness in my lower back, but the baby is so heavy I thought it was the strain. Also, Peter kept wanting me to pick him up . . ."

"You weren't supposed to carry him!" Chaim chided.

"I know, but how do I explain that to him?"

"Yesterday you had pains," Hannah recapitulated. "How often?"

"Once or twice an hour."

"And how frequently now?"

"Almost all the time."

"Isn't she amazing?" Chaim crowed. "She just sits here and talks right through them."

"Sometimes the early ones are fairly mild. Since you will need to have surgery anyway, there's no reason to suffer. I only wish you had called me sooner."

"I didn't want to bother you."

"But, Minna, you know that in your case if you don't have the operation promptly, you might place yourself—and the baby—in some danger."

"I didn't really think—" She stopped as something twisted her face into a grimace. After several deep breaths she was able to continue. "That one really hurt! Now I'm not sorry I missed it the first—" Her head fell back and she closed her eyes. "Ohhh!"

"*Gevalt!*" Hannah cried. "I've got to check her immediately." She scrambled to Minna's feet, parted them, and looked at Minna's panties, which were soaking. "Help me!" she ordered. Chaim expertly removed his wife's garments. "Now turn on that lamp."

Hannah positioned herself on her knees. "Can you hold her legs apart? That's it."

"Ahhh!" Minna groaned from someplace deep in her throat. "No! Stop! *Dray mir nit keyn kop!*" Don't bother me!

"Hush, I must. I will be quick." Hannah's deft fingers reached up to discover how far the uterus had opened. One glance at the blood-tinged mucus that pooled on the covers was enough to convince Hannah they would have to get her to the hospital at once, but her educated fingers came to a vastly different conclusion.

"My God! How could this have happened?"

"Is something wrong with the baby?" Chaim choked.

"It's almost here! We thought she could never deliver one naturally, and this one is falling out."

"What shall I do?"

Hannah looked around at the jumble on the sofa and the disarray of the room. "Not here. Help me move her to the bedroom."

"What about the hospital? The doctor?"

"Too late for that."

"But—"

"Chaim, do as I say. Now!"

"Can you stand?" he asked his wife.

"Yes." She swung her feet around. Then a pain gripped her. "No! Can't."

"Wait till it passes. Count with me: one, two, three . . . ten . . . twenty-five, twenty-six . . . better now? Yes? Chaim, take one arm. Minna, we're going to the bedroom. Now!"

They half walked, half carried Minna, and no sooner had her in bed when Peter started wailing, "Mama! Mama! Mama!"

Chaim looked anxiously from his prostrate wife to the other door.

"Go upstairs and get Emma, she'll help with him," his sister ordered.

"You said there was no time."

"We have five minutes, but not five hours." He seemed torn between his child and his wife. "Go!" the midwife demanded.

Calmer now herself, since with the head about to crown, the decision to deliver the baby was the only possible one, the midwife began to organize for a home delivery. Everything she required was in her bag upstairs, but she had not sent Chaim to fetch it. As soon as Emma stepped through the door, she gave her daughter instructions on where to find it.

By this time Peter was wailing so loudly Minna was becoming upset.

"Chaim, you go to the baby. Emma!" Hannah called her daughter into the room again. "You get my bag and tell your father what is happening. Come right back. Immediately! Do you understand?"

Emma shot one look at Minna's wide-eyed face, nodded solemnly, and burst from the room. In minutes she had returned and Hannah laid out the necessities. Chaim had Peter changed and perched on the foot of the bed. Even Minna seemed slightly distracted by her child's antics as well as the preparations. For the moment everything seemed normal, but Hannah's mind churned with the horror of what would happen if the scar were to rupture. She had no blood supply, no surgeon standing by. Were there any alternatives?

Another contraction swept Minna away. No, it was far too late to transport Minna. Hannah's fingers scanned her abdomen. The tightness was normal. "Does it hurt in any one place?"

"Just everywhere."

"Good," Hannah muttered under her breath. A localized pain might herald failing scar tissue. The midwife lathered her right hand in olive oil and began massaging the vulva, up into the vagina, and around the protruding portion of the head to hurry the child into the world and prevent more compression on the scar.

"Is that really hair?" Chaim asked with awe in his voice.

"Yes."

"You can see hair?" Emma asked. "That's disgusting."

There was no time to correct her daughter because Peter

was attempting to climb toward his mother. "Take him into the kitchen and give him some cereal," Hannah said. "And if he makes a fuss, carry him upstairs to our flat and keep him there."

"I have to get ready for school."

"Today you stay home."

"But, Ma—" Her protest was silenced by Minna's long, piercing wail. Emma leapt up, and in one swift movement she carried Peter out of the room under her arm. In her peripheral vision Hannah saw only the child's kicking legs.

Minna was oblivious. Chaim came around to the head of the bed. He cradled his wife in his lap, stroking her damp hair. "Darling, darling . . . it's almost here." Then he looked to his sister for an affirmation that this was true.

She nodded. "Now, can you push a little? Yes, gently. No, that's too hard. No, Minna, listen to me!" Hannah made certain she had Minna's full attention. "Softly, easy. Yes. Chaim, help her sit up slightly. That's right. Lean on him. Good. Now, hold your knees. Yes. Isn't that better?" One of the midwife's hands cupped the emerging head, while the other peeled the final folds of the perineum away from its scalp. "That's good, good," she coaxed as the infant's head moved two steps forward and one step backward with every strain.

"I can't—" Minna protested.

"Yes, yes . . . almost . . ." Hannah encouraged.

"No!" Minna's head snapped back and bumped Chaim's jaw.

"Ouch!" he complained, but nobody noticed.

"The head! It's out!" Hannah called.

Minna seemed not to have heard, and Chaim's eyes were closed. In the few seconds of transition between the uterine and external world, Hannah wiped the child's eyes, nose, mouth, and was rewarded by the appropriate gurgling noises. Without direction, Minna did what was necessary to expel the child from her loins. In concert Hannah guided first one shoulder, then the next, cupped the buttocks, and swung the baby up, around, and onto Minna's shimmering abdomen.

"But there's no—" Chaim stumbled. "I mean . . . it's a girl!"

Minna became more alert. She looked down. Her hands reached around at the same time as her husband's. Four hands clutched their daughter: a small yet perfect specimen who had defied medical prognostication by coming into this world in her own way, at her own time.

After the child had been bathed and dressed, after Minna had recuperated from her swift but unexpected ordeal, when Chaim had begun to recover from his shock, they discussed the events of the day. At that time her parents, her aunt and her uncle, agreed that Sybil, the newest Blau, was the littlest radical, for that day she had defied them all, as she probably would in the days to come.

∽ 7 ∽

The hour had come to leave Bellevue. Hannah had either missed, or ignored, the early warning signs. Dr. Starling had doubled his staff of doctors in training. He had assigned medical coverage for every shift. He had distributed a flowchart depicting how every staff member—nurse, midwife, even supervisor—reported to a doctor, even if only an intern. He had made himself Hannah's immediate superior until June, when the next class of students received their medical degrees. After that, the new assignments had Hannah reporting to a boy so green, he not only had hardly shaved, but had not delivered more than ten babies in his entire life!

This was intolerable. Dr. Starling knew it, as did the rest of the obstetrical staff. Finally, at last, Hannah did too. And she accepted it. Her resignation came as no surprise. From Dr. Jacobs she received a letter stating the hospital's gratitude for her many years of faithful service and wishing her well in her new endeavors.

Dr. Dowd organized a group to give her a plaque and a watch. At eleven on the appointed morning Hannah appeared in the amphitheater, anxious about having to be at Wendell's side through the public ceremony.

"We're sorry that Dr. Dowd's lecture schedule conflicted with this occasion," apologized Mrs. Church as she greeted Hannah. "He could not get back from Massachusetts in time."

"That's fine," Hannah said sincerely, for it was a relief not to have him orchestrating the last rites of her departure.

Dorothea Wylie asked, "Have you heard the latest about his poor wife?"

Hannah didn't respond, but Millicent Toomey filled in. "She's still resting at the seashore. Her whole confinement has been plagued with problems."

"I know," Dorothea added. "She was horridly ill in the earliest months of the pregnancy, and none of her husband's potions had the slightest effect."

"I heard that in the first trimester she was even hospitalized for violent vomiting."

"Where?" Dorothea asked.

"It must have been a private institution," Millicent sniffed.

Dr. Starling brought the group to attention, then completed the honors with surprising grace and good humor. Mrs. Clayborn Church was representing the Board of Managers, but nobody missed the coldness in her delivery of good wishes. The whole event seemed more like a medical procedure than a party, and Hannah's response was to steel herself for the interval, expecting the same blessed relief as when the dentist is done drilling.

Then it was over.

Then it was time to leave.

She began her last walk down the maternity-pavilion corridor. Hurrying along, she shook hands and accepted the well wishes of nurses, orderlies, and the other midwives, now a dwindling, almost extinct species. Dorothea Wylie and Millicent Toomey were crying, but they were the only two left with whom she felt an emotional connection. Hannah arrived at the main hall steps and began the long flight down. Yes, she thought as she paused at the landing, there were those she would miss, but the truth was that her favorite staff members had departed long ago. Out on the street, with the great monstrosity of the institution looming behind her, she felt free to turn in any direction. There was the clinic, the advice column, enjoying the antics of Peter and Sybil. Even though Benny and Emma were well on their way, she still needed to keep a watchful eye on them. Yes, there was plenty to do. Hundreds of letters a week had to be read and whittled down into seven excellent queries. At least another dozen or so required her private response. There was reading to do so she could analyze the problems of her patients at the clinic, as well as her correspondents. The extra time suddenly seemed like a vast inheritance. She walked up First Avenue without turning back for another glance. Her eyes were dry, and with each step Bellevue—its problems as well as its privileges—retreated into the past.

8

Experience had taught Hannah that every idea should be Lazar's idea if she wanted it to happen. In the early years she had resented his disparagement of her suggestions. Now she knew there were so many ways to trick him into believing that he had said it first that it hardly mattered what he thought, as long as—in the end—she had her way. Experience had also taught her not to get too soft when everything seemed to be going her way. Now that she was not at Bellevue, she knew that the bulk of their income came from the *Freiheit*. Right now the publication was healthy, but many such ventures collapsed after a few prosperous years. What if their readership became bored, began to prefer the *Forverts*, or wanted an English-language newspaper? Also, they needed to think ahead. If most of the children of the current subscribers were like Benny and Emma, they would reject Yiddish publications. In a few years the paper would lose its older subscribers and not have won any younger ones. What would they do then? Benny's idea of percentages was so appealing she began to think it would be glorious if Lazar would write a book and then continue to receive payment year after year, no matter what happened.

"What are you working on?" she asked her husband, who sat in his favorite chair writing on a tablet while she was opposite on the sofa surrounded by stacks of letters to the midwife.

"An editorial about Stalin. As you know, last month Lenin appointed him General Secretary of the Communist Party. My slant is to show that despite the significance Westerners

have attributed to this, it is a post of little importance and
that Lenin is as firmly in charge as ever."

"Nobody understands more about what is going on in
Russia than you. Too bad only the readers of the *Freiheit* are
benefiting from your wisdom."

"We're starting to get subscriptions from all over the
country. Chaim thinks we'll be up to thirty thousand by the
end of the year."

"And that's not just because they want to hear the midwife's advice!" Hannah said with a self-deprecating laugh.

Lazar removed his reading glasses, pretended to wipe
them, and stared at her to discern whether she was mocking
him. When he was convinced of her sincerity, he gave her a
wan smile, then sighed. "Neshomeleh, I think I've become
comfortable with my place at last."

"I'm happy to hear that, but if I know you, it won't last
long, at least not if your talents are wasted." Seeing Lazar
warm to the compliments, she decided to pursue her point.
"You could write a book. Not only does a book reach more
people than a newspaper, but it circulates for months, even
years. Also . . ." she continued hesitantly.

"Yes?" Lazar's brows arched with expectation.

"I understand that these publishing arrangements can be
lucrative." Seeing the confused expression on his face, she
spoke rapidly. "After the words are written, the book pays
something called royalties over and over, while you continue
on your regular work or begin another project."

"Royalties! Who's been filling your head with this nonsense?"

"Don't talk to me in that tone!"

"Who?" he asked in a voice he forced into a more pleasant register.

"Your son."

"What does he know about it?"

"More than you," she wanted to say, but halted herself.
"He was explaining about the different ways to make
money."

"Yes?" Lazar prompted, "Go on."

"He told me there are three ways to make money in this
world. The first is through labor, which is pure sweat and effort translated into dollars, like my work in the hospital, or
digging coal, or teaching a class. But he explained that the

problem with that is that if you are too old or sick to work, the money stops and you become dependent on others."

"That would not be a problem in a socialist state."

"Anyway," she said in a rush, "he said that most people would prefer independence, and I agree with him about that." She folded her arms to show this was not a point for debate. "He then explained one path to independence was to allow your money to work for you. However, the more risk you take, the greater the possibility of the rewards. I don't recall everything about interest and dividends and diversifying the risk, but he really does know what he is talking about." Ignoring Lazar's scowl, she continued, "He said the third way to make money might be the best, but the hardest to achieve. That's when he told me it's called 'royalties' because kings could force their subjects to pay them a percentage of their profits without doing anything for it. The point was that if you could invent or create something, then sell it, the person who buys it pays you a portion of the income forever after. I realized that I get a royalty on the *Freiheit* if it sells more than a certain number of copies every day, but once the day is over, so is any chance of making more money. If you wrote a book, though, you would be finished with it, but the money would roll in for every copy sold."

"That's not about to happen."

"Why not? This is not one of your lighter-than-air schemes. Lots of people make acceptable incomes from their writing. Most of your friends have written books. John Reed's is everywhere. And even before that, Louise published *Six Red Months in Russia*. Emma's articles on Russia for the *New York World* are coming out again in book form, Berkman has one in the works, many of those people who used to be at Mrs. Dodge's have written their version of events and . . ."

"That's because they are famous in their own right. People buy their books because they are curiosity seekers, not truth seekers. Nobody knows who I am, and I suppose that's been for the best, or I wouldn't be sitting here right now."

"But you knew everyone: Trotsky, Lenin, even Stalin."

Lazar's somber expression silenced her. "Nobody wants to hear what's really going on there, nor can I be the first one to tell it."

"What about Emma Goldman's articles?" she asked, knowing he would rise to the bait.

"I never thought I would see Emma Goldman, Queen of the Reds, recanting."

"They sold a lot of papers," Hannah said, recalling how the first installment had appeared in the *World* under the blazing headline—RUSSIAN REVOLUTION A FAILURE, SAYS MISS GOLDMAN, AND SLAIN BY THE BOLSHEVIKI THEMSELVES—as well as how Chaim had regretted not having enough money to compete for the series.

"E. G. did the most harm to herself with her one-sided opinion fashioned to save her skin. She is either blind or doesn't know the half of it!" he seethed.

"What haven't you told me?" Hannah asked in a honeyed voice to diffuse his ire.

"The reports, if they can be believed, are terrible." He shook his head morosely. "Hundreds of our people are in prison, every one of them in need, many suffering from scurvy. Alexander Shapiro has been arrested, others have been sent to the worst solitudes of Archangel." His voice choked. "Sometimes . . ." Tears streamed from his eyes. He could not continue.

Hannah reached out and clasped his hand, knowing the terrifying images that had to be swirling in his mind: the brutal murder of his family at the hands of Cossacks in Kishinev, the horrors he had witnessed during the pogroms of Odessa, and most recently, the grisly scenes of the revolution and the civil war.

As though he had received an infusion from the embrace, he was invigorated. "Don't be angry with me when I tell you that I feel I ought to be there."

"I know, I know," she soothed.

"But I could be another Shapiro case, another returnee arrested. Chaim agrees with me. The *Freiheit* is taking a collection. I've heard there are ways to send funds to our people there. Even so, it is a drop in an ocean because we cannot expect our comrades to be continuously contributing for the same purpose, not when the Freedom Fund proves there are important causes that demand aid here in America."

"How did it come to this?" Hannah asked shakily. "I don't understand why Russia is turning out so differently than we had hoped."

"I know why. We put our faith in the wrong men."

This was a shocking admission. Hannah wanted to question him further, but felt impeded, like a horse tethered to a post.

After a long while, Lazar closed his eyes and spoke in a hoarse voice. "Trotsky changed. He became obsessed with an almost Nietzschean litany, saying: 'We need to show our will to power,' by which he meant he had to prove his toughness by his willingness to use violence. He found it more expedient to order: 'Shoot them!' as if there was no other logical alternative. At first I saw that it took a toll on him, but soon it became a routine matter. Do you know what I learned?" His words were strangled in his throat. "If you shoot one, it is easier the next time. In the beginning you might limit yourself to military opponents, but then some civilian crosses your path and his comrades also must be taught a lesson. Soon you are murdering everyone who contradicts you." Lazar shook his head sadly. He closed his eyes, then his shoulders heaved and his whole body began to tremble.

"Lazar? What is it?"

"Nothing . . . a chill . . ." he lied.

Hannah was dismayed by this uncharacteristic display of emotion, but in a few moments he seemed in better control. "What about Lenin?" she asked. "Why didn't he step in to stop it?"

Lazar laughed ruefully. "Lenin encouraged ruthlessness. He knew what revolutionary power entailed, and urged his colleagues to take whatever measures were necessary to retain authority in the face of the civil war and intervention. He believed that the threat of starvation, forced labor, summary executions, concentration camps—in short, *terror*—was what maintained and expanded his power base."

"Why did you not tell me this before?"

"What good would it have done?" Lazar's hands stretched to cover his already closed eyes. "I never expected that Trotsky would become so talented in the application of these methods. In fact, I might say he distinguished himself, first by providing theoretical justification for Communist terror, then as an advocate for military methods in civilian activities."

"Yet you stayed with him," Hannah stated without accusation.

Lazar's hands fell to his sides. His eyes opened to reveal a film of tears. "You cannot imagine how conflicted I was.

I had given up everything to be at Trotsky's side. I had submerged my own feelings, beliefs, connections with my family and friends, even my status as a political thinker in my own right. And for what? Because I thought the cause greater than myself." There was a pause as he composed himself. "There was a time ..." he continued dreamily, "a very short time when I felt ennobled. But this passed swiftly."

"Couldn't anyone stop Trotsky?"

"Nobody wanted to. Trotsky's successes with organization and his zeal for punctuality and order impressed Lenin. Once, in the spring of 1918, he had me write, 'History is no indulgent, soft mother who will protect the working class: she is a wicked stepmother who will teach the workers through bloody experience how they must attain their aims.' And I wrote it. Without question."

"Don't be so hard on yourself. You thought you were on the right track. You had no idea how this would turn out."

"I should have known! I should have seen! Isn't it amazing how one's sight improves the farther away from the action one travels? From across the sea I can tell the false steps at once. There, in the midst of the revolution, everything was blurred."

As he stared bleakly ahead, Hannah did not probe. What was she to say? This was hardly the time to mention that she had always distrusted Trotsky, that he had been disagreeable and rude from the first.

While her mind wandered, Lazar continued down the same dismal path of confession. "I'll never forget the date: August 29, 1918. That's when Trotsky decimated a regiment that had deserted its post at Sviazhsk. Right away he called for a field court-martial, then held the executions on the spot. There were others, many others, but that's the day that has continued to haunt me. Why? Because it was the first? Because I was not convinced of their guilt? Or was it because he executed even the commissar of the regiment, a man named Panteleev?" Lazar's long sigh was an almost animal-like moan. "Yes, that is the day I recall, because after that day nobody ever felt safe again."

"Why?" Hannah murmured.

Lazar tried to respond twice, but no words could be heard. At last he managed to whisper, "That was the day our leader began murdering members of his own party."

"You must tell this!" Hannah insisted, then regretted the outburst as Lazar's face purpled.

"If you think the idea is so wonderful, why don't you write your own damn book?"

"What do I know from Trotsky?" she quavered.

"Forget that bastard. Thousands want your advice. Why not write a book for them and be done with this nonsense once and for all!"

Hannah refrained from mentioning that he had encouraged her to accept the assignment. Reluctant at first, even afraid of the responsibility, she now enjoyed the challenge. But a book? What could he be thinking? "I am finding it difficult enough to write letters in Yiddish. A book? It would have to be in English. Impossible!"

"Yes! Exactly!" he said, brightening. "It would be in English. For everyone. Women and men, but mostly women, for they buy these things. Remember when I had the bookstore?"

She nodded but didn't respond. How could she forget his disastrous failure when they had been starving during their first years in the city? Instead of a business establishment, the place had become a social club for his political cronies.

"Well, sometimes I became disgusted because the ladies rarely wanted to read about ideas. They either asked for romantic stories or helpful hints like cookbooks and medical advice. Who could give advice better than you?"

"A doctor."

"Doctors don't know the half of what you do. Besides, they're always attempting to find a scientific explanation for everything, even if one is not possible."

"Yes, that's sometimes true," she conceded.

He leapt up and strolled over to the sofa. Picking up a pile of letters, he began to thumb through them, checking out the categories. "I know you try to select the more interesting letters to answer, but you are neglecting the common, most often repeated questions. Right?"

"I suppose . . ."

"That means that people are more alike than we wish to believe. It means we share the same needs, wants, desires, problems."

"Of course we do."

"Why not give them what they want? Why not answer the

most ordinary questions in the form of a book? What are they?"

"What are what?" She was becoming befuddled by his agitation.

"What do people want to know most?"

"About having babies and not having them; about how a boy should be with a girl, how a girl should be with a boy; problems with parents, problems with children; conflicts between generations . . . You know as well as I do what they write!"

"Yes, yes . . ." He seemed distracted. "Can you distill that for me? Isn't there one basic question?"

Hannah shrugged. She was too tired for this game.

"Aren't they just asking how to be happy?" he blustered.

"There are no recipes for happiness."

"That may be true, my dear, but that won't sell books, or bring you your precious royalties either." His stare was penetrating yet not pugnacious.

"Well . . ." she began slowly. "When we worked on the survey, we divided the data by women who said they were mostly happy or unhappy with their marriages. There were many correlations between sexual satisfaction and general contentment, and so . . ."

"So?" He beamed expectantly.

"If more people were satisfied sexually, their marriages would be better, and possibly they would be happier for the most part."

"Or at least think they were."

Hannah drew a long breath as she deliberated on his meaning. Was he saying they themselves were happier than they believed they were and that their lack of a sexual connection did not affect their union as much as some would assume? "I still don't understand . . ."

"You understand exactly. Who knows more about how to get men and women to resolve their intimate problems than you? You should write it down, avoiding nothing for the sake of propriety."

"Nobody would dare read a book like that, let alone buy or sell it."

"Yes, they would, if it had an unthreatening title. You couldn't call it *How to Have Sex* or anything like that, but think of how many women are like Rachael, but would never admit it to anyone."

"How did you know about Rachael?" Hannah asked, aghast that the secret had been exposed.

"She told me how you helped her. She was proud of you and wanted me to know it."

Hannah shook her head in amazement at her friend's openness. Then another memory was triggered. She began to giggle.

"What is it?"

"I was thinking about the first time I discussed sexual matters with a stranger. It was when Mabel Dodge told me she had not yet achieved her goal in the search for the perfect orgasm. Do you remember? You were standing right there."

"How could I forget? Didn't I tell her you were an expert, and you shot me that look of yours, you know the one: I'll murder you when we get home. Anyway, you handled them brilliantly. From the moment you took on Freud and Havelock Ellis without skipping a beat, you won them all over, even Margaret Sanger."

"Nobody wins her over, but perhaps she was willing not to discount me after that."

"I suppose we can't title the book, *The Search for the Perfect Orgasm,* although it would sell millions."

Hannah couldn't help notice Lazar's inclusion of himself in the project, but let it pass. "How about something referring to health? Nobody objects to a book that will make them feel better."

"True, except if it doesn't allude to the true subject, it could be ignored."

"What's wrong with the word *marriage,* which at least shows the lawful association of a man and a woman?"

"Now you're thinking! How about: *How to Have a Happy Marriage?* Doesn't that say it all? Everyone knows that a marriage includes sex; everyone suspects that problems with sex would lead to an unhappy marriage."

Instead of cheering Lazar on, Hannah felt her heart sink. The idea was splendid, but she could not execute it. Words had never been her strength, at least not unless she were sitting face to face with a person. Answering a letter was one matter, putting her knowledge and experience into cohesive sentences, paragraphs, and chapters was another. Mentally she flipped pages in the texts in which she had sought information. Thinking about the documentation, footnotes, cross-references in works by people like Havelock Ellis further convinced her she lacked the scholarship to complete the task. "I could never do it," she admitted sadly.

"Of course you could."

"I'm not an expert. I have a hard enough time understanding what has already been written."

"If you do, so must everyone else. This is a book for regular people, not clinicians. Besides, haven't you told me a hundred times that these experts, these 'ignorant men' as you have called them—" Catching her disagreeable expression, he lifted his brows. "Come now, don't claim that you have not made disparaging remarks about some of the pompous asses who claim to know how a woman feels."

"All right, I'll admit that to you, but I wouldn't in print. I couldn't put any of it in writing. You know how muddled I get."

"It's easier than you think. I could help you. First, you would have to get organized." He retrieved his notepad, ripped the top few pages off, and came to sit beside her on the sofa. "A book is divided into what?"

"Chapters."

"And what are chapters? It seems mysterious initially, but they are merely sections to organize ideas for the writer as well as the reader. Now, what would be our—ah, your—first chapter?"

"Who knows?" She started to stand, but Lazar pulled her down. "This is ridiculous. We're not going to sit here and write a book this minute."

"Yes, we are," he said emphatically. "At least we're going to organize it. You love to organize everything. Order from chaos, right? Now, pay attention."

"You are sounding more like my editor than my husband."

"What's wrong with that? In fact, that's exactly what I shall be. You can't be expected to work on a project of this scope by yourself. Nobody ever claimed you were a stylist, or even a writer. You tell me what to say, and I'll put it down."

"Then you're the writer too, not just the editor."

"Okay, so we'll write it together." With his free hand he patted her thigh, one of the rare intimate gestures she could recall since his return. He asked, "Where do we begin?"

"With the marriage?" she offered.

"Before the marriage comes the selection of the partner."

"That's true."

On his pad he wrote: *How to choose a mate.* "Then what?"

"The wedding night, I suppose, which for some has preceded the event."

"That's fine. Nobody said you couldn't read the second chapter first!" he chuckled. "Next?"

"I think we should divide the next sections into separate discussions about male and female anatomy. You'd be amazed at how ignorant people are about their own bodies, let alone those of the opposite sex. Most don't know the correct names for any of the organs. They come up with the queerest ones," she chuckled.

"Good. How about 'The Female Body' and 'The Male Body'? I'll put the woman first since more women will read the book, although since Eve came from Adam's rib, perhaps it should be the man."

"Actually, there are embryological studies that may prove that the female organs were created first."

"You mean we all started as women?"

"Some scientists might agree with that."

"The rabbis wouldn't."

"I don't think religious leaders are going to be giving out copies of this book to their congregations."

"All the better," crowed her husband, the atheist.

"Anyway, if sales are our goal, we'd better minimize that point—which doesn't have much practical bearing anyway."

"Whatever you think best. You're the expert." He reached over and gave her a gentle kiss on the cheek. "I like the way you're thinking!"

Her face burned from the contact. She wished she could fling her arms around him and show how much she desired him. Flushing, she forced herself to glance at the list. "That covers the first four chapters. Now we should get the couple together, but how?"

"I thought we did that in the second chapter."

"Yes, but this would be more inclusive."

"I could name a half-dozen ways . . ."

"Yes, I'm sure you could, but how could you put it politely?"

Lazar pondered the question for several minutes, and as he did, Hannah clearly saw the task was not a simple one. An outline was one matter, the details were far more

complicated—not to mention more delicate—than he suspected. Soon he would come to the same conclusion: the
book was never going to be written. "Ah!" he boomed.
"Questions. You are good at answering questions. What if
the next section was in a question-and-answer format? The
first one might be something like, 'Who should initiate lovemaking?' and you could give an answer that either one, or
both, and demystify the belief that the man has to do everything all the time."

"But he does!" Hannah smirked as she recalled the moments long ago when she had mounted him.

"Does not!" Lazar threatened playfully with his fist.
"Anyway, what do you think of the question-and-answer
concept?"

For a moment Hannah could not respond. The crackle of
energy that had once locked them together was evident in
the room.

"Well?" he prompted.

"It would simplify matters . . ." she allowed as she came
back to the problem at hand.

"This is going to be fun!"

"You really want to do it . . . with me? How will you have
time?"

"I'll make the time. Think about the money this could
make!"

"Who would publish it?"

"We could print it ourselves, then find a distributor.
Chaim has lots of connections." Hannah shook her head.
"Now what's the problem?"

"You're sounding more and more like your son," she
dared.

"Don't say that! The boy's obsessed with money. I don't
know what to do about it," he replied soberly.

Now Hannah regretted her words. "Every boy that age
does something different from his parents. You did. Besides,
what's the most terrible thing that can occur? He can lose
money. Worse things happen in Russia, right?"

"Money, markets, governments, each is subject to the
laws of nature. What goes up must come down. I don't want
to see him hurt, that's all."

"Then you know about this investing of his?"

"I'm not blind. I've seen the book he is reading."

Hannah was glad he had noticed, for even she had been

alarmed by the title: *The New York Stock Exchange, A Discussion of the Business Done; Its Relation to Other Business, to Investment, Speculation and Gambling; the Safeguards Provided by the Exchange, and the Means Taken to Improve the Character of Speculation.* Nothing about it sounded kosher. After all, in the middle of the title was the word *gambling.* Was this how Benny actually had acquired his two hundred dollars last summer? Had his speech about hard work and being trustworthy been a ruse? Everyone knew that boys that age hid things from their parents and that their families were often the last to know of their difficulties, but Benny seemed to have his head on his shoulders. Her only complaint had been the clashes with his father, but on that score Lazar was as much at fault. The trouble was that Benny was fascinated by money: how to get it and multiply it. Was this abnormal? No, most men had to concern themselves with supporting a family. Another boy might have looked to his father for advice, but Lazar could hardly fill that role. So the boy turned to books.

Hannah shook her head as if to dispel her qualms. "You've always said no harm ever came from reading."

"If that is all he is doing!"

"You don't think . . . ?"

"He's like a sailor reading about navigation from a theoretical point of view. What does he really· know of what lurks in the treacherous waters of the business world?"

"He seems intrigued by this stork exchange."

"Once a midwife, always a midwife!" Lazar quipped. "It's the *stock* exchange, not the stork exchange."

"You don't think they would take a boy's money, do you?"

"Why not? Do you think these financiers care whom they hurt?"

"I admit you have been good at forecasting events in politics, but you will have to agree that this is one area totally outside your realm."

"On the contrary. I have always been a student of the evils of capitalistic exploitation. Anyone who owns a single share of a corporation is as guilty as its president."

"That's ridiculous! Just as you knew more than your father about say, socialism, you'll have to allow that Benny might know more than you about finance."

"Politics always takes economics into consideration."

"You should—" she corrected herself. "I'll talk to him."

"He won't listen." The spark of anger that had flared as Lazar thought about Benny's entrepreneurial explorations fizzled as quickly as a blown match. He grinned. "Any more than I would have listened to my parents at his age. The important point is not what he is doing, it's what we are doing," he prodded gently. "In a few years he'll be on his own, for better or worse. We'll still be making our life together." He tapped the pad. "Where were we?"

Hannah stared at her husband warily. *"How to Have a Happy Marriage* by—" she stumbled. "By whom? By both of us, or just by me, the midwife?"

"I don't know if we should put either name on the book."

"Why?"

"It's bound to be controversial."

"When did you ever avoid anything that was?"

"In the end I found it to my advantage to be the anonymous pen behind Trotsky, remember?"

Was this maturity, experience, or fear speaking? Hannah mused. For a moment she regretted the loss of the impetuous man who had brought her so much grief yet had always been exciting; then she reveled in his good sense. "What shall we call ourselves?"

"We could use our initials. *L* and *H* or rather *H* and *L*, since you should come first." He glanced to see if she would contradict, but his wife merely nodded.

"That's fair. I'm the expert, I suppose," she allowed with a modest glance to the side. He didn't disagree. Good. Another hurdle passed gracefully. "And for the last name?"

"Not Sokolow. But why not something with an *S?* Sok? Soko?"

"Sounds like a good name for a prizefighter."

Lazar laughed. "How about Low? H. L. Low."

"It's a bit short."

"If we add an *e*, it's more elegant. Lowe. I like it. Freudian too."

"In what way?"

"Lowe. Low. Down. Base. Common. Slightly sordid. The low down, low life, lower depths, lower yourself. Slightly dirty. Slightly sexual. Do you get the connections?"

"Yes, but no one else would."

"Perfect."

"What is?"

"The name. Our name. The title. The idea. Everything!"

⤜ 9 ⤛

The irony of Lazar and Hannah writing a book telling the world how to have a happy marriage was not missed by either of them, although they never discussed it with each other. For a long time she had tried to ignore the fact that she was writing about sex while living as a celibate, then realized that if she had been, say, widowed, she would not feel less of an authority, so why should she now? Also, she had a keen awareness that while she had hardly led a blameless life, her varied experiences allowed her to understand the foibles of others more keenly. Not that she mentioned this to Lazar. If there was one thing she had learned from her advice letters, it was that some matters were best kept private. So she also knew better than to question him about any women he might have known before her or even the ones he may have befriended in Russia. Why did one's own weaknesses seem so hard to understand when someone else's were so transparent? Maybe for the same reason she had worried about everyone else contracting influenza, never dreaming that she might be susceptible. Knowledge and experience did not confer immunities. No profession offered protection from pain. In fact, the most precarious perch was to hide behind the know-it-all pretense, for it took but one tiny slip to tumble into the churning abyss.

Yet if we had the perfect marriage, Hannah reminded herself, we would not know so many of the pitfalls. Soon she became more assured about what she had to offer. By recalling the transitions family and friends had gone through, she could make assumptions about the many variations from normal—from Eva and Napthali, whose union seemed more material than emotional, to Chaim and Minna, whose passion for each other was still palpable. Less traditional types, like Margaret Sanger, whose most recent lover was an expert at Karezza—an old Hindu method of prolonging sexual intercourse; and Mabel Dodge, who had reported she had found the ultimate orgasm with the Native American she was with in New Mexico; not to mention Louise Bryant, now cavorting with a diplomat in Paris, all provided fodder for her pen. Also, to steer her was the survey as well as the thousands of questions for "The Midwife's Advice." And since she had worked with women's intimate organs for so long, she had developed some practical techniques that brought swift successes.

For instance, a step-by-step approach she had formulated for problems like Rachael's had already helped many women. The key was to find the "music" that helped each relax so they could allow their natural inclinations to take over. After that they often required instruction on positions that might stimulate them better, techniques for the partners to employ, and large doses of general education about their bodies. Most extreme were her instructions on masturbation, which some rejected outright but seemed to bring many women their first knowledge of gratification. Much of this was too potent for the book, but she was working on the language that would say what she meant without offending.

There was a long list of questions she could not answer, and most of them referred to men's sexual problems.

"I don't know where to begin with these," she admitted to Lazar as they tried to sketch out those chapters.

"There are plenty of books," he suggested.

"Frankly, after I read them, I had more questions than answers." She told him about Malcolm Brody's case. "The cures the so-called experts suggest are almost as barbaric as those that poor man was subjected to by well-meaning practitioners."

"Then you'll have to find a consultant."

"Dr. Dowd is hardly any better. When I asked his help with Mr. Brody, he had some ludicrous suggestions. I shouldn't have expected a gynecologist to have more than passing knowledge in the male organs." She paused and looked up at her husband. "If you remember, you're the one who supplied the answer."

"I'd forgotten about that," he said with a wry smile. "To whom would Dr. Dowd refer a man?" Lazar asked.

"Dr. Blühner at Mt. Sinai."

"Why not see him?"

Would the haughty doctor, whose reputation was legion in

his field, condescend to consult with her? she wondered, until she recalled how he had joined with Dr. Dowd in the publication of "A Practical Treatise on Vaginismus" using her methods and giving her no credit. Wendell had said the *New York Medical Journal* would not have accepted it without Dr. Blühner's endorsement, nor would the editor have believed the work of a midwife. But the two doctors knew exactly whose case it had been. Later Wendell had told her that he also had shared the details of the squeeze technique for premature ejaculation and other of "their discoveries" with the eminent researcher, so Dr. Blühner knew that she had contributed some of the material. Since the survey, however—the one even Rachael referred to as the Dowd–Sokolow Survey—her own name carried some weight. Dr. Blühner would not only see her, he would be most intrigued with her questions.

Hannah asked Carrie to write a letter to request an appointment for a professional consultation. Since she knew the doctor had already published several books and she did not want to seem to be in competition with him, she decided not to mention the project. On the day of her appointment, however, her courage flagged. As she negotiated the corridors of Mt. Sinai, she recalled her last visit there had been escorting Minna to Dr. Rubin's laboratory. Look how successful that was! she reminded herself as she opened the door to the Chief of the Genitourinary Department's office.

Dr. Blühner stood respectfully and gave the midwife a jerky bow from the waist. "A pleasure to see you again, my dear Mrs. Sokolow." His thin lips formed a brief smile. "Now that you are no longer associated with Bellevue, I have not heard much about your work."

"My private practice keeps me busy," she replied silkily.

"And this is where you have encountered something you would like to discuss with me?" His voice arched in unison with his furrowed brow. Hannah suspected he was optimistic that she might have a succulent morsel like Stella Applebaum or Malcolm Brody for him to exploit. After offering her a seat, he took the chair behind his desk, ran his fingers down the leather cover of a notepad as though he were going to open it, but then folded his hands on top of it and waited. "How might I be of assistance?"

"My questions relate to the matter of male potency," she began with the briefest hesitation. The doctor stroked his salt-and-pepper beard, which tapered to what appeared to be a finely honed point, nodding for her to continue. "While I specialize in women's problems, I do have some male patients with this complaint. Mostly, though, the wives come to me with various ailments, but when the right questions are asked, allow that they are suffering from the effects of their husband's inattention."

"Very true," he said as he tapped one tapered finger on the pad's leather cover in a marching rhythm. "What do you suggest to them?"

"I will admit to several sorts of trial and error. If I can ascertain that the problem involves premature ejaculation, variations on the squeeze technique are often effective. But I am at a loss with other presenting symptoms."

"Well, my dear, if I could give you a tablet to offer the men three times a day, you and I would both be rich as Croesus."

"Do you think the difficulty is chiefly physical or psychological?"

"In my experience each case has a component of both. Unfortunately, there are some entirely incurable conditions. Our successes, though, are increasing."

"Why is that?"

"First, because the subject is no longer as taboo as it once was. More and more men are admitting the problem and looking for treatment. Second, since the war, we have had a wide variety of cases with different causes, some traceable directly to battlefield casualties."

Hannah leaned forward. "From injury?"

"Actually, the most frequent distress must be attributed to venereal infection, but then once the organic disease has been cured, there are often long-term effects that can not be readily explained."

"What are those?"

The doctor straightened his back to assume the posture of the lecturer Hannah recalled from the Bellevue amphitheater, but his voice was more reassuring. "After the war, almost every consultation hour brought at least one ex-soldier who had been successfully married before the conflict. On return, he rushed into the arms of his wife, but to his horror found himself impotent upon the first intimacy. Some of these subsided rapidly; others became permanently established as a result of autosuggestion, which created a fear of impotence.

But you know the pernicious effect of that cycle, don't you?"

"Yes. What you say explains why I am finding the problem so prevalent, yet I still don't understand the cause."

"One explanation says that in the face of death the sexual impulse recedes because the will to live supersedes it. On the other hand, Dr. Menasse, surgeon to a Russian regiment, reported that the sexual impulse sometimes flares up in the face of death. When a man faced a devastating battle the next day, he often was kept awake by irritating erections. To counter the manifestations of painful priapism, the doctor had to prescribe drastic cathartics."

"What happened to the men later?"

"Unfortunately, we don't have follow-up on those cases. Nevertheless, some of the impotent do report losing desire during the heat of war, which never returned after they were reunited with their families. Others may be tormented by guilt over masturbation or encounters with prostitutes. If they did acquire a venereal disease, they see that, as well as their inability to perform for the good women they married, as God's punishment for their sins."

Hannah could just imagine Lazar's response to that! For a second she was amused by the thought, then felt a stabbing pain shoot between her shoulders.

Misreading the distressed lines on her face, he prodded, "May I assume you take a modern view of autoerotism, Mrs. Sokolow?"

"Yes . . . well . . ." she babbled while her mind raced to stay ahead of the truth that was galloping to catch up with her.

"You should know that I consider it harmless, at least physically. Nevertheless, the fantasies associated with it can cause the man to become estranged from reality, whereupon there occurs that dangerous condition Freud has called regression, or the flight to the sexual ideals of childhood . . ."

Hannah was no longer listening. What had brought her to this illustrious man's office? Was it really a chapter in the book? No matter how often she told herself that she had accepted the end of her sexual relationship with her husband, she still yearned for satisfaction. Even though the idea of marriage to Wendell had always been preposterous, she had cradled him in her mind as her one last chance because she had assumed Lazar was incurable. Although she forced herself to repress her arousal to her husband, it had not evaporated entirely. In her dreams they were lovers but usually thwarted by the appearance of a child, the lack of a private place to be together, or some other disaster that kept them apart. Sometimes she found herself holding him at night, and would gently extricate herself without disturbing him. If she was honest with herself, she would admit that some of her irritation with him stemmed from her anger at his inability to love her properly. As though he understood this, he had been more empathic with her lately, but she had assumed that was mostly because of the book. Without cooperation and compromise, not a single chapter would have been completed. Now they were more than halfway through, which proved they could work together. And yet . . . yet . . . Dr. Blühner was speaking to her. She refocused her attention.

". . . Thus you see how the hostile attitude toward women may increase to a mortal aggression and awaken the homosexual component slumbering in every man."

"What about injury?" Hannah asked haltingly.

"My favorite cases!"

"Why is that?"

"Because with a simple test I can determine at once whether they are curable or not."

"Would you describe it?" She was unable to prevent her voice from sounding constricted.

The doctor stood, went to his worktable, and poured her a glass of water from a cut-glass carafe. "Better?" he asked solicitously as she swallowed.

"Yes, thank you."

"Now, where were we?" He did not take his seat again, but strolled the perimeter of the floral carpet at the back of his desk.

"The test?" Hannah gasped.

"Ah, yes! The first is a series of questions I ask the patient privately, then again pose to his spouse, who must be brought in if we are to achieve success with my procedures. The most important is: in the time the man has been home, has his penis been able to achieve any level of erection, or has it always been utterly flaccid? If they jump to respond negatively, I caution them to think about it. Ignore those times when they have tried to be sexual with each other. What about in the morning? Or after a bath? Or even the middle of the night?"

Hannah realized it was hard to remember. To spare them both the acuteness of the loss, she had purposely averted her eyes from his pelvic region. Thinking about it, though, she remembered believing that it was larger in the mornings before he used the toilet. "What difference does that make?"

"The goal is to categorize the man. As you may have read, there are levels of impotency ranging from those men who never in their lives have experienced an erection to those who lose capabilities later due to accident, disease, psychological causes, or merely the natural progress of aging. In my preliminary study—which, by the way, was published last year in the *Urology Review*—I have arrived at different degrees of performance competence."

"Is there a way to be certain that permanent nerve damage has taken place?"

"Absolutely. If there is any level of erection, at any time of day or night, the nerves are functioning. The on-off switch is in the brain, not the spinal cord. If the nerves were severed, the organ will never engorge. In my experience, however, that is the rarest case."

"Even with the many war injuries you have seen?"

"Especially with the war injuries! That is what is so fulfilling about this work. I've had successes with amputees, men riddled with bullets, their systems consumed by the effects of gas, and debilitated by constant pain. Once they believe that they might restore their sexual functioning, other improvements also follow. Some of the cures have been nothing short of miraculous. Of course . . ." His ebullience faded. "Let me not paint too optimistic a picture. There have been failures, even once the promise of a remedy seemed evident."

"There was a man I saw . . ." Hannah began cautiously, "who had a crushing injury resulting in severe pain in his leg and chest. I assumed he was incurable, so I did not suggest any therapies. Might I have been wrong?"

"I cannot say from that information alone, but in my experience the initial suffering during his convalescence may have blocked pleasurable sensations to that area, leaving him convinced he could never perform. Or, he may have had temporary swelling or bruising of the nerve pathways. These may take many months, even years to heal, but by that time the man feels defeated. In these cases you must examine the situation scientifically rather than emotionally."

"How can that be accomplished?"

The doctor's normally stony face relaxed into a beatific smile. He removed his glasses and placed them in the center of his blotter, then reached into his desk drawer and removed a set of five rubber rings. "The Blühner bands. You are the first person outside this hospital to see them!"

⸻ 10 ⸻

The set of rings went home in Hannah's pocketbook. To keep them from the eyes of her curious children, she placed them at the bottom of her medical bag, waiting for the time she might employ them. That evening Lazar was out at a meeting and returned long after she retired. The next few nights Benny was ill with a fever, and Hannah slept with the door open in case he needed her. They would require privacy for the experiment Dr. Blühner had proposed, not just in their bed, but to discuss it calmly. First she had to get Lazar to agree. For some reason she feared he would react negatively, spoiling any chance at a fair trial. Then she had an idea. She would not make this a personal issue. She would wait until the question came up in their writing. But then there were a series of delays—so many, in fact, she decided it might be best to leave well enough alone.

Because of all the ferment in the labor unions, Lazar was busier than ever with the *Freiheit*. In his editorials he was always searching for new vitriolic adjectives to condemn the anti-union actions of the militia and others who spurred sporadic violence. The only time he could put aside to read through her notes and rewrite them was late in the evening after he had put the daily newspaper issue to bed.

"Maybe we should put the book aside for a while," she suggested when he was rubbing his eyes at midnight.

"No, it's a welcome change from the grim news about the strikes."

Indeed, it was a relief to the nation as well as Lazar when the coal miners agreed to end a five-month strike after an appeal from President Harding, and railroad shopmen were given the green light to return to their jobs in mid-September. Despite Hannah's initial reservations, their collaboration continued smoothly. Maybe this unity also helped keep the peace at home, or maybe everyone was learning how to get along better with one another. Whatever the reason, Hannah found the sunny atmosphere as invigorating as the news of an international peace treaty.

That summer Lazar discovered that he and Benny had a common interest: baseball. Together they rooted for the Giants, exultant when their team entered the World Series against the Yankees. While they were not able to secure tickets for the final game, both father and son were hunched over Benny's precious radio on October 8, shouting in unison as the Giants triumphed in a 5–3 victory. Nothing more had been mentioned about Benny's financial exploits, which had probably been only a boy's idle speculation. The reading would be useful in the future she supposed, and secretly hoped her son would be better off economically than they would ever be.

Lazar also made routine trips to hear Emma sing at the settlement house. One day he came home to report he had seen her sitting with a boy. "They were so close that their hips touched."

"Who is he?" Hannah asked.

"Edgar Ross, her accompanist."

This sounded serious. "Her what?"

"He plays for her while she sings. He's trying to get her to audition for a place at the Institute of Musical Art."

"What's that?"

"A musical college."

"Is she good enough?"

"He thinks she is."

"Maybe he's prejudiced?"

"She *is* talented, Hannah," he said admiringly. "And she has spirit too. The boy was trying to talk her out of singing some lighthearted songs because they wouldn't make the right impression on a Mr. Damrosch, but she told him that not everyone was as serious as he was, and that this man might get tired of hearing the same somber tunes day after day."

"Good for her . . . but should we let her?"

"Emma's voice is very pretty, although untrained. If there

is enough talent there, they will be wise enough to see it. If not, there's no harm done either way."

"I don't know about that. Her eyes are filled with stars."

"Emma's loved music since she was a baby. Why not let her have her desire? What harm could come from it? If it were Benny, well, then we'd have more of a concern. He's the one who will have to make a living."

How practical Lazar was for a change, and yet how nearsighted. What was this myth that a woman did not need to work? Where would he have been without her skills? Hannah did not mention any of this.

Lazar, though, had not been transformed entirely. He still saw himself to be the great prognosticator. His editorial columns were filled with urgent warnings on everything from the collapse of the mark imperiling Germany to Mussolini's march on Rome signaling the death knell of that country. "I don't know why," he explained, "but once I see my words in print, I actually experience a sense of relief, even though nothing is solved."

"At least you have acted," Hannah suggested. "That must eliminate a certain amount of frustration."

"Maybe . . ." he allowed.

And maybe it has something to do with your contentment with both your work and . . . maybe your family, she thought, but did not voice. For a long moment she felt as if they had won a victory. Despite everything they were united. Their children were thriving and the problems of the world seemed far away. Unfortunately, her smugness did not solve her struggles with the book. The last chapters proved the most difficult. They were attempting to give advice about common sexual problems, from frigidity to premature ejaculation, impotence to sex during pregnancy, sexual inversions to men who preferred to wear women's clothing—almost everything that she had covered in her years in the clinic, at Bellevue, and in the *Freiheit* column.

"I have ideas, I have opinions, I know a few suggestions that have worked for some," she explained tensely during one siege with self-doubt, "but many experts would disagree with my points, and there's no way I can prove I'm correct."

They had been at work all one Sunday morning and were about to break for a meal. Lazar had already pushed back his chair. Hannah was about to boil water for tea.

"Just put down what you think is best," Lazar coaxed.

"What if I'm wrong? I could do more harm than good." She lit the fire under the kettle.

"How many times have you showed me an example of quackery in a book? What about those crazy electrical devices that were used to shock a man's testicles? A man might come to permanent physical, let alone mental harm. What about that doctor who hesitated to allow a man to aid his wife's satisfaction by touching her in a place that might increase her pleasure? If I had had the bad luck to read that during an impressionable age, I might have felt guilty for doing all the things that have made you happy over the years." He took a quick breath, then barreled on. "Then there was that doctor who maintained that intercourse during pregnancy would give the child epilepsy and other dread diseases. Or what about those so-called experts who think that children who fondle themselves should be bound with leather restraints? How could that make sense to anyone who knows that almost every normal child explores himself from head to toe? You could go on with more examples for the rest of the day. So far as I can tell, nothing you have written could be considered damaging to anyone. It may not be exactly right, or it may be disproved in twenty or a hundred years, but if you do your best to be straightforward and truthful, you won't have to worry."

"I agree, yet I can't help but—"

He cut her off. "Ask yourself one question: might this injure anyone? If you don't think it would, and if it follows basic common sense, then include it."

Hannah came back to the worktable and placed her hands on the rail of his chair. "What about testing some of the theories?"

"Why not? But you would need the patients and the time."

"Would you help me?"

"The kettle is boiling," he said, but she ignored him. "I don't see how I could."

She went to retrieve her medical bag. "Let me show you something." She laid out the five rings and then explained what Dr. Blühner had told her months earlier.

"We pick the size that comfortably fits over the flaccid penis. The man wears it day and night. If it begins to feel a little tight, he replaces the ring with the next larger size. Often, in the middle of the night, the discomfort from the constricting ring wakes the man."

"So what does that mean?"

"If it increases two sizes or more, the problem is not considered physical."

For a long moment she was unsure if Lazar understood her meaning. His face was blank. When comprehension flooded his features, they formed a look of astonishment.

"Well?" she coaxed.

"If you like . . ." was his whispered rejoinder as he took the rings and placed them in his pocket, then went to the stove and lifted the kettle without a pad, burning his hand.

≈ 11 ≈

There was a full moon that last weekend of October. A warm breeze crept over the city like a reprieve from the winter to come. The window was open. The drapes were pulled back to make the most of the fresh, dry air. After awakening to go to the bathroom, Hannah came back to bed and could not settle down. Moonlight filled the room to the corners, pooling on the quilt that had dropped off Lazar's shoulders. Hannah gently pulled the sheet up over him, but it came out from where it had been tucked at the bottom. He stirred and it moved away from his loins to reveal his undershorts slightly parted in the front. In the glimmering light, something caught her eye. The ring was in place! This alone gave her hope. Maybe he had worn it during the day and had achieved some degree of success, or maybe this was the first time.

Her hand grasped his soft organ. Holding it without any pressure, she examined it from the root among the patch of dense hair to the smile of the opening at the nub. With a fingertip of the other hand she stroked the end, then the sides, down the twisting loop of vein to the soft sacs between his legs, which parted at her approach, almost welcoming her investigation. Glancing at his face, Hannah was certain the rhythm of his breathing was unchanged. Then she checked the status of what she held in her hand and found it too was the same. The ring could easily rotate, and if it were not for the capped head, it would have slipped off. A pang of disappointment almost caused her to abandon her plan, then a gust of air ruffled her gown. Fresh smells from somewhere far away from the urban streets permeated the room. Without realizing it, she squeezed Lazar's penis and it slipped away in protest. He stirred, turned slightly, but did not wake up. Leave him be ... was her thought until she reached to cover him again and saw that his penis seemed larger than it had been. She tried to turn the ring, but it was held firmly in place by the engorged flesh!

She renewed her light stroking. The penis lifted from its flabby droop to a more impertinent angle. Was this merely an involuntary nervous response? She lowered her head and began to lick. No, this was not the confused reaction of stimulated synapses, this was a normal, excited male penis. Backing away, she watched with utter fascination as it waved in the air as if calling for attention. Lazar's eyes remained closed, although his breathing was more rapid. The ring looked miserably tight. She tried to slip it off, but it would not budge. Unfair to leave him like this, she thought. Well, she might as well make it as pleasant as possible by using her tongue to lubricate the shaft. At last the ring was free. His member arched and stretched as if in appreciation. She held it lightly in her hand, squeezing now and then as she pondered what he might be dreaming. From some memory long ago she was able to sense his imminent spasm. She slowed her pace. Her own body had long since passed its indifferent analysis and had begun to yearn to gather him inside for its own satisfaction. Must not think of that now, must do this for him, she resolved as she applied her last ounce of concentration to the task. The reward was swift. The spurting was absolute proof of health.

"Oooh!" Lazar moaned, rolling toward her.

"You were awake!" Hannah chastised.

"No, I was having an extraordinary dream."

"It wasn't a dream. There's nothing wrong with you."

"Ah! Just what the doctor ordered."

"I never told the doctor about you."

"I know, it's just an expression."

"But he was right. You just had some form of war impotence, only I was too ignorant to know it."

"War impotence?" he asked huskily. "What's that?"

"A broad term for men who returned with injuries—both mental and physical—that have affected their love life."

"What does the war have to do with it?" He sat upright.

"You don't want to hear about that now."

"Yes, I do."

"There are so many categories, from venereal disease to homosexuality to—"

"That's not it!" he said harshly. "What do those bastards who've never been there know?"

"Never been where?" Hannah asked, taking his hands in hers. "What is it? What is the part you haven't been able to tell me?"

"I don't know what you are talking about."

"It has something to do with Trotsky. Something to do with the train. Once, when you were telling me about the executions—"

"All right!" he cut her off. "You asked! Don't say I didn't warn you!"

"I want to know so I can understand," she murmured.

"Terrible, terrible . . . I can never forget . . ."

"Maybe it was the trying to forget that made it impossible for us to be together again. Maybe remembering will set you free."

"That doesn't make sense!"

"I know, but after what we just did, the worst is over."

"Over? It will never be over for me."

"Why?"

"The executions, Trotsky's executions. Always the same, like a choreographed ballet. If I close my eyes, it comes to me. Every night. Always. If I try to think about something else, like holding you, it comes faster, harder, in more perfect detail, like an endless movie in my mind."

"Tell me."

"The train would stop. We would all be expected to participate, otherwise our loyalty was in question. First they would round up the prisoners and force them to dig long ditches. Then they would pick out the victims, two by two. They would be made to stand side by side with their backs to the pit. Then—" His voice caught and he coughed on his swallowed tears.

She folded her arms around him and drew him to her breast, but he pulled away and cleared his throat. "The men would line up with their rifles. You would hear the crack of the fire. For a moment the prisoners would stand upright, then they would seem to be jumping in the air, but really it was their recoil from the hit. Always, always . . . they would fall back into the pit, and the men with the guns would walk forward and pump more rounds into the hole." He clasped his stomach. "I could feel it here. Terrible pains would shoot right through me. It never got better. Never!"

"Oh!" Hannah gasped in sympathy for her witness husband as well as for the victims.

"The bodies would writhe around for the longest time, even after the next group had fallen atop them, even as the dirt covered them . . ."

Her eyes had been shut tight, but she felt Lazar's hands on her arms, then sliding down to her legs, then tugging on her gown. His hands clasped her breasts almost roughly. As he twisted her nipple and began to suck hungrily, she could almost hear the crack of the rifles, see the twitching bodies in the hole, the very images that had haunted him now invaded her so utterly that she could barely sense the erotic feelings that he had begun to stir again.

"Oh!" he sobbed with such longing she drew closer. "See," he said as he forced her to touch his firm member.

So fast . . . how could he become excited again that quickly? It was like he had been many years ago, when they were first married, even before . . . He was spreading her legs and now his mouth found its mark. She reached to push his head back, but he dived forward, insisting with an animal-like grunt. "Hmmm! Nice. I've missed it," he said as he came up for air. This time she propelled him forward to her mouth while tilting to meet him halfway. His face strained with an intensity that was even more pronounced in the sharp moonlight.

Now they embraced fiercely, desperately. With his hand he guided himself into her. Had they ever made love so violently before? It was a wonder nothing hurt. The bed was shaking so hard she considered briefly whether the children would stir, but in a moment those thoughts were banished by the insistence of her own body to hit its mark. Their mutual shudder began slowly, then crested so fiercely she clutched him to prevent being swept away in the tidal wave. Together they lay locked in a desire they had not felt for many years. The intensity was far different from the tepid times of their final couplings before he returned to Russia. As they lay trembling together, the breeze quickly cooled their sweating limbs.

Instead of reaching for a cover, she climbed on top of him. "Is this better? Are you warmer?"

"A bit," he admitted with a smile that the white light wove into a silvery band.

Hannah's hips found the pace as her blood flooded into dry channels, filling, swelling, expanding. "Better now?"

"Getting there. Don't stop!"

Lazar, who had never failed to know where to touch, to probe, to stroke, proved he had not lost his memory. The pulse peaked as she surged over the top and felt herself spilling in the churning sea and swimming safely to shore.

"I didn't think you could," she said as she finally peeled herself away from him.

He covered her, then kissed her shining brow. "I didn't think you wanted me."

"Of course I wanted you, although I was afraid it would not work anymore."

"I was afraid too. Of my memories, the pain, and you."

"Me?"

"You avoided me. You never touched me. From the moment I returned, you seemed to find me distasteful."

"I didn't want to hurt you more. Even when I rolled over, you groaned. I wanted you to heal."

"When I would reach for you, you would spurn me."

"I didn't."

"You did. So I stopped trying. I understood why you felt as you did. First you were angry at me for leaving, then you were angry with me for returning."

"But—"

He placed his hand over her mouth. "No, wait. Let me finish." Sliding upward and rearranging pillows, he looked down at her. Hannah propped herself on her elbow so she could face him. The light from the window illuminated his eyes, which seemed as dark and fathomless as the ocean. "You did not think that I could have left you if I loved you. So, if you were to live with my departure, you had to divorce yourself from me, at least mentally. That's how you could continue to live with the strain. If I had gone to war, if I had promised to return, it might have been different. However, I was worse than a soldier. I never made any vows. You had no hope. Do you want to know how I am certain that this is true? I did the same, or I could not have left you. When I could not tolerate the pain, I would dwell on the bad times, the way you would nag me to work, how upset you were over the numbers money, how you hated Trotsky—"

"I didn't hate him."

"You did. Maybe not him personally, but what he meant to me."

Hannah was too tired to argue. Besides, what was the point? Never had Lazar been so conciliatory. How nice it was to hear him confessing the truth of his fears, talking sincerely about their life together rather than post-war depressions or Kronstadt or military maneuvers, which she now realized were partially a way to conceal his horror at where he had been, what he had seen, and what he had done—if not directly, then indirectly. "That's not why I stayed away from you."

"Then you admit you avoided me. Why did you?"

"It's complicated. I understand enough about men's problems to know that it is dangerous to push them, especially if they fear they won't be able to perform. I thought that you were frightened that your injury had permanently damaged you. If I had pressed the point and you had been unable to do it—even if you had the capability—you might have come to believe you were inadequate, and then you really couldn't have done it, even if the cause was in your mind, not your body. Do you follow me?"

"Barely. But that can't be the whole of it. I did try, but you would stop me."

"You did not."

"You don't remember."

Was that true? Fuzzy images of him reaching for her in the early months—sometime after he was feeling better but before he became thoroughly engrossed with the newspaper—rolled through her mind. Maybe she had misinterpreted everything. How could she have . . . with everything she knew . . . how could she have read the situation so utterly wrong?

"There was another reason . . . another reason you did not accept me and I did not challenge you."

"What is that?"

"You know. You say it."

Now something was wrong with her throat, and the words that would have explained about Wendell formed, then cracked, and fell away. "I don't . . ."

"Yes, it's simple. You didn't want me." A long, long pause. The moon was already over a different line of rooftops. The room had darkened considerably. Good. He could no longer see more than the outline of her face. "You wanted someone else."

"Who?"

"You never told me, but I would guess it's a doctor, or someone you met at work, or maybe someone you had helped. I suppose I could have found out. The truth is, I did not want to know. He existed. That was bad enough."

She should have denied it. Any illusions she once had about confessing now seemed preposterous. His pain was almost visible in the room. Any knowledge could do nothing but harm him further. None of this had been easy for him—not leaving her, living apart from her, the physical suffering from the accident, or the wrenching decisions about his return. Anyone with any sympathy would have wanted to ameliorate his anguish. All she had to do was to draw him close, tell him he was wrong, that they had miscommunicated, that each of them had been stupid, ignorant, too proud . . .

She didn't.

She wavered as the ideas blended and reformed. How to do this? What was right? After his revelation she owed it to be honest with him. She felt like she was heading down a road and had to swerve to avoid a collision. Was the brick wall better than the other car or the child in the middle of the street? Was one way quicker, less painful? Which would have the least calamitous effect in the long run? Reaching down to the depths, like the doctor spooning up the dregs of the rice pudding, she found a way to begin.

"There was a man. After you left, I loved him and he loved me. Still, I wanted you back. You. For yourself. I wanted to try again. He understood. He went away. In fact, he married someone else. So it's over."

"That's why you started with me again when I was asleep, when the risk was small."

"No. Well, yes, maybe. If you want to know the truth . . ." Suddenly she was convulsing with an odd combination of tears and laughter. "I wanted to discover if Dr. Blühner's bands would work. Really I did!"

"I've always been your willing subject, always will be."

"I know that, Lazar," she said automatically, and then she knew that her words, which had sprung from partial facts, were now the absolute truth.

∽ 12 ∽

By the end of November the rough draft of *How to Have a Happy Marriage* was complete. Chaim and Minna read it first.

"When you initially told me about it, I was going to print it like a pamphlet with maybe five thousand copies to sell for ten cents," Chaim began. "But this! It's incredible! What surprised me was how much I did not know. Even Minna learned something new. If we can place it in the right hands, it could set records in bookselling, but I can't promote it properly."

"Who could?" Lazar asked.

"There are any number of publishing companies who would dearly love to represent it. With your permission, I would be delighted to make the necessary inquiries."

"For a percentage?" Hannah quipped.

Chaim looked abashed. "Of course not."

"Why not?" she continued seriously. "I get my percentage of the *Freiheit.*"

"Well, in that case . . ." he allowed with the humility that was his strength.

The idea that someone else might want the work was flattering. At that moment she and Lazar suspected that they had a good concept, that they had written simple, easy-to-understand explanations, and that everyone was curious about marital relations. Exactly how curious they were, and how well written it was, turned out to amaze everyone concerned.

While they were waiting to learn how their effort would be received when it was placed in the stores early the following year, Lazar prepared the issue of the *Freiheit* on the fifth anniversary of the Bolshevik revolution. Looking at photographs of Soviet armed forces parading through Red Square, Lazar held up one, a close-up of Trotsky with a ribbon on his left breast taking the salute.

Seeing the yearning expression in her husband's eyes, Hannah said matter-of-factly, "You wish you were there, don't you?"

"No!" he retorted defensively.

Hannah shook her head. "It's all right, Lazar. I'd expect you to have some regrets."

"No, you have misunderstood entirely. What I was thinking was: why *don't* I wish I were there? I look at Trotsky and I see a cardboard figure, not the man I knew. I could not imagine being there"—his voice choked—"or not being here."

Was this true? Yes, she convinced herself when she thought about how often they now made love, as if they were newlyweds who believed they had just discovered something unique. Also, she thought Lazar finally understood he was better off commenting on the events of the world from a distance. He had a superb talent for synthesizing what he saw and heard and making it lucid for others. Working on the book together had been far easier than expected. Although he did not understand every technical detail, his suggestions on how to reorganize a section, reword a sentence, give another example to point up a solution were, for the most part, brilliant.

Months would pass before the final volume of *How to Have a Happy Marriage* was printed. Minna would suggest that a simple rose tied with a bow adorn the jacket under the title. "To make it look pure and natural." The effect was not only visually pleasing, but inferred that the material between the covers was delicate too. Even Emma admitted that she was not ashamed to see the book "at least from a distance." But Benny's concerns were directed at the arrangements for royalty statements, the rate of sales, the number of reprints. "You should have negotiated a higher royalty after the book sold a certain number of copies," he complained a bit prematurely, even if he would turn out to be right.

No matter their little—or great—successes, the world went on revolving and evolving. Nobody could ignore entirely what was happening in Europe. More and more Lazar was becoming alarmed by the vast audiences who gathered at National Socialist demonstrations in Germany, Mussolini's threats of censorship to the Italian newspapers, and warnings of fighting in the Ruhr. Yet in America, where the biggest problem seemed to be the naughty flappers who drank and smoked like men, persisted in cutting their hair, and wore too much rouge, all these rumblings seemed far away.

For a while Hannah worried about how their book would be received at a time when the mayor of Boston banned an appearance of Isadora Duncan because her costume exposed too much when she danced, the postal authorities were preventing the import of a supposedly lewd book by a Dubliner named James Joyce, and religious fanatics were trying to keep Darwinism from being taught in the schools.

"I hope we have half the controversy *Ulysses* did," Lazar responded to her concerns.

"Why?" she asked.

"Everyone wants to read what they are told not to," he claimed. "Nobody would have bothered to purchase a boring book like *Ulysses* without the dispute."

"I hope you are right," she responded without confidence.

On the afternoon of the last day of the year, a busy Monday, Hannah was seeing a few patients for Rachael because she had to get home to Nora, who was in a flutter dressing up for her first New Year's party at the settlement house. Emma and Benny would be attending the same one. Emma was going with Edgar, who was accompanying her while she sang her charming repertoire, including "Five Foot Two, Eyes of Blue, Has Anybody Seen My Girl?" and ending with the perfect finale for Emma: "All by Myself." Hannah would have loved to hear her, but it had been made plain that no adults were invited. Benny was going alone, but had promised to look out for Nora. Rachael had been hinting how delightful it would be if "something happened between our children." In her heart Hannah knew it never would. Benny was not ready yet, but when he was, she suspected he would fall for a very different type than the bookish Nora. There was so much they had yet to experience. If only there were peace in the world, life would be so much easier for her children. Benny belonged in business, not going through the dubious rite of passage of going to war. She hoped Emma would never have to suffer through having her beloved thousands of miles away on some foreign battlefield. Hannah also anticipated that no matter what sort of musical career her daughter pursued, she might also embrace motherhood someday.

Fortunately, there were no emergencies at the St. Mark's Place clinic. It was snowing slightly, so all her appointments were late. While she waited, she tried to finish some paperwork, but she felt the pen slipping from her hand as she thought about what 1923 would bring. Hannah was hoping to avoid discord when the book was published, even if that might sell more copies. At this moment her private world was unusually calm. From that stable center she could continue to try to mold order from the chaos that swirled in the outer maelstrom just beyond her doorstep.

Of course, there were situations that could never be changed, yet that did not mean she was defeated. Everyone could learn to be more accepting of their lot, and thus with themselves. The quest to always desire something bigger and better was a false undertaking. She supposed Benny eventually would learn that no matter how much money he amassed, he would want more, until he learned that it was not how much you had, but what you did with yourself that mattered. And Emma was going to be frustrated in her search for glamour. If she found happiness, it probably would not come as she stared out over the stage lights into a vast, dark audience. Where would it be for her? For Benny? For any of them?

Hannah was beginning to think that everything in the universe—all the chaos and confusion—did have an internal order, only there were no maps, no recipes. You had to discover it for yourself. Meanwhile, if you were lost, the best alternative was to inquire at the beginning, the way a newborn opens its eyes for the first time and locks into the gaze of its mother. How many hundreds of times had she witnessed that precious scene? Nobody who had not given birth would believe that the nascent vision actually saw, let alone processed, the face of its life giver. But every new mother was made a believer, and no midwife would consider discrediting the flow of information that passed during that bond, any more than she would discount the nourishment that had swelled through the cord which had just been severed.

Here was what it came down to: the mother as the island of safety for the newborn, the family as the protector of the species. No matter what horrors churned outside their gate, the family must not be allowed to become chaotic or the underpinnings of sanity would be lost—not just for the individual, but for society. And if Lazar was to exult that his idea had won them great fame, or Benny was to flaunt that his father had become rich despite his philosophy, or Emma was to regret that her mother was to be promoted as "America's expert on sex" during a time when this would cause her endless embarrassment, Hannah would not be troubled. No, not when the hundreds of thousands of people who were to read *How to Have a Happy Marriage* might find a few ideas to hold their families together more firmly. To her, each volume of her book was not the financial transaction of Benny's accounting sheets. It was as simple as her mother's recipe for glue. But—and she would never, ever tell Lazar this—this glue was far more powerful than any of his "isms." It was the adhesive that would prevent the world from disintegrating.

Of course, on that last day of the year, she knew only bits and pieces of this, but in the subsequent months, when blinding, confusing success came as swiftly as an avalanche, she was not entirely surprised. Instead of reaching out to the world that elevated her, she would turn inward to the core that nourished, to her family.

She heard footsteps. Her heart beat hard with anticipation. In her profession—why, in her life—you never knew who or what might walk into the room. She held her breath.

Carrie knocked on her partially opened door. "Mrs. Mandel is here with little Rebecca. Are you ready for them?"

"Send them in," Hannah called with gladness ringing in her voice. "Send them right in."

AUTHOR'S NOTE

Sex, its practice, problems, and prescriptions, are not recent developments. The issues of today have been common from the dawn of the species, and curious researchers have been pondering its mysteries for centuries.

For instance, sex selection has always been intriguing and controversial. The suspicion that Orthodox Jews produced significantly more male offspring than the general population was confirmed by Dr. Landrum B. Shettles in the 1970s. The biblical injunction that a woman not engage in intercourse during her menstrual cycle or for one week thereafter put most women at the most propitious time not only to conceive, but to have a boy because of several factors. First the smaller, Y-bearing sperm that result in a male are thought to be speedier, making them able to migrate through the reproductive system at the time of ovulation faster than the X-bearing sperm that result in a female. Second, male continence during the restricted time period is associated with an increase in the frequency of male sperm. Also, a third cause is the fact that X-bearing sperm seem to last much longer, so if intercourse takes place before ovulation has occurred, more of those producing girls will be around to effect fertilization. Interestingly, women undergoing artificial insemination, who must accurately pick the date for the procedure based on the time closest to ovulation, produced 62 boys for every 38 girls in one study, and 76 percent boys and 24 percent girls in another. Further, there is some evidence that the directions in the Talmud suggesting that since it was believed that sex selection took place at the moment of cohabitation (which is not exactly correct, but remarkably on target for that time period), a boy would result if a man waited until a woman experienced orgasm before he ejaculated. Dr. Shettles learned that female orgasm does produce more alkaline secretions, which in turn offer a more favorable environment to Y-bearing sperm.

The extraordinary case of Mrs. Czachorwski's examination is taken from observations by Dr. Joseph R. Beck of Fort Wayne, Indiana, while treating a retroversion of the uterus and duly reported in the *St. Louis Medical and Surgical Journal* in September 1872. Beck's findings, which contained some inaccurate perceptions, nevertheless were a milestone in the literature of early sex research.

Long before Dr. Alfred Kinsey started to investigate human sexuality from a statistical point of view, François Rabelais (*c.*1490–1553) began to correlate when people seemed most sexually active. In 1923, Paul S. Achilles, a psychologist, made the first study which included American women. Hannah's survey is loosely based on *Factors in the Sex Life of Twenty-two Hundred Women* by Katharine B. Davis and published in 1929 by the Bureau of Public Hygiene.

Various constraint devices, like the barbaric ones used for Stella Applebaum, were not uncommon, and the gruesome electrical treatments suffered by Malcolm Brody were popular therapies. In every case the more bizarre remedies and advice mentioned in this novel represent what was actually employed or suggested during this time period. Although it seems a safe assumption to think that doctors who counseled so poorly and destructively studied in the dark ages of sexual awareness, many misconceptions persisted far too long. While one may forgive Dr. Dowd's contemporaries for suggesting that premature ejaculation may be normal and represented power rather than disability, this fallacy was still being promulgated in the 1948 edition of *Sexual Behavior in the Human Male,* by Kinsey, Pomeroy, and Martin. "The idea that the male who responds quickly in sexual relations is neurotic or otherwise pathologically involved is, in most cases, not justified scientifically," wrote Kinsey. He continued: "Considering the many upper level females who are so adversely conditioned to sexual situations that they may require ten to fifteen minutes of the most careful stimulation to bring them to climax, and considering the fair number of females who never come to climax in their whole lives, it is, of course, demanding that the male be quite abnormal in his ability to prolong sexual activity without ejaculation if he is required to match the female partner."

Also, surgical cures for vaginismus are still employed to

enlarge the introitus. Even though a woman will be able to have intercourse, there are often adverse emotional reactions and her ability to respond may be impaired. Therapies, much like the one Hannah employed, that gradually desensitize the spastic vaginal inlet, have been very effective. Hopefully, Hannah's many intuitive, less invasive, and more practical solutions might have been employed by a few of the more enlightened or creative practitioners of her day, but these actually are more in line with thinking in the realm of modern sex therapy than knowledge disseminated during that period.

Dr. Isidor C. Rubin of Mt. Sinai Hospital presented his epoch-making uterotubal insufflation test to his peers in 1920, for the first time making it possible not only to visualize the status of the fallopian tubes, but to cure some cases of infertility by expelling the blockage. Women of the era, like Minna Blau, were the first to benefit from this revolutionary technique.

All characters, except those of historical note, are entirely the fictional creations of the author. When Hannah and her friends interact with people who truly lived, they do so in the approximate time and place the personages inhabited. When they speak or express opinions, they do so with wide artistic license, yet as much within the framework of their convictions as recalled in biographical material and other documents available to the researcher. However, there has been no attempt to quote verbatim, merely to express who they were and how they might have lived in an imaginary context. For instance, those who appeared at Mrs. Dodge's fertile evenings were really present in her salon, Margaret Sanger was a special friend of Havelock Ellis, and Trotsky lived in New York during that tumultuous pre-revolutionary period. Of course, no Minna Blau played a part in a hunger strike for birth-control rights, but another stalwart woman suffered a similar fate. Lazar Sokolow was not on Trotsky's train, yet someone was crushed and survived that famous wreck. A Yiddish newspaper, the *Freiheit,* did begin publishing at approximately the same time as in this story, but with a very different staff. It's no secret that Hannah is based on my paternal grandmother, Anna Bialo Weisman, or that Lazar is modeled after my grandfather, whose favorite newspaper actually was the *Freiheit.* Since writers of fiction have the ability to change history for a few pages in time, I'd like to think Louis Weisman would have enjoyed being its editor, if only in my imagination.

My gratitude must be formally extended to my vigorous researchers, Lesley and Adam Tunstall-Wiener, Ruth Chevat, Sandra Mandel; my assistants, Deborah Metzler Rector, Mary Ann Boline, Mary Wanke, Hazel Szfranski, Beverly Crane; and the following specialists: Jenny Clifford (sex therapy), Tom Davis (early aviation), James Kastberg (operettas), Lefty Mandel (the numbers racket), Dr. Ida Selavan at Hebrew Union College, Cincinnati (Yiddish translations), and Elise Roenigk (mechanical musical instruments).

Thanks also goes to Ralph Keyes for the loan of his Russian and sex-history collections as well as access to his eclectic files, Lorinda Klein of the Bellevue Archives, Barbara Niff of the Mt. Sinai Hospital Archives, and the Smithsonian Institution Air and Space Research Department. Medical advice was generously offered by Robin Madden, Ph.D, M.D., Joshua Madden, M.D., Mario Mendizabal, M.D., Dick Stewart, M.D., and Margaret Strickhauser, C.N.M. Other queries were fielded by Leonard Weisman, Leah Weisman, Marilyn Weisman, and Michael Corrigan.

I am especially indebted to Bob Singerman of the Price Judaica Library at the University of Florida, whose brilliant bibliographic scholarship is matched only by his intuitive grasp of a novelist's research requirements. The university's interlibrary loan department came through again, but this time even they enjoyed perusing the curious array of books they ordered from near and far.

Don Cutler remains my intrepid agent and friend. Especially supportive during some difficult days were Helen Stephenson, Maria Pallante, Alex Gigante, Carrie Camus, and Kathy T. Sperber. My mother, Elsie Weisman, is my very best reader. Our sons, Blake and Joshua, were brave enough to permit me to tackle this topic. Most of all, my husband, Philip, makes everything possible.

Lily

A LOVE STORY
by Cindy Bonner

Lily DeLony is the spirited but proper daughter of a hardworking, God-fearing father. She has no reason to doubt the rules of virtue and righteousness she has been brought up with—that is until she meets Marion "Shot" Beatty, the youngest of the infamous Beatty brothers who were the terror of McDade, Texas, in 1883. What happens when Lily and Marion defy all odds to come together makes for the most captivating and suspenseful novel of love that you will ever read—and for one of the most endearing heroines that you will never forget.

"The reader will cheer for Lily to the final page. A believable, engrossing tale of love and violence."
—*Abilene Reporter News*

"Absolutely spellbinding—a classic tale of true love against all odds—as supple and strong as a well-worked piece of leather." —*Booklist*

from ONYX